# OUTLAND

## M.C. COWARD

*Dedicated to the distractions.*

# PROLOGUE

*Bones*

If something wasn't wrong in the Outland before, it sure as hell was now. The dead man walked. Warner cocked his revolver, took aim, and fired. The dead man walked. Warner cursed and cocked the hammer. He shot again, hitting him in the neck. The dead man collapsed, twitching in the desert sands.

"What do you reckon it is?" Hijack asked, taking cautious steps toward the body. Holstering his pistol, Warner approached as well, the bones he wore rattling with each step. They hunched over the emaciated corpse. Where the skin wasn't charred, it was moon pale, like its blood had long gone blue. A black liquid trickled from the thing's neck.

Warner spat. "Smells like hell. If I didn't know better, I'd say it looks like Keller."

"Looks like him. But where'd he come from?"

Standing, Warner brushed a lock of his long hair from his face and surveyed the horizon. Save for their settlement just a few yards behind, it was flat fucking desert in every direction, matched only by the monotonous blue sky overhead. No clouds for Tombstone Warner nor the rest of the Infinite Bullets. He spat again and adjusted his shirt of bones. Scraps of sheet metal and wood constructed their settlement. Hide and canvas covered the makeshift shelters that clustered in their spot of desert. Other than his gunshots, it was a quiet morning, and most of his men were too hungover to care to investigate the noise. Hijack had been on watch and came to Warner about the dead man. They stood less than fifteen feet from the settlement, among the hardpan cracked earth looking at this pale thing that might have once been Keller.

"Left for Reaper's Cove a few weeks ago," Warner said. "Now he's come back."

"Word is Reaper's Cove burned." Hijack studied the horizon.

"Use your head, Hijack. More than three weeks ago, Keller says he's going to Reaper's Cove, say hello to some of his buddies, go whoring. We get word last week that the Cove's been burned. Look at his body."

Hijack looked back at the corpse. Its glossy black eyes stared upward, absent of life. "That ain't Keller, Warner. That's a dead man."

"It's a waste of two bullets is what it is," Warner said. "We ain't going to be the Infinite Bullets much longer if we start wasting ammo on dead men."

"What do we do?" Hijack asked.

Warner sighed and shook his head. He hated these sorts of decisions. The Infinite Bullets had been a grand idea. When the dark haired man calling himself Raven, had come to Warner, it had been all the luck in the world. He gave Warner more weapons than anyone in the Outland could have imagined. The deal was simple. Find the meanest, toughest men in the Outland. Arm them and teach them to shoot. They'd be the hardest outlaw gang there was, and if Raven ever needed their service, he'd simply call upon them. Ten years now and Warner reckoned Raven had forgotten them. Probably dead.

Guns alone didn't make a leader, Warner knew that much. In the Outland, bones made a leader. Every outlaw from Glenshore to Harbor wore bones, around their neck, piercing their earlobes. Half the outlaws had never actually killed a man, or if they did, they hadn't dared touch the corpse. Some thought they were clever and wore animal bone. Hard to tell the difference most of the time. But Warner thought he had been exceptionally clever. He had gone to Glenshore and he spent his metal on every bone he could afford. He even traded a gun. After a little string and wire, he donned his bones, and he called himself Tombstone Warner, making a name for himself as a killer long before he made a habit of killing.

He bought the loyalty of the hardest crew of brigands in the desert. And now that it came to it, he didn't like it much. There was always an order to be given, a question to answer, and when put to it, all of Warner's cleverness faltered. He spat toward the corpse. "Do whatever you want." He should have a better answer. Leave it, burn it, pour one out. He might have done any of those things with a dead man. But when the dead don't stay dead?

Hijack leaned over the corpse again, dirty, nimble fingers riffling through the tattered clothes.

"Find anything?" Warner asked.

"Nothing of worth, but look at this." Hijack pulled the man's shirt open. Deep wounds ran in parallel stripes, stitches lacing up each of the black trenches. "Crocotta got hold of him," Hijack said. "Then someone sewed him up."

"You know you don't stitch up a man when a crocotta's had a hold on him," Warner said. "Waste of time. He'll die of rot. Plus, that don't explain why Keller's half-roasted."

"There's more," said Hijack, ripping the pants away. More stitching ran all the way around the thigh, like someone had sewed it back on.

"What the—"

A white hand gripped Hijack. He jerked back, but the thing that had been Keller held tight. It lurched, flailing its other arm

3

towards Hijack's throat. He let out a yelp, trying to escape the corpse's grip.

Warner hesitated a moment, drew his gun, and aimed. He shot at the creature and missed. Blood sprouted from Hijack's torso. He screamed, knees buckling. The corpse pulled the wounded Hijack down and rolled over him. Warner's next shot hit it. Black liquid sprayed from its body, covering Hijack's face in tarry streaks. His mouth gaped and he flailed in horror, but neither he nor Warner's bullet had slowed Keller's corpse.

It began to bludgeon Hijack. One fist at a time, it beat down on the man's face. Warner might have rushed to help the man, but if a gun couldn't stop Keller, then there was little he could do. But that might look like cowardice to the men, and Warner couldn't have that. Hijack had stopped screaming, which was good. Warner looked back to the settlement and no one seemed to have made anything of the commotion. Just three yards away, the cluster of shacks and dilapidated buildings stood silent.

Hijack gurgled and twitched, hands weakly spasming as if still trying to find the will to resist. Keller's black eyes just stared at the man as he beat upon him. Hijack had been a good man. Not bright, so it was a small loss, but it always hurt to lose someone loyal.

Warner held the gun aloft. His earlier neck-shot had felled the dead man. He'd shoot it in the head this time, put it down again, tell the men how bravely Hijack had defended him, insisting that he fight it alone for the glory of it, and then Warner would tell the men how he had stepped in too late. They'd burn the corpses. If nothing else, that would do the trick.

Then Warner turned, looking back at his settlement. Standing just out front, not ten feet away, three of his men watched him. They had spectated as their leader let his man take a beating. There was Dirty Dan, Bry, and Pat. How much had they seen and what would they make of it? He decided he would address them boldly, as if his inaction had been deliberate. A lie came to him, and he opened his mouth to speak, but something in their faces gave him pause.

It slammed into his back. His knees struck the ground and the gun skittered across the desert sands. A cool, clammy hand gripped the back of his neck, pushing his face into the dirt. He flailed, trying to breathe, bone shirt digging into his beating chest. The sand gritted on his face. He pushed up, but it held him down.

The weight lifted off, suddenly knocked back. Warner struggled to rise, gasping for breath. He rolled over to see Dan and Bry pulling it off, and Pat beating it furiously with his crude sword. Picking up his gun, Warner stood shakily and rubbed his sore neck.

After an endless hacking, Keller's corpse lay in enough pieces that it seemed they had gotten all of the life out of it. Less worried about his reputation and more grateful to still be alive, Warner looked up and smiled at the men, ready to thank them. But yet again something came from the north. In the distance, on the horizon. He squinted at it, but it was no mere trick of light.

"Burn the corpse," Warner said. "Get ready."

They rushed about the settlement, the tumult of their preparations a constant rabble of clattering and shouts. Along with the gathering of blades, bludgeons, and spears, they loaded every rifle, pistol, revolver, and shotgun. The men drove rows of stakes into the ground. Warner's bones rattled as he shouted orders from the only building, the tall centerpiece they had built their settlement around. He called down to the scurrying scouts to ready them for what was to come. "For fuck's sake, Bry," he shouted down, "if that's all you can carry, you'd be more useful digging a trench. It's an ammo box, not an anvil."

It was too far to tell what sort of army came for them, but it was big, whatever it was, and would arrive by nightfall. The

Infinite Bullets would be ready. They may only be fifty strong, but they had the guns.

They stocked all of their ammunition on the north side of the settlement. The men with rifles stretched prone on rooftops. Shotgunners had the front line. Out of thirty-seven men, Warner had given Dirty Dan six of the best to hold in reserve should the enemy come at them from the side or penetrate their defenses.

Torches appeared at nightfall, ushering the mass toward their settlement. The Infinite Bullets lit no fires of their own. They sat restlessly in the dark, waiting for the first sign of combat. Now in his full bone armor, Warner ate by the moonlight wishing he were a harder man, that he could replace the knot in his stomach with confidence, and that whatever this was that approached them only meant to pass them by. Unlikely.

But he knew well that the thing that had been Keller had not been natural. The hands that had gripped his neck felt like they had been in a damp cellar, not the burning desert for as many days as it took that thing to make its way from the Cove to the Infinite Bullets. Whatever Keller had been or whatever had made Keller what he was came for them now.

Shouts called for Warner and he saw that the fires grew close. He walked towards them, the shadows of shacks and tents in their makeshift town lining the way. The men parted before him and he stood behind their spiked defenses, watching the group that approached.

In the dark their numbers were unintelligible, but many came. Torchlight revealed a motley gang of outlaws, bandits and criminals, some from outlaw gangs that Warner knew. They all wore their bones, some a single piece to show they had the killer in them. Some, a few to boast their record. But none so many as Tombstone Warner, whose bone shirt cascaded down his bare chest, making it seem less scrawny. He had donned every bone he owned and they bristled down his arms and back, jutting from the pads on his knees. They were his armor.

Further in the ranks, pale shapes moved, more like Keller than human. Unlike their armored counterparts, they did not clatter, nor did torchlight gleam off metal and leather, but rather cast a cold sheen to their sallow skin.

Yards away from the edge of the settlement a small group emerged. Along the defenses, a wave of guns cocked, ready to fire. Warner held up a hand to signal his men to hold, a sudden knowing of who marched upon them.

The black-haired man led the small company, a long dark coat tailored to his lean frame. Though short, he was too smart not to be dangerous. And next to a crocotta, any man looked small. It lumbered alongside him on four taloned paws. Its tawny hair bristled along its back like saw blades. The most terrible thing about it was its grin, exposing a jagged set of teeth glistening with hungry saliva. It sniffed at its surroundings, turning its head, the torchlight shining green in its eyes. And it stank. Like a poison-rotted corpse. Flanking them walked two women. Pale as the dead, but not like the others; they wore white dresses. Black, curly hair seemed to sway in a nonexistent wind.

Warner had been too silent as they approached. Their torchlight extended far, brighter than natural, and he knew they could see him plainly. His bones hardly felt intimidating. The approaching group was an army compared to the Infinite Bullets. He cleared his throat, reminding himself to speak strong. "Who approaches the Infinite Bullets? Friend or enemy?" It was a stupid thing to say, and worse, it hardly boomed.

"I am Raven. I think you know me." the neatly dressed man said in a familiar accent. "It's your choice whether I be friend or enemy. I have come to collect on our deal."

"We have no debts." After ten years this man came from nowhere, preceded by Keller—or whatever it was Keller had become. Warner had shown too much weakness of late.

"I believe you do," Raven said. "I believe those are my guns. We had a deal."

"You can't come demanding that we honor a deal over ten years old."

"Your man led us to you" Raven said. "Keller, he said his name was before he died."

"He wasn't dead when he came back to us."

"My point exactly," Raven said. "You can either honor our agreement or you can serve me as Keller served me. Giving you a choice is merely a courtesy that I am not obligated to extend."

The crocotta gave a light cackle, but the women remained expressionless. Raven's smile widened but his dark eyes showed no emotion.

"We don't respond kindly to threats, do we boys?" The question would get Warner's men involved, get their blood pumping. This was going to lead to a skirmish. They hadn't had a real battle in some time, and Warner was finding his confidence rising. But no reassurance came from his men. Silence and then footsteps behind him.

"Dan?" Warner said, smelling the man as he arrived. Dirty Dan smelled worse than a crocotta. Warner looked over his shoulder, the men he had sent with Dan stood around him. "We got this, Dan. These guys think they can bully us into soldiering for them. Well I say they'll give us little trouble once they see what we're made of. Give them fire."

His men had packed every empty bottle with an oil-soaked rag, ready to be lit and cast into this Raven's army. Warner pulled his own bottle, wet rag dangling from the opening. He struck a match and put it to the cloth. The fire went out. No one else attempted to light their fire-bottles.

"Just water in that one, sir," Dan whispered in his ear, the stench suffocating Warner. The knife slid in, grating against the bones he wore and then against his own bones. Something warm and wet flowed from his back and then from his pants. He shook, the bones rattling, pissing uncontrollably as he sank to the ground bleeding.

He trembled for a long time, trying to move his legs, but something had gone wrong. A voice spoke in his ear, Raven's strange accent.

"Next time grow a spine instead of buying one."

# CHAPTER ONE

*Marked by Fire*

"The boy is marked by fire. He shall go alone." The High Priest's tone prohibited dissent.

No one at the table would dare argue with Tasrael, but Liam replied to the priest's pomposity. "I am a *man* marked by fire, Your Eminence. And there is no reason for me to go alone. Several men have offered to join me."

"Those men have never left the City, let alone one *boy*, not since we closed its doors two hundred years ago. The prophecy speaks of one and only one to be marked by fire. You alone passed through the flames, so shall you alone go. Furthermore, I will not risk any more of Novum's finest than need be."

"And Chancellor Negosta?" Liam asked.

The High Priest's lip twitched, as if resisting a condescending smile. "This is a Church matter. Besides, the Chancellor believes this all to be a farce, and he is not alone in his notion. You're lucky he will even let us open the door for you."

Liam peered at the four other clergymen, one at a time, dismayed by their apathy. He met the High Priest's eyes. If Tasrael was intimidated, he didn't show it. Liam arose from his seat, feeling somehow small even though he towered over the sitting man. "So be it," he said. "I'll go alone. If I don't survive, if I don't find and warn Dorian, and this city falls—then it's on you. And if I return, it's only to spite you."

"You are dismissed," High Priest Tasrael said.

Liam turned, the echoes of his footsteps following him out of the room and into the hall. After a moment he remembered he was not alone. "It's not fair," he said.

"It is not what I would have wanted," Master Ferrith replied, walking alongside him. "I still have every confidence in you, but let's talk more about it when we get back to the apartment."

They emerged from the temple, the ancient brass doors swinging wide as Liam made his way down the marble stairs.

"Cool yourself, Liam."

Ferrith was right. Liam took a deep breath, slowing his thoughts and pulse. It smelled cleaner outside of the temple, but he still felt enclosed, stifled. He looked up at the walls of Novum, their slanted glass panes coming to an apex a mile above him, trapping him inside. Years of dust and sand added to their tinted hue, leaving the palest blue sky and desaturated desertscape. He would leave this place alone, the first person in two hundred years to see the great pyramid from the outside.

When they first built the City—Novum as it was properly called—they had deemed it prodigious in size and technology, but the closer it came to the time to leave, the smaller it felt. The Central Tower, its pinnacle almost reaching the peak of the pyramid they lived within, felt like nothing more than a needle amongst the greater world that extended beyond the soiled panes of the city walls.

At two bedrooms, Ferrith's quarters were large by Novum's standards. Had it not been cluttered with gadgets and half-finished projects, the living room might have been considered spacious, even if the kitchen was smaller. Between Ferrith and his partner's various endeavors, stacks of fabric hunched over sewing supplies, knives and short-swords lay next to a sharpening block.

No space was left uncluttered, save the couch, starkly bare with a neat collection of books arranged on the coffee table before it. That was Liam's space, where he slept and worked when he stayed with Ferrith and Standon.

Liam strode to the kitchen table, nestled among the counters and cabinets, the smell from the previous night's meal lingering stale in the air. Finding an uncluttered chair, he sat, elbows on the table, careful not to disrupt the sprawl of papers and his own work. While Liam fumed in silence, Ferrith made coffee. Stepping over a stack of books, he found his own chair at the table, steaming mugs in hand.

"It's bullshit," Liam said. "I wanted you to come with me. Perry too. Standon if he wants to come with us."

Ferrith ran calloused fingers through his short, wavy hair. The man was hardly forty, yet gray streaked his dark hair. "There's no way they're letting us out of here. I wish we could come, but like I said, I have every confidence you can do this."

Liam took a sip of his black coffee. Ferrith held that cream and sugar were far too limited a commodity to waste on the more expensive coffee, so Liam had grown accustomed to drinking it unadulterated. When he had found sufficient space for his mug, Liam picked up his own project from the table, a computer chip as old as the war itself. He examined the various circuits and mounts on the silicon board before deciding it needed a soldering iron and tossed it to the side. "Where is Standon? He has connections."

"Standon," Ferrith said, "is working late. As usual. He might get here soon, but I don't think he could do us much good, not without making his position fairly obvious."

"What's he doing anyway?"

From under the papers and instruments Ferrith retrieved a tablet and turned it on. After some swiping and tapping, he set it before Liam, who peered at the screen. Above the news article was a photograph depicting the pinnacle of the Central Tower, a ring of windows near the tip, one of them broken.

" 'Murder at the Tower'," Liam said, reading the headline. " 'The first time in twenty years.' So they know?"

"Thanks to you and Perry and your escapades. Of course, Standon couldn't tell them that it had been discovered by two teenage boys walking around the Central Tower like they belong there and discovering a mysterious room. Try to explain that one! He said he had to fabricate the rumor of mysterious sounds coming from the top floor so that whoever investigated it would find it for themselves."

The mystery had perplexed Liam for over a week now. Not long after he had been marked by fire, Perry had convinced him to sneak into the Central Tower and work their way to the top. "You at least deserve to get a view of where you're going," he had said. They found the room, dried blood on the remnants of a broken window distracting from the view.

"Something tells me," Ferrith said, "that there's more to this than we think. The High Priest may act like this isn't political, that the Chancellor wouldn't dare get involved, but I think there's more to this than we can guess at the moment. A mystery like this is sure to be a convenient distraction from Agnys Negosta's unpopular reforms."

"All the more reason I wish I wasn't the only one going," Liam said, ignoring Ferrith's political speculation. In a sense, Liam was almost glad that he was going alone, not so that he could have all the glory or credit, but because he knew his grandfather would approve. Yet, he felt isolated, like the sole responsibility was his and no one in the world could help him.

"When was the last time you saw your parents?" Ferrith asked.

"Days. A week. I don't know. They don't seem to notice when I'm there. I think this is sort of a relief for them. A way to please my grandfather and rid me from their lives. At least I have you,

Standon, and Perry," Liam paused and swallowed, "and my grandfather. But now I'm about to lose that too."

"Listen," Ferrith said. "For two hundred years we have been locked in this pyramid. The powers that be have either been too preoccupied or too scared to go out there. I think it's both. Why risk exploring what's out there when things are so set in here? They open those doors and new powers will rise, new conflicts, and perhaps danger. Who knows what's beyond those mountains? The last thing we knew before we lost contact was the war, and we know how devastating the prophet said it would be.

"But you and I have no vested interest in staying here or keeping things as they are. And you are brave enough to seize the opportunity. This was a task meant for us, not some quest for a bureaucrat's lackeys.

"You and I know damned well what happened three weeks ago. By however many greats he is your grandfather, his prophecy saved us over two hundred years ago, and I think it has saved us again. By whatever miracle he has lived so long, it's apparent he was meant to make this new prophecy. The priests didn't believe him, but you and I know what we saw at that fire. That was his proof."

Ferrith sipped his coffee, brow scrunched in thought. "I see the right of it now. You should go alone."

"I thought you said you wanted to come with me."

"I did and I do, but I see now that they were right."

"You can't be serious!" Had Ferrith gone mad?

"I'm very serious. Hear me out. The prophet Elijah, your grandfather, said this was for you and you alone. Now, you and I both know that prophecy is fickle. What little of it we've had has been nothing like we expected. Remember the prophet's words, 'he who is marked by fire shall journey to find Dorian' and you and I made the assumption that you only had to lead such an excursion, that you would be the catalyst by which Dorian was found. But after his prophecy, Elijah insisted that he meant you and you alone. And whatever their motives, the High Priest insisted as well.

"I'm not finished." Ferrith held up a finger, silencing Liam's objection. "Remember, we built this place to escape the destruction of the fallen. Now, we're sending you to ask Dorian, one of the very beings we built this place to escape, to help us, to protect us from Jacob. To protect us from worse. The priests likely think we'll hold just fine against any outside threat and the last thing we need is to bring one of *them* in here with us. They're playing along, but hoping you won't succeed. You want them to send someone with you? It won't be someone of your choosing. It won't be someone you can trust either. They'll be sure that whatever you discover out there is as benign as anything in here, or if you come back with anything, if you return with Dorian, that they can control it. This isn't something we want them to be a part of. It's yours and yours alone for a reason."

Liam opened his mouth to argue but words escaped him. His teacher was right. "I guess I'm just afraid," Liam admitted. "The desert and whatever lies beyond the mountains..." Beyond the walls of Novum, was the desert and then the ring of mountains, tall and sheer. The river passed from their northwestern walls, almost brushing against the City, and then trailing down to the southernmost point in the mountains, where the Pass stood. A ruin, the remnants of a long forgotten city, blocked the great gap. Beyond that might be anything. Uninhabitable wastelands, a lost civilization, the sea...anything. How was Liam to conquer that alone, much less persevere beyond it? There was a reason nothing had come from the Pass.

"I will not send you unprepared," Ferrith said. "Thanks to you and Standon, we managed to convince them to let me allocate the finances for this journey. Most of them, at least. Now that reminds me. Take a look at this."

Ferrith stood, searching among the clutter. He shifted a stack of boxes and then moved them back, muttering "Where the hell did I put it?" At last he found it, draped over the back of a chair in the adjacent room. "Try this on," he said.

Liam pulled the shirt on and over his dreadlocks. As Ferrith took several measurements, he talked at length of the virtues of such fabric, the way it quick-dried, its lightness of weight, the durability. Liam knew the necessity for the proper wear in the desert, but it bored him. When Standon came in, Liam sat shirtless in the kitchenette as Ferrith worked on his next alteration.

"Gentlemen," Standon said, giving a casual bow as he removed his suit jacket. His mannerisms, however formal, always had a wry tone, as if to relieve the stress of interacting with politicians all day. His properness was odd, but fitting to Ferrith, who contrasted his partner with a workman's attitude. Not for the first time, Liam worried what would happen if anyone found out that Ferrith and Standon were more than roommates. It would only take a rumor.

"How was your day?" Ferrith asked, not looking up from his work.

"Fine enough, though I got news of the meeting with Tasrael. Pompous prick, that one, but then again, priests usually are."

"*Puñeta*," Ferrith said regarding Tasrael. Liam was accustomed to Spanish expletives from Ferrith. A small group of Puerto Ricans had made it to Novum, and remained sequestered in a First Underground community that mostly worked in pharmaceuticals and electronics. A politician and his son, a young Standon, had visited in the interest of gentrification, and worked tirelessly with Ferrith to revitalize the community.

"Liam and I were just discussing the meeting," Ferrith said.

"And?" Standon asked as he loosened his bow tie.

Ferrith's glance told Liam that he was expected to explain their conclusions, though he himself had yet to vocalize agreement. "It makes sense, I guess." Liam said with a sigh.

"Well," Ferrith said, "if you have a better idea, you tell me."

"I get it," Liam admitted. "I just don't like it."

"Out with it," said Standon.

As Liam spoke, Standon started rummaging through the kitchen, listening to Liam's explanation as he made tea. He nodded occasionally as he set to boiling water and rinsing out a mug. Ferrith wrinkled his nose when Standon added the leaves, but said nothing as his fingers worked a needle in and out of the fabric.

"Tea?" Standon offered Liam.

He thanked him but shook his head.

"Well," said Standon after Liam's explanation. He removed a pile of fabric from one of the chairs and took a seat. "Sounds reasonable enough for me. There was a time when the people of Novum had a hope of one day leaving, of going back out into the world and restarting. We have vaults of data, embryos, things long forgotten for when that day came. I think they expected that Jacob's defeat would be absolute, not that he'd disappear and leave us afraid and wondering for two hundred years. It was the type of bastard thing I suppose he would do, and given the prophet's tidings, we were right to be afraid. But maybe, just maybe this is our chance, and this seems like the best way. You have the lineage to the prophet, but as far as they're concerned, you're no threat. Who knows what we have ahead of us, but we'll probably all perish in what's to come or finally emerge from behind our walls."

"But aren't either of you worried something will happen to me?" Liam asked. "We don't know what's out there."

"Very worried," Ferrith said, looking up from his work. "Beyond worried. I don't think the prophet would send you to your death, but that doesn't stop my concern. However, I have a great deal of confidence in you, and I won't stop saying that until you get some confidence in yourself. We must put aside worry and each of us play our part to whatever ends."

They sat for a time, saying little. Standon talked about his day and Ferrith had Liam try the shirt. After two more alterations, he remarked that he would need his sewing machine to get it just right. Standon invited Liam to dinner, but he declined, hoping that he might meet with Perry in the evening.

Liam walked the streets of Novum, the flashing screens and neon lights flickering on the concrete. Car traffic had once been more limited, but at this hour vehicles spilled onto the streets, coasting along the roads. He passed an officer casually standing on a corner, unwary and preoccupied. He carried no firearm, only a sword. Guns had been banned from the City, but some oversight had permitted bladed weapons, and their usage had become far too rampant to outlaw. The prophet still chuckled at that one.

In a back alley, Liam climbed a series of ledges. Before he had met Perry, he hadn't been one for heights, but his peer had torn him from fascination with ancient computers, and forced him to experience Novum as no one else had known it. Novum possessed a culture of complacency for which Liam cared little. The prophet predicted that Liam would be different, and Liam had hoped that he was right. But now that it came to it, his anxiety left little room for any anticipation.

Ferrith was Liam's teacher and mentor, more guiding than his own father had ever been. He would miss Ferrith and Standon. He would miss his grandfather as well, but Liam pushed that to the back of his mind, dreading that the man might die before Liam's return. Had he lived so long to give one last prophecy? Now that he had served his purpose, would he pass away?

As for the rest of his family, Liam found little affection for them. Their lineage gained them affluence but little more responsibility than to maintain the high reputation of the prophet's descendants. There was always an *event*—whether a ball, party, charity, or some other duty—and Liam was always too young to attend. He fell into the care of others, and much to his grandfather's wise design, they were good mentors and companions. When he turned nine—*a good age*, the prophet claimed—Liam met Ferrith and for the past eight years, had learned history, math, language, and even the sword.

Within his training he had only one peer, a slightly older boy who took an interest in the wars. Perry's parents were glad to finance his private education, having high hopes that their problem child would do better outside one of the government schools. Sure enough, Perry had done exceedingly well, but as he matured, the problem child never grew out of him.

"Want a smoke?" Perry asked, waving the pack his way.

This was their place, the easiest rooftop they could access without risk of getting caught. Most of the buildings toward the center of the City stretched far above them, but from this further ledge, the sprawl was theirs for the taking.

"No thanks," Liam answered. "You always ask that."

"You never know. In light of all this, you may not live long enough to die from it. Might as well enjoy what you can."

Even from their rooftop spot, the spire of the Central Tower dwarfed them, tall and ominous, jutting just beneath the apex of the pyramid's four walls. Their feet dangled from the edge of the roof and their necks craned to the tip of the edifice.

There might have once been a reason behind the city's layout—its scattering of condos and businesses, rooftop restaurants, and cafes—but they now spread in chaos, clustering and rising as their ranks gathered to the center. Ramps and bridges spanned between them at various intervals, paths that made the highest reaches feel like a metropolis in itself. Small vehicles navigated the streets, but for those who had business or pleasure higher above ground, narrow hovercrafts navigated between buildings, over and under the paths that linked them. Below ground, a similar system of trains and elevators snaked through the world beneath.

Gardens lined the southern walls, the most prominent view from their lookout. Green grasses and treetops stretched almost the mile of the southern border, vibrant colored flowers sprouting among them. Towards the center was a circular clearing of flat, engraved stone, a memorial to the world left behind. Liam guessed that the symbols carved into it were of some significance. The prophet had hinted as much about the round seal.

"You're really going," Perry said. It was not a question.

"I am," Liam said, trying to sound sure of himself. Night would fall soon, obscuring the distant mystery. Somewhere beyond them, Dorian lived. A month ago, Liam would have laughed at the idea that the fallen maintained any concern for them, if they even lived. Now, *he* was the one meant to go find one of them.

"You really think you'll find your fallen angel?" Perry asked as if reading his thoughts.

"I don't really think of him as an angel," Liam replied. "At least, Ferrith doesn't think of him that way. 'Spirit made flesh' he calls them. But yeah, I do think I'll find him. To what end, though, I don't know. I can't deny it's my purpose, as much as I wish I had help, but you saw what happened that day at the fire."

"You know I'm skeptical of that sort of thing. Even priests don't really believe it. They're humoring the old man. Politics." He lit another cigarette.

"My grandfather said it would happen and it did."

"Ha!" Perry said. "Your 'grandfather.' Your *great*—how many is it? Eight times?—great great great—"

"Shut up," Liam said. It was a calm command, but Perry listened, for once taming his incorrigibility. "I mean," he continued, "this isn't how I wanted to say goodbye."

"I wish I could come," Perry said. "It would be fun. Dorian's probably right at the Pass. We'd stroll up, fill him in on the old man's prophecy, and bring him back. We'd be heroes just for taking a long walk."

"Then Jacob comes."

"Come on," Perry replied. "That's just depressing. Maybe I can sneak out and join you."

Touched, Liam paused a moment, thinking. Who knew how far he would really have to travel to find Dorian? Anything could happen between now and then. He could die, a seventeen year old boy in the wild, though Ferrith was perhaps right that the prophet would not send Liam to his death. But if anyone else went with him and if anything happened to them, it would be his responsibility. Ferrith had been right. Liam had to go alone. "I can't ask that of you."

"And you're sure you are ready for this?"

They had prepared him as much as possible. Ferrith held nothing back, teaching him the sword, the horse, and schooling him in all of the classic subjects and then those of survival. Little was known of the Outland, much less surviving anywhere but the City, but Liam was as equipped as he could be. From their perch, they viewed the world beyond the tinted glass walls, the vermilion sands cut by the river, and leading up to the mountains' edge. From where they were sitting, the sliver of the Pass was barely visible. Liam gazed at his destination. "I'm ready," he replied. He would have to be.

Was it fear or excitement that took him as he said his goodbyes? Either way, he tried to subdue the trembling as Ferrith grasped his hand firmly, green-gray eyes meeting Liam's. He told Liam that

Standon regretted his absence, as work kept him from giving his regards in person. "You're a man now, Liam. Remember, I have every confidence in you and you should have it in yourself."

Liam went to Perry next and held out his hand, but in a rare dismissal of his usual flippant demeanor, his friend embraced him.

"I've never told you," Perry said, "but I think of you as my brother." He let go of Liam and faced him. "Come back soon."

It had been weeks since he had last seen his parents. They were strangers come to see him off. His mother, wearing precarious heels and a dress too formal for the occasion in the gardens, awkwardly hugged him. She pulled away, tears running down her dark cheeks. He had never known her to cry or show so much affection. She must have seen the surprise on his face.

"I care, you know," she said. "They tell you to get married, have kids, keep the prophet's line. They don't even know why. We don't even matter. But they spoil you for it, and you forget about the important things. I thought you were a boy, that there would be plenty of time to spend with you, but you're a man now."

His father put a hand on her shoulder, a forced comfort, as if he too had no idea how to the handle the situation. She leaned into him, turning her head away, embarrassed by her tears.

"I'm coming back," Liam said.

His father freed a hand and took Liam's. "I know you are," he said. "Maybe things will be different when you get back."

"They will," Liam replied.

Others had come to see him off. Friends of the family, a girl who had tutored with Ferrith for a short time, many more who were followers of the Church.

"It's time," a voice behind him called. He turned and nodded to High Priest Tasrael, and then looked back to those who had come to say goodbye. He should say something, but he thought he might choke on tears if he did.

His mother, who had stifled her own sobs, held out an envelope for him. "Your grandfather couldn't be here. He's so old. But he sent this."

Liam took it and then looked to Ferrith who gave him a nod. Liam returned the gesture and less ceremoniously than he had anticipated, he followed Tasrael from the gardens.

The way out of Novum had once been known to all, for it was by that door that they entered. However, once sealed, it had been a forgotten thing among the people, and became a secret among the high priests and administration. All Liam knew was that it was on the south side of the pyramid and at least partially underground. Tasrael led him into a nearby building. The unremarkable entrance yielded to a grand reception hall. The security guard waved as they went to the elevators. Among the fine marble and chic decor, the priest's robes appeared out of place, like the silly remnants of an age long past.

Liam, in his black shirt and pants, their synthetic fabrics hanging comfortably loose on him, supposed that he might look odd as well. A suit would have been more appropriate, as would have a briefcase instead of a backpack.

The elevator took them down and opened to a large hallway where bright lights lined the tall, white walls. "This," said Tasrael, in his usual pompous tone, "is the entrance hall. At one point there was a much larger elevator here, so that they could move anything they needed into Novum. Once the doors were closed, they reduced the size of the elevator for more space. They had planned to do the same to the hall, but like so many grand ideas for this city, it was forgotten. Come, right this way."

The other priests lined the end of the hall, hoods obfuscating their faces, though Liam probably knew them all. Here was the ceremony that had been missing in the gardens. No one had guided Liam regarding the order of things. This was unprecedented and accordingly the priests had cobbled together some sort of rite. Intuitively, he stood amongst the robed and hooded figures as they moved to either side of him. He had imagined a dim room with torches, but this was more like the Church in Novum with its bright lights and sterile walls.

Where the hall ended, it slanted sharply, leading up to a pale white barrier, the door that would soon open for him.

High Priest Tasrael cleared his throat, "May you who have been marked by fire endure the Outlands as you have endured the flame. Journey into the mountains and beyond to find Dorian, for he is our last hope against the Morning Star."

Liam stood in the corridor as Tasrael droned on, the priest's lofty and ceremonious tone only prolonging his anxiety. The door before him stood tall, silent, as if it had been awaiting this moment for the past two hundred years.

"And so concludes the Rite of Fire, foretold by the Great Prophet Elijah. Make haste and may the Eternal One bless you on your journey."

With that, the priests left, all of them filing out behind Liam, their footsteps pattering down the hall. Liam stood in the silence wondering what would happen next. Was he supposed to do something?

A clang caused him to jump. He clapped his ears and looked back to the door and the changing light. The door slid upward, slanting away, letting in sunlight. A gust of warm air filled the room and he held up an arm to shield himself from the dust that flowed with it. Dirt and debris fell through the open way as the stark white floor ramped up into the widening blue gap.

With another deafening sound, metal slammed against metal, and the door stopped. Liam walked up the ramp toward the opening, his eyes adjusting to the light, and for the first time he beheld the sky without the tint of Novum's glass walls. He had never seen a blue so deep, and he walked toward it in his trance. Warmth circulated around him, filling his lungs and swarming his fingertips, as if divesting Novum's insipidity with life and vibrancy. When he emerged from the corridor and his boots met the copper earth, the world splayed before him in formerly unseen, vivid detail. With another clang the door closed again, its trembling and grinding muffled in the open space. It slammed shut, isolating Liam from the life he had always known and forcing him into the new and unknown.

The silence of the City had felt muffled, but in the Outlands, it was an open sort of silence, like the quiet air itself teemed with expectation. It was, however, not silent. A new sound trickled near him, the soft laving of the river. From within the City, the rushing of its wandering waters had never found his ears, but now the wide stream flowed among the cursed land and up to the mountains, their sheer walls his distant destination. He took his first steps toward their southernmost point, towards the Pass and the ruins that blocked his way into them.

As he walked, the sun beat down on his skin, its warmth a reminder of the fire. They had not believed the prophet. He was a relic, his days of foretelling long over. When the old man had stood before the priests, he did not do so bent. He did not hold the pulpit to steady himself. He stood straight and spoke authoritatively, declaring that Jacob was on the move, at last ready to make his strike on Novum. Worst of all, he spoke of the Morning Star. He declared that Dorian was their only hope and that someone must be sent.

None believed the prophet and so he commanded the priests to build a fire and let any who would be willing to go to pass through it. The flame had blazed in the courtyard outside of the temple. Over forty men and women approached it, most seeking fame, others the few remaining zealots loyal to the church. None of them could come near to the heat, and so it seemed the prophet's miracle had failed. Then Liam was sent to the fire.

He had awaited the burn but it never came. When he drew closer than any of the others had, he thought surely the heat would deter him at any moment, but before he knew it, its light licked at his skin. Fear gave way to the warmth, not burning, but like the sun beating upon him now. Brightness filled his vision, coursed through his veins, and encompassed him. "The man marked by fire," the prophet had called him.

With that burning memory, Liam walked the cracked and flat dusty ground, eyes on the Pass, only glancing at his watch intermittently. When he petitioned to be sent with any sort of communication device, Tasrael denied the request. Prior to the fall, laws prohibited such advanced devices from exiting Novum. After the first year in the pyramid city, Year One, additional legislation banned outside contact all together. Standon had mentioned a recent attempt to repeal such laws, but the effort fell far short of coming to a vote.

It was midday when Liam finally turned around to behold Novum from the outside. Its great triangular walls rose, their sleek black surface glowing in the afternoon sun. It reached high, its peak jutting into the cloudless sky. What had felt small and crowded from the inside stood taller than he had imagined, impregnable, the last stand for civilization.

Years ago, when his grandfather had first told him about the fallen, he had thought of them as long lost—perhaps dead—beings of legend. As a boy, he sat by the amber glow of a dim lamp in his grandfather's quarters. The old man sat close in his own chair, his dark skin mostly blending in with the darkness. He puffed his pipe and its smoke curled in the light's soft radiance, spiraling beyond it into the void. "You wouldn't know it, Liam, but there was a time when all the world was like the City, but it was open to the air and sun. Great machines soared in the skies and vessels rode on great seas. Grass and trees covered the land and there was no desert. You've seen the videos. It was so."

Liam leaned closer as the old man spoke. Though well preserved, the last two hundred years had worn on the man, besetting him with frailty that left little doubt of the short time he had left. "It was more than two hundred years ago," he said, "when I first had the vision. There had been other prophecies and they all came true, but they were small tidings. The Prophecy of the Seven was different. I still remember it. 'Our ancient scriptures spoke of the *Grigori*, gods who served the Eternal One who were cast from his rule and dwelt among us. Their offspring were mighty and of renown. Such has happened again, as seven stars have found displeasure among the Eternal One. In his wise justice, he has given them a second chance. They may reject his grace. They will fall upon us and four will seek revenge. Their might will be terrible and their influence untenable. They will push the others to war and the catastrophe will be great. Yet, there is hope. An impenetrable, everlasting city shall be built. With all their strength, they will burn to bring destruction to us, but we will stand.'

"And it came to be, but all was not lost. We were able to build a city in time, this great pyramid in which we dwell, over a mile high and more-so deep, home to almost a million people. So few believed and it was too late for the rest. Novum was built and the doors were closed when those terrible spirits were cast from the heavens and made flesh among us.

"Jacob, chief of the fallen, had indeed conspired against the Eternal One, coercing the other six to unwittingly help. The Eternal One found them out, yet he pitied them and they were given another chance here in our world. As prophesied, revenge burned in Jacob's heart for he and three others sought to take the earth from its maker and claim it as their own. But Dorian led the other two fallen to oppose Jacob and to protect Novum. All else was lost, their war laid the earth to waste but the City was protected. Then, one day Jacob disappeared for no apparent reason and remains in hiding.

"Someday, I think something will come of all this and there is still the Tartarus Project. I haven't lived this long without reason. I can feel it in my bones. I have one prophecy left in me. Make ready, boy, because I suspect you may yet have a part to play."

Now Liam played his part. They had built their walls against the fallen, but now that Jacob marched on them again, their only hope was in another fallen, in Dorian who had saved them before by raising the mountains.

The memory assuaged his doubts and Liam wondered yet again what lay beyond the Pass and where he might find Dorian. The people of Novum had been so complacent that they sent a seventeen year old on a dire mission. They had called him a boy, they had ignored the prophet, but when Jacob came they would know that he was the man who had found Dorian in time to save them. For now, he could only walk. He would hope that Dorian was near, that he could get to him in time. He would remember that he was a man marked by fire.

# CHAPTER TWO

## *The Mercenary*

Maynard walked the Outlands. Through the crumbling highways and dust, under forgotten roads, through thickets and wild paths Maynard walked. Feet aching in rugged leather boots, and soiled cloak flapping in the stark breeze, he ran fingers through unkempt auburn hair. Traveling from Bowdton, under dilapidated buildings, overgrown and cracked parking lots, and dusty plains, he watched the horizon for Darsk, a town of life and hope.

Hope of fortune, safety, and rest. After pillaging and smuggling, laden with goods from Bowdton, he stepped amongst the ruins, alone save for the occasional rodent or stray dog. There was a time when the silence might have felt eerie, but Maynard had grown accustomed to the quiet.

In tough times such as these, silence—or the lack thereof—could tell a man much, particularly a man wary and laden with goods. Few made the trip between towns, but for those like Maynard, fortuitous and determined, the rewards exceeded the risks.

More than determination or the lucrative incentive, the broadsword across Maynard's back provided insurance on his journey. The ominous blade perturbed any threat.

In the nights, small outlets provided shelter during sleep and afforded a fire on occasion. He had watched the stray cats, ever ready at the slightest stirring from their sleep, and he emulated them inasmuch as a man could, always wary of approaching dangers in the night.

By day, his eyes, nose, and ears protected him, muscles eager to draw his sword at any threat. On this day, gray ruins of lost roads and forgotten buildings decayed under the cloudy skies, the eastern wind a harbinger of more than the skeletons of long fallen edifices.

From among the stones, dried weeds, and concrete ruins emerged the outlaws, their stench of sweat and old blood in the air. Maynard drew his blade, the sharpened steel ringing as he unsheathed it, half as wide as the length of his forearm and almost as long as he was tall.

"That sword is almost as big as you," one man said, perhaps the leader, bug-eyes searching him, leathered lips cracking to form a sour-toothed grin. He was one of the five before Maynard, eleven counting the other six ready to attack from behind. "Too big for you, I think. For any man, really." Had Maynard been unawares, they might have robbed him without preamble. They knew that he sensed them, and in their desperation they came out, surrounding him, hoping that perhaps their numbers could intimidate him into turning over his possessions.

"I am best left alone," Maynard said, hands wrapped around the hilt of his unusually large sword, anticipating the coming threat. "It wouldn't be a fair fight."

"You don't get a fair fight," the bug-eyed man said. "You get robbed. The end."

"You misunderstand me," Maynard replied. "It wouldn't be fair to you."

"You're all talk," the man said. He would have been right had Maynard been anyone else.

"Then enough talk," Maynard said. "Let me pass or get on with it."

Their circle began to constrict. Too impatient to coordinate with his comrades, one outlaw charged Maynard, sword swaying in his hands as he rushed at him. Through blade and flesh and bone, Maynard's sword sank into the man from shoulder to ribcage. The man fell, no sound other than the trickle of his blood and his maimed body thudding to the ground.

The rest came at once. Twisting and ducking, Maynard slashed. Two chipped and rusted swords came at him, their owners' bellies open before they could near him. He dodged a descending club, his blade slicing through the wielder's head before the bludgeon reached the ground.

More than the initial eleven attacked, mobbing him. Blood flew into the sky, intestines fell from his victims, as he blocked and dodged. Death and sweat surrounded him, their attack unceasing.

A jab took him in the back as he shoved his sword behind him, meeting bone and flesh. Bringing it back around, he felled three other opponents. He continued to swing, his speed and precision rousing agonized cries, yet they continued to close around him, more than he could defend against. If he could only fight his way through, but the circle thickened.

He blocked ax and sword, cudgel and dagger, but soon he would miss and their weapons would find him. Then the sound of the fight changed, new cries of terror arising from the outskirts. The circle broke and he maneuvered to the side, slashing his way from the outlaws.

Chaos reigned as a newcomer, a large bald man, fought bare handed, undaunted by blade or bludgeon. One dared to fight the big man, his head dashed against the broken asphalt after. Another nearby screamed, cradling the stump where his arm had been.

Away from the gruesome sight, another man, in all black, fought, sword moving with swift and fatal grace. The woman nearby slung a chain at her victims as a dog-like creature defended her, muzzle at the throat of one attacker.

Within moments, the dead lay at their feet, and as the shock of battle died, weariness took Maynard. He leaned upon his bloody sword, his adrenaline fading, each bruise and wound coming to life. Those who had aided him stood nearby, and he watched them warily, though he had no energy to defend himself if they meant him harm.

The man dressed in black, tall and thin, but broad of shoulder and commanding spoke first, his voice deep and punctuated. "That is quite the sword. Even a man as tall and muscled as you should have difficulty wielding it."

"Who are you?" Maynard asked between labored breaths.

"Call me Jacob," he said. "My companions are Amelia and Cain." Amelia stood in robes, pale skin and dark features, eyes fixed on Jacob as he spoke. The creature that had fought alongside her had vanished, like a magician's coin, but his memory of the part dog, part lizard, part dead thing would not fade. Cain stood even taller than Jacob, muscles exposed under a thin shirt, curving, ambiguous tattoos interlacing around his copper-colored shoulders.

"I am Maynard, and I owe you my gratitude." What reward would they demand?

"A strong name," Jacob said. "May I ask where you got such a sword?"

"After the war, there weren't any guns, so my family took on smithing."

"And you took up the family trade?"

"No, my older brother took up the trade. I am a mercenary, a warrior who does what's needed if the price is right. My father said I was the swiftest and strongest son born in generations and that I was worthy of it."

"Well," Jacob said, "we could use a sword like that and someone who can wield it." These were clearly formidable people. Amelia may have appeared young, but the agelessness in her keen eyes said different. Moments ago, Cain had menacingly butchered a dozen men with his bare hands, but now he stood collected, almost charming. His eyes were older and wiser than the rest of him appeared.

Jacob must have observed his trepidation. "We had been tracking these outlaws for days with little success." He motioned at the carnage before them. "You made quick work with a dozen before we had to step in. That kind of skill is rare."

"And if I hadn't been so skilled, you would have let them kill me?"

"You wouldn't have been the first," replied Jacob. "But you fought well and now I'm asking you to do so for me. There's a great opportunity in this for you." He meant it, Maynard could tell that much.

"Sounds dangerous," Maynard said.

"You took a dozen of them. What are you worried about?"

*Fourteen, actually.* "You flatter, but it's a tempting offer. What's in it for me?"

"What do you want? Money? Glory? Fame? I can give you those things. This will be the greatest event in two hundred years and those closest in my cabal will be greatly rewarded according to their desires. You have heard of the seven?"

"Stories for women and holy men," Maynard replied, though he knew little of them.

"The stories are true," Amelia said, offended. "They speak of an age of immortals and would-be gods. The war is far from over."

"You were headed west," Jacob said. "Give up your journey to Darsk. Follow us north to Gully. Seldom do your spices and goods reach beyond the swamp to the coast, they will fetch more there. I

33

have plenty of gold myself and will pay you. From there, we will hire a ship to the northern island."

"Who are you that I should go with you across the sea to the desert lands? There is nothing there."

"I am Jacob, one of the seven. So are Cain and Amelia and a fourth who awaits us. On the northern island there is more than desert. Beyond the wastes is the ring of mountains guarding an uncursed land. There is the City."

"You take me for a fool?" Maynard asked. "That's not even in the wives' tales."

"Come now," Jacob said. "You ask who I am, but I'll tell you who you are. You don't look a day over thirty, but you're going on fifty. Your father was well preserved too and his father only recently passed. Your family lives unnaturally long.

"There are few explanations to that. Perhaps two hundred years ago one of the fallen healed one of your ancestors and it gave long life to your family. They say it happened every so often. Maybe you're the descendant of one of our bastards.

"But look at you, Maynard. Your father did not give you that sword as some sort of birthright or reward for being a warrior. Your mother died during childbirth and he sent you away with that as soon as his conscience allowed it.

"You've been an opportunist ever since, and I find that a worthy trait. Forget these small towns; you'll never rise to greatness there. One day that will end for you, and I doubt it will be in the comfort of your own bed. No longer live as the wandering tradesman. Come with me. I have a plan. We will take this city and when the war is over, you will have peace and power. You may not be immortal like us, but you are the closest thing, and that makes you more than a mercenary. Listen, Maynard. I would make you a ruler."

This man knew much, too much perhaps, but he didn't know everything. Maynard took a breath, the air putrid. He had stopped leaning on this sword, and eyed it, the dried blood crusting along the blade. In Darsk he might find money, decent ale, and a woman to warm his bed. If he followed this stranger into the swamplands and to the flea-infested coastal town of Gully, they would sail to the desert.

Was this what it would take to get ahead in life? Was there glory on that distant island? Could he trust this man?

"I will come with you as far as the coast," Maynard said. "I pledge nothing further."

"That's good enough," Jacob replied. "You will come to see that I speak true. Let us turn north and be rid of this stench."

# CHAPTER THREE

## *Ghosts*

*Follow the river*, they had told him. Liam's shoulders sagged under the day's heat. As night neared, he debated as to where he would sleep. The river ran wide and deep, harboring the unknown beneath its placid stream. He would sleep away from there. He walked, Novum jutting behind him from the northern horizon, a distant, ubiquitous reminder of his trudging pace. Had he a horse or vehicle, he could hope to arrive at the Pass in less than an hour, but the City would spare nothing so rare and expensive. Had they taken the prophet seriously, had they more than humored him, they might have given him more, but it had been up to Ferrith and Standon to supply him.

The zeal that had been present outside of the City faded as the sunlight dissipated, the implications of his journey burdening him now that the chaos of leaving the City was behind him. The abrupt cessation of his education had given way to another duty, and the newfound busyness kept fear or excitement at bay as he prepared to leave Novum. They opened the doors for him, ushered him into this old world, but they would not come with him on what they considered to be a farce. Elijah kept faith enough in him, but even Liam's own parents showed little concern, demonstrating an unsettling apathy. Then again, his mother's tears had to mean something.

"To the Pass and back," the High Priest had told him disingenuously. "A short journey of no consequence." A few who took the prophet seriously thought that Liam would find Dorian after the two-day journey to the Pass and then return after another two days' travel back, Dorian with him. It seemed only the prophet and Ferrith had believed that Dorian might live far beyond the Pass, if he lived at all. And if he was not at the Pass and nothing lay beyond it...

Dorian lived and he could be found. Otherwise the prophecy was nothing more than the ravings of a man who should have, by all reason, died long ago. *I am marked by fire*, he reminded himself to parry the loneliness, but in the darkening desert such hollow thoughts carried little weight. Elijah had called for the rite of fire and it had proved the prophecy and Liam's call to find Dorian. It had been a miracle. It had to mean something. It had been a moment of surety, of confidence, and hope. Yet, now the doubt of the priests fell upon him.

Adding to his worries, his pack dug into his shoulders, and the sun sank lower with each of Liam's steps. He decided to make camp a few yards from the river. Unshouldering his pack, he dropped to his knees. Relief came to his feet that had never walked so much in one day, and he lay out his bedroll.

Even with his plethora of provisions, he ignored his hunger, stretching onto his roll and pulling a blanket over him. The Milky Way's arc cascaded in the soft hues of black and blue, nebulous pinks and radiant stars scattered throughout the spangled belt. He slept before he could think much about this new and possibly dangerous world.

He dreamed of an animal cackling and howling in the night, of the trickling of water, of hot desert days and cold desert nights, of that room at the top of the Central Spire, and of hope. He emerged from the convoluted sleep to the sun's rays stretching over the distant mountains, ushering in a new day. The sound of the flowing water made for a peaceful waking.

He pushed himself to his feet, muscles aching as he rolled his blanket and placed it in the pack. Before he continued, he splashed water on his face, filled his canteen, and ate a meager breakfast of jerky. Though sore, he was eager to continue his trek. In the daylight, the mountains had grown in daunting immensity, the Pass viewable in greater detail, but he faltered.

The ridge of mountains rounded the plains, halting directly to the south, giving way to one gap between their towering ridges, but at the foot of the Pass, the gap closed to a prodigious mound of rubble blocking his way. He had known it would be there, the barrier that obstructed any sojourner from entering the ring of mountains, but even so, it daunted him.

*Follow the river.* From the northwestern sea, it flowed through a labyrinth of caves under the mountains, through the sparse forest that sat against the northern walls, and into the desert around Novum. How long would he follow the river once it passed beyond the mountains? No soul had come beyond the Pass. Whether they deterred determined travelers or the ruins were warded by Dorian, no one could guess. Dorian had raised the mountains, so it was possible that he had indeed protected the City. Or the simple answer, the one Liam feared most, was that nothing existed beyond the mountains. Not even Dorian.

His spirits lifted later in the day as the mountains drew closer, their walls growing as Liam neared them. Alone and light-packed, his journey had been quick, leaving him hopeful that the ruins might not be as precarious as he feared. The river narrowed as it ran from the dry terrain and into the ruins, dipping beneath stone and debris.

Behind him stood Novum, the monolithic pyramid made insignificant by the distance. He returned his gaze to the edge of the ruins, the remnants of buildings, long fallen, sitting in silent and sordid mounds, their steel and brick crumbled things of old, sloping upward between the sheer, sentinel mountains. Broken stone and concrete trailed in memories of some dire last stand. Cacti and weeds sprouted along the cracks, naked vines climbing fractured walls and twisting around the fallen pillars. The path narrowed ahead, fading into a hill of gnarled metal, cracked walls, and dirt. Though the apex fell hundreds of feet short of the mountain's height, it still narrowed in a steep graduation between them, no less than two hundred feet from the ground.

Liam's feet ached more, never having walked so far in his lifetime. Nearly thirty-five miles had taken their toll, even with the best of footwear, but he might yet crest the ruins before nightfall if he persevered, and perhaps some respite awaited him on the other side. Better yet, he might retire early with a light supper and rest before climbing on the morrow. At age seventeen, he had done what no other man had done since the City closed its doors. He had emerged from the great pyramid and trekked to the foot of the mountains, and now he wanted his rest, leaving the mystery of the Pass for the next day.

However, there was time enough and even should night fall before he reached the other side, the ruins would be little less restful a place than the hard-packed earth where he stood. The river flowed freely into the ruins, as if from under the dilapidation it emerged into something hopeful beyond. Resisting whatever inkling told him to wait until morning, he placed his hands on the first slab of fallen and jagged concrete and began the climb.

Working his way up, he kept toward the center, just above the river that trickled out of sight under the weight of the rubble. He had never sweat so much in the City, but as the moisture leaked from his pores, he remembered his survival lessons. Dehydration was not always obvious, and Liam recalled that he would need to be deliberate about drinking water, while also rationing it. The sun glared off the wreckage, piercing heat without shade, a relentless enemy, but he carried on, drinking frequently to compensate for the moisture lost through sweat. The training only went so far, the City's gymnasium a poor teacher to face the slope of the wild. Tinted panes had protected him there, but in the Outlands each new foothold required another dry and hot breath.

Whatever he worked towards, he hoped his efforts would be rewarded. This subcontinent had been terraformed, a mass undertaking that made it hospitable for a place like the City. Great caverns ran under the entire large island, a permanent source of freshwater implemented should Novum or their small world run out of such a thing. Yet, deeply welled fresh water meant nothing if the outside humans had faded in the gods' wars or among the annihilation left by them.

For all he knew, it was a thriving land, long kept from the City. Outside of the northwestern wood, no flora or fauna appeared within the mountains, so if humanity did live beyond their walls, they either thrived or lived in poverty equal to the desert and ruin that surrounded Liam.

Looking behind, the ruin fell further than he had expected. He had made good time but his appetite had grown. He found a concrete slab that was near level and rested. From his pack he retrieved a can of food. "Spaghetti and meatballs it is," he said, popping the can open. The pack held every provision Ferrith could anticipate. Food was an obvious necessity. An assortment of metals, mostly in medallion or coin shapes, would hopefully serve as currency. If not, Liam would have to barter away some of his other amenities. A lighter, a small jar of lamp oil, tablets to purify water, a change of clothes, and other oddities that might be of help. It was halfway through his meal that he realized he had forgotten to read his grandfather's letter. How could he have? Dismissing his guilt, he found the envelope and broke its seal, opening the letter to his grandfather's scratchy penmanship.

# GHOSTS

*My dear Liam,*

*You are a man now, though the world wouldn't know it. But do not think that it makes you skilled or wise, for a wise man knows that he has much to learn. Be brave and courageous, but be humble.*

*When the angels fell, we learned much about God. It seems that we learned so much, all the more to forget. Some thought that he had forgotten us or even that he had cursed us. However, I do not believe that to be the case. I believe he watches over us, especially you.*

*And so, whatever Tasrael may intend, when I say that providence would have you go alone, I do not really mean that you are alone. My prophecy and the god who gave it to me goes with you.*

*Press on, no matter what dangers assail you, for so long as you live, there is always hope. The darkest of evils will one day be overthrown and I believe that day is nearly upon us.*

*Hold fast.*

Though the words were more homiletic than sentimental, they stirred Liam's emotions. He at once felt a longing to return home, but also a determination to see this through. He took a deep breath and steeled himself, rising to continue his journey. He had more confidence in his grandfather than Novum's god. So long as his grandfather's words went with him, he was not alone.

He climbed the ruin, never too steep, but still wearisome, and he hoped that those like the High Priest had been right. His grandfather had allegedly never been wrong, but he could not imagine journeying much farther beyond this wall and into the Pass without some success. There had been no speculation as to Dorian's whereabouts. If Dorian did not reside just beyond the ruins, perhaps Liam could find some indication or direction, and hopefully it was close. Whatever the case, he would have to be on his guard.

His muscles shook at times, his hands already callusing from the rough rocks. After what felt like hours, finding his footing amongst the rubble, he found that his determination had yielded less headway than he initially thought. The derelict path grew steeper, and the sun soon fell to the shadows of the mountains. Something about the coming dark unsettled him.

As the sun fell among the western reaches, evening coming too soon, tiredness overtook him. He paused a moment, standing in the growing shadow, debating on the best course of action. For some strange reason, the idea of sleeping in the ruins chilled him, a haunting and unshakable notion. Stranger yet, he felt compelled to go back, to make his descent, return to the City, and declare his failure. The su  n sank lower, its faint glow showing him the way toward the Pass. He moved upward, muscles and breath daring to fail him, but he navigated each stone and slab.

Each hand and foothold led to the next, and he gripped one jutting boulder, hoisting himself up and over. A stone gave way and he fell, knee slamming into the hard concrete as he continued to roll, each tumble awakening a new bruise. He stopped at the foot of a small dip in the ruin, gasping for breath, putrid air filling his lungs. He sputtered, dust and acridity billowing from his mouth. He pushed himself from the ground, looking to his watch, dismayed by the blank screen on his wrist. He tapped the screen and pushed the buttons. Nothing. His heart pounded with the realization, but not before he saw the source of the stench.

Liam stumbled back before the corpse. Its decay greeted him, wide eyes and mouth agape. Each step away pained his knees, bruised from the fall, but he moved from the body and then leaned against an old and broken concrete slab, rubbing a knee. Never had Liam witnessed a corpse, but the unsightly thing before him lay deteriorating, shriveled, almost as if mummified, the poor soul's failed venture beyond the Outland a bloody end.

The first sign of life in this world was decay. Ignoring the pain in his knees, he gave the body a wide berth and pushed up and over the next concrete slab, daring to turn his back on the corpse to move further away.

When the initial shock of seeing the corpse wore off, Liam took solace in knowing that life did reside beyond the mountains, a more certain hope that Dorian was somewhere out there. The corpse could not have been more than a few days old. Even as Liam left the city, this man might have fallen to his death, a realization that also served as a reminder that the ruins were treacherous. He was fortunate that he only had a few bruises instead of stumbling to his own end.

A compulsion urged him down, from where he had come, yet he climbed further up, letting the setting sun leave the corpse to the darkness. Within a few feet the decayed smell faded and he continued, but something else deterred him. A new sense found him among the eerie ruins, a chill in spite of the warmth, something terribly wrong. Climbing the rough stones, often using both hands and feet to pull himself forward, he persevered.

A tangle of hair among dried blood clung to a jagged, broken brick. Indistinguishable bones littered his path. Then came the whispers.

*Go back.* Inhumane and otherworldly tones filled his ears and soul, soothing yet stern. Was it his imagination? Liam took another step, careful not to lose traction, his hands pulling him up the next slab.

*Go back.* It was like something else was speaking into his mind. Liam shook his head, as if it might ward off the whisper. It wasn't natural, not quite right. Was it the ghost of the corpse he had seen? Was it some malignant spirit?

Liam fought fear. He had to press on, to find the man Dorian, to seek any hope of stopping Jacob. Or did he? They said the Pass protected Novum, a city walled with glass as hard as steel. Surely this was unnecessary. Dorian might be anywhere among the vast desolation sure to reside on the other side of the rubble. Liam was one person, no doubt inadequate at finding Dorian. He had stopped, standing among the sloping rubble. He should go back, undo the work of the afternoon's climb, and camp at the foot of the ruins. Tomorrow he could decide.

"No," he said aloud, willing himself to continue, recalling his grandfather's words to press on. The night sank in, the moon offering little light in the treacherous rubble. *Go back.* He found that he had receded a few paces, the previous moments vacant from his memory. He regained his willpower, and climbed back up the shattered concrete and jutting metalwork. He had to retain his senses, to follow the prophet's directions, to *hold fast*. He took another step, almost slipping on the uneven stone.

Mind fought body as he ushered himself onward. It would be better to give up, to return home and let someone else go in his stead. He should have brought Perry. He should have brought an army. These were not his thoughts. He had been chosen, the one who had walked through fire. Careful in the darkness he continued against the strain of his body's will.

*Go back. You will fail. They all fail.*

"No," Liam said, breathing heavily. "Not me."

The voice's incoherent screaming filled his head, its talons locked into him, drawing him back, compelling him to retreat. Fighting the urge that possessed him, he took another step. The voice abandoned reason, its soothing and caressing tone absent, replaced by impatience.

*You are not a man marked by fire. You are a boy.*

"Damn you," Liam said.

*We are the guardians of the Pass, the Last Saint, the siren to draw you away. No good can come of anyone's passing. Leave. Go back. No one has ever made it through.*

"I'm different. I am a man. I am marked by fire."

*You are a boy.*

When the next rush hit, Liam fought the obligating wave, the urge to go back, the madness creeping into his mind. Thirst and hunger took him, unsated by the remainder of his canteen. He pressed on against the madness, teeth gritted, firm steps one after another.

Hands griped the rough holds, the night sinking in. *Go back.* Liam crawled now, receding back at times, regaining control of his body, and then resuming forward. More than once he slipped, doubting whether it was by his own clumsiness or by the nature of whatever spoke to him, whatever haunted this place. Weary, he stopped and rested, the whispers creeping and cascading around him. The sourness on the back of his dry tongue reminded him that just a few minutes ago his lunch had splattered on granite slab as he hunched over in pain, trying to keep the vomit from splashing onto his shoes. With every moment more dizzying than the last, he wondered if it was the only time he had puked.

From the foot of the ruins, the climb had appeared shorter, and now every bone in his body told him that he would never make it. A small voice inside him—his own voice—told him to go on, a small truth to which he clung. Pressing on once more, pain shot through his knee, but he yelled, not in agony, but defiance. Eyes forward, ready to reach his next destination and whatever laid there, the man marked by fire ignored the torturous voice.

*What difference will you make? You are a pampered youngling. You will eventually break. We are the guardians of the ages.*

The voice terrified him. *We are the Last Saint.* Was it waiting for him in the distance or was it all around him? Had the corpse belonged to a man who simply tripped and fell to his death, or had this spirit been the agent of his demise? Or was this voice the spirit of the man who Liam had found dead?

So great was his concentration to resist the voice that he nearly tipped over the edge when he summited the ruins. Abruptly, he had made it. When he pulled himself upon the apex of the ruin, the Pass opened before him. The sloping desolation was behind him, and before him he beheld the expanse nestled between the great walls of the mountains. Their silhouettes loomed, a fissure of stars between them. Lights ran along the walls of each side, a marvel and a mystery illuminating the carved hollows of the mountains' feet.

Lowering himself over the edge with care, Liam began the climb down. Though tired and sore, he had to escape the voices, no resolve left for their temptations. Heavy of breath, he felt each step, careful as he worked his way down.

It felt like his descent was taking hours when he slipped. Momentarily weightless, falling back, his arms flailed in the air. Frantic fingers grasped the nothing rushing around him. With the impact the air left him. Gasping and chest heaving, he struggled to inhale. Each attempted breath pained him, like his body would never intake air again. It took long, painful minutes. When the cool night air filled his lungs, he opened his eyes to the stars spreading between the black mountain towers.

He stiffly felt along his body, hands finding the sore and bruised spots, but nothing broken. Letting his arms fall to his sides, he lay for a time, fingers digging into the dirt. He eventually found the energy to stand. The river flowed from under the ruins, cascading around the fallen rubble and out into the Pass. Strange lights lined the mountain sides, rising a few feet high before giving way to the dark walls on either side. The mountains made a looming corridor that ended some ways ahead, though in the dark, Liam could not tell how long it went, nor guess at what lay beyond the exit. When he at last gained his feet, he began to walk along the river, sore and tired, his bruised knees aching. Liam gauged that the mountains were likely several hundred feet apart, with the river winding more or less directly between them. Most surprising was the bridge that curved over the river. For a moment he hesitated, but then crossed it, staggering toward the western wall.

As Liam passed the first mysterious glow in the stones, he discovered that it was a window into a home. This was a town, its shops and dwellings built directly into the caverns of the mountains. Had the people carved this out themselves or was this Dorian's design? He passed the darkened windows of closed shops. He beheld the dimly lit abodes of the shopkeepers come home and their families. Cautious of intruding on anyone's privacy, Liam only glanced into the openings, glimpsing wooden tables, clay pots, and humble wares. For a space, a small alley opened up, leading to more homes. In the dim, he thought he saw the figure of a man watching him, but in a blink it was gone and he only stared into a dark alley. Liam pressed on into the Pass.

Though weak, he continued, fighting fatigue and hunger. The sound of boisterous laughter and music grew as he neared the brightest lit part of the western wall. A wooden porch framed the open door, a tavern like something out of the old western movies Liam had vaguely known. He made his way up the steps, slow but hiding his weariness. They did not sound hostile, but it was clear he was a stranger. He ventured inside. The cavern opened up, filled with old wooden tables and chairs, full of men and women too deep in merriment to notice him. Stairs led up to a mezzanine lined with doors. It was a foreign sight, but if nothing else he might hope to find food here. With a little luck, it might also be a place to stay, if anything they had given him in Novum was of worth enough to buy him food and shelter here.

The people at the tables reinforced the western notion. Most of the men boasted facial hair and brimmed hats. The women wore modest dresses, their hair tied in a bun or braided. Hands held cards or tankards, laughter and shouts erupting often, and the piano—slightly out of tune—played heartily to everyone's entertainment.

Those who did look at Liam grimaced. Here, as rugged as the last two days' travel had left him, he was the outlander, but he was more concerned that his darker skin might be the reason for the attention. Yet, no one moved to bother him. He maneuvered around the crowded tables, finding nothing available but a spot at the bar on the back wall. He almost ran into a bustling waitress as he made his way to the bar, the only piece of polished wood in the tavern.

The bar stretched before a row of oaken casks set along the back wall, oil lanterns hanging over the great round barrels. Other lanterns encircled the room, illuminating the old paintings and decorations along the walls, relics that might be long lost precious works of art. At the end of the bar sat the cash register, mostly made from plastic, out of place among the rustic and ancient world around him.

Liam pulled out a wobbly stool, ready to take a seat and rest, but a man two seats down spoke. "Barkeep, ale for the stranger. And food. On me." The man continued to look into the bottom of his mug as he spoke. Surely he meant food and ale for someone else, but he spoke on, plainly addressing Liam. "Some say Jacob didn't leave and that it's his ghost that haunts the ruins." He still kept his gaze down. "Others say they are the souls tortured by Cain. Some think they are superstitions, though even they don't dare climb the ruins. The few that do never return." The man looked up at last, a kind face, long and rugged, dark hair flecked with gray. "Come closer."

Reluctant, Liam moved from his rickety barstool and took a seat next to the man. The bartender set a mug of ale before Liam. Though wary, Liam took the libation, desperate for sustenance and thankful that this barstool did not wobble. Unsure of what to say, Liam took a sip from the ale in silence. He had enjoyed the occasional glass of wine with Ferrith, and Perry always had contraband, but he had never tasted beer. Bitterness filled his mouth, but sweet undertones warmed and relaxed him. He should be more cautious, but he had little choice but to find solace in the man's offer. Halfway through the pint, the soreness dulled and he looked to the man, who still remained silent.

The food came and Liam began to eat eagerly, forgetting his prior resolve to be cautious. He bit into the chicken leg, the juice running down his chin, and then he ate the bread, though it was a bit stale. The refined, too-perfect food of Novum was no match for this meal. After a while the man spoke. "Eat fast, young one. A few days ago a stranger passed through our town to venture into the ruins, years after the last unfortunate adventurer made an attempt. I do not doubt his fate. However, you are the first to come out of the ruins. I trust most of these people, but all the same, we cannot be too careful. We must leave soon." Was this man the figure he had glimpsed in the alley?

"We?" Liam said with sudden mistrust. "Leave?" He should have been more wary from the start.

"I don't mean to harm you. I wouldn't waste food on you if I meant to. You will have to trust me." Liam tensed at the man's words. "I wish I had more time to earn your confidence," the man continued, "but we need to leave before word reaches anyone that you came from beyond the mountains. They will think you a wraith, or worse, discover who you really are."

"Who I really am? You know who I am?"

"In a way," the man said. "I have been expecting someone like you. Eat and come with me. Then we'll talk." Still ravenous, Liam let the smell of the food tempt him and finished all but the remainder of the bread. The man talked for a while, filling the awkward silence. "Those who have braved the ruins never return. As I suspect you know, no one has ever come from the northern borders into our town. Those in this little town who dare climb the ruin to peer beyond speak of dark things. One would think that a mere boy could not pass one way or another among the ruins, but here you are. I have peeked beyond the ruins, just once, and it weighed on my heart so heavily that I dare not seek to view beyond them again. I'd not speak of it, so tell me what my glimpse could not. What lies beyond them? Does the City still stand? Did any of those brave men make it into the City?"

Liam set his mug down. "The City stands, though none have entered or departed it in two hundred years. I am the first since it closed its doors. I don't know its surroundings very well. It's mostly desert, though there's a small forest against the northwest mountain wall. The mountains surround the city, sheer and tall just as they stand here." He looked into the man's honest eyes, weighing the decision. "I think you want to help, but I won't risk it. I need to leave." This new world might be treacherous and his mission was too vital for him to compromise it with trust. If Dorian wasn't here, the man might know his whereabouts, but he had been too forthcoming, too bold for Liam to believe him wholly trustworthy.

He stood and shouldered his pack, turning his back on the man. A hand grasped his arm, firm and strong. He tried to pull away, but the man's grip did not relent. He looked to the man whose eyes held firm, though not unkind. Liam searched the bar, looking for help, but no one noticed them. "I'm afraid I can give you no choice," the man said, and before Liam could stop him, the man directed him behind the bar. He pushed Liam. "Come boy, I don't want to hurt you, but there are things we cannot talk about here. Just hear me out, and if you want to leave after that, I'll let you go in peace."

The stern grip compelled Liam to walk behind the bar. He reached for his sword, ready to fight the man, only to find it missing. The man held it like a cane, leaning on it, his other hand clutched around Liam's arm. "I'm afraid I'm going to have to borrow your sword. It's a good thing the City had the sense to give you that. Come now, on you go." How had the man gotten his sword without him noticing? The corridor was dark, but the man directed him, pulling Liam through twisting dark tunnels, down turns and paths. If the man left him here, he might never see the light of day again.

The sound of trickling water reverberated in the passage. "The river curves down into the caves," the man said. "It may be desert beyond our home in the mountains, but underneath is a system of underground reservoirs, a labyrinth of lakes, tunnels, and caverns. Not too much further now, and we'll be at my quarters."

After another turn they entered into an alcove, dimly lit by an oil lamp that revealed a small room furnished with a bed, nightstand, and small book-laden table. Two splintering chairs tucked under the table, which sat adjacent to a kitchenette. At the opposite end of the room, a quaint stairway led into the upper floor, a wooden door built into the bottom space for storage. The bolted front door, more rotted and splintered wood, fit the cavern's opening crudely, but enough to keep curious eyes from peering into this place where privacy was clearly cherished.

Liam trembled, though he managed to steady his breathing, controlling his fear. It was only a slight relief when the man threw Liam's sword on the nearby bed. He let go of Liam's arm and made his way into the kitchen with a limp. "Have a seat. I'll make tea. And don't bother with your sword. Just because I'm a cripple doesn't mean I'm inept. If I wanted to do you harm, you never would have come out of that tunnel." He turned on a small burner, though its source of heat was unapparent. Once the kettle began heating, the man turned to Liam. "Well," the man said, "sit."

Liam took a chair, never turning his back on the man, and put it as close to the bed and his sword as he dared.

"I should have brought my cane," the man said. "I left it in my haste to meet with you. Your sword worked well enough, I suppose." He was silent until the water began to boil and within

51

moments he had cleared a space on the table, stacking books on towers that already threatened to fall, and served them tea. He took a chair, stretching out his left leg as he sat. "We are safe for the moment," he said. "And for too long this evening we have forgone introductions. To the folks here in Avianne, I am called Ollie, a harmless man not quite old. I'm well-invested, but have kept a low profile. *You* can call me Oliver, but before we talk much more, you'll need to tell me your name and purpose."

Liam eyed the door and then his sword. The man Oliver did not react, but waited patiently. He had little choice but to trust the man. He took a sip of the tea. It was weak but soothing. "I am Liam, the eighth generation descendant of the Great Prophet Elijah. The prophet himself lives and sent me."

"The prophet lives?" Oliver asked, looking surprised for the first time. "That makes sense of some things. The histories of the seven…What else?"

"When I was young, he told me that all of my grandfathers had lived normal lives of normal length, but that he had outlived them to make one more prophecy." The details came vividly as Liam recounted the story to Oliver. Though the prophet was a *great* grandfather seven times over, Liam had known him only as Grandfather. To the rest of the world he was the Great Prophet Elijah, a mystery that had outlived its use, but nonetheless integral in Liam's life and training. The old man lived in chambers below the sanctuary, a modest room, but close to his place in the temple.

He summoned Liam one night, sharing bread and wine borrowed from the communion stores. "Tonight will be the night," he had said. "Tonight I will sleep and dream like I did so long ago." The old man had slept, Liam dozing by his chair. Liam emerged from sleep and looked over to his grandfather. His dark eyes were open, and Liam knew what to do.

Tasrael and the other priests came to the summons as a formality. Tired and irritated, they met the prophet in the sanctuary. They approached the pulpit, walking across the polished marble floor midst the vaulted, painted ceilings, and empty dark-varnished pews. Grasping disheveled robes, they knelt on the steps before the dais where the prophet leaned on the pulpit and Liam stood ready to support him.

The old man at the pulpit pushed himself erect, the age fading, and for a moment the Great Prophet stood before Liam and the high priests. "When I was young," he said, his voice echoing in the empty sanctuary, "I made the Great Prophecy that brought us here. Tonight I make my last prophecy. The seven rise again. The Morning Star unites with Jacob and they approach, bringing doom on us from the west. The shelter of Novum will no longer stand against the wars of men and gods. Our only hope is Dorian."

The high priests doubted but the prophet convinced them to build the fire. "This task is for you, my boy" his grandfather had told him. "I knew long ago that something like this awaited you. You will be marked by fire. You and no one else. You must go."

Now Liam was in the Outlands, telling his story to a stranger. At the time he had been a bystander, hardly aware of the implications of what this made him, but now he looked at this man Oliver and he knew that if Dorian was not at the Pass — Avianne, Oliver had called it — that something more perilous awaited him. If he could trust this man Oliver, then at least he would not be alone.

"The Great Prophet's descendant," Oliver wondered when Liam had finished the story of his journey. "I should have guessed. He had hair like yours when he was younger. He might still, for all I know."

Though old, the prophet hadn't balded, and still boasted a thick gray mane of dreadlocks. "How could you know what the prophet looked like? The City has been closed for two hundred years."

Oliver smiled. "Elijah saw true. The seven angels—in as much as they might be labeled such—did fall. Many mortals joined in their wars. They began as the City closed its doors. I had not entered the City. I didn't believe, even though I had seen the boy often in the media. I guess there was evidence enough, but not so much that it convinced me to pack up my possessions and go to some distant island. It was too big a risk. Many corporations invested in the City. If Elijah was right, they were safe. If he was wrong, they had the most lavish resort the world had ever seen. I was too cynical, you can see why.

"We all soon discovered that the boy prophet spoke true. By then it was too late for me. I lost much in those first months and then it was either run or fight. I was one of the first to join Dorian."

"And you've lived for two hundred years?" Liam asked.

"I wish I knew how myself. How has the prophet lived so long? We all have something we have to do, I suppose."

"So what now? Where is Dorian?"

"Not here," Oliver replied. "I'm sure you've gathered as much. Your journey is not nearly over. My leg makes it hard to travel by foot. It was injured in the war and Charis did her best to heal what she could of it. I often suspect it is the cause of my long life. You, however, are young and strong and I happen to have a hunch as to where Dorian went. I have respected his apparent wishes to be left alone, if for no other reason than the duties that occupy me here. But it's time we seek him out."

"What's out there?" Liam asked, trepidation growing that Dorian was not as close as he would have liked.

"Desert, my boy," Oliver replied. "Some dunes and patches of sparse growth, but mostly flat and dry desert. Towns are mostly scattered directly south of us, a central line down the island. Dorian's doing on his way south so long ago. There are other towns to the east and west, but they are harder to find if you don't know how to read the stars. The coastal towns are dangerous these days."

"It's all more desert?"

"Mostly. There's water, but it's hundreds of feet down, part of the terraforming. One of the few benefits left to us by the City. It's dry but not as hot as some deserts, as the terrain is the result of unnatural forming. You'll get used to it. The real question is, can you ride a horse?"

"There were lessons in the City, but the time and space with horses was limited. They are valuable animals, often used by the Enforcers to keep the peace. What time I spent with them went well enough." The need of a horse meant that Dorian was far, delaying his return to Novum. Had he thought finding Dorian would be that short and easy? Was the tension in his stomach anticipation or anxiety?

"That will have to do," Oliver said. "Tomorrow, I will buy you a horse. Being alive for over two hundred years makes it easy to make wise investments. Among other things, that tavern of mine has made me a small fortune. I will finance your journey south."

"I have gold and other metals," Liam said.

"That may be sufficient. Some towns insist on coin or bartering, but almost everyone takes metals. They usually deal by the gram, so be wary and make sure they have an honest scale. Some towns work by trade alone, but often a box of matches or handy knife will get the basics. I have a better sword, so you can trade the flimsy piece of steel they gave you. I'm surprised they even gave you one." Liam eyed his blade, the fading hearth's fire a faint gleam on the metal. There had been archives in Novum, but the sheer amount of information made it almost impossible to know what made one sword better from another. The nobles carried them as a status symbol, but they had rarely if ever been used.

As Oliver and Liam discussed a plan, Liam learned a great deal. Dorian had spent the first few decades after the war making peace and establishing townships, digging wells, and hunting outlaws. The fallen angel had suspected that Jacob hid on the southern island—of which Liam had no prior knowledge—so after a relative peace, Dorian became a hermit in the canyon at the southern tip of their northern island.

Oliver gave Liam a gun and showed him how to use it. "A 1911. These things will make it to hell and back." Oliver looked at the gun in his hand before handing it over. "They practically *have* made it to hell and back. Not to trade. Far too rare. Use it only at your greatest need. One clip holds six rounds and you can keep one in the chamber, giving you seven total. Here's another loaded magazine." Liam ran his fingers along the barrel, fingers brushing over the engraving. *.45 ACP*. Banned from the City, a gun was something Liam had never held. He was careful not to point it anywhere dangerous, just as Oliver had instructed. "Guns are rare," Oliver had said, "but this is the most likely type of gun and ammunition you could come across. I have one myself." Liam wanted to fire it, to see what it was like. Instead, he applied the safety as Oliver had shown him, and forced himself to put it away.

The doorway in the stairs yielded a pantry and storage. From it, Oliver gave Liam more food, matches, a flashlight, a small dagger, and a better sword. Indeed, the sword was lighter and nicer than what Novum had given him.

"The desert is harsh, but it's flat. Water flows in the deep caverns, but that doesn't make it readily available. Any town that's survived this long will have tapped into it, but you will have to ration it as you journey between them. Carry as much water as you can, but not so much that it weighs you down. Assuming you make good time, the trip is a fortnight."

Oliver took out a roll of paper, three feet in length, and splayed it across the table, its curling ends dropping over the sides. "It's crude, I know," Oliver said, finger at the center of the landmass, depicted in burnished orange among a sea of faded blue. "After two hundred years, I'm still not much of an artist.

"This circle is the ring of mountains. Your city is somewhere near the center and here we are at the southernmost point. Anyone who's dug deep enough has freshwater, but that didn't stop people from flocking to the shores. However, sea life as a source of food quickly attracted criminal opportunists looking to trade along the coast, though I doubt most of them know of the southern island.

"That said, tribes in the Eastern Pan have discouraged settlers from that area. The main towns seem to run along this central axis. Like I said, Dorian gathered and established them on his journey south, and so he just planted them on his most direct route. When you make it to the—"

"I thought you were coming," Liam said. Less than an hour ago, Liam had believed that he would make the journey alone, that he couldn't trust anybody. Yet, something told him to trust Oliver.

"No," Oliver replied. "I could not travel so far. With my leg, I'd only slow you down. I have a journey of my own, hopefully not so far, but one that will bring us Charis and Nathan."

"You mean to find the other fallen."

"Don't call them that. Not Dorian, Charis, or Nathan anyway. But yes, we have to get back here and to Novum before Jacob."

"I thought the mountains were closed to them," Liam said.

"So did I, but as your prophet says, Jacob has a plan and with the Morning Star involved, who knows what they are capable of? The supposed protection Dorian put on the mountains and Avianne has never been tested. Jacob is clever and wouldn't do anything rash. He likely knows that Dorian watches for him from the south and he will come prepared. Where there is Jacob, there is sure to be Raven, Cain, and Amelia following, wherever they might have been hiding.

"What guards the Pass?" Liam asked.

"Avianne is guarded by a magic Dorian laid here. It is warded by a great sacrifice, a man we suspect knew Elijah better than he let on. Only Dorian could say more."

"Is the Avianne named after him?"

"No," Oliver said, and he cast his eyes down. "Avianne was my wife," he confessed. There was a silence, Liam not knowing what to say, before Oliver continued. "As I was saying. There's this southbound route. You don't want to find yourself in the Eastern Pan and if you deviate too far either way you'll be either in unfriendly territory or too far in the wilderness to survive to the next town. There are cults in the west, though I know nothing of them, save that you want to stick to the towns Dorian established.

"This center path can be tricky. It's not exactly a straight line. Even on flat terrain, you won't be able to see anything more than a few miles into the distance, save for perhaps the highest buildings of the town a bit sooner if you pay attention. But," Oliver noted small dots on the map, "these are formations and markers that can help you on your way. If you think you've deviated too far, try and find a higher ground to give you a better vantage.

"Water, not just for you but your horse, is the most important part in getting you to the southern coast. Dorian spoke of heading towards a more secluded piece of shore. There are sea caves here and two towns. The one slightly north of the shore—Dali—I'd ask about him there. Avoid Glenshore. Like most of the coastal towns, it's held by criminals. Now, let's look at your pack."

They took inventory of Liam's packs, noting that Ferrith had done well to provide him with a utility knife, vitamin packs, and other useful supplies. Going horseback meant that Liam could carry more, so Oliver gave him additional packs, filling them with additional provisions, and placing them among Liam's other things.

Oliver made a pallet for him, apologizing that he lacked the facilities for a proper bath, but Liam was grateful to have a roof over his head on his second night in the Outland. He laid down, ready to sleep when he thought of something.

"Just one more question," Liam said.

"What's that?" Oliver asked, rolling a blanket and stuffing it into a sack.

"Why Dorian? It's bothered me for some time, and I suppose it seems obvious, but why him?"

Oliver looked up from packing. "Dorian is the only one strong enough to stop Jacob. It's not just his power but his ability to persevere, to so often do what many of us cannot or will not. As a leader he knows that it's more important that he surround himself by great people than it is he be great in himself, and we can expedite that if we find Nathan and Charis. Only then can we hope that Avianne survives, though it may too late for my home here. Honestly, Dorian is probably only the beginning. Elijah's prophecy is merely the first step."

Oliver continued to rustle about the room preparing for the next day's journey. Liam fell asleep to the rhythmic thud of his cane.

Liam awoke shortly before sunrise, a small lantern glowing in the dark room as the smell of bacon and eggs filled it. Bruised and stiff, he pulled himself up, rubbing at his sore arms and legs as he made his way to the table for breakfast. The grits, which Oliver said were somehow made from corn, were new to him and he liked them so much that he consumed two generous helpings. As he ate, Oliver reviewed his journey and gave him more advice. Some Liam already knew, some he did not. "The heat is not so bad up here, but once you are out from the shadow of the mountains it gets hot. You may think to take off your clothing to keep cool, but when your skin is blistered and you're dehydrated, you'll think different."

Oliver left to buy a horse and Liam rechecked his bags as sunlight crept through the windows. He was sore, bruises aching with every movement, sand gritting under his clothes. Liam inspected his watch again, anxious that it had stopped working, but thankful he had Oliver. He liked the man, even if he did refer to him as "boy." When Oliver returned, he excitedly motioned Liam to meet him outside. He left the stony inlet and saw the Pass in the morning light. Avianne was a broad stretch between the mountains where carts, horses, camels, and people bustled about their morning business. Dirt roused into small clouds with each footstep on the dusty ground. It was a post-apocalyptic montage of the Old West, Arabian culture, and desperate survival. The townspeople, many whose skin was as dark as Liam's, wore simple clothing, most of the men wearing brimmed hats. Horses led wooden carts laden with foodstuffs, building supplies, or odd wares. Though dull of color and mostly dry, a surprising amount of vegetation flourished in the valley, nestled in sparse patches along the road.

"Camels?" Liam asked.

"It's perfect," Oliver said. "They're less skittish than a horse and they have a little more of a mind of their own. You'll have to learn to ride it, but once you get used to it, they'll be far more useful in the desert. I almost didn't check the eastern side, but Tate had them."

"He didn't have horses?" Liam asked.

"You'll find that most towns have horses and camels alike, though horses can be skittish around camels. It's not different here. Camels are more expensive, as they take more training, but they are quite worth it. Take Lucy," Oliver said, giving Liam the reins of one of the camels.

Liam was cynical about the animal with its smug grin and lackadaisical expression. He took the reins, a simple leather strap, and led it closer to Oliver's home nestled into the rock of the mountainside.

"I'm not sure it likes me," Liam said.

"*She* is a dromedary camel, as indicated by the single hump. I'm not even sure the two-humped Bactrians exist anymore." Oliver gave his own camel a scratch on the neck, which he, or she, seemed to like. "You will need to feed and water her as often as possible, but if you find yourself in a stretch between towns, you can worry more about yourself. She has plenty of sustenance stored in that hump. And, she just gave birth a couple of months ago. Her milk can buy time in a stable in most towns and if you're stranded in the desert, it is high in nutrients. You will also find that wood is somewhat of a commodity, but camel shit is so dry it makes for a decent fire."

Liam's eyebrows scrunched. "You can drink its milk? Light its shit on fire?"

"I assume the City probably has to be more conscientious of its animal resources," Oliver said.

For the first time it occurred to Liam that the chicken and bacon he had eaten was from a real animal. He decided to change the subject. "Will a camel be as fast as a horse?"

"If you end up in a short chase, a camel might be a disadvantage, but over a long distance, a camel can keep a smooth gallop for long stretches."

Lucy's insipid expression was not convincing, however Liam had little choice but to accept. It took half of an hour to saddle and ready the camels. Oliver had not expected to find the beasts and had packed for horse-travel, so it took some reorganizing. He would ride south with Liam to the first town and then they would part ways.

"We're going to Bronton, where I hope to find passage to a town I hear has ale to rival my own, and I have a feeling I know who owns it." Oliver secured another strap as he talked.

"One of the fallen? I mean, one of the angels?" Liam asked.

"Charis, to be specific. I have long wanted to visit, but her city is only rumored and what rumor there is indicates that it is difficult to get into."

"I assume you have a way to get in," Liam said.

"Not at all," Oliver replied. "I was hoping to secure that in Bronton."

Mounting the camel took some time. At first she did not want to let him on, but Liam's stubbornness won out in the end. Oliver showed him how to climb on top from behind the camel, but he slid off twice before succeeding. Once mounted it was only somewhat comfortable. Even with brief horse lessons in the City, the camel would take some adjusting. He expected the bumpy gallop of a horse but was surprised with the camel's smooth gait.

Oliver led them from Avianne, beyond the sparse farmland just outside of the Pass, and Liam saw the true Outland for the first time. It was not so different from the desert around the City, but no mountains loomed in the distance. Only flat, hard-packed, burnt orange desert extended before him, meeting with the cloudless morning sky.

They rode out from under the shadow of the mountains, passing the occasional rolls of rock and sand, formations, and even distant bunches of trees. Through the dry and warm air, they rode to Bronton.

# CHAPTER FOUR

## *The Necromancer*

The boy was inexperienced, but well enough trained with a sword. They had broken from their riding and Oliver proposed they spar to test the boy's capabilities. He moved with a natural fluidity, even if it a bit clumsy. More impressive, Liam did not once blame his mistakes on the days in the saddle, though he was a novice at riding and surely sore. Of course, Liam wasn't adept enough to beat Oliver, but the older man found that he had underestimated the boy.

Oliver had spent his long life mastering as much weaponry and combat as possible, learning to work the forms around his leg pain. At first it had felt pointless, darting around his spacious upper room, waving his sword or ax at the sprawling stacks of books. It slowly came more natural, though Liam was the first person in a long time with which Oliver clashed weapons. The ringing of steel sounded refreshing, but he already missed his books.

With the war came the looting. They raided the markets and electronics stores. The people, desperate and delusional, thinking that things would soon be over and return to normal, did little to preserve themselves. The chaos had fed them, catalytic to their own pandemonium. Oliver's own hometown had suffered burnings and pillaging. Other towns had it worse. Rumor had it that little of Detroit was left for the war to demolish. Jacob had leveled it all the same.

While the people of his California town had busied themselves in the sacking, Oliver had to break the glass windows of the bookstores himself. Had he the time, he might have set fire to the religious sections, having been angry with God in those days. Instead, he loaded a stolen moving truck. Just like the moving truck, no one would miss the books.

He had tried not to grab at random, but time only afforded him so much delineation. So he hoped that he took what he would need to preserve himself and anything that remained of society. He hoped he collected the words that would rebuild the world if the City failed. Small business, urban survival, culinary arts and agriculture, medicine, zymurgy, weaponry, combat, the classics, engineering...

There were jars and bags of other things he hoped would ensure his survival. Seeds, precious metal, and two hard drives that both held the entirety of Wikipedia, music from Bach to the Beatles, and another library—this one digital. If one hard drive hadn't survived, hopefully the other still functioned, though there wouldn't likely be anything to which to connect it in his lifetime. It had cost him everything to preserve it during the war and eventually move it to Avianne.

With two days of travel ahead of them, Oliver took the opportunity to teach the boy. He taught him how to load, aim, and fire a gun, though they could not spare the ammunition and there was only so much to be learned from dry-firing. There was more, too much to remember, like he was teaching the boy to pack for a long trip and neither of them knew where he was going. It was easier and safer to run from bandits than to fight them. Inns with electricity were more expensive. The sheltered teachers of the City could only have instructed him so much, though the boy spoke affectionately of two of them.

They rode with less haste than they should have, but the afternoon sun had taken the energy out of Oliver. He thought, and not for the first time, that the complexion he inherited from his Irish ancestors wasn't doing him any favors. Sweat might have beaded his brow had it not evaporated so fast. He took a drink from his canteen. Whenever Oliver drank, Liam did likewise, perhaps trying to gauge how often it was wise to take water in order to stay hydrated but also ration his water.

"Most just think the prophet's old and mad," Liam said. "He was my grandfather, though, and I believe him. Master Ferrith believes him too. He taught me most of what I know. There are books and videos, if anyone cared to dig them up, but Ferrith knew it all. He taught us history, all about the war, and he trained me with the sword. He said I was a natural."

"Did he?" Oliver asked. "You are good with a sword, but don't get cocky just because an old cripple like me said so." Liam would have to learn caution over confidence, which he hopefully would not have to learn the hard way. They rode in silence a while before Oliver asked Liam of his family.

"Since we descended from the prophet, we are held in high esteem, but not that much is expected of us. Supposedly, my family's job is to keep up prophet's line, but for what I don't know, and they don't seem to care enough to find out. They're young enough that if something happens to me out here they can always have another child, not that I think they'd want that burden."

"They don't care for you?" Oliver realized the camels had slowed and ushered his to pick up the pace. Liam followed his example.

"I don't know," Liam replied. "I knew they didn't want kids. As soon as I was born, both of them underwent the sterilizing process. They said it was for the tax incentive, but it was like they didn't want another me, another inconvenience. When it was announced that I was leaving they showed the usual indifference, but on the day I left, my mother…"

Wealth and comfort had rendered the people of Novum apathetic. The dust had settled and now they acted as if they were never in danger, and now that problems faced them again, they believed that if they ignored it would go away. Perhaps the boy's mother was the first to realize a terrible reality.

They stopped again after two hours, too soon, but riding bothered Oliver's leg. Stiffly, he let himself down from the saddle. They watered and fed the camels, Liam still appearing reluctant to warm up to Lucy. Oliver's camel, who Nate, the seller, had called Herman, had already grown accustomed to him. He scratched Herman on his slender neck.

Four animals trotted in the distance, cackling as they scampered along the desert, mangy and razor-backed.

"Hyenas?" asked Liam.

"Of a sort," answered Oliver. "The locals call them crocotta based on an old African myth and the hyena's Latin name. Devilish creatures and quite unlike their extinct cousins. These are no scavengers. They're aggressive and fiercely smart, a product of the Cloning Revolution. You probably know about that. I'm sure the City's food supply still depends on it.

"In the case of those monsters, when scientists started breeding extinct animals, the pachycrocuta was conceived, not in its prehistoric form, but modified for sport hunting. Big game hunters wanted something smart, something vicious that few would see the need to preserve. Suffice to say, it wasn't a popular decision, but some geneticists went ahead with the project.

"They're nasty creatures. You'll want to avoid them at all costs. Even a scratch is a sure infection. Their bite is loaded with tetrodotoxin, a bad way to go. It causes paralysis, but the victim still feels pain. They were supposed to be sterile as a safety mechanism, to either be hunted or die out. They sure as hell didn't die out. No one knew they would be so resourceful, so resilient, but they've survived."

Oliver put a hand on the gun at his hip, ready to fight or flee if necessary, but to his relief, the crocotta clan wandered off. After a short snack of jerky, Oliver urged them to mount again and continue riding south. Far from the shadow of the Pass, the hardpan desert sands stretched before them, meeting the faded blue sky at the horizon, ever distant before the camels' trotting.

They endured the afternoon heat, and Liam appeared visibly relieved when the sun set and it started to cool. They rode into the night, stopping only at the point of exhaustion. They unsaddled, making a small camp. Along the ride, Oliver had taken the time to save camel dung. Liam obviously thought him out of his mind, but when they stopped for the night, Oliver gathered some brush. He showed the boy how to grind the dung down to a mealy texture and then one match was all it took to get a fire going.

"Whether or not you light a fire is up to you," he told Liam. "This will keep away crocotta but it may catch the attention of thieves." With the cool of night, they hunched near the flames, chewing on dried meats. "You did well today. I suppose I shouldn't be surprised. You made it through the ruins. You'll do just fine."

Liam had protested more than once that he disliked their coming parting of ways. "What if something happens and I can't find Dorian? Wouldn't two of us be safer?"

"As I've said, Elijah wouldn't prophesy you to your death, nor do so without ample time for you to find Dorian." Oliver did his best to sound sure. Prophecy had a funny way of coming about, but Liam needed reassurance. "However," Oliver said, "we must part because I get the impression that Jacob's arrival is imminent. We have to expedite this any way we can. We must be prepared. To amass an army, make plans, preempt whatever it is he's planning. I know you don't like it. Dorian wouldn't either. He always preferred us all together, like something terrible might happen should we separate. But it has to be so."

Oliver sighed, empathizing with the boy's anxiety. Already, he had grown up too fast, on the cusp of manhood, fearful and excited, with unrefined bravery. He would exceed his peers in Novum, finer and stronger than their pampered men and women. With that in mind, Oliver changed the subject, distracting the boy from his angst.

"You said they carry swords in the City."

"The wealthy do. Ferrith says that it's a status symbol. The gun you gave me is the first I've ever seen in real life. But not fifty years after Novum closed its doors, there were political assassinations. Swords hadn't been outlawed like guns. No one thought to ban them, and so those who might have made laws against them were the first to bear them, and now it's common for those who can afford it."

So, the great sanctuary of divine peace had assassinations? That led to more questions than answers, but he somehow suspected that Liam had said as much as he knew.

"Do you miss the City?" he asked.

"I miss my grandfather. I miss Ferrith and Standon. Perry too. My parents. I don't know."

"I mean the City itself. The amenities you had there."

"As I prepared to leave, I started to kind of hate the place. Maybe it's because this is all so new, but I actually like it out here so far. In the City, the sunlight comes in, but it's not enough. There's some artificial light, but it's stale just like the air. Here the air and the water are fresh and the sun feels so real. And out here in the desert, I can say whatever I want."

"What do you mean?" asked Oliver.

"I don't know. I guess it's just that if you say anything people don't like, they just resent you instead of even considering it. Everything the prophet has said has come true and I guess that means there's a god, but in Novum you have to follow their god the way that they want you to follow god, and they don't want that questioned. Sometimes I wonder if God even cares about us."

Oliver looked to the boy with a raised eyebrow. "Deep words for a seventeen-year-old. I once asked Dorian the same thing."

"What did he say?"

"Nothing very satisfying. You can ask him when you meet him." Even after over two hundred years of pondering that mystery, Oliver had no inclination to tell the boy what he thought.

"What about you? Is there anything you miss from before the war?"

*Everything.* "This way of life has shown me how very materialistic people can become. To me, my family, my house, my job, they were everything. Disasters always happened anywhere but where I lived, never in my country. Even the earthquakes in my region were never too bad. Then it came. I learned that what I had thought of as moderation was really excess, what I had called necessity was amenity. I have grown to appreciate the simple things. There is less work and less to worry about, though things are changing now."

"What happened to your family?" asked Liam.

His wife, Avianne, her smile, those eyes, the memory never quite in focus. He might stare at her faded picture for hours and still the details of her effigy escaped his memory. His children, Amy and Aaron—yes that had been their names—their faces escaped him as well.

"Gone," Oliver replied. There was little talk after that. Not long after, they retired. Tomorrow was Bronton.

Little had changed since Oliver's last visit to Bronton. No wall guarded the rugged sandstone and wooden structures, bare and dusty in the afternoon sun. Their well was known to run deep, providing better irrigation than most towns. With their richened patch of land, they had managed to meet their basic food needs and even had a few trees.

Oliver's fondness for the town came mostly from his recent discovery that a local farmer had a unique hop vine. He had purchased it from the farmer, but found it difficult to grow in the cooler shadows of the mountains in Avianne. However, the Kettle Bar & Inn promised a brew made from those very hops, and so he led them there.

The owner was a kind man, known for asking few questions so long as his guests were also inconspicuous. It was close to the town's stables, so soon after finding accommodations for their camels, they saw to their own needs at the Kettle. As they made their way there, residents bustled in the streets, and Oliver guarded his pockets, warning Liam to do so as well. The denizens of Bronton wore a hodgepodge of light colors, shirts and trousers or robes. One person, Oliver noticed, had even procured sunglasses, an impressive feat in this barren world.

Inside the quiet tavern, the bar sat mostly empty, and a few card players in the corner passed around a bottle of whatever it was that kept them in their merry state. Thom leaned against his bar, hand-rolled cigarette between his lips and a book in his palm. He noticed them, snapped his tome shut, and greeted them with a smile.

Oliver knew him well enough to secure rooms and meals at a fair price, shortening the usual negotiation. After Liam and Oliver stored their packs in their rooms, they returned to the tavern and took two barstools. It was their first time sitting at bar together since that first night in Avianne, but they looked like natural customers, side-by-side, elbows on its wooden counter.

"It's just been so long," Thom said, excited fingers tapping the spout, beer foaming into a mug. "Wondered how things were up there in Avianne."

"All is well," Oliver said, taking the pint from the man's wrinkled fingers.

"Finally got some help around there?" he asked, nodding at Liam, giving the boy a pint of his own.

"Aye," said Oliver, going along with Thom's own assumptions. He took a large gulp from his beer and held it aloft, saluting Thom's brew.

"I've got a cellar that keeps it nice and cold," the old barkeep said. "As for your food, give me just a bit. I'll have it right out."

"Could you hold the meat?" Liam asked. Oliver raised an eyebrow at the peculiar request, but Liam only shrugged, so Oliver returned to studying his beer. Its darker amber color was not quite as bitter as Oliver's own brews. Though Oliver preferred a more bitter beer, Thom's brew suited him just fine. Even if it was a bit sweet, it was also stronger.

Over supper, he continued to direct and encourage Liam, whose worried quietness had overcome his usual inquisitiveness. "You told me that this Ferrith of yours said he had every confidence in you. Well, I'll tell you the same. I have every confidence in you." The words seemed to mean a great deal. Though inclined to have some measure of faith in the prophet and Liam's apparent competence, Oliver feared that it would only do so much good in light of the boy's inexperience. But Liam did not need to know Oliver's trepidations. He needed hope and support.

"This might have all been easier if people only believed in the prophet," Liam said.

"It was no different back then," Oliver replied. "When Elijah foresaw the coming of the fallen, it took little time for the factions to develop. There were those who didn't believe your grandfather. He was just a boy after all, and even after the fall, a surprising amount of folks refused to acknowledge that it had anything to do with any god. To complicate matters, these weren't simply angels. That's the best word we have for them. They were great and diverse celestial beings. Dorian himself had stewardship over an entire planet. The word 'angel' is an approximation."

"Spirit made flesh," Liam said.

Oliver nodded. "Some listened to the prophet. Corporations seized the opportunity and built the City, doubtless looking to capitalize on the situation in any way they could. It was probably the only way such a technologically advanced metropolis could be built, but it also ostracized those who believed, but hadn't the money to make the move. It was a big enough gamble as it was for those who had the money." Oliver drank deeply from his mug, his muscles relaxing under the alcohol's influence, the tension from the day's travel slowly softening in his shoulders.

"The known world was well established," he continued. "To move to a distant island and on some leap of faith pay to live in Novum: such a thing was unheard of. They terraformed the island, utilizing its resources for the City, but that didn't stop people from moving here. Many of the people here are the remnants of those who waited too long, who made one last move to get away from the Graylands."

"Is that what's out there?"

"I guess so. I was here before the major migration happened. A few leftover soldiers established what lives they could here, but then more started to come, bringing the last vestiges of mankind with them. Thankfully they brought camels, though I can't say the same for the crocotta."

"They weren't here all along?"

"I'll never forget when that boat came to port," Oliver replied, shaking his head. "I've seen a lot of war but I've never seen something so bloody. We may have killed them before they made land, but we were too busy running for our lives. Four died that day on top of however many died on the boat. Once the crocotta deserted it and we came back, there was no telling how many people had died. The body parts didn't add up, too unintelligible."

Oliver's stomach churned, remembering the look of horror on what was left of their faces. He took another sip of his beer, wanting nothing more than to drink away that memory, but he would need his wits about him.

"How did Jacob get so far? How come you couldn't stop him? Isn't Dorian more powerful?"

"One on one, Dorian might be able to take Jacob. But Jacob was a more charismatic leader and faster to act. He played on the fears of the people. By the time Dorian might have countered his influence, it was too late. Jacob worked his ruin, Dorian tried to stop him, and in the end just these two islands survive, though who knows if anyone lives on the southern island.

"But Jacob's tenacity wasn't all. There were the abominations."

"Abominations?" Liam asked.

"Undead things."

"Zombies?"

Oliver chuckled. "Who knew, right? I guess that's as good a word for them as anything, although zombies are said to be contagious and these were simply being raised from the dead by Raven's methods. But they couldn't be controlled. They just attacked and killed all in sight."

They talked at length, another round of beers relaxing their conversation. Apparently, those in the City had little appreciation for classic rock or movies, but Liam knew his books well enough. However, it was surprising what had survived the war. Oliver's eyes grew wide when he learned of the thousands of religious texts that the City had banned. He should have guessed, the world's understanding of God having changed after the fall, but no *Inferno*, no John Calvin. Sterile renditions had been contrived in their place, mere bookmarks in the place of history. Surprisingly, they had allowed C.S. Lewis. At least Tolkien had managed to slip in.

"Most of the old music," Liam said, "is archived, readily accessible. A few people collect vinyls, but they're expensive and so are the machines that play them."

"You ever listen to any older music?"

"I don't like music."

Oliver raised an eyebrow. "And why is that?"

"It's only for entertainment. It doesn't have any real value. The people who listen to music are the same people going to parties and balls—people like my parents."

"Then you haven't heard good music. Had you only taken some time in those archives of yours, I'd bet you find that music quite different from the aristocratic pop those people listen to."

Against his better judgment, Oliver allowed one more beer, welcoming the ease that it brought him. Afterward, he assigned the boy to a bath and bed. He gave Liam the extra key and told him to lock the door.

Oliver went back down to the tavern. There was work yet. Lights burned low at the now quiet bar. Thom with his usual hand-rolled cigarette and his book. "A pint for you, Ollie?" he asked, looking up from the pages of a worn paperback.

Oliver never did like the nickname, but rumor of his proper name would not do in the Outlands. He had been next in command under Dorian and the other angels. On Jacob's side, Solomon served as the highest ranking mortal. Unlike Solomon, Oliver had survived the war and lived on, but no one need know that just yet.

"Yes," replied Oliver. "A pint if you will. And a question."

Thom rose from his stool, dog-earing and discarding his book. He hobbled over to the tap, taking a mug, and filling it with beer. "And what would that be?" Thom asked as the mug foamed to the top.

"There's a rumor of a city in the east. A garden city."

"Just rumors," Thom said, shaking his head as he sat the beer before Oliver.

"I would agree, save for the strange folk who travel from those parts. Surely you've seen them. Maybe around town?"

"I suppose I've seen such folk. I reckon some sort of city out east does exist. But there's all sorts of crazy religious types in the desert. Nothing I'd say is worth bothering with. People around here know better than to get tangled up in religion. Our town priest is more a beggar than a holy man."

"Still," persisted Oliver, "have you seen any of these people, the ones rumored from that eastern city?"

"They come and go, I suppose. A couple folk dressed like them rode in this morning. Probably at the other inn, unless they were just passing through."

It was probably too late to catch them tonight, but that was promising enough. However, if they were just passing through, they'd likely leave at daybreak. He would have to take his chances. Thanking Thom and finishing his beer, he took his cane and decided to make his way over to the other inn.

Oliver knew more than he let on. There *was* a garden city in the east, the name unknown, but the rumors of its majesty spread in whispers, and so did a name. *Charis*. Some claimed to have seen the garden city with their own eyes, but none were allowed to enter. According to the hearsay, a denizen of the garden city had to vouch for one's entry, the rarest of things.

The rumors indeed circulated. Some believed the garden city to be the last remnant of civilization other than the City itself. On one hand, reports said it was a city that survived the war, while others claimed it had been raised out of the ashes of the waste, a restoration of the old world. Yet, no one quite knew enough about it to say one way or the other.

Such theories all agreed that entry into said city was near impossible, and so Oliver had left it alone, in spite of a deep desire to find it. But he had known better. He had known that his place was at Avianne and that it was better that he respected Charis's wishes to remain hidden.

Through the dark streets, Oliver walked to the other inn. In contrast to the dimmed and darkened windows of the shops and houses, the Harvest Inn's light and laughter spilled into the street. The small tavern sat nestled into the larger inn.

Patrons sprawled across old wooden tables and chairs, their plastic renditions cropping up at random intervals. Among the leather vests and tweed jackets, torn and dirty from the outlands, two people sat apart at their corner table.

Their dress told all, the silk and colors standing out. Her tawny skin complimented his ebony complexion, and as they pushed their empty plates from them, Oliver approached, cane tapping on the splintering planks.

He sat at their table casually, ignoring the pain in his leg. Though they showed no surprise or puzzlement at a stranger's boldness, they remained silent as Oliver signaled for another round of drinks to be brought to their table, ordering water for himself.

People spoke of their strange fashion, but to Oliver, their style and colors were familiar. She wore a sari, the customary wrapped linen dress from India. The men's fashion varied, but he wore a blue silken robe. Unlike the homogeneous outlanders, who were most often lighter skinned, most rumors from the garden city spoke of those like this couple, colorful and exotic.

They eyed him warily at first, but then sat in the awkward silence as the barmaid distributed three pints before them. Oliver took a large gulp of the water, gathering his courage, and then spoke.

"I hope," Oliver began, "you'll pardon my rudeness, but the matter is urgent. My name is Oliver." He paused, giving them space to introduce themselves.

"I am Obi," the man said. "And this is Lem."

"A pleasure to meet you both. You'll forgive me if I cut right to it. I need your help. I need to get to the garden city."

Obi appeared neither surprised nor upset. To Oliver's surprise, the man did not deny the existence of the city. "Many seek passage to our city," he said, stern but not unkind. "But we do not allow such things."

"But it's urgent. I must speak with Charis. I know her."

That made their eyes widen. "You know her?" Lem asked.

"I do," replied Oliver. "It's important that I speak with her."

"It is urgent, you say?" Obi asked.

"Yes," allowed Oliver. "It's sensitive information."

"How do I know you are not like the others that so often come to us? They know of a city, and a lady, though not their names. They want her hand in marriage, they want to trade with us, they want our wealth."

Oliver had hoped this would be easier, but this was not going well. "Does the name Jacob mean anything to you?"

Lem startled, the smallest of flinches. "That is an evil name."

"It is an evil name," Oliver agreed. "And this matter concerns him. We are in danger."

Obi held up a hand. "This is not for us to decide. We have two more days here and then we ride back to our city. We will discuss it with the Lady Charis and if she deems the words of this man, Oliver, important, we will send word back to Bronton."

"There's no time for that," said Oliver, incensed by the man's mechanical, unwavering approach.

"There will have to be. We cannot make exceptions. It is for our safety."

"Don't be a fool," Oliver said, exasperated. He held his tongue, trying not to show his temper. "This is imminent. It's no matter for discussion; we need to act now. Don't you know the histories? Do you know what threatens you?"

"We are well-guarded," Obi said.

"Your walls won't protect you. Charis can't defend you against him. Not alone. And what about everyone else? What about the people of Bronton? Of Novum?"

Lem tugged on Obi's shirt. "If what he says is true," she said, "then we would do well to heed his words."

"Our city has prospered for two hundred years because we have kept its rules. This very conversation is risky enough as it is. This man knows the name of Jacob, but it means nothing. He boasts the name Oliver, like he is the hero come back from the dead. I do not trust him."

Oliver stood, his chair scraping against the floor. He steadied himself, a hand on the table as his leg spasmed. "This is the biggest threat in two hundred years and you think protocol is going to save your city?"

"I will do as I have said and nothing more."

Oliver took his cane, stomping out into the night. He was angry, in pain, and at a loss. One bureaucrat's stubbornness would doom them all. What did he expect? The plan would have to change. There was always Nathan, wherever he hid, or perhaps he was destined to aid the boy in finding Dorian. It might take too long, but it was also the easiest route to discovering the other two angels.

Or he could just wait for a response from the garden city. He could follow Obi and Lem there and bang on its walls until someone opened it up. Perhaps it didn't even have walls. If only he could contact Charis.

He let out a sigh, realizing his fatigue. At first light he would talk it over with Liam, two rested minds a better alternative to his tired disposition. He had to admit that the beer had gotten to him as well. He walked back to the inn, waving at Thom as he made his way to the room where he had his own bath before bed.

The tumult awoke Oliver in the night. Cries of pain and calamity. Amber light flickered in through the window and smoke filled his nostrils. Bronton was under attack.

He rushed into the hall, a bustling of confused patrons, half-drunk and asleep, stumbling in a panic from their rooms. To his relief, the inn itself was not afire. He returned to their room to find Liam already rousing. They packed their things, Oliver's fingers fumbling over straps and drawstrings, fearful of an attack on the inn.

"Forget your sword. Keep it sheathed," he told Liam. "Get your gun and remember how I taught you to hold. Keep it pointed down and don't raise it unless you know you're going to shoot."

Most of the inn was empty by the time they were headed out of the back door, pistols in hand. Warily, Oliver led them toward the stables, damning his need of the cane. Women and children cried among the blazing fires. Laughter and shouts of pain filled the night. Then came another sound, gunfire echoing in the dark. Oliver cursed. This was getting bad. Though the alley itself was empty, Oliver had to step over the occasional body. The raiders had worked their way further into town, seemingly victorious in taking it.

Liam coughed behind him, choking on the dust and smoke, but they pressed on. Within a few feet from the stables, a woman crashed through a back door. Oliver almost cried out. *Lem.* But a man stepped through the doorway towering over her. With a slash of his knife he cut her scream short. Oliver's shot rang out, too late to save the woman. The man fell dead, but Lem lay on the desert sand, blood gushing from her throat.

She reached out for them before her arm fell limp, and her body lay in a pool of dark glistening liquid. Oliver steadied himself on his cane and began to walk on, but Liam lingered, staring at the woman's body. "There's nothing we can do. We have to go." But then Oliver stopped with a realization. This was the back door of Harvest Inn. "Hold on."

He put his back to the building, peering around the door frame. The fires cast ghostly shadows among the flickering light, ever closer to their side of town. The gunfire sounded nearer as well. It was a wonder that the raiders who had already come through hadn't put it to the torch. Bronton had never been a target for raiders, yet this would be an unprecedented sacking for any town. This was either something big or an ill-timed coincidence, and given that the raiders had guns, Oliver suspected the former.

At a glance, he saw the lifeless bodies strewn about the room. He surveyed the bandit he had shot, a well-equipped man, not like the usual desert clans other than the bones he wore. Oliver looked back to the open doorway, into the death and darkness.

"Follow me," Oliver told Liam, stepping into the back door of the inn. "Watch behind us and watch the fires."

They stepped over debris and bodies, and though no threat appeared imminent, they remained quiet as they climbed the stairs, each step a throbbing pain for Oliver. It had not hurt this bad in years, decades perhaps, but it bothered him now, the feeling that something was out of place and twisted inside him.

He peered into each of the rooms, searching any sign of life among the torn and broken furniture. He almost didn't see Obi, his ebony skin difficult to spot in the dark, face down unconscious. He felt for a pulse, finding the man to be alive, but breathing shallowly.

He shook the man, hoping he would come to, but he didn't stir. This was Oliver's best hope for the garden city. He shook the man again. "Come on," he said.

Footsteps thudded up the stairs behind him, and an unfamiliar voice shouted something, before a loud crack shook the room. Oliver ducked to the ground, his ears ringing. He waited for the floor to cave in, for the collateral damage to splinter at him. But it was still. He looked up, trying to still his heart, to gain understanding. Liam stood at the doorway, gun before him, a stunned expression on his face. Two boots poked into the room, belonging to a body that had not been there before.

"I'm sorry," Liam said, too shocked. The poor boy probably had no clue that he would have to kill anyone on this journey, much less this early on.

"You did the right thing," Oliver said, though if Oliver's ears were ringing, the boy was surely momentarily deafened.

The man beside him stirred, Obi coming awake.

"Lem," he said, dry-voiced. "They took her. I tried—"

"I'm sorry," Oliver told him, helping the man to his feet. He looked into Obi's eyes and tried to push the urgency and panic from his mind. "I'm sorry," he said again. "They killed her."

Obi shook his head.

"I killed the man who did it," Oliver said. More shouts rose anew, and it felt as if the room had grown brighter, that those twisting shadows were giving way to a new and malicious fiery flicker. "The fires grow. We need to leave. Help me with him, Liam."

The boy put the gun away, hand shaking, and ran over to support Obi. They helped the disoriented man down the stairs, Oliver groaning with each step. When they got to the back door, Obi saw his wife's body, throat open, coagulating blood seeping into the desert sands.

"No," he said, tears falling. They had to pull Obi away from her body. The stable sat a few yards away from the row of buildings. They would have to run into the open to get to the stables.

They leaned Obi against the building and Oliver turned to Liam. "Listen," he said. "I'm going to cover you while you make a run for it. Get him a horse or a camel, whatever they have. Steal it if you have to. Now, on my mark."

Neighs and hoof-beats came from the stable, beasts nervous in the commotion. He hoped their camels were still in there.

He glanced around the corner into the street. Few remained in defense against the marauders. It was all laughter and flames now, chasing down the stragglers and doing whatever it was they did to them. More gunshots echoed in the distance. Oliver signaled, and Liam helped Obi across the clearing, safely arriving at the stable. Oliver followed, gun in one hand, cane in the other, and then he was spotted.

Through the distant flames, no more than ten yards away, a man emerged from the shadows. Oliver knew that thin, dark-haired man, and his perpetual sneer. He met Raven's menacing, sadistic eyes with an equally cold gaze. Raven stalked towards him and Oliver ran for the stables, almost falling from the searing agony in his leg.

Raven would get to them long before they could even mount the camels and he would take them to whatever horrors he had in store. Oliver had almost gotten to the stables, but the fallen was close as well. A shot resonated. Oliver recovered from his instinctual duck and saw that Raven had stopped as well, holding his arm as black fluid streamed down it. And then Oliver looked to the door of the stable where Liam, cold and still, held his gun. He fired again and missed.

"That's good enough," Oliver told him. "Let's get the hell out of here."

They entered the stables and started to mount their camels. Obi had recovered enough to pull his own horse over, where he made his own preparations. With a clatter, the stable door opened and two men rushed upon them, swords swinging. Oliver and his camel both almost took a hit, but the close quarters made it unwieldy and one blade locked into a piece of wood. Oliver's own sword flashed out and pierced the man up to the hilt.

Liam stood off against a man who seemed unsure if the boy was capable or not. He never found out. Obi came up behind the man, wringing his throat, before he could strike at Liam.

After the tense moment that Obi strangled the assailant, the black man stood, chest heaving with deep breaths. Liam had gone back to shocked silence. Obi was barely dressed and Oliver felt remorse that they had not taken some of his belongings with them. He had an extra change of clothes that might suit the man. They nodded to each other, a mutual understanding that they were escaping together.

They secured their packs within minutes, and Raven was apparently too preoccupied to pursue them more. Liam struggled to mount his camel, until Lucy finally complied and they were all ready. Oliver had unhitched the main doors and they burst from the stables toward the southern border. The camels kept their composure as buildings crumbled, burning around them. Shouts followed as they exited the town, Raven's riders coming for them. Oliver grunted, twisting in his saddle, and fired a shot into the night. The riders faltered at the threat of a gun, and their half-hearted pursuit died quickly.

They rode for near half an hour when they finally stopped, the camels, the horse, and the men weary.

"That was one of them," Liam said. "One of the angels."

"It was," Oliver replied. "And that was a damned lucky shot."

"He's terrifying," Liam said. The angels could have that effect on people. Raven looked like a small, bony man, sickly and pale, but his prodigious presence even overwhelmed Oliver, who was accustomed to the angels and who physically dwarfed Raven by at least a foot.

"So it is true," Obi said.

Oliver nodded. "Take me to your city."

"I will take you both to Mere. I owe you my life."

"Not both of us." Oliver looked to Liam. "The boy is from Novum, and was sent to find Dorian. We part here."

"I can't do it without you," Liam said, fear in his voice. "I need help."

"You're stronger and braver than you think," Oliver told him.

"How will I find you?"

"If nothing else, I will meet you at the Pass. Or I'll send someone to meet you and tell you where to find Mere."

Liam, accepting the terms reluctantly, only nodded his head.

"Godspeed," Obi said, locking eyes with Liam. "Be careful out there."

Into the night they parted ways. The boy to find Dorian in the south. Oliver and Obi to Mere, the garden city in the east.

# CHAPTER FIVE

*The Garden City*

Unsettled upon seeing Raven, Oliver found no relief from the memory of their confrontation. Aback his camel, he rode the bright desert sands, haunted by that cold moment. He should have known that something was amiss when the unlikely bandits assaulted Bronton. They rarely invaded towns, content to nip at the fringes, if not avoid them altogether.

Yet those black eyes still pierced him, Raven's look of menace and surprise, but something else, something mysterious. It was always the same with the fallen, like they harbored some deeper understanding. He had not seen eyes such as those for two hundred years, but they found him in Bronton.

If Jacob marched on the City, then he would have to breach Avianne, the Pass. That made Bronton the perfect base from which to make the siege. The fact that neither he nor the boy had been pursued with any enthusiasm made sense enough. Raven was taken by surprise. He had not come to Bronton in search of them, but was rather preoccupied with bigger things. He knew no inkling of their mission, nor did he find them a threat, but such was the arrogance of angels.

As he ruminated, the sun rose higher, and Obi rode silent as usual, guiding them to the east. Oliver had protected Avianne, Dorian watched from the south, and Charis had her eastern province. But Novum had boasted no vigilance. If the boy was right, they were complacent, timid even.

Dorian had fought for the people of Novum, even if from outside its walls. They shut the world out and the world died for them. Had it been worth it? Dorian seemed to think so, though not without a hint of guilt. As for Oliver—what *did* he think? Now, Jacob came a second time and once again the City let the outside do the work, sending but one boy. The one boy gave hope and confidence that preservation was worth fighting for.

The coming conflict would be over more than the City. Humanity had reestablished itself beyond its walls. Dorian desired solitude, but Oliver convinced him to help establish order in the various townships on the northern island. Now it was home to a string of towns down its center, gleaning water from the depths of the terraformed reservoirs. The coasts thrived, though Oliver's commitments at the Pass kept him from the vibrant fringes of their small world.

Obi interrupted his thoughts. "What happened?" It was the first time the man had spoken in hours and even then he only gave short directions. For all he knew, the sack of Bronton was coincidence. Lem was the victim of a senseless crime. Oliver had contrived a dozen ways to tell him, but never found the right words of consolation. He could not empathize with the man. His own wife had died, true, but that grief was far gone, a long soured and decayed part of him.

Perhaps if he started at the beginning. "How well do you know your history?"

"I know of the seven and I know Charis is one of them, though few in Mere are aware. If I didn't know better, I would say you are the legendary Oliver or named after him."

"Thanks to Charis, I'm still alive. The boy from the City says the Great Prophet Elijah still lives. He foresaw Jacob's return and sent

Liam to us. The man—the thing—responsible for Lem's death was Raven, one of the fallen and a follower of Jacob."

"This does not bode well," Obi said, shaking his head, but showing no sign of surprise.

"Not at all. I worry about the boy, but we have to stay ahead of Jacob. He moves fast."

"The world is changing," Obi said. "I can feel it."

It was indeed changing and the people of Bronton were only the first victims of the coming threat.

"I'm sorry," Oliver said. "About Lem." After two hundred years, he still didn't know how to console people.

"She was my wife. We had traveled to Bronton to see if it was viable for the expansion."

"The expansion?"

"Lady Charis dreamed of allying another city to us, to cultivate it into what Mere had become, to extend our beauty elsewhere. It was a dream I shared, but there was none as passionate as Lem." He sighed at that, and silenced for a moment, only the clopping hooves of horse and camel breaking silence. "I will miss her," he said. "I am not a man of vengeance, but I cannot help but pine for justice."

Obi spoke more after that. He talked little of Mere, often hinting that it was better to see for oneself, but he told Oliver of their eastern spot in the desert. Oliver relayed his own doings, comparing notes, and discovering a little more about this island than he had known having been restricted so close to Avianne.

Within a few days, Mere, the garden city, appeared in the distance. He longed to be within its walls, to behold its beauty, but most of all he thought of Charis. How she fared, how she would react to the news, how she would react to him. She was a strong woman, though never the warrior, but rather a healer and creator of all things beautiful.

So long ago, she spoke of founding a town in the east with fertile soil and deep wells, a place for the world to begin recovering, a beacon of hope in the bleakness of the Outlands. Within a few years of the war's end, rumor spread of a place in the east, led by a woman whose beauty never faded. Then those rumors decreased and save for the seldom and shy denizens of the city, most idle chatter about it faded. Oliver should have sought her sooner.

Mere's vast wall, running miles around in dark brick, loomed tall, with sentries on the parapets, their attire earthy tones of leather armor and green cloth. The city was prodigious enough on the outside, though in the expanse of the desert, one might travel for days and not find it. Even if someone did come to its doors, they risked being turned away, with little food and water on the journey home.

Trees and spires jutted from above the walls. Green leaves sprouted over the bricks, bundling into the blue sky. Shingled roofs and stone towers spiked into the air, the hints of things behind those doors.

The doors themselves faced directly west, surely one of many entrances, their impenetrable arches closed to the outside world. Thick wood, reinforced by steel bars and rivets, blocked their way. A narrow slot opened, the porter glaring at them.

"What's your business?" the man asked, eyes shifting in suspicion before seeing Obi. "Ah, Obi, yes. You return sooner than expected." With a squeak and a clang, the lock lifted and the porter opened a door wide, beckoning them to enter. "Welcome."

Those suspicious eyes and furrowed brow belonged to a man with a kinder face, old and generous. He would have stood little chance against an attack, but the guards that flanked him stood at attention, spears in hand.

Townsfolk bustled amid the vivid architecture and flora. After dismounting, Obi led Oliver through the town. Wood and stone buildings complimented structures of harl and stucco, windowed with stained glass. They towered and wound, intermingled with lush vegetation and vines. A network of bridges and stairs connected the buildings, a multilevel pathway of ancient garden beauty.

There was nowhere in the Outlands like this place. Beyond its beauty were the people, bustling in a veritable metropolis, so diverse and energetic. Bright clothes complimented their varying skin tones. The smells of spices filled the air. Cilantro, tamarind, chili powder, cardamom, ginger. Hellenism and India met in a resplendent clash. The garden city epitomized its whispered reputation. Trees and plants—budding with lively flowers—lined the streets and structures of Mere. Rich, green vines twisted and crept along columns and walls, intertwining with the lattice.

They passed a stunning tree, its brown, spidery roots twisting into a trunk, culminating into slender branches with small, violet flowers. So taken, Oliver almost forgot his purpose. "Obi," he said, recalling himself, "Where are we going?"

"First, we stable the animals. Then I will take you to Charis. I will leave you then. I have yet to mourn my wife." The man had not shed a tear, yet he did not seem apathetic. He was merely awaiting the right time, and he was bound to his duty before he could grieve. He may have been stubborn, but his motives were pure. He really did want to do the right thing, to put honor before his whims.

The stables, finer than any Oliver had ever seen, refused his pay, declaring him a guest of honor. He left a generous tip with the stable master, and allowed Obi to lead him, wondering the streets. Their path of marble walkways and cobblestone streets twisted around massive buildings, each a work of art in itself. Once in a while, Obi commented on a structure. "They say that two hundred years ago, when this city was founded, that this building was the first to be restored. They called that time the

Great Redemption, when from the ashes and sand, this place was built." It was a church. Spires jutted up, surrounding a bell tower at the center of the massive building. Lion statues perched on each corner of the tower. The church's bronze doors splayed open, inviting all in, their arches pointing to the great round stained glass window under the peak of the roof. Laced with intricate stonework, the carvings of saints spun and twisted around the transparent, colorful display. Oliver recognized one of the statues, its graven image a reminder to him, and he stopped.

"It is the Last Saint," Obi confirmed. "But come."

Wrought iron gates protected the walled estate that housed the Lady's mansion. Past the guards and into the gardened grounds, Oliver spotted the dogwood tree, its flowers like a cross-shaped snowflake. Great white columns upheld the building before them. "Its true name, *Fusang*, never caught on. The locals simply call it the mansion," Obi said. "Out of the eastern gate is the Garden Saloon, also run by Lady Charis. The finest beer in Mere. The whiskey's good too."

Trepidation filled Oliver as they entered the great house. He should have come a long time ago, he should have sent word to Charis. It might have been reckless, but he should have done it anyway. Obi led him from room to room, across creaking hardwood floors. Crown molding lined the tiled ceiling. The painting coursed through the walls as if the vines and flowers outside crept through the windows, extending into the house. They came to a door, and with a quick, but not discourteous nod, Obi left him. It was a single nod, but it meant two things. It was time for Obi to mourn his wife, and there was no need to knock. Oliver opened the door.

Tall, thin windows lined the far wall. The bar in one corner boasted a shelf of assorted liquors and a beer tap. In the center spread the round table, regal chairs awaiting those on important business. It dwarfed the desk in the corner where a woman of earthen beauty worked, head down and pen in hand. She looked up, smile ready to greet her guest, but then her eyes widened. Was that anger? No, there was something else there, like fear mixed with astonishment, and then the expression turned to discrete joy.

Oliver forced himself to meet her gaze and he couldn't help but smile. She rose, steadying herself and then walked to him, poorly hiding her eagerness. She looked at him, a brief moment, eyes traveling from his feet to his eyes. He hesitated, but she wrapped her arms around him. Pain spasmed in his leg as he leaned in, but it was soon forgotten in the embrace. They held each other, perhaps longer than was appropriate, but as far as she was concerned he had come back from the dead, and so he let her process this as she might. She parted from him, and he saw her face clearly now, unaged, save for her eyes. Older and wearier, but the same compassion in them.

"I mourned you over a century ago," she said. She was beautiful as she always had been, her thin figure and dark brown hair still breathtaking. Tears filled her eyes and she choked on whatever she was going to say next.

"I'm sorry," Oliver said. "I should have come sooner, but I thought it was better if I was presumed dead. I feared that Jacob or one of his allies would come for me and I thought it would be better if I took them by surprise if they ever did come back."

"But, how are you alive?"

"I think I owe that to you," he said, holding up his cane.

"I never could heal your leg in full," she said.

"No," Oliver replied. "But it seems that one way or another we have an advantage. I'm still here."

"And you haven't aged a day."

"I doubt that's the case, but none of that matters now. I'm here on serious business."

"What do you mean?" she asked, then paused. "But wait, your leg. Let's sit." She motioned to the small bar in the corner, four empty stools of their choosing. She guided them over, pouring small glasses of a clear liquid. With the help of his cane, he took a barstool and she set the glass before him. "They probably told you the whiskey was good," Charis said.

"And the beer," Oliver said.

"But sake is what I do best."

Oliver hadn't tasted sake in two centuries, and he let its smooth burn caress his throat and work its way to his belly where it lingered like the sun shining through a window on a warm spring day. Charis had once told him how humans and other species had become common on the rare life bearing planets. Humanity was every bit as diverse, and, she had said, alcohol was the transcendental unifier. It had certainly unified those who stood against Jacob, and her fairness and her craft showed him how Japan's beauty manifested elsewhere.

"Charis." Oliver cleared his throat. "I've been at the Pass all this time, and a few days ago, a boy emerged from the north, from the City. I'm afraid it's bad news."

"He made it through Dorian's wards?"

"I don't know how. No one else has. But he did and he now speaks of Jacob's return and the aid of the Morning Star. I am not the only one to live so unnaturally long. He has it from the prophet. From Elijah." He told her all, including the sacking of Bronton, Lem's death, and how Obi led him to Mere.

"I see," she said when he had finished. "This is troubling."

"I know you always hated the war, but you will be needed. I've sent the boy to find Dorian. We need Nathan. We need a plan, an army, many things."

Charis pondered it a moment and then spoke. "I knew this day would come. When I fell, all I felt was hopelessness and shame. I had been deceived. I was innocent, but I was sentenced here nonetheless. I felt even more hopeless when Jacob started the war.

"We weren't supposed to be different. We were to live our life here just like the other fallen did millennia before. But then there was Jacob's despair and destruction." She sighed, and her voice quavered, but she remained strong. "When Jacob disappeared, we had nothing. I was finished. Nathan left to whatever end. Dorian went south to be a hermit. I could not follow you into the Pass, but you were the only one of us who could go. I assumed you to have died a long time ago. Then, I started something new.

"I became a warden in the east. Out of the ashes I began to hope again. I will help you, but I hate this. I built this city of peace, but war and blood have found me. If I leave here, I may never return. It may fall like before."

"It may. But if we can stop Jacob this time, we can restore it all." Oliver looked to her earnestly. "The City can be opened up and the world rebuilt. We have to try."

"I don't know what difference it would have made," Charis said. "But I wish you had come back. I wish I had known that you were out there."

"I—" He faltered. "Everyone left and I had failed. Once my guilt subsided, I just sort of thought I was forgotten. I'm sorry. I am. We can't fix the past, but we can do something now."

"We can." Charis paused a moment in thought. Her brow furrowed, eyes wandering. "Mere has a military. It's not battle-seasoned. It's only subdued the occasional outlaws. But they are well-trained. I wouldn't take any man from here against his will, but they will come if I ask. First, I'll convene the consulate."

"You have a consulate?"

"In a matter of speaking. It's a small council formed by six members: one military commander, three viceroys, a priest, and myself at the head. The commander is on the brink of retirement, we are without a priest, and one of our viceroys was Lem, who passed. You will be on the council, second only to me. We have to make a plan, mobilize the army. You will be vital to that."

"This is overwhelming. I fear my days as a general are over. My leg still pains me."

"You will lead them." She did not ignore him, but she spoke as if there was no alternative and Oliver supposed that was a good point. "I think I can find Nathan, and maybe while I'm at it, find this Liam and make sure he knows to rendezvous here. Meanwhile, you can work with the commander to mobilize the army. They are meant to defend walls, not march into battle. You will have to prepare them."

"That's all a bit overwhelming," he said. She expected him to lead an army again, to sit at the right hand of immortals.

"You'll do fine," Charis said. "We'll centralize here and I'll make sure you have everything you need. In the meantime, spend some time at the baths. It would do wonders for your leg."

Such was her gift, the grand scheme of things, knowing what must be done and doing it. Such systematic thinking had built this town, had put this oasis in the desert. He hated that they had been united only to part so soon. Surely this was how Liam had felt, but like Liam, he knew it was for the best. He wanted to know so much more, the details of the past two hundred years. She had evidently built Mere. But how?

"We will have to catch up soon," she said. "Right now there's work to be done, starting with a visit to the baths. It is good to see you again, even in these desperate times."

Charis was right about the bathhouse. After riding more than usual and the dire flee from Bronton, Oliver was in desperate need of their healing waters. As much as he might have complained about the pain in his left thigh, he was grateful to have survived the severing of his femoral artery on that day long ago. Medical sciences could have done nothing for him, not in so little time, but Charis had been different.

The soothing springs bubbled in man-made pools, frequented by residents to cleanse or convalesce. After selecting a book from her vast library, he made his way to the baths, finding an empty room, old stone columns between the few steaming reservoirs. He undressed, submerged his legs and cracked the book. Had he witnessed someone else bathing with the rare book in hand, he might have scolded them, but he assured himself that he was more than equal to the task of soaking his leg and keeping the book dry.

Henry Talmas had been a popular public intellectual, the bulk of his work on the angelic wars, but Oliver had thought it long lost. This edition of *Cruel God* was a copy of a copy, surely curated by a printing press within the town. It was unlikely that it was the only edition of the book, but all the same, he held it with care, well above the water.

*There are still detractors who believe that there is a perfectly scientific and rational explanation for these beings. While I cannot rule out the possibility, it seems evident that something supernatural, or at least extranatural, is among us. While it does not prove the existence of a deity, nor the Ultimate, it certainly presents evidence of some power that is beyond the natural or that is centuries away from scientific explanation. What better term to call this power than "god"? It is with great regret that I am inclined to review the current evidence and admit the probability that such a being or force does exist. But should my theist opponents consider that a victory, they are wrong. For though god may exist, god is not good. He has spited his own creation. He has given us seven new plagues.*

There, on the page, was the source of some of his old bitterness. Liam had inquired about this very thing, and though Oliver wanted to answer, it was not his place. The boy needed to learn

95

for himself, or at least talk with Dorian enough to decide that it was a long, dark road he didn't want to follow.

The water soothed Oliver's aching muscles. Not just his leg, but his back and feet. He flipped a few more pages into the book, skimming the passages for more memorable remarks. They weren't all so different. Whatever the case, Oliver was not here to be bitter, not as he had once been, and god or no god, he would give his every living breath to human survival.

"Reading Talmas?" her voice asked. Charis had allowed herself in, gentle and quiet as usual. With any other woman he might have covered himself, but it was *her*. She was a fallen goddess, a healer, and though she was beautiful, he tried not to think of her sexually. The thought of her that way tread on ground he knew well would frustrate him. A forbidden territory. Too sacred, too set apart.

She walked in and smiled at him. Was that medical sterility in her eyes or did that smirk show more? Now he knew why he had avoided her for two hundred years. She was proper, compassionate, so deliberate, but when it came to moments like these, he sensed something else. But he was jumping to conclusions. Once he had a wife and in some ways he would always mourn her. Did he still feel that loss or was that an excuse?

Charis knelt, inspecting his leg. Nothing appeared unusual about it, but inside he felt the twisting wrongness. She was so medical about it, so factual, and he tried hard to feel little else as her fingers dipped beneath the water and felt his inner-thigh. He set the book aside, well out of the reach of the lapping water splashing outside of the pool.

Her touch was a gentle, that of a caring physician soothing the pain. She was an immortal, neither romantic nor sexual, or so he reminded himself.

"It was an ugly battle," she said. "I didn't have a choice. You were going to bleed out any minute. I'm surprised you made it so long. It would have needed days to do it right." She paused, rubbing a thumb on the spot, and the pain disintegrated, reducing to a dull sensation. "It's the same problem," she went on. "With more time, I think I could put it back to right, but it would take far too long. Months. I'm sorry."

"I'm just grateful—" Oliver began to reply, but she had removed her hand and the pain returned. He hid it, trying not to garner more of her already generous sympathy. Her compassion, beyond the typical female affection, was like that best of counselors or friends, too genuine and caring to be wasted on him.

"We can work on your leg more when we have time. I need to call a meeting before I leave to find Nathan."

"I can be finished shortly," Oliver said.

"I'm not leaving yet," she replied.

She had risen, standing over him. She took the Talmas book gently and set it on a nearby windowsill. She came back then and, before he could protest, removed her dress. There she stood before him, under garments clinging to her soft figure. He might have spoken then, but she removed those too, and he choked on his objection.

When she stepped into his bath, he found words. "Charis, I didn't mean for you to take it this way." This was more than a woman, something divine, amongst whom he was unworthy.

She kept silent, coming down to him, legs brushing his torso, lips close to his ear. His resistance to her faded, impossible to counter, and after two centuries without intimacy, he wanted to disregard judgment. He could feel her breath now.

"What is this?" he asked. It was too strange, too unexpected, but nestled in the water, their skin touched, and he knew what it was.

She looked at him, eyes so sure, all of their compassion funneled into true understanding. "I know," she said.

"Know what?" But he knew. He cared for her, more than he had anyone else since the war. That day she had healed him he knew he wanted her. He had felt her life, her vibrancy, the way she healed all. She acted selflessly, putting her own desires aside, forfeiting peace for the war she hated so much. He wanted that woman, someone who understood.

"Why?" he asked. He had resisted it so long in the name of wisdom. But the foolish facade fell away, decades abandoned to the want he knew to be there all along. He lost himself in her eyes, his chest tensing as she smiled at him. Nothing was supposed to be this good, not without some hidden loss, but he surrendered to her. They embraced, meeting one another in something more ethereal than human love. He felt it, but tangibility escaped him as astral ecstasy filled his soul. She was him, he was her, they were one, they were each other, coursing lights intertwining, energy transcending this barren planet, and soaring into other worlds.

Amid the euphoria their thoughts coalesced.

*Why…*

*The world is ending.*

*But why us?*

*It was there all along. I healed you.*

*You healed me but I left you. And now the world is ending.*

*That's exactly why I won't lose you again.*

Charis left Oliver to his thoughts. He had suppressed his feelings for her. That trepidation was the heart of why he had avoided the garden city for so long. Though he possessed unnatural long life, he was still a mortal in ways she was not. The angels could die, or so the first fallen beings had, but they were difficult to kill, and until someone or something did the deed, they lived on. Before her fall, Charis had been a goddess, a steward over her own planet just like Dorian.

Charis reciprocated Oliver's love. She said as much and so did he, over and over, aloud and in the lacing of their thoughts. At the end of the world. There was hope that Jacob could be stopped, but no guarantees that Oliver or Charis would survive. He had waited too long to find her, to know and accept that she could love him, and to act on that. He now knew, when it was perhaps too late, that he was worthy of her. Or that she at least believed that he was worthy of her.

When she parted from him, the pain returned. It reminded him of all of the aching he might have saved himself if he had been intimate with her all these years. When she had saved him that day, when he found that he loved her, he shouldn't have repressed it. He should have known how close they had come to losing each other then.

On that day in Chicago, they knew that Jacob led them into a trap. They outnumbered his forces four to one, and the odds convinced him that they could counter Jacob's snare. Dorian consulted with him on it and Oliver assured him that they had every advantage.

Those were the latter days of the war, but before the front lines had moved to the island. They marched into the heart of a city, downtown buildings towering above them, the sun peeking between their shadows.

The forces crowded around the buildings. Few guns remained. This battle would be fought with the blade. The ground shook. The beasts poured into the streets with reckless fury. Crashing through building and wall, they came, unstoppable forces summoned and sent by Amelia. Jacob's militia followed them, war cries the harbinger of their turbulent rush.

Oliver looked to Dorian, his usual solemnity a steel disposition, gritted for battle. Their army held steady. The ground shook harder, the rumble deafening. Jacob's army met theirs. Steel rang. Victorious shouts turned to screams. Beasts roared. Spears and arrows flew into the air, sinking into flesh like the teeth of the monsters that also assailed them.

Dorian had not been idle. One hand guided his sword, another worked a tapestry of magic. He was a blur, too fast to follow, a whirl of flame and light. All who opposed him fell.

Oliver issued commands, surveying the carnage, bewildered that the match was more even than he had anticipated. The enemy quickly surrounded his position, and he led his men into the foray. Ringing steel and grunting, they made fast work of the dirty battle. He felled two of Raven's soldiers and then met one of Amelia's beasts.

Claws scraped at him, teeth gnashed, but Oliver's rapid strides carried him out of danger. An ogre-like creature dealt a smashing blow and Oliver rolled to the side, springing back to his feet to face the creature. It roared at him. Like a god, Oliver leapt into the air, sword held high. A flash of his blade and his sword came down swift, through flesh and bone. The beast's howl fell short, and it crashed to the ground, its cloven skull lifeless.

The battle raged, more enemy soldiers coming at him and his men, the world falling down around him. Then the foray parted and Amelia emerged, facing him. He froze. There was no defeating a fallen. His only hope was help from another angel. Nathan, formed as a giant tiger, fought another beast in the distance. Dorian's light flashed, too far away to hope. He searched for Charis, not finding her at first, but then he saw her. She ran towards him. Could he hold Amelia off long enough?

He held up his sword and met Amelia's cold eyes. Her black leather armor clung tight to her slender body, contrasting her alabaster skin. Her sanguine smile was terrible. He readied himself for her attack. With one step, Oliver realized that something was wrong. Then he was in her grip, sword knocked from his hand, and her bony fingers locked around his neck.

*Too fast.*

The pain screamed on his inner-left thigh. He might have shouted, but her grasp cut him short. Hot liquid soaked his pants. Had he pissed himself? No, it was blood, he realized, fighting through the delusion of shock as agony became intermittent numbness and spasms of pain.

"That was easy," she said to him.

*Too easy*, her whisper came to his mind.

The artery was cut. This was how he died.

With his blood, thus flowed his existence. She let go of him, and he slumped to the ground, the pain exacerbated by the fall. He gasped for air, watching Amelia flee.

The beasts and soldiers were once more upon him, ready to make his death even more painful. The rumbling surged. The world shook, darkening. Battle stopped as man and creature looked around them. Then they ran.

He lay to the side, hoping they wouldn't trample him. He wanted to die in peace. That's when Charis had found him.

She knelt down, hands attending to his leg. Flecked with dirt and blood, she was beautiful against the blue sky. Her eyes were all he wanted to see as he died, but her workings hurt, and he squeezed his eyes shut. A roar filled his ears, like a terrible wave.

"Not like this," he heard her say. "Not like this."

*Not like this.*

Eyes back open, he looked down the narrow street. Buildings collapsed, crumbling to the earth. They would all die. They would be crushed.

The waters came.

The deluge reached them, catching their bodies in its current, demolishing everything around them. Charis's grip held him tightly, swimming against the torrent. He held his breath, each second begging him to breathe in, but he would die either way, and it was better for Charis to get away. He wanted to fight free of her, to let her save herself.

The surface gleamed above them, rays of light shimmering down, their shafts illuminating the silhouettes of the sinking rubble. A bold shadow blocked the sun and he beheld the great crocodile. It swam, serpent-like above them. It dove.

It approached with astonishing speed, and Oliver wondered why Charis did not flee. Surely this was not Nathan, not even he could shift into such a monstrosity. Charis swam toward it, and his heart pounded, blood pulsing from his wounds. Whatever healing she had managed before the flood had staunched some of the flow, but he still felt life leaking away. It didn't matter. He would die. Blood seeped from his leg, water threatened to fill his lungs, and now this beast—surely one of Amelia's pets—came for them.

With a rush it swam past, its wriggling body ushering waves around them. It darted beneath them. Oliver wished he could see it, wanted to look at his fate as its gaping jaws came up and closed upon him, to anticipate the moment.

He let the air from his lungs, its oxygen long spent, and he readied himself for death. Charis looked to him, and he looked to her, blue and floating, and he wished that even in his unworthiness that he could have had her just once. She looked so sure and hopeful, and he weakly put an arm around her, hoping that wherever she bade him off to, that she would find him there.

As water filled his burning lungs, the impact came, but no teeth closed around him. He was rising, faster now. They were upon its back, nestled in its ridges. Within moments he was coughing water while trying to gasp for air, fingers clutching at the rough terrain. The panic subsided, but he writhed in pain. Charis held him down on the scaled back of the creature. They broke from the flooded area, the great crocodile taking them through the shallows.

Through his faint vision, he saw the church, Dorian and the others awaiting them before its doors, wet and grave. He let the delirium take him, ready to die among his closest friends. They reached the dry steps and hands seized him, half-dragging his limp, bleeding body into the sanctuary, their panicked words a blur to his ears. The chapel was dimly lit and all he remembered was the old wooden cross just above the pulpit. He fixed his eyes on it, craning his neck back, beholding its inverse image. Charis worked the wound.

After that day, those like Talmas had little influence on him. He had chosen the book to reminisce, but those words held little weight for him after Chicago. He didn't know what he thought about God, but not all seven of the fallen angels had been plagues.

The events had been blurry. He still did not fully understand everything. Whatever Jacob had done, he had commanded the elements beyond even Dorian's abilities. Was that the limit of Jacob's power or had he held back to preserve that which he sought to rule?

There had been the question. Were they really saving the world from Jacob? Surely he would want anything he conquered to be the sort of place he would want to live. Jacob appeared to have other motives, and Dorian had been right to resist him. Jacob had done terrible things. They underestimated his wrath, the bitterness that he demonstrated right up to the walls of the mountains.

Amelia and Raven's armies had been used to bait them into Chicago. None recalled if Cain had been present, but whatever the case, Oliver seemed to have been targeted. While the motives were unclear, it was guessed that the attack on Oliver had been a distraction to keep Dorian, Charis, and Nathan unaware of the coming flood, and thus eliminate them without direct confrontation. It had nearly succeeded, and even the loss of Oliver alone would have been a substantial loss. Oliver's injury crippled him as well as their resistance, but at least it remained intact. With the most minor of successes, Amelia and Raven had survived the flood. They knew it was coming and evacuated before the worst of it.

Two hundred years later, Oliver still cursed the day of the fall, but he did not curse all who fell. He realized that he loved Charis, even if only too late.

Oliver climbed out of the bath. His leg felt better, but he knew the relief was temporary. Once dressed, a servant notified him that he was expected at the council dinner that evening. That left him a few much needed hours of relaxation, and so he decided to revisit the library for any other nostalgic gems.

The library, an extension of the mansion, was a large room of old stained, mahogany shelves, lined with books from floor to ceiling. Sunlight poured through vast windows, natural light illuminating the rustic leather-bound spines and tawny pages. He beheld it covetously, uncertain where to begin his search. When he found her copies of *The Chronicles of Narnia*, he retrieved the first book, eagerly flipping through its pages. Even the illustrations had been preserved. Charis loved those books. He should have known she would have such well-kept editions in their order of publication.

In the end, he chose to browse the more poignant parts he recalled from Dostoevsky's *Brothers Karamazov*. Almost late for dinner, he closed the book and left the library. He had been instructed as to where they would dine, but he wished he could meet the strangers one at time. It proved more painless than he had anticipated.

They did not meet at the round table in Charis's office, but rather in her solarium at an oval table. Other than Charis, he knew Obi, but the others who rose to greet him were new faces. The first was an older man, tanned skin, standing ridged as he extended his hand to Oliver.

"Jaked Mari," he said, his voice forceful, but surprisingly soft. Oliver shook his hand.

"This is the consulate. Meet Vicereine Adivee Sumtra," Charis said, beginning with a middle aged woman with tanned skin. "You already know Viceroy Obi Dan. Lem was a vicereine until her passing, may she rest. You will serve in her place."

"Do the people not elect their viceroys?" Obi asked.

'They do," said Charis, "but the matters at hand require an emergency governance."

"It has been more than a century since such a thing has happened," Adivee said. "What has come upon us?"

Charis told them. Apparently Oliver had been somewhat of a hero in Mere, memorialized among the greats in the war. There was even a statue of him in one of the squares, though Charis said it didn't look much like him. It was probably the better for his pride.

It felt bewildering to learn how much he had not known about this place, much less Charis. He stifled his longing to know her more. That could wait, but in the meantime, he needed to know more of her city. Mere had been a secret, for general security as much as to hide from Jacob. Nearly twenty-five thousand people lived within its walls, larger than he had expected, but well-populated outside of the urban center. The walls encompassed the pastures and farmlands. A nearby oasis was home to nearly three thousand people, densely populating condominiums among the shops and offices in the area. The scope of the walls encompassed more than ten square miles of living space, public buildings, pubs, and shops. He would have to explore later.

"This," Adivee said upon Charis's news, "is grievous." She was a teak-skinned woman, dark-haired with an upright posture.

"Indeed," agreed Jaked.

"Then," said Charis, "does the consulate agree to an emergency governance?"

"I concede," Obi said, formally, "so long as we send no one to battle against their will."

"So be it," Charis said, though Oliver saw that the concession was not without reluctance.

"Aye," Jaked said, and Adivee agreed thereafter.

"Then the matter is settled," said Charis. "We can welcome Oliver as our interim viceroy. In my absence, he also serves as Council Leader. I hope none of you will take this as a slight. You have worked close with me over the years, but Oliver's experience is paramount to our success."

Jaked stirred. "There is no man more respected than Commander Oliver. I consent."

"My lady," Obi said. "He may know the ways of war and leadership, but he does not know our ways."

"That I can learn," Oliver said, speaking for himself for the first time. "Your ways are derived from cultures long forgotten, ones I have lived long enough to know well. From Rome to France, these are historically rooted in things of which I am well-learned. I will not accept power unless it is freely given, but I assure you I am worthy of the task." He wondered that his own reluctance had faded.

"We have persevered for two hundred years," Obi said, "by our ways and traditions. Will we simply hand them over to an outsider?"

"Obi," Charis said. She put a hand out toward him and met his eyes. "You must remember, Oliver was a part of this before Mere was ever built. Can we not welcome him into our trusts once again?"

For a moment Obi appeared reluctant, but his expression softened. "As you wish," he said.

"You all have a say on this council," Charis said. "Do not acquiesce just because I ask it. Our utopia is at great risk, and while we cannot allow division among ourselves, dissent can be useful to balance." She looked to Obi again. "Do not do anything because I wish it, but because you believe it to be right."

"You are gracious, my lady," Obi said. "From little I know of this man, I know him to be honorable and competent and experienced. If you, who are of that much greater experience, also believe the same thing of him, then I will trust your judgment, and also trust that Oliver will do as he says."

"You are gracious," Oliver said.

"I thank you," Charis said, looking to her military commander. "Jaked, will you postpone your retirement for the time being?"

"Retire?" he said. "At a time like this?"

She smiled. "Thank you, sir."

"Once again," Oliver said. "I'm not here to disrupt your way of life."

"Jacob has disrupted enough already," Charis said. "You're in charge, by their consent as much as my own, because they are the wisest people I know. Take your place, Oliver. I'd sooner not put a man in charge who isn't wise enough to know his place, so do not be fool enough to refuse me."

"Well, when you put it that way—" Oliver said.

"It's settled, then," Charis said. "Let us eat and plan."

It was the finest food he had tasted since the war, just the right fusion of seasoning. The spiced mashed potatoes complimented the exquisite lentil curry, bringing back long-forgotten flavors. He noticed that no meat was served, but he didn't miss it. It reminded him of India, as if reflecting that past's influence on the strange amalgam of forgotten cultures. Charis hadn't appropriated them here, but rather preserved them.

It turned out that Commander Jaked Mari was well-versed in the ways of battle. He was strict, yet a well-loved commander of a sizable force of men and women. "There's place for everyone here," Jaked said. "Mere is an inclusive place, that goes for our military. A good soldier is a good soldier." Oliver respected that, and when Jaked said it, it became apparent that he meant it about himself, as if at one point he questioned whether he belonged.

Bottles of saison circulated the table, and when everyone was merry and full, they talked logistics. Charis would ride out and find Nathan, foregoing a guard in order to remain discreet. In Shima or Lavyn she would find someone trustworthy to watch for Liam if she could not find the boy first along the way.

"Are you sure this is wise?" Adivee asked. "Shima has a dark reputation."

"All the more reason to find someone there should Liam return that way. It is the most likely stop along the way and it's not too far from Mere."

Oliver was to work close with Jaked in preparing the army. The soldiers were trained, but inexperienced, and battle was imminent for them. Their longstanding peace was about to come to an end. Adivee, appeared to share Oliver's thought, and suggested that the threat might extend to Mere and that they needed to protect themselves from Jacob. "If this man is as ruthless as you say," she had said, "then he will come here first."

Obi, by the book as usual, an asset as much as a shortcoming, spoke next. "We were not meant for outside battle. Our forces are not offensive, they are defensive."

"That," Oliver said, "is correct, but this is going to mean serious battle on our part one way or another. We might as well prepare ourselves for anything. War is ugly. It is not gallant or pleasant, it is bloody and painful. It is also the last resort. But Jacob will bring against us that which does not compromise. It cannot be reasoned with. It will seek beauty only to destroy it. Jacob may very well march on Mere before he marches on the City. He may do so after. Either way, he's coming for us and we know it. But if it's not too late, if we can defeat him, then not only will Mere be safe, but at least the whole world has hope. One day Mere will extend what they've done here to the rest of the world as we know it."

Perhaps it had been the saison, maybe his eagerness or energy from his newly elected seat, but he wanted to do right by the responsibility. After the meeting, they moved from the table to the living area with its couches and chairs. They talked and drank well into the night, but Charis dismissed herself early. She had a long journey in the days to come. Oliver went back to his own quarters, having drank a bit too much. He wanted to find her in his bed, ready to be alongside him, but of course, she would want to be well-rested for the next day's journey.

At dawn he awoke, ignoring his aching head and limbs. She stood ready just outside the gate. With her parting embrace, she clung to him a moment, a whisper of love in his ear, and then she mounted the horse. She had disregarded her dress, giving it up for pants tucked into leather boots. A cloak protected her from the sun, and she bid him farewell as she climbed into the saddle. It bothered Oliver that she was alone, but he did not doubt in her wisdom. Not only was she capable, but she could travel faster alone and more inconspicuously than with a company. She rode into the Outlands, leaving Oliver in charge of Mere. He had the aid of the consulate, but if he was honest with himself, he was afraid.

# CHAPTER SIX

## *The Wayward Crew*

"Like flies swarming a pile of shit," Jacob had remarked of Gully's inhabitants. Their northward travels through swamps were bad enough, but Jacob had been right. It was a shit town. Between the backwater and the shore, mud caked each step, inescapable however far Maynard wandered inland. The miserable people buzzed about, covered in muck. The touts unceasingly pestered him, proffering useless trinkets, which he continued to reject. As Jacob led them to the inn, Maynard turned down old toys, dinted unlabeled cans of food, and mangy puppies.

The inn turned out to be little more than beds and chamber pots, so Maynard put his things in the assigned room, and went in search of as good of a drink as he was bound to find in Gully.

Seeking the driest spot between the swamp and the sea, he discovered the Quarter Ale House, where the watered down beer cost more than a quarter. Currency was ambiguous at best in such parts, but Maynard knew when he was being swindled. The bar was dry enough, and Maynard drained a pint and signaled for another round.

He wasn't surprised when Jacob found him there. "You have doubts," he said, sitting across from Maynard, knuckles rapping casually on the splintered table.

It was true. Though Maynard had kept silent through the swamps, Gully was too much of a letdown. And he distrusted Jacob. Furthermore, his clothes were ruined by the mud and he still had marks from the leeches. The alligator had been of little challenge, better tasting than intimidating. Sure, the goods he had brought from Bowdton sold at a fair price, better than he would have gotten anywhere else, and Jacob had already rewarded him handsomely. But no amount of money in his pocket could promise him that a future with Jacob was worth his efforts.

"I want to hear it from the beginning," Maynard said as the barkeeper set down another ale. "I may have an old family, but what I know is a patchwork of foolishness and mysticism. Jacob has never been a name spoken of highly."

Warped wooden chairs and tables littered the dim, smoky bar, patrons packed within its walls. The ale might have been a bit sour, but he found it just relaxing enough to challenge Jacob. Deep in conversation or drunk at their games, the other patrons paid them no attention. In one corner, a ragged group of men hunched over a game of cards. In another, they talked and laughed loudly amongst themselves. No one paid the occasional flicker of lights any mind.

Jacob sighed, glancing about the room, ensuring that no one eavesdropped. "You would be surprised how much foolishness and mysticism there is to it. The stories are always about the Eternal One and the Morning Star. God and the devil. Angels and demons. It's far more complicated than that, but those are basically the two sides in a war between what you might describe as spirits." Jacob cracked a proud, clever grin. "I thought, why not a third? Their little war was a nice enough distraction from my plan. I coerced six others to aid me, though they had no idea what they were doing, unknowing pawns in my little coup."

That was an uncomfortable thought. Jacob was a liar, not just against man, but against God. All men lied, but Jacob made a practice of dishonesty. Though not religious, Maynard was more so wary of a man who would defy a deity. He had asked for the truth, yet he wondered if he wanted to hear it. He could leave now and live his life in peace instead of being another pawn in Jacob's war.

But he liked battle, on the edge of chaos and death. No thinking, no talking, no strategy. Just the sword and blood. Morals concerned him little. He was a man of the sword. Someone had once given him advice: *You've got to do whatever it takes to get ahead and don't let anybody stop you.* It had become creedal to him, even if he had become so accustomed to living by it that he seldom recalled it. He would either die in battle or live long enough to grow rich from it. Then he'd live an easy life. Jacob's confidence was persuasive. Was this his path to victory, the way to the easy life?

"You were found out," Maynard said, deciding he wanted to hear more about Jacob's coup.

"Yes," Jacob replied. "The others were unaware, yet implicated. The Eternal One took pity on us, of all things. He couldn't bring himself to condemn us, but he couldn't forgive us, not like he did the humans. So, he sent us here."

"Knowing what would happen?"

"Oh, he believes himself to be a god of benevolence, of second chances, and mercy. Love and all of that stuff. He has great faith in humans and spirits alike. If there's the slightest potential for goodness, it's a risk he's willing to take. Of course, he knew how bitter I would be, but I think he underestimated my wrath. And perhaps Dorian's competence. And it wasn't an uncalculated assumption on his part. We were not the first to fall. Many before, particularly in the ancient times, chose life on earth. Others displeased the Eternal One, but they didn't want to side with the Morning Star. They were called the *Grigori*, and they lay with humans, their descendants the Nephilim. Which I reckon you are.

We were just a few more *Grigori*, spirits made flesh. The word 'angel' is the closest approximation, but we're hardly how the Catholics thought of us."

"The Catholics?" Maynard asked. It was a familiar word, but an ancient ambiguity.

"One of the many factions that worshiped the Christ. That's beside the point. What I'm getting at is that we fallen have always been rare, but this was still nothing new."

"But you were bitter."

"I *am* bitter." Jacob furrowed his brow. "I cannot be God, so now I want to rule the thing he loves most. This little planet in the middle of millions of planets is his baby. Why? I don't know, but he's certainly given it special treatment. But I want it for myself and I made the mistake before of trying to do it alone."

"But you have Amelia and Cain."

"And another. On the northern island. He's called Raven. Followers. All of them. I need a partner. For two hundred years, I have patiently seethed, waiting for the right time, and it's coming. I found a way to get what I want."

"Then why do you need me?" Maynard almost thought Jacob wanted him to be the partner, but he hardly saw how that was possible. There was something else to the scheme.

One of the men playing cards yelled, accusing another of cheating. When the commotion died down, Jacob continued. "Make no mistake. I do not *need* you. But you are valuable. Like I've said, I think in some way you are one of us. I've had my share of women. Cain too. Who knows, maybe Raven fathered a few bastards. I think I'd have noticed if Amelia bore a child, so you can at least rule her out.

"There are other possibilities. Raven healed a man and supposedly he still lives, though not without side effects. Maybe one of us healed your great grand-something. Whatever the case, few Nephilim discover their roots. The ones that do rarely live up to their potential. The fallen are few and far between as it is, most of their living progeny generations removed. But there's more in you. I can tell."

Maynard had often contemplated the possibility that there was something unique about him. On the outside he was an ordinary man. He was broad-shouldered with dark, red hair and a close-shaved beard. He should be an old man, but felt as quick and strong as ever, quicker and stronger than anyone he had ever known, save for Jacob and his fellow fallen. His sword was light enough for its size, but even still a normal man could not wield it so agilely as him. It had been more than that. Strength, after all, was of little use if one did not also have some cognitive advantage. While perhaps not exceptionally clever, his wits were partially creditable to his survival.

Understanding came natural to him and he often found his instincts served him better than most. And right now, his instincts told him that Jacob's point of view would get him what he wanted.

"Have you ever heard of Achilles?" Jacob asked.

"Can't say that I have."

"How even the great become forgotten," Jacob mused. "He was the mightiest of fighters, invincible, and victorious in all that he did. He was called to war, but his mother prophesied him two fates. If he were to stay home, he would live a long and peaceful life, fall in love, have a family, maybe never die. But he would be forgotten. However, should he go to war, he would die, but his name would be immortalized in legend. He could either be immortal in life, but not in name, or immortal in name, but not in life."

"And what did he do?" Maynard asked.

"He went to war. He died. But even now, when so much is lost, I tell you this story. Hear me, Maynard. I would not have you

114

choose between life and legend. I offer you both, with riches to match. If you follow me."

In all of his long life, his energy and competence had never faded, but strength meant little to a tired mind. And Maynard was weary. When his stamina and determination failed, what then? One day his fortitude would abandon him and to what end? An old man with nothing to show, all his endeavors wasted. Or perhaps he would die first, and in the Outlands, there was no good way to die. It was all or nothing, as the saying went, and Jacob offered all.

"I am not a pious man," Maynard said after a pause, "and I have little interest in getting back at your god. But if there is a hell, I'm sure to find it when I die anyway. I want battle and after that I want wealth and peace. If your little war can guarantee that, I'm in."

Jacob smiled.

The next morning, they searched for a ship. The overcast, damp weather closed in around Maynard, its sticky warmth like a swamp under his clothes. They walked the docks, rickety things lined with boats, most too small to do more than fish, but a few large enough to make a real voyage. The ships likely circled the large island, traveling and dealing among the southern archipelago.

To the other known landmass, the northern island, no ship sailed. Maynard breathed the salty air. Each captain gave the same answers. It was rumored one could circumnavigate the southern island twice in the time it took to sail to the northern land. There was nothing there. Not a single port, but a vast desert. There was rumor of one mad captain who would make the voyage, but he had not been seen in some time.

To make matters more difficult, Jacob wanted to voyage to the northwest side of the island, where he claimed they could follow a ring of mountains to a pass.

Nervous at the idea of sailing, particularly of a long voyage, Maynard's surety gave way to reservations of the daunting task ahead. What exactly did one do on a ship? Did it storm on those northern waters? It was said that the northern island was cursed and dry, but it was wet enough here in the south. Whatever the case, it sounded like more trouble than it was sure to be worth.

The sea, calm and quiet, lapped at the docks, caressing the hulls of the ships. Seagulls squawked overhead, fighting for the scraps from the morning's catch, though the real feast would be later when the other fishing boats returned.

Jacob ignored the fishermen, going to the captains of the bigger ships, their great, slackened sails drawing Maynard's wonder. Each captain turned them down, all for the same reasons. If Jacob was as powerful as he claimed, it was strange that he did not simply seize a ship. Perhaps taking a ship was one thing, but crewing it was another. Was Jacob scheming at something more grand?

As Jacob haggled with the next captain, Maynard caught Amelia glancing at him. She stood rigidly, wearing her usual black cloak. Jacob had called her a follower and it was apparent in what little she talked. She was attractive, but cold, almost pitiable, as if permeated by loneliness. He had seen that odd beast with her on the day they saved him from the outlaws. Jacob had said that she once summoned the creatures of the heavens, but now she summoned them from hell. As they went from ship to ship, Cain remained mostly silent during Jacob's interactions. He was the man for Jacob's dirty work, sadistic and fond of inflicting pain.

That left Maynard, also standing quietly as Jacob was turned down by yet another captain. Jacob wove a convincing web, but it seemed these sea-wizened men would not play the pawn, and neither would Maynard. He resolved that he redouble his efforts to disregard his reservations. He would follow Jacob. That was the way of mercenaries and they don't ask questions. But he had asked questions, and he found his niche in Jacob's war a vexing one.

When it was all said and done, what would he do? He was a simple man, driven by the same things that motivated anyone. Money, power, companionship. He was no fool. But this was big. More substantial than any of the other wars in which he had fought. The risks were great, the payoff more promising. Yet, both the risks and the payoff were far too vague to be convincing.

They had found their last hope of reaching the northern island. If Jacob couldn't convince this captain, they would have to wait for another, more willing ship to come to port, or find their own means. As far as Maynard was concerned, it was high time that Jacob showed some of the legendary power of which he had boasted.

"I'll tell you what the others told you," the captain said. "There's no way."

Jacob was clearly frustrated, trying to maintain his cool demeanor. "Did you hear how much I offered you?"

"They say you could circle our island twice in the time it takes to get there and then you want to go even further up. I can make more trading here."

"I doubt that," Amelia interjected.

"Well, no is no. So fuck off."

Jacob nodded at Cain and they turned and walked from the captain. By the time they had returned from the dock, back to the muddy bank, Cain had caught up with them, having paid the captain in kind for his rudeness.

For whatever reason, Jacob maintained the necessity of a fully crewed ship to take them to the northern island. Because Jacob was determined to pay for what he could more easily take, they would have to check the docks each day for new ships. Until then they were stuck in Gully and Maynard was not looking forward to days of soured ale. He had resigned himself to finding better beer, when a man from the docks hailed them.

"Wait," he said, waving his hands as he ran toward them. "A ship, *The Northern Lady*, is due back in two days." The short and stocky man appeared sea-worn. "They say she sails to the north, to the mountains, to mine it for whatever precious stones and metals they can."

Jacob studied him and gave him a nod. "You know this?"

"Aye," said the man. "Name's Harry. I've been known to sail north with them when times are tough for the traders."

"And," said Jacob, "how would you like to sail north again?"

"Why not?" Harry suggested. "Nothing for me here. Bad season for fishing and trading. Wouldn't mind a few of those gems myself."

"Gems?" asked Amelia with a condescending smile. "You look like you'd be more apt with a war-axe than a pickaxe. Maybe you should go with us into the desert, to war, and glory."

"Into the desert?" asked Harry. "Beg your pardon, but I'd rather be in a dark, cool cave looking for precious stone."

"Very well," replied Jacob. "But if you find anyone else who wants to come, I'll pay well for their passage. They can either follow me or go to the mines when the time comes. I'll pay either way. Tell that to your friends."

With the prospect of their coming voyage, Maynard spent the afternoon at the market. Between the sale of his own goods and what Jacob had paid him, he had sufficient funds to buy new clothes and supplies. Once in the desert, he doubted he would have another chance to restock, even if the merchants accepted the eclectic mix of coin and metal that passed for currency on the southern island.

The market streets were more stone and less mud, but the stench of the meat was enough to make Maynard think less about ordering the stew at the Quarter Ale House. He ignored the meat, thinking about the clothes he would need to replace those smelling of swamp.

Though he had never been in love, there had been women in his life. There were the regular whores, and other, more serious relationships with the conniving sort of lady one found in the mercenary business. There had been one woman in particular, a smuggler with whom he had shared the road for a season. She told him to buy clothing that complimented his eyes, which were brown around the edges, but faded to gold-flecked green closer to the pupils. She had loved his eyes, and though she was long gone, he continued to take her advice. When he had the option, he preferred dark greens, browns, blacks, and the occasional yellow. Appearance, however, was second to durability and function, but finding clothes proved easy enough, and he even purchased a sturdy pair of boots with a nice tread.

After acquiring suitable clothing, he sought a new pack. A replacement pack had been long overdue and the swamp had only exacerbated his need to replace it. It would have to feel balanced on the shoulders, the right size for his build, and durable. Few materials compared to leather, but preferable, pre-war synthetics still existed.

Within the mercantile district, two vendors showcased travel accoutrements, but their featured gear was unsuitable. The shop-made patent leather packs appeared expensive, however, their thinness testified to their lack of endurance. He searched the stocks, the rickety walls of their shacks shading them from the sun, but also blocking out any useful light.

On the verge of giving up, Maynard then spotted a small pile of well-used packs in the back of the second shop. He searched among them, some pre-war, but soiled and thin, others like the shiny sacks on the wall, having been too easily worn and discarded.

"Come now, my friend," the shop owner said over his shoulder. "Wouldn't you rather a new bag for your travels? I know you can afford it."

"So you'll make a bigger profit from that cheap, thin leather? We'll see what you have here." Maynard picked up a bloodstained pack and set it aside.

He found two usable bags. One of canvas, which would be good for the desert if it survived the sea. Thinking that likely, he shouldered it to see how it felt. It held a little less than his current pack, but it felt light and had various clips for bedrolls and other attachments.

The other appeared more worn, but the tag inside read WATER RESISTANT and that would be worth quite a bit. Had the shop owner been able to read, he might have noticed the label. Maynard hid a grin and shouldered the pack, finding the ventilation in the back comfortable. It was nice, bigger than his current bag, but he would have to sew straps on it for his bedroll. Simple enough.

"I guess this will have to do," Maynard said, as if settling for less. However, it was always the same with these shopkeepers. At first the man refused to part with it. "How did that get in there? That's not for sale!" Maynard's sword would have been handy. Had it been strapped to his back, the owner would have been less bold.

It took half an hour to settle on a less-outrageous price. In their haggling, two other patrons, clearly locals, had come, bought their wares, and gone without such difficulty. Maynard had coins, most with the face of some dead asshole on them. He also had rough metals, which if veritable as gold were worth more. The real value was in the gems, which ranged in color from piercing greens to deep reds to crystalline blues. Somehow, no combination thereof would satisfy the shopkeep until Maynard feigned surrender and made to leave. Only then was a price settled upon.

"Here's your money, motherfucker." Maynard said, putting down twice what the pack was worth. He turned and stormed from the shack.

In the market, Cain bargained for a set of knives. Dozens of blades were splayed on a cloth-lined table. The owner, a scrawny man, was somehow not intimidated by Cain's tall, muscular frame.

"That's twice what the knives are worth," Cain said to the keeper, jabbing a finger at him. Maynard stood behind him, watching his shoulders tense, tattooed glyphs and symbols spiraling from under his shirt. Maynard wondered at the intricate patterns a moment, but then decided to save the shopkeeper some pain.

"That seems to be the way they treat guests around here," he said to Cain.

"Can you believe this shit?" Cain replied.

Maynard motioned to the shopkeeper. "Give him the local price and he might let you keep your arms." The shopkeeper looked into Cain's depraved eyes, and decided to cut his price in half.

They walked together among the swarming market. Though taller than most men, even Maynard had to look up at Cain.

"Why'd you have to stop me?" the bald man said with a chuckle. "I was looking forward to tearing those arms off."

"I don't doubt it," Maynard replied. "You lot could be ruling this southern island if you're half as powerful as you say. I don't know why you even bothered bargaining."

"The southern island isn't what we want. God doesn't even want this shit-hole. I wasn't about to let the shopkeeper fuck me over, but money isn't much of an object to us. It was easier not to make a scene."

"Since when is killing not worth your while?" Maynard asked.

"You think I'm a monster, but I'm not."

"Then what are you?"

"I am chaos. As soon as people think they have things under control, everything goes wrong in life. We've gotten preoccupied, obsessed even, with control. The spirits, the humans, we all want to know what's coming next. Boring. There was an age of paradise and humans ruined it. Because you can't have control and know anything. To know something, you have to turn it upside down. Shake it up."

"So you hurt people," Maynard said.

"That's only one manifestation," replied Cain. "I delight in watching people lose control, to show them that they are going to die a horrible death and there's nothing they can do. They lose control. Of their bowels, their ideas, their will. Spill a man's intestines while he's still alive and he will pray to any god that he thinks will save him. The best part is the final moment when the praying stops and they realize the futility of it all."

Though Maynard liked battle, he never enjoyed human suffering. He had ended the pain of his fair share of men on this principle alone. Cain made him uncomfortable, made him lose faith in the world. But truth be told, were they so different?

"I know what you're thinking," Cain said. "But one day you'll have your choice in salvation and destruction and you will appreciate Jacob even more."

*Followers.*

*The Northern Lady* ported at Gully as promised. Harry was already at the docks when they arrived, grinning next to the captain. Judging by the captain's morose expression, the prospect aboard *The Northern Lady* was far from hopeful.

Jacob, normally calm and relaxed, matched the captain's stern countenance. He was a broad-shouldered man, weathered by the brine, with a long curling beard like some forgotten sea-god. His haggard and scarred face tightened at the sight of Jacob.

"I recruited forty men," Harry said. "They'll meet us at the Farthing Sour tomorrow at noon." Maynard thought he might need to try the beer there.

"Captain," Jacob said, ignoring Harry. "I hear you might be able to take us north."

"That would be Captain Reed to you," he said gruffly. "No passage. We are a mining ship. Not a passenger vessel."

"I will bring Harry and forty more men and pay for their passage as well. I mean to make for the northwest where the desert meets the mountains and then follow it around to the Pass. If these men want to come, so be it. Otherwise, you'll have an extra set of already-paid miners on your hands."

"You'd be wasting your time and mine. Once we get to the mines, our hulls will be too crowded with goods to carry the men back." Water splashed against the dock, gentle laps among the seagulls' cries.

"Then leave us in the desert," Jacob said. "We'll be content to starve there."

"And the forty men?" Captain Reed asked.

"No more than a handful will deny my offer, I assure you. You'll be compensated either way. Name your price."

The captain pondered a moment, crow's feet deepening around his eyes. Then he looked at Jacob and named his price. If Jacob had that kind of money, he could not have carried it with him through the swamps into Gully.

"Cain," Jacob said. "drown Harry."

Harry squealed backing away. "What the fuck, man? I didn't do anything, I swear." His shrieks echoed the gulls for a moment, before Cain forced his head underwater, bubbling for a few seconds.

"Care to come down on your price, Captain Reed?" Jacob asked after Harry's gurgling had stopped. He still squirmed and kicked under Cain's hold.

"Without his commission, it's fifteen percent less." If the captain was intimidated by the spectacle before him, he didn't show it.

"Half now and half when we get there," Jacob replied. Harry stopped squirming after a moment, but as Cain started to let go, he began to spasm again, albeit weakly. They all paused a moment, awkwardly watching Harry's last moments.

"Two-thirds now," the captain said.

"Deal. I will have it delivered." Harry stopped squirming and Cain let his body slump lifelessly into the sea.

Where Jacob acquired the money or how he had it delivered, Maynard never knew, but they were scheduled to set sail in two days.

# CHAPTER SEVEN

## *The Priest of Shima*

Once positive that no one followed, Liam rested. The intensity of the desert had tested even the camel's endurance. For all of Oliver's preparations and advice, their hasty flight had left him short-supplied. Though sore, he felt too anxious to break longer than it took to stretch and take a small amount of water. In theory, he knew how to follow the stars, but in practice he could only hope that he was on the right track. He headed south, but how far to the east or west had he deviated? The next town should have been Shima, unless he was off course and had passed it unknowingly. If he was more than a few miles off course he could have missed it. There were more towns after that and then the shoreline caves where he hoped to find Dorian.

He feared being alone in the desert, but then again he wasn't alone. There were raiders, crocotta, and other mysteries. A town meant safety, or so he had thought in Bronton. Liam had little sense of what had happened the previous night. The vision replayed, a man with a knife, a woman bleeding out from her throat. Oliver killed that man. And then Liam killed a man after that.

Oliver had led them there to save the dark skinned man. He was apparently important and as Oliver roused him, someone came up the stairs. Liam felt indecisive, hoping the approaching man was a fleeing innocent, or that Oliver would be the one to kill him. But the silhouette coming to the top of the stairs held a gun, raising it as he hit the landing. What had the man yelled? "Infinite bullets, motherfuckers!" Then he lay in a puddle on the floor, never anticipating Liam's gun. The sound had been deafening in the small room and in the following ringing, Liam's thoughts fell into chaos.

In the dim, he saw the bullet hole, nestled between two murderous, vacant eyes. The point blank shot had splayed the rest of the man's head down the stairs, slippery as they ran down them. Liam had almost vomited then, and would have, had he the time.

He shot another man that night, the one that Oliver recognized. It had been no ordinary raiding. The memory of Raven's eyes, unforgettable and ageless hatred, still made his stomach knot. Liam held the gun, steadied and breathed as Oliver had taught him, and something felt right. He gently pulled the trigger. Raven had not cried out, only broken his stride, and his hand bled.

They fled and parted ways. The man with Oliver had said something: *Remember, people like us have to be careful out here.* That was the thing about being black. He always had to be careful, even as a member of the prophet's family. It was no secret that one reason many did not flee to Novum was because Jacob played on their fears and prejudices. The City itself wasn't exactly free of those things. Every time someone slighted Liam, even the insistence that he go alone and the ambivalence on part of both the Church and government, left Liam wondering if the heart of those things went back to the color of his skin.

Now Liam was in the desert alone. Every rocky outcropping and dune harbored the unknown. There might be bandits, crocotta, or perhaps the desert hid worse things. His newfound world had pushed Novum to the back of his mind, but as he rode in the stark desert, its heat bearing down on him, his thoughts turned to home. Had it been home to him or a construct of false solidarity? In his few days outside of it, he hardly thought of what lied within the walls. The monolithic pyramid was the last stand for civilization. It was four triangle walls, glass dark as obsidian, towering up at the center of the mountains.

What little comfort lay within came from those like Ferrith, Standon, and Perry, but it did little against the smothering air, cloying words of High Priest Tasrael, and the contrived contentment. The prophet had spoken of an age of immortals and a city that would protect mankind from them. But what did that city protect? Corporations seized the opportunity to save themselves. Had the prophet been wrong, they still would have the world's most advanced, self-sustaining resort on their hands.

And what had religion become? There was no longer the Christ, but rather an institution with its own corporate concessions. The lines between the sacred and secular were blurred, but at the abstraction of the sacred. Liturgy and tradition persevered, but Elijah claimed that the details had fallen into obscurity. Orthodoxy was a method of control by which the prosperous reigned.

Novum had been open to all, but affordable to so few. Oliver had confirmed as much. How exorbitant might it have cost to live in Novum had the angels not fallen? What a relief it must have been that they did; a backwards sort of comfort at the end of the world. By satellite and the airwaves, Jacob's propaganda circulated the City, his attempts to convince them to let him in. Failing gentle persuasion, Jacob's pursuit turned to war. He landed on their island and marched on Novum.

Dorian had been thwarted at every attempt to stop Jacob and even in the distance, the prophet had said that he could see Jacob's armies approaching the last city. Jacob's anger burned. What field or forest was left after the terraforming had been put to flame, scorching all that it could in bitter conquest. Jacob's victory had been imminent.

Until, from the ashes, Dorian came, lifting his hands in anguish. The wall arose. The ground trembled and deep in the bowels of Novum, a mile deep, the tremors echoed as Dorian made his last stand. The mountains—the ring, the wall—grew and after that, nothing threatened Novum. The last radio calls promised finality, that with the mountains, Jacob had given up. Year one was over, and the City severed its outside contact. By whatever power and wards Dorian had raised the mountains, he had also protected the Pass.

Novum's sigh of relief was short-lived, for the abandonment of outside communication did not keep the darkness out. The only thing more degenerate than that of a fallen angel is the pride of men. Though the sun's light, darkened by the tinted glass, shone on the city gardens, and though their roots ran deep, Novum only grew to be a place of manipulation, shallowness, and pride.

So few of these memories were Liam's own. His grandfather, the prophet had guided him, teaching him the true histories. Ferrith had taught him as well, knowing the old ways. Though he had not been there, Liam could almost envision the fiery swirl of clouds expelling a fallen angel, the smell of brimstone, the vibrations from the impact, the pain of the people.

For all his growing cynicism, Liam did miss Novum. He longed for its safety, for the light warming the gardens, the rooftops he would climb with Perry. He felt guilt for not missing his family, wishing he understood those last moments with his mother and father.

The sand and rock baked in the heat. He had to worry about the camel, where he would fill his canteen, and finding Dorian. At times the desert stretched in hard-pan earth, a flat and orange plain as far as he could see. Other times, hills loomed in the distance, and Liam rode towards them, rock and rubble in hues of grays and browns, scattered with sparse patches of vegetation, weeds and desert flora nestled within them. Sometimes a cropping of trees would surprise him, too withered and thin to be more than firewood once dead and dried. It was a wonder any wooden structures existed.

Liam found the heat more bearable than he had anticipated. It was uncomfortably warm, but this land had been manufactured, and so it was not as hot as a true desert, if any of those still existed. However, Oliver had warned him to be wary of the heat, that the dryness would evaporate his sweat, leaving him dehydrated without warning.

By nightfall, he was too exhausted to make a fire. He nearly fell from the camel the second time he drifted to sleep in the saddle. He had wanted to find a town with an inn, but he would have to camp in the desert for the night. The crocotta were clever, mostly scavengers, only exerting themselves to hunt fresh meat when necessary. As for outlaws, they were seldom subtle, and he would hear them long before they neared him. These were the thoughts that comforted him as he dismounted the camel.

He took a little time to unroll his blanket, sore and stiff from the day's riding. The events in Bronton had left him short on rest, and though its horrors still plagued him, he was too tired to let them trouble his sleep. As he drifted into a slumber, he thought about how dirty he was. As every nick and bruise came to life, he thought about a warm bath. He would be lucky to get a quick rinse in the desert where water was so sacred.

He awoke the next day with a dry throat. He opened his eyes to the morning sun's yellow light on the desert sands. Laying on the desert floor, coming to his senses, he exhaled, disrupting a dusty cloud of sand. The cool ground told him it was early. Rising stiffly, muscles still aching, he took a sip from his canteen to clear his throat. The water sloshed in the bottom, a concern if he didn't find a town soon. Shima should be close. He hoped.

He looked to his camel, her unworried expression somehow soothing. "Well find a town today," he told her. Once mounted, he rode at a steady trot, wanting to find a town soon, but not wanting to push the camel too hard. Often on the journey, he spoke reassurances to her. Had he thought about it, it made him feel better as well. "Today," he told her, "we'll find water. Not that you're worried. I'm sure you could use the rest, though. All said and done, they'll tell stories about us. The man who was marked by fire. And his camel." He cracked a dry smile at that.

Lucy continued her trot, but she gave him a glance. Her large eyelashes fluttered, and a wry smile seemed to agree. To the Liam of the City, talking to a camel was insanity, rubbish. To Liam of the desert—of the Outland—it was the way to stay sane and keep hope. Eventually, the hope was rewarded, and with heavy footfalls, Lucy bore him into a town. It had slowly grown on the horizon, the shabby structures appearing and, with gradual progress, drawing near. Though the water had been out for a short time, Liam felt as if days had passed, though it was only an afternoon. It was in his malnourished, overheated, and stupefied state that he first witnessed Shima.

Oliver had told him of the different towns. Wandering streets composed some, while others were centralized by a main road cutting through the center. Towns that were not walled tended to have a main drag with stores, inns, smiths, and taverns at either side, and homes on the outskirts. For most, a population of more than a few dozen was considered large.

A drag of desert cut straight through a small group of mostly flat-topped clay buildings and huts. Liam followed it up and into the town, looking for the nearest inn among the clustered structures. At the center of the town, the public square, a crowd stood before a platform. Dismounting, he tied Lucy to a post and saw the man on the wooden stage.

His robes were black. His hat was black. The round lenses of his sunglasses were like onyx. He wore white bandages on his face and hands, covering all but the tips of his shriveled and burned fingers and the chapped lips through the hole in his facial wrappings. He stood upon the wooden platform looming over the crowd, a weeping young man before him on his knees, wrists bound and bloody. The young man was naked and dirty, unshaven and bruised. He was also dark skinned, and Liam remembered the parting words of the man in Bronton.

"People of Shima!" the black-robed man spoke, motioning behind him. "We have burned the whore." The corpse of the woman clung to the nearby pillar, her gnarled and burned body the color of the man's robes. Liam shuddered, the faint smell of char in the air.

"The whore has paid," the black-robed man continued. "But what of her lover?"

The crowd responded, a blur of angry shouts.

"People!" He held bandaged hands spread wide, his body a twisted cruciform. "You know that I am merciful. This man is a victim. The poor soul could not resist the temptress and it is but his first trespass. His punishment should be lenient. But this is a man of the temple. A personal embarrassment. Is it not enough that I am afflicted? That I have a condition that impairs me. I need dependable and honest people in my service. I've been used," he rasped. "Andrew, my own acolyte, has sinned egregiously. He must be punished accordingly. What say you?"

The crowd roared in indistinguishable cries, all of which seemed eager for Andrew's demise. The man silenced them with a wave of his hands. "And you, Andrew? How do you plea?"

"Mercy," the naked young man begged. The tumult rose again as the crowd opposed him.

"He shall have mercy," the black-robed man shouted over them. "He shall be absolved for his sins, but only after requital."

He looked to Andrew , hand extended in contrived compassion. "My child. You can be saved, but you must pay for your sins." He looked back to the crowd. "God may forgive Andrew, but forgiveness is not enough. He must turn from his ways. I cannot judge his heart. I cannot tell if he is truly repentant. So, let the spirits decide." The black-robed man clenched his fists before the crowd. "Take him to the box."

"No," Andrew begged as two men dragged him from the platform. "Please. You said I'd be spared."

"And if you are truly repentant, then you shall be. Only the spirits know your true heart."

"I'm innocent!" The men continued to pull him away as he struggled.

"Yes," replied the man. "By this you may be made innocent."

Andrew shouted more, but it was lost in the noise of the gathered crowd, their cries rising above his pleas. They had been zealous for Andrew's punishment. The black-robed man had manipulated them to get what he wanted. Did he really believe the spirits would judge Andrew or did the priest have another motive, something to do with this box? Behind those bandages were secrets, Liam was sure, but weariness and dehydration were more pressing.

He turned to the nearest inn, but stopped when he felt that he was being watched. He looked back. From behind those round, black spectacles the man stared at him. Liam turned away from the unsettling glare and made his way through the crowd and to an inn.

Carl's Stop was almost empty since everyone in the town had gathered to see the judgment. It was a small inn, nestled between a large general store and some sort of office. The wood was old, splintering among the cracked clay patchwork. The small commons boasted little more than a bar and mismatched furniture. Stairs led to a second floor, where Liam assumed were additional rooms. Tables sat vacant, scattered with half-empty beer mugs among a littering of cards, chips, and dice. An old acoustic guitar leaned against the corner wall, a wonder to Liam who had seen so few wooden instruments and most often in the hands of the very wealthy. Other remnants from the past hung from the walls or sat on shelves, some of which Liam knew, other relics too old and forgotten to recognize. One sign bore a Coca-Cola logo, another five interlocking rings of various colors, the most curious of which limited the speed to sixty.

The square cardboard pieces mounted on the wall must have been the sleeves to vinyl records. He recognized that much. One album cover depicted an old man, hunched over with a bundle of sticks on his back. Was that what the world looked like so long ago? Another had a dark-skinned man lounging on his side in a white suit. From the other side of the room, it was difficult to discern the cursive writing on the cover.

"Can I help you?" a man asked, presumably Carl the owner. His voice was quiet, as if hiding behind his handlebar mustache.

"I'd like a room for the night," Liam said. "And some water and food and ale."

"All right," the man replied, "the wife can see to your room, we have a vacancy just down the hall. I'll get your food going. Let me get Lyn."

He called for her and she came bustling into the room, smoothing her apron, and for all of Carl's reticence, she chattered on about available rooms and the inn. "We'll take just about any good silver for a night's stay, so long as you don't cause trouble. There's always food if you want, but the hot meals are at sunrise, noon, and around six o'clock. Last call's at midnight and then we lock the doors. It's a small town, but we aren't taking chances."

As she talked, the townsfolk began to wander back in, resuming their drinks and games, their murmurs returning warmth to the old tavern.

Curiosity regarding the priest's mysterious box nudged at him. Perry and he had explored every inch of Novum, even the top of the Central Spire. It had been Perry leading the way, Liam the reluctant follower, but in the Outlands he had found his own curiosity. For now, Liam needed a room, water, and food, though he lost his appetite at the events in the town square. Hopefully, hunger would return by the time the food was ready. Lyn escorted him to a simple first-floor room with a bed, a table, and an oil lamp. She gave him the key, told him where to find the lavatory, and left to fetch the water.

He examined the key, rubbing the brass teeth. According to Oliver, not all inns had locks. It was strange coming from Novum where it seemed every door had a lock. Their keys were not like the relic he held, but plastic cards or fingerprint readers. For this particular lock, he was grateful, the gaze of the man in black still lingering in his memory. He would tuck a knife beneath his pillow.

From his pack, he took his valuables and stashed them under the mattress and deposited what remained in the corner. Even with a lock, he knew he could not be too careful. Any thief would hopefully steal his pack, not thinking that he had other possessions stashed elsewhere. Liam would not be without his gun or tradeables. Whatever else was stolen—his change of clothes, blanket, light cooking gear—could be replaced.

Lyn returned with a pitcher of water and a ceramic cup before leaving him alone again. He drank heartily. Once settled in, he felt better. Andrew's fate still bothered him, the short nights of sleep had left him lethargic, but the hydration had gone a long way in reviving him. Whatever happened in this unnerving town, he would restock on supplies this afternoon and be rid of the place the next morning. He decided he was hungry after all and that stabling Lucy could wait.

Other than simple tables and chairs, there was a small bar. It might have once been a deep blue, but the years had left it faded and chipped. The tables were mostly full and the idea of sitting at a bar had grown on him. Besides, there was no use in him taking up a whole table to himself.

He ordered ale while waiting for his food. A few days ago, Liam had never tasted beer, but now he found that he liked it a great deal. The innkeeper stood at one end of the bar, hand-rolling a cigarette, and Liam wondered what he knew about the black-robed man.

"The beer's good," Liam said, raising his glass, though he knew he hadn't really developed a palate enough to distinguish what exactly made good beer. Carl perked up at the compliment.

"Yep," Carl continued, "The stuff down the road's good and all, but I'm a simple man. Don't need anything more than this." He paused and his expression turned ponderous. "Say, I don't want to get into none of your business, but we don't hear a lot about wider doings. Any news?"

Liam trusted the man, but he could not tell him about the prophet, Jacob, and the City. "Looks like you have enough going on around here."

"You can say that again," Carl replied.

"Who's the man in black?"

"The priest," Carl said, his face souring. "Came years ago to save the town. Or so he says. Things were well enough without him if you ask me. But he's gone about purificating us. That poor girl of Andrew's must have had it coming or I don't reckon the priest would find a reason to burn her. All the same, not the type of thing I'm liking to see. I could hear her screams from here and that was bad enough."

"What's the box this priest speaks of?"

"The box," Carl began, "was something the priest brought with him. He says that a man stays in it overnight and whether he comes out dead or alive is the way we know if he's guilty. The spirits judge him."

"Has anyone ever come out of the box?"

"Sometimes, but most of the time not."

"And the people that don't?"

"Look like a wild animal got a hold of them, they say. All torn up. I don't like to think about it really."

"Where is the box?"

"Like I said, I'm not the sort to like that kind of thing. Father Solomon does his thing out there and the town gathers, but that's when me and Lyn stay inside. We like our quiet life and it seems the quieter folks are around here, the less likely they are to end up inside that damned box. Any news of the outside, boy?"

Liam cringed at being called boy, but held his tongue. "Bronton was sacked and I'm fleeing. I knew a guy that went south some time ago and I'm looking for him."

"Revenge?" Carl asked.

"Nothing like that. I think he can help me. I just need to find him."

"Everyone's looking for something, I suppose."

Lyn came in from the back kitchen, a plate in hand. "Beans, mutton, and cornbread," she said, setting it before Liam.

"She's the best cook I ever met," Carl said.

"Did you say Bronton was sacked?" she asked.

Liam nodded, swallowing his first bite. The food was good. "Bandits put it to the torch. I barely made it out alive."

"Oh, poor Thom," Lyn said. "Bronton was a safe place, too big a town to have to worry about bandits much. It worries me."

"Thom was a fine man," Carl added. "Made good beer too. I think I saw the bandits you're talking about pass by a few days ago. Never seen a group so big, and I'll tell you, I was sure they'd come for us. They went right by without trouble. I thought maybe they weren't bandits after all, maybe one of those crazy religious groups or nomad tribes around the Eastern Pan. I'm sorry to hear about what happened in Bronton. It worries me. We could be next. I'll tell you, the world's changing."

It wasn't long before other patrons called on the innkeepers, and Liam was left alone to his mutton. He wasn't sure what mutton was, but it tasted good. It also bothered him. This was not the lab grown meat of the City, but rather that of a once living animal. It's why he had requested a meal without meat back in Bronton, but he was so hungry that he could hardly ponder it as he bit into the flesh. Perhaps he should have felt guilty, but he had bigger things to worry about.

After stabling Lucy, Liam restocked on water, dried goods, and other supplies. As the sun set, he retired to his room. He checked to make sure that all was where it belonged and blew out the candle as he nestled into the sheets of his bed.

When he wakened in the dark room he lay still a moment. He calmed his breathing, listening between heartbeats. No smoke in the air, no flickering fire, no screaming in the streets. Again he regretted his lack of a watch, something he should have procured somewhere in the town's market, but he guessed it was near three o'clock. He stretched as he got up from the bed, rubbing sleep from his eyes. He wanted to know what was in the box. What was happening to Andrew?

The nail-tip of a moon provided little light, particularly through the dirty and hazed window. He lifted it, stepping into the dirt-packed alley. No light filled the windows of the homes or shops. The town slept. In the square, the faint stars lit the platform. From there, Liam wandered the grouping of buildings, searching for the box. For Andrew.

His extra set of clothes warmed him in the desert night. He pushed a stray dreadlock behind his ear, wishing he had thought to tie his hair back.

Perry and Liam had scaled every part of Novum at their disposal. For a time he expected they would be caught, but trouble never came of it. Master Ferrith figured it out, and to Liam's surprise, encouraged it. The buildings of Shima clustered together, boxes and barrels stacked at their sides. He worked his way up the nearest roof to gain a better vantage. He surveyed the town, the platform at the center and the silhouettes of the buildings down the main drag. He walked along the conjoined buildings, feet falling light on their roofs, until he came to their edge. He let himself down, deciding to work his way around the outskirts of the small town.

Creeping along the edge of a building, a sound came like a quiet chuckle. Liam gripped the hilt of his sword, back pressed against the nearest wall. The inhuman laugh came again. The darkness hid the desert beyond, where anything might stalk him. The cackle came close. He risked a peek around the building's corner. Its eyes glowed in the dim light of the moon. A single crocotta stealing into Shima. Then came the human voice. A pleading. "Oh God. No. Please."

Crouching low, Liam dared to move closer. A nearby stack of crates let him up on the nearest roof. He inched his way to the edge, looking down on the source of the noise. This close, it was bigger than he had realized. It looked more like a buffalo than a hyena, though it stepped gingerly up to the small shed. "Please," a voice begged from within. It was Andrew. "I won't tell anyone. I swear."

The *box* was a shack of equal proportions. It was perhaps eight feet in width, length, and height. The creature approached it, using its paw to lift the wooden plank that barred the door. "Please. I'll go away. Never come back." The door cracked and the over-sized hyena wedged its snout into the shed, sniffing at its prey. *No* and *oh, God* interrupted Andrew's sobs. The repetition grew louder as the crocotta came closer.

Liam should do something. He drew his sword, careful not to let it ring out as he pulled it from its sheath. The beast was so big, so terrible. Liam's body felt stiff, but his hands shook and his breath ran shallow.

The crocotta lunged at the shed. It rocked. Shrieks echoed in the night amid growling and gnashing. The smell of blood and shit solicited nausea in the back of Liam's throat.

In less than a minute the tumult ceased. It stopped and from the shed's door, two burning eyes peered from the darkness, reflecting the moonlight over a bloody snout, like the priest had looked at him earlier that day, like the same eyes that had lurked behind those black-disked sunglasses.

He wanted to run. Had it seen him? Should he stand and fight? With a shiver, he fled, sheathing his sword as he ran. As light-footed as he could, he hurried along the rooftops, jumping between them. The night obfuscated each building. Fear clouded his mind. His stretch of buildings ended and he stopped, clearing his thoughts. Breathing hard, he crouched down, wary of being seen. Something was wrong. He had made enough noise to wake the neighboring houses, but no one stirred. He held his breath, but the sound of breathing continued, coming from below. It pursued him.

He ran again, back the way he had come and along another line of roofs. He worked his way down one side, into the dark alley, and up another roof, fearing the claws in his back. He made his way closer to the square. He stumbled, sliding down a roof, catching himself before its edge. The inn was close, but the moonlight was too dim. He finally spotted its sign by its shape. He paused, holding his breath again, listening. Nothing. Had it given up? A fainter sound. Not breathing. Sniffing. He needed down from the roof and across the square to the inn.

He should have brought the gun. He should have taken his sword to it before it killed Andrew. He felt a chill in the desert night, an unsettling rustle in the sands. The man marked by fire. *Or the boy?* He hardened his will, gathering his resolve. He dropped from the rooftop stealthily, but dangled, holding the ledge by his fingertips, waiting for any sign of danger.

He let go, dropping in the dark quiet. His toes struck the ground, and he dashed for the inn. His fingers reached the door, and he tugged at it. It was locked. *Of course.* Scuttling around the building, fingers running along the wall, searching for his cracked window, he thought he heard something pursuing him. Something near.

His digits found open air, and he squeezed in through the open window. His body halfway into his room, he shook as the fear took him. Jaws would lock down on his leg at any minute, tearing him from his journey, sealing him to Andrew's fate.

Long seconds later he was inside his room. He slammed the window shut, locking it down, and wishing he had a curtain. He tried to slow his breathing, but watching the tremor in his hands just made it worse. Nausea crept upon him, but he pushed it down. He had been stupid. He should have done more. But then he might be dead and what of Dorian and Novum? Bravery was a hair away from stupidity, and he had been foolish to investigate the box in the first place.

Sleep eluded him as he turned in his bed, sticking to his sweat-soaked sheets. For a time he sat up in his bed, the faint oil lamp illuminating the bare wall. He stared at it. What was the priest's game? He found people he didn't like, subjugated them to the "spirits," and then fed them to the crocotta. That was strange sport. It made no sense.

His frazzled nerves yielded no sleep, but the matter was best forgotten. In the morning he would leave, too early to worry about the night's events. He had evaded the crocotta, and now the locked doors and safety of the walls protected him for the night.

He didn't bother to remove his clothes. When he had enough of staring at the wall, he extinguished the oil lamp and lay down, hand under the pillow, finding the safety of the knife. He slept.

There had been a smell at the platform. As the priest spoke, a strange odor pierced the air. It was not the smell of burning. It was something else. Something metallic. He did not recognize it, not consciously, but it was the same smell that led him to the box. To the crocotta.

Why did he smell it in his dream?

His eyes opened, the confusion brief. Then he knew the smell was in the room. The odor of blood, like the smell in Bronton after Liam had shot the man.

The oil lamp burned, though he had blown it out. In its light, the man leaned close, the smell coming from his breath. He had a rugged face, hard wrinkles at the corners of his eyes. He wore the priest's black robes, but no bandages. His ears stuck out under a nest of hair, absent of the black hat he had worn earlier. He hunched over Liam, his nose flaring as he sniffed at the air around him.

Liam gripped the dagger under his pillow.

"A pity," the priest said, his voice wild and raspy, deep and velvety, but also grating.

Liam fixed on his black eyes. "What do you want?"

"To eat you," the priest replied. "Unfortunately, I can't."

"Please don't eat me," Liam said, the previous fear returning, a meekness in his voice.

"No," said the man. "*He* wants you alive. To question you himself."

"Who?" Liam asked, finding courage in his hidden weapon.

"So many questions. All will be answered, but the short of it is, kid, you're coming with me."

This man was not like Oliver. He was not a good man and did not want to help Liam. If he could help it, Liam would go nowhere with this priest. Contemplating his move with the dagger, Liam tensed. The priest sensed it and made to grab him. Stunned by his own quickness, the dagger met the man's side.

Warm blood poured over Liam's hand, gushing over the bed. Nausea found him again, but he struck once more. He looked into the priest's eyes, no surprise in his vacant expression and apparent bloodlust.

"Why would you do a thing like that?" the man asked, falling from the bed and stumbling to the floor, dagger just under his ribs. Liam leapt from the bed and kicked the man, bare feet striking his first wound. He then searched for his sword.

"Don't bother," the priest said, removing the dagger from his chest and staggering to his feet. Blood dripped to the floor, but not as if the man continued to bleed. "I took care of the sword already. The dagger was an oversight. Should have searched you and the room better. A minor setback."

The priest tossed the dagger to the floor away from both of them. Liam eyed the window.

"You can forget that too. I lost you between the buildings earlier. That's only because you surprised me at the box. You can't outrun me." The priest had been at the box. Had he been spying on Liam? What did this man want? The dagger hadn't slowed him down. Someone wanted him for questioning. His stomach turned as he feared Andrew's fate would be his own. Certainly it was. Liam stopped his thoughts. Liam, the man marked by fire, looked at the man, mustering his defiance.

"Now, kid," the priest said. "You and I are going to have to come to an understanding. You're a wanted man. There's a bounty and all. My job is to make that happen. I can outsmart you, outrun you, and find you. It'll be easier if you just come." The man gestured at him with thin and burnt fingers. He loomed against the lamp's light, swaying slightly.

The man approached, and Liam readied himself to fight, but the priest did not assault him. He laid a hand on Liam's shoulder. "You're not going anywhere. I have you."

# INTERLUDE

## *The Fallen*

*In the days that we traveled and warred together, I spent a great deal of time with Dorian. He would visit me during the alone times, knowing, I suspect, that it was a welcome distraction from the pain in my leg. It started with the talk of ordinary things—as ordinary as they might be given our circumstances. It did not take long before Dorian began to speak wistfully of his world, a fantastical planet much like our Earth, but with rings like that of Saturn.*

*When he discovered my efforts to preserve his tale, he warned me, riven from Elesonia as he was, that it did not have a happy ending. However, the story fascinated me so, that it became cathartic for me to put it to paper, much of it in Dorian's own words, in as much as I can remember them.*

*When he first began his tale, it started so naturally that I hardly realized what was happening. Dorian was often captivating in that way, somehow able to extemporaneously conjure immense joy or sorrow, fear or courage, and weave a tale that thrilled and terrified me. I doubt that I have done the telling justice, but I believe that it must be told all the same. I had no pen or paper at hand on the first night, but it is perhaps the most memorable part of his story, for it answered a great deal of questions about what had happened in the Outlands and in Novum.*

*—Oliver*

They called me Dor and I was a god. I was not *the* god, but I was a god, the revered steward of a world that I created. I gave lesser spirits their dominions, authority over the places of my world, but one nation found my favor, and I smiled upon it, defended it, and kept it safe. They were a resourceful people, immensely efficient on their own, the only thing that gives me hope that they survived my absence. Their country was a beautiful place of lush flora, brilliant architecture, and rich culture. The closest thing to it on Earth might have been Southeast Asia, and the people, like me, did not look so different from the people of India.

I made my dwelling upon the rings, my palace of rock, ice, and crystal, a cool rainbow arching around the planet, fading into ghostly white. I frequently deigned to descend, to take a closer appreciation of what I had created for them, marveling at how they had shaped it. I still recall the rings' beauty from the shores of Seabridge.

Then Jacob visited me. I still remember his form, coming before my throne, and he told me that the Eternal One was in danger. I had known Jacob for as long as I had existed, familiar with his wisdom, but also his cunning. I had no reason to distrust him, but I was wary of his words.

"Brother," he called me. "Great tumult rises upon Earth, demanding the Eternal One's intervention. Balstone was commissioned to guard his High Palace, but instead has seated himself upon the throne, declaring it for himself. He claims he has done what the Morning Star could not do, and usurped the Highest God."

I had known Balstone all of my long existence as well, a noble spirit of renown, comparable to Michael and Gabriel, but even after millions of years, the fall of the Morning Star remained a constant reminder that even the best of us can be consumed by darkness. I was of a skeptical mind. The Eternal One could defend himself and could easily sort out Balstone and I had pressing matters on Elesonia. Then Jacob said this: "The Eternal One summons us himself to tend with the problem. Cain, Charisen, Nathalian, Amlyca, and Revenar are called to aid us."

Of course, you know them by their other names. Just as I was Dor and came to be known as Dorian on Earth, thus did Charis, Nathan, Amelia, and Raven have their celestial identities before their fall.

I remember my last glance at my world, the way my eyes scanned the doings, searching the hearts of beloved and enemy alike. I saw the threat in the north and my best hope against it and I told myself that whether or not I was there, the mechanisms had been set into place, and that no intervention of mine would make any further difference. I hoped to return before the other coming threat arose, before Callianeira could make her mischief.

I allowed Jacob to lead me, and we traveled the celestial highways, faster than light, and we passed into a realm beyond time and space. I had been there many times and it was as glorious as the gates of hell are terrible, each equally indescribable. We entered its halls of light and crystal and even over the millennia the marvel never dulled. It was a garden of life and light, of ageless beauty. There we found Balstone and his defenders. How he had amassed so many spirits to fall with him was beyond me, but the seven of us were the best. We destroyed them all, and I dare not tell you what that means for a spirit of our caliber and being, for we are not the ethereal things thus conceived in human tales, nor are we flesh.

Having slain Balstone and his followers, the seven of us gathered, battered and tired, the High Palace a massacre, but one I believed to be of justice. I was ready to allow Jacob to be the steward of the High Palace until the return of the Eternal One, and when I suggested as much he laughed. By now, you have probably heard that laugh, but I assure you it was nothing so terrible as it was that day in the Eternal One's court. He called me a fool, among other things, words in the tongues of angel's that could crack the earth, bring fire from the skies, and strike fear into the bravest man.

Yet, we were in another world, the realm of the Eternal One, and I stood strong as he accounted himself to me.

"The Eternal One quests to save his precious planet of Earth. Why it ever needed special attention or why the Morning Star took such an interest in it, I'll never know. Whatever the case, the Eternal One became preoccupied. He thought only of the *love* of his creation and forgot the important thing. He forgot *power*. Whatever battle he fought on Earth, he lost to the Morning Star. I am *the* god now and this your opportunity to reign instead of serve."

Charisen had gasped then and I saw something in her that broke. Though not naive, there had been an innocence to her. She was a spirit of creation and beauty, unlike any other, the delicate and artful one who made things grow, for form as much as function. She never lost that, but it has been jaded ever since, something for which I do not expect to ever forgive Jacob.

As for Nathalian, his eyes burned fire then, deeper red than his hair even, a righteous anger that travailed within his mind, that might burst forth at any moment. One look from Jacob and Nathalian's defiance passed into something I had never seen in him and never saw again. Fear and doubt crippled him for but a moment, but then he looked to me.

It took perhaps too long for me to realize that Amlyca, Revenar, and Cain looked at me too, but in a different way. I knew that I had Charisen and Nathalian on my side, and I am sure they knew where I stood, Charisen's loss and Nathalian's defiant anger matched in my own expression. But when I looked to the others, they looked at me from Jacob's side.

"Charisen, Nathalian," I called. "You are with me?" They assented.

"What of you Cain?" I asked. He looked at me, not a hint of shame as he shook his head.

"He has abandoned conscience," Jacob spoke for the bigger being. "For I will give him what he wants: No restraint. He may have all he desires, however he desires it. Those who oppose him will fall victim to his malice, much to his delight."

"Amlyca?" I asked. For her answer she only walked up to Jacob and put her arm around him, like a succubus, and I saw by Jacob's expression that he would lead her on for a thousand years if it meant her loyalty, and her expression told me that she would continue to fall for it. For all of her strength, Jacob would be her vice.

"And you, Revenar?" I asked the muse, his small form still intimidating, like an ominous aura clouded about him.

"I'm on the winning side," he said.

Jacob looked at me, as if it were only him and me, and I met his stare. "The Eternal One is not coming back, Dor. Your servitude and honor mean nothing to him now. Reign with me." He even had the audacity to hold out his hand, as if to offer me freedom with him, as if I did not know that it would just as soon grip me in his snare. I thought of Balstone and his fate among the other palace defenders, their gore still tainting the High Palace around us. I thought the end would be different, that the Eternal One would battle the Morning Star between a host of angels, but somehow the Eternal One had fallen on Earth, leaving his courts bare and susceptible to a being who thought he could do what the Morning Star had failed to do all along.

For my answer I drew my sword. The ring of steel is seldom noticed by anyone who uses his or her blade frequently, however, in that moment it sang with such particularity that all other sounds became dull memories.

"It's four against three, odds in my favor," Jacob said. "Perhaps you would like our friends to step aside and just leave this to us. A fair fight. Shall we duel for the throne?"

"No," said I. "We shall duel for justice." No fight between beings such as us could be deemed fair, but the odds were better if it was just the two of us, so I assented.

I felt his malice as our swords first met and as they continued to exchange in attacks and parries, his ire only grew, like another weapon against me. His sword flashed, meeting mine. I twisted, maneuvering his blade around, striking then at his neck. He dodged it. We became a single blur of motion. Steel clattering, flourished by jumps and rolls. Quicker than thought. I blocked his sword, punching him with my free hand, but his fury remained undaunted. He brought a furious swing. I took the opening, launching at him, using all my momentum to bring my blade swiftly upon him. His own thrust came at me. Barely had I summoned the deflection when his foot sent me back, skittering across the tiled palace floor. Had I breath in this world, it would have been knocked from me, but I otherwise felt excruciating pain. When I at last found the willpower to arise, I also found his sword at my throat.

Nathalian and Charisen held their swords out to Jacob's three followers, outmatched yet ready to meet in battle. Charisen dropped her sword first, Nathalian shortly after. Jacob grinned then, and the words that I spat at him, awaiting the deathblow, were a glossolalia he understood. For I too knew the deep words of insult, the ones that cut to the heart of a spirit. Yet, whatever accusation of evil I directed at Jacob, his smile only widened, and I saw unquenchable pride within his ageless eyes.

Then Revenar dropped his sword, Amlyca and Cain thereafter, startling Jacob from his reverie. Jacob retained his sword, though he backed away from me. I looked and there stood the Eternal One. I had seen him many times and in many forms, and even when he had taken a new shape, I knew it to be him. This was no exception, though this form had a wildness about it I had never seen in him. Emotions are rarely easy things to describe, and to behold God is a far more complex experience than can be conveyed. His form might have been called 'human' though not without its own divine deepness. I saw the usual love, joy, sorrow, anger, wrath, justice, mercy, grace, and compassion, but something else manifested in those eyes, something I would learn later was empathy, though not for us.

He met Jacob's eyes, who then dropped his weapon. By some impulse, we knew to stand in a line to await his judgment. Jacob and his followers stood slightly apart from us. The Eternal One surveyed the palace and the massacre we had left. He shed tears then, as he was wont to do, though whether they were drops of anger or sadness I never could tell, but they were the noblest tears ever shed.

I dared glance at the others and saw that some of them shared my fear. I had been implicated in a lie, but surely I would not be annihilated, surely all blame rested upon Jacob. I knew better in my heart, that whether intentional or not, that an evil thing had been done by my hands. I realized that in all of my wisdom, earned over thousands of years, that I had been daft. Balstone was no usurper, but had been a good and true guardian. Jacob's ruse had been easy, convincing all of us to aid him on not his word, but the word of the others. We had done irreparable damages and no claim of ignorance would deliver us from justice. For the first time, I felt guilt.

The Eternal One knew our transgression. There had been times when I had seen him ask questions of those who offended him. Not for his benefit, but to make clear his case, not just to any witnesses, but to the recipient of his justice. There were no witnesses that day. The bodies of the spirits, in all of their strangeness, do not hear the living of spirit or flesh, nor bear witness to even the Eternal One. All was known to all present and no explanation or excuses were needed.

He spoke directly to Jacob. "My son, my son, you do not know what you have done." Jacob looked at him in revolt, as if he might still succeed in his insurrection. "I was away for but a time, but I always intended to return. Why do you trouble me so?" There was pity in his words, as if he understood something Jacob did not.

"This isn't over," Jacob said.

"It is," the Eternal One said. "Do not mistake my humble form for a lack of power. Even now my host regathers and they are but a fraction of what I can do." He then walked over to me and put a hand on my shoulder. Why I felt comfort from the words that came next, I do not know, for nothing so sorrowful has ever befallen me.

"Dor, my bright one. Were that your folly not so great, but do not fright. There is a place for you." He stepped back from me and looked at all of us. "There is a place for all of you. There's hope for you on Earth. The Morning Star may be cursed, but others like you have gone to Earth to redeem themselves. It's more possible now than ever. Go there. Live in peace. Take your second chance."

"I will not live in the filth of that precious planet of yours," Jacob said.

The Eternal One was not unkind in his response, but stern nonetheless, "Would you rather me give you over to the Morning Star? I can tell you that he is not in a bargaining mood and you can either join him or suffer however he deigns to torture you. Do not be bitter Jacob, for it unbecomes you. Take this chance and see where it finds you when this is all over."

Something changed in Jacob's expression. Sudden piety and shame. "You are right and just. I will do as you say."

Though his newfound demeanor was strange, I believed then what I later found to be another lie. I do not know what the

Eternal One believed. But it was sufficient enough, that he made Jacob's fate no worse than ours.

*Longness* is a relative term, something that was only extended by what was to come. I do not know the mind of the Eternal One, but Jacob did not heed him, and accordingly continued to prolong whatever plans he had.

As I fell, I recall that I was not alone in my sorrow, but that was the last I knew of the Eternal One.

# CHAPTER EIGHT

*Therianthropy*

The cell was dark and cold. In the dim, he found a blanket in one corner and a bucket in the other. A small, barred window, high in the wall, let in a shaded afternoon light. For two days this had been Liam's world. Unlike the rest of the Outland's stone, clay brick, or wood, these walls were concrete, closed by a single door of bolted steel.

Trapped with nothing and no one, he was just a boy after all. His resolve had varied during his imprisonment between bouts of dismay and determination. The initial cries for help had been answered only by the reverberations in his own confines before he gave up. The food, always cold, awaited Liam whenever he woke from sleep. The trays remained uncollected, so he stacked them by the door. As for the bucket, sitting on the pail's thin edge was impossible, but hovering made Liam's legs ache. He had finally thought to use the wall for support.

The isolation and impenetrable confinement exacerbated his fear. It was clear that Liam was being held for a reason, but the unknown of what would happen next instilled a madness. He had known loneliness before, but this feeling was different. It was hopelessness. There was no Elijah, no Ferrith, no Oliver. Not even Lucy, the stupid camel. His grandfather and the damned High Priest Tasrael had claimed by faith that Liam would succeed alone. His grandfather was old and the priest knew nothing of true faith. Liam was too negligible for them to risk their egos. They let him be the solitary hope in the desert.

Perhaps they were right not to risk more. Maybe this was a farce. Jacob could destroy what was left in the Outland, but it was unlikely he could breach the City's impenetrable walls. Liam would have been safer inside with everyone else. At least, he would not have been alone.

He again paced between the cell's walls, looking for any possible way of escape. Even if it was hopeless, little else occupied the time and it distracted him from the filthy state of himself and his cell.

"You need to calm down, kid." The voice came from the outside, sounding like the lit end of a cigarette, but somehow musical. Liam stopped when the lock turned with a thud and the door creaked open. The priest took a moment to remove his sunglasses and unwind his bandages. Revealing a mess of short, wild hair, he hung his hat on something just outside the door. He came into the cell and Liam faced him, determined not to show desperation.

The priest looked at him with the same deep bloodlust, but it was not malicious. "You look pitiful," he said. "Not that pity means much to a man like me." The man chuckled. "What's your name, kid?"

"Liam."

"Well," said the man, "These days I'm Father Solomon Glass. Most around here call me Sol. Now, Liam, what's the story?"

Liam shook his head, silent.

"Here's the deal," Sol said. "My boss is the secretive type, so I don't know why you're wanted, but I know that he's looking for you and I know that he wants you untouched. It so happens that I'm a little curious, but limited in my methods of persuasion. You surely have your own questions, so I thought maybe we could both talk, be mutually beneficial. How about it, kid? Tell me a bit about yourself."

Liam did not want to confide in this man. "You start," he said. "Why do they call you a priest?"

"Fair enough. As you can see I have..." Sol paused and held out his hands, "an affliction." With shriveled and scarred fingertips, Sol pulled at his black cassock, which covered all but what the bandages had hidden. "I find the best way to deal with it is to garner sympathy without coming across as a beggar. What better way is there than to be a priest? Religion is a great way to make a living. Apocalypse or not, it always has. There's your answer. Now, how do you know my boss?"

"I don't know who your boss is."

"Curious. Then why is he after you?"

"I don't know your boss, so it's my turn to ask the questions," Liam said, finding some gumption. He had to ask the broadest question he could that would still get specific answers. "How are you different?"

"In lots of ways." Sol could apparently play stubborn too.

"If you won't answer that one," Liam said, taking a different tactic, "what's in the box?"

"It's complicated. People do bad things. I put them in the box to await judgment from the spirits."

"There are no spirits. I saw the crocotta. You're being vague."

"So are you. I've given you much more information than what you've given me. I feel I'm losing this game. What does my boss want?"

"I told you, I don't know who he is or why I'm wanted."

Sol took a piece of folded paper from his black robes and handed it to him. Liam unfolded it and found his face crudely printed with a considerable bounty written below it. There were other dark-skinned young men in the Outlands. Andrew had been a testament to that much, but Liam knew he must stand out. If these posters were circulating, it was no wonder he was so easy to find and capture.

"Who is your boss?"

"Raven."

"Oh," replied Liam. "I shot him."

Sol raised an eyebrow. "No offense, but I find that hard to believe."

"I can defend myself. I stabbed you, didn't I? Why were you following me last night?"

"Fair enough. I wasn't following you. You followed me."

Yet another answer as perplexing as the priest himself. Now Liam was giving more information than he was getting. He asked the wrong questions. Sol had entered Liam's room through a locked door. He spoke of an affliction.

"Why did you shoot Raven?" Sol asked. A good question. Liam sat silent.

"Look," Sol said, "why don't we be open with one another? This game is pointless. I'm not fully human. I'm also not an angel or whatever they are. The crocotta you followed to the box was me. It's called therianthropy. Thanks to Raven, I have this unique ability, but the sun sensitivity is an unwelcome byproduct.

"As for the priest thing, I do it because it works. I don't talk much about the Christ. No one does anymore. Just sins and hellfire. Seems to do the trick. Andrew, one of my rare aspiring acolytes, discovered my secret and he told his girlfriend too. He tried to blackmail me and came to regret it. It was all the excuse I needed to feed my hunger, something not often sated out here."

The whole thing was creepy. Liam was trapped in this dim concrete chamber with this beast. He shivered, though it was warm. "You're terrible," Liam said. It felt like an obvious statement, but he could not contain the truth of it.

"Aren't we all, kid?" Sol said. "So, let's hear your story."

"I am from the City. It was prophesied that Jacob was returning to finally take it. They sent me to warn everyone. I made it to Bronton, and it was attacked by Raven. He caught me on my way out of town and that's when I shot him." It was not the whole truth, but Liam could not risk saying more.

Sol looked amazed, "Jacob returns. So, that's what Raven is up to. These types are so arrogant, they don't tell us anything. I'm surprised Raven hasn't killed you already.

"Don't look so surprised, kid," Sol continued, apparently having noticed Liam's expression, "I serve Raven and have for a long time now. Furthermore, I have done worse things than kill the likes of you. You live today, but only by Raven's orders." Sol started to bandage himself again with leathery burnt fingers, "You're interesting, but it changes nothing. Just remember how fast you came here and how fast that news traveled ahead of you. You can't escape me, and if you try, Raven's orders or not, I will kill you. Either way, you should probably get used to the idea of dying. If you're going to die you might as well do it like a man."

Sol turned from Liam and opened the door. "One more question, kid." Sol paused. "What is the Tartarus Project?"

It was not an unfamiliar name, but Liam could not recall where he had heard it, much less any details regarding the Tartarus Project.

"I have no idea," Liam said.

Sol left and the loneliness returned. It was more hopeless than before, but Liam stifled his sorrow. A new resolution awoke, a determination. To overcome the priest. With his newfound peace, Liam felt confident enough to sleep.

When he awoke, night had fallen. The faintest moonlight found his cell, and in it, Liam saw the small loaf of bread and water left for him. He ate heartily, hunger still plaguing him after he finished.

It was after his meal that it occurred to Liam that he had not checked the floor. It was dark, but he worked at the shallow layer of dirt all the same until he uncovered more concrete. There would be no digging his way out of this prison. He resolved to pay close attention to Sol's routine with his meals and visits. Sol was clever, more so than Liam, but he was also arrogant, something of which Liam could take advantage. The fall of the most brilliant people was so often the assumption that those of lesser intelligence could never outsmart them.

It was impossible to track Sol's routine. The window indicated day and night, but it proved difficult to find a pattern in the priest's sporadic comings and goings. Before Liam could discern any routine, the day came when Sol brought him out. How many days had it been? He attempted to count the nights—five perhaps, maybe six.

"Come on, kid. He's here."

Liam's joints ached from his confinement and the stairs from his small cell opened up between a shadowed alley leading to the outskirts of Shima. There were nearby buildings, but it still felt isolated.

Sol, smelling of blood as usual, wore his customary robe, hat, and sunglasses, all black. White bandages wrapped the rest of his skin, save the mouth-hole and fingertips. Faint smoke curled up from beneath his sharp nails.

Against the yellow sand and blue sky, just beyond the alley, stood a shadowed figure: the man Liam had shot. They approached, Raven's features becoming more apparent. The spirit made flesh wore two small swords at the waist of his slim, darkly-lined robe. Black embroidery slithered up the charcoal colored linen sleeves and down his torso. His jutting, black hair made him appear taller, but still shorter than Liam or Sol. Had Liam not known him as an immortal, he might have mistaken him as youthful, but his eyes carried a dark eternity.

"So," Raven said. "This is the one who shot an angel." He held up his sickly white hand, more pallid than the rest of his already pale skin. Black veins spidered around a single wound. Liam clenched his jaw, looking from Raven's grotesque hand and into those eternal eyes. Instant fear tightened in Liam's chest, but he hardened his resolve, showing none of it to the fallen.

"Who are you?" Raven inquired. They were almost at a level, the angel slightly shorter, but Liam felt small before his gaze. Had he expected more? Perhaps something bigger or more threatening. Something with wings? It seemed silly now. This was more ominous. Heavier to be behold. But Liam would not answer to him.

"He told me—" Sol began.

"Silence, my pet." Raven held aloft a bony finger. "Can you tell the truth from a lie as I can?"

"I would like to think so," Sol said wryly.

"You can't," Raven snapped, eyes still fixed on Liam. "But blood tells. Cut him."

Without faltering, Sol obeyed. He gave Liam no time to evade. Sol grabbed his wrist, running a finger across his right forearm. It cut through cloth, sinking deep, more like a talon than a nail. The vastness of the desert swallowed Liam's cry. He wanted the pain to stop, to will it away. The red liquid seeped from the wound, flowing too fast to find where the gash stopped and his arm began. Sinking to his knees, tears blurred his vision of the growing pool of black on the desert sand as it drank his blood.

"It hurts. Doesn't it?" Raven said. "I should have known Oliver was still alive. What were you doing with him?"

The world continued to sway and shift under the pain. Liam held his arm, blood running between his fingers. He wanted to look the angel in the face, to defy him. The agony held him down. "No," he said. It came out a rasp through clenched teeth.

Raven seized him by the neck, drawing Liam aloft. Breath left him and he squirmed, clutching with his uninjured hand at the fingers that clenched his throat. Raven tossed him to the ground, like he had grown bored of Liam. He struck the ground, sand rousing around him. Its heat burned where his exposed skin touched it. He writhed, trying to push himself into the shadow, falling back feebly, gasping for air, for the pain to go away. Raven hunched over Liam, gripping him under his chin, thumb and forefinger clenching at his cheeks.

"Tell me," Raven said, "What is the Tartarus Project?"

"Is it safe to do this out here?" came Sol's voice from behind Liam.

"It doesn't matter," Raven said. "Shima won't be around much longer anyway." Raven slapped Liam, the sting hardly noticeable compared to his throbbing arm. "Where are you going?" he asked more adamantly. "Answer me!"

Liam struggled to catch his breath through the agony, every movement another pang in his right arm. He clenched his left fist, weak as he felt. He struck Raven. His offhand slammed into the angel's face. Though Raven appeared undaunted, Liam's hand shot with pain.

"You little shit!" Raven drew a dagger, raising it. He would have stabbed Liam, but Raven toppled over, dagger falling from his grasp. Liam snatched the short blade as Raven was wrestled to the ground.

Liam arose on shaky legs, gripping the dagger, witnessing the dusty fight before him.

"Don't do it, kid," Sol said coming beside him. "Never meddle in the affairs of angels." Sol put a restraining hand on Liam's shoulder, making Liam wince as the movement sent pain down his injured arm.

Raven kicked, sending his assailant back. The figure, who Liam saw to be a woman, took the blow gracefully, landing in a defensive stance. As if propelled upward by an invisible force, Raven arced into the air. The woman shot up after him, katana screaming from its sheath. Raven bared his own short swords. He crossed his blades, deflecting her blow, launching his own attack as they landed. She parried his strike, the battle gaining speed. Their swift movements, too fast to distinguish, generated a series of grunts and ringing. They continued to fight in leaps somewhere between jumping and flying. Swords swiped and clashed. They twisted away from one another, then resumed combat.

Sol's eyes transfixed on the fighting, but his hand remained on Liam's shoulder. He dug his fingers into an imprisoning grip.

Raven fought the woman, a graceful accelerated dance. Each clang of their blades resonated musical and rhythmic. Raven dealt a series of blows. She blocked each one, so close she took the chance to knee him in the stomach. He fell back but a moment, then returned her fury. Their match was a wonder, each attack blocked or dodged with incalculable speed. Liam lost all comprehension of the fight.

Raven crossed his swords at her strike, locking them for a moment. "You're tiring, Charis," Raven said, grin spreading. "You never were a fighter."

Charis looked hard at Raven, but her shout was for Liam. "Run!"

Sol's nails dug in further, but Liam wrenched back, loosening from the grip. The pain ripped through his shoulder and wrist, but he took the dagger, and slammed it under Sol's ribcage, directing it toward his heart. It was harder to pull the knife out than he anticipated, but he managed to rip it away. Sol fell to the ground, just out of the shadow of the buildings. His sunglasses fell from his face, revealing wide eyes.

A torrent of blood gushed onto the desert ground. Though it pained his hand, Liam ripped the hat from the priest's head, smoke rising from his scalp, embers flickering in his hair. He began to scream, clutching at his head. Remembering how quickly Sol had recovered before, Liam made haste. He ran, taking the hat with him. Sol had underestimated him, too transfixed on the fight to think Liam would take the dagger to him. Dashing down another alley, Liam threw the hat to one side and tucked the dagger into his belt.

The townspeople peered at him as he ran, bloody and scared, but no one attempted to stop him. He found Lucy still stabled and started to saddle her as best he could with an injured right shoulder and wrist and a left hand sore from punching Raven. It was taking too long, his shaking fingers fumbling at the straps.

"I hope you're planning to pay for that," a gruff voice said. It was the stable owner, a portly man, greedy-eyed and standing firmly at the entrance.

With no other choice, Liam drew his dagger and directed it at the man, the threatening tip coming close to his jowls. "Water," Liam demanded. The man's eyes grew big as he pointed to a canteen and then to a bucket. Liam found a canteen and filled it. It was dirty water, meant for the horses and camels, but it was better than going thirsty in the desert.

His adrenaline faded, as weariness took him. The world spun and he steadied himself against the camel and he noticed the blood—his blood—which continued to seep from his wound. He staggered as he led Lucy out, past the startled stable master who began to call for help.

There were some supplies in the saddle-packs and the canteen was hopefully enough to reach the next town. He mounted the camel, grasping his saddle as she rose. He urged her on, riding hard out of town, hoping in his delirium that he had guessed the way south.

Feverishly, Liam rode with little food and water, his injuries treated by strips of cloth cut from his shirt. He attempted to tie a strip between his upper-arm and shoulder, tight enough to stop the blood flow, but it was impossible to do with his offhand, particularly injured as it was from his blow to Raven. With the rest of the cloths strips, he tried to bandage his wrist and shoulder. Blood soaked through within an hour and he cut more strips, wrapping them tightly, and applying pressure. The pressure helped the pain in his right arm, but the work exasperated his left hand's bruised knuckles and sprained wrist. The blood continued to flow. He pushed harder and by nightfall it had slowed, but the blood loss left him dizzy.

After the first agonizing night, the wound began to smell, but he resisted taking the bandages off, knowing it could start the bleeding again. The next day, when he had depleted half of his water supply, he resolved to be more sparing, only taking the smallest of sips when he thought he would go mad with thirst.

How little he had cherished water in the City, running the faucet for as long as it took to do dishes. After a long day of sparring with Master Ferrith, he would take an extra long shower. Perry, Ferrith, Standon... he missed them.

The pain grew to be perpetual, joining the throbbing in his arm. The wound was possibly infected. Definitely. Whatever the case, it needed stitches. The shallower claw marks in his shoulder emitted an odor as well. His left hand felt wrong, as if broken in places. Such was the price of shooting an angel and stabbing a werecrocotta.

A spell of delusion clutched at him again. He took a small sip of water, careful not to spill a drop. At times, he had talked to Lucy to keep alert, but his throat ran dry, and he dared not spare the moisture.

The second night, exhaustion overwhelmed him. When he attempted to dismount, he fell from the camel, and slept there on the desert ground. No peace came to his slumber. In his dreams, Sol found him. Raven's fingers gripped his neck.

He ran out of water the next day, the last drop almost evaporating before it struck his tongue. They had milked Lucy back in Shima, but she yielded enough to sustain him a little further.

Fear of Sol and Raven dissipated. A new terror plagued his thoughts, the greatest and cruelest enemy he had known yet. The desert. She was relentless.

If only the pain would end, even if in death. Fatigue, blood loss, dehydration. Each was enough in itself to kill a man, much less the severity of the combination that Liam endured. He closed his eyes, slumping in the saddle, wavering in the camel's smooth gate. Then he fell.

He awoke in the dark. A faint light burned around him, amber flame flickering soft. It was warm, he realized, not the cold of the desert's night. This was death.

No. It was the warmth of a bed, soft sheets against his skin. It was a candle on a nearby nightstand. A faint rustle disturbed him and he saw the man, sitting in a chair close to the bedside. Liam's gut tensed, soreness awaking his pain. The man wore black robes. *The priest.* Liam's eyes traveled up to the man's face. He was older and his skin was light brown. He was different.

"My dear boy," said the man. "You made it. Here. Eat and drink. Then we shall talk."

The man helped Liam sit upright and placed a tray upon his lap. Liam took the large clay cup and drank the water eagerly. "Not too fast now," the man said. The bread was warm and soft, as if it had arrived in time for his waking. He added a prodigious spread of butter. It melted into the loaf's flesh. Liam would always remember that bread, its perfect flavor and texture satiating. For but a moment he forgot his dire flight into the desert.

The respite fell short as pain returned to his arm, each movement like a fresh cut from Sol's talon. He had been adorned in a light, comfortable shirt and matching bottoms. He pulled back the white sleeve and found the stitched mark, running across his wrist.

"You are lucky to be alive," the man side. Liam looked up to him, inspecting his old, kind features. "It will heal in full with time, though you will surely bear a scar. Your shoulder, at least, seems well on the way to recovery. Crocotta are nasty things. You are lucky Charis was able to treat the infection."

"How did you find me?" Liam asked. It came out quiet and raspy, like he had not used his voice in too long a time.

"I didn't," the man said. "Charis brought you and your things as well, which Carl and his wife were gracious enough to turn over to her. She brought you to me. Said you were important and that I should take the utmost care of you. She stayed until she was sure you were well on your way to recovery."

"Where am I? Are you a priest?"

"You are in Lavyn," the man said. "By your camel, it's five days south of Shima, and as far as I'm concerned it would be nice if it was further. That is not a town I care to have in any proximity. I am Father Barker Stoke. Call me Barker, of course. I have no business demanding formality from a descendant of the Great Prophet Elijah. Alas, I ramble, don't I? The Lady Charis told me of your journey. I admit that I was reluctant to believe that I had met *the* Charis, much less that you were who she said you were. I never imagined meeting one of the fallen, the *Grigori* as tradition calls them. I imagined them dead, but I guess they are the closest thing to immortals we have."

"What happened?"

"Her fight with Raven was evidently rather dramatic. She said you were heroic yourself. Anyway, she fought him off well enough, and it didn't take long to track down your lodgings and recover your belongings. What wasn't at Carl's was in that so-called priest's defiled parsonage. He had fled, for the time being at least, so she found your other effects there. It wasn't hard to guess the direction you were headed, so she followed. Oh, and, she did pay the stable master for his troubles." The man was older, crow's feet sprouting from the corners of his eyes and joining a network of wrinkles. His eyes were kind, assured by a perpetual expression of peace.

"Thank you," Liam said, also relieved that the stable master had been compensated.

"Think nothing of it. Rather, I am honored to play a part—however small—in these happenings. You are to recover, for Charis is the master of healing. Another day will do it, I think, and then you will be on your way.

"Raven retreated to the north, and I am confident that you are safe here. However, it is only a matter of time before he sends others to pursue you. The wanted posters are already circulating."

"Where did Charis go?" Liam asked.

"She was apparently on another errand, though she meant to cross paths with you," Barker said. "She had intended to find someone here that she trusted and set them to watch for you, but she was fortunate to find you in Shima and deliver you from that abomination. Such a blessing is something you can seldom count on in your journey to come.

"Speaking of your journey, once you find Dorian, you are to rendezvous in Mere. I was tickled to find that it really did exist, and I can show you on a map where to find it. This little church has its share of resources, but the maps are old I fear. They will have to do."

"You're different," Liam said. "From the priest in Shima."

"What is a priest really? Is it the robe? The title? Anyone can possess these things. I fear your acquaintance in Shima has taken on a role of which he is very much unworthy. I am too old to investigate, much less do anything about such things. Once again, I ramble. You should sleep."

With that the priest bid Liam a goodnight, blew out the candle, and left the room. Slouching beneath the sheets, Liam sank his head into his pillow. Given his recent, prolonged rest and all of the excitement, he doubted he would find sleep, but soon a peaceful slumber overtook him.

Liam awoke refreshed and discovered that he had recovered faster than expected. He desired a longer respite, but finding Dorian was more crucial than ever. He set about readying for the coming journey, exploring his surroundings in the small parsonage and adjacent chapel.

The sun poured through the stained glass, casting warm hues on the old brick walls. Rustic pews stretched among the aged sanctuary, a contrast to the newer parsonage's patchwork of stone, clay, and scraps. Liam looked into a few books, the old tomes smell of must and vanilla filling the air with each turn of a page. Illuminations rendered around ancient languages, their bold, Gothic lettering holding its sacred secrets.

He visited Lucy and found her equally rejuvenated, her usual wry look greeting him. Among the town's stores he restocked on necessities. One shop had ammunition to match his gun, for which he traded his old sword, ignoring the shopkeeper's suspicious glare. A little extra silver bought his discretion.

Cans of food, water, and other supplies filled his pack. When he returned, Barker showed him the map, directing him to the fresh mark where he would supposedly find the garden city.

"I will see you when you get there," Barker told him. "Lavyn is no longer my place. Mere is in need of a priest."

By sundown, Liam had completed his work, ready to embark on the next morning. For the first time since Shima, he settled into the nearest public house and had a much deserved pint.

The next morning Barker shook his hand. "Farewell, young man," he had said. "Safe travels." As Liam departed from Lavyn, he remembered the look in Father Barker Stoke's eyes. Hope.

# CHAPTER NINE

## *Nomads*

Taesa laid on the beach as Argon stroked her scaled skin. The great crocodile was the largest of her congregation, stretching nineteen feet. She lay half-submerged in the water and Argon sat upon a rock petting her neck. The afternoon sun beat down on the eastern hills, their rocky terrain rising in gray rubble and falling into the muddy oasis of the Eastern Pan. Argon's long black hair stuck to his bare bronze skin, wet from the recent swim. He now sat in the quiet, relaxing in the day's warmth.

"All those years ago, Chief Belriah was right," Argon said, "This is good land. Never have our people been able to stay in one place for so long." The crocodile made no movement. He felt connected to her and often talked to her in this way. Every day that he could, he made his way to the small lake where he and Taesa could swim and play together, and when they were tired, they would sit like this, sometimes into the night under the moon. When he could, he brought her food. He was of the People of the Moon, and they sacrificed to the crocodiles to appease the moon god, for his people did not fear the crocodiles and the great reptiles were no threat to them.

Henmad the slave boy disturbed them, "Belriah asks you meet him at the witch's tent." Argon's irritation must have showed, for the boy cowered at his glare. He told the boy he would be there and then proceeded to dawn his cloak.

"Perhaps tomorrow, Taesa, I will see you again," he said as he wrapped the cloak around his tattooed and scarred torso. "They say they are going to sacrifice much livestock for the Moon Feast. You and your brothers and sisters will eat well." He strapped his curved sword to his waist and walked back to the busy village. The tents and stands smelled of incense and spices. He stopped to satisfy his hunger with some figs before finding the witch's tent on the outskirts of their settlement.

The witch once had a name, but she had long outlived it. Most knew her to be a charlatan though there had been times that her divination was useful. Argon found Chief Belriah, a shorter and bald man, just outside of the tent. "It is not good for us to be seen here," Argon said. "We are not men of such superstition."

"Maybe not," replied Belriah, "but she claims revelation from the moon god. Hear what she has to say before you oppose her."

"As you command," Argon said as he stepped into the tent. The incense was overpowering in the dark tent, the haze held in by all but the smallest tears in the canvas, which also allowed in traces of light. The witch sat cross-legged by the small blue flame barely illuminating the pale gray scales on her eyes and thin matted hair. "The doubter!" she said as she crushed an egg in her hand. A mixture of yolk and blood seeped from between her fingers. She flung it at Argon's feet with a toothless smile. He suppressed a grimace.

"Show him what you have seen," said Belriah.

"As you wish, my chief. We shall see if he can be made to believe."

She took a small sack and emptied its contents onto the floor. They were coins, small round medals, their faces etched with various animals. Argon recognized some. The goat, the crocodile, the sheep, the tiger, the raven, dog, horse, and others common to their zodiac. She raked the tokens back into the bag and shook it before gesturing for him to pick one from it. He withdrew a coin, a crocodile. She motioned him to take another. A tiger.

"Now," she said, "put them back and draw two again."

And he did, drawing the crocodile and tiger again. He put them back and drew from the sack thrice more with the same results.

"Every time," the witch said. "Do it as many times as you please but you will always draw the omens."

"Omens?" asked Argon.

"Tell him," said Belriah.

"I dreamed," she hissed. "A tiger and a crocodile journeyed north and west to the mountains. It was there that they fought a great battle and the moon god gave them the promised rain."

"We are the People of the Moon, kindred to the crocodile," Argon said. "Our bothers in the east The People of Fire are kindred to the tiger. Your dream is a mere chance. You miss your kin in the west," said Argon.

"It is by this sign you know I tell the truth," declared the witch holding up the sack and rattling the metal contents.

Argon looked to Belriah who spoke, "I trust your judgment, Argon. You are second only to me in our clan and chief friend to the queen of the crocodiles. What say you of these omens?"

"He need not say anything now," said the witch. "Sleep tonight among your beloved pet and you will see a sign for yourself."

Throughout the rest of the day Argon pondered the meaning of such happenings. He had kept the tokens and now turned them in his hand. A tiger and a crocodile. To venture north and west by the divination of an old fraud was folly. But the signs gave edge to the witch's credibility. Her tricks were simple and these signs were not. He supped with his family but toward sunset withdrew, taking the finest sheep from his personal livestock to the lake. As the sunset and he stood at the shoreline with the frightened ewe and the crocodiles edged forward. Then Taesa, their queen, made way among them and she watched and waited. He knew the ritual: the finest parts of the sheep for Taesa and the other parts for the rest of her congregation. When they had finished their meal, the other crocodiles departed and Taesa joined Argon next to their rock. As the final faint rays of the sun glowed Argon gazed north and west as he told Taesa of the witch.

"Nomads we are but the harvest is soon and we have water here. Could we leave these lands? Could I leave you all for a witch's farce?"

Curiously, Taesa bellowed and she turned in the water to point to the northwest where Argon gazed. In the distance as the sun's last rays sank beneath the horizon he saw it. He blinked his eyes, willing the mirage away, but it was no hallucination. A great tiger ran through the desert and disappeared behind the hill. It was brief but he knew he had not mistaken its great fire and smoke pelt. Argon was astonished. The crocodile then looked to him and he felt a sense of mourning from her.

"I must go, mustn't I?" he asked, "And when the promised rains come will you follow? One day will you find me in the north?"

Argon slept little and at dawn left her to find Belriah. The chief sat outside his own tent boiling eggs in an old pot over the fire. He was older than Argon with slightly darker bronze skin. He looked upon Argon with delight.

"My most trusted friend, what say you now?" he asked.

"The Queen of the Crocodiles has shown me the way. Last night upon the north and the west she did show me a great tiger, the likes of which I have never seen. I like it not, but the witch speaks true."

"I hoped she was wrong," said Belriah with understanding, "This is too good a place to leave. The harvest is soon and the land is still fruitful. Yet, the omens do not lie. We dare not tell the people on empty bellies. Set up a feast for the midday supper and when they have had their fill we shall speak."

"It will be done."

"Before you leave, we must settle the details of this matter. Call the others and let us discuss it."

Those closest to Chief Belriah met and discussed it at length. In the end, they agreed to the move. After he had made arrangements for the feast, Argon went to his tent to sleep. There he found his wife. "My sweet Gardelle, where are our children?" he asked.

"It was said that there is to be a feast, so I sent them with Henmad to help," she replied. "Do you know why we feast? Are we to start the Moon Feast three days early? And do we not usually fast until sunset?"

"I'm afraid this feast will bring more somber tidings," Argon said, "We have lingered here long and it is time the nomads moved. Belriah is making the arrangements now, and all will be announced at tonight's feast."

"Somber tidings, indeed. This is all our children have known and we have yet to outlive the land. Why should we move?"

"To war and then the promised rains."

"Woeful is this news," she said, "That the prophecy should be fulfilled in blood! We are no warriors."

"We were once. In my heart, I have feared the same, but we are a strong people. Though we have warred little, we have trained warriors who hunt the most dangerous beasts and endure the harshest desert. Take heart, my wife, for the omens have all spoken true. Our people will soon be nomads no more. There is a place for our people. A land of long rest."

He took his wife and made love to her and then rested until she awoke him for the feast. In the late afternoon, they gathered in the meeting tent and a great meal was set out. A fat boar had been selected from the livestock and roasted, a cask of pomegranate wine tapped, and small peppers stuffed with goat's cheese. The chief and his consorts sat at a table upon a mound. Argon joined him there.

"Argon, my friend," Belriah said. "This is a splendid feast. Surely the people will be inclined to favor us."

"There are always those who find not their fill in food but in power," said Argon.

"Don't speak of that. Ever the pessimist, but I suppose that's what makes you a damn good adviser."

"Where is your son?" Argon asked.

"As you know, Baran does as he will, wild boy that he is. It is worse than usual and he will not see reason. I do not yet know if that will make him a great or terrible chief. Perhaps both."

They feasted and they wined, though Argon had little appetite. It was just before nightfall when the peoples' bellies were full and their thoughts merry that Belriah finally silenced them. The drum and pipe music ceased and the crowd hushed. He stood before them upon the mound. "My people," he began. "For centuries we have called ourselves nomads but for the past generation we have truly been agrarians. I am sad to say that this could not last, for in our hearts we are still nomads. There is a promised rain and it is not here but in lands beyond. Our soothsayer has shown us the omens. We must go west and join our brothers of fire and then we must move north and west. There we will fight the war that will bring us the promised rain."

There was a great murmur at this and it was sometime before Belriah could continue, "My most trusted adviser, Argon, has also seen the signs for himself. My people, I tell you the truth, that I am reluctant to leave such a place. But I know the promises of the gods."

After more mutterings from the crowd a voice cut through, "Has Elah, our moon god, not led us here? The ground is fertile and we have water. Is it a coincidence that we found our kindred brother, the crocodile?" The man stood at his table close to the front. He was a short, hairy man, known well for his contrary nature. At this Argon replied, "My dear Gaezar, you know that I am closest with our kindred beasts, but I have seen the omens, shown to me by the Queen of the Crocodiles herself. People, hear me! The omens of the witch were the crocodile and the tiger. Behold, last night as I sat with Taesa she pointed me into the desert where I saw such a tiger as I had never seen before."

"Is that all she showed you, Argon?" said Gaezar. "Chief Belriah, I do believe you take council from a man blinded by love."

At this Argon's anger flared, "You speak out of turn, filth. Shall I show you my whip or must I sacrifice you to the kindred beasts to silence your insolence?"

"I am not the one defying the gods for a witch's farce. I declare this apostasy," spoke Gaezar. At this the crowd broke out into more discord. Some cried out for Gaezar, others Belriah or even Argon. Others declared apostasy. Belriah seized his whip, snapping it in the air with such a fierce crack that the room dropped into silence.

"What have I called you?" asked Belriah, "*My people*! That is because our forefathers taught us that the gods ordain the chief. The gods led me to bring you here and the gods are guiding me to take you from here to a better place. There are those of us who will die in the desert and those who will fall in battle, but their reward will be greatest. We can stay here, but one day the water will run out. One day the crops will fail. One day our crocodiles will leave us. And what will be left? I say unto you, *my people*, the time is now." With that he won them and great cheers erupted and they chanted to the north and the west. Gaezar quietly left, sulking and bitter.

"Shall I have him imprisoned?" asked Belriah.

Argon shook his head, "We have overcome his doubt with the people, and it has made us stronger. The time will come to silence the naysayers, but today let him walk in peace." Argon resolved to watch Gaezar closely. Not only was he quick to express and breed dissent, he was too close with Baran, the chief's son. Argon would not trust the man.

The moon feast was in three nights and they were to leave ten days after. The village was in a bustle of packing, harvesting what they could, preserving food, all the while readying for the feast. They would not be able to take all of their food and livestock with them so the feast was to be grand and the sacrifices many. After the feast they would muster every man, woman, child, and animal and prepare to make way west to the other nomadic tribe.

"You have met with them more recently. Do you think we can convince them?" asked Argon.

"Serj remains my spirit brother," Belriah said, "and we have always been of like mind."

"Yes, but he will not yield power to you. What were his numbers when you visited not more than a year ago?"

"Last I saw, his clan was over two thousand strong in warriors alone, more than our men, women, and children combined. But he need not yield power to me but to the tiger, whatever it may be. Until such a time, I will be subservient to him as long as we are of one mind: North and west and the promised rain."

"North and west and the promised rain," answered Argon.

The Moon Feast was the greatest the younger generation had seen. Poultry, pork, and mutton were set at the tables with peppers and other vegetables. The stronger potato wine was provided and the people celebrated well into the night. "To the north and the west and the promised rain" they all toasted many times over until they were too full, drunk, and tired to celebrate any more. The crocodiles were fed leftovers, which were in abundance, and Argon was sure to sacrifice his purest and fattest bull as he said goodbye to Taesa.

On the tenth day after the feast the People of the Moon departed. Animals pulled carts and carried sacks of food and supplies. Everyone, young or old, great or small carried what they could and they set out at dawn in a great trail of people heading west.

Argon looked to the oasis one last time, to his beloved kindred beast. *Farewell, Taesa.*

# CHAPTER TEN

*They Called This America*

"A customer! And it's early yet," the shopkeeper said from behind the gray-haired mustache. "What can I get for you today, young man?" Liam said nothing and handed the man the piece of paper. The man's eyes flicked down, skimming the list. "I can do all of it, but it will cost you."

Liam put a small stack of gold coins on the splintered wooden counter. He hoped it was far more than the goods were worth, enough to buy the man's cooperation and discretion as well, but Liam didn't understand the currency system in Outland enough to be sure. Oliver had said that some towns bartered while others had their own forms of paper currency. The surest form of payment was gold, particularly if in the form of coins. Whatever the case, it appeared sufficient for the man behind the counter. With a nod, he went to the back of the store.

In the quiet of the morning, the store stood empty of patrons. Sunlight bathed the dusty shelves, the shadow of the windows' bars striping the room. Liam walked among the shelves, surveying the cluttered relics. In the City, movies had been of little interest. They represented a world too far removed, depicting a primitive society whose only commodity was the limitless sprawl of the earth. As far as Novum was concerned, the bygone world had hardly utilized that resource. Movies were a waste of time when one might be working their way up in the societal ranks.

However, Ferrith had an affection for film, and through them Liam had learned much of the past. Liam recognized the disco ball hanging from the ceiling, the toy race car on the shelf, and the jukebox in the corner. A dozen other things garnered his attention, but his caution never wearied. He avoided putting his back to the door and he kept his hand close to the gun hidden in his shirt.

Lavyn had been safe, but he had known well to avoid other towns. He had circumvented the previous two, sure that the wanted posters and their gratuitous promised reward had reached them. Though more accustomed to the desert, he had yet to conquer his thirst. The days between towns left him empty of food and water, finally desperate enough to drink the camel's milk. In his delirium, he hardly noticed the taste at first, but as it satiated him he noticed the taste was not unlike cow's milk, perhaps sharper and saltier.

Eventually, even Lucy had grown tired, and when he sighted the next town, he knew he needed to stop. And now he found himself in the shop early in the morning, hoping to be in and out before the town began to wake and bustle. The morning sun had shone through a tattered American flag, its metal pole long and rusted. Small gardens, likely of beans and corn, sat in patches on the outskirts. Next to the store, Liam had given a coin to a young boy to bring water and food to Lucy. He tied her to the post and entered the store, passing a dog that yawned on the porch, too old and tired to pay him any mind.

Liam's caution bordered on paranoia as he now waited for the shopkeep to return with supplies. When the man returned, Liam's stomach tightened and he moved his hand closer to the hilt of his pistol. The shopkeep held the wanted poster in hand. "It's him, all right."

"A reward like that, you must've done something real bad," said the deep voice behind him. How had they slipped in on him? "Another boy gotten into too much trouble. Well, son, turn around slowly."

Liam turned, facing three men. One held a sword and the others bludgeons. This he could handle.

He guessed they did not work for Raven, but rather sought the reward. He would avoid hurting them, but if it came to it, he would do what was needed. He pulled out his gun and pointed it at the man with the sword, stepping to the side to put the shopkeep in his peripheral. "You know what this is?" he asked holding his hand steady. "That's right," he continued. "It's a gun. I have two bullets for each of you, so here's how this is going to go. The shopkeep is going to get the items on my list. He has five minutes to come back alone. After that I shoot one of you. Every five minutes, I'll shoot another. Is my camel still out there?"

The man with the sword nodded.

"Good," Liam said. "Don't make me show you why the bounty's so high."

The shopkeep scampered away and Liam hoped he wouldn't have to keep his promise. He wasn't sure that he could. He held steady, determined not to show weakness. They would not see his uncertainty.

Without a watch, Liam kept time in his mind, counting the seconds, perhaps too slow. The shopkeep returned with two minutes to spare, two sacks in hand. Liam made him show their contents and nodded in approval, hoping with a glance that it was everything. "Drink it," he said.

"What?" the shopkeep asked.

"The water you brought me. Take a sip, a big one."

The man, shaking a little, took the flask and put it to his lips, swallowing a mouthful of water. If it was poisoned, there was no telling how long the effects would take, but Liam would have to take this man's state of health as promise enough.

"Okay," Liam said after the man sealed the flask and replaced it in the bag. "Everyone in the corner." He glanced out of the window, confirming that his camel remained at her post and no one else waited for him outside. "I'm leaving and you won't be following. If I see you in the distance, I'll shoot, and they say I'm a good shot."

"Come now, boy," the lead man said. "You know you won't get far."

"Believe it or not," Liam replied, "the people after me are the bad guys." With that, Liam backed out, passing the disinterested dog, and maneuvering to his camel.

He untied Lucy, who appeared well watered and fed already. He tucked the bags into the saddle-packs, watching closely for anyone else to challenge him. The townspeople had already started milling about the dusty street, but he kept his head down and his gun inconspicuous.

He headed north out of the town, riding far, hoping he had fooled them. After a time he turned southward, keeping a wide berth of the town. But within an hour, riders appeared in the distance, a cloud of dust in their wake. Whatever the reward, it outweighed their fear of his gun. Liam cursed, ushering Lucy faster.

Hoping that whatever sustenance she had gotten in the town was enough, Liam pressed the camel onward. Her smooth gate carried him, and he thanked Oliver that he hadn't gotten a horse. He rode hard, hoping that even if the horses were faster, Lucy could endure longer.

As the pursuers gained on him, four more figures emerged on the eastern horizon. Crocotta. As Oliver had said, they preferred to scavenge, however they were aggressive as well. If they decided to pursue him, it might turn ugly. Could he use this complication to his advantage? The idea that came to him would either be his best hope or a slow death.

He directed his camel eastward, galloping toward the crocotta. Their cackles greeted him, excitement growing as he drew closer. To Lucy's credit, she didn't shy from the massive hyenas. Even in the heat, Liam's skin prickled with a chill. Their sinister smiles awaited him, crooked teeth ready for fresh meat. One of the crocotta let out a cackle and they engaged him in unison. He directed the camel away, curving left to loop back northward toward his pursuers, hungry crocotta in tow, their barks and whines close behind him. The thud of their paws felt ever-closer, but he dared not look behind him. Lucy ran with an energy to match Liam's new vigor.

The men on horseback startled, turning from their pursuit in retreat. Something lurched into Liam's periphery, racing alongside him. Nearly as large as his camel, muscles taught as it ran, it snapped jagged teeth at him. Liam maneuvered away, nearly retching from the crocotta's smell.

Another two appeared alongside, threatening to leap ahead and trap him. Instead all three on either side ran ahead, chasing the men on horseback, leaving one for Liam to face. A crocotta for each of them. Smart indeed.

He shifted Lucy into another arc, pulling away from the northern trajectory. If the other three could outrun his camel, so could this one, and he had to take evasive action. Liam pulled out the gun, twisting awkwardly in the saddle for a better shot. With vicious apprehension the crocotta closed in as Liam fired, the discharge resonating. The gun kicked, the odd angle shifting his position in the saddle. He grasped attempting to regain his seat, but his fingers met air. He faltered, unbalanced, and the desert ground drew closer. The impact jolted him, his skin burning against the rugged sand. The wound in his shoulder reawakened, pain and shock seizing him. His hand clenched and opened as he writhed in pain until he forced himself to stop and focus and search for his fallen gun.

A growl alerted him, and he stilled himself, listening as its footsteps padded toward him. He looked over, muscles aching in his neck. Blood matted the hair around the crocotta's head. Though daunted by the injury, it staggered toward him, red saliva dripping from its mouth. Its rancid odor filled the air.

Still prone, Liam held the gun awkwardly and fired. He missed. It continued to lumber until Liam fired again. It lodged into the beast's shoulder, but it pressed on with a pained whine.

Then it leapt, coming down on Liam, the gun tumbling from his hand. His dagger flashed, stabbing up at the descending snout, the point finding the creature's throat, piercing the soft tissue. Tearing into the flesh, the dagger sank deep, blood gushing from the wound. It gurgled a howl, writhing as Liam rolled, avoiding the talons that scrapped at him.

Gasping for breath, he watched its death throes, until it finally lay in breathless spasms. He approached the twitching carcass and retrieved his dagger, slick with blood. Something snorted behind him. He turned, ready to face another crocotta. It was Lucy, looking at him as if she had been ready to run should he fail.

In the distance three men on horseback skirmished with the crocotta, maneuvering their skittish horses in an attempt to round on the creatures and stab them. He hoped they would only scare the men off, and not harm them. He found his gun on the desert floor. He attempted to reload it with the bullets he had gotten in Lavyn, but for some reason they did not fit. He cursed himself for not comparing them to the bullets Oliver had given him, but at least he had some of those left. After reloading, Liam mounted the camel, thankful that she had stayed, and continued his ride south.

The desert's monotony was often broken by strange hills, rock formations, and small valleys with sparse vegetation. Small enclaves offered sheltered or cozy spaces. As night fell, Liam led the camel into a small valley, up a series of hills and rocky steps, and into a formation. The rock curved around, leaving an entrance into a space large enough for Liam and Lucy to camp for the night. It opened up to the night's sky, the moon offering enough light for him to settle and start a fire. One side of his enclave sloped enough that he could climb onto the formation's ridge and survey the desert.

The shadowed desert stretched to the horizon where it met the black sky, stars spattering the dome above him. Nothing across the plain threatened him. He climbed down, sharing some of his water and a meager meal with the camel. Laying his blanket down, he found sleep quickly.

He awoke to the embers of the dwindling fire, the cold of the desert penetrating his blanket. At first, he thought the odor was the camel, but he knew this smell. Decay filled his nostrils, fetid and metallic. They were close. Liam might have found a place to hide, but he would not abandon the camel. Not only did he need her, but he had grown attached to her. She was more than a means of transportation. They had to look out for each other in the desert.

He scaled the wall of the cave, crouching along the ridge, and surveying the desert. One crocotta crept along the side of the formation, edging its way toward the entrance. Lucy stirred. It lumbered into the opening, the dim remnants of the fire casting the shadow of its razorback on the rocky wall. He would not need a gun for just one crocotta. Just a little closer and Liam could bring his sword down on it in surprise.

The smell grew worse, smothering, as if from something closer. He surveyed the Outlands, sighting nothing, until he saw the two eyes gleaming next to him on the ridge of the formation.

For a moment he gazed at the yellow-green glowing eyes. Then it lunged. Teeth prickled from its gaping jaws. He jumped, nearly falling over the edge. He grappled for purchase, evading another strike from the beast. Drawing his sword, he met the next attack, its blade slicing at the creature. It yelped as the edge bit into skin and bone. Liam dodged a clawed lash, and jabbed with his sword, putting his weight into the thrust. It sank into flesh, deep and true. The crocotta fell, snapping and clawing at him as he yanked the sword free.

The other crocotta had not been idle. No sooner had Liam pulled his sword free, than it had come to the aid of its partner. With a leap, it bounded up the ridge, growling, and Liam gave a yell of his own. He raised his blade.

It lunged and Liam rolled. As he gained his feet, he brought the sword around. The swing met flesh and dug deep into the beast's shoulder. It cowered at the blow but a moment. It sprang, but Liam's sword met it again, a slice across its face. Blood sprayed as it hacked into the crocotta's eyes. It struck him blindly, knocking both of them from the ridge.

With a shock, Liam landed, fall broken by the flailing beast. He rolled from claw and tooth, found his feet, and drove his blade down. He thrust, down and down again. He hacked at the wretched creature, striking it long after all life had faded.

He returned to the enclave and once again climbed the slope to its ridge. The other crocotta, the one that had ambushed him, lay breathing raggedly. When he had struck the life from it, he stood in the dark of night, fatigue sudden upon him. He did not recall sinking to his knees, but when he found the energy to move, he arose, maneuvering slowly down the slope, careful of his footholds. The day had not been kind to his wounds, exacerbating his arm and shoulder, compounding them with new injuries and soreness.

There had been four crocotta and so far he had only killed three. He hoped the men had slain the fourth, but he dared not risk it.

Lucy looked at him wryly, perhaps upset that he had left her alone in the enclave, like bait for the crocotta.

He gathered his things and took her reigns, leading her from the formation. They walked into the night and when the dawn came they walked more.

It was on the nineteenth day that Liam spotted them. He had been cautious among the southern towns, often entering in the dead of night to steal whatever water and supplies he could find. Wanted fliers riddled posts and boards throughout the towns, many with his face on them. Though in Novum, he had felt indistinctive, this artist captured well his prominent cheek bones, dark skin, and dreadlocks. Anyone would recognize him.

His thievery came with some guilt, so it was with relief that he found a town without the posters. It was perhaps ten days after the ordeal with the crocotta. Most of the soreness had left him, and the quiet days did much to restore his strength and confidence. Killing three crocotta was no small feat.

Metal scraps composed most of the wall that surrounded the town. He took several days there to recuperate and let Lucy have the rest she needed. He visited her every day, and whatever grudge she held dissipated as rest renewed them.

The town itself, Backlund, was the first town in the Outland where Liam found the girls attractive. The City had its fair share of attractive girls his age, but what few women he had encountered in the Outlands had been homely. Buckland, however, boasted many that turned his eye, and he felt some guilt for his shallow interest. Youth had been seldom seen in the Outlands, mostly visible among the beggars and street rats. In Backlund, however, the walls provided enough safety and the children played freely among the town.

Some towns were richer, others begrimed. Each town possessed its own personality, whether it had walls, electricity, or law enforcement. The variety astonished him, but so had his own adaptability. In Backlund, he found more consistency and cleanliness than in previous settlements, and he nearly found himself spoiled.

There was a poor side of Backlund, but they seemed more content, working hard among the land, and enjoying good drink when the day was over. That prospect was what lured him. No comforts tempted him, but rather the life that a place like Backlund offered. His wants had been ambiguous in the City, and in the Outland, his quest to find Dorian proffered its own share of uncertainties.

He had grown accustomed to the heat, and the dust and grime started to make him look like an Outlander. This was a merry people, and he saw himself living a simple life among them. Hard labor was better than complacency in the City or the threat of crocotta. He could work until his muscles ached, so long as he had a community like Backlund, where a good drink and companionship awaited him.

He knew well that no life was truly simple. These people suffered their own troubles, even if they dulled them with spirits. Not to mention that the wanted posters would catch up with him. Knowing that he already lingered too long, he reluctantly left after a week.

When Backlund was behind him, he watched for Dali, the final town before the southern shores where Dorian was said to reside. When he found another town, he waited until dark. Upon nightfall, his reconnaissance revealed the town to be Dali. Relieved at the last segment of his journey, he rode in high spirits the next day, the nineteenth day since he had encountered the crocotta. His relief was short-lived for that night he saw a campfire to the north.

Its distant flame flickered in a small encampment and he knew they pursued him. What worried him more was their confidence, that they felt no need to hide their fire. He allowed himself little sleep and continued to ride into the night. When the morning came, the rising sun told him he had drifted from his southern direction. He corrected his path, hoping he had not given his followers any ground.

The following two days were rigorous. He slept restlessly for a few hours, rode on, and still his pursuers seemed to gain. Oliver had told him to run in such a situation, but he may have no choice but to fight. How they had found him, he did not know. Perhaps he had been foolish in Backlund or he had been spotted in one of his nighttime escapades. Unlike his previous pursuers, he had the feeling that these men worked directly for Raven and Sol. If his unfounded sense was right, these would be trained men with the swiftest horses.

At noon the thunder of their hooves caught up with Liam. He pushed Lucy harder, but three men on horseback surrounded him, a cloud of dust stinging Liam's eyes. When he drew his gun, something hit him. Lucy toppled, throwing him to the ground. New and old bruises came to life as he rolled in the sand. He tried to breath to no avail. It felt like death and he clutched at his throat, as if it might bring the air back. He caught his breath suddenly, gasping heavily between coughs.

The three men trapped him in, their horses circling close and swords drawn. Liam felt the warm wetness on his lip and found blood. Lucy moved away from the circle, a look for helplessness in her expression.

A bearded man hopped from his horse, holding forth his blade. "I do believe, boy," he said, "you are the first person I've seen worth more dead than alive."

Liam felt for his gun. If he was no longer valuable to Raven alive, surrender wasn't an option. His heart sank as he found the gun missing, but he steadied his courage and drew his sword. They laughed.

"Have it your way," said one of the men still on horseback, smiling beneath his mustache. He seemed to be the leader.

The bearded man approached Liam warily, but their fight was short. Within two strokes the man faltered, and Liam's blade found his belly, spilling its contents open as the smell of his bowels filled the hot air. He fell to the ground, reaching for his two comrades.

"Should have stayed on his horse," the mustached leader said. Something struck Liam's head, agony ringing out. He fell to the ground, fingers squeezed in blood-wet sand. Darkness crowded his mind, flashes of light forcing him further down.

"Take everything."

In the City, beneath the gardens and buildings, Liam drifted through black, glossy halls of marble and into the temple. There at the pulpit stood his grandfather, Elijah the Great Prophet, old and frail. He spoke fervently, but Liam could hear nothing. The prophet was arguing with someone, the high priests who stood before him. They spoke back with equal zeal, spit spewing from their angry mouths. Back and forth they went, pointing fingers, sneering with exaggerated, twisted expressions. The prophet stepped from the pulpit and raised his hands and upon them burned a fire and Liam heard his words, "By this sign, he lives!"

Dorian grasped a handful of sand from the flat desert ground. He rubbed the dark orange grains between his fingers, each of the coarse particles telling its story.

*I am from the stone that slew Goliath*, one told him.

*They called this America*, whispered another.

Then one told him what he wanted to know. *A boy came here.*

Liam gasped for breath, eyes blinking as they adjusted to the sunlight. A weight on his back stifled him, pushing on his lungs. Body pressed fast to the earth, his bare skin seared against the sand. He might have cried out in shock at his nakedness had he the strength to do so, but even as dust curled up under his shallow breathing, his voice abandoned him.

There was a man lying nearby, his entrails sprawled from his body. It was the man Liam had struck and to his horror the man still lived, shallowly breathing. A crocotta buried its snout in the man's abdomen, the sound of gushing as it feasted upon its prey. Liam might have gasped had he the breath. With a groan, the man's head lulled to the side, eyes rolling up to meet Liam's. Amid the crocotta's slurping came a crunch. The man did not flinch, but something about his eyes said that he was in agony.

Liam averted his eyes to the vacant leagues of dull sand that merged with the cerulean horizon. He struggled to take another breath, and then realized the pressure on his back. Raven's men had stripped him nearly naked, and padded, clawed feet rested on his bare, hot skin. Short sniffs trailed up his spine, punctuated by a sudden exhale. Its ominous shadow stretched across the desert floor, its jagged, dog-like shape resting on Liam's body.

He had no gun, no sword, no hope. With horror, he realized why the man, still alive, couldn't move, because he did start to move. At first, it was a twitch, and then it turned into convulsing. He didn't spasm, but rather trembled. The crocotta perched on Liam's back let out a small cackle, as if delighted to discover Liam still lived.

Oliver had said that their bite was paralyzing and eventually fatal, but that it didn't cause numbing. When it started to eat him, he would slowly loose control of his muscles, unable to resist or scream as it consumed him alive. If the wounds inflicted by the crocotta didn't kill him first, it could take minutes to hours for his lungs to fail or his heart to give out.

He was so close. He had traveled leagues from the City into the Outland. He fought his way into the last stretch, only to fail. He wanted to shake, to wince at the pain of his sunburned skin. The painful strike would come at any moment. He longed for the numbness of death, but the crocotta granted no such death. Slow and painful, just like the man before him. He tensed, waiting for the torture to begin.

A shadow moved. Steel rang. The crocotta before Liam lurched, then collapsed into halves, its insides spilling over its victim as a gleaming sword severed the beast.

The silhouette filled his vision, a tall man in a long coat, sword in hand. With sudden pressure on Liam's bare back, his crocotta lunged. The man in the long coat stepped to the side easily and clove the monster in two, its body thudding to the desert ground.

With aching lungs, Liam drew a deep breath, skin tightening and burning. His ribs screamed as he tried to rise, but he collapsed as his arms failed him. He lay, staring at the soulless, dead eyes of the crocotta before him in a pool of blood-soaked earth.

The stranger had just saved him, reigniting Liam's last embers of hope, but as the dirt-caked boots approached him, he braced himself for any coming threat. Had he the energy he might have sobbed, but the life had left him. Only the ache of his body and burn of his skin remained. Something enveloped his naked body, sheltering him. The man's coat a comfort after the trauma.

"I'm sorry I didn't get here sooner," the man's voice said.

The world turned blurry, then faded into darkness.


The trickling of the river filled his ears as Liam returned to consciousness. He cracked his eyes, finding water running in the shadow of a luminous cave. Heat emanated from his body. "I've done everything I can," the voice said. "But I know it hurts. The most I can offer is more sleep."

"It's not that bad," Liam said, but as he tried to sit up, he winced.

"You'd better rest. But can you tell me who you are?"

"I am Liam. I seek Dorian." The words just came out. He had no other choice but to hope this man could help him.

"Well," said the man, leaning over him with a smile. "I'm afraid he's found you." Liam found new energy. Here was Dorian. He had done it.

"Dorian." Liam said the name aloud.

"And why did you need to find me?" Those ageless eyes searched his.

"The prophet lives. Oliver lives." Another wave of burning pain surged through Liam's body, taking his energy with it. "Jacob lives. The Morning Star—"

"That's good enough. You can rest," Dorian said. "That is troubling news, but for the time being we're safe here. I'm going to get your things back. I doubt your attackers knew what you sought, much less do they anticipate retaliation. I think I can track them and recover whatever was lost. There's plenty of food and the water here is fresh deeper back in the caves. For now, sleep."

Dorian laid a gentle hand on Liam, who resumed his peaceful slumber.

# CHAPTER ELEVEN

## Dorian

He waited with Liam until dusk and then Dorian rode his camel north into the desert. He could have taken the young man to Dali and bought whatever the boy had lost, but just as easily he could allow him the much needed rest and pursue those who had taken his things and left him for dead.

It had been too close. Dorian sensed Liam's coming, but did not arrive in time to spare him from his assailants. He was nearly too late to deliver the boy from the crocotta. It would have been a lamentable and painful death, foreshadowing Jacob's coming rule. Once Liam healed, Dorian would hear the details of Jacob's reemergence. He anticipated a full accounting of the news of the coming threat.

That the prophet lived was one thing, but Jacob's return disconcerted Dorian. It amplified the guilt that had plagued him for so long, already ingrained by his solitude. Two centuries of cogitation had dulled his shame, but Jacob's return revived old compunctions.

So long ago, Dorian tried to help the resistance against Jacob. Not only did he fail, but he let most of the earth go with it, preserving only Novum. He had never entered its doors, nor did he know a single soul within the pyramid. Yet, he saved the people within and it only cost the world. Raising and warding the mountains had a price: the life of the Last Saint.

The deep scars that lay upon the earth, both in the Outland and on the distant continents, were Dorian's fault as much as Jacob's. The world slowly gave way to Jacob's destruction, his tumultuous wrath seeping into her cracks. The kingdoms could not withstand the waves of despair and ruin; they could not contain his terrible greatness. Every effort of Dorian's was thwarted with such clever malice that it only lay more to waste.

The city had been right to fear the fallen, for Dorian's best intentions were inadequate, provoking Jacob further. Had he left the world to its own devices against Jacob, had he given up when he fell, would it all still stand? He wondered what would have come of Jacob's reign. What little power Jacob seized prior to the war was evidence enough. He claimed, and perhaps believed, that all he wanted was to rule, but he sewed too much chaos and destruction for it to be true. The old dissonance replayed in Dorian's mind just as it had since the end of the war.

And now that Novum, of all places, turned to him for aid, he wondered further if it would be better off without his help. Jacob's agenda was surely of dark design, but any attempt to stop him could be just as catastrophic. The wards that protected the mountains were powerful. If Jacob could breach them, then surely his power had grown great.

Dorian rode steadily in the quiet of the desert, his hair rousing with the camel's strides. The waste and deprivation opened before him, the mountains too far north to peer over the horizon. The two islands, large as they were, were their small known-world. Charis had found her place in the northeast and Nathan was to guard the west. Dorian had watched from the south. If Jacob had gone to the southern island as rumored, then this was where he would most likely strike first. Where had that left Oliver? Liam said that Oliver still lived, and if he knew that, then surely the boy had spoken with him. If Oliver was smart, he would be at the Pass, where no fallen angel could stand as guardian. Though they guarded the proverbial four corners, it turned out it was the prophet who predicted Jacob's new pursuits.

Dorian returned to where Liam had been attacked. He took little time to survey the bones and dried gore. More to his interests were the camel and horse footprints. They did not trail to the north toward Dali, but rather southeast toward Glenshore. It was closer, a coastal town of nefarious reputation. Dorian had long meant to clean the settlement, but it was more a benign slum than criminal hub, so he had let it alone. More important, Dorian consulted a contact there on his infrequent visits, in case he might gain word of Jacob or the others through Glenshore's criminal underground. Liam's attackers would likely find the coast and take it toward the sunrise until they found Glenshore.

Anger for Liam's assailants burned in him. The great injustice of their deed coiled in his stomach, a profound bitterness reserved only toward the most selfish and cruelest of men. How many had Glenshore's marauders left dead or raped or beaten? How many had they impoverished? The downfall of the world had not incited the least bit of unity among humanity. They turned their attention from the obvious: preservation in helping one another. Like animals, they fought for their own survival, resorting to fulfilling their own needs instead of seeking the greater good. It was the few who held onto hope, not just for themselves but for all of humanity, who worried about the future more than their own successes, who made the difference.

Sheer luck had kept Liam's pursuers from killing the one person who could save them. In these lawless lands, who could give them what they deserved? Dorian had enough blood on his hands, yet something had to be done. Liam was his responsibility and because of that he wanted justice. Those men would have killed Liam, and Dorian desired to take from them what they had surely done to so many others. That much was not his place, not unless he had to, but he would recover Liam's things if nothing else.

Nightfall brought him to Glenshore, the lights reflecting on the small bay, a deceitfully welcoming sight. He waited on the outskirts until the raucous laughter reached its peak. Good drink had done its job, ushering in the nightly celebration. When all other towns might have slept, Glenshore came alive.

He led his camel into town and found the stableman sprawled in the shadows, the smell of sour beer dense around him. With a kick he awoke the drunk man. "Up you go, master," he said.

With a groan the man roused himself, wavering even as he used the wall for support.

"What'd you want?" the stableman said.

"Some men came in here earlier. Had at least one camel with them."

"I've got one camel," he slurred. "Over there. Left it here last night."

"Who?" Dorian asked.

"Don't remember." The man put a hand to his forehead, as if the name might come to him or he might puke.

"What did he look like?" Dorian asked again.

"Mustache. Dark hair."

"Half of these men have mustaches and dark hair."

"But they ain't got a gun," the drunk replied, slinking to the floor.

His eyes fluttered a moment and then fell shut, followed by snoring. Dorian was surprised he had gotten as much coherent information out of the man, but also imagined he would be fortunate to get much more from anyone else in the town. Unless, of course, Ink was still in business and open late.

Two signs tethered together labeled the Bone Shop under amber light. Where Ink, the owner, had found the new sign that said "bones" Dorian did not know, but he entered all the same. Though years since Dorian had visited, it had changed little.

Ink sat behind the counter, tattoos running along his exposed skin. Intent on his work, the man didn't bother to look up as he greeted his customer with an indifferent wave. Bones lined the walls, dangling from the ceiling, and scattered on the floor. Human and animal skulls sat on shelves amongst jars of tarsal and carpal bones glowing in the neon and black lights.

"Haven't changed a thing have you?" Dorian asked.

"Got a new sign," Ink said, still fixated on whatever it was at which he scrubbed. "Bone shop. Shop of bones. Shop which sells bones. However, you like to think of it."

"Business good, old friend?" Dorian asked knowing well that the demand for bones in the Outland continued to exceed its novel facade.

Ink waved a colorfully tattooed hand at Dorian. "Someone drop you out of the sky? We've got thieves abound in this place. Marauders, bandits, brigands, however you like to think of them. And not one of them isn't sporting a bone of some kind. All the fashion for these criminal types.

"Everyone around here knows. You find a bone, you bring it to me. I'll clean up the bones you want to keep and buy the ones you don't. I pay good money, particularly for skulls. Believe it or not, smaller is better. Ain't never saw no one going around with a necklace dangling full-sized skulls."

The shop was open under the pretense that it was primarily where criminals could bring the bones they won to be cleaned or decorated. However, Ink kept the shop open late for the more discerning customers who bought the bones to boast as their own winnings. It was one of those things that everyone did, but to which no one would admit.

At closer inspection some of the bones had intricate patterns on them. That was new too. Ink had painted them in a variety of ways. Some had subtle markings, like pale henna. Bold stripes, flowers, and designs decorated others.

"Oh, fuck," Ink said, having looked up. "It's you."

"I'll admit that it's been a while," Dorian said with a grin. "Other than the sign, what's new?"

"The leader of the Infinite Bullets, once toughest clan there was, Tombstone Warner they call him. I don't know that he ever killed a man in his life. Never brought me any bones of his own, but he sure as hell bought them. Wouldn't tell you, except he's dead now. The end of the Infinite Bullets was the end of a good bit of my business."

That was a name Dorian knew. "Who killed him?"

"Don't know for sure, but there's a name going around here and I don't like it."

"What name?"

"Raven."

Dorian hid any sign that this was meaningful to him. "Tell me about the man with the gun," Dorian said quietly.

In return for Ink's information, Dorian gave him a small ruby. Firearms had not been seen in Glenshore since Tombstone Warner met his end weeks prior. According to Ink, the boastful cocksucker had it coming and there was a new man with a gun. Ink directed Dorian over two streets and down an alley, dimly aglow in hellish torchlight. The scarlet-lit lane ended at the tavern door guarded by two burly men. Dorian showed no sign of intimidation as he approached them.

"Password," the one on the right said.

"Kaidin," Dorian answered as Ink had instructed.

They allowed him into a room where some remnants of electricity bathed the space in gaudy multicolored lights and shit music. Most of the faces bristled with hair, mustaches prevalent among them, but only one boasted a gun laid out on the table before him. The woman danced for the man who had no coin but only the threat of the weapon. Unlike the more egalitarian world above, women here clearly had a lower place.

Dorian stepped between the man and his dancer.

"What the fuck?" the man asked reaching for his gun.

Dorian's sword came down, blade falling just short of the man's reach. The hand trembled, almost pulsating in sync with the jukebox's distorted drumbeat.

"What the fuck?" the man said again, weakly this time.

"That gun yours?" Dorian asked.

"What do you think?" the man asked.

"I don't think it belongs to you."

"I got it fair and square, asshole."

"Then I'd like to take it from you," Dorian said. "Fair and square, of course."

The man seemed to make himself relax, shifting his shoulders as he eased back into his chair.

"Listen, man," he said, the slur more evident in his drunken words, "I'm just enjoying a little dance here."

"I can wait until you're done," Dorian said.

"What business could you possibly have with me?"

"You have a gun. I have sword. How about we duel?"

"In the fucking dark? Are you crazy, man?"

"Tomorrow. I'll even give you time to sleep off the hangover. Noon, at the main drag. Bring your friend, the one who was with you when you got that little toy of yours." Dorian lifted his sword, leaving a groove in the table between the man and his gun. He flipped a coin to the girl. She had stopped dancing and only uncovered herself long enough to catch the gold piece.

Dorian left the man. He was likely too drunk to put it all together, but even if he did in the morning, his confidence would get the best of him. He would meet Dorian at noon. It was better this way. If Dorian recovered Liam's belongings outright, he would cause a scene and the town would turn on him. If he won it in a duel, it was considered fair. Furthermore, the man might just get what he deserved.

At a quieter place on the outskirts of town, Dorian nursed a neat glass of whiskey. He drank it like vengeance. Whatever comfort mortality had denied him, it at least afforded him solace in strong drink.

For the first time in years, Dorian awoke after the sunrise, a tender pillow under his head. He rose from the bed, stretching, and rubbing the sleep from his eyes. He splashed his face in the basin, rubbing the tepid water against his skin. To anyone else, this inn was far from luxurious, but compared to his shoreline cave, it was an unusual comfort. Breakfast in the commons consisted of eggs and polenta, other amenities his seclusion had not afforded him. He settled with the innkeeper and left, stepping into the dusty streets.

By morning, Glenshore resided in relative quiet. It had been a nice town once, the stone and clay structures untainted by the grime and smoke. However, the criminals who infested it had not bothered with upkeep. The town thrived on the fencing of stolen goods. On a visit decades ago, Dorian had almost bought a motorcycle, but decided against it, knowing how the seller had come by it. Once, not so long ago, Glenshore trafficked humans, mostly from the southern island, but demand had declined as more shoreline towns dissipated. Indeed, most of the coastal towns had become dangerous, more so than Glenshore. At first, they offered wealth, but greed soon made them only hospitable for those willing to fight for what they wanted.

As the afternoon drew near, the townspeople roused themselves, half-drunk or hungover. The shops were mostly open, and Dorian browsed among them. Some had electricity, surely paying a premium to whoever controlled it. In settlements like these it wasn't unusual for manual labor to be the means by which to generate power. When noon came, Dorian went to meet the man.

"How do you want to do this?" the man said, stepping into the street. By daylight his mustache was ratty, accentuating his disheveled and malnourished appearance. He set a pack to the side and rested a hand on the butt of the gun at his waist. Dorian wondered if the pack indicated that the man meant to flee once the duel was over.

"Where's your friend?"

"Ain't here," the man said.

"Went to tell Raven that you killed the boy?" Dorian asked.

If the man was surprised, he didn't show it. Perhaps he had suspected that Dorian wanted more than the gun. "Fifteen paces," the man said. The terms of the duel. They were as good as an answer. Somewhere in the Outlands a man journeyed to tell Raven that Liam was dead, and that was likely for the better. If Raven thought the boy dead and that Dorian had no knowledge of his machinations, so much the better.

"Fifteen paces?" Dorian asked with a smirk. "My sword is not that long, friend."

"I'm not your friend. You missed your chance to call the shots. If you don't like it, fuck yourself."

"Fifteen paces it is then."

"Mark it." The mustached man spat, every bit as confident as a man with a gun should be toward an opponent with a sword.

They walked. Fifteen paces by the markings on either side. Dorian completed it in twelve strides, the kerchief dropped, and he spun.

The pistol fired, bullet rifling over Dorian's shoulder, traveling into the distant desert. Dorian jumped at the man, gliding into the air in a wide arc. He landed, skidding on the ground. A wave of sand sprayed behind him. His blade glimmered among the dusty column, drawn from its sheath like a demon's talon. It struck the man from shoulder to hip, clean through, and left Dorian's sword slicked in the deepest red.

The halves of the man fell with a sickening sound, spraying a streak of blood into the street. His mouth moved and his limbs twitched once, twice, three times. With an ethereal gasp, death claimed him, and his fingers relinquished the pistol with lifeless finality.

After cleaning and sheathing his sword, Dorian took the pistol. He then examined the man's pack, its synthetic fabric long forgotten by the Outlands. It contained bullets, though for a Colt .45. The recovered 1911 had shorter rounds. Also in the pack, there was a broken watch, some comestibles, and a letter. The pack belonged to Liam.

Dorian looked up from his search. A dozen men and women watched him, eyes squinting in the sunlight.

"Do you know who that was?" an older man said, pointing at the corpse's halves.

"Someone who robbed the wrong man," Dorian said shouldering Liam's pack and putting a hand on his sword hilt.

"He was one of Raven's men," a woman said. "What sort of shit is this?"

"My kind," Dorian replied. "Anymore of Raven's men around here?"

"A few," the older man said. "They won't be happy." They would report back to Raven who would recognize Dorian's work.

"Tell Raven's men that the boy they killed is avenged," said Dorian. "And tell them to warn Raven. I'm coming for him."

"Who are you?"

"A vengeful god."

The afternoon's kill gave Dorian a thirst. The tavern had electricity and boasted an old air conditioning, which worked but made the place feel more dank than anything. A disco ball hung from the wooden rafters and a stereo in the corner played music from another age, it's neon lights flickering. A Tom Waits song blared as Dorian found a spot at the bar.

A ubiquitous fear permeated the air and he knew their eyes fixed on him. He had been inhumanly fast in the duel, and they were intimidated by his show of sorcery. They might turn on him after all, but at least the duel didn't give away Ink's cooperation.

He ordered ale and food. "A shot of whiskey too," he said as the barkeep served his beer. It reminded him of those years just after the war. On his journey south, he had found what makeshift settlements there were and turned them into real towns. Digging deep wells, he tapped into the labyrinth of reservoirs beneath the cursed Outland desert. He showed them how to use it to make clay bricks, to develop some semblance of agriculture, and cultivate peace. He whispered things into the earth so that plants might grow where the soil was otherwise deficient.

One important element, in his estimation, was that they have good beer. Things changed little in these places, and so the art of zymurgy had survived. Of all the discomforts of the past two centuries, at least they had beer.

"Damned good, isn't it?" asked the barkeep, his belly pushing up against the bar as he served Dorian a plate of potatoes and beans.

"That it is," replied Dorian, raising the beer in salute, welcoming back his inner-cerevisaphile. The whole meal might have overall been enjoyable were he not preoccupied with Liam's news. His thoughts turned north, wondering if he might find Charis and Nathan in time. He would need them. Even with them, Jacob would be formidable.

Dorian ate his food and opened the letter that had been addressed to Liam. He wondered a moment if he should mind his own business, but when he saw that it was from the prophet himself, he gave into his curiosity. *Press on, no matter what dangers assail you, for so long as you live, there is always hope. The darkest of evils will one day be overthrown and I believe that day is nearly upon us.* Words even Dorian would do well to take to heart.

He drank another beer, downed another whiskey, paid the barkeep and left the town with Liam's camel and his own. Word had reached the stable master, and whether out of sense or fear, he made no fuss in turning over the second camel. Dorian rode into the Outlands.

It was not Mars, though it looked like it. Dorian had been there before, to a dozen planets like it, but this was none of them. This was Earth. It had not always been like this. There had been cities, jungles, forests, swamps, life. Yet, Dorian suspected much of that was gone. He almost imagined that across the seas in the Graylands, beyond the two remaining islands, that the continents still burned. How they smoldered in ruin, nothing more than carnage and smoke. In the midst of it all, little did they know what was coming for them. Indeed, the prophet had spoken, but the planet had survived every preceding threat. Through nuclear war, maniacal dictators, disease, and famine, it had persevered, but it could not match Jacob's divine wrath. What was the largest anthill against the plow?

The fault did not lie solely with Jacob. He had wanted the world, and had Dorian allowed it, Jacob might have been content to rule instead of simply ruin. The prophet had said that all but the city would be destroyed. Was that a prediction that Dorian had fought or fulfilled?

The sunlight beat upon Dorian, its afternoon warmth a harsh distraction. He drank from his canteen and decided against removing his duster jacket. Liam's sunburn was bad enough to remind Dorian of the sun's dangers. As much as he might have resented this heat, he knew there were more pressing matters. Liam had muttered the name: The Morning Star.

The collaboration between Jacob and the Morning Star should have been obvious. Jacob loved the shadows, springing from his snares with venom. Furthermore, it explained Jacob's sudden disappearance. Dorian guessed that he had truly thwarted Jacob, and that his last resort was to make a literal deal with the devil. But that bargain would take time. Jacob's patience had paid off. He could turn any truth around, undo any goodness, breathing out destruction with an effortless infliction of malady. Dorian felt ill just thinking about it. The pursuit was a sick addiction, an irresistible desire to itch at the wound. Attempting to stop Jacob was like sucking in the water as one drowning is desperate for air. He felt as if he was clawing at the surface, hoping he might grasp something that could lift him up. Then Liam had come.

Two hundred years of hurt remained, a reminder of Jacob's lies and of his fall, and every memory a curse. The flames had lashed at him as he entered the atmosphere, knowing his punishment was what he deserved. His anger was not at God, but with Jacob. At his fall, Dorian desired cruel revenge, but by the time the shards of dirt and rock scraped and gnashed his body, he awoke in shame. The ire had been spent as had the burning, and then he lay cold and naked in the crater.

He remembered his hands trembling for the first time. He pulled himself from the pit, alone save for his sword. He did not recall it being with him in the fall, but he had discovered it next to him. His hand grasped the edge of the crater and he pulled himself up, muscles aching. Earth, in all its advanced technology, would know. The satellites would have seen the anomaly, seven falling stars and then someone would come for him. This was not like other fallen before.

Though shaking in unbearable pain, Dorian knew he needed to move. Each breath hurt. He had felt pain before, but nothing ever so mortal. Naked, sheathed sword in hand, he surveyed his surroundings of bare terraformed earth. He knew that he needed to hide, but this world and his newfound mortality daunted him. He did not recall how they found him, but they said he had been catatonic and with little effort they handcuffed him and ushered him into a helicopter. Strangest of all, no one seemed surprised to have found him.

As it turned out, there had been a prophecy. Elijah predicted it all, but Earth's affairs were so distant that none had heard the prophecy, much less thought it about them. Had Jacob known and ignored the warning signs?

He had landed on an island and he learned that its pyramid city was meant to protect the world from him and those like him. That is all they told him. They were afraid of him, as if their worst fears had come true. There were cells, questioners and their questions. He talked little.

They extradited him to the mainland, whoever *they* were. Earth had long been overlooked by Dorian because his celestial duties warranted his attention elsewhere. It was changed but not unexpectedly. Civilization had birthed cars and buildings, a digital age.

He could have broken from his high security facility, but his stupor continued. They might have tortured him, but the media had their eye on him. The questions stopped one day and they gave him a television. It was a small handheld screen and he bothered little with it, turning it on sometimes just to hear something other than his own breath and heartbeat. That was when he first discovered Jacob's rise.

Earth, with its unique history and divine preference was the perfect place, the place of second chances, an unheard of possibility in the spiritual world. Dorian expected the others to simply give into their situation as he had, but it seemed that Jacob had not learned from his failure. He sought power and somehow Amelia, Raven, and Cain had chosen to join him.

Dorian could have easily escaped his confines but he was unsure of what would happen if he did. He might be pursued, though he could likely go into hiding with ease. He sensed Jacob's quest for power was more than political, but it did not seem imminent that he do anything about it. Then Nathan found him. Before Dorian could think much of it, he was free from his cell, given new clothes—a long coat of which he was rather fond—and then sat in a pub with Nathan. How Nathan had arranged it, he never did find out.

"We have to do something about Jacob," Nathan had said. The very thought of it overwhelmed Dorian, who sat at the bar, staring at the various bottles with disinterest. "Didn't you hear me?" Nathan asked. "We need to do something about Jacob."

Dorian sighed and took a sip of his whiskey. "What would you have me do?"

"I don't know, but something more than sitting in a cell. I didn't procure your sword and break you out of there so you could come get drunk. Not that you can't get drunk. You just have to do something about all of this too." Nathan had always dealt with these things with some levity, but Dorian found he was not in the mood.

"Why does the expectation always fall on me?" Dorian asked. "Why am I the leader? You're clearly the mastermind here. You're the one who had the idea to break me out and take on Jacob. I don't see why this is my burden."

"Listen to me, Dorian," Nathan had said. "You were fooled by Jacob. We all were, but there are consequences. You know this, if you'd only think about it. Had we all been privy to his plan you know what would have happened to us, but since we acted in ignorance, we were pitied, even Jacob who knew damn well what he was doing. There have been many fallen in the last, what, sixty thousand years? More? In less than three months Jacob has convinced the world that the prophet was wrong, that he was sent by God, and that he deserves their following. He engineered a disaster on the American west coast just so he could come in and appear to be saving the day. It's only a matter of time before matters get worse."

"So, what are you going to do about it?" Dorian asked.

"*We* are going to stop him."

"How?"

"Charis is on her way. Novum shut its doors the minute we landed but there are those on the outside who don't buy Jacob's lies. There are people who know that if they don't fight they will lose everything. They'll follow us, we just need to find and recruit them."

"And how would you suggest that?"

"We already have one and he's promising, experienced, and intelligent."

"Then have him lead you," replied Dorian.

"You don't understand," said Nathan, "This is our fault and our responsibility to fix it. You are a great leader and that's what we need."

And now Dorian would be needed again. He still recalled the pub, the wooden bar, the absence of a television, crummy beer on draft. The sign on the door read "No Smoking" but it didn't stop anyone, not even the bartender. It was there that Dorian had been convinced that it was his responsibility to stop Jacob. Here in the desert he would return to Liam and inevitably they would depend on him once again. But to what end?

# INTERLUDE

## The Boy Prophet

*When, just over two hundred years ago, the boy now known as the Great
Prophet Elijah, first gained fame, I gave it little credence. I confess, I was
a preoccupied atheist living on America's western coast. As far as I was
concerned, the City, which they later named Novum, was a distant
thought and likely the product of a charlatan that knew how to coerce
religion and corporations. It was not that I dwelt on these thoughts. In
fact, had I pondered them, I might have come to very different
conclusions and saved my loved ones and myself a great deal of pain.*

*By the time I realized the truth of it, I was too late, and while I take
pride in my assistance to Dorian outside of Novum, I often wish that I
had possessed the sense to really weigh the issues at hand back then.*

*Though I had the privilege to meet the prophet, I gleaned very little
personal history. The annals that I acquired were of the most help,
though Liam was able to recount the more personal nuances of Elijah's
story.*

*—Oliver*

"Why do you care? You don't give a damn about him," Elijah's
mother said, the phone to her ear. "No," she continued, voice
shaking. "They are showing it for the eighth time today." The boy
knew without looking that tears streamed down his mother's face.
He sat on the couch, the television quietly playing the clip again.

Elijah had seen it over and over, the man on the phone, his father, saying the same hurtful things every time.

"He's just a boy. Nine years old," his father said into the news anchor's microphone. "I guess he just wants to take after his old man."

"And does he?" the reporter asked.

"Honestly, I don't think so. I think it's the fantasies of a child who wants to impress his father. I regret that I don't see him as often as a father should. Maybe this is his way of reaching out. In a way, I blame myself."

"What do you say to the prophecies that have come true? It is unprecedented that the mainstream media would report such things, and yet they are. Don't you think there's something to that?"

"No," his father shook his head. "He's a fake, a phony. He is not like me."

*He's a fake, a phony. He is not like me.* Elijah's stomach turned and bitterness filled his mouth.

"You know who the charlatan is here, Ron," his mother said. She paused, his father's response on the other line indistinguishable.

"You know what?" she yelled. "It's ironic that a man who has been a *fake* and a *phony* all his life would be the one to go on TV and announce to the world that his son was all those things. You know the truth. You know he's real. As usual, you put power before everything else. The world could be ending, people dying, and you'd still lie through your fucking teeth to get five minutes on the news.

"Let me tell you something," she said, her voice shaking. "I will cry when his prophecies come true. I will mourn every soul that doesn't make it to the City. But you, Ron, you will get what you deserve." With that she hung up, sniffling away the sobs.

Elijah had dreams. He would wake up and know the future. Sometimes they could prevent the future. The first time was when Elijah's prophecy stopped the bomber. A refugee in Minneapolis was going to go into the Target Center to blow himself up. Elijah did not live in Minneapolis, much less did he know anything about the sports stadium. They had questioned him and his mother after that. She was scared, but Elijah knew everything was going to be okay. They stopped the man, Elijah and his mother were cleared, and from there the government had kept a keen interest in him.

Some predictions could not be avoided. The hurricane last year had devastated the Caribbean and Florida coast, though thanks to Elijah, most of Miami had evacuated. The warning of a viral outbreak in India had not reached them in time and most of Rajasthan suffered in the epidemic.

*They* started and funded a church in his name. *They* hinged on his every word. But *they* were the leaders of corporations, denominations, some with the best of intentions and others saving themselves. It pained Elijah to know that the city they would build was not for the true believers. It was not even for the people who did not believe but deserved to be saved anyway. It was a city for those who were willing to capitalize on the risks, to preserve themselves and their vested interests for as long as possible.

"That asshole," his mother said. "Don't say that word. Don't listen to me."

He turned and looked at her, the phone held limply in her hand and tear streaks down her face.

"It doesn't matter," Elijah said.

"Of course it does," his mother said.

They moved that year to a parsonage where they would be away from danger. Elijah had been safe, but not from the attention garnered by his status, and soon the wealthy—celebrities, politicians, and corporate heads alike—began to probe at him. Some genuinely believed, he could see it in their eyes, but in others he only saw greed. It was a terrible thing to see that animal hollowness in their gaze that would never know love. The greedy ones reminded him of his father, though even at age nine he knew better than to speak of his father as his mother spoke of him.

Over the next few months, he met with various world leaders, corporate executives, and religious leaders. Some begged him to recant his prophecies. Some attempted to extort him. Some seemed to think he was a blessing. But none of the people that he met in those months was so unnerving as his father. It had been perhaps a year since he had last seen the man, and Elijah trembled at the thought of coming face-to-face with him once more. When his father requested the meeting, his mother had given Elijah the choice, and regardless of his fear, he assented.

They sat in his modest living room, an old, unused tube television in one corner. A tattered quilt draped over the couch on which he sat, and his father faced him, leaning forward in his chair.

"You haven't registered to come to the City," Elijah said.

"No," his father answered.

"Do you really think I'm a liar?"

"No," his father answered, "I think you mean it, but I think that you're fooling yourself."

"Then why did you call me a liar?"

"That's not what I'm here to talk about."

"It's what I'm here to talk about," Elijah said. "You called me a liar and your words could cost people their lives if they choose to believe you."

"Elijah," his father said. "It's time you learned something about people. They're not worth saving. What did they ever do for us? When they couldn't put us in chains any longer, they made damned sure we'd always be on the bottom, poor and starving. It's time we did something for ourselves."

"Bullshit," the nine year old said, startling his father.

"Elijah, listen to me, because no one else as self-serving as me will be this honest with you. I called you a liar because it makes me look good. We live in a world where if you don't take advantage of other people, they will take advantage of you. Might makes right, lust trumps love, and you need to act on that. I'm a televangelist because my conviction is that religious persons are weak, and it makes my life easier to extort them. If they're dumb enough to fall for it, they deserve it. At the heart of every so-called selfless person is a selfish motive, whether they know it or not. Most people are like me and they're too afraid to admit it."

"I don't believe that," Elijah said.

"And I'll tell you this," his father continued. "Most aren't worth saving. So take your own sanctimonious bullshit and face reality."

"You should go," Elijah said. "This was a mistake."

"Maybe," his father said, rising from the chair and standing over his son, "but maybe it's how you'll survive the mess you'll have made for yourself when this all turns out to be a delusion."

They called his city *Novum*. In Latin it meant *new thing*, but Elijah never liked the name. It was not a new thing, but rather a way to continue the old. Another opportunity for the rich and a catalyst for corruption. He had asked them to call it anything else. *Initium* had been the compromise he offered. "Beginnings." They rejected it.

His father's words stayed with him, even as they had moved into Novum. The power grabs began as soon as they shut its doors. The doors were not to be reopened until they were sure the angelic wars were at an end, or had never begun, but within a month, a religious grab expelled a large amount of Hindus and

Muslims. There was a witch-hunt for the radicals among them, fear gripping those in power that their religion was at stake. Of course, they were really threatened by the prospect that their own positions might be compromised.

Elijah had never wanted this, but the only compromise they had given him was that if he was right, then they had built the city according to his prophecy. They had even acquiesced to his bizarre request to build an alleged memorial to the fallen world. A stone disk was put in place, glyphs and runes drawn on it to his specifications. Of course, it was no memorial. It was called the Tartarus Project. It was something out of a dream, and Elijah had no idea what it was, just like a dozen other things around Novum. The reactor was buried deeper than necessary, their reservoirs tapped into a system of caves, there was a secret room at the top of the Central Spire. Whatever the case, he now watched as the world on the outside burned. If there was no hope in the city, surely hope was dying out there.

# CHAPTER TWELVE

## *The Northern Lady*

After a few days on the water, Maynard grew bored with the ship. He ate, he drank, he slept. At first Maynard feared he might be lumped in with the recruits, not fitting in with Jacob, Amelia, and Cain's familiar triumvirate. But Jacob delegated most of the duties to their forty hires. He had been prepared to insist that he was more like his angelic superiors, but once Maynard saw the ragtag group of men he didn't worry that he would be ranked with them. Nor did he protest when most of the work was assigned to them.

He did, however, take it upon himself to train the willing. Jacob talked of war, and Maynard would fight alongside trained men if at all possible. When the days grew hotter, the eagerness to learn waned. Only Devan kept interest. The dark-skinned man had become a sort of a leader among the hired men, respected among them. He was skilled at combat and Maynard found he had little to teach him, but they continued to spar if only to stay practiced and avoid the ubiquitous boredom.

It was in these days that Maynard had taken to leaning against the rail of the ever-rocking ship, looking out to the horizon or deep into the waters. For the most part it was dull except the afternoon when he saw the giant crocodile. At first he thought the emerging dark spot was the rum but soon other men spotted it. The great reptile swam up under the boat as men loaded their harpoons and bows. The very body of the creature was the length of the ship, and it seemed sure to rise and capsize them, but instead dove deep out of sight. Though most of the men were excited, Jacob was infuriated. "How dare he!" Jacob spouted just after the crocodile descended into the deep. Jacob stormed off and Maynard hadn't seen him in three days.

Now Maynard leaned over the rail, breathing the salty air and gazing over the rich blue waters. Amelia had walked up beside him quietly. "Captain says we're bad luck," she said leaning over the rail next to him.

"Men of the sea are superstitious. I would worry more about that giant crocodile if I were him."

"It was the most excitement the men have seen in days," she said with a chuckle.

"It is also the angriest I have ever seen Jacob," replied Maynard.

"I hate to see him like that."

"What was he so upset about? No harm came of it. It left us well enough alone."

"It was not just any crocodile," she said.

"Obviously not. I have never known them to grow so big. Then again, I've never been at sea. I'm sure there are many mysteries in the deep."

"I mean it was no ordinary beast at all," Amelia said, "It was the Leviathan, a daemon who is meddlesome in our affairs."

"A demon?" Maynard asked.

"A daemon." She offered no further explanation.

"Not on your side is he?"

"He would claim not to take sides," Amelia replied, "but he certainly favors Dorian."

They were silent for a moment and she moved nearer to him. She was beautiful with porcelain skin and eyes as crystal blue as the churning waters. It gave her a bold, royal look but there was a coldness to her as well. She leaned toward him, lips close to his ear. "It's lonely here," she whispered. Her breath tickled his neck and a strand of hair fell, brushing against his cheek. "I have a private cabin."

"And what about Jacob?" Maynard asked.

"He doesn't mind," she said. That was not what Maynard had meant. It was a possibility that one of these fallen had fathered him. Most likely she was looking to love the closest thing to Jacob, who only expressed as much romantic interest as it took to lead her along. Maynard liked little the idea of being the substitute.

"I better not," he said, "It may satisfy me now, but there will only be trouble after."

At this she retreated back, offended, "Am I not beautiful to you? Or do you prefer a different kind of love? Perhaps you'll find some of the men aboard more to your liking."

"If you actually fought alongside some of the men who do find other men more to their liking, you would know that's hardly an insult." She turned and left. Maynard resisted rolling his eyes, and watched the ocean as her angry footsteps faded away.

Moments later, Cain leaned on the rail at Maynard's side laughing, "Turned her down, did you? I have a private cabin as well. Mind you, I'd be on top."

"Very funny," Maynard said, though he didn't laugh. "I wasn't lying when I said she is beautiful, but I imagine when this is all over I can have as many lovers as I like without all the complications."

"You speak true, sir," Cain said. "She's just looking for the closest thing to Jacob. It's been a while for her."

Maynard laughed, "Aye, I guessed as much."

"Don't worry. She's used to rejection and gets over it quickly. I turn her down all of the time. Honestly, I don't think it would do any harm, at least not in my case, but I just like watching her frustration at the fact that I'll get with just about any woman but her. Of course, I have needs she could never meet."

If a beautiful immortal like her could not please Cain, Maynard did not want to guess at the sort of needs she could not meet. After a brief silence he changed the subject, "Jacob seems to have a plan, but he's talked little of it to me. What is our course?"

"He has spoken little to me as well, but I can guess his mind. Unless the land has changed, up in the northwest corner is a ring of mountains. I suppose the captain usually pulls right up to the caves, lowers the boats and they go to work. But we are to have him drop us at the point where the land meets the mountains. From there we will march east to a town south of the Pass where we will meet Raven. Then we will go into the ring of mountains where the City lies. Here's what I can't guess. That pass is guarded from us by a deep magic and the City itself is an impregnable pyramid."

"Why did he hire forty men?" asked Maynard.

"There are sure to be more than forty," Cain said. "Raven is on the mainland and if he meets us as planned he will have amassed more men. Of Amelia's many gifts she can come to people in dreams. Dreams are funny things. We can forget them within moments of waking or we can disregard them as wishful thinking. Raven, however, is keen-minded and Jacob seems confident enough that he received her message. Also, I have a feeling much of the ship's crew will join us."

"Is that so?"

"The captain is not a likable man. He goes about grumbling. There are too many people aboard, our folks are bad luck, the guy with the big sword drinks all the rum."

"I suppose that's fair," replied Maynard.

"You are not alone. Don't suppose you have any?"

"That I do," said Maynard, producing a flask. He took a swig and handed it over.

Muffled by the heat, Maynard almost didn't register the shout from the crow's nest when the lookout declared land in sight. It had only been one swig of rum, but it was stout enough, and his senses were somewhat dull. The boat lulled and he felt light, even merry, at the idea of land. Maynard followed Cain toward the front of the ship where they saw shore in the distance. It was not what Maynard expected. The blue sky and bright sun faded into a gray cloud prevailing on the horizon. The land was ashen, ridden with the smell the centuries' old rot. "The Graylands," Cain said. It was an appropriate name, as if the golden beaches in the South Outland had lost their color. In the distance, the hazy water lapped at the shores of the gray sand that faded into fog. Even in the heat a chill seized him, a silent warning. *The dead are here.* It was likely his imagination, but he almost saw slate-colored figures of skin and bone, their hollow black eyes gazing at him from the shore. Nothing was visible, but he felt them nonetheless. It was not the place he imagined and he did not want to go there.

"This is North Outland?" Maynard asked quietly.

"No," said Cain. "This western land is not where we are going. Our destination is to the east. What you see here is the Graylands, what's left of the world outside of our two islands. It's called a continent, a land many times the size of either of these larger islands. You could walk well over two thousand miles from coast to coast, but there would only be ash."

"You've been there?" asked Maynard.

"Yes," said Cain, his eyes showing some elation. "We made it what it is." Cain took a swig from the flask and passed it to Maynard. He drank, the mellow haze growing, and returned the flask to Cain.

That was it. Jacob, Cain, Amelia, and Raven; those they had rallied to their cause. This was their work. He had walked across the South Outland many times. It had taken weeks. Yet this was thousands of miles. What would it take to traverse those lost lands? Months. More. Among the ashes and the dead. It had happened two hundred years ago, and whether by slow or short death, it had been painful. He imagined leaving the footprints in the ash, moving through the fog. No life could survive such a thing, but intuition told him that something had survived. It might have been the few progeny of the desperate survivors or perhaps their wraiths. The ship slowly turned from the Graylands, the sad sight of a power struggle gone wrong. It might have been Jacob's fault or Dorian's, but Maynard knew something beyond his understanding of the world had been lost and now its wraith lingered. Cain elbowed him, handing him the flask. The Graylands were soon forgotten.

They drank into supper time, Jacob and Amelia joining them at the table. By all appearances, Amelia had gotten over the altercation with Maynard. With their merry making came such stories as Maynard had never heard. They spoke of men and war machines and the tallest buildings. They told of battles at the gates of hell and of the war after their fall. Later they were joined by Devan who had already imbibed his fair share of the ship's rum. The evening livened in laughter, drunken bitter remarks, and more rum. Well into the night, Maynard found himself sufficiently tired and drunk.

He awoke the next morning with a hangover, the sway of the hammock nauseating. It being like any other day, he had nothing to do but lie in his bunk and recover. He put an arm over his eyes, shutting out the ship, willing himself back to sleep. But Jacob roused him. "Get up, there's work to do." Then the angel disappeared, leaving Maynard barely awake in the stinking hole of the ship.

Gathering his wits, he dressed. Splashing his face and drinking water seemed to help enough but he had to be sparing with his rations. On the deck he found Jacob, Amelia, and Cain awaiting him. The sway of the ship and the bright sun made him feel nauseous but he did his best to ignore it. Jacob shook him by the shoulder. "Feel better, there's work to do," he said, and Maynard did feel better. If nothing else, Jacob could at least cure hangovers. "We're approaching land soon," Jacob continued, "and when that time comes we will need a way to move across the desert. We would be lucky to find a town on the western border where we can buy horses, gather more men, and stock up on water. That is too optimistic. We need this ship and we need blood." Maynard was confused as to how taking the ship would help them in the desert but he had little time to wonder because the captain and the crew approached.

The captain and his crew found the four of them on the deck, unarmed. "It's a funny thing," Captain Reed said. "It was my intention to alter our deal and go to the mines first. If your men could see the wealth to be had there, they'd likely stick with me instead of following you into that damned desert. But in spite of my best efforts to make for the mountains we seem to be ever on the path to your desert. Maybe it's your bad luck or maybe you're up to something. But I don't like it and I think we'd be better if we were rid of you."

"I would rethink that," replied Jacob. "You may kill us, but I don't doubt that Cain here would rid many of your men of their heads and limbs before you could overtake us."

"You're outnumbered five-to-one," said the captain, raising a hand. The conversation ended. With the stretch of his arm, the captain bade the crew to attack.

Maynard never confused intelligence and courage. The crew held swords, knives, and clubs. The four of them had nothing. Damn this! Damn Jacob for convincing him to come die at the hands of a greedy captain and his wayward crew. The men rushed at them. Jacob had yet to show any real power and this would be a good time for it, but nothing seemed to come. As they met in combat, Jacob gave one command. "I want the captain alive!"

Cain bellowed, meeting the battle. Near Amelia, a strange growling ended in men screaming for mercy.

Maynard's first opponent wielded a dagger. Dodging a strike, Maynard shifted to one side, taking the man's arm. He brought the man's limb backwards, using his own forearm as leverage against it. The arm snapped, bone shattering and blood spattering. He relinquished his grip, kicking the man and the dagger overboard. Another assailant cleaved at him. Maynard ducked, the ship's railing splintering as the ax met the wooden beam.

At least Maynard would die in his element: blood and sweat and battle. The assailant slashed at him, Maynard sidestepping it with ease. Unarmed he failed to duck the next swipe. Maynard raised his fists, blocking his face, but a blow from Cain intervened, sending the man to the ground.

Cain moved on, leaving two other men coming at Maynard. He dodged a sword, directing its wielder into the other man. They clashed, falling aside, as two more men rushed at him. A spiked club from one and a dagger from the other came at him. He tackled the dagger-wielding man to the ground, forcing him down and grasping his dagger hand. Muscles straining holding it away, Maynard straddled him, clutching at his opponent's neck. A shadow came over the deck, the second man, raising a spiked club. Maynard tensed for the blow. Instead a cry arose, like a small army rallying. Armed and sweeping upon them, Devan lead the forty hires, rushing into the skirmish.

Maynard found his senses. As the spiked club descended, he rolled. The man under him stiffened, Maynard pulling him over. The club struck the dagger-wielding man's back. He fell limp, gurgling as blood leaked from his body and mouth, and his blade clattered to the ship's deck. Pushing him off, Maynard rolled away from the second blow, grasping the fallen dagger. He sprang upward, plunging it into his attacker's belly.

He made quick work of his other opponents. With the help of the forty hires, the battle turned, and the captain and his crew were soon dead or subdued. All four of them came out of the skirmish unharmed but for some bruises and minor wounds. Somehow Maynard had bloodied his lip. Of the forty, only six were seriously injured or dead. Maynard had thought them as part of the crew. They ate, drank, and slept as one of the crew, and when the captain gathered his men to confront Jacob, he must have made the same assumption. A grievous calculation.

The blood sloshed on the deck of the rocking of the ship and Maynard stumbled over to Jacob and the rest. "Well led, Devan!" Jacob praised. Then he spoke to the whole crew. "Throw no man overboard. Put the dead or dying on the rear deck. Bring me Captain Reed." The hired men bore a bloody and beaten captain before Jacob. The captain met his proud stare.

"Cain," Jacob said, "You know what to do with Reed." Cain took the captain by the arms and dragged him away. Though too proud to beg, the captain's eyes showed fear.

"You saw this coming," said Maynard with a smile.

"Of course," said Jacob, "Whether the captain likes it or not, this ship is headed for our destination and I knew it was a matter of time before he realized it wasn't just a bad wind that thwarted him. In less than two days, we'll come upon the shore as I have willed it. Now, I have work to do while the blood is still fresh."

On the second day, the ever-roving waves yielded to the distant land. Instead of throwing the dead men into the sea, the crew had stacked the bodies on the rear deck. Maynard would be glad to be rid of them once they hit land and left the ship behind. Why Jacob insisted on keeping them until they landed was beyond him, but it was fetid, right down to the living quarters, even with the bulk of their stench trailing behind them. For those days, he had slept in an uncomfortable nook at the front deck, but at least it was away from the stench.

The ship's men were either assimilated or slaughtered. The captain himself was given no grand execution, but disappeared with Cain, who remained unseen since the skirmish. Rumors of muffled screams and pleas from Cain's quarters circulated among the crewmen. One night Maynard had put his ear to the cabin door, but heard nothing. Still, Cain's prolonged disappearance was strange, unsettling even. Maynard did his best not to think on it.

As they neared the land, there were questions among the men as to what would happen next. With no horses or camels, who would carry the supplies they needed? Rumors circulated that the forty men had been hired as pack-animals to carry unreasonable burdens across the desert. Devan assured them otherwise. Maynard hoped that this Raven awaited them.

Maynard expected orders to ready for their landing, but none came. When Jacob could be found, he spoke little, muttering mysteriously of the necessity of the blood that had been shed. Maynard decided not to trouble himself with the matter and spent the day lounging at the front deck in an attempt to ignore the smell. Dolphins, as Devan had called the sleek, gray mammals, darted in and out of the water.

At some point, he was wondering at the cheerful creatures when the land appeared too imminent for his liking. The blue waters gave way to the deep orange and brown hills that leveled into a single continuous terrain. Far to the right, the water morphed into a different sort of ocean, a sea of sand that spread into the horizon. In the distance, to the north, the mountains loomed in a straight vertical rise and stretched into a curve towards the east. They were unlike any mountains he had seen, a single continuous ridge that rose and flattened at the top. There were no slopes or ledges along the sheer walls. If a person were to attempt to climb it and find footholds along the way, they would tire long before the top. If anyone could reach it, they could walk atop it, perhaps many abreast. How he longed to see the top and walk along it and survey the desert and the uncursed lands from on high.

The most peculiar thing was that the shoreline did not yield a harbor. There might have been a town there once, but the scorched terrain and dilapidation looked more like an old burned garbage heap than a town. Had it still stood, they could have amassed supplies, transportation, and formed some semblance of a plan. Instead, the desert spanned in one direction and the mountains towered in the other. His musing was interrupted by a great commotion from the men and Maynard soon realized that they were approaching the land with rapid speed. The land drew near, so close they should have run aground. The crew cried out, pulling ropes, shifting the mast but there was no stopping the ship. They braced themselves and Maynard receded from the edge and held tight to a rope. At any moment the ship would beach.

The wreck never came. The great ship ceased to tread the water and instead broke through the sand. The transition was smooth and the rocking of the ship faded as it glided through the dunes. Instead of surf at the helm, a wave of sand crested at the front of the ship. They dipped in and out of the small dunes until the terrain flattened, and then it continued to cut through the dirt. Half of the men cheered and the other half remained speechless with terror. Maynard knew. At last Jacob had demonstrated his might and here they had all the stores they needed for their journey. The ship was magnificently sailing through the desert. It rolled as it plowed through the ground, pushing onward amongst the Outlands.

Maynard peered over the rail and instead of the rolling blue waters he found the desert's hardpan terrain. The ocean was long behind them and at last they had arrived at North Outland. Below the deck, he found Jacob, who appeared morose.

"Are you sulking?" Maynard asked.

"Not exactly," Jacob said, "Just pondering."

"You should have seen the men. They hardly knew what to do with themselves. What next, are we to fly over the mountains? Is that your plan?"

"Were that I could," said Jacob, "but nothing would come of it. I grow impatient, Maynard. You would think that having waited this long, I could wait a little longer. But as the time ripens, the sweeter it grows and the more I desire it. I should have been wiser before. Had we thought of it, we could have made our way through the Pass back then. It was too well guarded then anyway, but Raven has been clever as usual and he has found our way."

"And that would be?" asked Maynard.

"You will have to see," replied Jacob. "If I told you that I would make this ship sail across the desert what would you have said of me then? And if I told you I could raise the dead you would say that even I have limits. Today I do but one day I won't.

"In the mean time, we are not headed first to the Pass. We are to meet Raven in the first town just south of it. At this speed, it's another couple of days travel, but we may stop if we find towns along the way. This land has changed, so it is difficult to say. Raven is gathering an army there and we will gather more at the Pass. If we can, we'll make our way into the City from there. If Dorian finds us out and we have to battle him, the Pass will be our most strategic point. Otherwise we make for the City."

Maynard departed and went back to the top deck. Everyone was in good spirits and a bottle of rum found its way to him. He spent the evening merry making with Devan and a few of his men. The smell was not even that bad. Supper was excellent as Jacob had allowed extra rations to be used and ordered that if they came in sight of a town to stop there for more provisions. The sun set and the chill of night set in. The sky felt different here but Maynard could not guess at the distinction.

# CHAPTER THIRTEEN

*Prophecies*

Liam emerged from sleep to a sound he could not place. He opened his eyes to the shaded cavern, finding himself nestled into one of the many recesses. The sun glimmered on the pool's surface, its waters flowing into the cave, crystallized light cascading reflections down the stone walls. It was hard to tell the cave's deepness but his immediate surroundings were apparent. This was Dorian's home. It was modest with few blankets, some crates, and other tools. Liam's body ached and his skin burned, but not so bad as before. The memories came to him: Sol, Barker, crocotta. He shivered. He heard a sound and, though familiar, he could not place it. It reminded him of the rushing river outside of the City, but it was different. Instead of a trickling stream, it oscillated. He remembered the previous days, fading in and out of the fevered dreams. Orientation dawned on Liam as he recalled the way the sound permeated his dreams. He turned stiffly to see the source.

Before this journey, Liam had only viewed the desert through Novum's glass walls. There had been the sparse northwestern forest and the ring of mountains, but now he had finally beheld his share of the outside world, right down to the southern shore. There were old videos and pictures, but nothing matched the real thing. They never quite captured the vivid way the sun beat down on the harsh red and orange ground. Never did they depict the vastness of the waste. No picture came close to the ocean he now viewed. Liam made to arise but found he was naked beneath the blanket. Of course, the men had taken his clothing, but he improvised, wrapping the blanket about his waist. Liam walked to the mouth of the cave and stepped onto the beach. A picture could not replicate the smell of salt in the air. Film hardly captured the sound—which Liam now recognized—of waves washing upon the shore in their lazy rhythm. Nor could those things depict the foamy crest of waves receding into the glossy waters that stretched into a rolling blue expanse. Liam, though stiff, knelt and dug his fingers into the wet sand, allowing the waves to rush upon his dirt and bloodstained legs. The water was not frigid, but rather a cool, crisp contrast to the warm air. Fish darted in the shallows, seaweed swayed, and Liam thought he could never leave.

"It's good that you're awake," a voice said.

Liam turned. Dorian led two camels down the path nestled between dunes, a brief respite from the steep shelves that housed the caves. The rocky pathway declined into the sandy beach that stretched for some small portion of what appeared to be a narrow bay. Liam recalled Oliver's map. He had been right about where to find Dorian. Liam studied the spirit made flesh. His skin was darker, but not like Liam's. It was a dark tan, but more natural. The tall man wore a brown leather coat that came down to his calves. His hair was long and dark and he kept a short beard. His brown eyes shared that same deep look that he had seen in Raven, yet they were kind and studying.

"While you recovered, I went and got your things back," Dorian said handing Liam the pack and then taking his own from the camel's saddle. Liam stood motionless. After all he had been through, here was Dorian. For the first time in weeks he felt peace, like everything had come together. He had held fast.

"Not talkative?" asked Dorian. "Come over here and have a seat." He motioned towards two large stones, seats by which to converse or watch the ocean.

Liam was not afraid of Dorian, nor was he at a loss for words. Rather, it was as if he felt he had little to say, that there was nothing he could tell this man that was worthwhile. The fallen angel carried himself in the same curious manner that he had briefly seen in Raven and Charis, but even Dorian was something different. He certainly was not what Liam expected.

"It's not that," Liam finally managed to reply as he sat down and faced Dorian. "It's just that I have nothing to say."

"That's interesting" said Dorian with a small laugh. "I would think you have plenty to tell."

"Well, I suppose I do," said Liam and he soon found that he indeed had much to say. He told Dorian everything. He told him of being the eighth generation descendant of Elijah, of the new prophecy, and of finding Oliver and his journey south. Dorian did not interrupt him, but merely listened patiently. When Liam had finished, they sat silent a moment.

Dorian sighed, "Oliver lives, Jacob comes, and you arrive to tell me in time. Still, more bitter than sweet, I fear."

"What now?" asked Liam.

"I don't know," said Dorian.

Liam was surprised. The prophet had sent him all this way to find a man who could supposedly save them and now he did not know what to do.

"What do you mean?" asked Liam.

"How could you understand?" asked Dorian shaking his head. "I was one of many implicated in Jacob's deceit and yet the duty to stop him falls on me just as it did before. Before, when I failed."

"You didn't fail," Liam said incredulously, "You stopped him. You raised the mountains. You kept Novum safe."

"The City, yes. Do you know how many people were in the world before the war? How many people can Novum hold?"

"It has grown to well over a million they say," Liam replied, "We are near capacity."

"Before the war, the world was reaching a population of eleven billion. Your city is a few square miles of subterranean levels and skyscrapers and the population of this subcontinent is hardly noteworthy. I wonder if you could even pinpoint it from space."

Liam was confused. "Never mind," Dorian said. "Suffice to say, much more was lost than was saved."

"And if you had not intervened, all would have been lost."

"I suppose so. At least, that's what I told myself."

"So, there must be something we can do now?"

"If the prophet is right, then Jacob means to take the City. Who knows to what end? There's nothing else here for him. He has made a deal with the Morning Star, another mystery, though I suspect it might have something to do with his prolonged disappearance. I also suspect that he has ways of amassing an army that we do not. We might be able to rally a few men from town to town, but we can't hope to make it worth their while."

"What about the Tartarus Project?" Liam asked.

Dorian's eyes widened in surprise. "A rumor that you would know more about than I do."

"Sol and Raven asked me about it. I knew I had heard it before, but I couldn't remember where. I'm pretty sure my grandfather mentioned it right before I left Novum."

"If we don't know what it is, I don't think we can rely on it. The Tartarus Project could be anything."

"Look," said Liam, surprised that he was the one giving the advice. "You heard what I said. We meet Charis in Mere. She is going to find Nathan and bring him there. Oliver will be with us then too."

"And what then?" Dorian asked.

"Raven has taken Bronton, so forget about that. Mere is in the east, Jacob is coming from the west, and the Pass is somewhere between. We make haste, get to Mere, and ride out to take Jacob before he can hope to meet with Raven. How much of an army can he gather between the shore and Bronton?"

"A lot, if he's coming from South Outland. He could bring a fleet of ships."

"Across a desert?" Liam asked.

"I have to hand it to you," Dorian said with a smile, "you've thought this through. Jacob is persuasive. He has a way of always being one step ahead. But, no doubt, he probably isn't as strong as we think."

"You've been down here all this time should he return. Well, he has. We should go to Mere and figure it out from there. Oliver's there. Charis and Nathan will also know things we don't. Unless, I came all of this way for nothing. You could stay here, for no apparent reason, and when Jacob wins you'll know that it's because you did nothing to stop him."

Dorian furrowed his brow. "I never said I wasn't coming. Believe me, I fully intend to fight this with every breath I have. The years have just made me a little cynical." Dorian paused and then sighed. "How are you? Can you ride?"

Liam nodded even though he still felt considerably sore and sunburned.

"Good then," said Dorian. "I have most of your things. We will ride at first light."

Most of Liam's things were packed, and he was a little too stiff to do much else than check his bag. He waded into the shallows that afternoon and bathed. It was salty, but refreshing, and when he was finished, he sat on a rock near the shore, wearing nothing but a cloth around his waist, watching the waters as he dried. Dorian moved about packing, and soon the sun began to sink in the west, falling behind the small cliffs of the bay. Once dry, Liam put on his spare set of clothes and contemplated the journey as the sun set. After making a fire, Dorian set his coat to the side and sat next to Liam. They sat in silence for some time before Liam spoke, "What was it like?"

"The war?" asked Dorian.

"No, I mean, being an angel. You're not what I expected. None of you are."

"It's hard to put into words. It's another dimension, another realm from us." Dorian spoke into the night. He spoke of battles at the gates of Hell, of the demigods and the stewards of the celestial bodies, of ages before known history, and of things Liam did not understand. As it grew later, Liam began to fall asleep and Dorian had turned to more abstract topics. He spoke of the great cosmic dance and the ways the stars moved in constant harmony. The constellations existed only to live in a single, perpetual motion, repeating the rhythm for millions of years, because the thing in itself was so beautiful that it bore repeating to the end of days, so that everything that had lived would live on to behold the beauty of their glowing patterns. The heavens resounded in a deep song that preserved the cosmic order.

Dorian had once participated in that order, the steward of a distant planet, a god in his own right. He governed it, subordinate only to the Eternal One, and he was beloved by its inhabitants. Such were the ways of celestial beings, doing all that they did for the great creator. Dorian told him how it had not been so different from earth, for the heavens and the beings who dwelt within that realm were generous.

"Take for instance the horse," Dorian said. "A magnificent creature. When the Eternal One created Earth, one being fashioned the creature and gave it to him. Think of it as a housewarming gift. Such a creation was indeed used, but also shared. Thus we have horses on my planet." His voice grew mournful, "Or what *was* my planet. That was so very long ago.

Ages have surely passed. And more are sure to pass, but tonight we must rest."

Liam fell asleep.

The next morning Liam felt less sore and his skin was cooler than it had been in days. The morning sun reflected blood orange through the pool in the cave. After splashing some of the soothing water on his face, Liam was ready to set out. They packed the camels and gathered fresh water from the depths of the cave's inner pools. Liam checked his gun and decided to keep it on his person instead of his pack. "I noticed that gun of yours, Dorian said when he saw it. "It's a good thing Oliver gave that to you. It will be handy. Guns in themselves are quite scarce, as before the fall they were increasingly banned, but this particular model was possibly the most common in the world. So common, in fact, that I have one myself and happen to have a good supply of ammunition."

"I have bullets too, but they won't fit," Liam said, showing Dorian the ammunition he had bought.

"You're right," Dorian said. "These are for a Colt revolver. Do you see how the base has this little disk? See how they are too short? We'll trade them if we get a chance."

They finished what little packing remained and led the camels up the steep trail. It was a bit difficult for them to get their footing, but after a little work, they were level with the desert again. Behind them, the sea stretched in every direction. Liam saw how the bay curled up at the tip of the land and then the rest extended beyond sight. It looked like the land eventually leveled out and that the caves were the only formations nestled into the southern tip. Dorian confirmed as much. Before them stretched the immense desert, and they started out with their camels in a steady gallop. At first it was a little hard on Liam's bruises but eventually he grew accustomed to it. Dorian explained that the less they were seen within towns the better, and so they agreed to stay in the desert as often as possible.

This would be another sort of journey. Dorian was with him, but no matter what came next, Liam would hold fast.

"You know how to get to this garden city?" Dorian asked.

"I remember the maps," Liam said, and they began their trek to Mere.

# CHAPTER FOURTEEN

## *People of the Fire*

"We should have stayed at the oasis," Gaezar said. "It is too hot here and my skin burns."

The nomads journeyed through the desert, strung across the sandy terrain. Argon's burden was the heaviest. He would not ask anyone to bear anything he was unwilling to carry himself. Gaezar had caught up with him toward the front of the procession, his unwelcome, unburdened, and sweaty appearance one more thing to tire Argon.

"You should wear more clothes," Argon replied.

"But then it's hotter still," said Gaezar.

"One would think that you had not lived in the desert your whole life, Gaezar. This is our way."

Gaezar cleared his throat. "You misunderstand me. I do not complain on my own behalf. I'm content to endure the sun and heat if it is the will of my chiefs. It's the others I worry about."

"They follow more loyally than you. None gripe so much as you. I do not worry about them."

"You are correct. There are none who are disloyal to you, save for the ones too weak to make the trip. Of course, they would not dare to deliberately betray you or Belriah, but they cannot help but die. I fear we have already lost a score to dehydration, overheating, and weariness." Gaezar could barely keep stride with Argon's gait.

"I am dealing with these matters, but you must understand that this is the people that we are. We were the first men of this land, exiled here only to be overtaken by the engines of other men and the magic of the gods. We are a people born out of war, heat, and death." Argon liked little the way Gaezar complained, appealing to the misfortunes of others. There were others who were perhaps not so well-fed or rich as Gaezar, yet they bore suffering with more grace. Argon wiped the sweat from his forehead as Gaezar continued. "Please, Argon, if we could only slow our pace or find another oasis for just a short time."

Argon stopped and stepped from the procession looking at Gaezar, towering over him. "I will hear no more of this," Argon said. "We are slow enough as it is and there is no other oasis, not that you or anyone would be allowed more than a day's convalescence." With that he walked over to an old woman whose back hunched under the weight of her pack. Others, too poor to own livestock, pulled their own carts or had almost no possessions.

"Woman," Argon said, "Give me your burden. From now on it is mine to carry. You can make camp with my family and we will provide your needs as best we can."

She looked at him timidly, but shook her head. "I thank you, but I will carry my share." She gave him a short bow and continued on her way.

Gaezar glared at her before turning his contemptuous gaze to Argon and stalking away, leaving Argon glad to be rid of the greasy man.

Belriah found Argon a little after Gaezar disappeared.

"What is this I hear?" the rotund chief asked with a grin. "Offering old ladies into your service?"

"No," said Argon thoughtfully. "I serve them."

"Humorless, as always," Belriah chided before sighing. He paused a moment and continued, "Argon, when matters like these, like this journey, arise who do I consult?"

"The small council, the gods, others," Argon said.

"Humorless *and* humble. No, Argon, I consult you."

"It is true, you often seek me for council."

"Baran is almost of age, yet I never consult him, nor does he learn from me."

"You have let him sit on some of the councils, though not lately. He takes lessons like any young chiefling."

"Yes, in principle, he is getting everything he needs," Belriah replied, "Everything except my guidance. I have withheld my hand. Do you understand?"

"I am not sure I do. You would want your heir to know all things as you know them. You would want him to know them better, in fact."

"Yes," said Belriah, "my son does not know these things, but my *heir* does." They were walking a few feet away from the line. In the distance a small clan of crocotta scavenged. Argon guessed Belriah's meaning but it was unsettling.

"These matters were of little importance before," said Belriah, "But with the coming war there is a chance I will die. My son does little to please the gods. He does not make sacrifices or consider our kindred beasts. He does not visit the tabernacle for repentance. I worry about him and his friends. They are unwholesome plotters."

"The gods have smiled on the less pious before," said Argon. "After all, Elah allies with Xu."

"Yes, and they have been strong and wise rulers. Not Baran. He would use the power for his own gain. He keeps unsavory company and belittles those around him. He does not care for what it takes to rule, only the wealth that comes with it. He does not understand the sacrifice."

"We have laws, Belriah."

"And if I don't change them, Baran is sure to break them."

"You may lead, but remember that these people trust your guidance. They will turn on you the minute they see you politicking as you please."

"Then they are sure to turn on my son," replied Belriah.

"What then would you suggest?" asked Argon.

"I'm thinking on it," Belriah replied.

Argon thought on it as well. It was not beyond his observation that Belriah's son, Baran, had recently been absent from the councils. Nor had he missed the boy's perpetual look of boredom whenever Baran attended. Argon had thought it a mere phase, yet this was no time for a young chiefling to have a season of apathy. Would he even follow his father into battle or would he preoccupy himself with the usual indulgences? Belriah should have been sterner with the boy, but that was all too late now.

Hot and dry days passed. Even the camels grew weary, and if they should come upon a town, it was unlikely they could afford the amount of water needed for so many. The People of the Moon knew how to barter and trade, each according to one's resources or skill, but the townships in the Outlands possessed little sense of economy. One town might take a mismatched assortment of coins, another gold. They might trade in goods, but not consistently. There was little hope that anything save that Elah alone would restore their dwindling provisions.

It had been months since the last rain, but Argon hoped that their god would provide. There were no clouds, only the clear blue heavens above. They had separated from their tribesmen in the west many rains ago. It was a happy parting, but it was obvious that the single oasis in the Eastern Pan could not sustain the size of their people. The presence of the crocodiles was sign enough that the People of the Moon remain. The People of the Fire moved into the west to seek another rumored oasis. They seldom visited each other and Argon wondered what they would be like now.

The People of the Moon worshiped Elah who favored her people and the crocodiles. Yet, Elah seemed to be leading them from their kindred animals, guiding them into the dry desert and eventually war. Would they ever be joined with their kindred again? The People of Fire, who served Xu, the sun god, were kindred to the tiger. It was rumored that long ago they lived in harmony with their kindred beasts, but no longer. It was a wonder that Argon had seen one in his lifetime, as he previously believed them to be extinct.

They traveled over a fortnight, crossing the southern portion of the small continent into the west. His family owned many camels but he had loaned them all to the less able-bodied, those who needed them more. If this was simply an army, it would have traveled with more efficiency, but this was more than a march to battle. It was a migration. Argon was tempted to worry about Chief Serj's reaction when they presented themselves to the People of the Fire, but at the moment, he knew how important it was that he put all of his efforts into getting to the western settlement. At least Gaezar had not been seen in the hot and trying days.

"Shouldn't we be there by now?" Argon asked Belriah one hot afternoon.

"They settled almost directly west of us and a little to the north," replied Belriah, "If we are reading the stars right, then we should arrive any day now."

"Do you really think Serj will be open to this?"

"Who knows? I have my people and he has his. If he will not listen to the will of the gods, what can I do?" As Belriah spoke, a rhythmic thumping sound filled the air. The drums played a beat Argon knew well, hearkening hopeful news.

"A settlement," Argon said.

"Let us go see it," Belriah said.

With that they took quick strides to the front of the lines. In the distance stood a settlement.

"That is not the town of an outlander. Those are the tents of tribesmen," said Belriah. "Send messengers ahead."

Soon camels galloped across the desertscape toward the sprawl of tents, leaving clouds of dirt in their wake. Argon and Belriah continued to lead their people toward the settlement and then another set of dirt clouds appeared to be coming back their way. One scout returned, "Chief Belriah, it is the People of the Fire. Chief Serj opens his lands to you."

Belriah and Argon chose camels for themselves and rode ahead. Argon found himself excited and hopeful as they approached. It was much like their oasis in the east, though their small lake looked less clean. Small tents lined the outskirts, smoke rising from fires within the camp. As they passed the rough border of the settlement, Argon held his breath, trying not to take in the fumes from the latrine. They arrived at the tents on the fringes, and passing between them, they met Serj. Argon recognized the bony man, though he had grown older. His tattoos sagged a little more and gray patched his hair. Belriah and Argon dismounted their camels and each in turn embraced Serj.

"It is good that your arms once again fall upon my neck, my brothers. It is good that you have come," said Serj. "But look! You bring a host with you. What am I to make of this? Tell me plainly of what your messengers speak."

"My brother," said Belriah kneeling. "The time of the promised rain has come. Our gods bid us to the north. We ask you to join us."

"It is as I was told," said Serj, troubled.

"Your gods have spoken to you as well?" asked Argon.

"In a way, but that is not of what I speak. Come," said Serj.

He arranged for their camels to be taken and directed Argon and Belriah to follow. They entered a large tent, the cushioned seating and fine wares indicating that it was a place of meeting for important tribesmen. In the center stood a thick wooden pillar to uphold the tent, smaller supports lining the walls and corners. By the wooden beam stood Baran and Gaezar.

"Your son, Baran, came ahead of you with his servant," explained Serj. "Gaezar here has told me that you brought lies regarding dreams of gods in order to gain my subservience. Is this thing true, Belriah?"

"This thing is not true," said Belriah shaking his head. "Depart, my son." Defiance flickered on Baran's expression, but Belriah's disposition hardened. Baran poorly hid his resentment, yet he left the tent as if belittled. "Stay there," Belriah commanded Gaezar before he could move from the wooden beam. "Come," he said to Serj. "Let us talk about this."

"There is no need for talk," said Serj walking over to a weapon rack. Argon's hope sank. Was Serj going to believe this pest of a man instead of his friends? And what of Baran? Had not the gods spoken to him too? Argon and Belriah were not armed. Even if they could defeat Serj, they could not escape his camp alive. Argon was ready to surrender when Serj took a spear from the rack, examining it, testing its weight as he hefted it. He threw it. Argon tensed, ready to defend his chief. But it was not directed at him or Belriah. It drove true and fast into Gaezar's gut and pinned him to the large wooden beam. The room immediately filled with the stench of bowels.

"You!" Serj bellowed toward the shaking and bleeding Gaezar, "You would come here and set me against my brothers. You would defy the will of the gods. Hear me now small man, as you die. Not a fortnight ago I dreamed of a tiger and a crocodile journeying to the north. I thought it was only a dream until you came to me. You insult me!" Gaezar bled from his mouth, gurgling as he tried to speak. The smell grew worse. Argon wanted to cover his nose but he did not flinch.

"Guards," Serj called as several soldiers burst into the tent, "Unpin this man and drag his body beyond our borders. Leave him for the crocotta."

The guards saw to the orders, though one of them vomited as they approached Gaezar's twitching body. Serj lead Argon and Belriah from the tent, away from the smell.

"Serj," Belriah spoke, "I apologize for this man's insolence."

"No apology is required," Serj said, "for this was not your doing. I doubted his words and it gave me time to think as I anticipated your arrival. You must tell me everything and we will make a decision together."

Serj led them to another tent and they sat at a broad table with a map laid out on it. They spent the afternoon in deep discussion. Belriah and Argon recounted the omens and visions and Serj listened closely.

"My brother," said Belriah. "I keep my chiefly power out of duty and not greed. It is the way of our people. If we can be of like mind, I will surrender my chiefdom to your command."

"We are of the same mind, but there is no need for you to bend the knee to me. We will work together," said Serj.

"That is good," Belriah said. "Still, let it be said that given my son's betrayal, that Argon will become chief in the event of my death."

"Do not speak of such things," Serj said.

"Things are changing," Belriah said. "The promised rains come. You must support Argon, if he is to be my successor."

Argon stood, giving a slight bow. "Please, my chiefs. There are more pressing matters."

"Argon speaks true. It shall be as you wish, Belriah," Serj said with finality. He stood, scanning the map spread on the table. "I have been thinking about this for many days now since my dream. We are nomads and this map is what our forefathers have known. Look here." He pointed to the Eastern Pan, the People of the Moon's former home. He slid his finger up. "Follow that west and a little north and here we are. It was said that you are to go north and west. Xu, the Sun God, has shown me to go north, for you have already traveled far enough west. If we follow straight north we will find the mountains. Perhaps our destination is beyond them. Who knows?"

"Yes," agreed Argon. "We have always considered the People of the Fire as our western brothers, but look, this is really where we are." Argon gestured more toward the center of the landmass. "If we go straight north," he continued, "We will find ourselves at the eastern border of the mountain where the chain seems to meet the salted waters. If there's not a way beyond the mountains, we can march along the range until we find a way through. It may take time, but it prevents us from missing a path."

"This is a very old map. Who is to say if it is accurate?" said Serj. "Only once when I was a child did I see the mountains and very few times have I seen the salted waters."

"You both speak true," said Belriah. "This map is very old and I myself have seen the mountains but once. Yet, it is all we have to go on. I say we start by following Argon's suggestion and let the gods lead us where they may."

"And what of water and provisions for such a large group of people?" asked Serj.

"We take what we can," said Argon. "Build more wagons from the remnants of this camp, use the livestock to pull water and food. We should not delay, but there is no reason we cannot take the time to prepare."

Serj and Belriah both looked at Argon and nodded.

"This man," said Belriah putting a hand on Argon's tall shoulder, "always speaks wisdom. Should something happen to me, Serj, you would do well to heed his words."

Argon even let out a humble smile. They broke the meeting and set about making preparations.

# CHAPTER FIFTEEN

## *The Falling Star*

Jacob sent a summons that morning, and Maynard found the fallen angel in a small, dim cabin with a bunk, a wooden table, and two old chairs. It was apparent that Jacob had been thinking on something for days, and on the seldom occasion that Maynard passed by him, he often spoke with little awareness of his present situation. Yet, Jacob possessed deliberateness. He did not seem the type to take any action without first considering the matter from all aspects.

"I've been thinking," began Jacob, motioning Maynard to sit across from him. "As I've said, you're one of us, or at least partly so. I want to do an experiment. I want to teach you what you would call magic. If you are willing."

It surprised Maynard but he was curious, "Magic?"

"Well, that's what you would call it. Do not assume that because the natural is so apparent and tangible that the supernatural does not exist. The term 'supernatural' doesn't quite capture it, and it is not magic by *our* standards. 'Extranatural' is perhaps a better term, as what we do is more an extension of the natural rather than the breaking of it. It is actually just the manipulation of our current reality. You perceive this world by seeing, feeling, by sensing. Running parallel to your perceived reality is another dimension, or aspect, of it. You can't use your senses to detect or understand it. It is like arithmetic. There are formulas and complexities to learn, but even a child understands it at its most basic.

"Everyone's gifts are different. You have innate abilities that you will have to discover for yourself. I can help you hone them, teach you the formulas, so to speak. Cain has unnatural strength, Amelia can summon creatures of the underworld, and who knows what you might be able to do."

"What can you do?" Maynard asked.

"Move boats," Jacob said. "Now, close your eyes and clear your mind."

Maynard obeyed, trying to push away the collage of thoughts as Jacob put a hand on his shoulder. The smell and sounds of the cabin faded. Maynard felt the world shifting, as if he were going somewhere he sensed all along, but never knew how to find.

"Now, open your eyes and turn around" Jacob said.

It was black in every direction, a hollow abyss, a void. Upon turning again he found a clear pane of glass, glossy and still. Somehow an unseen light reflected on the surface, fading into the dark behind it as if it possessed a subtle, tranquil fluidity. Jacob's voice spoke in his mind. "Your body is here, but your mind is now in the Darkworld, the other dimension I spoke of. How does it feel?"

"Like nothing," replied Maynard.

"Interesting. It is unlikely you will find yourself here often. Mortals and fallen see it this way because it's another kind of existence beyond our own. Before I fell I saw it differently, but I can't explain it. Touch the surface."

Maynard tapped the glass. It turned out to be placid water, and concentric wrinkles rippled out from his finger.

"Magic is extranatural. It bends the rules of the natural. Whenever you do magic, think of yourself as tapping into this world. Meditate in this place and soon you will unlock its secrets. You will—"

Jacob's voice fell short. The Darkworld faded. Maynard was falling. High above the earth he fell. Upon its atmosphere he burned. Fire and flames licked at him in unbearable heat as he plummeted into the clouds. The burning faded into tenacious cold. It was no mere descent, it was a soulful downfall. But he would not scream. He would defy his punisher. This was not pity, it was pain and he would have vengeance. With his growing velocity, his anguish and maleficence also burgeoned to a degree previously known only by the Morning Star. Beyond the fiery clouds the world once again came into view, a scape of water and green lands. He loathed all he beheld.

He met the surface with violent force, chaffed by dirt and stone. The hole grew deeper under his impact, a crater of his ruination. At last he lay there, a vanquished celestial being, and a vengeful dead star.

The cabin came into view as Maynard regained consciousness.

"How did you do that?" Jacob gasped.

"I thought you did it," replied Maynard.

"It was not my doing, but it was my pain. You saw it didn't you?"

"Yes," said Maynard, fearing he had upset Jacob.

"You are starting to understand," Jacob said. "Perhaps that is enough for the day. You know the way now. If you practice, you can meditate on it and find it on your own."

Maynard departed, his thoughts dwelling on the vision. The ship and world around him now seemed surreal compared to the burning, cold pain, the remaining tremors of Jacob's dark thoughts overcoming his own. The sunlight and the deck of the ship welcomed him but the smell of burning permeated his nostrils. This was Jacob's world. The promise of more wonders as a harbinger of death. Maynard did not desire the showmanship, but only the honest battle of steel on steel, and sweat and blood.

The call came early the next morning, alerting the crew to the upcoming town. All aboard the ship came to see the small wooden and clay structures emerging on the horizon. The settlement appeared small but they could buy and trade there. Maynard was curious regarding the people of this strange new land. Jacob emerged before the crew and called their attention.

"All the riches of this town are yours," he said. "It is there for the taking so long as you keep the bodies."

The men cheered but Maynard's stomach unsettled. As Jacob left the men to celebrate, Maynard caught him by the arm.

"You cannot possibly mean to kill a whole town," Maynard said to him. "There are men there that would gladly fight for good coin."

"Since when did that matter to you?" asked Jacob pulling away from Maynard.

"If you want me to kill a man in battle, I'd happily do so. But women and children?"

"Come, Maynard. This is a chance to prove that you care about the greater good. And if not for the sake of the greater good, then just remember that if you follow me, you'll be able take care of yourself in the future. You'll take orders from no one and be beyond wealth. And if that does not tempt you, then at least you will appreciate the kind of security that money can buy for a family that might not otherwise survive in these harsh times.

"I know you better than you think. You never took a wife because the idea of her being raped and killed before your eyes horrified you. It is true. It likely would have been her end. But now you're old and you've done things and you don't like it. This is war and this is our conquest. Do your part. Do what it takes to survive, and when all is said and done, none of this will be of your concern." Maynard weighed his words. Jacob, as always, had a point and Maynard made ready for the reaving.

Though the crew of *The Northern Lady* had grown bored of the wonder, the people of the town started to gather at the border to see the ship sailing through the sands. The spectacle was not the only reason. When they got closer it became apparent that it was a collection mostly of men who had various weapons at the ready. Pitchforks, clubs, and the occasional sword awaited them at the town.

"Looks like they're going to put up a fight," Cain said. It was the first time Maynard had seen him since he had taken the captain, and his eyes gazed at the townsfolk with a particular soullessness.

"Why would they fight?" Maynard asked. "How do they know we mean them harm?"

"If I had to guess, a magical ship carrying a stack of dead bodies isn't exactly seen as friendly."

This particular town had nothing more than shacks, yet their population was surprising. They lined the outskirts of the town, weapons in hand. *The Northern Lady's* crewmen secured ropes along the bulwark, shimmying down them from the deck and onto the desert sands. The crew ran at the townsmen as soon as they landed. Maynard took a rope and worked his way down, following the men. He drew his sword. The town was prepared, probably having drilled often in case of bandits.

There was a war cry from both sides as the crew met the townsmen. They locked in battle. Maynard made quick work of all who assailed him. His sword hacked and hewed. The familiar feeling of battle crept in, but for the first time Maynard knew of its source in the Darkworld. The energy to wield such a heavy sword with such speed, the intuitive motion, and the endurance. Men cried and fell. Among their dying agony, the weeping of women and children echoed in the wastelands.

He locked swords with a bearded man about Cain's size. Maynard was tall, but this man towered above him, with more bulk and muscle. They clashed in battle, the bearded man anticipating Maynard's swiftness. Their swords rang and exchanged swift blows, blocking each strike, matching every move. Teeth gritted and muscles tensed. The opponent's strike reverberated through Maynard's blade, quavering in his tense arms but Maynard yielded not. He dodged and blocked, maneuvered and attacked. They relented for a moment and he could see that his opponent tired.

"Yield," said Maynard. "Come with us!"

"So I can go make another town of widows? I think not."

The man came at him with renewed furor, but his blind anger was his undoing. Maynard rolled and slashed at the man's legs, cutting clean through his shins. As the man fell with a cry of pain, Maynard brought his blade down. Blood spewed into the air, flecking Maynard's boiled leather shirt. Turning from his lifeless opponent, Maynard took on four other men. Usually in battle, Maynard was lost in himself, but the large man had been his only formidable opponent, and he fought the rest of the battle with ease. He took the opportunity to study Cain and Amelia. Cain maneuvered and ducked every blow, using his bare hands to smite his opponents. One unfortunate man assaulted Cain who easily stepped from the dash and with a bare fist knocked the man's brains from his skull. Maynard was so shocked he almost failed to block a hit from a determined young attacker. He dealt with the young man quickly and then looked for Amelia.

She stood back in a trance-like state. From the ground had emerged a strange creature. It was almost a wolf, but the skin was a tense and twisted black that glinted red in the sunlight. The oxblood color was unsettling but not so much as the way the creature reduced its victims to a gory heap within seconds. The hellhound's dexterity with its claws and jagged teeth brought each unfortunate soul to an agonizing death.

Within minutes no one opposed them and Cain led the crew into the town to raid and pillage further. Soon the rooftops were aflame. Women's cries of sorrow turned to bellows of pain. Maynard walked among the burning village with a cold surveying eye. In the square a single building stood, yet to be touched by the flame. The group of men forced the remaining townspeople into the wooden town hall. He joined Jacob and Cain who stood to the side.

"Who will put them to the torch?" asked Jacob, displaying his customary grin.

The men, who had just bolted the door, did not waver. They knew what came next. They knew damned well the fate of those they had locked within. So long as they did not strike the match, they harbored no guilt. A weakness or strength?

Jacob came to Maynard, speaking softly. "I know this is just the beginning, but we're at war. We need the bodies." Maynard stared at him, and Jacob turned back to the gathered crew. "So, I ask again, who will do what is required?" Jacob walked to the nearby fire and picked up a torch. He held it out to Maynard, meeting his eyes. He considered taking the torch, but in his moment of reluctance Cain stepped in and took it, walking to the chapel with an amused expression. "Listen to me," Jacob said, again quiet so only Maynard could hear, "I mean to take this world from God and give it to the people it rightfully belongs to. This is necessary."

When the screams and smell of burning flesh arose, Maynard did not waver, but only stood with a hardened look. Yet, he questioned everything.

He did not return to the ship where the stench of the dead would soon reek even more. Rather, he found a well just outside of the town and sat there with his back against the short stone wall that encircled the deep hole. As the sun's glow faded, the illumination of the fires lit the night, the smoke filling Maynard's senses, burning orange fires casting stark and flickering shadows. The cries and screams were more ragged now and he longed for it to be over. He shut his eyes and tried to meditate. His mind followed the path and took him into that place.

In the Darkworld the screams faded away and he sat before the serene wall of water. It was fluid, yet stagnant, and silent. Jacob had been so vague about this place. Would he be taught more? Before he could contemplate it he fell from the darkness. Once again he found himself in smoke and flame but this was in an old wooden room, glowing in Jacob's fire. He did not know how, but he was aware that it was one of the shacks in the town. The heat and smoke stifled him. There among the flames stood the woman, naked, with blood running down her legs. He did not know her, but she knew him.

"Maynard!" she cried in profound anger, "I name thee the bane of wives and the maker of widows. May severe vengeance fall upon you."

Maynard tried to reply but the smoke was too great. "It was Jacob." He coughed. "It was Cain—" but she only burned and screamed.

"Wake up," a voice said.

It was daylight and Cain stood over him, covered in dirt and blood. Not his own blood. "Having a bad dream?" Cain asked. The chill of the morning lingered and Maynard welcomed it after the vision. The bodies, many charred, were gathered and stacked at the rear of the ship among the others. The thought of helping collect the corpses sickened him. Cain left him, and later in the afternoon, Jacob found him still sitting at the well. "We'll be leaving soon. Did you have fun?" Ignoring Jacob's sarcastic tone,

Maynard got up from the well's stone wall and stretched his legs. He dusted off his pants and looked up. Jacob had gone.

Maynard enjoyed battle, but the spoils were a mere byproduct. He spent the day surveying the wreckage. Most of the buildings had been leveled by the burning and he could see the massacre beyond the smoldering ruins. The sand around the town was black and red.

"How did it come to this?" Maynard asked when he found Cain.

"What?" asked Cain. "You mean people willing to slaughter and burn man, woman, and child? Feeling guilty?"

"You mock me," said Maynard.

"No more than you do yourself," responded Cain. "You follow orders, which is the excuse you use to absolve any guilt you might feel. It doesn't just cleanse your conscience. You take pride in following the orders, in not looking weak. You tell yourself that it's for the greater good."

"I thought it was," said Maynard.

"And who is to say that it isn't? Or that there's anything wrong with pride? Don't do the right thing. Do the best thing."

Back on the ship Maynard found a bottle of rum and a place to drink alone. He had spent his life killing but not in cold blood. Taking this town hadn't felt right from the start. It was one more step to money and comfort. Could he even take a wife now? If he was honest, he could love no one, much less anyone love him. He blamed Jacob. He blamed himself.

Maynard feared that meditating again might bring another vision but he tried it anyway. There was something peaceful about the Darkworld and his soul felt calm there. It was as if he could take a break from life and truly experience nothing for moments at a time. At first he could only do it for a few seconds but eventually seconds became minutes and then he could spend an entire hour in the void. Jacob found him there, appearing out of the darkness, walking on nothing. The air grew cold and Maynard's breath puffed in a gray cloud before him. With Jacob's presence, the water-wall started to freeze and solidified into a smoky sheet of ice.

"You've gotten good at this," said Jacob.

"I like it here," replied Maynard.

"The raid on the town probably seemed a bit much and for that I'm sorry," said Jacob. "You are starting to understand."

"It's getting cold," said Maynard.

"Yes, it is. This is how we see it." Jacob gestured at the icy wall. "This is the bridge through which all things pass. Others are gifted in using this to send messages over long distances, such as Amelia when she visited Raven in a dream. Yet, it's still a fickle thing. For most of what I do, I simply need this realm to manipulate reality. Before the fall Amelia could summon such mighty heavenly creatures, but her bridge to that has been cut. And when she summons them from hell it is here that they pass. She is proud of her power, but it destroys her."

"Her pride or her power?"

"Isn't it always both?" replied Jacob, "But I'm not here for these musings. I want you to see something." Jacob put his hand to the wall of ice and it seemed as if the opaque fog gave way to a clear frozen portion. "One can't just summon creatures from anywhere one likes. We obtained permission. We made a deal."

There in the ice stood a most unsettling figure. It was tall and hooded with a ragged black cloak. Maynard felt as if he could see into the being's soul, deep down into the cold and black hole of its hood. Anger festered within, ageless beyond the eons, a place of deep pride and loathing. It desired to inflict suffering. Its snare was carnal passion, and with that temptation, it would swallow the world piece by piece. Its depths were like that of the ocean, a darkness able to crush the souls of men with effortless malice.

There resided a complex knowing, a consciousness of the ways of manipulation and the intricacies of darkness. The surface of the knowing was like that of a sadistic child, ready at any time to degrade and humiliate. It was eager to tempt and then mock the very sin it had tempted one to do.

Maynard felt despair and darkness, as if it searched his soul as well. It found his pride and guilt and bloodlust, and whispered into his very heart on these things. He was nothing and to be something he must have power. He must oppress the world to truly know his own worthiness. *Lament not the name widow-maker. Rue your weakness. Overcome it by taking your place above the games of mortals.* Maynard heard the susurration and longed for these things before the ice became a gray shadow again and it was gone.

"The Morning Star," Jacob named it. "We see it through a glass darkly but this is the way we win. We don't just win the City, we win life and death."

"He has a way into the City?" Maynard asked.

"Dorian's magic is deep but there is deeper still. The Morning Star is not bound by such nonsense. He is already there in the City whispering into the weak hearts of men, ensuring our victory.

"Continue your meditations but do not dwell here long. Soon enough it will show you your power and then you need only tap into it to use it. You are strong and swift of sword. You have visions. These things may or may not be significant. Learn to call upon, resist, and control them. Then you practice them in the real world and try and find that place between. You want to brush with this dimension, not enter it."

With that Jacob faded into the darkness.

# CHAPTER SIXTEEN

## *The Shapeshifter*

Liam reserved most of his questions, not wanting to pester Dorian. Their journey consisted of riding by day and sleeping in the desert at night. Dorian seemed to relish the straightforward approach. He wore his coat that both protected him from the sun and served as a pillow. The stitched patchwork of his well-worn boots was likely Dorian's own doing, furthering the impression that he was reluctant to change. They seldom stopped in a town, mostly to restock on food and water. After three towns, they found a shop where they could trade for ACP ammunition to suit Liam's gun.

Once back on their way, Dorian seemed to be in one of his talkative moods. He could be as solemn as he could be cheery. They spent the afternoon in their saddles and Dorian spoke lightheartedly of his time in the desert. "After the war there was little left to do. Many had lived on this island prior to the building of Novum, and few had entered the City. This was home and always would be. There were the transplants. Some were decedents of colonists. Others moved later. There are inhabitants at the Eastern Pan and another oasis just west of that, exiles from the City."

"I thought no one had left the City since it closed its doors," Liam said.

"Is that what they tell you?" Dorian asked. "Once it was obvious that it was no mere resort, but rather a religious harbor, they started kicking people out. The laws between religion and corporation blurred, each using the other for its agenda."

"How could they tell what religion a person was?"

"I wasn't there, but there will always be those ardent to their faith, relishing martyrdom. I also suspect that much of it had to do with where a person was from or the color of their skin. Xenophobia perseveres. Ironically, upon exile, they formed a tribal band and adopted a religion all their own. I know later, after the war, Nathan went missing, but I suspect he had something to do with their formation. I'll have to ask him when we see him."

"And what about you?" Liam asked. "After the war, I mean."

"I was spent, ready to give up." Liam knew that guilt still haunted the fallen angel, but he didn't mention it. "Oliver suggested that I put my resources toward reconstruction and order," Dorian continued, "and so I did. We dispersed after that. Since he was not a fallen, it makes sense that Oliver went to the Pass, should something happen there. I suppose Charis found her little city in the east and it wasn't long before Nathan disappeared. Some of us seem to have done well for ourselves."

"So, you went south?" Liam asked.

"For a few years I waited in anticipation of Jacob's next move, but to be honest, by the time you showed up I had rather dismissed the threat. Life as a hermit was simple and I have grown accustomed to it."

"I suppose that will take some readjustment," said Liam.

"Perhaps, but I've been around a long time. Tens of thousands of years, maybe more. I'm used to a little change after a couple of centuries."

They stopped for a break. Liam's soreness was wearing off, making the long hours of riding a little more bearable. Once dismounted, Liam took a swallow from his canteen. Dorian retrieved something from one of the packs and walked over with Liam's gun.

"Let's see how you shoot," Dorian said, holding the grip of the firearm towards Liam.

"We can't waste the bullets," replied Liam.

"It's not a waste," said Dorian, "Give it a try."

"All right," Liam agreed, taking the pistol. "What should we shoot?"

"You should shoot this," said Dorian, walking a few yards away, and setting an empty can on the ground. It was small and distant.

"I can't hit that," Liam said.

"Probably not," replied Dorian. "Try anyway."

Liam gripped the gun. It felt right, just like the time he shot Raven. Liam had chambered a bullet and then filled the clip giving him eight rounds total. It was a trick Oliver had shown him on top of keeping the firearm "cocked and locked" as he called it. Dorian stood back, well away from the can as Liam took aim, thumb disengaging the safety. He squeezed the trigger and the gun erupted with a kick. The bullet thundered into the air. Miss. A cloud of dirt puffed where the bullet had landed.

"Try again," Dorian said.

Again Liam pulled the trigger. He could smell the gun powder and the sound reverberated in the open desert. The can bounced back in a flurry of sand as the bullet met it.

"Impressive," Dorian said. "That's enough for now."

Liam wanted to fire more, to keep pulling the trigger, and feel the kick and hear the crack in rapid succession. He wanted to watch each bullet hit its target with the same precision. He put it away.

"You have a talent," Dorian said. They rode again, camels keeping a smooth, but steady pace. "It's times like these," he continued, "that the earth seems to reawaken."

"What do you mean?" asked Liam.

"You would call it magic," Dorian said, "but it's the simple fact that there are other forces at work than what we can see and touch. Some people have a better sense of those things than others. I daresay you have a gift. Don't take it for granted."

Liam nodded thoughtfully.

"Really," said Dorian. "You are the son of the prophet and that's something. His gift is no coincidence. This is not the first time the Eternal One has cast beings from his realm."

"It's not?"

"Well, consider the Morning Star, for instance."

"Was that the first fall?"

"On Earth, yes. Most of the cosmos was created by the Eternal One, though some planets and much of their contents have been created by some of the ancient and powerful created beings. The point is, Earth isn't the only option. It is, however, a rather special planet. Some beings that displease the Eternal One are sentenced to non-existence. Some are cast into places of suffering, others marooned on empty planets. Some have actually come out very successful as a result. Others wallowed in the barren wastes. But a select few have been cast down to Earth.

"The Morning Star was the first. They were close once, the Eternal One and the Morning Star. I think the Eternal One really had hope of redemption. You see, when I say that Earth is special, I mean that it's not only the Eternal One's prime creation, his favorite, but also that this is known as the place of second chances among the celestial beings. The Eternal One really does love this place. After the Morning Star did his damage, the Eternal One considered never casting a fallen spirit here again.

"Why he gave it another shot, I'll probably never know, but he did. Tens of thousands of years ago. Here's where it gets interesting. Those fallen didn't cause any trouble. They married normal humans and had their children. Their progeny grew up to be some of the most powerful people in early civilization. Their talents passed, only slightly fading between generations. There were descendants. Most didn't know their power, others had little sense of what to do with it, and almost all of them kept it a secret. Though their powers were weak compared to their ancestors, there were those who could slightly manipulate the world around them or see elements no one else could. It might be as simple as high intelligence or persuasiveness, but it could be a person with a gift for prophecy or extrasensory perception.

"The fallen have many of these gifts in abundance, but the descendants of the second fall are so far removed that their power has waned. Yet, sometimes the resonance of the past magics come through in odd ways. Hence the prophet."

"Are you saying I have some sort of power?" Liam asked.

"It's difficult to predict how it passes. The genetics are complicated. The gift isn't always the same either. But it's likely you have something, whether it's resilience, which magic or not, you certainly have—or having keen aim, or something undiscovered. Much of it is innate but if you discover what it is, I can teach you how to control and amplify it."

Liam wondered at that. He expected to feel the power, but experienced nothing. When he recalled the day he was marked by fire, he had felt a small kindling in his chest, but he suspected that was something wholly different.

"Let me ask you," Dorian said, "What did you expect?"

"Of what?"

"You said that none of us were what you expected. What did you have in mind?"

"I don't know. You just seem so very human and so very different at the same time."

"Should I have had wings? Would you like me better if I was a chubby baby like in the paintings?"

"That's not what I mean."

"I know," replied Dorian with a laugh. "I shouldn't give you such a hard time. You'd never guess how many people say they thought I'd be a white guy."

At that Liam laughed. On one hand, he thought about the color of his skin all of the time. He always had to second guess his actions, how they would be perceived, and the motives behind the actions of others towards him. On the other hand, it could drive a man mad to try and figure it all out, and so he tried not to think about it. "When it comes to that," he said, "I try not to make assumptions. I guess I make other assumptions. I just always thought of angels as sort of royal and perfect. I'm not making any sense, I know."

"You are," said Dorian. "Some angels are proud beings who take themselves too seriously. They can be too solemn, too canny. However, *we* are the fallen."

"But you are powerful."

"None of us are as powerful as we were. We are beings who have witnessed greatness. We have seen great mirth, great tragedy, great love, and great hate. I have feasted with the Eternal One himself and marched on the gates of Hell. But our fall was deserved. We fell far and hard. I have no delusions."

"What do you think will happen when this is all over?"

"If we win? We will rebuild. The secrets of the past have been preserved."

"And you?"

"I'll die. Someday. I don't know what happens after that. This is the place of second chances." The conversation stilled and Dorian looked to the horizon. "It's going to rain."

Liam looked to the cloudless sky and then to Dorian in confusion. Even if Dorian could predict the weather, this was odd.

"It hardly ever rains around the City. Does it rain more here?" asked Liam.

"Believe it or not, more often than you would think. Thanks to the terraforming the surface of this place is as good as cursed. It rains but nothing grows. Farmers have a tough time of it, though I did my best to renew the soil around the towns that I founded. We should be grateful for anything at all."

Dorian paused looking in the distance. "That town should be Timberton. I have business there."

Liam could not guess what business Dorian might have in a town he obviously had not been to in quite some time, but they rode toward it, plodding through the barren wasteland. Liam had bypassed the town on his way south. He recognized the wooden spikes jutting out from around the settlement, red banners towering above the circling defense.

"I didn't name the place," said Dorian, resuming the conversation. "But suffice to say, it used to have quite a bit of wood at its disposal. It was one of the larger towns and had a substantial store of dried lumber. I think it was imported during the war by someone with a very bright idea on how to get rich in a post-apocalyptic desert."

"Do you really think it was?" asked Liam.

"What? A bright idea?"

"No." Liam shook his head, "I mean the apocalypse."

Dorian laughed, "I can tell you with certainty that it is not the end of the world. That, I imagine, will be a whole other ordeal. I mean 'apocalypse' in the loose sense of the term. Everyone thought it was the end of the world, and I wouldn't be surprised if some people get to thinking that again when things here start to gain momentum. But, no. It is not the literal apocalypse. You wouldn't have to ask if it was."

Dorian's description of Timberton was accurate. Though most towns used little lumber, opting for brick and clay structures, wood composed most of this town. There were fewer camels and more horses, several general stores, brothels, shops, and taverns.

It was also big enough that it had a rich side and a poor side. Dorian took them to the poor side, an area more dilapidated than anything Liam had seen in the Outland. Huts consisted of old signs and tarps. Almost everyone begged or sold some useless trade. A boy solicited Liam to buy a bracelet that was no more than a knotted leather strap. The desperation and the audacity took Liam off guard. He barely uttered a kind refusal before moving on, trying to keep up with Dorian.

Dorian pretended to ignore the touts, but Liam glimpsed compassion in his expression. Dorian's eyes paused as they glanced at the huts and small buildings lining the dirt road, most with no windows or doors, covered with old tattered curtains or nothing at all. Liam did buy a box of matches, although he now knew how to make a fire with flint, but the little girl who sold them, glassy-eyed and silent, looked to be starving.

"Don't buy from children or those with apparent disabilities," Dorian said.

"What do you mean?" Liam asked.

Dorian stopped and turned, his broad figure blocking out the sunlight. "Kids and those with disabilities are as good as slaves," he said, lamentation in his voice. "Their owners send them out to beg and then collect at the end of the day. The beggars are given nothing in return save for their own lives. If they run or attempt to keep anything for themselves, they are most often found and maimed. Then they are sent back to begging, their newfound malady a welcome point of compassion for would-be donors. They most often refuse food, finding scraps where they can at the end of the day. They have no home. They have nowhere to run, and if they did, they'd starve before they got a day's walk into the desert."

"Why doesn't someone stop them?" asked Liam.

"The pimps, you mean?" asked Dorian. "You have to find them first and then you have to take the law into your own hands. For most, it's too big of a task with too high of a risk. For some, they don't feel it's their place."

"Is there something we can do about it?" asked Liam.

"Not today," replied Dorian, "but if we manage to stop Jacob, we might rebuild for these people."

They continued along the narrow road between the beggars and poor merchants. Dorian stopped, crouching to talk to a woman, her face aged and wrinkled by the sun. Through a toothless smile she spoke to Dorian in whispers. Occasionally, he nodded and whispered back. He thanked her and stood.

"I have something I need to do," he said gesturing at a large hole a short distance away. "Take the camels into town. Just follow this path toward the clock-tower. Meet me at The Bricks, or at least that's what it was called a long time ago. The locals will know it either way. Wait for me there."

Dorian took a rope from a nearby pile and walked toward the hole, lacking explanation. With little choice, Liam did as instructed and made for The Bricks, if he could even find it.

In spite of Dorian's directions, it took some asking before Liam found the inn. He arrived, somewhat chagrined at his difficulty locating the only brick structure in town. First he stabled the camels, making arrangements to exchange Lucy's milk for a discounted rate. He entered the drab, two story building, finding the inside just as unembellished. Tobacco smoke filled the tavern and the wooden floorboards creaked as he walked. His own pack hung off his shoulder and Liam carried Dorian's in-hand. He acquired a room, relieved to secure the weighty packs before returning to the main tavern and sitting at the bar for a drink.

The barmaid was the most attractive girl he had seen in Outland. Unlike the petite, polished girls of Novum, the barmaid's subdued, almost organic look captivated him. She could have rolled out of bed, thrown on a dress, come to work, and been prettier for it. Yet, she took care of herself, not the malnourished or emaciated contrast that Liam had seen in the towns. Nor was her hair the usual mess.

"Boy, do you want a drink or not?" she asked. He had not realized she had been talking to him. His eyes shot down to the counter, a bit embarrassed.

"Ale," he stammered out.

"What kind? We have three. Brown, pale, and something else. All I know, it's sour."

He felt stupid for a moment, unable to decide, blurting, "Your pick," before quickly adding, "Not the sour."

"Pale, it is," she said pouring the libation and setting it down. "Name's Trish."

She went about serving the other patrons and Liam sipped from the foamy ale while eying her. She was graceful and her voice pleasant. When she came back to his side of the bar, he resolved to order food without looking like such a fool.

"Hungry?" she asked.

"What do you have?" he asked.

"Lots of things," Trish said. "Depends on what you're in the mood for. There's mutton, chicken, potatoes. Hell, just look at a menu." She slapped a piece of paper down in front him and went back about her business. Most places boasted so few choices that they lacked a menu all together, making this selection relatively distinguished with its list of handwritten items accompanied by prices in three different currencies.

"So, what's it going to be?"

He looked up from his menu to her leaning over the bar, smirk aimed at him, exposing her cleavage a little more.

"Your pick," he said. *Stupid.*

"A guy who appreciates adventure. I like that," she said before running to the back.

Dorian had not returned when Liam had finished his meal and ale. He wanted to stay at the bar, to watch her, but he did not want to drink more, and had no excuse to stay. Having paid, he reluctantly went upstairs to the room, sitting on the bedside closest to the window. There was still plenty of daylight left, and down in the dusty street, carts, horses, and people came and went, but he thought of *her*. He had been attracted to girls before, being a teenage boy after all, but for some reason he took an immediate liking to Trish. He imagined that he could stay in this town, eating and drinking at the tavern for every meal, getting to know her. She seemed graceful and fun. Having found Dorian, his part was finished.

Of course, that was not all that was expected of him. Dorian, at least, assumed Liam would join them in Mere. Had Charis not said the same to Barker the priest? When all of this was finished, perhaps he would come back. One day. Not for Trish, who would surely be married or gone by then. But the Outlands offered him something true, something that drew him.

A woman walked the street, turning into an alley. For a brief moment he couldn't place her, but then realized it was Charis. It might have been the ale, but her elegant walk, dark hair, and smooth features were unmistakable. He pulled on his belt, buckling the sword to his waist, as he left the room. Down the stairs and through the tavern, stopping to glance at the barmaid, he left the inn.

From the window, he had watched the woman pace down an eastern alley toward the more destitute side of town and he followed her path. Dorian had told him to stay at the inn, but if it was Charis it couldn't be ignored. Surely it was her. Worried of losing Charis, Liam worked his way through the press of people. The figure ducked into a small, unmarked structure. He approached and pressed close to the building, hiding from any view within. The structure lacked a solid door, a tattered curtain hanging in its place. He drew close to the opening and ventured a peek between the curtain and the door frame.

There sat a tiger, stunning as it was terrifying. The vivid orange coat rippled with jet black stripes fading into a clean, velvety white underbelly. It was wild and awful at the same time. It saw Liam. Panicking, Liam drew his sword, stepping back from the door. Then he heard a peculiar thing: a laugh.

Liam remained wary, standing slightly to the side of the doorway, ready to strike.

"Come now," a manly voice said from inside. "Nothing to be afraid of."

"A tiger?" Liam asked aloud, forcing sarcasm through the fear.

"Don't be silly," the voice replied. "Come in, come in."

Liam was not going to enter but a hand reached out of the doorway and drew back the ratty sheet that covered it. It was not a tiger but a jolly faced man with a red, shaggy beard and savage hair. He looked just as wild as the tiger, but with a strange mirth. "Come on," the man said. "In with you. You're safe."

Liam reluctantly entered, ready at any moment to unholster his pistol. He had expected to find the tiger, but it was nowhere in sight. Liam gaped.

"You won't find your tiger here, but you should tell me why a young man such as yourself, though keen-eyed no doubt, feels the need to go chasing ladies in the alleys instead of minding his own business."

"I thought I saw someone I knew," replied Liam.

"Curiosity will get you killed," the man said with a smile. "And who might you be?"

"Well," started Liam, but he was interrupted by a voice from behind.

"It's him!" It was a female voice. "That's Liam."

The man looked up and a woman entered. Two pretty women in one day. Liam was feeling a bit overwhelmed, but he recognized her.

"So, this is the boy then?" the man asked. "Where's Dorian?"

"You're Charis," Liam said.

She smiled at him. Her eyes were like the others, but deeper set, curving upwards in a slim teardrop shape. "Yes, I am. I'm glad to see you well. I'm sorry for the scare. I knew I was being tailed, but I didn't realize it was you so I told Nathan to stand guard."

He could see now in Nathan what he had seen in the others. "You can shape-shift," Liam said.

"You didn't tell me he was smart," Nathan said to Charis. His lip twitched, a brief half-smile showing his sarcasm.

Charis ignored the joke, looking to Liam, "Where is Dorian? Did you find him?"

"I did. He was with me, but went to what looked like a well and sent me to The Bricks."

"Mighty good ale at that place," Nathan said. "Cute barmaid, I daresay." He gave Liam a wink.

"He's gone to the mall," Charis said. Liam was confused. In the City, the mall was a giant shopping center. What was a mall in a place like this?

Nathan gave her a raised eyebrow. "What business does he have there?"

"You know him," she said. "He has to know these things for himself."

"All right then," Nathan replied. "I say we wait for him and travel together. It will be safer."

"That would be best," Charis said. "What should we do while we wait?"

"Well, times like these are always good for a pint," said Nathan. Charis rolled her eyes.

"He has a point," said Liam, "The Bricks?"

Trish was not their waiter this time. It was a young gentleman who was nice, but of course, not as pleasant to look at as the barmaid.

"I daresay, this is a mighty good pint," Nathan said as they settled into a booth.

Now that they were comfortable, Liam was able to take it all in. Nathan was a red-haired burly man with a wry sense of humor. Charis was not without levity. In fact, her smile was infectious. Her mere presence put Liam at ease. They sat in the curved booth, the bench arching around the table, with Liam on one side, Charis on the other, and Nathan in between.

"So, what brought you here?" asked Liam.

"It's quite simple," said Nathan. "Charis went around asking for the merriest, drunkest ginger on the west side and found me. I've been all about this damned island, so it's a good thing she found me. This was but a stop on our way back to Mere."

"It's not a total coincidence that we're here," said Charis. "This is a special place for Dorian. We decided to stop through and see if there was any word of the two of you. We have been here three days and were nearly ready to give up when you arrived."

"Dorian didn't say where he was going," said Liam. "What's this about a mall?"

"He can be a little mysterious," said Nathan. "The whole island is chambered with caves and reservoirs. We hid some secrets down there, including a large stock of supplies. We call it the mall, because it's where we go shopping."

"It's not just a mall," said Charis, "Dorian's *zero* is probably a quarter of a mile away. I think he's checking to see if it can be used against Jacob. I doubt he'll like the answer."

Nathan must have seen the puzzled look on Liam's face, "I guess most don't know, but we call the places where we fell our 'zero' as in ground zero. Dorian's is here, which we've always found odd. Of all places in the world he happened to fall, on the one large island in the middle of nowhere that just happened to be where the City was built. Of course, he was taken immediately to the mainland. I miss having a pint with that guy."

"I'm sure you'll get your chance," said Charis.

"Where were your zeros?" asked Liam.

"Damn my luck," said Nathan, "the ocean. A cold one."

"The land has shifted since," said Charis, "but I landed in South America."

Trish appeared sometime in their conversation and Liam watched her as he listened to Nathan and Charis. He could find a girl like her and go live in the southern caves, making trips to Dali for supplies as needed. As ridiculous as that was, Liam was becoming increasingly aware that he did not want to go back to the City. But Nathan's next words told him that he might be too idealistic.

"We're in for rain, I fear."

# CHAPTER SEVENTEEN

*Abominations*

Metal clashed on wood and Devan stumbled back. Devan held the only shield Maynard had seen aboard the ship and suspected that Devan had fashioned it himself, using what wood he could find to craft it during the boring periods between towns. Cursing as Maynard deflected yet another strike, Devan stopped to catch his breath.

"You think the enemy will stop while you rest?" Maynard asked.

"You can't say you don't present a unique challenge," Devan said between huffs. "Most men with a sword that big are more cumbersome."

"Some men carry little swords and they don't know how to use them. Others carry big swords with surprising swiftness. Every opponent brings his own unique challenge. You need to worry less about what you see in your opponent and more about your own competence. I watched you use the same maneuver at the last town."

"And it worked," replied Devan. He was seasoned for his age, with hardened muscles and scars to prove it.

"Because you were smarter than your opponent, but it could fail in your next battle, just like it did against me."

"All right," said Devan. "You have a point."

"Maynard let his sword down, giving Devan time to catch his breath. In all fairness, the dark skinned man was more skilled than any opponent Maynard had fought in the last twenty years. Deciding to give Devan a rest, Maynard brought up their journey. "How do you feel about all of this?" He looked over the railing as the ship eased among the golden-brown stretch of desert to the south.

"What?"

"We just head east, go from town to town, and wipe it out. That's all not to mention the unfortunate smell."

"Any man who can take the captain is no laughing matter," replied Devan. "That guy was tough as they come. Then, this Jacob has our boat plowing through the sand smoother than water. Now, that's something. So he asks me to do some killing. I've spent my life on odd jobs, but I'm no stranger to a good fight. So, I do it. Doesn't matter what it's about or whose involved. At the end of the day, I'm richer for it, and that's enough for me. What about you, Maynard?"

"I suppose I share your sentiments."

"Why wouldn't you?" Devan asked. "You're close enough with Jacob. Surely, you reap all the more reward for it."

"Surely," replied Maynard, blocking the image of the slaughtered townspeople from his mind, "I do."

The imposing wall of mountains towered to the port side of *The Northern Lady*, their steep—almost vertical—walls stretching high above. Sometimes Maynard would crane his neck, looking to the sky, and fathom their height. At some times of the day, the shadow would extend hundreds of feet beyond the mountains' roots.

"The Pass!" a crewman yelled. Maynard searched the great stone walls, but saw nothing. Several other crewmen emerged from their stations and Maynard found them looking ahead at the wall. Men pointed and murmured about it, but Maynard still searched the north.

"You can't see it either," a voice said. Amelia joined him at the rail. "We can't," she continued, "just as if we were to try and scale these mountains, we would never find the top, we cannot see this pass. If only we could have found a plane, but then again we would have needed a fleet of them to get an army into the city."

Maynard surveyed the flat desert ground that stretched around them. "Looks like a plain to me."

Amelia let out a small laugh. It was endearing, almost girlish, and for a moment Maynard thought he liked her. Then her smile faded, and though the beauty remained, the darkness returned.

"An airplane," she said. "A craft unlike anything you have seen. Think of it like a boat with wings. Jacob searched high and low for one. All we ever found were scraps. A hull or wing here and there. And who's to say it would have worked? It is good that the men see the Pass, though. We need to know that it really does exist and where it is."

"So, we can't see it but they can?" Maynard asked. "This Dorian really doesn't want you or anyone like you getting in."

"You could say that," she said.

Maynard surveyed the port-side mountains before them, looking for any break in the monotonous wall. "The Darkworld is different for you. I see a wall of water while the fallen see a wall of ice. Yet, we both cannot see the Pass."

"So, Jacob has shown you the Darkworld, and apparently with results? Were you a full angel you would see no wall in the Darkworld. It would look very different altogether. As for the Pass, I imagine that Dorian must have willed that his magic would keep out anyone with enough power from seeing or entering it. The fact alone that you can enter the Darkworld is likely enough to keep you from seeing it."

"Is the plan still to turn south or will this ship magically just wedge us in?" Maynard asked, half expecting it might be the case.

"No," Amelia laughed. "We turn south from here."

"Away from this pass I've heard so much about?"

"Oh, we'll be back," she said. "But first we go to meet Raven."

"You know this?" Maynard asked, but the sailors' enthusiasm had died down and with it, Amelia had quietly left him alone again. The momentarily forgotten smell of rotting, dead flesh came back to him. Some towns were small, some big, but all of them had yielded the bodies, gathered for Raven's plan. In their wake they left destruction. All had been slaughtered, bodies for Jacob's plan. That was the way of the Outland, the way to be on top.

Jacob spoke of Novum as if he had been there, but apparently his information was from before the war. "Air conditioning," he had said. Great machines that allowed one to feel a cool breeze in the desert heat. He made it sound better than that. Jacob seemed to assume that they would win this war and Maynard would come out of it alive. Maynard supposed it likely, and if he did, he would be one of the new leaders. It was not the power that appealed to him so much as what came with it. Too much power and he would still find himself looking over his shoulder. But just a little power meant that people would respect him, and as long as no one knew what it took him to get there, he might just find a woman who would have him. *You will be able to take a wife,* the quiet voice told him. *Take.* He would not have to ask. It rang hollow for just a moment, but then he reminded himself that it was what he really wanted. It was part of the principles by which he had lived his entire life. He could not turn back now, not on himself, not on Jacob.

The ship creaked as it turned to run perpendicular to the mountains, away from the unseen pass. Over the next two days the ship treaded the desert sands, sailing the flatlands, the occasional dunes, and the wastes. It never faltered, but drove on, steady and smooth. The mountains shrunk behind them and the smoldering remains of a town appeared before the ship, reminding Maynard of their prior path of destruction. The bodies aboard the ship stank of rot and smoke. Stacked so high at the ship's rear, Maynard suspected a normal vessel could not have balanced under such a weight.

During the journey, Maynard took to meditating often but found himself in the Darkworld less and less. He now sensed the power without entering it. If he concentrated, he could conjure a faint glow in the palm of his hand. After a time, he managed to manipulate the color. He could produce a warm blue, amber, green, or anything between. He was first cognizant of connection to the Darkworld back at the first town. He could orient his strength in a different way now. It manifested in a single blow, the swiftness of his muscles feeling as if they pulled from that other world. It was more of what he had all along. With that thought he awoke from his trance and went to his cabin where he stored his sword. Once there, he pulled it from under his cot. It felt lighter than before and he pondered it. *"My birthright was this sword"* he had told Jacob the day they met. No, it really wasn't. Was most of his life based on a lie?

A knock roused him from thought and he heard Cain's voice, "We're here."

Maynard strapped the sword to his back and left the cabin in time to follow Cain to the deck. The men acted as if they were readying the ship for harbor, even though there was nowhere to port. Jacob and Amelia met them.

"Maynard," Jacob said. "It's time you meet Raven."

"It is important that you understand something," Jacob said as they walked the desert, leaving the ship behind as it rested in the sands. Amelia and Cain walked with them.

The town had long been sacked before their arrival, but ash still fell about the black frames of burned houses smelling of smoke. They walked among the ruins, and Maynard, glancing back at the ship, noticed that the men were throwing the dead bodies off of the deck and onto the desert ground. He pondered it before turning his attention back to following Jacob and the others.

"You must understand our ways. Dorian's so-called magic is a magic of life. I won't bore you with details, but I assure you his view is delusional. To him, everything is good or bad. Light or dark. Life or death. There's no middle ground. Do you believe in middle ground, Maynard?"

"The way I see it," Maynard replied, "there'd have to be middle ground. We're all trying to get ahead, and sometimes if you want to make progress there will be sacrifices along the way. You can't have it all, so you have to make do with what you have."

"My point exactly," said Jacob. "Dorian's sense of honor will be his downfall. He's under some delusion that his way is somehow noble, but I assure you it's not. I get things done and that's what matters. It is for this reason that his magic is predictable and therefore I can counter it."

Within minutes, they had walked through the town to a small unburned building. It bore scorch marks from the surrounding fires, but the actual structure remained uncompromised by flame. It was little more than a shed. Jacob opened the door, ushering them in. Amelia stepped ahead, walking into the building. As Maynard ducked in behind her, he spotted the metal door in the ground.

"This town was Bronton, and like many towns, they tap into the wealth of caverns and reservoirs below. One such cavern made a perfect base for Raven's operations."

Jacob opened the metal hatch with ease. Stairs descended into the dark corridor, Jacob leading the way. In the pitch dark, even the walls of the downward stairwell could not be seen, much less

Amelia, who was the next person in front of him. He was the last to enter and took his time stepping down the uneven stairs, feeling the cold walls to help navigate. Eventually, a pale blue light outlined the silhouettes of the others. He soon found level ground. The others marched ahead into the room, but he stopped, observing the chamber. Darkness filled the cavern, swallowing the walls and ceiling.

The source of the blue light horrified him. Uniform glass tanks, held by bolted metal frames, sat in rows as far as he could see and in each one a pale naked corpse floated upright, illuminated in the blue glow. Some of the bodies were intact, others grotesquely burned or maimed. Exposed and stitched wounds alike amplified their macabre, contorted appearance. The glowing tanks sprawled in uniform rows throughout the cavern on either side of a single lane down their center where the others walked ahead. Maynard followed briskly, uncomfortable in this strange graveyard. When he dared to glance at the horrors, it felt as if their gaping eyes followed him, their pale black and dilated pupils shifting beneath the sagging eyelids of men, women, and children. At the end, a man lounged upon a chair. It was more like a jagged throne, illuminated with blue glowing runes. The lounging man, who Maynard assumed to be Raven, was accompanied alongside his throne by two ghostly pale women in once-white, tattered and stained dresses. The women appeared dead, but they stood nonetheless, casting morbid smiles at Jacob and his company.

Though the throne's frame dwarfed the fallen angel reclining within, he demonstrated his confidence with a morose smile. "Jacob," he greeted in a strange accent. "Amelia, Cain." Without getting up he gave each a short nod as if to bow.

"Raven," said Jacob looking him up and down. "You're still dressed so seventeenth century. Always a bit theatrical."

"Late nineteenth, my friend. British as my accent. Do you know how hard this was to come by?" He gestured at his outfit, perhaps as sincere as he was sarcastic.

"Spare me," said Jacob, looking around at the sprawl of glowing tanks. "This place is quite the operation."

"Yes," said Raven. "I am quite proud of it. This batch should be ready shortly, then we can put those bodies of yours to use."

"So you know about my present?" asked Jacob.

"Of course," said Raven, "but who is this you have brought with you?" Raven eyed Maynard.

"One of our own," said Jacob, "Likely a bastard descendant of one of us, and he shows prowess with a sword and our art."

"Not one of my bastards, I wouldn't think," said Raven, giving Maynard a knowing look. "Too tall."

"Never mind that," said Jacob. "What news?"

Raven gave Jacob a grave look and held up his hand, pulling back the sleeve to expose his wrist. Marring his pale arm, black veins spidered from a central black wound, webbing out around his forearm. "A boy," Raven said, "shot me."

Jacob cocked a cynical eyebrow.

"A boy from the City," Raven continued. "Discovered by Oliver and sent south to find Dorian. They happened to be staying here when we took the town."

Jacob cursed. "So, Oliver is still alive after all this time? And Dorian knows?"

"Come now, Jacob. I'm better than that. The boy gave me my fair share of trouble, but my men found him and dealt with the situation. I would have done it myself, but I needed to return here."

"Good," said Jacob. "Dorian will figure this out soon enough, but we need more time. What of Oliver?"

"Don't know, but he wasn't with the boy," said Raven. "And my arm's just fine thank you. Took a page out of my own book."

Raven flexed his fingers in and out of a fist before pulling his sleeve back down, covering the unsightly wound. His skin was already fair, but his hand was as pale and blue as that of his accompanying women. They stood still in their haunting white dresses, eyes trapped in the thousand-yard stare.

Ignoring Raven, Jacob looked to Maynard. He gestured at the rows of tanks, "Impressive, isn't it?"

Maynard felt the whole thing was a bit saturnine, but he had guessed the plan. "This is your army."

"Yes," Jacob replied. "They do not eat, drink, sleep, tire, or complain. They are also rather difficult to kill. They will do well for my *path*. The Morning Star has provided for us well."

"How many?" asked Amelia.

"I can produce about twenty-five hundred at a time," said Raven, "I had the Infinite Bullets—don't let the name fool you, their ammunition is rather limited—raid most of the surrounding towns and this is batch number two. How many did you bring, Jacob?"

"At least enough for a half-batch," he replied. "Once we take the Pass, assuming our own losses are minimal, I wouldn't be surprised if we were able to get our number over eight thousand. Now, I believe we have a subject of rather special interest. Cain, would you care to talk to Raven about the fate of our captain?"

Cain nodded, remaining behind as Jacob cued the rest of them to leave. He clearly intended to keep his secrets, so Maynard did not bother to ask questions. Turning from Cain and Raven, and the two silent, mysterious women by the throne, Maynard followed the others back down the rows of vessels. He focused on the exit, ignoring the horrific, unsettling rows of cadavers. Only when they returned to the surface, did Maynard realize how cold it had been down below. He welcomed the sunshine and warmth.

Maynard spent most of his time on the ship, which sat on the edge of town, now free from the dead bodies, but not their smell. Raven had supplied them with some rather decent liquor. It seemed rare but Jacob had been flippant about it, urging them to drink it freely. Not one to argue on that point, Maynard found a bottle of rum to his liking. It was difficult to tell exactly when it was from, but the label read 1824. That was a pre-war date, but he had little concept of why it ranged in the thousands. Before long, he was a little too drunk to care about much of anything. Raven's bodies left his thoughts, and instead he found himself musing on what power the Darkworld might offer. He closed his eyes, mildly inebriated, feeling his way down those strange corridors of his mind, tapping into that other universe.

"So you're the one they're talking about?" a voice asked pulling him from the Darkworld. His eyes returned to the desert, ears hearing the voice. It was raspy and deep. Maynard turned, recognizing the man who had been about the camp. The peculiar figure wore a black cassock and a black, brimmed hat. What his clothing didn't cover, bandages obscured, leaving only his fingertips and lips exposed. The most unsettling thing was the pair of glasses the man wore, the two dark disks behind which Maynard could only guess were eyes. "The name's Sol," the man said, extending a hand. "Don't worry. I'm not contagious."

Maynard shook his hand, the rough finger tips gripping his own. "Maynard," he replied.

"They told me some great bastard of a fallen was out and about. They didn't tell me he had good taste in rum. Do you mind?"

Maynard hesitated. "Really," Sol said gesturing at his bandages. "Nothing to worry about. I'm sensitive to the sun."

Maynard passed the bottle, deciding to trust the man. "You work for Raven?" he asked.

"I am in his service," Sol replied, after a swig from the bottle. "We've worked together since the war."

"But wasn't that two hundred years ago?"

"It was. I was mortally injured and made a deal with Raven. I survived and have been better for it, save for this damned sun sensitivity. Raven says I'm fortunate to have survived the transformation without more side effects, so I suppose I'm lucky. Don't worry, I'm not a vampire, though I doubt you've even heard of such a thing. I'm a therianthrope, which is really just a fancy way of making my condition sound exciting. In reality, I'm a werecrocotta."

Maynard had heard of vampires, legends of the old world that he suspected never existed in the first place. However, a werecrocotta was a foreign concept. Of course, he knew crocotta well and had killed his fair share of them in South Outland. He had seen them prowling the horizon from the deck of the *Northern Lady*, but this was a new concept.

"It means I can shapeshift," Sol clarified. "At will, I can become a crocotta. There, the truth is out. Everyone always wants to know what's up with the bandaged guy. I suppose you now know why I work for Raven. I owe him, and to be honest, it's been rewarding for both of us. I'm sorry friend, I talk too much about myself. What about you? Tell me about yourself and why you work for Jacob."

"Compared to you, there's not much to tell really," Maynard replied. He wanted to know more, but it did not seem the time to ask. "I've been a mercenary all my life. I've been a sword-for-hire in a couple of wars. Some I believed in, others I just wanted the coin. I've been on the winning and losing side, but at the end of the day it's about coming out alive and being richer for it. Until Jacob found me, I had taken to smuggling between towns. The way I see it, this is my best shot at giving up all this mercenary nonsense. One day I'll be too old for it or die doing it. If Jacob tells the truth, I'll be able to retire when this is all said and done. Maybe then I can get with a woman who I don't have to pay."

Sol chuckled, "They said you were interesting. You will have to tell me more. But alas I must continue on with my errand. It was a pleasure to have met such a man as yourself. I don't doubt we will work together in the future. Another before I go?"

Maynard realized he wanted another drink of rum and passed the bottle. Sol took a large gulp, handed it back, and left with a nod. Crocotta-shapeshifter or not, he was indeed an odd man.

Maynard had fallen asleep on the ship's deck, looking out over the Outland. He awoke, and from the heat. The sun might have been up a couple of hours. He found Cain sitting next to him with the remaining rum. "Morning, sunshine," he said.

Maynard shook his head, coming out of the alcohol-induced sleep.

"Hungover?" Cain asked.

"I don't think so," Maynard said.

"Good," said Cain taking a swig from the bottle.

Jacob could be secretive, but he guessed that Cain might be open, especially since he was apparently drinking rum instead of eating breakfast.

"So," began Maynard, "what did come of the captain?"

Cain let out a laugh, "You really want to know?"

"Sure."

"He's a special *abomination*." Cain said.

"Abomination? Special?" Maynard asked.

"Yeah," Cain replied, "I don't know who first called them abominations, but it's a fitting name. Raven is a necromancer of a sort. *A sort*, mind you. He can reanimate the dead. They aren't quite alive. Undead, rather." Cain's matter-of-fact tone gave Maynard the impression that this had been done before. "The problem with the undead is that they, having no soul residual from their former selves, are completely unintelligent. We all have better things to do than worry about pseudo-zombies. They were out of control during the war, not something even we want to happen again. But, you saw Raven's women? They're something different. That's a gift from the Morning Star. Jacob told me to break the captain, but keep him alive. Raven is doing something special with him. I have my guesses, but let's wait and see."

Abominations were horrific but Maynard was growing accustomed to this type of thing. In fact, it fit rather well with Jacob's grand scheme. It was a little dark, but nonetheless effective, much like his other actions. The cries from the burning chapel and the burning woman flashed in his memory. Was it remorse? And if so, what was the reason for it? It was, perhaps, remorse for standing by during such a terrible thing. Yet, he also felt pangs of guilt for being so subservient to Jacob. Why had declination not seemed like an option? He might have taken it and burned those people had Cain not taken it upon himself.

This was what an old commander would have called the devil's work. That was, after all, what was the Morning Star.

"How long have you been in with the Morning Star?" Maynard asked.

"Since the war, but not nearly to the degree we have now. Amelia was formerly able to summon beasts from the heavens, but when that was barred, we worked out a deal for her to summon them from Hell. I think the Morning Star just wanted to see some good, old fashioned chaos and destruction, but he has other motives now."

"You speak of his *gifts*," Maynard said. "I take it that since you're using these abominations again, that it's somehow related."

"Blood magic, my friend," Cain said. "Dorian and his followers won't touch the stuff, except once, but that's another story. Two hundred years in the making, and the Morning Star has given us what we need to do the impossible."

Amelia came up to them. "It's time," she said and walked off.

Maynard gave Cain a puzzled look, but Cain just got to his feet and started walking to the other end of the ship. Maynard followed. It was there that Jacob and the others waited. Sol stood coolly to the side and gave Maynard a nod. Raven's women were abnormally strange in the sunlight, their pale skin exposing cold and blue veins. Among them stood the former captain, his skin sickly, stitched, and grisly. His beard had faded from brown to white with splotches of faded red. It looked as if two bones, almost horns, curled from his bushy hair. There was a woman, alive but sick and malnourished, supported by Raven's women.

"I assume this is all new to you, Maynard," said Raven. "In short, abominations have had their disadvantages. On one hand, they are easy on the resources and hard to kill. The problem is that they aren't exactly sentient. Attempts have been made in the past, but the problem is that sentience often comes with a rather unfortunate self-awareness. That is, they can make their own decisions and often the reverberations of their past self give them rather undesirable inclinations.

"Thanks to the Morning Star, we have some new ways of working around that. You need a mediator, someone in between. Something as undead as the abominations, that can lead them, but that can also follow orders. This is quite the task. Hence my two ladies here, and presently Captain Reed. To start our demonstration, we must first kill the prisoner." Raven stepped back.

"Any volunteers?" asked Jacob, eyes shifting towards Maynard. The woman could barely hold her head up, but Maynard saw the pleading in her blue eyes. She hung limply between the two women, loose skin sagging off of her malnourished, naked body. Maynard looked away.

"It's not like you've never killed anyone before," Jacob said snidely before walking over to the woman. He pulled a knife and taking a fist full of the woman's hair forced her out of the grip of her captors and onto her knees. He slid the knife under her throat and pulled slowly. The woman gasped and gagged, blood flowing from her neck onto the deck. Her body fell limp and Jacob held her up by the hair as life flowed from her. Long moments later the life faded from her eyes and he let her body thud to the deck. If Jacob felt remorse or discomfort from his actions he did not show it. Maynard retained his composure.

"Captain," said Raven, "Raise her."

Captain Reed walked over to the corpse. No matter where its eyes looked, they seemed to be staring into the distance, as if his body acted of its own accord. He held a gnarled and scarred hand out over the body and opened his mouth. The skin stretched, revealing holes in his cheeks. A tension filled the air as the captain's hand trembled and he emitted a prolonged and raspy croak. A moment passed and the corpse flinched. Maynard had expected it, but he still jerked a little at the movement. The corpse pushed herself up with rigid movements and soon stood upright, her black pupils dilated, only the faintest blue left of her irises.

"Captain," said Raven, "Have her fetch us some wine."

The captain pointed a finger and flicked it at her. They watched silently as she walked to the other end of the deck, disappearing down into the cabins.

"It's a rather beautiful thing," Raven explained. "She's never been aboard this ship, but the captain has. Thus, by him she knows exactly where to find the wine."

"This is unprecedented," said Jacob. "He can reanimate the dead and give them orders, all while being subservient to us. What happens if he's killed?"

"Well," said Raven, "assuming 'kill' is the appropriate phrasing for a thing already dead, it would take damned near a beheading or inferno to *kill* the thing, but suppose someone managed that. This much is in theory, but I think those he commanded would go on carrying out their orders. Once carried out, I suppose then is when it would get messy."

"It won't get messy like it was before," Jacob said. "Even if it does, we won't have to worry about it."

"What do you mean?" Cain asked.

"You've done a fine job," Jacob said ignoring Cain. "The Morning Star has truly made it worth the wait."

"Yes," said Raven, "My girls made a perfect test run, but with our combined energies we have done the unimaginable. Cain broke the captain in a rather special way. He is capable of independent thought, meaning we won't need to worry about him on the battlefield. He is subservient, yet independent, and he can learn. But he serves us and us alone. Finally, the *lich* has become a reality.

"Girls," Raven said to his women, "Go get the others. It's time they marched. Sol, you know what to do." Raven's women left, over the deck of the ship and down the rope ladder, their ghostly white dresses swaying as they walked among the blackened buildings and orange sand, Sol following closely in his black cassock.

The reanimated corpse returned, holding a tray of full wine glasses. She was nude, the wound in her throat still wet with blood that dripped down her bare breasts and body. Jacob and the others partook of the wine, but Maynard abstained under the excuse of a hangover, though he felt fine. They all walked to the edge of the boat's deck, looking south over the pillaged town.

On the opposite side of the ship, the mountains loomed in the distance. Beyond the orange desert ground a single dark ridge ran along the horizon. Maynard turned from that view and looked out with the others. He heard the distant, faint sound of marching. It reminded him of a battle long ago but he focused his attention on the source of the marching.

"Oh, Dorian" said Jacob, "How you used the blood of the fallen and spirit of Earth to protect the city. The mountains arose and thwarted my every move. I tried to penetrate them but alas my every step was frustrated. You were clever but I have made a path. The Morning Star has provided souls to line my passage. Your spell on the Pass is cheapened and the City's doom is imminent. I will take everything from you."

The otherwise silent desert echoed with their steps. From the smoldering town emerged the abominations. They marched, at least five thousand strong, their maimed and burned bodies reminders of the massacres. They approached through the ash and rubble, stopping before the ship facing toward the mountain. With a nod from Jacob, the captain descended down the side of the ship and stood at the head of the procession. He then pointed a finger forward and led them on. It took minutes for them to pass, their blank expressions staring ahead and their tattered clothing dragging the ground. Some walked easily while others staggered. Even those with no wounds often had rope marks on their throats or broken bones. This was the result of, not one, but multiple massacres. They had died a horrible death, awoken to die again, to face a life of ignorant submission, involuntarily bearing the pain for someone else.

Maynard watched in part wonder, but hid the horror he felt. Only when he broke his stare from the procession did he realize that the *Grigori* smiled at it. This was not utilitarian. This was not a means justified by the end. It was their way. Whose side was he on? The way of this world was that to rise, one had to use others as their stepping stools. He had to be detached. This wake of destruction was not new. Only now, he could not ignore it as he had before. His excuse was worse than ever. He was not vying for livelihood, but power. What was power? Was it happiness? He could *take* a wife, but could he really take love?

Maynard then came to a realization. In the grand scheme of Jacob's antagonizing work, he was the destructive vengeful force come to destroy the world, and Maynard was on his side. Jacob looked at him, as if to read his thoughts, and Maynard pushed it from his mind.

The procession had passed, now marching into the distance toward the mountains. "What now?" Maynard asked, feeling numb.

"We wait. There's a town in the Pass," Jacob replied. "I do not know what lies beyond it other than the City. They will make the way for us and we will be able to march right up to its walls.

"And then?" Maynard asked.

"The ways of the Morning Star are mysterious." Jacob replied.

"You trust him?"

"I almost tricked God. I am not easily fooled. Trust him as you trust me."

The Morning Star. In the end, Jacob had made a deal with the devil and now asked Maynard to trust the devil. Maynard wanted to settle down and live comfortably. He wanted to stop watching his own back, put the sword away as he grew old, and have a family. That was what one was supposed to do: settle down and have a family. He would have to deprive so many others of those things to have them for himself, only to find that what he had was contrived, an imitation. Yet, he was trapped. He had come too far to go back. There was no return ship to Gully, and if there was, what would lie for him there? Perhaps he could settle in some town on this northern island. It would be better to be miserable there for the rest of his life than be miserable and inflict misery on everyone else. He felt the impulse to start drinking. It was not even midday. *No,* he told himself. *This demands a clear mind.*

The day passed. Maynard eyed the mountains and for some reason longed to be beyond them. Was this Novum a place of peace? Were any of these towns such a place? He started to ponder a life of his own. No more battle, no more smuggling. He could be a smith like his grandfather, like his brother. He did not have to do these terrible things to follow in their footsteps. He had left home thirty years ago. The blade had not been his, it had belonged to his brother. He coveted it and took it. The wrong way. He pondered this as he sat in his cabin, polishing the sword. The steel rippled with beauty. His brother could barely wield it, but Maynard had found it easy. It was broad, wider than any sword he had ever seen, as if it were fit for something otherworldly. A knock interrupted his thoughts. *What now?*

The captain's room, stuffy wood paneling the walls, was now empty save for some lamps and the small gathering. Jacob, Amelia, Cain, Raven, and the two lich women that accompanied him. He hadn't thought it necessary to bring his sword, but he wished he carried it now.

"You wanted to see me?" asked Maynard.

"Yes," said Jacob. "We did."

All eyes in the quiet room fell upon Maynard, amplifying his discomfort.

"We need more abominations and another lich to oversee them. Of the forty hired men who joined us at Gully, twenty-eight remain. Pick the best to turn into a lich. Kill the others."

"That's what this is about?" asked Maynard. "Those men have fought for you and will continue to do so. There's no need to kill them."

"Paid mercenaries cannot be trusted," said Amelia. "They flee in battle or betray you. This is a good way to prove yourself."

"I've proved myself just fine and so have they. I see no reason for this."

"The others are starting to draw some conclusions about you, and I'm afraid I share their concern," Jacob said glancing at the others in turn before continuing. "You showed great promise when we first found you. You were sure of yourself as a mercenary and killer, but I am beginning to sense that you have doubts about those things."

"I joined you to fight men in honest battle, not kill women and turn their corpses into these abominations. Nor do I think we should make it our business to kill our own."

"As if it makes any difference to you," said Jacob. "Since when did you develop such lofty morals? You would think that you are somehow justified in killing a stranger just because he is on the other side of the battle lines, but you know that is not true. That stranger is no different than you, rather another man with hopes and dreams. You know as well as I do, that it is a justified means to an end.

"I'll tell you something now, and you'd do well to remember it. There are no good people. All men are selfish and self-motivated. The best of deeds is ultimately the means to pat oneself on the back. Altruism is a lie. Who gives a fuck if the world is burning, so long as you aren't the one on fire? When it's all said and done, there'll just be more for you. That is what every man truly believes. The difference is that some people aren't as honest about it as others. So here's the question. How honest are you willing to be about yourself?"

"You misjudge me," Maynard said. "I have no delusions of morality. The blood cannot wash from my hands. The stranger on the other side likely has more right to live than I do. Let him strike me down. What hope do I really have? If I make it out of this alive, I will be rich. But I will ever be whispered as the widowmaker wherever I go, and furthermore wary of a knife to my back. Can I buy a lover who will not loath the shallow man that I am?"

"How very humble and valiant, Maynard! I have seen the afterlife, and I tell you that nothing is there for you. This is life. You get rich, you find affection in whatever way you can, and you hold onto it until you cannot anymore. You are so very human, so let me make it simple. It is not about love or goodness. It is about you living the best life you can by taking advantage of those who are not as good at life as you."

"Well, you're doing a damn fine job of it," said Maynard, "Taking advantage of us."

"Watch your tongue," Jacob said before pausing to gain his composure. "You could have gone the way of the captain. I could have had ultimate subservience from you, but I gave you your autonomy. Partly because I liked you, but also because I thought I could break you the easy way."

"I may have followed you to whatever end, but I will always be my own man."

"Will you? Have you been your own man? The fight with the captain and his crew was a setup. We had long been off course, and I knew it was a matter of time before he picked a fight. I intended to kill him and take the ship all along, but I let the captain come to us. Raiding the towns was partly for the morale of the men, but it was also for you. Your occasional compromises were promising, but now I see that they only perpetuated your doubt."

"And what now?"

"This. Our effort to reason with you. If you go your own way, there will be nothing for you. You will never return to South Outland, but be forever doomed to walk the deserts of this godforsaken rock. You will be lonely here and you will always have to watch your back. After what you've done, you might as well accept that there's nothing for you other than this. You might as well be on the winning side. You can surpass Achilles. I am giving you the choice."

It had come to it, sooner than Maynard hoped. He had spent decades doing what Jacob now asked him to do. The habit of that worldview now pleaded with him to follow it, to survive. But something felt different. His conscience pulled him the other direction. It reoriented his survival instinct. It told him that Jacob's course was hollow, that he could never be happy, and that it would be better to fade away alone than live as a miserable legend who inflicted misery on others. Jacob had just offered to let him go his own way.

"Alone it is," Maynard said, almost to himself as much as anyone. "I will leave now."

Everyone in the room glanced at one another but remained silent. Raven crossed his arms, directing a cynical look at Maynard.

"That's not how this works," said Jacob, coming close and meeting his eyes.

"It is," said Maynard glaring back. "For once you don't get your way." For the first time in his life, something felt right, as if he had taken a stand for something worthy and made a difference. Then he felt Jacob's fist slam into his jaw.

The surprising hit sent Maynard to his knees. He felt and heard the crack in his face as he lost his balance and steadied himself with a hand to the ground. No sooner was he about to rise when Jacob kicked him. Though normally strong and swift, Maynard had lost control. He fell over, rocking on the wooden planks of the room, gasping with acute pain. He told himself to fight back, but every time he tried to rise Jacob kicked him down, something else in him cracking or breaking with each strike. He told himself to just wait until Jacob was finished, and he would crawl out of this town in the morning, find a place to recover, and live the rest of his life in peace. The next kick made it feel like a stupid thought.

"Damn you, Maynard!" Jacob said. "I am no mere man, I am not to be trifled with. I will not have you waste my fucking time."

Maynard's sight blurred and he heard Jacob call to Raven. Cold hands locked around his arms in a surprising grip. They dragged him on the rough wood as they took him from the room. He tried to fight, but his muscles fell limp. Amelia and Cain stood watching alongside a furious Jacob. Then Raven came into view and picked up Maynard's legs. They led him out and all went black.

The stone ceiling came into focus. He tried to move but he was bound. The chains were tight, burying into his ankles and wrists. They chaffed, biting into his bones. The concrete room was small, most likely underground. He somehow knew they were down the hatch. As he became lucid, a searing pain erupted from his stomach.

"Now, Livia," a female voice hissed, "That's too much."

"I can't help it, Sissy," another replied in a similar scratchy whisper, "His flesh is so nice. Look, he's awake."

Maynard breathed heavily and, for the first time in a long while, he was afraid. Their pale faces came into view and Raven's girls smiled with blood colored lips.

"Hello," said one. "The others have left already, but we will catch up later. They thought you'd be done by now, but you are quite resilient." Her white skin was almost opaque and crawled with patches of blue and black veins. She did not seem human, but rather like some dark creature attempting to act human. *Liches.*

"If he's awake," said the other, "we can get the real work done."

The sensation in his stomach worsened. Fear faded and Maynard could only think about one thing. Pain.

INTERLUDE

*The Girl Who Fell*

*Though Dorian spoke wistfully of his home, particularly regarding the nation of Abriel, it was not always well on his planet. Dorian initially talked disdainfully of Callianeira, who—in as much as Dorian and the others like him were angels—was a demon, well known for her artful and disruptive meddling. Considering her role in the days of Jacob's return, Dorian's former vehemence towards her faded into reluctant appreciation. Her part in the story begins on his planet, Elesonia, where she played a key manipulator in a rival nation's ambitions.*
*—Oliver*

Callianeira leaned on the balcony railing, admiring the Oradar Sea. No water adorned its sandy waves, only the ringlight, painting it a cool blue. The rings themselves arced in the sky, a splendor that paled the stars. She had seen many worlds, few of which could match the beauty of this one.

Without disturbing the sleeping king, Vesuvia had come and gone with the news, the spiritual essence of her whispers a fresh burden. Callianeira had protested that the mission on Elesonia was not complete, that surely the task on Earth could fall to another. As she learned from Vesuvia, things had changed.

A cool breeze caressed her naked body. How would she tell the king? How long did she have before she had to go? She would tell him tomorrow and leave. There was no other way.

The king stirred. "My dear? Are you well?"

She turned from the ringlight, walking through the sheer curtain, back into the king's chamber. King Soni sat up, looking to her. The violet darkness enveloped most of his lean torso and handsome face.

Laise stirred from the foot of the bed. After a quick stretch, the cheetah gingerly leapt from its cushions and left the room. The great she-cat made the best of guardians, but sensed the privacy of the matter.

"My king," Callianeira said.

"What is it my love?"

"I must go."

"I say when you go," the king said, not unkindly.

"I beg your pardon, but things have changed." She lit a series of lanterns, washing the room in a flickering, golden light.

"How?" he asked, rising from the bed. Lean muscle showed on his youthful body. As he approached the age of thirty, he had become a great king, all at her machinations. Much to Dor's frustration, she had made Gipar a country with which to be reckoned. Were she staying, King Soni would rule all of Elesonia. But his fate was his own now.

"I am called elsewhere," she said.

"Did a messenger come? Was his word more powerful than mine?"

"Yes." She would play the clever woman with him. It would do no good to pretend at coyness or fear.

"Tell me who he is, so that I may conquer him and win you back."

"My sweet king and lover," Callianeira said with a smile. "Were it that simple, I'd have you ruling the universe."

"Speak plainly to me." The king's tone was that of a man on the verge of judgment.

"I am more than I have revealed to you."

His face grew grim, anger rising.

"Peace," she said, holding up a calming hand. "I have always been loyal to you. Lay down your anger and hear me."

"Continue," he said after a reluctant pause.

"The world is bigger than your dear planet and its gods. There are conspiracies within conspiracies and I am one of its weavers. I am your mistress. I make you laugh with my wit. I take you to bed like no other woman. You love my ferocity. It helps that Laise likes me. But all this time I have whispered in your ear. Think of all you have accomplished from my mere suggestions. They are playful things, but they turn in your mind, either out of your want or satisfaction in me."

"You have deceived me, woman!"

"I have only made you more powerful."

"Are you a Pyrsati sorceress? Shall I feed you to the lions?"

"I am not even from this world, and I am worse than a sorceress. However, I only ever intended to aid you to victory."

"And what now?"

"Ah," she said, and chuckled. "At first I say that I am helping you and you accuse me of deceiving you. Now that I would take it away, you fear."

He opened his mouth to speak, searching for words.

"I only ever cared about you," she said. "I wanted you to succeed. Is that so bad? But now I must leave. Fear not, my king. I believe we've already accomplished much together. Abriel has lost its god."

"Dor has abandoned his people?"

"You're more right than you know. It's difficult to explain, but your enemy is no longer protected. You don't need my help. This you can do yourself."

"What if I don't want to do it by myself? What if I want you by my side? Do you not love me?"

"Soni," she said, and she drew near to him, placing her palms upon his face. "I care for you deeply. I want you to succeed with all of my heart, and were that I had a normal life, I'd be content in your company. But I do not know what love is."

"Love is—"

"Love is nothing. It is a contrivance that holds us back. It tames ambition. It weakens the hearts of men and women. And worst of all, it is false. Do not love, King Soni. Rid yourself of all passion save ambition."

"I love you. There is no falsehood in that."

"Isn't there?" Callianeira asked. "Why do you love me, Soni?" She ran her hands over her body. "Is it for this?"

"There is none more beautiful than you, but that is not all that draws me to you. I would grow old with you."

"Your concubines are forever young."

"That's not fair."

"You know what's not fair?" She leaned close to him now, almost at a whisper. "You may not have known who I am in that head of yours. You're clever, but I've hidden it well. But your heart knows. You have loved me and your subconscious has rewarded you well. It does not do that for most men. *I* do not do that for most men. Most of the time I am called to ruin them, not make them great."

A single tear slid down his otherwise dry cheek.

She felt his nakedness, her hands finding him wanting, desiring her.

"One last time," she said.

When they were finished, she donned her garments in silence. She felt his brokenness and hoped it made him stronger. As she walked toward the door he spoke. "Send Laise in."

She reached the door, hand ready to open it, and she paused. She knew the words would come and she would allow him to say them.

"I love you," he said

She could not say them back.

Outside of the king's chambers, she found Laise waiting. The cheetah looked up to her, silent and knowing. She knelt and wrapped her arms around the cheetah, pressing her ear close to the great cat's comforting purr. She dug her fingers into Laise's hair, feeling the soft pelt around her slender body. In one moment, they neglected both of their dignities, parting ways as if they always knew this was the way it would be.

She regretted that she had to leave. King Soni surely cried alone in his chambers now, but he was not a weak man. He would be a great man, but with her he would have been magnificent. She did not love him, no more than the previous tasks given to her. But she had wanted to see this through, not just to succeed in her mission, but to see his rise to power.

That was impossible now, and so she found relief in knowing that she could be herself for now, something that her work never afforded her.

She met Vesuvia outside of the palace walls and took the hand of the other demon. Then they were off, traveling the celestial highways towards its darkest corners of the cosmos. The collar had returned, a reminder of her master. She could take it off at any time, but it represented her loyalty to him and to the bond that they shared. So long as she wore it, he protected her, endowed her with whatever she needed, and guaranteed that one day she could be done with this dirty work and live a higher existence.

Every planet had at least one major religion that believed in Hell. None of them had gotten it right. It was not an eternal place of torture—at least, not for *most* souls. It was the capital of a spiritual empire where the Morning Star reigned over all loyal to him. The ethereal dimension of the Eternal One remained unattainable to those like her, those who had chosen to leave his service. But Hell resided within an interdimensional plane.

Earth's realm was close. Callianeira had been there before, always bemused by its people. They had strange conceptualizations of the Morning Star—who they called the Devil or Satan or Lucifer, all misnomers—and Hell. They also held a strange obsession with the idea of love. Over the eons, the Morning Star suffered a few defeats when humanity did the unexpected. It reminded her of the conversation with Soni. Those like the Christ had taught love. It wasn't supposed to succeed, and certainly not persevere for two thousand years. Though it was all but forgotten now, the people of that planet seemed to have a special connection with the idea of love. It made them as impervious as it did susceptible to her manipulations.

This would be a difficult job. If it was a matter of gullibility, they would have called anyone else. With Earth's war of the fallen, who knew what awaited her. That had been an oddity as well. Who would choose pseudo-immortality over service to the Morning Star? He was the realist, the one who saw practicality in immorality. The Eternal One's rules were arbitrary. Why prohibit lying, when a lie could accomplish so much? What did morality and love ever give anyone other than a broken heart?

Hell was a general term for the main city that bustled in their realm, which was home also to various other municipalities and suburbs such as Jahannam, Xibalba, and Bardo. On their plane, the toxic clouds twisted overhead like swirling paints, greens and oranges streaking and spiraling in the sky, but their city was an eloquent sprawl of spires and buildings, red stone contrasting the green oxidized copper, complimenting the patterns above. Of course, many souls did come here to perish, the engines by which Hell existed safely among the tumultuous atmosphere.

Vesuvia had left Callianeira to the path that she knew so well. Fellow spirits, all followers of the Morning Star, bustled among the streets. Many creatures, great reptilian or gargoyle-like beasts, either sentient and on their own business, or dumb animals under the care of their masters, roamed among them. By Earthen standards they were hideous and befouled, but only per their association with the Morning Star and all things undesirable, ugly, and wicked. Before that, they had been as praised as any other creature of beauty. They say darkness is evil, but among it they marvel at the stars.

She had let her mind wander, worried at what was to come. Pandemonium awaited. Every capital has its palace and Pandemonium stood tall at the heart of the city, a collection of Gothic spires and bell-towers. The bridge led her over the river, through the portico, and into the palace. She was young, only in her hundreds, but already she knew every step of the palace and where it led her. She fixed her garments before entering the courtyard gardens, fingers feeling the collar around her neck. It served as a reminder that had been so absent when she had duties that required her to obfuscate it with a glamour.

Sagtyx stood by the pool, pious robe hiding the scars that Callianeira knew were there. She had given some of those scars. Sagtyx had begged for them. She looked into the pool's placid, dark waters, and they reflected back her sharp features and olive skin. "You know your orders?"

"Vesuvia told me," Callianeira replied. "Stop the catalyst. The usual problem."

"Yes," Sagtyx said, reaching down and tapping the waters at her feet. Her gray hair almost touched the pool, but then she righted herself and looked at Callianeira. "What of the Soni boy?"

"He's no boy. Not anymore," Callianeira replied. "With the loss of Dor, the nations cannot hope to withstand Soni's conquest."

"Consider that mission completed. I will report it as a success, regardless of the outcome. You did all that was necessary."

"I thank you."

"Now," said Sagtyx, "see what comes next."

Callianeira peered into the pool's reflection, its glossy dark surface dimly reflecting the green clouds floating among a jaundiced sky. With a ripple in the water it shifted, and she saw the boy. He transitioned into a man, auburn haired with green eyes like the skies above them.

"This man resides in the company of Jacob, one of the fallen. So long as he does, he is corruptible."

"Sounds easy," Callianeira said.

"He will not remain in Jacob's company."

"That's where I come in, I take it?"

"The oracles don't foresee much these days, but our power is reawakening on the Earth. The Morning Star moves and we shall as well if all goes according to plan. What they have foreseen is that this man will fall into Dorian's company. We don't know why, but we do know that as far as Dorian's intentions and motivations go, this man is a lost cause. We think the change of sides has to do with his motivation to be in the winning camp. You can use that to your advantage."

"When do I go?"

"Immediately." Sagtyx said.

She wanted some respite from the years she had spent on Elesonia. She needed some time to herself. Alas, this was the life she had chosen. "Of course, I'll be wanting compensation."

"The usual and a potential place directly under the Morning Star. This is his operation and he asked for you by name."

"Good enough for me," Callianeira replied, keeping eagerness from her expression or tone.

From the shadows of her dimension she watched the boy turn to man. She saw what he was like, and at first, she identified with him. Much like her, he saw profit in everything. In the end, what matters is one's success. Had she been mortal, she would have thought just like him. If he was going to die, might as well enjoy life.

She made sure he got the sword, a gift from her world. He fought among the armies in the south, he took his cut, and he squandered it. Then he would go back out, fight in more battles, strip the corpses for loot, and take his pay just to spend it all again. After a while, he wizened, saving his money, finding less dangerous and more lucrative jobs in smuggling. He was clever there, shorting his delivery where he could, skimming the payments.

When he joined Jacob, she saw the fulfillment of his desires. He would burn an entire village if it made him rich enough that he never had to do it again. Jacob made him promises, ones she knew he had every intention of keeping, even if he was a liar, and the man gave his loyalty further with every word.

Then one day the man did something strange. He showed remorse. He came to believe in the value of goodness, to know that he could never attain it, and to still desire it anyway. Whatever success had meant before, it reoriented itself now. She saw his mind, his delineation. Above all else, he wanted love, and he knew that his deeds would never warrant true love, nor could he ever give it. Suddenly, his path seemed meaningless, for he saw the frivolity in serving Jacob, but knew well that any good he aspired to was sanctimonious.

Callianeira had spent that day in a daze and the next day screaming.

Whatever Sagtyx had seen, this was not it. Callianeira was the best, but this was not going to work.

Then the man suffered under Jacob's wrath. This was not a man who changed allegiance because he wanted to be on the winning side. He had come to realize something. The same realization came to her. Slow, but fierce and true.

"I'm out," she told Vesuvia. In the middle of the Outlands, they were alone, desert in every direction.

"There is no *out*."

Callianeira held up the collar, its loose shackle dangling.

The frizzle-haired demon rushed at her, suddenly close enough to kiss.

"We are not the fallen," Vesuvia whispered. "We are the ascendant. We are free from the Eternal One."

"Yet, here we are. Hardly free."

Vesuvia released Callianeira, spreading her hands wide. "Are the rewards not sufficient?"

"No," Callianeira replied. "They aren't."

"What do you lack?"

"Love."

Vesuvia laughed, like sanity had abandoned her, cackle rising. "The great Callianeira, the Morning Star's highest ranking slut, says she believes in love all of the sudden? Are you trying to bullshit your way to kingdom come?"

"I don't—I didn't—believe in love. I think I do now."

"And, please tell me, what does it mean to *believe in love*?"

"I don't know. I just think it matters."

"You *think*?" mocked Vesuvia.

"I do," replied Callianeira.

"You want to fall?" Vesuvia spat. "Then fall."

The world quaked. Vesuvia took her by the neck and flung her. She sailed into the air and landed. The earth gave beneath her, like a consuming vortex, and she felt the pain of falling, the burning of the underworld lashing up at her.

"I could send you to Pandemonium," Vesuvia said.

From her pit, Callianeira cried out. "Only to be exiled."

She clambered from the crater that engulfed her, pulling herself over its red, glowing ledge, the cracks running along the earth. She took the collar and flung it at Vesuvia.

"Tell your master to find a new slut. Leave me!"

"You want to follow your new suitor?" Vesuvia bellowed. "He's in Bronton, dying as we speak."

Then Callianeira was alone in the Outlands, risen from the bowl of earth, and she was free. Somewhere out there was this man, and if Vesuvia was right, he may not live long enough for this to be worth her while. She gazed out at the desert. She had grown accustomed to its soft moon and spattering of stars again. She knew the nearest town. From there she would use whatever wit, resourcefulness, or determination left to her to find this man.

She had a feeling, fate would weave her way.

# CHAPTER EIGHTEEN

## *The Sigil*

*Elijah could remember the day of the fall. He stood at the highest observation deck of the City as the clouds gathered over the land. No mountains blocked his view of the desert, the storm shadowing it in a night-like darkness. At first, the occasional flicker of lightening flecked the ominous dark-gray clouds with white flashes, illuminating the land for a glimpse and then darkening again. The Great Prophet knew this was the day.*

*The clouds began to swirl, an organic funnel forming. They stretched and shifted, churning streaks of orange and red appearing among them, fiery wounds rippling across the sky. The fire twisted into a funnel, and as if a volcano was erupting from the sky, it expelled a single figure. Even in the distance, Elijah knew it was a man. No. Not a man, but rather a being, spirit made flesh, a fallen angel. A* Grigori. *The shock of it hitting the ground vibrated throughout Novum and Elijah knew it was only the beginning.*

Though his zero held little hope of use in Jacob's imminent confrontation, Dorian needed to know. He needed to know what this newly awakened earth would bring and its capabilities. The well opened up into the usual caverns that interwove underneath the landmass, but he also knew of another place. Deep within was a special cavern, an unearthly crater that for a few brief moments had been all he knew of this planet. He had been back once since—and only briefly—to hide their stockpile, but he knew his zero to be here, and though obfuscated by time, he knew the way.

He walked the stone path, wide and then narrow, surrounded by great pools of dark waters. Holding his hand out, a small ball of flame ignited in his palm, the soft blue light illuminating his way. He took little note of the creatures that lurked in the underground, disregarding them without fear as he maneuvered the dark and winding caves.

Dorian had used his zero as an underground stockpile, a homing point for the provisions needed after the war. There were mounds of supplies should the world ever want to rebuild and should any of them be in need.

He wandered through the various openings and pathways until one let out to a vast dip. The cave domed above mirroring the terrain beneath. He found his crater still hidden, the surface above restored, leaving a deeper place in the caverns. Apparently, Novum had not taken any chances of their underground water supply being contaminated or utilized, and even after the fall, their deep pockets secured a solid covering of this site.

Dorian increased his light, revealing the cracks and lines etched in a spiraling glyph right down the center of the crater and before Dorian dared step foot on such a wonder, he removed all but his trousers. Shirtless and barefoot, light in hand, he climbed down into the massive bowl. He overstepped the grooves and shallow trenches, knowing their design. It was the sigil he had known for so long and the likeness tattooed into the back of his upper-right shoulder burned with a faint blood-orange glow, bared to solicit but one of the magics it revealed.

He stood alone at his *zero*. Cold stone on his feet, he stood a moment not knowing what to do. He sank to his knees, placing a hand on the ground and he tapped into the other world. The tremors began. He could again sense the hum of the earth, the echoes of her great tragedy resurgent. Would she be wounded again? Would the ancient scars be opened anew? The power that had faded in the two hundred years was returning, resurfacing. The immortals were unsettling and with it awakened the deep and mighty magic to war yet again.

His bare skin soaked in a knowing, that things were indeed coming to a peak. It could not tell him the future, but it groaned in anticipation. The vision came, overwhelming his senses, flashing almost too fast to comprehend. A ship sailed upon the desert, a man endured torture, and the dead walked towards his precious pass. Among these strange, flickering images, the Pass perturbed him most, arousing the suspicion that his ward had been broken.

Yet he did not find all he sought. Was it that he hoped to use this place against Jacob? It was a small hope that the crater would be enough to bind a *Grigori*, a fallen angel, but it held little magic. He would have to find another way to stop Jacob. Such sigils graven into stone could potentially trap Jacob, either killing him or transporting him elsewhere, but it would take a significant amount of power for them to work. If his own sigil didn't hold such ward, then he couldn't imagine that he would know such a glyph if he saw one. Furthermore, he wasn't sure that he was equal to the task of activating such a ward, not with the sacrifice that it would require.

After redressing, he took another series of tunnels, and after another half hour he found the narrow passage. Rats scurried down the cracked and moldy path. He entered what they had deemed the Mall, a damp, cold, and dark place. Dorian drew his sword, holding it in one hand, and continuing to light his way with the other. The cache had fallen into decay, metal boxes rusting and plastic crates slumping under the weight of their contents. A few precious items remained secure from the elements, but otherwise the smell of ruin filled the air.

He decided he could use new clothes, boots, and perhaps anything else that might be helpful. Other than one stack of looted boxes, nothing of real value was taken. It had possibly been an animal, or perhaps someone did come down here, but not finding their initial search fruitful, gave up. Perhaps Charis or Nathan had come here. He wandered the boxes until he found clothing and shoes to his liking and fit, sufficiently free of decay thanks to the durability of the plastic bags that preserved them.

Dorian loathed shopping and spent little time worrying over fashion. Fit and function were all that mattered. In the end, he left with some good finds. Comfortable socks, moisture wicking underwear, trousers made from a quick drying blend of fabric, and a shirt that would help keep him cool under the desert heat. The boots he found were a better fit than what he currently wore, and he knew they would be even better once broken in.

On the return trip, his mind wandered. His zero brought up memories of the war. There had been sacrifices. Two hundred years ago there had been the Last Saint. Jacob had been ruthless. Was all lost? Dorian was unsure, but the world had been demolished. Only a few remnants stood on the two islands. A cropping of trees here and there, a few clusters of people beginning to form settlements. For all of Dorian's efforts, the island came to ruins. It infected the land, poisoning the life, leaving only the cursed desert sands right up to the front lines. The refugees came, immigrants from the Graylands. They brought memories from the old world, and in each meager township, restored what pieces they could of the past.

Jacob burned their ships, leaving the immigrants alive. He might have destroyed them too, but instead, he focused his power on Novum. If he could breach that one place his revenge might be satiated. Of course, Jacob could not be soothed and even if he were to hold the City he might break the thing itself, not out of petty revenge, but out of the covetousness that only a fallen god might harbor.

And so, the front lines had clashed before the City, a pyramid on the northern horizon. Dorian remembered that day well. The clouded skies were bronzed by the piercing sunlight, a bitter silver lining that held so little hope. There was no rest for those outside the City, just the few and brave souls who knew their deathly fates, who fought onward, believing that one day the human race might prevail because of their sacrifices. Perhaps they fought because there was nothing else to do.

However, matters became dire, and such beliefs turned tenuous. Jacob pressed on, his vengeance too fierce for their dwindling forces. The first time Sachin Pendharkar came forward, Dorian had turned him away. He would accept no such sacrifice on the part of one person, and was even surprised that anyone could know that such things were possible. Dorian's magic manipulated the natural, but somehow this man had heard of blood magic. He was no operative of Jacob's, but he knew their ways, and most curious of all, the man who came to be known as the Last Saint offered his life.

After turning the man away, the army continued to endure days of bloody battle, and Dorian tired. He wearied of fighting, stretching the ends of his magic to war against Jacob. Amelia's beasts savaged soldiers on the front lines before Raven led a battalion to slaughter the rest by sword and spear. Einstein had said that the fourth world war would be fought with sticks and stones, and indeed they had resorted to more medieval battle, but it also came with tooth and claw.

If it would have mattered, Dorian might have sacrificed himself, but he could not both oversee such a ritual while also being dead. Sachin came forward again and offered himself. He knew it was the only way and so did Dorian. In more than skin tone and facial features did Sachin remind Dorian of himself. The man was depressed, not because of some unknown melancholy, but because he truly knew the state of the world. However reluctant, they agreed and made their plans.

If Dorian wasn't present, Jacob might suspect something and increase his efforts, but Nathan's absence could go unnoticed. Dorian was always present, commanding and fighting, moving earth and fire to help in any way he could. Oliver was ubiquitous as well, but Nathan and Charis were often behind the scenes. That was when Dorian first found out that Nathan's power to shapeshift was less limited than he thought. Nathan, in the likeness of Dorian, held the lines.

The sacrifice took place far behind the lines of battle. In the distance, perhaps not more than thirty miles, the black pyramid stood. Defeat was increasingly inevitable and then Jacob would march on Novum. Its walls were said to be impenetrable, but so far Jacob remained one step ahead of them. He would find a way.

And then what? That was always the question. Jacob claimed he would have been content to rule outside of Novum, but his ceaseless grasping for power had undone much of the world, and Dorian mused that it was not out of pure greed or incompetence, but rather in deliberate spite. The evidence cast little doubt that Jacob would be content to merely possess power over the City.

Dorian looked to Sachin. They stood in the desert, the sound of battle a distant susurration. Whether or not by Dorian's hand, Sachin would fall to cancer if Jacob's army didn't kill him first.

"I'm ready to die," he said in Marathi, the mother tongue of his Indian state.

Dorian nodded at the frail man and then gestured toward the City. "For them? The people that will not come out to help us, nor give us shelter?"

"They will be all that's left of humanity when this is over." He was right. It was why Dorian fought.

Dorian had drawn the runes in the sand, circles filled with writhing ancient symbols, crude and ancient glyphs that belonged to a time long passed. Blood spells were of dark magic, remnants of a time when tribes sacrificed the unwilling for the blessing of their gods. Blood magic was the Morning Star's domain, but when one gave life willingly it was something wholly different.

Dorian drew his sword. This man deserved more ceremony, but at least he would die by a noble blade. When Sachin knelt, Dorian noticed that he shook, but his eyes remained strong and sure.

"I'm sorry," Dorian said, walking behind Sachin.

"I am not. Have you ever seen someone die of cancer? It is a meaningless, undignified way to go. After weeks of more agony, I would finally waste away in my bed, frail and dead in my own filth. I would rather my death have meaning." Sachin began to repeat a *ram* mantra and Dorian raised his sword and buried it in the innocent man.

Sachin Pendharkar would be remembered as the Last Saint. By the sacrifice, Dorian appealed to the mountain to the northwest. There stood, on that easily terraformed landscape, a loan peak. He stretched every limitation of his magic, calling life from that earthly void. Summon it he did, and it flowed, curving around the quaking landscape. Lava coursed in circles, hot and blood red. It layered and compounded, laving across the landscape. Thus did the earth burn and rise, like a particle in the memory of the creation of the universe itself. Dorian was the worldmaker once again.

By rock and fire, the ring of mountains arose with a single and inhabitable pass. Dorian worked fast, but he allowed for the inklings of a forest to grow in the northwest corner of the mountains. He directed the waters to trench through, channeling their way from the forest and into the pass. The Last Saint's death warded it so that no one with *Grigori* blood could behold or enter sole gap in the mountains. Dorian walked from between the towering walls and turned to see only steep stone, he too being blocked from entering.

After the raising of the mountains, Dorian expected to die on the front lines, warring against Jacob and his army. Men were smashed against the mountain walls, and others fled into the Pass that was obstructed from the angels. But Jacob left sooner than any expected. One day there was battle, and in the night they rested. The next morning, Jacob and all his might had disappeared.

Of course, Dorian had some suspicion that Jacob was biding his time, that he knew the futility against Dorian's ward, and left to find another way. Never did Dorian dream that Jacob's scheme would take two hundred years, nor did he foresee the plan. They waited for Jacob's return, vigilant and wary for a time, but he never came.

After a time, it was agreed that Jacob would be long in returning. Shame plagued the fallen, knowing how much of the destruction for which they had been responsible. There were always the questions, always the puzzles. Had they not tried to stop Jacob, would he have been content to take the City and rule it peacefully? Would he have been so hell-bent on destroying the world? But Jacob's burning desire to lay the Eternal One's favored planet to waste was evidence enough that he would take everything he could. Had Dorian simply stood aside, and had the others—Nathan and Charis—allowed it as well, the City would merely be Jacob's first distraction before doing as he did.

Jacob's power was awful and calculated, something only Dorian could rival. When the fallen angel set his will to it, the earth would cry in agony and all before him bled. Dorian could feel that power resurrecting. The earth hummed, a persistent vow of fear and blood.

Dorian walked into a cavern and found a congregation of crocodiles. Realizing that he had not come that way before, he quietly backed out, and tried another passage. He eventually found the end of the rope he had used to climb down. He had paid the old lady dearly to ensure that no one tampered with his way out. A small side of him had feared she would fail at her job, but considering the handsome payment he should have had more faith.

The rope ran along a wall that, though jagged, proved difficult to climb. Dorian had tried to stay in shape the last few decades, but cave diving was not something he practiced. Though bearing the strength and skill, it took him a while. The opening came into view, giving way to the unusual sight of a gray sky. As Dorian pulled himself out of the hole it began to rain.

# CHAPTER NINETEEN

## *Inner Demons*

"Where the hell is Dorian?" Nathan asked with a juvenile smirk.

Liam wondered the same. In the rare storm, Dorian's prolonged absence seemed ominous, not that the angel couldn't take care of himself. Rains occurred less than a handful of times a year, and from the City it had always seemed less dramatic. The charcoal clouds rolled in, prematurely turning the day to dark, trickling rain at first and then gushing the downpour.

The tavern's roof leaked but the patrons paid it no mind. Buckets caught the larger breeches, dripping water creating a sporadic tin rhythm. It took Liam longer to adjust to the tobacco smoke in the humidity. For the most part, all sat quiet. Nathan gazed at the lanterns along the wooden wall, Charis sipped her ale, and Liam tried not to make it obvious that his eyes followed Trish wherever she went. He did a poor job.

"She's a pretty girl, she is," Nathan said. Charis shot Nathan a glance.

"It's true," he continued. "A boy finds a pretty girl attractive, is that so wrong?"

"It's not that," Charis said. "Just allow him some dignity, that's all."

"It's okay," Liam said, though he was thankful for Charis's defensiveness on his part. "She is pretty, but it's not like I should care."

"What do you mean?" Nathan asked.

"With the war and Jacob and all," Liam said. "I'm not going to have time for any distractions."

"I won't deny that there is work to be done," Nathan said, "but you've done more than your share. No one would blame you if you went your own way."

"To what end, though?" asked Liam. "You'll be off fighting wars and I'll be down here—or wherever—doing nothing. There's work to be done."

Nathan gave Liam a look of fascination. "I think I know what you're getting at. There are a lot of folks who don't understand it. They think they can go about life making money, doing things their own way, and dying happy. But the man who dies rich, still dies. And then what of his riches? I'm not bashing wealth. I'm just saying that there's more to life."

"Though Nathan is right," Charis said, "you're no longer under any obligations."

Liam took a sip of his ale, thinking on Nathan's words. Perhaps that was what Liam had meant to articulate all along. It felt somehow wrong to abandon them, but now that things were coming together, weariness crept on him, and he found himself wishing it was all over. In fact, it occurred to him that up to this point, he had given all of his energy to this mission, with little regard for his own interests or desires. He was fully entitled to give up, and honestly, how important was he in a war between gods? However, he knew he should see it through. What was it Ferrith once said? *All that is necessary for the triumph of evil is that good men do nothing.* Likely he quoted one of the old philosophers.

"It's not selfish to want something for yourself," said Charis. "Not after all you've done."

"Do you know what you want?" asked Nathan.

"I think I do," replied Liam. "I want to find what it means to be normal."

"Oddly enough," said Nathan, "normal can mean different things to different people."

"I know," Liam said. "Before I left the City, it was all I ever knew, yet it never felt normal to me. It was like I didn't fit in. My family was apathetic towards me, except Elijah, of course. I had friends, but they're so different."

"Is this an improvement to you?" asked Charis looking around the leaky tavern.

"After seventeen years in the City, I never felt used to it. I'm getting used to this, out here."

"You should come as far as Mere," said Charis. "I think you'd like it there."

"I want to stay with you all anyway," Liam said. "For as long as it makes sense. I may go with you in your pursuit of Jacob, but when it's all said and done, maybe I will just stay in the Outlands."

There was a movement next to Liam and a wet Dorian sat next to him in the booth, causing Liam to scoot in surprise, the water soaking the seat and his pants.

"Where the devil did you come from?" asked Nathan. "Better yet, where have you been?"

"Don't worry," Dorian said to Liam. "These pants are quick drying. Said so on the tag."

"You took your time shopping," said Nathan.

"Call it what you will," said Dorian with a smile.

"You went to your zero," said Charis.

Dorian grew serious, "I had to, to see if it was of any use. I thought maybe if I could lure Jacob there I could bind him. It's not that simple. There was something unsettling about the place, like the whole earth is coming alive. I should have known it would be this way again."

"The earth is coming alive. This is certainly the worst storm I've seen in some time," said Nathan.

"It's not just that," said Dorian. "The old ways are returning. I can even see it in Liam here. You should see him shoot."

All eyes went to Liam. "I'm pretty good, I guess."

"Oliver said he shot Raven in the arm," Charis said. "And I saw him give Raven a pretty good left hook."

"Wait," said Liam, "are you saying I can do magic?" His prior conversation with Dorian came to mind.

"Not really," said Dorian. "But we aren't the first fallen spirits and our predecessors surely had progeny and passed along some power. It seems to come to life in times like these."

"But I doubt I'm the descendant of one of them," Liam said.

"Sure you are," said Nathan. "How else do you think the Great Prophet came by his power? That was not a god-given prophecy he had. No, he divined something unexpected. Whatever you have is small, far removed from the greatness of even the prophet, much less whoever he inherited it from, but you likely have something nonetheless."

"Well," said Dorian, "we've made old friends again quick enough and we have a lot of catching up to do."

Soon everyone's piece of the story had been told. What surprised Liam was Nathan's part in which the City had opened its doors once after closing them. It was after the fall, but prior to the front lines reaching the island. Two groups were exiled for supposed religious differences. In reality, most had been associated with their respective religion in culture only. After all, many had fled to the City on the promise of something external to their native religion. However, it did little good that they were two very different cultures, and after the war, Nathan found them quarreling amongst each other.

"With the aid of the Leviathan, we gave them something else to believe in," Nathan said. After that he traveled in the west, a nomad among the towns, playing the drunk, but always on the lookout for information. Apparently, he derived his income from gambling. Liam told of the prophet and the City, Charis told of Oliver and Mere, and Dorian spoke of his tenure in the south. More ale was had, stories were told, and Liam tired. Charis must have noticed it, for though they all spoke lively as ever, she was the first to suggest sleep.

"We have a long journey and we should get some rest," she said, "Weather permitting, we leave at first light and ride north."

It took some time, but eventually her advice was followed and everyone found themselves in their beds. By the morning, the storm had gone, leaving a muddy and pocked terrain. They took a quick breakfast, paid for their rooms and retrieved their camels from the stables. As they readied their mounts, Charis whispered into each camel's ear, her words too quiet to distinguish, but apparent in their reassurance of the beasts.

"I always preferred a good horse to a camel," Nathan said.

"He's only goading Charis," Dorian said to Liam in a whisper.

"Fine," said Charis, her tone matching Nathan's sarcasm. "You bring your horse. We'll see who makes it to Mere faster."

"That shit town?" Nathan said. "I don't know if I could get so noble a creature as a horse to even trot towards it."

Charis laughed and Dorian packed as she bantered with Nathan. Once saddled, the jocularity ceased and they rode into the drying desert.

For the next two days, the terrain moved from a flat plain to rocky hills and then back to flat again. It would turn from orange red rock to brown and gray sand. Liam learned much along the way. "So, you're a therianthrope?" he had asked Nathan.

"No," said Nathan. "Nothing of the sort. Your werehyena priest was nothing like me. I can take on different shapes at will. Some take more time and practice than others. A tiger is my preferred shape. Agile, large, fast, intimidating, beautiful, and not to mention a creation of my own." Liam could see the likeness from Nathan's shaggy orange-red hair. "You should see my Dorian impression," Nathan joked.

"You created the tiger? Didn't the Eternal One create everything?"

"Not necessarily," Nathan shifted in his saddle. "He has commissioned his created to be creators as well. Child bearing isn't some magical process. It's a biological event. The cosmos is not idle. We have our mandates to be stewards, to create, to serve a function. At the foundations of this very planet, some of the celestial beings gifted the Eternal One their creations. Think of it as a house warming gift."

They went on to talk about other things, a welcome distraction from the blinding sun and heat. Liam tried not to ask too many questions, but he wanted to know so much. His inquisitiveness did not seem to bother Nathan or the others who rode nearby. Occasionally Dorian and Charis would strike up a conversation, like old friends reminiscing. What struck him most was the way they treated him. These were not the pompous attitudes he had expected from immortal angels. They were respectful and understanding. They really listened to him and took the time to answer his questions. Yet, he feared that it was contrived, a small kindness. They did not seem condescending, but long experience with indifferent parents and Novum's clergy had made Liam suspicious.

The best part was that traveling with them meant that he was well protected from danger. He did not have to worry about the elements, Raven, or starvation. They all had to be conservative with food and water, but at least he knew that they would not let him die of thirst. That was reason enough to continue on.

"How many days has it been without a pint?" asked Nathan. "Next town, I say we stop in for at least one, if not two." Liam thought he heard him mumble "or three or five."

"See here, a man after my own heart," said Dorian. He was never as mirthful as Nathan, but in the company of the other two angels, Dorian was less morose. He was preoccupied, almost distant, but it appeared more manageable when they were around.

"Now this is a shit town," Nathan said as they entered Graegon, a town Liam had previously bypassed on his flight south. "What did the sign say? Population 372? Well, I'd like to think one in 372 people make a decent ale. Maybe we'll have some luck."

From the outside, the Graegon Tavern and Inn seemed as uninspired as its name. Nathan, Dorian, and Charis led the way and Liam followed behind, always taking in the surroundings. Even after almost a month in the desert, so much remained new to him. They walked into the tavern, the smoke immediately assaulting Liam's senses. He began to look for an empty table, but it was crowded with dirty townspeople.

Liam's three companions drew their swords. The metal rang as each of them unsheathed their blades. Nathan no longer looked merry, but fierce, and let out a quite growl. As Liam looked for the danger he drew his own sword, awkwardly holding it at a room full of drunk men. And one woman, feet propped up on a nearby table. Dorian stood at the head, steel-eyed, pointing his sword at her. The unsettled patrons' eyes fell on the four new strangers and their drawn weapons. The room went silent.

"I'm tempted to fight all four of you just to see how I'd hold up, but I suppose I'd best surrender" said the woman. Her pants were tucked into her calf-length leather boots. She had straight dark hair, sand-colored skin, and a wry smile.

"What are you doing here, Callianeira?" Dorian asked.

"What business is it of yours?" she asked taking a casual sip of beer. "You really should relax, maybe sit down for a drink. You're scaring the patrons."

"Jacob returns, the Morning Star is at work, and you want to dispute whose business it is if you want to hang out here?" Nathan asked.

She sighed, "Can't a girl relax?"

"No," said Charis. "Take it from me."

"Look," Callianeira said."That stuff you're all talking about, I got out of it a while ago. I've been doing well for myself here and I'd like to continue to do so. Move along and I promise not to make any trouble."

"That's not going to happen and you know it," said Dorian.

Callianeira looked around the tavern, all eyes on her.

"Fine, but if you won't sit and talk it out over a drink, let's take it outside." she said gesturing to the door.

Dorian nodded. "She's a wanted woman," Dorian said to the tavern.

By some authority in his voice, that seemed to be enough for the tavern's customers. The room came to life again, patrons doing their best to make it plain that they had no intention of interfering.

They stepped into the dusty street, Liam blinking as his eyes readjusted to the light. As soon as Callianeira walked out of the tavern, she tried to run, but Dorian and Nathan grabbed her arms.

"Afraid not, sweetheart," Nathan said with a smile, contrasting Dorian's serious disposition. Liam trailed behind as the men escorted her, puzzled by the situation. They were attracting attention and Dorian seemed intent on finding somewhere less conspicuous. They ducked into the stable. Lucy was down the way among the other camels.

"Can't we go some place where it doesn't smell like shit?" Callianeira asked.

Dorian ignored the question. "What are you up to?"

"Seriously," she said. "I got out."

"You don't just get out," said Charis.

"No, you don't, but the boss was a little preoccupied."

"You," said Nathan, "of all of your kind, wouldn't want out."

"That was true at one time." Her attitude calloused.

"You're telling the truth," Charis said with wonder.

"You'll have to get used to it," said Callianeira. "Can I go now?"

"Why did you leave?" asked Dorian.

"What would you prefer? That I was back on Elesonia fucking your Giparese king to victory?" She smirked, but then her expression grew serious. "All I want is to go to Bronton."

Dorian exchanged a look with the others. "Bronton has been sacked. What is your business there?"

"Can't a demon have a change of heart?" she asked. "I've discovered love."

A demon. Just who was this woman?

Nathan laughed. "That's a new one."

"It's not like that," she said. "It's not romantic really. The way things were before were easier for me. I used people to do what needed to be done. I see that I was wrong and I've chosen the harder path to do the right thing."

"That's not how this works," said Dorian. "You have a past and your going to Bronton is suspicious at best."

"I've done horrible things, I know," Callianeira said. "Against you and your beloved planet. I know that I don't get a clean slate. But if no one is putting me on trial, I might as well try and be better going forward."

Was that a look of compassion from Charis? Even Nathan furrowed his brow in careful consideration.

Callianeira gave Dorian a cold look. "Can you judge me, Dorian?"

Dorian dropped his gaze and sighed. "No. I can't."

"These are strange days," Charis said.

"Strange indeed," said Callianeira. "Strange that you three find me. This is not how I would have liked to have met. I was shocked when I heard what had happened to all of you. Jacob's a real bastard for what he did. What's he up to now?"

"We're still figuring it out," Dorian said. "All we know is that Jacob is on the move again and that he has help from the Morning Star. I would think you would know more, Callianeira."

"First off, call me Calli. You people butcher my name. And no, I don't know much more than that. Like I said, I got out a long time ago. What I can tell you is that this thing with the Morning Star has been in the works for a long time. Ever wonder why one day Jacob just stopped? That was the day he got desperate and he made a deal."

"With the Morning Star," said Charis.

"Yeah," continued Callianeira. "They were already in league, but this pact was something bigger. I don't know what it was, but I know that Jacob had little hope of breaching the mountains, much less getting into the City, until the Morning Star offered it to him. All he wanted in return was patience. I honestly didn't think that was something Jacob had, but apparently it's about to pay off."

"This is bad news," said Dorian. "We need to make haste."

"Go then," said Callianeira.

"Come with us," said Charis.

"I'm not sure that's a good idea," said Dorian.

Callianeira ignored him and looked to Charis. "Well, you lot do seem like more fun. Care for a stop in Bronton? I have a feeling it will be worth our while."

Dorian gave the others a look of silent disapproval.

They were on their way from Graegon soon after, Nathan complaining that he never did get his pint, and Liam still somewhat confused about the whole situation. Callianeira rode a horse, which stuck out among their camels, but it didn't take long to warm up to the other beasts.

After riding an hour, a wind picked up. Though somewhat refreshing at first in the hot desert, the gust began to blow sand their way. It was subtle but bothersome, even after wrapping a cloth around his face. Liam rode up beside Callianeira, hoping to talk to her and distract himself from the wind.

"Who are you?" he asked.

"You heard them," she said with a cunning smile. The wind and sand apparently didn't bother her. "I am—or I suppose I was—a demon."

"You weren't being figurative?" Liam wiped the grit from his face, adjusting the kerchief over his mouth and nose.

"I'm afraid not," she said. "And you are?"

"Liam," he answered. "I'm from the City."

"Oh?" she said raising her eyebrows. "Things really are getting serious."

"What are you doing here?" Liam asked.

"I could ask you the same," she said. "You might say that I wasn't the right fit for my previous occupation."

Liam shook his head, "I mean, I thought you'd be more reluctant to tag along. Dorian hasn't given you a kind look since we left."

She looked serious, as if pondering his question. "I'm searching for something, someone rather. Being a lone woman in the Outlands isn't easy. My travels are constantly interrupted. Let's just say the potency of many a man was in question after I stopped them from taking advantage of me." She smiled.

Liam suspected there was more to it, but he did not press. He liked her. The others were kind and respectful, but she was the first to treat him like an adult, and he liked that.

Liam realized the others were having a serious discussion and listened in.

"I'm telling you," said Nathan, "we should scout Bronton and see what exactly is going on there."

Ever since Callianeira had joined their company, the detour to Bronton had been a hot debate. Her presence was tenuous at best, Charis having come to her defense against Dorian whose over-suspicion cast a certain tension among the group. It was agreed that Callianeira could travel with them, but that if they decided against going to Bronton, she could abandon her destination and stay with them, or travel on her own again. Nathan had accepted Callianeira by the fact that he was a proponent of stopping in Bronton. He seemed to lend credence to Callianeira's suggestion that there might be something or someone of use there. However, her attempts to be specific had been mystifying at best. She said they would find someone with answers.

"There's no time," said Dorian. "We go to Mere, and if Callianeira wants to go get this person herself and bring him to us, that's fine by me."

"Oliver seemed to think Raven was really up to something," said Charis. "Ignoring it could cost us more than time in the long run."

"I really wasn't looking forward to going alone," Callianeira said. "We should all go."

They looked puzzled at her adamant tone, but Dorian sighed, "It appears I'm out-voted. Bronton it is."

# CHAPTER TWENTY

## *The Survivor*

Callianeira ran her fingers down her neck's smooth skin, knuckles brushing against soft, dark hair. Sometimes she could still feel the collar. She had again woken from her sleep, imagining a burden at her throat. No scars or marks indicated centuries of bearing the band, but its icy sensation lingered. She withdrew her hand and pulled the blanket to her chin, but no further sleep came. What did she see when she closed her eyes? Her former master's burning rage, the collar falling from her neck as she breathed freely for the first time, the faces of the men she had corrupted, her bloody and naked body emerging from the darkness.

There would be no sleep. Someone snored, the fire crackled, a faint wind persisted. Leaving her blanket and pack behind, she walked to the fire, the ground growing warmer on her bare feet as she neared it.

A sleeper rustled. By the shape, it was Liam. When the others had inadvertently ostracized her, Liam had talked to her, telling her his story. It was difficult to tell if he was humble or unaware of his abilities, but the young man was strong.

"Can't sleep?" asked a voice. Charis sat down.

"I can't remember the last time I slept well," said Callianeira. Charis didn't reply for a moment.

"You're brave, you know," said Charis. "Really. You went against your very nature, and at great costs."

Charis was so different from Callianeira. Where she was tan and rugged, Charis was fare and delicate. Where she was wry and cynical, Charis always seemed compassionate and hopeful.

"One day everything I had done and believed felt wrong," Callianeira said. "Yet, I often doubt if I should have left. I know you would be better off without me, but since I've been in the Outland, I've been lonely." Callianeira had thought herself calloused, too cynical and hardened to need the company of others. She certainly did not like the idea of being vulnerable, yet she relaxed as she confided in Charis. "I guess I've always been lonely, no matter my company. I can't ignore it like I did once, but I thought it would be easier. Doing the supposed right thing didn't change things as much as I thought it would. I was suddenly so uncertain."

Callianeira sensed that Charis's look of compassion was not one condescending pity, but rather true sympathy. It shamed Callianeira. "After the fall," said Charis, "I wanted to wrap up inside myself. I mean, I wanted to abandon responsibility and go die somewhere. I lost everything because I took orders from a liar, and I couldn't have back what I lost. The world has come and gone, the prophecies are over, and nothing but a small sliver of hope remains. I'm no warrior, but I fight anyway. I don't fight for the innocent. I fight for those like you. Like us, really. It is those given a second chance who have the greatest potential to act."

It was a peaceful thought, but almost too idealistic. After a quiet moment, Charis rubbed Callianeira's shoulder and then quietly left, returning to her blanket. Callianeira sat by the fire a little longer. Clouds, ushered by the unusual winds, moved in the distance. Lightening flickered in the desert night. Clouds would cover the sky once again by the morning. The campfire's embers burned low, hardly brighter than starlight. Callianeira watched the fire die, and after a time, the sun rose.

The clouds came again, promising a second rain, a rare phenomenon in Outland. Nathan rightly deemed it unnatural.

In the first ghost-town, char crept up every structure, leaving nothing but death in the gray dusk. The ash flitted upward, winding its way into the breeze until it dissipated into the gloom. A drizzle began, doing little to cleanse the black and smoldering pillars of buildings long given to the flames. The grave of a town extended from one end to the other, but no person or body could be found. Charis grew upset, and that regal face shed tears, something Callianeira would have never imagined. The town had been called Lavyn.

When next they arrived in Shima, Liam spoke little, as if haunted by memories at which she could only guess. She learned a little of his unfortunate tenure there, regarding the false priest who could turn into a crocotta and his little box. Unlike Lavyn, most of Shima's buildings stood intact, except for the occasional broken door or window. Other than the occasional blood smear, no evidence of humanity lingered save for the sweet, metallic, and acrid smell of decay. Callianeira helped the others scavenge supplies before they settled in and stayed the night. Liam's obvious discomfort drove them from the place early the next morning.

"Where did they all go?" Callianeira asked, her horse plodding alongside the others' camels.

"I don't think they left alive," Dorian said. From the smell of Shima, he might be right.

"It could be abominations," Charis said.

"If they had abominations," Callianeira said, "they'd be out of control, crawling all over those towns, probably out here too."

"If not abominations. It's something else," said Dorian. "Bronton's next and I'm starting to suspect that you were right to suggest we go there."

Bronton was the worst of all. Though the rain had been brief and the clouds receded, the somber canter of the weather remained. Callianeira left her horse with the camels on the edge of town and they walked among Bronton's smoldering ruin. Any ash not dampened by the earlier rain floated under the light wind, gray flecks drifting in the light of the sinking sun. Burned and black frames of crumbling houses and stores hunched over the scorched desert ground. Dusk came. It felt colder as they walked among the ghostly main strip of town. The black remnants loomed in the growing darkness and the smell of smoke reminded Callianeira of things passed. She ignored the memories. "Looks like someone's been playing with matches again," she said. It wasn't funny, but she had to say something to manage her emotions. Sarcasm was her habitual mechanism. No one laughed.

Dusk faded into night, the stars and moon casting a faint light. Dorian led the way, a blue flame glowing from his outstretched palm. Occasionally one of the company would peer into a charred structure.

"There's nothing here," said Nathan. "It's empty just like Lavyn and Shima."

"These seems more desolate," Liam said. "What happened to this place? It feels wrong." Callianeira put a hand on the hilt of her sword.

"You're right. Something is wrong," said Dorian.

The ship at the end of the road was the most mysterious thing. Unlike everything else in the town, it was unburned. It sat half-buried in the sand, cocked to one side, a long trench behind it running into the darkness. It was as if it had sailed the sands to settle here and be left behind. Dorian was right. Something felt wrong. The burnt smell had another scent to it. Was it decay? The rustling sound from among the town broke the silence. Callianeira drew her sword with the others. Nathan motioned for them to group together. They clustered with their backs to the ship. Dorian stood, his stone eyes flicking about the remains, searching. Though she expected Liam to fall back behind the protection of the others, he stood at the forefront, blade ready.

The silhouettes of the buildings ran jagged below the starry sky, slate ash-flakes glided in the acrid air, and silence perpetuated the tension. A pale white thing, a glimpse of a ghost, darted between buildings. Something cried out in the night, a terrible howl reverberating throughout the darkness. Then they came.

It thumped behind them, followed by more jumping from the ship. They poured out of alleys, rushing on the company. The things ran, pasty white with blue and black veins spidering around their uncovered bodies, wounds exposing organs. Some had burns or rotten black scars running along their skin. They lacked genitals, androgynous abominations coming upon them.

The tiger attacked first, Nathan slashing wildly at the oncoming creatures. Dorian stabbed and hacked with his sword, wielding flame at intervals. Callianeira took on those that had jumped from the ship. One was hairless and missing an eye, fiercely slashing a serrated bone. She stepped back, evading the weapon, bringing her sword down. Her blade drove into the shoulder and through the chest with sickening ease. The revenant fell to the ground in a pile of dead organs and black blood. She pivoted and downed two others with blows from her blade. More hands reached out and she cut at them. Weapons of bone shattered under her blade, howls of bloodlust and anger came at her.

There was a moment of respite before the next wave. Breathing hard, she propped up on her knees with hands splattered by dark red blood. A few yards away, the tiger spilled the intestines of a remaining creature. Liam's sword pierced the ribcage of another.

A breath later, the abominations burst forth again in horrifying numbers and she emerged from her rest, striking them down.

The blood and bodies turned the ground to mud. She swung her sword, missing her target. Under the strike's momentum, she slipped, falling amongst the rot and entrails. Then they were upon her. Cold hands groped her legs and arms, and pulled her hair. She tried to scream but her breath caught. They fought to tear at her. Something bit her leg and her shriek came. She kicked, its teeth scraping as it jerked back. She would not be overtaken. Not like this, but their grips held her. A foot slammed into her sword hand, the mud softening the impact, but excruciating all the same. Among the pain, the sickening smell, and the groping, she could only think that she was stronger than this. One broke the circle of tugging and leapt on top of her. Its knee jabbed into her groin and she screamed again. It closed its undead fingers on her neck and leaned in with exposed sharp teeth hissing. She looked into its black eyes and knew fear.

A blade separated its head. It rolled onto her chest. The groping hands loosened and she fought free pushing the dead thing off. Charis spun and slashed, striking the abominations down with fierce grace. Callianeira recovered, her sword hand aching, but she fought on, back-to-back with Charis.

When it was over, Callianeira's breathing softened, her adrenaline fading to pain and exhaustion. She stumbled among the bodies and joined the others away from the carnage. She trembled from fatigue as she sat in the dirt next to Liam. The black blood that covered him shocked her, but she knew she was also tarred by the gore. Liam sat straight-backed, as if trying to remain strong, but the young man shook. She put a comforting hand on his shoulder, but he continued to stare, jaw clenched.

Liam was likely the only person present who had no idea of what he had just faced. "Abominations," she said, calling them by the best translation of a word she dared not utter. Liam didn't look to her, but she knew he listened. "Up until Jacob's war, they hadn't been used for thousands of years. No one has been that desperate. They're tedious to harvest, impossible to control, and morbid. It didn't stop Jacob from giving them a try two hundred years ago, and the results were catastrophic. He soon learned that nothing he could do would control them and much of what was lost is because of it."

"We should have seen this coming," Nathan said, returned to human form. Like the others, his injuries appeared minimal compared to Callianeira. Charis came to her and began to tend the bite on her leg.

"You don't want an infection," she said. "There are few pains worse."

"I suspected abominations," said Dorian, "but never that they'd be capable of a surprise attack."

"Most foul," said Nathan. "Should we check for more?"

"I don't relish the thought of dealing with these things any more than we have to," said Dorian, "but he harvested them somewhere. Calli, you're injured. You look a bit dazed, Liam. You two want to stay here?" She nodded and Liam did as well.

"If I may stay as well," Charis said. "I will see to their wounds."

Liam sat quietly and Charis continued to tend Callianeira's wound. Charis dressed the shallow bite with ease before minding Callianeira's aching hand. Dorian and Nathan returned a few minutes later.

"You should see this," said Dorian.


The shack was the only thing other than the ship left unburned. Inside, a metal hatch took up the small floor-space.

"What do you think is in there?" asked Callianeira.

"I'm almost sure it's where they harvested those things" said Dorian. "But I have a feeling Jacob and the others are far from here."

"There's only one way to find out," said Nathan, gripping the handle. He looked to see if anyone would stop him. Callianeira stepped back behind Dorian, sword at the ready but too exhausted to be much use in another fight. Nathan opened the hatch to a dark descent down concrete stairs.

Callianeira went last, following Dorian's blue light down the narrow stairwell. Soon the blue light grew as the stairs ended and the corridor opened into a giant cavern. The light did not belong to Dorian. Empty tanks glowing cerulean stretched throughout the cavern with a single path between them. As Callianeira followed the others down the pathway, she lost count of the tanks around the eighteenth row, distracted by the black and twisted throne at the end.

"This is Raven's work," said Nathan.

"Over here," Charis called. She had gone beyond the malformed throne and found a door, old and wooden, a faint light running along the crack at the bottom. A muffled, raspy female voice sang behind it.

Dorian looked at the others and motioned for them be silent and ready to fight. He kicked the door and it broke free, swinging open. A hiss came from the room and Dorian rushed in, sword first.

A man lay chained to a stone table. The two grotesquely pale women hunched over him straightened and glared at the intruders before attacking. One jumped with a hiss and Dorian cut her down, dark blue blood spraying on the walls. Another lunged and he decapitated it with ease, head thudding to the concrete floor with an unusual squish. Abominations were not supposed to be sentient. Had she imagined the singing? They entered the room, stepping over the corpses.

"Those were not normal abominations," observed Charis.

"She was singing until we interrupted," said Nathan. "Abominations don't talk. They don't think. Sure as hell don't sing."

"They don't," said Dorian. "This is something different. This man has been tortured, methodically." If Dorian guessed more, he didn't elaborate.

Charis looked to the man on the table. As he took shallow, rapid breaths, his green eyes stared widely into nothing. Though shirtless, yellow sweat stained what clothes he wore, and from the smell he lay in his own excrement. Multiple wounds festered at his torso, some poorly stitched, others infectiously gaping.

"Poor soul," said Nathan. "He's been down here for some time."

"I doubt he could recover from this," Dorian said. "I'm surprised the man's lasted this long. Is there anything you can do to ease his passing?" He looked to Charis.

"Please," said Callianeira. Dorian looked to her, cocking his head, questioning. "He can't die," she added weakly. This was what had brought her to Bronton, both a hope that this man on the table would either validate her decision to leave everything behind or confirm this a farce.

"There might be hope for this one," said Charis, glancing at Callianeira.

"If this man is broken," said Dorian, "it will mean serious trouble."

When Nathan moved a finger in front of the man's face, his eyes followed.

The man grunted, as if trying to plea through motionless lips. She cringed at his sallow tone.

"Look," said Dorian, "we don't have a way to get him to Mere, and even if we did, I doubt he'd survive the journey."

"He can ride with me," said Callianeira. What was she saying? She was going to share a saddle with a dying man who smelled of shit and death? "I will tend to him," she added.

"And I will help," Charis said. While Callianeira was prepared to undertake this task herself, she appreciated the aid and solidarity.

"I have to admit, Dorian," Nathan said, "there's something about him. I say we give it a chance."

"I don't like it," Dorian said, "but I suppose this is what we came here for. We need to get him cleaned up as much as we can before we leave town. When we searched the ship earlier, we found medical supplies that might be useful. You know where those are, Nathan. Will you grab them and anything else that's useful? Callianeira, you'll need water to get him cleaned up. If I help, we can probably get enough for our camp and to fill our canteens."

It took some time to unchain the man and carry him up the stairs. He was heavy with muscle and slippery from the sweat and blood. Callianeira ran ahead and brought her horse over so they wouldn't have to carry the man all the way through the town. She led the horse near the ship, spread her blanket on the ground, and with help from Dorian and Nathan, laid the man on it. Charis began to see to the wounds while Nathan went to the ship to find anything useful. Liam offered to help, but Callianeira could tell the whole night had disturbed him and did not want to exacerbate it. She commissioned him to make a fire, figuring it would be an easy distraction.

Dorian went to the other end of the ship, to the site of the battle. He began to pile the bodies a little farther away. It was not long before a cool blue flame arose, smoke trailing away on the wind, and Dorian returned.

"Once down, I've not known abominations to come back," he said gesturing toward the now cremating corpses, "but we can't risk it, not when these are so different from what we know." He stood back and watched as Callianeira and Charis tended to the man. His eyes were closed, and Charis cleaned one of the many wounds.

"They broke a collar bone and these cuts were deliberately placed," Charis said. "Calli, they tortured him. This may be bad."

She looked to Charis. "Dorian said himself that this is why we came here. I'll explain more as we go, but this man is why I gave up the life I had. We have to try."

She helped Charis pull off the man's soiled clothes, revealing his maimed body. The women had tortured him in every way possible. After cleaning most of the excrement off of the man, they were tending his wounds when Nathan looked over the deck of the ship. "I found some medical supplies, blankets, and a good bathing tub."

Nathan brought down the amenities and Dorian went to the well to get water. It was hard work, but when they were done Callianeira suggested that the others retire. "You've all done enough. I can take care of the rest."

Dorian joined Liam by the fire and together they heated some water for the tubs. Having found decent wood among the wreckage, a campfire blazed. Charis continued to help, though Callianeira had gone through great lengths to let Charis go if she wanted. For a time Nathan helped and they worked well into the night. They warmed water and bathed him and dressed his wounds. Discarding Callianeira's soiled blanket, they wrapped him in a fresh blanket taken from the ship, placing the man close to the fire.

When Charis and Nathan went to bed, Callianeira bathed herself. A single trip to the well was exhausting, and she took a cold bath, too tired to bother with warming the water. She finished, tossing most of her clothes and dawning her backup outfit. She did not join the others in sleep. Rather she sat up next to the man, warming by the fire. Though still pale and feverish, shivering at times, he seemed to be resting at more peace than before. She reached over and ran a hand through his hair. In the firelight it was a dark red, almost auburn. Now cleaned up, he was handsome. She knew him, though he did not know her.

Callianeira awoke to a moan in the night, heart beating as she searched for the coming abominations. Her heart continued to pound, even after she realized that the sounds came from the man. She sat up and looked over at him. Beneath his sweating brow, his eyes moved with a new lucidity. "Sword," he croaked.

That got her attention. "Drink some water," she said, putting the canteen to his lips. "You still have it?" she asked. After all this time, she thought that sword long lost. If nothing else, Jacob would have taken it with him.

"No," he said when he finished drinking. "On ship... second cabin..." He closed his eyes.

She did not want to leave his side, nor did she like the idea of searching the ship at night. His remaining effects were likely gone altogether, yet her curiosity bettered her reservations and she stood, stretching as she eyed the vessel. It took a few moments to find and climb the rope ladder Nathan had used to mount the ship.

Much like Dorian she could produce a light to guide her. After emitting a soft amber flame in her hand she surveyed the wooden deck of the vessel. Though Nathan claimed to have searched the ship well, she navigated with caution around the mast and down into the belly. It was a large ship with several living quarters. The second cabin was a simple room with a single bed, a night stand, and an unlit lantern. She burned her light a little brighter. No sword. There was a pack, which might belong to the man, so she shouldered it. Without success, she looked behind the door and dresser for any type of blade. It was only when she went through the trouble of peering under the bed that she found it.

338

Her fingers felt the cold blade and careful not to cut herself she worked her hand down to the hilt. She gripped and dragged the immense sword from under the bed. Though not heavy, it was cumbersome due to its length. A harness accompanied it, made to strap it to one's back. When she got back to the deck she attempted a better look at the blade.

She knew the man had been in Jacob's company, so Jacob was aware of the blade, and wouldn't leave without such a treasure in his possession. Did Jacob really not think to look under the bed? A startling figure interrupted her inspection.

"Running about at night?" Dorian asked.

"Walking really," she said. "You know. A casual evening stroll."

"With a big sword?"

"A girl can't resist." She realized she must look suspicious. "It's not mine. The man woke for a moment and spoke of it. Here, you hold onto it." She laid it on the ground, hoping the gesture would prove her innocence.

He approached with caution and picked it up. "I suppose it doesn't make a difference," he said, looking over the blade. "After all you have a sword of your own. If it's all same, I'd like to take a closer look at it."

"Sure," she said, though she wanted a closer look too. If Dorian knew its origins, he may suspect her even more.

He started to walk away.

"Dorian," she said stopping him. He turned. "I'm sorry for your home. For Gipar, for Soni and Abriel. For all of it."

He gave a short nod and jumped from the side of the ship. She had known Dorian a long time, having been at odds with him more than once. She could not blame him for his mistrust, but things had changed. Though he could not know now, she hoped he would come to learn. He was a good man and might even be able to help her, give her some direction. She took the rope-ladder down.

Back at the camp, she went to tell the man that the sword was safe, but he slept. She searched the pack, relieved to find clothes. She had not been looking forward to sharing a horse with a sick man wearing nothing more than a blanket. She also discovered a bottle of a brown liquid, which upon smelling she found to be rum. She took a gulp and set it aside. Other than a blanket, she discovered little else. Though Nathan had recovered more blankets from the ship, she decided to use the one from the man's pack. It smelled well-used but pleasant and she laid with her back to the man, feeling his occasional shiver, hoping she was doing the right thing.

As the sun peered over the horizon, Callianeira awoke from a fitful sleep. Charis was the only other person awake and she was attending to the man. Callianeira wet her throat, emptied her bladder, and returned to help Charis. "He's already looking better. Faster than I would expect" Charis said quietly. "Pigment is returning, the wounds seem to be healing, and his fever should break soon. Travel will be hard on him. What he really needs is rest. I wouldn't have said anything so optimistic last night, but he possesses an unexpected resilience."

In the rising sun Callianeira took her first real look at him. He was muscular, and in addition to his recent wounds, seemed to bear multiple older scars. His thick auburn hair was not long, but wavy and a little wild, giving way to a lighter-colored beard. Charis placed the blanket back over him. "Now," she said, "We need to figure out the situation with you two sharing a horse."

The man stirred. "Sword," he said in a dry voice.

Charis gave him water.

"We have it," Callianeira said, "It's safe."

The man fell back out of consciousness. Charis gave her a puzzled look.

"Last night," Callianeira said. "He did the same thing and gave a cabin number of the ship. I found his pack and sword there." She showed Charis his things, except the sword, explaining that she had given it to Dorian. They fit the man with his extra set of clothes and then repacked Callianeira's horse, redistributing some of her supplies among the camels.

"This is going to slow us down no matter what," Charis said, "but I think the horse can handle both of you."

The others soon woke and they shared a small breakfast. By the second hour of sunlight they had all mounted. Their detour concluded, they made east for Mere. Callianeira shared her horse, the man slumping in front of her. It was uncomfortable and she did not welcome the extra body heat, but she was determined to endure it. After the first hour she had gotten somewhat used to it.

"What exactly is Mere?" she had asked.

"My city," replied Charis. "It is a place of peace. If this man makes it there, he will find much healing."

They rode towards Mere, the best fortified city in the Outlands outside of Novum itself. The walls were of rock and mortar. If any other town boasted the fortune of being fortified, it was with rusted chain-link fencing or scrap metal. The company approached the city and a resounding horn bellowed from within. The townspeople welcomed them in celebration and Callianeira had difficulty taking it in. Everything from the skin color to dress varied. This was a melting pot, but also a harmonious tapestry of culture. Vivid lavenders, blues, reds, and oranges streamed from fabrics, flowers, and buildings. The place was alive, organic.

Servants helped her and the man from her horse. A tall and slender gentleman embraced Charis. He greeted Dorian and Nathan like old friends. Charis led him over as Callianeira unsaddled her pack. He leaned on a cane as they made their way a few steps over.

Charis introduced him as Oliver. When Charis identified Callianeira, she didn't do so with any apprehension. Charis had been nothing but graceful, but all the same, Callianeira expected some level of suspicion now that they were in her beloved city. *This is Callianeira, the demon, the bane of our existence since she started steering the hearts of good men down the wrong path.* But there was no hint of that. Had she been accepted by Charis truly and wholly?

"Call me Calli," she said to Oliver shaking his hand. He smiled but his attention turned to the man.

"It's a pleasure, and who is this?" he asked as two men moved the man to a stretcher.

"We don't know," said Charis. "All will be explained."

Charis arranged for the man to be taken to the infirmary and guarded. She then led the others through the winding streets. Traditional hard-packed sand lined some of the thoroughfare, but stone paved some of the others. Foreign smells, simultaneously sweet and spicy, piqued her hunger.

Callianeira, awestruck by the mansion, stood for a moment, mouth gaping at the thing of worlds past. It was a building of old wood, like an elegant aged tree. She had not seen such architecture since before her fall and she longed for the days of columns and domed ceilings. They gathered in what appeared to be the living room. Light poured through the stained glass, giving the room a multicolored warm glow. Dark wooded tables and stands accompanied the fine, plush seating. Callianeira plopped down upon a loveseat, sinking into its cushions with the convalescence for which she had longed. Her fingers rubbed the velvety material and she thought she might nap even though she did not feel tired.

Charis called for everyone's attention, "Before we get down to business, I believe we should get settled in. Servants will show you to your rooms, where you can leave your things. There is a bathhouse down the way, if you care to go through the trouble, otherwise baths will be drawn here." Charis gave a sniff and added, "I don't care where you bathe, so long as you do it." Charis looked around the room with a warm smile. "Afterward there will be a meal. We've been so busy getting here, we've barely had time to catch up like people who haven't seen each other in two hundred years. That's not to mention the new faces."

The servants went about helping everyone to their room but Charis approached Callianeira. "Our stranger is not forgotten," she said. "I am having my healers look at him and then take him to the baths where I will help you see to him. You could probably use a little medical attention and would do well to join me."

Inside a building of arches and pillars holding up a high ceiling, Charis led her beside a large cistern of steaming water and into a narrow hallway. "That," said Charis pointing behind them, "is the public room. There are smaller private rooms, usually reserved for those in specific need of their healing properties. Here we are."

Their private room contained three small pools, each about six feet long and three feet wide. The man was already in one, laying unconscious, the water coming up to his shoulders and his head laying on a towel on the edge. He was naked save for a single garment covering his manhood. The night they had found him she had seen most of his body, so it was nothing new, but it felt different to see him so refreshed and peaceful while almost naked. The two attendants who had been watching him left the room.

"If you want to go ahead and get in one of the baths, I think you'll find it just the thing you need," Charis said. Callianeira hesitated. "Just relax and I'll be with you in a minute," Charis added.

Callianeira removed her clothes. Anything that had been white was yellow from sweating in the desert heat and they smelled musty. She piled them in a corner with her boots and put a toe in one of the unoccupied pools. It was hot, but not unbearable, and as she slipped her entire body into the steaming water she felt overcome with relief. The dull thud of pain in her hand and leg wound dissipated. The soreness of battle and sharing a saddle left her muscles. As the heaviness in her chest lifted, she began to breath in peaceful bliss.

Charis faced away, hands working at the man's wounds. Her dress revealed her shoulders and the customary tattooed sigil. After a few minutes Charis turned her attention to Calli. Her hands were gentle, and whenever she worked at something painful, she would distract Callianeira with small talk. "If it wasn't for these baths," Charis said pressing on the bite mark, "it might take this man months to recover. Now he might wake within the week and soon gain some mobility." Charis's touch was firm, painful before a numbness spread. Charis lifted her hands, revealing a faint mark on Callianeira's skin where the wound had been.

"What I can't do," Charis continued, massaging Callianeira's hand, "is fix his mind. Let's hope they didn't break him. There," she said, letting Callianeira's hand fall. "I will bring you some soap and you can get cleaned up. I'll have servants bring you new clothes. There's a shop a couple of blocks away that does your style. We can get your measurements later and have some outfits properly tailored."

"I don't know what to say, Charis. You've been so kind. I caused so much trouble for you in Camira."

"I suspected as much," Charis said, "but that is not my realm anymore. This is my world now, and you are here, and I believe you mean to help."

"I'm sorry all the same."

"Whatever there has been between us in the past is forgiven."

"Thank you."

Charis left and returned with soap, servants trailing her with fresh clothes. One of the men glanced shyly, setting a change of clothes on a dry windowsill. Callianeira smirked at him and raised an eyebrow. He blanched, turning his head, and helped the other servant pull the Bronton man from the pool. They strained as they lifted him onto a gurney. They wheeled him out, Charis following them with a kind farewell, and leaving Callianeira to finish bathing in privacy.

The clothes fit rather well. They were simple and modest which she liked. Though her days of seduction were over, she liked to flatter her body. The pants fit the curve of her slim waste and the shirt was not too tight or billowy. It draped over her breasts and muscular body, complimenting her form without exposing too much of it. She put on her boots and found her way back to the mansion.

Everyone else had finished bathing and dressing about the same time, and they lounged in the living room in casual conversation. Nathan had brushed his hair and trimmed his beard, looking less wild. In fact, he reminded her of someone, but who? Sitting in a chair, Dorian had discarded his customary trench coat, now wearing clean and casual clothes. The rest sported similar attire, more suitable for normal living and not desert travel.

A servant offered her a glass of beer and she accepted. It reminded her of some beers she had tried long ago on a mission in France.

It took some time, but soon everyone had situated. Charis, Dorian, Liam, Oliver, Nathan, and Callianeira all sat in the same room, appearing equally hungry and tired.

"Well," said Dorian, looking somewhat commanding in a large chair, "We all made it, and it seems we picked up a few along the way. Now that we're not so busy, I think it's important that we get on the same page before anything else. While we wait for the meal, shall we begin with Oliver?"

Oliver was tall and slim, almost lanky, but not awkward. He stood, leaning on his cane, and spoke, "It's hard to know where to start. While Charis was away, I had time to inspect and ready the militia. Commander Mari has done a more than efficient job with the soldiers. There are several points on which we will most likely have an advantage on Jacob and whatever army he might gather. Also thanks to Commander Mari, we have a camelry. Even if Jacob has a cavalry, it's likely he will use horses, which in my opinion, are inferior. Second, we have trained fighters. From what I understand, these creatures—the abominations—provide their own set of obstacles, but competence in battle is not one of them. He will surely have us in numbers, but not in skill. Do not mistake me. His numbers far outweigh ours, a problem we'll have to address as we plan."

He talked more at length. It was not that he was uninteresting, but rather Callianeira found little of it relevant to herself, and her stomach growled. She let her eyes wander the room as she sipped her beer. Liam looked bored and Charis preoccupied. Only Dorian and Nathan gave Oliver their full attention. They exchanged talk about the coming war, regarding Jacob's tactics, and before long, supper was announced by a servant. "It's about time," Callianeira said, her usual levity returning.

A similar conversation continued over the meal, but she was distracted by the lavish food. Gravy, seitan, and ale to match.

"What do you think, Calli?" a voice asked. She looked up, Nathan had asked her a question.

"About what?" she asked.

"About the man," he said.

"Oh," she said and paused a moment in thought. This was not the time to tell her story. "I don't think we can know anything until he wakes up."

"And whose side do you think he'll be on?" asked Dorian. "Should we keep him under lock and key?"

From someone who distrusted her as much as Dorian, it was likely a trick question, but she answered with honesty. "A man who has suffered at the hands of Jacob's undead is going to wake up ready to kill his saviors? I doubt it."

"What of the sword?" asked Dorian.

"Give it back," she said.

"Obviously," Dorian responded. "Assuming he won't use it against us. Assuming he can even use it."

Nathan laughed, "He just keeps it around to fool the ladies." Callianeira and Liam were the only ones who gave a chuckle. Not only had she made a similar joke, but had since seen the man naked when they tended his wounds, and it was hard to resist informing Nathan his error. "It's extraordinarily light for its size," she commented.

"That it is," said Dorian with a ponderous look, missing the innuendo. He might have said more, but went back to his dinner. If he knew the sword's origins, he might know that Callianeira was more involved than he could have guessed.

The meal continued with more discussion. Liam described the food in the City and how it was bland and overly healthy. As it turned out, Charis's cuisine was inspired mostly by Asian culinary arts, even if this particular meal was reminiscent of Southern Comfort Food from the United States. Interestingly, the whole city was vegetarian. After the plates were removed more talking and planning bored Callianeira and she excused herself.

Charis's mansion was beautiful. She wandered the greenhouse gardens, the sun room, and library. It was in the sun room that she found the piano. She rubbed her fingers on the ivory key, longing to strike a note, to feel the vibration resonate. *Not today.*

# CHAPTER TWENTY-ONE

## *Getting Lost*

Liam survived the desert, Sol, Raven and the abominations. Charis had worked her wonders on his arm a week ago, and though the fight with the abominations had exacerbated it, Mere's baths brought full healing. The remaining scar was another memento of his time in Outland, one wound after another leaving him stronger once it healed. Rejuvenated, Liam explored Mere.

Stepping off of a waste bin, he shimmied a pipe up to the roof, careful not to touch the surface as it baked in the hot sun. Skipping across two rooftops, he pulled himself onto a tree branch, navigating further to a series of arches and ledges up to the bell tower. He scaled its rigid wall, resting once he reached the top, taking in the view. The structure was the tallest in Mere, overshadowing the intricate sculptures and stonework, its crenels accented by lions on all four corners. He found them unsettling at first, but as he spent more time atop the tower, they became more like companions than threats. Their stone faces were terrible, regal, and compassionate all at once. He fought the impulse to ring the bell and instead sat at the tower's edge, cooler in the shadow of the massive bell. He had been to the highest point of the City once.

"Are you sure about this?" he had asked Perry. Their escapades about the City seldom led to anything dangerous, yet this felt precarious. They had taken the elevator as high as security would allow and entered into a corridor. "Confidence is the key," Perry said. "As long as you look like you know what you're doing people will assume you belong. If we pass anyone, just act natural. Confident."

"Maybe for you," Liam said. "But they might recognize me. They know I'm not supposed to be here."

"All the more reason to act confident. Trust me."

The corridor wound around the building, one side belonging to the various rooms and offices of the Central Tower, the other side a window to the City. They seemed so close to the apex of pyramid's sloping wall, its windows close, but clouded by age. Around a curve, their outside view ceased and a wall began. Perry led them to a door, as Liam glanced from side to side, watching for anyone.

"You ready?" said Perry, looking at Liam with his bright green eyes.

Perry swung the door wide. "Come on," Perry said, ducking out into the open air.

Liam nervously stuck his head out from the door and saw that Perry hung on a ladder that led up the side of the building.

"You've got to be crazy," said Liam.

"Look, there's a carabiner and some rope," said Perry. "It's for the maintenance guys. It doesn't look like it's been used in a while, but it should be safe. Hook it to your belt and then hook it on as you go, and if you fall it will catch you." Perry began to climb the ladder. Liam took in a breath and followed.

The city sprawled below, stretching to the four corners. Buildings, apartments, the train, and the gardens intertwined and festered below him. The sight was dizzying, and he turned his attention upward as he continued the climb, hooking the carabiner to each rung as he went, less and less sure of the old rope, as he ascended. They passed another two doors.

"Shouldn't we be at the top? I thought there were only two more floors," said Liam shakily grabbing another rung.

"Two more floors that you know of," replied Perry.

He could see now that the building sloped at the top, like the pointed end of a rocket. Various antennae jutted from the peak. They came to a strip of windows that ringed the top and the ladder ended. The door to the top floor was locked, but a nearby broken pane let them in. Shaking, Liam pulled himself in. They walked around the room, glass crunching under their feet. Liam studied the scene, shocked by the massive amounts of blood near the broken window. There was something inauspicious about it and Liam wanted to leave.

"Come on, Perry," he said. "We've seen it. Now, let's go."

Perry lit a cigarette and casually walked away from the dried blood. He sat against the glass, his back to a fall of several thousand feet. There was nowhere else to sit, so Liam, also attempting to impress his friend, sat next to him.

"Do you know how thick this glass is?" asked Perry.

Liam shook his head.

"This is less than an inch thick," Perry said passing the cigarette, "but it's also some of the strongest stuff in the world."

"How do you know?" asked Liam. He took a drag from the cigarette and coughed. He regretted it every time he tried to smoke.

"All of the windows in this building are made out of the same kind of glass. It's even stronger than bulletproof glass."

"Why would you need bulletproof glass?" asked Liam. "Guns are only in the movies."

"It doesn't matter," said Perry. "The point is that this is strong stuff and it's broken."

"I'm sure there's a perfectly reasonable explanation," said Liam.

"Which is why you're so eager to leave? Because it's probably nothing? The blood is just a coincidence?"

"So, what do you think it is?" asked Liam.

"It could be anything. I heard once that if you sit in the dark with two mirrors while holding a candle that you can talk to the spirits."

"That's nonsense," said Liam.

"Perhaps, but think of all that was lost from the war. For all we know, people did it all the time," said Perry.

"You obviously haven't been coming to lessons with Master Ferrith," said Liam. "Besides, that doesn't explain this."

Perry cocked his head, putting the cigarette to his lips again before answering. "The lessons are boring. I want to hear about the angels and wars. All he wants to talk about are dead leaders, prewar culture, and sword fighting." Perry tossed the butt of the cigarette against the door. "All I'm saying is that there are lost things he doesn't know about. Whatever did this knows something no one else here knows."

"I thought you liked the sword lessons," said Liam.

"I do," replied Perry, "but back then they had guns and bombs. What about those?"

"We're barely allowed the swords," Liam said. "And there simply aren't guns anymore."

"Maybe," said Perry.

"I see you found my favorite spot," a voice said, startling Liam from his memory. Liam turned to find Barker Stoke.

"You made it," Liam said, happy to see the priest who had helped him recover in Lavyn.

"I suppose I did," the priest said. "I was reluctant to leave my parsonage and I lament Lavyn's fate. I wonder if I should have been there. I cared for those people. But the work here has kept me occupied."

"I'm sorry to disturb you. I just like the view of the city from here. Is this your church now?" asked Liam.

"It is my parish now. It seems to have been without a minister for quite some time, so I am content to shepherd and maintain it." Barker looked over the city, eyes following the twisting and colorful roads. "I come up here to pray every day. So very long ago it was common for the church to be the highest point of a city, and the ministers would go to their bell towers to announce the hour and pray for the people."

Liam pushed away the bloody memory of the highest point of Novum. "What do you pray for?" he asked.

"I should think a boy of the City could tell me what I should pray for," replied Barker.

"I don't know," he said. "I've heard my grandfather pray. He prays for peace and compassion in the hearts of men. He prays for safety in the City. Then I hear other people pray. They pray for themselves."

"And what do you pray for?" asked Barker.

"I hardly ever pray," said Liam. "When I do, I try to be like my grandfather, but I don't really feel anything. It seems to me that we always pray for things that we end up doing ourselves. Why do you pray?"

"Hope," the priest answered.

He left the priest to himself. The man was kind and patient, but Liam still felt guilty interrupting his routine. The tepid boy from Novum was disappearing and he thought that he would have made Perry proud. He maneuvered the rooftops and alleys with boldness, and stopped in at the first tavern he could find. Unlike the unpredictable bartering standards in the Outlands, Charis's city boasted a currency system, out of which she allowed Liam and the others a generous per diem. With little else to spend it on, Liam found fine food and beverages his preferred expenditure. He found that in Mere he did not have to reconcile his cognitive dissonance over eating once living beings. In Novum, animals were things meant to be preserved, and meat was lab grown. Most in the Outland didn't seem to think twice about butchering an animal and eating them. He wasn't sure what he thought about it, but it was easier to eat food that comforted his conscience, and Mere provided just that.

Welcome to Goose's Wild," the burly barkeep said. "It's a penny a pint. Minimum of two drinks. We got a red, brown, and sour. Your pick."

Liam had learned the hard way that he did not like sours, though when he had said as much, Dorian gave him a pitied look and claimed that sour ales, like the bitterness of hops, were an acquired taste. Liam ordered the amber and the barkeep set the frothing mug in front of him. "Eyes off Aster, son."

Of course, Liam had not missed the young barmaid skipping from table to table, drinks and food in hand. She took orders with an infectious smile, carrying herself ladylike and confident. In the other towns, the men rarely showed the women respect, touching them inappropriately, cursing them when they took too long to bring drinks. The men here, even those that appeared most unsavory, spoke to Aster politely. Yet, she might have been the prettiest girl he had seen in the Outlands.

"Did you hear what I just said, boy?" The barkeep waved a hand at Liam, who shook himself from his lustful gaze and gave the barkeep a nod.

For the most part, Liam had other things on his mind. He had spent the days exploring Mere, a tangled city of alleys, shops, homes, gardens, and taverns. He made it his goal everyday to get lost and then work his way back to the mansion. By this method he found the most interesting and often quite beautiful places. The multi-tiered complex of stained glass, wood carvings, vivid colors, and flowers never gave way to poverty or dilapidation. If there was anywhere in Outland that Liam had wanted to stay, it was Mere. It was a marvel that a single oasis in the desert could produce such life, but then the lake had been larger than he expected. Among the other bathers, Liam had dipped into the crystal clear water, the cold spring refreshing in the hot arid desert. Toward the center he could see the deep, reaching down into the unknown caves. That was day two when he had also talked with Dorian.

He had found him on the porch enjoying one of Charis's famous saisons, which Liam acquired as well as he sat next to Dorian, who gave him a nod, but said nothing. It seemed like a rather inopportune time, yet Liam had questions.

"It's a nice day out," Dorian said after a long pause.

Liam nodded. "It is," he said. "How much longer do you think we'll be here?"

"It's hard to say," Dorian said. "Jacob's man sleeps and he may have answers yet. We've guessed that Jacob has marched north, somehow finding his way into the Pass. A battle there would be hopeless. In the end, I figure we could potentially do more harm than good, just like we did last time."

"You always talk like that," said Liam.

"Like what?" asked Dorian.

"Like you've done some great wrong, and are scared you will do it again."

"We did do great wrong," Dorian replied.

"Oliver, Charis, and Nathan don't seem to feel guilt," said Liam.

"They aren't responsible. Or maybe they are and just hide their guilt," said Dorian lackadaisically.

"Then why try? Why even come all this way across the desert?" asked Liam.

"Because of who I am," said Dorian. "I may feel guilt for my failures and have fear of repeating them all over again, but I know my duty."

"I think everyone here knows their duty. At least, I think that I do. But will that be enough?"

Dorian raised an eyebrow, "It's funny. I lived for thousands of years as an angel and I was so sure of things. I had transcended the problem of evil and fought with valiant enthusiasm at the gates of hell. Two hundred years here and I don't know much of anything anymore."

*So this is what Oliver meant,* Liam thought.

"Is it enough, you ask?" asked Dorian, "Is it worth it?"

"You must think so," answered Liam. "You're here, after all."

"You're the boy from the City," said Dorian. "Is what's in there worth it?"

Liam thought about it. Even if Jacob had a way into the City, he would inevitably get bored and then it seemed unlikely that he would be content to let a place like Mere exist. If he had known about such a place, he would probably have marched on it first. While Oliver's criticisms of the City and its people were legitimate, even he thought they were worth saving. Of course they were. They had to be. Vines and flowers, vivid and bright, surrounded the lush patio. Without the threat of Jacob, the whole world might be restored to something like it. Perhaps that was bold optimism, but if nothing else, at least without the threat of Jacob, the world could wake from its stagnant state and grow anew.

"I think it is," said Liam. "If it's so hopeless, then we'll die either way, but at least we will die fighting. And if there's hope, even a little, then this is our chance to stop living in fear and grow again."

"You sound like Nathan," Dorian said with a sigh. "You sound like Oliver too but at least he says it with a little cynicism. Yet, you say it with refreshing humility, and despite my own doubts, I know that you speak true. These are sad times when someone as young as you has to wrestle with these questions, but the worst is yet to come, and it is good to have someone like you on our side."

"It is," said Charis as she stepped onto the patio.

"Welcome," said Dorian. "We were just discussing if this is all worth it, if it will be enough. The usual afternoon casual conversation."

Charis pulled over a chair and sat, her kind smile containing some subliminal joy. "Of course it is," she said.

"Normally," said Dorian, "hope is fleeting for me. I have to remind myself, and force myself to believe in it even when I don't want to. But your city instills it in me."

"The credit is not all mine," Charis said. "It's amazing what people can accomplish."

"You provided the tools and the motivation," Dorian said.

"I wonder," said Liam, "if the people of Novum could ever understand a place like this."

"They're human," said Charis. "They can."

Dorian tapped his fingers on the arm of his chair. "Don't let my fatalism get you down."

"You weren't always fatalist," Charis said. "We knew something during the war even if we didn't know we knew it. Hope is empty if it is vain. Our hope wasn't empty then, and it's not empty now."

"It's not," said Dorian, "but I can't put my finger on it. It all made sense from afar, when I was a god. Humanity is a peculiar thing. Humanity will force you to deconstruct."

"Then deconstruct your fatalism," Charis said. She met Liam's eyes, and he felt that she saw something in him. There was an excitement to her gaze, as if wrapped up in his humanity was the perfect gift.

"Fate is fate," said Dorian. "The cosmic chain reaction disseminates into our everyday lives, until our experiences dictate our most minuscule decisions."

"That's where humanity comes in," Charis said. "Fate makes a person the way they are, but they have the incredible ability to overcome it if they will it."

"Is that what hope is?" asked Liam. "The ability to fight our nature and circumstances?"

"Perhaps," said Charis. "I think it's what love is, and that hope is a byproduct of love."

"Tell me, Liam," said Dorian. "You're the human. Is she right?"

On the seventh day, Liam found Aster.

It was not that he had not noticed girls before, but now his confidence had changed. Not that the opposite sex didn't intimidate him as much as a crocotta. He kept his eyes down as she passed behind the bar and into the back. He had been quite successful at ignoring her until he heard the voice of a young woman. "Where'd you get the scar?" He looked up and she smiled at him.

He stammered a moment, regained his composure and with his best smile replied, "Crocotta."

She raised an eyebrow, her expression a mixture of respect and incredulity.

"No, really," he said, realizing the futility of trying to cover such a long scar down his arm.

Her flirtatious grin faded, her eyes going to something behind him.

"Who's this stranger?" a young man asked, sitting next to Liam.

"You leave him alone, Max Pike," she said, "We were just talking."

"Looked like more than that to me," Max said putting a firm hand on Liam's shoulder. He had two stout friends in tow to complicate the situation. Though he was armed and they were not, they either didn't notice his sword or they weren't intimidated by it. Were they really so protective of Aster that they would fight Liam over it? Liam resisted rolling his eyes.

"Aster," said Liam, holding his voice firm, "it has been a pleasure talking to you. I don't want any trouble, and these three gentlemen seem to take offense to our innocent exchange. Why don't you be on your way, I'll be on mine, and these guys can rest easy."

She gave him another smile before bustling away.

"Satisfied?" Liam asked.

"The hell I am," Max said. He stood, kicking a stool to the side.

Max swung, and Liam leapt from his own stool, grasping the seat to bring it around. It broke across Max's side, splinters sailing into the air. Max sank under the blow, grunted, and lunged. He gripped Liam around the waist, taking him to the ground. Max's friends made a charge, but two other bar patrons held them back and another tried to pry Max away. He resisted them and swung at Liam who blocked the punch and landed a blow of his own. The fat of his cheek rippled under Liam's fist and Liam felt something loosen under the hit. Max fell to the side, spitting out a tooth and blood. Liam climbed to his feet, standing before a silent room, the patrons staring at him in shock.

Without a word, he tossed three silver dollars on the bar, enough to cover the two drink minimum and a gratuity, and left the stunned patrons, slamming the rickety wooden door behind him. He stormed into the street, cheeks burning. He stepped into the alley, trying to still his shaking hands, wondering how much trouble he might be in. Surely they were just looking for a fight. They saw an outsider and thought he would be an easy target. Aster was all the excuse that they needed.

"I've never seen anyone stand up to Max like that," he heard Aster say. She stood in the alley, hand on her hip. She no longer wore the barmaid's dress, but a loose off-white shirt and dark pants.

"You shouldn't be here," he said.

"It's all right," she said. "I convinced them I needed to get some fresh air after all the excitement. They think I'm in one of the upstairs rooms. Are you okay?"

Liam calmed his breathing and wiped the sweat from his face. "Fine," he said. "I'm fine. I don't know what the hell their problem was. You should get back in there. I don't want you to lose money on my account."

"I tell you what," she said, twirling her blond hair between her fingers. "How about I be done for the day and you take me for a walk around the lake."

Liam chuckled, relaxing. "Okay," he said. "Anywhere but here." She went back inside for a moment, likely to let someone know she was done for the day and collect her tips, and returned a few minutes later. Though he knew the general direction of the oasis, it might have taken a half hour before he found it. Aster, however, having lived there her whole life, knew the quickest way and they arrived in half the time.

"So, you're the Aster they warned me about?" Liam asked.

"They're just overprotective and Max is jealous," she said. "He has emotional issues, and a bully turned protective lover-boy is a dangerous thing. Had I known he was there, I would have kept my mouth shut for your sake. You're not the first fight he's picked over me, for all the good it's done to try and stop him. You are the first fight he's lost. My boss says he's banned for good. Took him long enough."

They walked in silence for a moment before Liam changed the subject. "Tell me about yourself," he said, having little to talk about.

"Me? I've lived here my whole life. I'm not interesting. You're the stranger. Tell me, stranger, what brings you here? Tell me of the happenings in the world beyond. Tell me how you got that scar." She said it, not in an ignorant sort of way, but almost daring. Not only was she beautiful, blond haired and bright eyed, but the way she spoke was magnetizing. No wonder she was so guarded. Why had she decided to pursue him of all people?

Liam realized that he was no longer the lanky pale boy who had left the City, but a tan and hardened young man. To her, he must look the bold adventurer. He wanted to tell her of his fight with Sol, where he had gotten the scar, but thought better of it. They arrived at the small lake, and began to take the worn path around its clear blue waters. It was still but for the occasional ripple of a fish.

"You're lucky," said Liam. "Most towns have a well and can barely sustain a single crop. Some are bigger than others, but most no more than a few hundred people. You have the cold spring here and then the hot baths on the other side of town. That is quite the luxury."

"They say it's all Lady Charis," Aster said.

"What else do they say?" asked Liam.

"That far away the crocotta grow restless. The nomads are on the move, there's a reward for a boy from the City. The silly things men talk about." Liam felt uncomfortable at the thought. "Where does an exciting man like you stay in this city?"

"The mansion," he replied.

"You're staying in Lady Charis's mansion?" she asked.

"No," he lied. "I mean the inn next door. I can't remember the name."

"The Garden Saloon," she laughed, "It's easy to remember."

"You have pretty eyes," he said trying again to divert the subject from himself.

"And they tell me pretty everything else too, though they have to keep their hands to themselves," she said pulling Liam's arm around her waist. He forced himself to relax and smile casually, but the new feeling rose in him nervously.

"Come," she said. "There's some beautiful shade over here."

"I can't believe you've never kissed a girl before," she said after they parted lips. "You're good."

"Thanks," he said.

"I have something to confess," she said.

"Don't tell me you already have a boyfriend," Liam said with a smile.

"No," she said, her tone serious. "I have a habit of stealing."

"Should I check my pockets?"

"It's not like that. I collect memories from other people."

"Do you?" Liam asked.

She smiled then. "There are so many happy memories in the world. I want them all."

"Have I said anything worth keeping?" Liam asked.

She shook her head. "I haven't found the memory I want. Not yet. Alas, I think it's time for me to go. I'll have to get that memory some other time, sad boy." It didn't bother him that she called him a boy. He knew she meant it as a term of endearment. Night had come and with it a chill. He liked her taste, his arm on her side or his hand in her hair. He wanted more but resisted. Even if she would let him, he knew better. Nothing good could come of more. He would eventually leave this place.

Yet, he couldn't resist. "Let's go somewhere," he said. "I'll buy you a drink."

"Charming," she replied. "Alas, I will be missed. I can skip out on work, but not my family. I'd have you stay with us, but I doubt my father would approve. Kissing all afternoon and then staying the night. What would the neighbors think? No, I must be off." With a peck on his cheek she stood, brushing the grass and sand from her clothes. Liam got up as well.

"Farewell, Liam," she said. "Will I see you again?"

"I should hope so," he said. "Where can I find you?"

"The blue house, same street as the butcher's. I know where to find you."

"Well," he said, "then I'll see you again, Aster."

"I hope so," she replied, her fingers rubbing the scar on his forearm. The moon glowed in the night sky and Liam realized he had little concept of how to get back to the mansion. His clothes were light and with the lake, it got cooler than usual.

"This wasn't from a crocotta," she said with strange certainty.

"It kind of was," Liam replied. "But it's hard to explain."

"A man who can turn into a crocotta," she said. "Who ever heard of such a thing?"

Liam retracted his hand from hers. He had learned to control his fear, to resist panic, and to find the best way out of a situation. Yet, this was unknown. There was no barrier to break through, no beast to face, but rather an unfamiliar sort of danger. She might have been sent to lure him away, and as evening came, so would the trap. This world was so new to Liam that he figured she might turn into anything herself.

She took his hand back. It was warm.

"I'm sorry if I scared you," she said. "I can explain."

"I have to go," said Liam. He wanted to know how she knew, but he was too scared, distrusting. To his surprise she did not pressure him.

"Fine," she said, "I'll see you soon." Her tone was not ominous, rather it seemed understanding of something Liam didn't know. He wanted to ask about it, but he left. At a glance over his shoulder, Liam saw that she watched him with a soft smile. He wondered if he should take it as sly or reassuring.

How would he explain this to the others? He had spent the afternoon boyishly getting to know this young girl, but there was something about her, a knowing that haunted him. Every path of relative safety had been denied to him. Sol the priest left him with a scar on his forearm, the deserted town of Bronton had turned into a deathtrap, and even a demon had joined the people he supposedly trusted.

At night, Mere did not shut down in the usual shades of gray and black, with dim amber lights creeping out of the windows. Instead, the light, hued by the customary stained glass, spilled across the streets, illuminating the paths in cool greens, blues, and pale reds.

After a time, Liam found Charis's mansion. He took the walkway into the estate, through the gates, and briskly walked up the steps. Entering the solar, he fell into a cushioned chair and sighed. It was dimly lit, relaxing, and smelled of old books. He almost didn't hear the servant approach with the beer. As he took it, wondering why the servant had thought to bring it, a familiar voice spoke. "Not Goose's Wild," said Charis.

"He's a boy," said another voice. "What did you expect?" Nathan similarly stood in a spot Liam could have sworn was empty moments ago.

Oliver walked in, "So that's what our little adventurer has gotten himself into."

"Am I in trouble?" asked Liam, startled and looking at the three people in the room previously thought to be empty.

"Heavens, no" said Nathan with a smile.

"We were worried about you, that's all," said Charis.

"But I go out every day," replied Liam.

Oliver gave a short laugh, "Yes, but you're normally easier to follow. One minute you're in Goose's Wild, a bar rough by Mere's standards, and the next minute you disappear down an alley. And not without quite a commotion."

On reflection, the superfluous rooftop jumping and alley running felt embarrassing. They meant well in following him, making sure he avoided trouble, but given his desert survival, giving him a tail felt condescending.

"It's nothing," said Nathan seeming to read his thoughts. "He just met a lady." Charis gave Nathan a look. "Not that kind of girl," added Nathan.

"I heard," said Charis, "that you started a fight with Pike's son."

"No," said Liam, "He started it. I did finish it."

Nathan laughed.

"You are a man yet," said Oliver smiling. "I suppose you got the girl."

"I did," said Liam. "Is that it then?"

"More or less," said Oliver. "We were having a chat when we heard you come in, decided to give you a scare."

Liam took a sip of his beer. "By all means, carry on," Liam said, debating on whether or not to relay the matter with Aster. He should have known better than to get close with a stranger.

"We were just discussing our mystery guest," said Nathan. "The man we found in Bronton."

"Yes," agreed Oliver. "We've spent the last few days trying to figure out our next move. If the man wakes, we might gain some useful information regarding rumor of the army at Avianne. By our scouts, it seems Jacob and his abominations would hold at my pass, though we don't know why."

"How much could this man really help us?" asked Liam. "An army is an army. We could just march on the Pass and be done with it."

"We know too little," said Oliver. "We know that Jacob has likely taken Avianne using the abominations. Dorian thinks his wards at the Pass have been undone by some sort of death-based power. We suspect Raven's necromancy has something to do with it, but we don't know how or if Cain and Amelia are involved. For all we know, this man is a random prisoner, but more likely he has some information, perhaps about these unusual abominations. Jacob has a reputation for being brutal, but he usually doesn't go out of his way to be so unless it's personal."

"And," added Nathan, "we don't know how much time we really have here. It's quite possible Jacob knows about us and this place."

"Speaking of which," said Liam, deciding to disclose the meeting with Aster. "The girl I met. She knew about me. She knew where I got this scar."

"My people shouldn't know," said Charis. "Who is she?"

"She goes by Aster," replied Liam.

"I know her," said Charis. "Daughter to Kevin Balter. A good man, and from what I've heard she's a nice girl. It would be impossible for her to be working for Jacob, but it's strange she would know such a thing."

"We stay prepared and wary," said Oliver. "Leave the girl alone for now, but stay vigilant."

A servant interrupted their conversation. All looked to the man, dark buttoned shirt tucked in and gray hair receding. "Pardon me," he said, "But the man has awoken."

# CHAPTER TWENTY-TWO

*Of Nephilim*

He was careful not to slip on the algae as he stood on the river steps washing his clothes. He was fourteen. Or was he forty-nine? He could not remember. He took another shirt from the gently flowing river and put it in the woven basket. Squinting in the sunlight, he observed his surroundings. Children played in grassy yards, men bathed in the river, women came to do laundry. If his mother had been alive, it would be her cleaning his clothes instead. Wooden apartments two and three stories tall lined the river.

When the boy was finished, he took the basket and made his way back home. Out of the river and up the steps that lined the bank—some locals called them ghats—he left the shore. His bare feet led him down the familiar streets of rock and dirt. This was a nicer neighborhood. The homes were in better repair, the shops sold finer linens. He passed these things and soon entered his neighborhood. The stairs of his dilapidated apartment building took him to the third floor, each step creaking as he raced up them. On the third level he went to his own door.

Rivers was home. "It took you long enough, Maynard," his brother said. "We'll never get this place cleaned up before Dad gets home."

"I worked as fast as I could," he replied, "but I still have to hang them out to dry."

"It's okay, I'm a little behind as well," Rivers replied. "I've been down to the shop. I have a surprise for our old man."

Maynard would have liked to pry but there was too much work to be done. If Father returned and so much as a spoon was unclean, there would be hell to pay.

He always felt a little nervous on the balcony, as if it might fall out from under him at any moment. He braved the crumbling platform, draping his clothes over the line, careful not to let his feet drag on the planks. It had taken help from Rivers and half of an hour to remove the previous splinter.

Ducking back inside from the balcony, Maynard felt relieved to be on solid ground. Rivers peeled potatoes while Maynard, on hands and knees, scrubbed the kitchen floor.

"How come you always get the easy work?" asked Maynard.

"Because I'm older," replied Rivers throwing a peeled potato into the pile.

"Only by two years. Besides what does that have to do with anything?"

"When Ma died, guess who had to scrub the floors *and* do the dishes until you were old enough? On top of that, I'm apprenticing with grandfather."

Maynard could not recall a time when he did not have chores. Could he remember a day that he did not fear his father? Maynard did not broach the subject. Their mother's death, their father's temper, these were not things of which to speak.

As usual, Father arrived home in the late afternoon. Maynard and his brother had spent the last hour scrambling with the finishing touches of cleaning and cooking. The apartment was clean, the floors swept. Dinner was ready. This was the most immaculate home on the west side of Kal. The old man came in with the usual smells of smoke, iron, and whiskey. He stopped in the doorway, and though drunk, he did not sway. Rivers and Maynard stood at attention as their father's eyes scrutinized floor and wall. This was the moment.

Maynard spotted a scuff on the floor, just inside the door. How had that gotten there? How had they missed it? He looked away, daring not to draw attention to it. Father looked at him and then to Rivers, stroking his red beard. Had he seen it?

The man nodded in approval. Maynard dared the quietest sigh of relief as his father entered the home. "How was your day, Father?" Rivers asked.

"It was okay, as these days go," he replied opening a cabinet near the door and extracting a brown glass bottle, unstopping it, and tilting it to his mouth.

"Supper's ready," Rivers said.

"Aye, good," Father replied. "First things first. You boys wash up and set the table."

The table was set. A father and his two sons joined hands as he spoke the words they knew well. "Lord, we thank you for this bountiful meal. We pray it will nourish us 'til the end of our long lives. Amen."

After their father picked up his fork, the sons followed. Maynard took a bite of his greens. They always made him want to gag, but he suppressed it and swallowed the bite.

"You're quiet today, Maynard," Father observed.

*Act natural*, Maynard thought, knowing that that he did a poor job hiding how that day was different. "I'm sorry, Father," he said. "I was enjoying this meal so much that I forgot my manners. How is our grandfather?"

"I see him so little. He spends all of his time with the apprentices," he replied, shooting Rivers a look. "But he fares well. Never did know a man so well preserved. I'll remind you boys again that the Smith family lives long, and you would do well not to waste such a gift. Your grandfather has his own smithy and is gracious enough to allow me to earn a living there. And he speaks highly of Rivers, his favorite apprentice. Maybe he'll have his own shop one day."

"Yes, Father," said Rivers. "Which reminds me. After supper, I have something to show you."

Maynard needed an evening that appeared routine, but whatever Rivers had in mind was unusual. He feared it would interfere with his plan. *There's always tomorrow night.* No. It would be this night.

After supper, their father lounged in his usual chair, bottle in hand. Some nights the old man got more drunk than others. This would be one of those nights when he finished the bottle. Maynard sat on a stool, awaiting Rivers. He came into the room, a long object wrapped in a sheet. Maynard had already guessed that it was something forged by Rivers, but it was too large. Whatever was under the sheet was big, bigger than the odd horseshoes and daggers Rivers had boasted in the past. Upright, it might have been as tall as Maynard and wider than his hand. Rivers began to pull the sheet away. A hilt was revealed and slowly the steel blade was uncovered.

Maynard had never seen that look on Father's face. It was reverence, envy, and pride all at once. He could guess Rivers's intentions. The old man's reaction was unpredictable, depending on where the drink led him. If the man expressed jealousy, Rivers would flatter him, offering the sword as if it had been intended as a gift all along. If the man could find it in himself to be proud of his son, Rivers might even be bold enough to ask to leave, to go on his own as a master smith. The sword was not one of an apprentice.

"Tell me, son" the Father said. "How did you come about such a blade?"

"I made it, Father," Rivers replied.

"Tell me no lies. Did you make it, or your grandfather?" asked Father.

"Grandfather has been teaching me the art, but I found a way to make a better sword. His advice was minimal. This is my creation."

"And what do you intend to do with that? It would take a great man to wield a weapon such as that," Father said with apprehension.

"Hold it for yourself," Rivers said. He held the sword out and the man rose, taking it in his hand. Maynard saw that Rivers quivered. He did not want to give up the weapon. If the man wanted it for himself or to sell it, would Rivers simply leave or submit himself to their father's demands?

Father lifted the weapon and wrapped both hands around the hilt. There was a wild look to his eyes as he paused, holding the sword. After a moment, he smiled.

"Well done, my son," Father said, handing the sword back and sitting down. "You've got me beat. Hell, you surpassed your grandfather. What will you do with it? Sell it?"

"I've thought about it," said Rivers. Maynard's brother had his own exit strategy. "Remaking one of these would take another eight months in Grandfather's forge. As long as I'm borrowing tools, I have to share them, or else stay up into the nights doing my own work. But then I couldn't be here tending the home and Maynard."

He had a way of talking and Father was starting to see his reasoning. "If you sold it," Father said, "you could afford a forge of your own."

"Exactly," Rivers said. "I could make swords, armor, hire apprentices of my own and teach them the secrets behind this alloy. It will revolutionize metallurgy and—" Rivers stopped. Father's eyes drifted from the room. Maynard was so anxious about Rivers leaving that he had stopped worrying about his father's temper, but the mood could suddenly take the man, and then it was just a matter of time before he found the minute detail that gave excuse for his anger. Maynard searched the room, looking for anything that would incriminate him, but things were just the way Father liked them. Had their father seen the scuff on the floor after all? That was hours ago and in another room. Father did not look around the room, but rather gazed out the window onto the balcony.

"Whose clothes are those?" he asked. Not tonight, this couldn't happen tonight. For once the man just had to drink himself into a stupor and go to bed. If he was angered, his rage could last for hours. What could be wrong with the clothes hanging outside?

"Mine, sir," said Maynard.

"And what are they doing hanging up out there like some peasants rags?" Father asked.

"They are drying, Father," Maynard answered.

"Are you being smart with me, boy?" The man's face grew red.

"No, sir. I did laundry today and hung them out to dry. Just like always."

"Did you think I really want your rags hanging out there, showing the whole neighborhood how poor we are?"

Father could not see reason. He could not understand that Maynard wore those clothes every day, so whether they hung to dry or not, they were seen. Nor could he understand that had Maynard not hung them to dry that they would have been damp and moldy the next day, and their father would inevitably have been angry at that. He needed to be soothed at all costs.

"Father," pleaded Maynard, "I will take them down. I will go begging tomorrow and earn enough to buy new clothes for myself. You are right, I am an embarrassment."

His father rose from the chair, towering above Maynard. "You're damn right you're an embarrassment. New clothes, old clothes, everyone knows who you are. Thanks to you, I lost your mother, and what are you now but another mouth to feed? Where is your sword? Have you forged a single thing?"

"I will learn the forge, then," said Maynard, "and I'll do my chores as well. I'll—" but he was stopped short as he was pinned to the wall. Father held him there and Maynard struggled to breathe.

Menace filled his father's eyes as his broad forearm loosened off Maynard's chest, letting him sink against the wall. The relief passed when the blow came. There was a crack in his ribs and he gasped, trying to breathe through the pain. Maynard curled against the wall at Father's feet. There was a time when fear of pain restrained Maynard, but now it had come and it would come again regardless. He could not wait until the man was asleep. The time was now. The man picked Maynard up and hugged him in a malicious crush. Breath left Maynard again and his hand, barely free under the grip fumbled for his pocket. This was the father's way, to suffocate. There were less bruises.

Maynard's hand was almost in his pocket when his father let go. He fell to the floor, heaving, his knees scraping the wooden planks. A hand gripped his underarm and a thumb dug into the pressure point. Maynard made no sound. He had learned that it only made things worse. His hand fell from his pocket and he clenched his teeth. Rivers stood, sword in hand, and did nothing. He never did anything.

The grip loosened so the man could take a swig from the bottle. Maynard shot his hand into his pocket and gripped what was inside. The man picked him up again, this time putting him in a headlock. His world became an intense desperation for air, but instead of scrambling as usual, he took the knife in his hand, using his thumb to flip the blade open. He stole a glance and met Rivers's eyes before stabbing down into Father's leg. The grip loosened but he soon found the man falling on top of him. The weight crushed him and the knife fell from his hand. His father moaned as Maynard tried to pull free.

"You son of a bitch!" Father said. "You ungrateful bastard!"

His father grabbed the knife from the floor and waved the knife at him, struggling to keep his footing as he tried to strike. Maynard made no sound but only panicked as he stumbled up from the ground and staggered out of the room. The floor shook under the stomping of his pursuing father, but Maynard outran him. He flew out the door, down the stairs, and into the alley. He ran aimlessly through the various alleys before the pain in his cracked rib overtook him and he had to duck behind a pile of refuse. His best clothes were on the balcony, he had no money, no shoes, and his plan had failed. The dream ended.

When Maynard awoke it felt as if he had been underwater and only as his last hope of breath ran out, he reached the surface gasping for air. His eyes opened to a dim room and two women stood on either side of his bed. The liches. But, no. One was soft featured with a gentle look and the other appeared genuinely concerned for him. The torture and nightmares were over and this was the most plush and soft bed he had ever laid on. He made to sit up but pain shot through his side.

"Be still," the fair one said. "You're recovering faster than I could have guessed, but you still have some work to do."

Maynard calmed his breathing, "Where am I? Who are you?" Flashes of the dark concrete room, the door crashing open, and the strangers. He could recall the pleas for his life, the desire to speak, and a pain that prevented it. Memories of gentle hands and warm water.

"I'm Charis," the fair one said, "and this is Callianeira." She gestured to the other who had smooth tea-colored skin and dark hair. "This," continued Charis, "is Mere, the garden city."

"The City?" Maynard said, somewhat disoriented.

"Not *the* City," said Charis, "But it is a city. It is my city."

"And who are you?" Callianeira asked.

"Maynard. I was with Jacob and he betrayed me."

"Such are his ways," said Charis.

Though he had many questions, he reserved them for later. Surely they had questions for him as well. He needed to recover, and his body felt like it had been through hell. Needles punctured his side, razors ripped through his muscles, and his dexterity failed. His body was stitched and bandaged.

They helped him don a robe and then, like an old man, they led him out a back door and to the baths. He marveled at the structure, though the wall lanterns only revealed so much. It was unlike anything he had seen, but the task of walking was such a chore that he had little time to appreciate his surroundings. Each step led to new pains. They helped him into the warm pool and relief came in places he had not known hurt. Charis seemed to have some training in healing but Callianeira was there to help and otherwise stay out of the way. Both were beautiful, though in different ways, and had Charis been anything less than professional as she poked and prodded him, he might have been aroused, though he probably found Callianeira more attractive.

"What are you doing?" asked Maynard as he felt more unexpected relief.

"You might call it magic," Charis said, working intensely.

"You're one of them," Maynard realized.

"A *Grigori*?" said Charis, "Yes."

"You too, Callianeira?" Maynard asked.

"Call me Calli," she said. "And, no. I have my own problems." She smiled but he could tell it was a painful subject.

"How long have I been unconscious?" he asked.

"We found you in Bronton nine days ago," said Charis. "Two of those days we spent coming here, and the rest have been here where you've received care in these baths, from me, and my best physicians. You have recovered quicker than you should have."

"I tend to do that," he said. "Apparently I'm not so different from you." Charis gave him a searching look but said nothing and then continued with her work.

When they were finished, he managed to dry and garment himself without any help. Half way back to what they had called the mansion, the stiffness and soreness returned, and they helped him once again. This time, they led him through the front and accommodated him in a rather lush living room, muffled discussion coming from the nearby room. The voice was not angry but it was firm, "I can't risk that, Dorian." Charis poked her head into the unseen room and said something too quiet to hear. Soon, Maynard had company.

Compared to Jacob's venom, he expected Dorian to be different. In contrast, Dorian was a solemn and stern man. It was as if he carried the weight of the world on his shoulders, each gesture tentative, but genuine. He smiled and sat nearby without saying anything. Six people filled the various sofas, loveseats, and chairs in the room. All eyes were on Maynard.

"I know it's late and I'm sure you're feeling overwhelmed," said Dorian, "but it's important we get to know one another. I'm sure you've heard a lot from Jacob, but if you pay enough attention, I think you'll find that we don't operate like him and are very different from how he might describe us."

Dorian pointed at a tall man, "Oliver here was a general during the war and has lived an unexpectedly long life. This young man is Liam, who journeyed from the City and is largely responsible for bringing us together. Calli is a demon we picked up along the way. As you can see we're a rather diverse lot, but we stand together. We would like to know where you stand. So, Maynard, it's time you told us about yourself."

Eyes remained on him. No gentle prelude. Only questioning, judging, probing. Under the directness, Maynard sensed an eagerness as well. Maynard took a deep breath and began, "As you may know, there is another large island south of this one, though not cursed like this one. It is not all desert. There is forest, swamp, river, and rain. I was a mercenary. One day, a man named Jacob promised that my dreams of wealth and comfort would come true. I was a death-bringer and widow-maker in his plot. I led, followed, and aided in the slaughter of thousands. From town to town we went killing, until we came to Bronton. Then I saw that it was more than a means to an end. I saw the bodies of people I had slaughtered come back to life and march on the Pass. I knew that they could and would slaughter thousands more. If they made it into the City, it wouldn't just be a conquest, but a massacre. I quit and Jacob didn't take it well. He left me in the hands of Raven's lich women and they endeavored to make me more like them, but I resisted. I'm more resilient than the average man because, at least according to Jacob, I'm a decedent of one of you. And here I am.

"As for my side, I don't know. I thought I was on my own side, but it turns out I was just following Jacob under some delusion that I could kill my way to a life of peace. Suddenly, neither my side nor Jacob's sounds worth a damn. I suppose for now I am at the mercy of you all, and as such I'm willing to do my part. I don't yet know how I feel about fighting—much less dying—for your cause, but I can tell there's something different about you and I want to know it."

The red-haired man who Dorian had called Nathan spoke, "No one here is asking you to do anything. Stay here, recover, tell us more of your story. We'll tell you ours. There's not a person here who has any judgment for you. The best of us is that seventeen year old boy over there," he gestured at Liam, "and he's the least judgmental of all of us."

"Well, I think there's some level of trust to be had here," said Oliver, "so I think we can retire for the evening." There were nods and sounds of assent, and soon they were bidding him farewell, encouraging his rest, and leaving. Callianeira and Charis helped him back to his bed. Part of him was wakeful, wanting to know more about this new world of which he was a part, but the short evening's events had worn him out.

The next morning a servant brought him coffee and a tray of food. He was familiar with the drink, but as a luxury, and though bitter, he drank it. Once he had finished the meal, the servant returned, and parted with the tray. As he began to wonder what he should do next, someone knocked on the door. After Maynard bid them to come in, the red haired angel stepped in, the one who had called himself Nathan.

"Morning to you," Nathan said.

"You as well," said Maynard.

Nathan took a chair, moving it closer to Maynard's bedside, and sat. "You'll have to pardon my eagerness," he said, "but I had to come to you first thing."

"About what?" Maynard asked.

"I want to hear your story," Nathan said. "From the beginning."

"Well, I was smuggling spices into a town when Jacob helped me fight off some bandits," Maynard replied.

"No," said Nathan, "The beginning."

"My beginning," said Maynard.

"Yes."

"South Outland is different from here. The plants grow green, the populations are denser, water is easier to come by. My family was simple. After the war, guns were so rare they had become mythological, so my great grandfather—however many "greats" removed he might be—became a smith. The idea was simple. Make the best armor and weapons one could buy. He passed it on to his sons and they passed it on to theirs and so on. Such were things when I was born."

"My grandfather still lived and had his own forge. My father worked in the forge, but as the years went by, he spent more time drinking. Even when he did work, it was usually small and independent things away from the scrutiny of my grandfather. My grandfather was not a harsh man, but my father did not want him to see his only son squandering his talent away. Father made a lot of horseshoes, which he sold for next to nothing, and then had enough whiskey for the day.

"As for my mother, I know so very little about her because she died when giving birth to me. All I really know is that I got my darker hair from her, even though it's still a little red. My brother was only two years old when she died, but he said she was a loving mother and good woman. I learned from a very young age not to broach the subject with my father. It was the quickest way to invoke his frequent fits of rage. Rarely was my older brother, Rivers, the target of such outbreaks. If he did anything that would set my father off, I was somehow implicated and made the target. Rivers never meant for harm to come to me, and often went through great lengths to see that Father remained subdued, but if he made any obvious attempt, then he would likely take a beating, though less severe than mine.

"I seldom saw my grandfather due to his long days in the forge, but my brother was an apprentice under him. My brother learned the art of metallurgy, but he also learned a little of our past. Apparently, my father had quite the aptitude for metalworking until my mother died. He changed after that, working just enough to support us and his drinking habit. I would have become an apprentice in the forge like my brother, but my father retained a strong conviction that it was my duty to do what my mother wasn't there to do.

"I learned the hard way that it was pointless to try and deny Father alcohol. He always kept whiskey in a cabinet by the door. We were expected to be ready, standing at attention when he walked in, the place cleaned and dinner prepared. He would walk in, usually already a little drunk, and survey the place, take out the whiskey, and if he was satisfied we would sit down to dinner. If he wasn't, well, the beatings started earlier. I make it sound like he beat me every night. The truth is, it was only about once a week. Some nights he would just start breaking things and making a mess, causing a rather time consuming clean up the next day.

"I had not imagined that my life was much different from anyone else in our situation. Like I said, we were poor, and though we lived in a large apartment building, it was still in the ghetto and safer to keep to ourselves. Who could I go to about the beatings? My grandfather was too weak and we didn't have any friends. I rarely had proof. My father's beatings were unusual. He liked to crush, to suffocate. He didn't want anyone to see bruises, not that they would have cared, but he had a very adamant complex. We were poor but he hated the idea of anyone knowing. It was obvious, but he lived in a strange denial.

"When I was fourteen I had had enough. Our kitchen knives were all dull and Father did not allow weapons in the house. He claimed it was because he didn't want to bring work home, but Rivers and I both knew that he wanted us defenseless. I acquired a small, but very sharp pocket knife. Suffice to say, I stole it. My brother was home that day and we cleaned the house together. It was going to be spotless, I was going to be on my best behavior, and he would go to bed and pass out drunk. I thought about simply escaping, but I wanted the man dead. I hated the bastard.

"He came home and things were perfect. The meal went well enough, he got drunk as usual but sometimes he just had it in him to get angry. My brother had forged a very special sword. I had never seen anything like it. He presented it to our dad, offering it as evidence that he was ready to go out on his own. It was a big risk if for no other reason than the fact that my brother had brought a weapon into the house. My father acted proud, but the moment was cut off. He began to be beat me, all because I hung my clothes out to dry. Remember, he had a real complex about our poverty, and I guess it suddenly occurred to him that hanging my clothes out to dry was a display for all to see how poor we were. Of course, he would have beat me anyway. He really had it in him that night. I think he was genuinely proud of Rivers, but I also think that he was jealous and even upset to see his favorite son leaving. He took it out on his second son instead. He hit me first, which was rare. After some abuse he put me in a headlock and things started to go black. I should have let him finish the punishment and just killed him in his sleep, but in my panic I stabbed him in the leg and ran.

"I don't know how long I ran, but I remember coming to my senses behind a garbage pile. My adrenaline wore off and I calmed my breathing. I had learned not to cry, to be strong, but for what was probably the first time in ten years, I cried. When I was done I just sat stupidly staring at my bloody hands. My side ached from where he had hit me and it was getting dark. I had nowhere to go. I took some time to think and knew what I needed to do.

"I waited. I waited for hours, until I knew the old man would be drunk asleep. I went back to the apartment. I had cleaned the place inside-out hundreds of times and I knew ways to break in. I knew every creaking plank and how to avoid them. I stood in the room that had belonged to my brother and me. He slept soundly and I took what I came for. The sword. It was wretched, I know. I wanted to wake him, find out what happened after I left, see if he would come with me. We could have left together, and he could have started his own smith somewhere, and I could have learned from him. I should have done that, but I didn't.

"I stole the sword. I lied to Jacob about that, told him it was my birthright. The sword wasn't as heavy as I expected. God only knows how he had the talent to build such a weapon. I took it into my father's room and found him snoring loudly in his drunken state. I wanted to wake him, to make him feel it, but it was too risky. Instead, I raised the blade and brought it down on his neck as hard as I could. The sound haunts me to this day. The sound of my first kill. The sight of his severed head and bloody sheets didn't even faze me like that sound, of a blade slicing through human flesh. Even still, the kill felt right.

"A boy shouldn't kill his father. That is the way of things. Yet I did, and I do not regret it. I left Kal and I never went back. I had been drinking from the river and stealing food when I could. There were merchants and farms along the way. Some eggs here, a loaf of bread there. I was probably eating better than I ever had. Though light for its size, the sword was burdensome to a fourteen year old boy. I had thought to sell it, but I grew attached to it, though it was tough to carry on the road. I stole some reigns from a stable and fashioned them into a harness to carry it on my back, since it was too large to sheath at my side.

"Following the river, it was only a matter of time before I happened upon a group of unsavory men. I approached them by their night fire and asked to join them. They laughed at first, but when they realized I was serious, the leader, Gerald, actually took me in. To this day I wonder what convinced him, but he was a good leader and taught me the *arts*. He taught me thievery, battle, and survival. I learned to pick locks, use that big sword of mine, and hunt. I suppose it was from him that the idea of not being poor, of actually having money, first came to me. He started including me on jobs, and soon, I could afford shoes, clothes, and food. "One day, you'll be rich. You'll find yourself a woman, and you'll be the happiest man alive. That's all there is to life." He often said things like this to me. Those were good years, but the details are negligible. The problem arose when Gerald was killed. That's the thing with these mercenary types. They are always trying to rise in the ranks. Gerald's men loved him, but he was growing old, and wouldn't retire as fast as they would have liked. His second in command betrayed and murdered him. They knew I was close to the old man, so I fled, fearing they would come for me too.

"I wanted revenge, but I knew I was powerless. Gerald had taught me much, but I had barely gained any real experience, particularly in battle. I was seventeen then, old enough to join the army. It seemed like the thing to do. At the time, South Outland was broken into three main provinces and two of them were at war with one another. At the time, it was a distant thing that didn't concern an outlaw like me, but with nowhere to go, it made the most sense. It was there that I found my element. After training and two years of war, few people could rival the twenty year old with a big sword. Several important battles were won and soon the war was over, my side victorious.

"The war made me somewhat wealthy but I was young and stupid. What wasn't spent on whores and booze was squandered away in gambling. It took me five years to grow out of that and by that time I was in debt to a very intimidating man. Cino, however, was reasonable. I smuggled goods between a few towns, he gave me food and a room, and slowly but surely we were square. Even after that I stuck around, working odd jobs for him, making a decent living.

"That eventually got boring and I decided to go out on my own. I had a few connections and started my own little illegal business. It was simple and effective. I made the commute between Darsk and Bowdton, smuggling goods, made my own money, and no one bothered me. The problem was that I wasn't under anyone's protection. Before, if bandits found me on the road I would only have to show them Cino's mark and that was enough for them to leave me alone. On my own, I couldn't do that anymore.

"One day I was ambushed by a rather large group of bandits. I had valuable cargo and was not about to give that up. I fought well, but there were too many, and that's when Jacob showed up. He is persuasive and it didn't take much for me to join him. He promised money and comfort and kept me in just enough supply of both that I jumped on a ship with him to North Outland. It was through him that I learned that I just might be the decedent of one of you, some bastard-born nephilim. It never really made sense, because none of them owned up to the fact that I likely descended from one of them, but Jacob showed me magic. It made sense of my youthfulness, ability in battle, and some small feeling I could never put my finger on.

"Jacob simply made sense to me. He appealed to my wants, proved his power, and seemed to have a plan. He told me the story of a man, Achilles, and it resonated with me, the idea that I could be the mighty warrior he was and die happy as he might have. The problem came with slaughtering innocents. It wasn't a highway robbery, it wasn't war. It was going from town to town and killing. Then he made the abominations. It was too much. I always expected bad guys to be more maniacal and devious. Jacob was beyond those things. He wasn't some contriving villain. He wants something and he's going to do whatever it takes to do it. He was so matter-of-fact about the abominations and the killing that it disturbed me.

"I still don't know what to make of the whole thing. There's always been this underlying ideal that I would get rich, settle down, and find a wife. I never had any reservations on how to go about that until then. Part of me just wanted to go through the gritty mess and then forget the whole thing. The other part of me realized that I was with the bad guys. I've never been a good person and I'm not pretending that I'm good now, but he tortured me, and I got a taste of my own medicine. The pain was beyond anything I have felt before. It was as if they were killing me slowly. Jacob intended to break me and then turn me into a lich. I suppose I would have been the most powerful thing completely subservient to him. Jacob left, taking most of the abominations with him. He left a small contingent behind. Once I was ready, I suppose I would join him at the Pass, but then I woke up here."

Nathan had not spoken the entire time. It was an odd thing to have anyone care about his story. He was not much of a storyteller, yet Nathan had listened with intensity. Maynard felt a little shame. He had never spoken about his life aloud and now that he told his story he saw how despicable he had been. He was selfish, shallow, and absurd. He envisioned a simple life, but complicated it with petty doings.

"You are not the descendant of a bastard," Nathan said.

"What do you mean?" asked Maynard.

"Think about it," said Nathan. "Jacob nor Cain acknowledged you as theirs. I doubt you're Raven's and you're definitely not Dorian's. Yet, you are certainly one of us."

"It has to be Jacob or Cain, they were the only others in South Outland," replied Maynard. He paused, thinking. Nathan implied something. "Wait. Are you saying it's you?"

"The hair says it all," said Nathan gesturing at his red mane. "Whose side had long life?"

"My father's side," Maynard replied.

"What color was his hair?

"The color of yours," Maynard admitted.

"Now look at my eyes," said Nathan leaning in close. The thin rim was brown, outlining a deep green iris, with flecks of bronze turning gold toward the center.

"Shall I call for a mirror?" asked Nathan.

"No," Maynard answered after a moment. He knew those eyes. Every time he saw his own eyes in the looking glass, he saw his father's eyes. He had always thought them as the cold and brutal inheritance from his father. Yet, Nathan's eyes were warm.

"She was beautiful," said Nathan. "After the war I left North Outland. It's the gift of a shape shifter. I took on the form of a dolphin and went to the southern lands. She would come to the docks, beautiful and lovely, and I would watch her. I transitioned back to my human form and got to know her, and she got to know me. It wasn't long before we married and had our first child. Our daughter Aubrey was red of hair, precious." Nathan's eyes grew dark, "But it could not last. Jacob had disappeared by then, but I can't help but think it was his doing. Something killed my wife. It was an awful sight, unnatural. It had Jacob written all over it. I took our sweet Aubrey and hid her with another family and I left, hoping to lead whatever it was away. When I was sure that Jacob did not know of Aubrey's whereabouts, I left the South Outland and returned."

"Why didn't you get revenge? Why didn't you try and find out what it was?" asked Maynard.

"I have made a long story quite short. The details are for another time. I intended to come here, find Dorian, and go back and seek out that evil. I admit that I did not handle my sorrow well. I spent many years at the bottom of a bottle and when I came to my senses it was too late to get my revenge. But I guess it wasn't too late to find you. I'm not proud of what your father did to you, but I'm proud of you. My progeny, turning out better than I could have hoped."

Maynard scoffed. "Didn't you hear my story? I've spent my whole life working for my own means. I've deluded myself that I could ever settle down and be content. I told myself that the bloodshed was a means to an ends, but now I know better. I know what I've wasted."

"Did *you* hear your own story?" Nathan asked. "In the end you did the right thing."

"I cannot disregard my long bloody path just because I arrived to some half-cocked righteous conclusion. I'm not even sure I've come to any real absolution. If Jacob had not found me, I would have continued my life as a mercenary."

"Perhaps," said Nathan. "But you didn't. There is nothing you can do to take back what you've done, but you can be grateful for the man you are today and use it for good."

"Nathan, I'm a killer. It's what I do. If I do it in the name of good, I'm still feeding the bloodlust."

Nathan made to reply but he was cut off. At first it was a faint, single soft keystroke. Then the music flowed. Without saying anything Maynard and Nathan rose, following the sound into the parlor. Callianeira sat at the grand piano, back to them, flawlessly playing. He knew little of music, but this shook him to the core. Each note and chord, in perfect rhythm, resounded with such emotion.

"Chopin," a voice said. Dorian had joined them. Each resounding note captivated Maynard. The notes played by each hand seemed to drift apart and come back together, sometime subtly dissonant, and at others in odd unison. They never ceased to be complimentary, but they never quite aligned. The lower notes kept a gentle cadence, while the treble notes meandered with arousing grace. It might have lasted days, garnering his unceasing attention. But it only lasted minutes and when she finished Callianeira turned, surprised to find an audience.

"I'm sorry," she said. "I only meant to play a few notes, just to see what it sounded like."

"My dear," said Nathan, "why would you ever apologize for something so beautiful?"

She flushed, "That's kind of you. If you'll excuse me, I should go."

Maynard wanted to stop her, to beg her to play more, but he said nothing as she left. He realized Dorian was not the only one to join them.

"Rarely have I had the privilege of hearing something so beautiful, much less in my own home," Charis said. "Were that these times were better." She and Dorian left.

Nathan put a hand on Maynard's shoulder. "You're not the only one here with a past."

Then he left Maynard alone in the parlor. The black grand piano took up most of the tile floor. The windows opened to a garden. It was a beautiful, sunny day. Yet, Maynard did not know what he felt about anything. He needed time.

Maynard was free to roam the mansion and spent his afternoon exploring, resting as frequently as he needed it. There were more books in the room than Maynard had seen his entire life. Gerald had taught him to read, but it was not something he particularly enjoyed and he often only did so out of necessity. He had read one book all the way through in his lifetime. All he remembered was that the hero died at the end.

He had found the library, not because he wanted books, but because it was a quiet place. The shelves ran, flowing around the room, lined with books. A spiral staircase wound up to the mezzanine. He had walked the lower floors, glancing at titles, running his fingers along leather bound spines. Spinning up the wooden steps, griping the iron railing, he ascended slowly to the balcony where another line of shelves curved along the walls. The floors creaked under his footsteps, subtle squeaks breaking the silence. Engraved brass plaques labeled each section. He stopped at the history section, surveying the vast and strange subcategories. Asian history, United States history, and the like. The American Civil War, the French Revolution, the Ming Dynasty, all peculiar names to him. The next section caught his attention: Post Year One. He pulled out a book, careful to remember its place. *The Rise of Jacob*. He opened the book, the thin binding revealing a small print. He flipped the first few pages and read at random.

*While most had anticipated that some would refuse the guidance of the prophet, none thought that any would actually side with the* Grigori, *much less Jacob. Yet, his political prowess gained in popularity, much like many human dictators before. Therefore, the war was not merely between a handful of* Grigori, *but rather a full scale geopolitical conflict—*

He closed the book, putting it back in its place. He needed to think, not read. He made note of the section and then sank into a worn, padded chair back on the first floor. Just climbing the steps had hurt and the small amount of activity made him weary. The smell of the library was new to him. It was that of long worn paper filling the room. It was a woody, complex, and—he breathed in—relaxing, yet it hurt his side. The pain awoke the memories. Cold white hands, dull blades on his skin, hisses in the dim. The faint taste of blood haunted his tongue. He opened his eyes. He was not in the dark, cold concrete room. He was not the tortured subject of two undead women. He was in the strange company of people who seemed to care for him. It eased the trauma, though he could not gauge if his resilience had only made matters worse or protected him from the same horrors the captain had surely endured.

For some reason, telling his story made a difference and settled some of the trauma and his unease about the event. Yet, he was also thrown off by the relation to this Nathan. The resemblance was undeniable, but the story felt unlikely. Even if he accepted it, what then? Then again, his tenure with Jacob did not seem coincidental, not that he could have known. Or did he?

"This is my favorite room," a voice said. Maynard looked up.

"After the war," the man called Oliver continued, "I had my own little library. This puts it to shame."

"Meeting's over?" Maynard asked. They always seemed to be in a meeting.

"For the moment," Oliver replied, pacing the room. "They tell me you suffered under Jacob."

"You could say that," answered Maynard.

"They also tell me that you are a decedent of Nathan."

"They tell me that as well," Maynard said.

"You don't believe it?" asked Oliver.

"I think Nathan means it, but that doesn't make it true."

"I suppose it doesn't," said Oliver, "though I've known the man a long time and I have to tell you, it's rather uncanny."

"I can't argue with that," said Maynard.

"What's troubling you?"

"Lots of things, I suppose," said Maynard. "I've been rethinking some things. For a long time I knew who I was, and slowly they took that away from me. Then I find myself here and now I'm being given a new self. I don't know what to make of it. You'd think I'd know who I am by now, but I don't even know whose side I'm on. And what happens if I'm not on your side?"

"It matters, yes, but less than you think," Oliver said. "A long time ago I was employed by a man that said everyone was replaceable and he had no issues reminding employees of it. I had another boss later who acted liked every employee was crucial to the success of the business. To be honest, you may very well be the little bit of help we need to succeed. I wish you would stay, even for selfish reasons, but also because Nathan seems drawn to you. I think you have great potential. On the other hand, if your conscience would have you go, then fine."

"Just like that?" asked Maynard.

"I suppose," replied Oliver. "You're not a prisoner, you know."

"No more than I was with Jacob."

"Quite a bit less, actually," said Oliver. "I mean it. Recover here and go. I'm sure some will be sad to see you leave, but we'll manage without you." Oliver had paced the room, made his way up the spiral staircase, cane tapping on each step. At the landing, he leaned down at the history shelf where Maynard had been at earlier. He picked a book and standing up, cracked it. "Charis really did document everything," he said, and started reading.

"Here's a bit about the Genetic Revolution." Oliver closed the book and placed it back on the shelf. "It's rather dry stuff," Oliver said making his way down the stairs. "Fascinates me, of course, but I don't expect you care. Suffice to say, centuries of core systemic changes and cosmic wars have brought us here. I admit that I have a hard time being sympathetic to the City. Is it really the last stronghold of mankind? We're doing just fine out here, not that we're defensible worth a damn. Sure, I've never been in the City, but I have my guesses. Do they have a library like this? Is their culture remarkable at all? Is it a thing worth preserving? But then I think about the fact that these are peoples' lives we are talking about. The agenda is not power, it's not some idealistic quest to save the world. It's preservation." Oliver sat in a chair next to Maynard.

"All Jacob wants is the City. Why don't we just give it to him?" asked Maynard.

"You and I both know better," Oliver replied. "He won't settle for a throne. On the outside he acts like his only desire is to have power, but the truth is that he desires holocaust. If you don't believe me you can read these books. The pattern was simple: Jacob tried to destroy, Dorian tried to stop him, things usually got worse. We're going to try not to repeat that this time."

"I have mixed feelings," Maynard said. "On one hand I want revenge. On another I want to do the right thing. I struggle with my own tendency to be self-serving. I want glory, I want to be left alone. There's always been this delusion that I would settle down one day, yet my battle-lust would never let that happen. It's like I've been fooling myself all along."

"I'll tell you something," Oliver said. "You can spend a lot of time waiting for your motives to become pure, but they never will. If you're remotely concerned with doing the right thing, you should act on it. Wealth won't bring you comfort or peace of mind. I'm not saying doing the right thing will either, but at the end of the day, at least you have something to show for it."

They sat in silence a moment.

"You should talk to the girl Callianeira," said Oliver. "I think you'll find something you've been looking for."

# CHAPTER TWENTY-THREE

*Hunters*

Ear pressed to the ground, Argon sensed vibrations. The sand sifted in barely visible tremors. He sat up, squinting in the light of the noon sun. Once again stopping for a brief respite from the march, Argon took the time to check for any sign of wildlife. It was becoming the difference in sustenance and starvation, and fortune favored him at last.

"To the west," Argon said. "Less than five miles."

Camels were brought, spears sharpened, and they rode out. Argon led the small envoy and soon the vibrations that had been so subtle with his ear pressed against the ground became audible over the gallop of the camels and the wind. The cloud of sand billowed in the distance, massive bodies stampeding in their midst. Some seasons were better for hunting than others due to the migration of the wildebeests. This was not the season in the south, but he gathered that this must be in proximity to some route that the creatures favored this time of the year. Having hunted by horse and camel, Argon favored the latter. Horses were useful for shorter bursts but camels endured, able to keep a steady run for much longer. They also offered a smoother gallop, making for a more accurate strike with spear or sword. Archers rode with them as well, skilled at shooting from the saddle, useful for slowing a beast for the deathblow.

Ratik, who was of a comparable position to Argon for Chief Serj, rode alongside him, spear in hand and they nodded as they approached the herd. Working in unison, it was as if their tribes had not been apart for so long. They matched the stampede's pace, careful not to get too close. An arrow from afar pierced one of the herd's rear stragglers and Ratik broke off to finish the kill. The rush of the hunt rising in him, Argon urged his camel faster, relishing the rumble, the sand sticking to his sweaty skin. He drove forward, ignoring the way the grit dug into every crevice of his body, the way it seemed to permeate his being. Coming alongside a bull he readied his spear. It knew the danger and swung a horn at Argon's camel. He guided it away, and thrust the spear to ward the wildebeest off. It withdrew its attack, dodging the spear-point. They were racing once more. Argon took a breath. The moment felt right, the earthquake of their hooves distant reverberations in his mind, the path between his spear and the bull clear. He threw the weapon, hitting his mark. The animal snorted with a cry as the spear pierced the fleshy part of the wildebeest's shoulder.

Throwing itself at Argon, it clashed into him, a horn piercing the camel's neck. Argon rolled from his camel before the bull fell upon it with crushing force. Sore and weary, Argon stood, blinking the dirt from his stinging eyes. The bull had recovered, the spear still impaling its shoulder, facing him. It snorted again, stomping its hoof. To the left, the stampede raged. If the bull charged, Argon's best chance was a roll to the right. It stomped again. Argon readied himself.

The wildebeest rushed, the injury only amplifying its strength and determination. As Argon rolled, he saw that the animal anticipated it and was almost upon him, a black shadow in the afternoon sun. Another shape clashed into it. The beast veered, leaving Argon in a spray of blood as Ratik buried a spear into it and shoved it to the ground.

Even then the bull survived, maimed and kicking on the ground. Bloody and panting, Argon got to his feet and put the beast out of its misery with his blade. He looked to Ratik. "You have my thanks," he said.

Ratik shook his head, "No, brother, this is our way." And so it was. It was mutual understanding, one that could mean life or death in battle. The stampede rushed away, taking its dust-storm into the distance. Between the six hunters, nine wildebeests were slain. It was an unusually good hunt, and Argon would have been embarrassed by his shared kill had it not been such an adventure. He now had a story to tell.

The fires were set and the wildebeests finished roasting as the red fringes of light sank over the horizon. Argon bit into the meat. Though chewy, he took pride with each bite. It had been a good day.

"It was all Ratik," said Argon. He took another bite from the massive rib. A fire illuminated the small gathering.

"No," said Ratik. "Argon dealt the vital blow. I only shortened its inevitable death."

"Either way," replied Argon, "it is food in our bellies and for that I am thankful to Elah."

They went to bed, the sweet smell of roasted meat still filling the air. A wise man would remember their days of wandering the desert. A wise man would not take safety in numbers for granted. Yet, satiated by their bountiful meal, the nomads slept with little concern for the ways of the desert. It was moments like these that she would betray them. The smell of blood and cooked flesh, caught on a faint wind, could bring such unsolicited malice that the Morning Star himself might tingle from some inconspicuous delight. Thus the crocotta came, desirous, but not delusional. Their primal instincts coalesced into chaotic want, but a strange — almost mystical — part of them restrained just long enough to utilize their cunning.

It was for this reason that Argon did not wake at first. They came upon the camp with such unstoppable apprehension that when the cackles and cries awoke him, it was too late. The claws ripped through the tent and the baleful snout broke through the slashed curtain. It was upon his family before Argon had a spear.

Henmad, the servant, was more alert. He took the whip to the beast. It half-barked, half-yipped at him. The distraction was all Argon needed to find a spear and sink its tip into the crocotta's skull. It collapsed to the dirt as Argon ripped the spear from the fell beast's head, blood and brain spattering the ground.

He looked to Henmad. His servant was no longer a boy, but a suitable tribesman. By Henmad's confident nod, Argon knew that his family was in worthy hands. He looked to Gardelle. She held their children close, none of them injured or in apparent danger. "Go," his wife said. "Defend us."

Through the tear in the tent, Argon leapt and followed the screams. One crocotta kicked a fire's dying embers upon a tent, spreading the flame. Argon launched himself at the beast, striking it down. Another crocotta, a few paces ahead, pounced on a man. A single slash from the crocotta, and the man's expression turned to horror, permeated by death as his bowels fell to the ground. Several arrows struck the creature, but they did little to pierce its skin. It bellowed a cackle and charged the small group of archers. A whip wrapped around its neck and Serj pulled, jerking the beast forward. Using the momentum, Serj launched into the air, arching and falling upon its skull with a short blade. The crocotta jolted, twisting, dragging Serj under it. Its claws clambered at the chief. But Serj held true, dodging the talons, and drew his knife across the crocotta's jugular. It tried to howl but gurgled instead as blood sprayed from its neck. Serj was covered in the black liquid, but unscathed.

Another crocotta appeared among the flame and the carnage. Without hesitation, Serj charged it. With its mocking laugh Argon saw its trick. Another beast approached Serj from the side. Argon threw his spear with all his might and it pierced the crocotta in its ribs, sinking deep into the abyss of its heart. Argon rushed to the fallen monster, retrieving his spear just in time to thrust it into the throat of an oncoming crocotta. He ripped the spear free and struck another beast as it mauled a hapless victim. The spear jutted out the other side. Jumping over the arched back of the dead crocotta, Argon seized the other end of the spear, pulling it free as he faced another. It feigned a frontal attack and maneuvered to the side. Its jaws were almost upon Argon when he used the butt of his spear to deflect the bite. With a lunge he twisted in the air and brought his spear down the throat of the monster.

A crocotta paced at an unarmed Ratik with anticipation. It was out of throwing distance, so Argon charged at it, hoping to take it in time. Another sideswiped Argon, taking him to the ground. His skin gritted against the desert sand and its rank breath filled his nostrils. It outsized him but a punch forced the beast's head away. He took the opportunity to sink his fingers into its eyes. It yelped, its frantic claws barely missing Argon as he pulled himself out from under the animal and mounted its haired razor-back. He clung around the neck with crushing force. He could feel the bones popping and the windpipe crushing under his deathly embrace. It jerked and rolled and gasped, but Argon held on. At last, it collapsed, its black tongue sagging from its unbreathing mouth. Ratik was locked in a similar battle, and Argon, recovering his spear, launched it at the creature. His adrenaline sent it further than he could have anticipated. It took the crocotta in the hindquarters and squealed in pain, lurching away from Ratik. It was just the advantage needed. In a single, swift punch, Ratik pummeled the crocotta and it collapsed to the ground, its skull an unrecognizable jumbled of broken bone and blood.

"They're organized," Argon said as he helped Ratik to his feet. "If we don't do so as well we won't stand a chance."

They ran through the camp together, gathering more men. When they had a group assembled they acted quickly to make a strategy.

"We work our way to the edges in groups of two and three," Argon commanded. "Protect the women and children. Use fire or any means necessary to establish a perimeter." The group took to the task, rushing among the fires and tents. Argon took his spear, twirling its end in the cloth of a nearby burning tent. Three crocotta enclosed on him and Ratik, but Argon waved his newly-made torch at them. They backed away, hair bristling. Argon crouched, picking up a nearby rock. He threw it at one. The crocotta sidestepped the projectile and lunged. Argon shoved the burning spear-tip into its face and it howled. The smell of burning hair filled the air as it raced off, flames traveling across its body. Chaos ensued as two other crocotta attacked. When Argon and Ratik emerged from the skirmish, the black blood of their kills painted their bodies. Ratik sustained a gash on his chest, but was unfazed.

When they came upon Belriah, he stood alone on a mound of dead crocotta, their massive carcasses gnarled and twisted things. The steel of Belriah's sword was wholly black, yet he appeared unwearied.

Just before dawn, the fight ended, the surviving crocotta retreating into the desert. The remaining bodies burned in a heap on the edge of their encampment, while the tribesmens' own dead became a sad pile on the opposite edge of the camp, soon to be their own pyre.

It was bittersweet. Though relieved to find his own family safe, the casualties were otherwise high. He held Gardelle tight and then each of this children. He thanked the servant Henmad, who would be rewarded.

Later Argon met with Belriah and Serj. "Thirty-nine People of the Moon, twenty-seven People of the Fire," said Serj. "This is indeed lamentable."

Argon cursed, "How could such a thing happen?"

"We have forgotten the way of our enemy," said Belriah. "The souls of the wicked possess these creatures. It is the doing of the dark one who opposes Elah. That is why they are so clever. They picked out the guards and killed them first. They were upon the camp before we stood a chance. The witch says it was Gaezar coming for revenge."

"I hope his cursed soul lies with the dead crocotta," replied Argon.

Though sore from the previous night, Argon saw to the burning of the dead and then spent the afternoon with his family. That night, he slept restlessly, dreaming of cackles, growls, and black liquid. He awoke to another sound, a loud rumble. Thunder. Perhaps there was hope after all.

The rains continued into the morning and the camp rushed to collect its water. Argon stood in the downpour, naked save for the cloth that covered his waste, letting the waters wash the desert dust and dirt from him. Other difficulties came with the storm. The ground turned to mud and the tents that were linen, rather than leather, soaked through. Argon robed himself and went to help collect the water, however Henmad came to him. The desert and crocotta had made the boy less timid. He now looked into Argon's eyes when he spoke, "It's Ratik. He is sick."

The rains softened as Henmad led Argon through the mud and bustling camp to Ratik's tent. They had managed to keep it dry inside, but an unbearable smell flooded the tent. Ratik lay, heaps of skins and blankets stacked on him. The witch hunched over the injured man, her pale eyes moving restlessly over the bowl as she muddled her potion.

"There might have been a time," she said rasping, "when we knew how to heal this. But it has been a long age since our tribe suffered a crocotta attack."

"My healer will know what to do," said Serj, words giving little credence to the hopeless tone by which he regarded his closest friend. Belriah was present too, as well as a weeping woman assumed to be Ratik's wife.

"It will do no good," rasped the witch. Ratik's shallow and rapid breaths faltered a moment with a guttural cough and then resumed.

"Are there more wounded?" asked Argon.

"There were fifteen others," replied Belriah, "but they die by the hour."

The flap opened and a man, wet from rains, stepped into the tent. He glared at the witch. Unlike the twisted and wrinkled crone, likely older than anyone else in the tribes, Serj's healer was a small man with hard and knowing eyes. He remained silent as he disregarded the old woman and approached Ratik's bed. The witch cowered to the side. Serj's healer shifted the blankets back. The claw marks ran down Ratik's chest, the torn skin festering with malodorous, deep black streaks. Ratik had not been bitten, but the claw marks left little resembling a torso.

"This man is as good as dead," the healer said.

"Isn't there something you can do, Haron?" Serj asked.

"I can mix a potion that will ease his passing and nothing more. The crocotta carries decay in its claws and toxin in its bite." The man paused, a look of horror in his expression. "What did you do with the other victims?" Haron asked.

"Burned them," replied Belriah.

"Damn it all," Haron said. "You didn't know? Have you forgotten?"

"Forgotten what? It has been many generations since we have dealt with the crocotta. Our encampment was always well protected and they left us alone."

"A crocotta bite carries a toxin that paralyzes its victims while leaving all of their senses intact."

"Where did you find this learned man?" Belriah asked of Serj.

"I have traveled far and wide," Haron said. "Never mind that. Assuming there's no infection and bite itself wasn't fatal, a person that survives the first day can usually make a full recovery in less than a week."

"What are you saying?" asked Serj.

"I'm saying that we may very well have burned people that were alive."

"By the moon," said Belriah.

"There is blood on our hands," the witch said. "The gods are angry."

"Silence," Belriah said, anger flaring. "Where were you woman when we burned those people? You knew no better than we did."

Argon's stomach soured. Most of the bodies had been torn to pieces. The massive jaws of a crocotta were likely to be fatal in any case, but he did remember a few of the bodies that were only missing an arm or had a bite on the leg. They might have survived but instead they burned, unable to move or scream. Even in the rain-soaked desert heat, he felt goose bumps.

"We will appease the gods later," Belriah told the witch. "Right now, we need to worry about those who live." Belriah then turned to Ratik's wife, weeping in the corner. His expression softened and Argon thought he saw the chief's eyes water. He knelt before her and gently took her hands into his. "Sweet woman, I am sorry for this. We should not have forgotten the ways of our fathers. Your husband cannot be saved, but we can ease his passing."

She tried to respond but only choked on her words, omitting a sob instead. She nodded her head. Belriah looked up at Haron, "Do what needs to be done."

Haron bowed and left the tent. Belriah offered more words of consolation before stepping out and urging Argon to join him. The witch left, bitterness in her hunched posture.

"We're in a bad place," Belriah said, ignoring the rain.

"Listen to me, Belriah," Argon said. "Haron is a wise and learned man, but he may be wrong. I did not want to give false hope to Ratik's wife, but if we find a town we may be able to find a healer who knows."

"We would be lucky if they would take us," said Serj, coming out of the tent to join them. "To them we are savages."

"Then I will be savage and put a knife to their healer until they help us," replied Argon.

Belriah weighed it a moment. "You speak true. This is our best hope. We should continue north until we find a city or town. By then we may need more water and food anyway. We have stayed here as long as we can. The rains will stop soon and we must move on."

Three weeks later, desperate once again for water, the nomads caught sight of a city. For days the distant walls never seemed to draw closer, until at last its battlements were significant even in the distance. Belriah and Serj agreed to send an envoy to the town to solicit a healer for Ratik and also food and water for the people. Riches to trade were scarce, but no other options offered promise. However, Belriah's son, Baran, sowed dissent, suggesting that this was their great conquest, the promised rains. Why Baran, who had been otherwise absent, opted to lend his voice in this particular meeting not only eluded Argon, but irritated him as well. He wondered if he could ever serve Baran as he did Belriah.

Baran had called for scouts, and on that much Belriah and Serj obliged. In the night, their swiftest men had ridden by camel to investigate what came to be known as a city. They had found the walls difficult to scale and well-guarded, but they had managed glimpses. An oasis, greater than the Eastern Pan, and a land of beauty. It was enough to tempt Belriah, but Serj held fast to coming by this land's wealth honestly.

"It is not yet the time for battle," Serj said.

"Will you forgo the promised rains when it is there for the taking?" Baran asked.

"My son speaks true," Belriah said, siding with his son.

"My most trusted adviser is fallen," Serj said. "And my best hope of recovering him is that city. I will not risk his life on your conquest."

"And my most trusted adviser," said Belriah, "thinks that we should—" He stopped, a realization that he had not once asked Argon to speak on the matter. Baran had spoken loud and clear, ostracizing Argon with his zeal for battle. "What do you think, Argon?" his chief asked.

"My counsel lies with Serj," Argon answered. Opposing Belriah was one thing, but coming between the chief and his son was another. Belriah may have given his blessing to Argon as his successor, but Argon meant to be true to primogeniture regardless of Belriah's intentions, and here he was dividing father and son. Torn between loyalties, Argon tried to give an answer that would speak to all. "Perhaps," he said, reading the men who waited on his wisdom. "I am not worthy to weigh in such a subject, but I suggest that we make our presence known. If they treat us as allies, we will buy and trade with them, and hopefully find someone who can help Ratik and any other survivors. But if they show any aggression at all, I say that we raze their city."

The next day they moved their camp closer to the garden city. The warmth of their reception would dictate whether the People of the Fire or of the Moon had their way.

# CHAPTER TWENTY-FOUR

## Visitors

She had allowed herself one note, and before she knew it, she sat at the piano playing Chopin. Now she was nothing more than a showoff, and a poor one at that. Though not unaccustomed to playing the piano in front of others, she hadn't allowed herself the satisfaction or indulgence for some time, at least not without an ulterior motive. Carried away, she had forgotten that she might garner an audience, when it was something she preferred to enjoy alone.

Back in her room, Callianeira fell to the bed, its plush mattress and blankets absorbing her fall. Her fingers tapped on the top sheet, dancing on imaginary keys. What was she doing here? The sun bathed her in the spot on the bed, warming her as she took deep breaths.

This was unlike her. She was the funny one, flippant at the most serious times. Ever since the skirmish in Bronton she felt out of sorts. *I've got to get it back*, she thought. There in the warmth of the sunlight, her chest rising and falling gently, her lids felt heavy, and she slept.

The curtains rustled in a gentle, yet unsettling wind. It was not the stuffy evening cool of the desert, but a sharp chill that jerked her awake. She felt the familiar coldness around her neck.

"Callianeira," the voice hissed. It was little more than an icy whisper, but it cut through the air. Sitting up in the bed, she saw the shadow standing in the darkness. With a smirk she extended her hand, conjuring a soft orange glow, illuminating the sinister figure in the corner. This was something she could handle.

"Vesuvia," she called the woman. "Miss me already?"

"Sagtyx would have you back," Vesuvia said. She was fair skinned and stately, save for her frazzled black hair and malicious gaze.

"You can tell the Dark Bishop," Callianeira replied, "that I'm just fine here."

"Callianeira, you are young yet. It's common for a woman in her hundreds to go through such phases. Your future is full of regret. Look around you. Would you really deny yourself the luxuries of the master for all of this?"

"Would I deny a cold collar, one loveless relationship after another, and a life in fear?" asked Callianeira. "This may be a little less comfortable, but at least I'm my own person."

"You fool yourself, young one," Vesuvia said. "I have seen the new masters you have taken on."

"I am here by my own will. I am free to live and love on my own terms. You are far from convincing."

Vesuvia hissed and her frayed hair shook. "We will give you many lovers."

Callianeira laughed, not a forced chuckle, but rather a merry sort of laugh as if reminded by some forgotten joy. "You mean I would be Sagtyx's whore to pimp out as she pleases. Your promises are hollow."

"You are a fool," said Vesuvia. "You will pass from this place and then you will serve instead of reign."

"I will take my limited time here, savor it, and in the end, likely suffer at the hands of the Morning Star. Forever will I remember these days, holding onto them and knowing that no one in all of

Hell has what I do and no one there can take it away. As the flames lick at me and the teeth gnash, I will smile. The Morning Star will suffer all the more for it, more so than he could ever make me suffer."

"You will not laugh. You will not smile."

"You're just mad because I've saved the man from Jacob. Was he to be so pivotal in this little war of yours?"

"He's nothing to us. It's you we want." Vesuvia lied.

"Be gone," said Callianeira. "You are unwelcome."

Vesuvia hissed, but she faded, her black shape curling into the night.

Callianeira sighed, letting the light from her hand fade. It had been tiring, but she had succeeded and did not expect another call for a long time.

Her eyes flickered awake at the sound of a knock. It was daylight, perhaps two or three hours after sunrise. She sat up, still in her clothes from the previous day.

"Come in," she said. Maynard entered, and she was glad to see him. A talk between them was overdue.

"Hi," he said. "I didn't realize you were sleeping. It's just that we seem to be wanted at the next meeting."

She gave him a small smile in return. "It's okay," she said.

Though a relief to see him well, his presence surprised her, tall and strong, yet with a gentleness.

"Um," he said with hesitance. "They said you were the one responsible for saving me. I wanted to thank you."

"Oh," she replied. "It was nothing really." She felt maladroit for the cliché response.

"No, really," he said, awkwardly standing in her doorway. "You saved me from something terrible. Nathan tells me that the others almost gave up, but for some reason you insisted on trying. I'm truly grateful."

She could see it now: the reason. She had known at the time, or perhaps known since she had been given this task, but there was something special about this man. It had escaped her and now it returned, the reason behind her extemporaneous notion to save him. Within her heart, it was very core of her prodigal parting from the Morning Star. It was the man who could love. She hardly knew what she meant by the notion, yet she had indeed left under the thought of something little more compelling than a whim.

The thought had manifested in her mind centuries ago. She considered the intellection a cancer, metastasizing in her mind. The more she pushed it away, the more it haunted her. The more she scratched the irritant, the more it spread. Over time the idea prevailed and it turned out to be, not a cancer, but rather a pearl.

It was true that God himself could love greatly, and so could the greatest heroes. It was they who gave their undying affection to romantically love their maidens, die for their people, and sacrifice themselves for the greater good. But what of a man who had fallen terribly? A person was capable of great evils, and she had mused at just how far a person could fall before they became unable to love. The proud hearts of men so often concede to their darkest desires. The obvious manifestation was always death, ruin, and chaos. Yet, men could also do great deeds for their own gain, pride, and desires. She had spent the ages manipulating that, turning the truest hearts until they cannibalized on the souls of others. She had done it to Soni on Elesonia, much to Dorian's chagrin.

Then the pearl was borne. A man could fall far, but in the end, resist those things. Just as a good soul could so easily be corrupted, a wretched soul could be redeemed. A fallen man could love. The idea thwarted her very concept of evil, and in taking root, it disarmed her. It was only a matter of time before one day she would whisper in a man's ear and at first he would listen. He would betray those around him. He would betray himself. Only, then he would betray her. He would upend her malice and he would go forth and love. He might even use her very work to do so. At first it drove her mad, then it terrified her, and finally she clutched onto it because she knew that it was the true thing she possessed.

"Are you okay?" Maynard asked.

She put a hand to her neck. It likely appeared a ponderous pose, but she knew what it meant. It meant freedom and the terrible risks that came with it. She looked at him. He knew so little of his own journey.

"I'm fine," she said, "You just reminded me of something."

He knew better. He wanted to help. She could see it in those eyes in all their complexity. For a moment she dared get lost in them, but receded her gaze. It was tempting to invite him in, to simply be with him, but she dared not tax him for her selfishness.

"I am in your debt," he said and then sighed. "The meeting is in a few minutes."

They would talk at length later she decided. She stood and walked toward him. He started to move from the doorway, to allow her to accompany him to the meeting but she stopped him.

"Wait," she said. "You should know something."

He looked at her, brows knitted.

"Your sword," she said. "It's stolen."

"I know," he said. "I stole it from my brother who made it."

"Your brother didn't make it."

Maynard cocked his head. He truly believed that his brother forged the sword.

"I'm sorry," Callianeira said. "It fell into your hands by my design."

"Do I know you?"

"In a sense," she said. "I've been keeping track of you for a while, Maynard." It was time she told someone. Dorian and the others already had vague notions. Even she did not fully understand things until they came to a head. "I am, or was, a demon. Before you, I was stationed on a planet far from here, of which Dorian oversaw before he fell with the others. It was my job to maneuver events so that his world was undone. I was reassigned to you. That sword came from Dorian's world and I ensured it got to you. I think he suspects it, but hasn't said anything."

"I find it hard to believe you've orchestrated my whole life," Maynard said. "There are certain things I wouldn't thank you for."

"I didn't cause your father to abuse you, if that's what you're suggesting. I did use it to urge you to leave. I can't cause or predict the future, but I had it on good authority that you would fall into Jacob's company. I was tasked with making sure you stayed in it."

"Could have saved me a lot of pain," he said.

"I could have saved many people a lot of pain," she said. "We're both here now and there's no going back."

He looked at her, mouth twitching as he sought understanding. She wanted to sit with him, to tell him how she had come to give up everything because of him. He had every incentive to continue service to Jacob and against all inclination, against any hope that his life might be worth living going forward, he chose the unselfish path.

She put a hand to his face, cupping his gruff cheek and meeting his eyes. "I realized something," she said, "when I had any sort of influence on you. I can't explain it, not right now. But we should talk."

The meetings had mostly been between the angels and Oliver. The consulate also attended. There was Viceroy Obi Dan, who had lost his wife in a diplomatic mission in Bronton. He was a rigid man, but well liked. The commander, Jaked Mari, seemed most content with the practical, often leaving the tactical side of the military to Oliver. Commander Mari's wife, Adivee Sumtra, sat in on the meetings, and spoke regarding financial concerns.

Sometimes one would come or go, but for the most part Callianeira, Liam, and Maynard had been uninvolved. All except Commander Mari were in attendance at the long mahogany table which had a large map of the island at the center. Beverages and comestibles were served as they settled in. Maynard sat next to her.

Obi commenced the meeting and gave the floor to Oliver. "I suppose we're all here," said Oliver. He stood, leaning on his cane. "Hopefully you have gotten the chance to get to know one another better. Here's what we have so far. Jacob has gone to Avianne, the Pass, and seems to have breached it. Scouts have returned with little news. This is partly because it would be dangerous for them to get too close. If captured, they would likely be tortured for information. Most recently, Commander Mari led a scouting team himself and reports that Jacob has taken the Pass and apparently quite a stench comes from it. Other than that, we're still trying to get more information.

"It is difficult to say why, but none of us feel that he has made it into the City. We also do not think that he is cognizant of our current whereabouts. This gives us some advantage, but given Maynard's estimation of his numbers compared to our own much lesser militia, we are having difficulty deciding on a course of action. Though we have tried not to bother you with the boring details, we all think it's time we brought you in. Liam has come from beyond the mountains, Callianeira from the service of the Morning Star, and Maynard under Jacob. You all have a perspective we don't. Furthermore, fresh eyes—so to speak—on this situation would be much welcome."

Liam spoke first, "Won't the ruins stop them?" Oliver looked to Dorian who appeared to be interrupted from deep thought.

"The ruins," Dorian said, rubbing his chin. "This island was chosen for its cave system. Vast underground caverns are home to a rather complex system of freshwater pools and lakes. There were some mountains before the subsequent terraforming. When I raised the ring of mountains, I implemented the river, but stopped it short at the Pass. It dips down into these caves. I wonder if he's found a way to get around the ruins."

"Why have the Pass at all?" asked Obi.

"It's one thing to keep things—us—out, but another to keep them in," replied Dorian. "I honestly thought the day would come when Jacob would be finished and a solid ring of towering rock would be rather inconvenient. The ruins were the remnants of our last stand and I left them as an unfortunate necessity." Dorian gave Liam an apologetic look before continuing. "I knew the time would come for someone to go beyond the Pass, but I thought I'd be present for it, and therefore able to lift the wards I had placed. It was agreed that Jacob and any of his agents should stay as far away from the City as possible. I placed a ward, thanks to the Last Saint, to deter anyone from coming or going. There might have been a better way, but we were desperate."

"Would that ward deter Jacob?" Liam asked.

"Sachin Pendharkar sacrificed his life on the guarantee that it would. Jacob lies within the Pass, so he beat it somehow. For all we know," said Dorian, "he's beaten the ruins as well."

"But there's no way he can get into the City," said Liam.

"Why not?" asked Nathan.

"It's impenetrable. It's like the stuff they built spaceships out of, and that doesn't break."

Nathan laughed. "You mean 'space shuttles' and they were mighty durable, but that won't necessarily keep him at bay."

"All right," broke in Oliver. "Liam and Dorian have been good enough to assist in updating this map. Are there any insights to be gained from it? Maynard, I know you are as yet undecided on your course of action but you may be of help."

"There's not much I haven't told you," replied Maynard. "Or, at least, nothing of which I can think. However, I might have a suggestion. You've been fighting Jacob reactively this whole time—at least from what little I understand. I suggest you take him head on."

"Jacob is strong," said Dorian. "Probably stronger than me."

"Bullshit," said Nathan. There were some chuckles but Charis subdued the commotion.

"I think Maynard is onto something," she said. "Sure, one-on-one Jacob might be able to take us. But if we fight him together, we stand a chance."

"The problem," said Oliver, "is that there's no systematic way to do that. It's a battle. In a pass, maybe three hundred feet wide. History will show that geography favors him."

"What about magic?" asked Maynard.

"What you call magic," said Dorian, "takes time. Less than tunnels, I suppose, but I'm afraid there's little I can do. Were it that I had known before, something preventative could have gone a long way."

"Well," said Maynard standing and hunching over the map, "these caves have to count for something."

"Yes," agreed Oliver. "There are tunnels. There's one advantage we have discussed. People have made homes and shops in the various hollows in the Pass, but there is a network of tunnels. We can use them to attack the flanks. The problem is that the passages are narrow. It wouldn't take much for Jacob to find them and use them to sabotage us before we ever entered. We can't depend on them."

"Maybe," said Maynard. "But put a good man at the front and he can hold the opening long enough for plenty of fighters to break through. It might be worth the risk."

"Well," said Oliver. "That is something. Any other considerations?"

Maynard shook his head and sat down.

"Calli?" Oliver asked, "Anything?"

She had been dreading this moment. All eyes were on her.

"I like the tunnel idea," she said with a smile. "Put me at the front and I'll hold it long enough for plenty of our fighters to break through."

There was an astonished silence and at last Charis broke it with small laughter.

"Aye," said Nathan laughing as the others joined, "Didn't see that coming from you."

When things settled back down Liam spoke, "I'll hold an opening as well."

"The hell you will, boy," said Dorian.

"I'm not a boy."

"Come now," said Nathan. "Oliver says he's a good fighter."

"I didn't say we should put him on the front lines," said Oliver.

The room resounded with Maynard's knuckles rapping on the table. All eyes were on him.

"I'll tell you something, Liam. I've had things done to me that I wouldn't wish on anyone else. But I'll tell the rest of you this as well. You have a man willing to fight on the front lines. You've got a lot of willing men, but how many do you have eager to go out there and really fight? Sure, don't let him defend something so dangerous as an opening. He'll get himself and others killed. But let him do something."

"There are other ways in which he could better serve," said Dorian.

"Well, I guess it's no business of mine," said Maynard, "but if I were you, I'd be grateful you have anyone worth a damn in the first place. I'll tell you first hand that Jacob isn't the type to take prisoners unless he means to hand them over to Cain."

"All the more reason for an inexperienced young man to not go." Dorian let out a breath. "But you have a point. Besides, it is Liam's decision and not mine. However, he won't be at the front lines. Onto other things." Liam gave a contented nod.

Callianeira raised a hand. "I think Maynard was onto something about the tunnels." She gave him a glance and raised an eyebrow. She looked over the map. "Look," she said. "The main army can take on whatever waits us at the Pass. We wedge ourselves in and then take these tunnels. We can surround them if we come out the other end."

"The problem," said Dorian, "are our numbers. And what if Jacob uses the tunnels too?"

"Aye," said Nathan. Oliver nodded.

"Perhaps he's taken the army beyond the Pass," said Obi.

"Unless he has found a way into the City," said Oliver, "that would put him at a disadvantage."

Something about all of this didn't add up for Callianeira. "I don't understand," she said. "What use are the abominations to him? He's amassed a primitive army to take on the greatest technological advancement in history. Did he expect more resistance at the Pass? Maybe he thought we'd be there waiting for him."

Oliver's brow furrowed. "This is our problem. We keep coming back to where we started. We don't have enough information. If we attack and he is at the Pass, he will hold the advantage, even if he hasn't managed to clear the rubble, it's not enough to corner him. Yet, we need to act."

"I say it's worth the risk," said Maynard.

Oliver opened his mouth in what Callianeira suspected was dissent, but a servant entered. Oliver seemed like he was going to speak anyway, but Charis held up a silencing finger. All eyes fell on the young man.

"I'm sorry, but we may be under siege."

*We may be under siege.* They walked through the mansion and down the wandering streets and given Oliver's reaction, this sounded like bad news. Callianeira knew that Charis had trained the militia well enough and Oliver had even drilled them according to his own knowledge. They were ready to fight, but not withstand a fully armed attack on their city.

They marched up the stone steps and mounted the wall. Liam looked inquisitive, Maynard serious, and the others anxious. Overlooking the desert they saw the gathering in the distance.

"What do you think?" Oliver asked when he saw Commander Mari.

"It doesn't make sense," he said. "They came from the south."

"And," said Oliver, "it looks more like a migration than an army."

"They have not shown any hostility," Mari said. "The question is what to do next."

"Those are not the pale bodies of abominations," Dorian said. "That is the dark skin of the nomadic tribes."

"Do you think Jacob convinced them to join him?" Oliver asked surveying the distant encampment in the desert.

"I doubt they are any more likely to join him than join us," replied Oliver.

"Then how would you explain this?" asked Mari.

"I think we should ask them," Callianeira said.

# CHAPTER TWENTY-FIVE

*The Tiger and the Crocodile*

The walls of the unknown city stood in the distance, pale against the orange sand. "I'm worried," said Belriah.

Argon worried too. The rains saved them from a sure death in the desert, but their supply had not lasted. Perhaps it had only prolonged the inevitable. Furthermore, the crocotta had taken more lives and might still claim Ratik. All others had succumbed to their wounds.

"Before the rains, at least we had food," continued Belriah, "but now we are almost out of that as well. It's not just our short supplies. We run out of the peoples' patience. For all of our faith, we ask much of them." The sun beat down as they stood on the edge of their encampment. The morning had come and the question remained as to what they should do with this city before them.

"What of the witch?" asked Argon.

"As old as she is, I'm surprised she has made it this long," said Belriah. "I thought she might be of more use, but nothing."

"Perhaps this city can offer us the resources we need. Maybe it can save Ratik," said Argon.

"We have nothing to offer them and I would not beg."

"Perhaps your son was right. This is the battle we are to fight and this is the place of the promised rains," said Argon.

"That is not our way. I think the gods would give us the rains fairly, not by that kind of force. It would be a pointless endeavor. Look at the walls."

Indeed, the walls stood high and solid in the distance. The buildings arose behind them, old and unharmed. This city could withstand a siege. If the gods meant for them to take the city by force, they would need a better sign.

"Look," said Belriah. "They come to meet us." Something moved from around the walls, a group of people on horse and camelback.

"At least the matter of what to do next is settled," said Argon, expressing hope, though he had reservations.

"Maybe," said Belriah. "Get Serj. Ready the guards. Bring me my spear."

The guards assembled and they stood waiting a few yards away from the edge of their encampment. The strangers approached from the distance and Argon allowed himself a swallow of water, hoping there would be more in the near future.

Three riders on camelback, accompanied by a riderless horse, came into view. But it was no small horse, it was something else. Argon's heart leapt at the sight of the tiger. Belriah had seen it too and had a look of wonder on his face.

"What do you think this means?" asked Serj. "Is this who we are to war with?"

"No," Argon said. "Not these people.

The three strangers dismounted their camels. Strapped to the back of one man was the largest sword that Argon had ever beheld. The second man was tall and slender, now approaching on foot with a cane. Both followed the darker skinned man in the long coat. They were openly armed and their wariness obvious. The tiger sat on its haunches, intimidating but not threatening. Tension and questions loomed between parties.

"Greetings," the tall man said. "I am Oliver. This is Dorian, Maynard, and Nathan." He gestured at the tiger with the final name. "We come inquiring about your business with Mere, the garden city."

The accent was strange, but they spoke the language. It was a peculiar scene, the teak skinned tribesmen and the three strangers with a tiger.

"You bring the omen," said Serj. "We have not seen one of our kindred beasts since before there was desert. Surely, this is a sign for us."

"I think you're right," said Dorian. "What do you think, Nathan?"

The tiger began to change. Serj jumped, and Argon stared at the shifting creature. It did not contort, but the light around it shifted and bent until it finally stilled in a human form. He was a fiery man, tall and fully clothed.

"I think," said Nathan, "some demigods have been at work."

"I'm sorry?" asked Oliver.

"What is this talk about gods?" asked Serj.

"I can explain," said Nathan. "For now, the important part is that you are here by design. We are allies."

"How do we know this?" asked Belriah.

"For one thing," said Nathan, "it hardly seems a coincidence that I came to you as a tiger. Second, and probably more convincing, we came to you. We are at your mercy."

Belriah nodded. "I see it now. It seems we have much to discuss. If you will, I would have you come with us."

It was cooler in the tent as they sat in discussion. Argon thought that the strangers would have found their story hard to accept, yet Nathan claimed to believe them, Dorian nodded in agreement, and Maynard had little to say. What had been more fantastical was their claim, that they were the legends of old and had known Elah and Xu.

Nathan leaned forward and smiled. "I can take you to the king of your kindred beasts."

"Is Taesa not the greatest?" Belriah asked.

"I'm sure she's magnificent," said Nathan, "but I don't think you'll argue with me once you see this one."

"Let's see it," said Argon, feeling a little challenged.

"That's the trouble," said Nathan. "The best place to do that is rather protected right now. You said your god called you to fight a battle, right?"

"We believe so," said Argon.

"Well, I have a battle for you," said Nathan.

"Why should we fight for you?" asked Serj. "Who is to say yours is the right side?"

Dorian opened his mouth to say something but Maynard interrupted, "I can tell you that I have been on the wrong side and it almost killed me."

"We believe," said Dorian, "that our enemy holds the Pass and intends to march on the City. I think the Pass and what lies beyond it may hold some answers for you."

"The promised rains?" asked Belriah.

"That I cannot say," answered Dorian, "but I'm quite sure that you'll find the direction you seek."

"And what if we do not want your help?" asked Serj.

"It's up to you," said Oliver. "Our help is available to you regardless of whether or not you will help us. We have food, water, and medical care."

Belriah looked to Argon. Everything made sense to him, as if for decades, perhaps centuries, this had been a plan. His people survived the war, the people who worshiped the moon and the people who worshiped the sun. One the people of the crocodile, the other people of the tiger. In some strange way, the signs led to this unexpected path. That or the whole thing was a farce.

"Shall we consult in private or make our decision here?" asked Argon.

"I have nothing to hide," said Belriah. "It seems suspicious, yet it also seems the obvious path. What say you Serj?"

"Show the people. Let them decide. That is the way of the People of Fire."

The strangers consented to stay until the people could be assembled. They were given the best accommodations possible, though it was relatively little given their situation. Only Maynard left to update those back at the city. Argon found the man-tiger and asked to speak with him in private. They walked among the fringe of the encampment.

"Tell me, if you will, how we are to meet this king of crocodiles?" said Argon.

"You may not like it," said Nathan.

"I am more open minded than most," said Argon.

"Do you understand who I am?" asked Nathan.

"Your god was displeased with you as his servant and cast you away. That is your story," Argon said.

"In a way, yes," Nathan said, "But it wasn't just a god, it was *the* god."

"There are many gods, otherwise how could our gods lead us here."

"You are clever, indeed," said Nathan. "There is but one supreme god, the Eternal One. He created many spirits, some more powerful than others. These spirits have different rankings, classifications, and designs. Elah and Xu, as you know them, are — or were—among his most powerful servants. They are demigods, stewards of the light and day. Why do you associate the kindred beasts with your respective gods?"

"It is said that at the beginning, when all of the gods gave their gifts to the earth that the moon so loved us that it took a part of itself and out of it formed the crocodile from which all scaled animals have descended. The sun would not be bested by the moon, and so it gave us two gifts. First it gave us fire. Then it gave us the tiger, from which all haired animals have descended."

"Ah," said Nathan. "Why the crocodile and the tiger?"

"Because they are the mightiest of their kind," said Argon.

"That you know of," said Nathan.

Argon felt irritated. "It has been said among my people since the dawn of time. Are there greater beasts they did not know of?"

"No," said Nathan. "And I am sorry. I did not mean that to mock you. Though powerful, these demigods are just one kind of spirit. Some are in the service of the Eternal One, others have established themselves. Some have beings in their own control. These servants can manifest themselves in various ways, and they are called daemons, for they often prefer a certain form. When the Eternal One formed the earth, the demigods and other beings gifted its creator with creatures by which to fill it. Often these forms were that of the demigods' favored daemons."

"So," said Argon, "there is the god, the demigods, and then their daemons."

"You understand the hierarchy. Some daemons were also demigods or angels, or angels subservient to demigods. It's all rather confusing, but you get the idea. The point is that the daemon in the service to Elah is a quite active servant of his and he can be found."

"And what of the tiger?" asked Argon.

"I am afraid that daemon fell from Xu's service quite some time ago," Nathan said. "So you do not have the fortune of meeting him in his true form. But I tell you that you speak to him now."

Argon stopped and turned towards Nathan. Their eyes met. "You are asking us to believe quite a bit. We are not a gullible people."

"I'm not asking you to believe anything," Nathan said.

"This feels right to me," Argon said. "Then again, what choice do I have but to trust you?"

"About as much of a choice as I have to trust you. Oliver was telling the truth when he said that our aid is freely given. I know you need it. As for us, we need your help just as much.

"I am sorry," Argon said. "If you are who you say you are, I have dishonored you."

"It's not about me and my honor," Nathan said. "It's about working together to survive and then flourish."

The masses were gathered at a makeshift platform that had been raised. Argon was chosen to speak, but he intended to keep it brief. The man-tiger would be enough in itself. Judging by the sun and its shadows, the time neared. He looked to Nathan. The plan was simple. No theatrics, a straightforward demonstration for all to see. There was no simple way to explain the matter. He rehearsed different speeches in his head. If he were nothing more than a man in the crowd, how would he understand such a thing? He climbed the platform and surveyed the thousands of faces, staring intently. Serj and Belriah joined him, as did the strangers. It must have appeared an alien scene to the audience. Belriah gave a nod. It was time. After the crowd quieted, Argon began.

"You have wandered the desert in good faith. Through starvation and drought you have followed us. We have at last come to the next step in our destination. Before the promised rains, the gods would have us battle, but they would not have us battle alone. They have sent us men of greatness. We have joined with them to do what neither of us can accomplish alone. I was unbelieving at first but I cannot ignore the sign."

With that, he ushered Nathan forward who stood with a small smile. Once again the light bent around him and he transformed into a tiger. Argon took a step back. The tiger leapt from the stage and the crowd gave it a wide berth. It did not look menacing or threatening, rather regal and assuring. It pattered between the parting crowd and ran along it. Marveled gasps and cries of astonishment broke their fierce silence. The tiger returned down the path and jumped back upon the platform. Before it landed it retook the shape of Nathan, clothed, and smiling.

"This is what the gods have sent us," said Argon to the crowd. "Shall we ally with these people?"

There was a stunned silence. Argon's stomach tightened. They had inspired fear more than awe and the people would not assent. Then the crowd erupted, shouting in joy. Argon's heart beat faster. They had done it.

The camp was permitted to move closer to Mere so that the supplies might be made more readily available. Within a day it pressed against the wall and provisions came in full. The city could not host all of the tribesmen, but the higher ups like Argon were permitted to come and go as they pleased. Meetings and discussions were had. Plans were made. Water and other provisions were delivered to the people and Argon was beginning to better understand this strange group that had taken them in. There was a mutual respect, a working together that contradicted everything Argon had heard about the non-tribesmen. He had been taught that they often frowned on the way of the nomads, that they considered their civilization inferior, but these people appeared to have high regard for the tribesmen. In fact, if anything, they seemed genuinely grateful for the help, even though the relationship was equally beneficial.

It had been up to Serj and Belriah to worry about the logistics and planning. Argon sat in some of the meetings, but mostly he was consulted after the laborious conferences had sorted through the details. He and his family were given a suite near the oasis. The serene pool itself reminded him of the Eastern Pan, but the small guest house was a different type of accommodation altogether. The wooden walls replaced the tent flaps and the plush beds substituted for mats. He had quiet days to spend with his wife and children for the first time since the start of their journey.

Everyone referred to the meeting house as the "mansion" and Argon found himself there one day enjoying an unfamiliar fermented drink. The man Dorian found him pondering the beverage.

"How do you like it?" asked Dorian.

"It is a strange thing," said Argon, "At my first sip, I did not like it, yet now that I have tried it again, I can't seem to get enough."

Dorian smiled. "Such are the ways of beer."

"So, that is what they call it," said Argon. "Tell me, Dorian, how will Oliver lead us in battle with his injury?"

"He won't," said Dorian. "In fact, he is mostly logistical, behind the scenes. The frontline usually falls to me."

"You say it like you do not like it."

"It's not that I like it or dislike it," said Dorian. "It's my duty one way or another."

"Yet something about it troubles you?" asked Argon.

"I just don't want to do more harm than good," replied Dorian. Belriah might have been critical of Dorian, but Argon did not think lesser of Dorian. This man was caught between idealism and realism, duty and wisdom.

"That is a wise fear, but a man can let it drive him away from what he was meant to do. It can also drive a man to do better. My people would tell you that it is time your soul awakes."

Though days had passed, little word of Ratik reached Argon. Upon inquiry, little was said. Ratik was with their healer, the woman who started this city. She was one of the fallen and a capable healer, but even her progress was uncertain. They had almost been in Mere a week. He had been teaching his youngest son how to string a bow when the knock came.

He ran a hand playfully through the boy's hair. "It appears we have a guest, young one," Argon said. "Run along and try it yourself. And remember, no arrows until you get this part right."

The boy ran off into a back room and Argon opened the door to find a smiling Ratik.

"Argon," he exclaimed, throwing his arms around him.

Argon was surprised but delighted to see this man. He had been on the brink of dying, in and out of sleep as his wounds festered and putrefied, but now he stood bright and energetic.

"Ratik, my friend. I am so very glad you have recovered."

"You wouldn't believe it," he replied. "I was in pain and I dreamed the darkest dreams. Then their woman took me and lifted the decay from my wounds. She stitched me up. You should have seen the look on Haron's face. I am still sore and stiff, but I feel great. I must thank you."

"Thank the healer," said Argon.

"They say you pushed for them to find and approach a city. They say it was you who said there was hope for me. It was you who didn't give up."

Argon and Ratik agreed to sit out on the shore of the oasis. He had to help Ratik down since the man was still sore from his injuries. Argon sat next to him and for the first time really took in the beautiful blue waters. He wished a congregation of crocodiles lived there and that they could stay forever, just like they did back on the Eastern Pan. But this was not their city and they had a battle and journey ahead of them. His heart ached for Taesa, the crocodile that was more than a pet.

"Tell me all," said Ratik. "I have slept too long."

Argon told him of the rains, the dilemma of approaching Mere, and of meeting the fallen. He did his best to explain what Nathan had told him about the gods and Ratik seemed to understand.

"So, we are to battle," said Ratik.

"It is believed that our journey will carry us to what they call the Pass. A ring of mountains stands to the north and west and there is one way through. Beyond there, they say there are the promised rains."

"And you believe these people?"

"He is a man who takes on the form of the People of the Fire. He says he can show us Elah's chosen daemon. I believe him."

"I think I believe them too." Ratik said. "I will fight again."

"You should worry about recovering."

"Argon, my friend, you always think in this way. It's not about the promised rains."

"Then what is it about?"

"It's about hope for our people."

INTERLUDE

*A Crocotta's Story*

*I knew of Solomon Glass as the closest to my counterpart in Jacob's opposition. I was a commander under Dorian. He was a high-ranking dog closest to Raven, who, of course, served Jacob. It took a long time for me to connect that the man who called himself Sol was also the seemingly sentient crocotta that plagued our lines of battle. We learned of his nature from Liam. The rest of his story explains a great deal about his cruel disposition.*
   *—Oliver*

The crocotta was in his sight, the stock of the rifle pressed tight to his shoulder. The beast ahead had been standing still for some time, sniffing the ground, oblivious to his presence just a few yards back in the bushes. It was nice to get away from the war, if only to hunt in the woods a few miles away. He remembered the breath, the single inhale and the gentle pressure of his finger on the trigger. Before he could squeeze, before the kick of the rifle, something knocked him back. Breath left him with a heavy pressure on his stomach. Had the gun blown up in his hands? *Just like the fucking cartoons*, he thought. But he had not pulled the trigger. And there was that smell, the one that would follow him the rest of his life after that moment. When the world came back into focus, he still struggled for breath, but he saw the massive crocotta holding him down. *Smart bastards*. Indeed, they had been the ones hunting him. How had he not known? For two centuries he had looked back on that moment shocked by his own ignorance. He thought he would die that day, and looking back, he should have.

It raked its claws across his stomach, one of the cuts opening his belly. The moment let him gasp for air, but the pain sucked it right back out. He would not die in a war, but be eaten alive by this massive hyena. In a desperate attempt he pulled the knife from his belt and brought it down on the animal. The first blow glanced off the thick hide, but caught the animal's attention. He had to act quick, though the pain tore at his belly. He struck the creature again in the soft part at its neck. It dug in and the beast reared, jaws snapping close to his arm. Sol screamed and cursed as the beast thrashed, its saliva spraying about. It collapsed on top of him, its final death throes suffocating Sol and ripping at his wounds. After it died, it took Sol the better part of an hour to drag himself out from under the carcass. If any of the saliva touched his wounds it would be over. He'd die in paralyzed agony. After moments of unbearable pain, of pushing and pulling, trying to keep his insides in, hoping that the other crocotta was not patiently waiting nearby, he freed himself.

As he pulled away, he turned to the sound of shifting foliage, and the other crocotta appeared, cackling upon eye contact. Not a foot away lay the rifle, his best hope. Feeling his innards squirm and ripping pain, he took the gun. It pounced. He fired. It landed on his hand, crushing it, but the shot had maimed the animal. It squirmed, pulling itself from him, dragging its back legs. Everything in his hand felt wrong, like the bones had been arranged in their most uncomfortable positions. But Sol willed himself to hold the gun aloft and fire again. It struck the half-paralyzed beast in the neck, and it slumped to the ground, breathing heavily, dark blood squirting onto the foliage. Sol laid, breath heavy, staring the crocotta in the eye as it bled out.

It would have been a two hour walk back to camp. After wrapping his abdomen with his jacket using one hand, he dragged his way back to camp, sore and tired, waiting to just collapse and die. In battle, he had seen men die this way, uselessly trying to reattach limbs or hold their innards in, slowly dying in quiet hopeless sobs. He sometimes paused for moments on end and simply screamed. After a few hours he wasn't sure if the pain had subsided or if he had grown accustomed to it. He made more progress then, but more pain and delirium soon overtook him. By dawn the next day they found him, staggering through the woods. When they took him back to camp, dragging him into the medic tent, Raven came personally to check on one of his best soldiers. The words were lost in his memory, but he remembered Raven making an offer. Sol begged for it, begged for anything to make his hell go away.

He had fought the rest of the war surrounded by rumor. He would take off his shoes as he entered the battle, running and discarding them, and then the change would begin. Hair, claws, mass. He grew through his clothes, ripping them away. His yells turned to roars, laughter into cackles, and with the growth of his body, thus increased his bloodlust. Each kill filled his mouth with flesh, juicy with blood, and he grew, not only to like it, but to need it.

# CHAPTER TWENTY-SIX

*Hunger*

Sol dreamed of Shima. It was long abandoned, but a memory that he still contemplated. It was right after the boy, Liam, had gotten away. Crouching naked in the dark, his keen eyes surveyed the carnage. As usual, he felt no guilt at having done what was needed, what some urge deep down had told him to do. He licked his lips and tasted the still warm and fresh blood. Blood lined the walls of the back alley, stained the sand, and sat in pools glistening under the moonlight. It was dried beneath his nails, smeared on his chest, and the dirt clumped to it on his feet. Having just fed, Sol felt the wounds restoring themselves. The boy had made them deep and the healing would still take time. One meal was not enough.

He needed to return to his quarters. It would not do to be seen like this. The mess would be disturbing to whoever found it in the morning, and he contemplated making some effort to clean it, but the horror of his kill would be short-lived compared to what was to come to Shima. He began to rise.

"A good kill," a voice said. Sol squatted, jerking around, seeing Raven.

"Why Master Raven," Sol said. "Did you decide on an extended stay?" Unashamed of his nakedness, he rose from his crouch. "Enjoying the sights no doubt. We have sand galore."

Raven stood somewhat short but nonetheless noble, his skin porcelain in the moonlight. His hooked nose and black hair gave him a cold, raptorial look. Sol wondered how the fallen angel had acquired a long coat from the eighteenth century. It was Gothic, morose almost, but well fitted to him. "There's more sand in our future," Raven said. "We leave soon."

Sol licked some blood from his lips and sniffed, "For the Pass?"

"Not yet. First Bronton and then the Pass."

"I thought you said Bronton was laid to waste," Sol replied.

"It is, but we will rendezvous with Jacob there. Besides, that's where most of our work is being done."

"And what part in that work would you have me do?"

"You know exactly what I mean for us to do. We are not the only ones leaving Shima."

Sol awoke a long way off from Shima, the dream bringing back the events of the prior weeks. Raven's orders, the slaughter in the dark, the journey to Bronton. All of Shima came, bodies on wagons, pulled by the horses that once belonged to them. On the first day, the smell of flesh nagged at Sol's hunger, but after another day the rot nauseated him. Raven had suggested they travel at night for Sol's sake, but he suspected that Raven also disliked the sunlight, his pale complexion an obvious sign.

The stay in Bronton was brief and the bodies from Shima went with them. They did not leave Bronton on carts as in Shima, but instead reanimated. The town, the man Maynard, all of that was behind them. Before them gaped the Pass. Sol had always seen the mountains in the distance, but up close their magnitude was immense. While Jacob and the other fallen angels could not behold the Pass, Sol saw it well. It was warded against their sort, but not a bastard therianthrope like Sol. Thus, instead of holding back and waiting with the others, he went into the Pass with the abominations. They were disturbing, haunting even, and Sol felt awkward approaching the opening as the one sentient being amongst the host of zombies. Of course, the captain was there, with some presence of mind and control over the undead beings.

Jacob and the others had set camp behind, but Sol, the captain, and the abominations marched into the Pass at night. Jacob was sure the plan would work, adamant that Dorian's tenets would fail. *Love, life, all that other bullshit.* Sol was not convinced that such magic would be undone so easily, but who was he to turn down his hunger?

Perhaps fire might have stopped him. Those instinctual resonances plagued Sol, amplified in his reaction to sunlight, but even fire in a place like this held little intimidation. They entered the town quietly, and then the screams began.

After massacre, carnage, and slaughter, Sol returned to his master. He was the great hyena, powerful, cunning, and swift. No spear, arrow or blade stood against him. His giant form emerged from the dark crevasse, between the great walls of the mountains. The saliva dripped from his mouth, saturated red with blood. Emerging from the predawn glow on taloned claws, Sol approached Jacob and the others. Amelia, Raven, all of them stood, almost stupid with awe as they looked to the Pass. Jacob had been right. They saw it.

Sol the crocotta escorted them into the gap. He would not take on human form before them, he would not be naked, but a noble animal. He did not cackle like his brothers, but walked silent, his masters behind him. Jacob, Cain, Amelia, and Raven looked in wonder. The inhabitant's bodies lined the walls on either side, splayed from beginning to end. The river ran red. The abominations stood at attention, the captain at their head. This was their way in.

"I wish I had been here for this," Cain said.

"It worked," Jacob said, a grim smile spreading across his arrogant face. "It worked."

"A path of the dead," said Amelia.

*A path of the dead.* Stretched from the supposed impregnable entrance to the ruins. They had overcome the obstacle of the Pass, only to face the ruins, but Sol wasn't worried. If Jacob could stop Dorian's deep magic, he could overcome anything. The method was sinister indeed, but not without credit. Sol grinned, his sharp jagged teeth showing a little more. Raven came alongside him. "I brought you a change of robes if you prefer."

Sol nodded his head a little. Raven threw the pack on the ground and Sol picked it up, holding it delicately in his mouth. The others would have to decide what to do next and, in the meantime, Sol would return to human form and clothe himself. The homes and shops were built into the walls. They ran the length of each side, separated by the river. He had to push through the ranks of abominations and then over the line of dead bodies. Toward the end, Sol dipped into an alley, pack in mouth. He was alone in the darkness.

When he returned, he found the others talking.

"It's one obstacle after another," Raven said.

"Come now," replied Jacob. "We didn't journey all this way to be stopped by a pile of rubble."

"If we had been thinking," said Raven, "we could have used the townspeople to take it down."

"We don't know how far back it goes," said Cain. "It could take ages."

Jacob's mouth tightened. "We are gods, are we not? We have undone Dorian's deep magic and we will undo this as well."

"And what would you propose?" asked Raven.

A silence fell. Eyes shifted, and though Jacob did not look uncertain, he delineated. It was Amelia who broke the silence. "Give me two days and three living humans."

As they considered the conundrum of the ruins, the camp moved into the Pass and there was ample celebration at the tavern.

Thanks to the captain, abominations were set to clearing the bodies out of the tavern and soon the beer was tapped. They also discovered Oliver's quarters, library, and healthy stock of libations. Sol drank whiskey. It was not that he disliked beer. He was prone to a pint when struck by the mood, but there was nothing so stately, so simple yet refined as whiskey. One could drink it at an uppity party or in the dingiest dive, and it had a lovely effect on the mind, relaxing it in all the right ways. Sol sat at the table eying the short, half-full glass of liquor. He turned it, fingers on the rim, looking deep into its amber color, but pondering something else.

*Why?*

Of course, the question nagged at him with more frequency than he cared to admit. Perhaps it was due to his *condition* that he had given up on anything resembling virtue. He answered to the hunger and nothing would change that. Every man may have any number of masters. All are slaves to greed, self, sex, some or all of those things. Sol could have many a thing subservient to him, but he was content to serve in whatever capacity allowed him the solidarity and efficacy to feed his needs and live comfortably. He had done it for the past two hundred years and it worked well. He took another sip of whiskey. It burned a little, cheap stuff or poorly made. And so he told himself once again that perhaps the question was not why he did it. Sol downed his whiskey. The better question was why would he do anything else?

Two days in the Pass might have proved a luxurious stay had it not been for the odor. It was as if by some power, the fallen could turn off their olfactory, but Sol's curse gave him a more powerful sense of smell. He could not decide which would have been worse, staying in the camp outside of the Pass with the abominations or staying within any distance of the stench. Sol saw no reason for the dead bodies lining the Pass to remain. The deed was done and Dorian's ward was broken. Cain confirmed it when Sol said as much, yet no one seemed compelled to do anything about it. Nor did it appear that there was any hope of Amelia completing her task sooner than expected.

In his boredom, he took to frequent walks, exploring the Pass. It was perhaps one hundred yards wide with the river flowing closest to the western wall. Though the water passed under and through the obstructing rubble, it seemed clean enough so long as everyone did their business at the south end of the river where it dipped into a cave. Sol had tried to explore this cave, but it was not nearly as deep as he had thought. Just at the entrance the walls narrowed impossibly thin, the river having carved out a lower tunnel. Sol did not like the idea of swimming, so he searched no further.

Though the prodigious walls were rugged, they were more or less flat, jutting straight up. Sol could not guess their height, but it was at least three times that of the width of the Pass. The homes built into the walls did not go higher than two stories. Some of the previous townsfolk had carved the rough and uneven openings into proper, glassed windows. Others did not have so much as a door. Shops boasted signs, sometimes wooden, others carved and painted on the rock in white letters. It was clear from Jacob's comments that the rooms and recesses were Dorian's work. He intended for people to live here.

Early evening on the second day, during one of Sol's walks, he revisited the alley in which he had changed the night they taken the Pass. The alley had not been sacked as much as the rest of the Pass and Sol took the time to search the homes. He smiled when he discovered someone's stock of whiskey.

When he found the hiding boy, shaking timidly upon his discovery, Sol almost did not kill him. He felt somewhat sympathetic to the poor lonely soul, but then also felt compelled to rid the boy of his loneliness in the only way he knew how. He had comforted the boy with a game of hide and seek, so the boy felt nothing when Sol took on his crocotta form and interrupted the boy's counting with a claw to the throat. Dry stuff, really.

Sol searched the nearby homes for clothes that would fit, keeping in the shadows whenever possible. He liked that the Pass was abundant in shadows. The towering walls not only kept it cooler, but shielded him from the burning sunlight.

The homes were filled with relics from the past. He had almost forgotten daisies and lilies and daffodils until he found a book on gardening. One person had a stock of bullets but no gun. He got excited when he found an old music player, but the battery had faded. He then searched for batteries or a power source but found nothing. There was a bloodstained suitcase in one house where he discovered rusted and bloody tools. *Either a shit doctor or someone like me.* He smiled when he entered another home and saw their record collection. There had to be power nearby for people to keep such treasures, but he could not guess from where it came. Some of the musicians he recognized such as Led Zeppelin, Roy Orbison, and others. He thought he kind of looked like Tom Waits. Some of the musicians were new to him.

After exploring the alley, he left and visited the wall of rubble that stood between them and the City. He had never seen Novum in real life, but during the war with Jacob he had seen video clips. Once the mountains were raised there was little hope of ever beholding it again, and now a great wall of ruin stood before him. Amelia was expected to do something about it but she was nowhere to be found.

He began to scale the ruins. Though not much of a climber, he knew he could survive the fall. Sometimes he had to let the crocotta part take over, never in full, just enough to give him the strength to pull himself up and balance. He called it parshifting, the act of indulging his crocotta ability and senses without transforming into the entire beast. At the top of the wall, a steep slope fell into more ruins and in the dusk stood a black pyramid that must have been the City. He also saw, or perhaps felt, other black shapes. They loomed closer and he felt them pressuring him to leave. The push was so quiet, yet so compelling, he hardly knew what he was doing when he found himself working his way down. Something up there was wrong, terribly wrong, and it was only when he stopped a few feet down, heart pumping, and breathing heavy that he realized what he was doing. Such foreboding seldom had any effect on him, and yet he found himself anxious to descend. He contemplated climbing back up but decided to step down.

Amelia now worked at the bottom, organizing a pile of wood for a fire. She stood coolly, arms crossed around the sticks, her gaze searching the ruins. Sol could not decide whether or not he regretted that intimate night with Amelia. She had propositioned him, their soulless eyes meeting. He accepted her offer. There had been no romantic evening, just a time and place to meet and begin where her naked pale body and dark hair waited for him. It had been good. She played to all of his primal desires and even seemed to relish it. All of his desires except one. "No," she said when he made to bite her, "I can heal well enough from those little human teeth of yours, but you carry the crocotta's venom. I can't take my chances." She made it up to him in ways he had not imagined. He came out of that night with a thirst unlike any he had before. As a man's passions peak after a bloody battle, thus did Sol's carnality feed his desire to kill.

It had indeed been good, both times that night, but Sol wondered if it had been wise. Nothing obvious changed between them, but the little things were there. She was distant in some ways, as if she respected him a little less, as if he had come like a dog to her beckoning and it made him a little beneath her. She had become playful with him, but that was condescending as well. Sometimes he thought he understood it, as if it had been this way all along and she just needed to prove it. Sometimes he felt guilt, a foreign emotion that seldom bothered him. A kill never bothered him.

"Are you okay?" she asked, smiling as she leaned a broken chair leg on the woodpile. "Need another go?"

"Not today," he said. But he did want another go. He wanted to know how she tasted.

"Why so sour?" she asked.

"The ruins make me uncomfortable."

"Did you find something up there?" she said, looking up at the massive accumulation of concrete and rubble.

"Just a bad feeling," said Sol. "A very bad feeling."

"Did you see any dark shapes?"

"Yeah, but I didn't stick around long enough to see much of anything else. Why?"

"When Dorian raised these mountains it wasn't enough. Costly wards were also needed."

"Raven says you draw your power from another dimension. Is there really enough to raise these mountains and ward them?"

"There are other places to draw power, like the body of a man."

"A human sacrifice?" asked Sol.

"And what's more, a willing one. That's the only way Dorian would do it. To his credit, it makes the magic all the more powerful. Life is not death's rival. Love is, and as you can see, it was not strong enough." The pride in her voice was almost chilling, but Sol reminded himself that he had never loved and would never love. He might find a friend like Raven to care about in some capacity, to stay loyal to, but in the end, Sol did all he did for Sol.

Before all of this had happened, he did not believe in gods or angels. Love had been a mechanism, not inherently bad, but an outdated evolutionary trait that was most often a weakness. After the angels' fall, he had no choice but to change his perspective, and he learned quickly that there was a spiritual side to love, but he never changed his opinion. Love was a weakness.

They said that this god conjured love as a representation of itself, to instill in its chosen beings a sense of emotional and spiritual attachment. Sol could not help but wonder if this deity had gone dreadfully wrong in the creation process and had to instill the element of love as a way to keep an entire species from wiping itself out. But why would such a being care if its creation wiped itself out or not unless it truly loved as well? Sol's answer was simple: because the creator was wrong. The creation would not wipe itself out. It would do just fine without love, and in fact, it would thrive.

"Lost again, Sol?" Amelia asked.

"Two hundred years ago I didn't believe in a god and now there's an angel in front of me," he said. "Two hundred years ago I should have died, but here I am now and none the wiser."

"What is your insecurity?" she asked gently.

Sol might have never called it an insecurity, but it was just that. He wanted to ask her to meet with him that night, to challenge his sense of degradation, to prove himself by fucking her again. But instead he asked, "Are you going to get us over these ruins or not?"

"The others will be here soon. Help me arrange these for the fire."

The others arrived moments later. Amelia conjured a fire and lit the woodpile. Sol studied the odd lot. Cain looked ready for battle, his body covered in light leathers that fit tight around his bulging muscles. He brought three people with him, walking in chains with bags over their heads. Their crew of the living was dwindling and Sol wondered where Cain had obtained the prisoners. Raven's eyes shifted like he was in on something nefarious that no one else knew about. Jacob was slightly shorter than Cain but his presence was more demanding. There was a terrible confidence in his face, a lurking danger and determination. As comfortable and protective as his priestly garments might be, Sol felt out of place in them. Yet, looking at everyone, he was confident that they really could rule this shrunken world. The real mystery was what Jacob would do with the world once he had it.

They stood back, staring at the great mound of debris in front of them. It sat cold in the shadow, the rusted metal and dead wood sprouting from among the broken concrete. Amelia took the first of the prisoners and led the man forward. He smelled awful and looked as if he had been kept in the bottom of an outhouse. Amelia brought the other two forward, both women in a similar state. Not appetizing. She did not remove the bags from their heads, but Sol could hear the sobs and quiet pleas. They were not pleas for life, they were begging for the cold mercy of death.

Amelia granted the man's wish first. She grabbed him by the neck and drawing a knife she struck it up under his rib cage. The man's legs gave out, and holding him by the neck, she lowered him to the ground. The blood flowed and the stench worsened as she worked the knife. His legs twitched and he shrieked, but she held him down as she withdrew the knife. She reached into the wound and the man screamed louder. After a moment, she withdrew the man's beating heart. The organ throbbed in her outstretched hand, its beat almost audible. It took him longer to die than Sol would have thought. Amelia threw the heart into the fire and the smell of burning flesh filled the air.

The other two were visibly trembling and the bags on their heads were wet from tears. Sol almost felt sorry for them as Amelia did the same as she had done to the man. They screamed too. With the second heart, the fire turned a vibrant blue, and Amelia smiled at them before she faced the ruins with the third heart still in her hand. Sol could tell that she did not delight in the killings. They were a means to an end, the necessary steps to what it was she really wanted.

She raised her hands, and for a moment, all was silent, save for the crackling fire. It was but a murmur and then the rumble of grinding stone and squealing metal roared. Wood snapped and steel whined. A tremor ran through the ground. Small bits of rubble began to float and then the great broken slabs lifted as well. Amelia spread her hands further. The stones moved, hovering away from the Pass, settling on either side of the gap. When she was done, there remained a wide path and the river.

The river ran from the northwest greenery, coursing through the center of the ring where a great black pyramid stood in the distance. The sun glistened on its obsidian smooth surface, and even from so far away, it was beautiful. Jacob broke the silence. "Show yourself, steward."

Charcoal shadows appeared in the blurry shape of a man. It was like looking at a figure so out of focus that it appeared to be many.

"You are not the man you once were," Jacob said.

A voice whispered, *"No."* Except it was not a whisper, or at least it was not audible. Sol realized he had only heard it in his mind.

"Show yourself."

The voice hissed and the shadows slowly came into focus until it was one, solid dark man, a single void where the sunlight had no presence. Light began to trickle through the shadow until it coalesced into a man. He was naked, a single wound on his chest. His eyes stared into nothing and his ragged beard pointed down to his torso.

"The riddle of the Last Saint solved at last. What is your name?" Amelia asked.

"Sachin Pendharkar." His eyes uncrossed, focusing on Amelia, but the wildness remained. He stepped forward.

"Who bound you?" asked Amelia.

"Dorian," the man said, his voice croaking.

"You are bound again, but to another. Do you know who binds you?"

"Jacob" said Sachin Pendharkar, "And I will not be bound." His next step was defiant.

"Correct," said Jacob. He smiled. "You won't be bound to me, but you will be bound to her."

Amelia threw the third heart into the fire. The man seized for but a moment before the rigidity left his body and he knelt, gazing at them. The vacancy returned to his eyes and a grin spread across his face.

Jacob inspected the man a little and said, almost to himself, "Again, Dorian, I have used your own magic against you. It is only the first fruit of your undoing."

"Can you be a little less mysterious for five fucking seconds?" Sol asked. "What do you mean I'm not going?"

"Just that," said Raven. They sat in what was once the tavern. Jacob and his men had depleted most of the beer, but the whiskey remained. After pouring and serving them both whiskey, Raven broke the news.

"I've been your man for two centuries and you're just going to leave me in the desert?" He wondered, and not for the first time, if Raven could be trusted. Raven was nothing if not calculated, and Sol thought highly of his loyalty, but he worried that he was being disregarded. Sol didn't know if it was more terrifying that Raven might dispose of him or that Raven would more likely kill him once he outlived his usefulness.

"It's just for now," Raven said. "I need someone I can trust out here. I need you to do something."

It was more likely that if Raven was going to kill Sol, he would make use of his death. "Is it to do with this Last Saint? What does that even mean?"

"It was a rumor leaked to us about the time Dorian raised the mountains. We knew it had something to do with the wards in place."

"Is that why you quit?"

"No, it's not why we quit," Raven replied, agitated. "We never quit. Jacob made a deal with the Morning Star. We knew it would take time, though not this long. Jacob is patient nonetheless." Raven took a breath and continued, his tone more soothing. "Enough questions for now. I won't abandon you out here. You'll come to the City in time. You are to sack the garden city and you will use our newfound ally."

"We don't even know where that is," Sol replied, increasingly amused by the task before him.

"We do now. Before we got to the Pass, their scouts found our camp and we followed them back. With our reconnaissance and some old maps in the upstairs library we pinpointed the location of this city. You and the Last Saint will go there and target the important people. This is where it gets interesting. I saw Oliver when we sacked Bronton. I had no idea he was still alive, but I'm betting he's there."

"I had heard that I was not the only human survivor."

"Still a cripple from what I hear."

"Can I also take your little gang of gunmen?" Sol asked.

"Not the Infinite Bullets. Just the Last Saint."

"I think it's going to take a little more than me and whatever it is that you turned the Last Saint into."

"He's more than he appears. He can manifest in multiple locations, and he'll be able to find those you'll need to kill. He's an army all his own. Your job is to get in, make as many easy kills as you can, and then get out and return here."

"Give me some of those abominations and I'll just take the whole city down."

"Certainly do your worst, but I doubt it's a battle you could win. They are sure to know we are here and bring a battle to us, but we're going to do it on our terms. Your attack will hopefully bring down some of their more valuable players. It will also spur them to come sooner, which is easier for us to predict," Raven replied. "In the Pass will wait the captain and his abominations. Amelia is sure to summon her own little army."

"And you intend to fight them here?" Sol asked.

"That's just the thing," Raven replied. "We won't be here."

# CHAPTER TWENTY-SEVEN
*To Change the Man*

The stone chafed at his skin, abrading it layer by layer. At first it was a dull sensation. Then it burned, becoming unbearable. The lich rubbed with intense patience, but Maynard was beyond the pain. It was almost welcome among the lacerations and burns he had suffered. Anything was better than the suffocation. The coarse rubbing had gone on for hours, lightly grinding on his forearm, when the undead woman stopped. Maynard opened his eyes and saw the ghastly pale woman, her white dress covered in blood, most of it his. She looked to her companion, but the chains kept him from seeing her.

"It's time," she said. "Get the tetrodotoxin. The other woman came into view with a dropper and held it to the abrasion on his arm.

"Only a little bit," she said. "Just enough to keep him still." The tiniest drop fell into the wound. He was unsure what he expected, but this was wholly different. Over the next half-hour he lost function of his lips and tongue. His head pounded and he convulsed, losing control of his muscles and his bowels. The room stank worse and he wanted to cry out but could not find his voice, much less catch his breath. At last, the effects subsided and he found himself in his own waste, taking shallow breaths, unable to move. He tried to make a noise, but nothing came out. This was his fate worse than death. To be broken, and then to become one of them. Powerless.

"There you have it," said one. "This will be easier without the chains."

Maynard awoke in his chambers, cold sweat trickling over his muscles. He ran his fingers along his chest and sides where the abrasions and cuts were healing. The skin was scarred and stitched, but otherwise fine. It was just a memory. The worst had come after that memory and he was glad to have woken. He calmed his breath. Taking a blanket, he walked to the porch, relieved to have the open sky and stars overhead, though the clouds in the distance seemed closer. Sleep would not come, but perhaps this was better.

"Am I interrupting anything?" a voice asked. The shadow was Nathan's, standing in the dim light. Maynard shrugged.

"Good," Nathan said. "I've been meaning to talk to you. How are you holding up?"

"Just fine," Maynard said.

"I doubt that," said Nathan. "One doesn't recover easily from what you've been through."

"I've always been resilient," replied Maynard.

"Even a resilient man has bad dreams. Every time you move you can feel the memories, bits of pain with every step. How are you really?" Nathan held out a hand and an orange light hung in the dark before them. It gave gentle illumination to Nathan's concerned expression and Maynard's hardened resolve.

"The same. Bitter, confused, angry. I don't know," said Maynard.

"The plans have been made, much of them thanks to you. Two tunnels on each side of the Pass basically lead from the entrance and around to the back. We will take the army head on while two companies sneak through the caves and cut them off at the rear. I was hoping you would lead a group."

"Why me?"

"I'd bet you're a good warrior and a better man. We could use you."

"I don't know how I feel about fighting anymore," said Maynard.

In the soft glowing light Nathan pulled out Maynard's sword, sliding it from behind his broad shoulders. "Don't tell me you've forgotten this," he said handing it to Maynard.

How could he forget? The lightness in spite of its size, the way it seemed to cut through the air itself. He wanted to stand with it now and practice his forms.

"You know that sword was not your brother's making," Nathan said. "He cannot be blamed for the lie, for he hoped to escape your father. Had I been there things would have been different. They would have been better. I did not have that choice. But take it. Keep it. After breakfast, meet me at the practice field. I want to see what you're made of."

As it turned out, Jaked Mari was quite the swordsman. He came alive in combat, fighting with a practice sword against another man who Maynard had gathered was named Keye. Mari and Keye exchanged attacks in the practice yard, a hard-packed earthen patch lined by the armory and barracks. Jaked blocked one parry and attacked. Keye, who had a sword and a shield, barely recovered from the move and only after a quick maneuver avoided Jaked's thrust. With each strike, Jaked grunted through gritted teeth. Down, block, up, over, block.

"Do you think it will rain?" Maynard asked Nathan, looking to the north. They leaned over the railing of the veranda, enjoying the shade, and watching the melee.

"Those are no rain clouds," Nathan said. "Jacob awaits us."

Jaked's sword clanged against the other man's armor and Keye yielded. He was good, but he was no match for the Commander's lithe and graceful movements. "Not bad, soldier," Jaked said. "Adaptability will be your greatest asset and you're getting better at it." Good advice.

"Thank you, sir," Keye said before walking towards the barracks. Jaked Mari gave them a nod and left as well. It was their turn.

"Come," said Nathan.

"With live weapons?" asked Maynard.

"I trust you," he replied.

They stood in the circle, and Maynard realized they had spectators. He took out his sword, holding it before him, ignoring the whispers and gasps. Nathan wielded a simple wooden staff, a curved blade at the end. They nodded at each other, beginning to circle in slow calculated steps.

Though reluctant to strike first, he had a feeling Nathan's patience would outlast his. He decided to get it over with and made the first attack. He brought his sword down and the tip of Nathan's staff glanced it aside with ease. It was not unexpected. This sort of swordplay was different than battle. In warfare, the goal was to kill. Here, it took a certain finesse to mark the opponent without doing any real damage.

With the tension of the first move broken, Nathan took the offensive. Each end of the rod made to stab, trip, or hit him. Maynard ducked and blocked these with ease, but narrowly missed the slash of Nathan's clawed hand as Maynard brought his sword up to deflect another swing of the staff's blade.

"Come on," said Nathan. "Make an honest attempt."

Nathan might have been the hardest opponent he had yet faced. He defended each strike, countering with an offensive attack. The staff served Nathan well. Maynard sidestepped a swipe from the rod, blocked the other end that came around behind him, and brought his sword down in what would have been a fatal blow. Nathan met it and parried his sword down. As his rage built, Maynard countered the move, finding an opening, and brought the sword rushing for Nathan. Maynard stopped himself before the sword met the man's neck. Maynard was stunned at himself, but Nathan smiled.

"You might be able to take Dorian," he said. "Just don't tell him I said that. I'll admit defeat. It's a hot day out. Let's go find a quiet corner and a drink. There's something I'd like to talk about. I promise it's interesting."

They were soon enjoying a pint, sitting at an old splintering and wobbling table nestled in a tavern nook. They made it a point to sit out of notice of the patrons, most of who preoccupied themselves with games, discussion, or even the occasional book. Maynard took a sip of his beer. He preferred Charis's beer, but this ale was decent enough.

"As usual, Jacob tells just enough of the truth to hide the lie," Nathan said. "I knew a boy once. His father didn't teach him to swim. He took the boy on a boat to the middle of a lake. He threw the boy in. The boy learned to swim. Aye, he had little choice. Now, another father took his son and he showed him the ways of the water. The boy learned that without water, he would die. He then learned that too much water would kill a man. This father then taught his son the various ways to swim. He learned the difference in paddling like a dog and strong strokes. Which son became a better swimmer?"

"The latter, of course," said Maynard.

"Aye, right you are," Nathan said. "Now a man, on a whim, throws you into the Darkworld. Granted, there's slim chance of it being life-threatening, but you get little sense of the thing when someone just throws you in. I reckon you'll have to unlearn some things, but nothing we can't handle. First things first, it's not magic. You'd think two hundred years after the downfall of civilization folks might forget the stories of sorcerers and magic, but I suppose when the reason for said downfall is what appears to be magic, that's what you get.

"Well, the point is, when things go bad, you can't just conjure up stuff to fix your problems. I'm sure Jacob makes a good show of it, but it takes effort. Think of it like this. When you joined the military you went through training. You clearly had a gift, already had some experience, and then you had an education. Only then did you see combat. You block the first guy who waves his sword at you. It's a rather simple maneuver for a trained combatant, but it took a lot of work. You learned, you trained, you practiced. Who is to say how much time, sweat, blood, and energy went into being better than your opponent? It all made for one simple move that saved your life. Now, imagine taking a boat—a big one—and making it plow through the sand like it was water."

Maynard was beginning to understand Jacob's strange disappearances and behavior during his tenure on *The Northern Lady*.

"Or," continued Nathan, "reanimating the dead. Sure, there are the little things like conjuring minor fires or lights in the palm of your hand. You probably feel it when you fight, but if you want to do anything big you have to work for it. The catch is, you may have reached your limits. Eons ago, other angels were sentenced to earth and they laid with humans. Among their offspring some were greater than others. The fact that you can enter the Darkworld says much, and it's likely you can do great things.

"Now, I am a shapeshifter." Nathan took a swig of ale before continuing. "I prefer the form of a tiger as it is a being of my own creation. However, I can become just about anything. The issue is that it takes time and a great deal of knowing it."

"You can be anything?" asked Maynard.

"To a degree," said Nathan. "Raising the mountains took more time and energy than Dorian or any of us possessed. So, when it came to it, I did double duty as myself and him."

"And no one knew?"

"Well, Oliver and the lot knew, but what was left of our small army didn't know. It wouldn't have been good for morale or for Jacob to find out."

"How do you do it?"

"How do you know to wield that sword so well? Part of it is innate. Otherwise, you simply learn and you practice. Knowledge is power, in this case. You learned swordsmanship inside and out, and when it came to it, that's where this stuff really benefited you. You could stretch beyond our realm and feel the inner-workings of the thing. I learned forms because that was my job. You've already felt Charis's healing touch. You should see Dorian's command of the elements. But first things first. I'll teach you to make fire, because it's easy. Have you ever used flint?"

"I could start a fire with my eyes closed. Once, I did conjure a small flame in my palm."

"Ah," said Nathan. "That will make this easy." Nathan held out his hand and a small flame began in his palm. "I was there when the foundations of earths were formed, so I know the inner-workings of these things. If you feel into the Darkworld, you can probably find the way. At least give it a try."

Maynard held out his hand in the same fashion. He thought about that sensation he always felt when he started a fire. Sometimes there were the unsure strikes of the flint, but for some reason there was always the one strike that felt right as he did it. With it came the flame. Then he thought of the Darkworld and in some strange way, it made sense. He had to stifle the rushing sensation and push it back, only allowing a small bit to come through and sprout in his palm. Nathan's grin spread wide.

"Not bad," he said. "Eventually you'll be able to make it even bigger."

Maynard decided not to mention the feeling that he could.

Nathan sighed. "Alas, I wish there was more time to train you on these things before the battle. The first, at least, will aid you in the tunnels. It takes a lot to conjure enough to actually burn anything, but they make great torches."

"Who said I was going to go to battle?" asked Maynard with a smile.

"Whether out of duty, revenge, or anger, I have a feeling you'll go. I think you want to do the right thing."

"What if I don't think it's the right thing?" asked Maynard.

"Then I suppose you wouldn't go, but I'm not here to manipulate you."

"You got the nomads to join us well enough," said Maynard.

"It's a damn miracle," said Nathan. "And mutually beneficial. We need them."

"Do you really know everything you said you did?"

"And more," replied Nathan. "These are a very old people. Our meeting with them really is the machinations of the gods."

"Where are these people from?" asked Maynard.

"Back at the founding of the City, if the prophet was wrong, Novum would have been the greatest resort in the world. The prophet was right, and that made it not only the greatest resort in the world but also the largest religious institution. Certain outliers, those considered too unorthodox, were exiled, usually by their ethnicity or the color of their skin more than their actual religion.

"They felt they had been rejected by not only the City but by their gods. It was before Dorian raised the mountains that they came into the desert headed for the front lines of war. I diverted them well away and they kept many things associated with their former religion and culture but also took on a new mythology. I helped them discover a place to reside in harmony."

"Where did everyone else come from then? Wouldn't the islands have been empty?"

"The nomads are the City's exiles. The others are probably the descendants of former soldiers. They are likely from both sides, mind you. Others probably lived here, particularly on the southern island. They survived the razing of these lands and had no where else to go. There was a small group of refugees that came by ship, bringing many supplies with them that are still among the island today."

"What of the people beyond these islands in the Graylands?"

"They," said Nathan, his eyes darting to the ground in a hint of shame, "suffered a worse fate, I fear. Disease, famine, holocaust. Many followed Jacob blindly to their own demise. Those who resisted had the luxury of meeting their fate sooner. I fear the City will undergo the same thing if nothing is done. As for places like this, they would fall as well. We would be like the sprouts of life, coming through the cracks, only to be uprooted once and for all."

There was a short silence, a finality to the subject. In the end, it seemed Nathan was right. It was not a sense of obligation or even Maynard's usual thirst for battle that compelled him, but he would indeed fight. It was about time he did the right thing, yet his motives were *backwards.* The list of reasons mounted, but at the heart festered revenge for Jacob, Cain, and the captain. He only wished the lich women who had tortured him had died by his hands.

Callianeira provided some incentive to stay, but he did not imagine that he would ever be anything but alone for the rest of his life. At least, this battle might give him one last chance to do something good, even if it couldn't redeem his prior actions.

"I still don't know," he said.

Nathan met his eyes.

Maynard continued. "I feel like I've spent my life trying to satisfy my own delusions by following the delusions of others. I'm done with it."

"This is your opportunity to make a difference. I can't promise glory or anything like that," replied Nathan. "But I can promise you that it's worth it."

From the honesty in Nathan's tone, he meant it. In a sense, things had been more straightforward under Jacob. Do the dirty work, get the glory, acquire the wealth. When Maynard had followed his reasoning to that hollow end, he found himself the subject of torture. Now he was a potential key player on the other side. This worldview, though more substantial, was also more complicated. He could fight for the cause of these people, but deep down revenge motivated him. In the end, any altruistic motives were questionable. Was Dorian doing it for the greater good? Surely most fought out of obligation, perhaps even Nathan.

"Why do you do it?" Maynard asked, bringing his glass to his lips.

"As with anyone, it's complex," Nathan said. "I guess you could say that I don't like the idea of living in Jacob's world. There's so much potential in humanity, so much opportunity for love and beauty, and to watch that burn under his power goes against everything for which I stand and believe. But, I suppose part of it is revenge, that he has wronged us and I can't let that happen again. Now that he took away someone that I loved, I hate him even more. Humans see the spiritual war simplistically, as good versus evil. There's God and the devil, angels and demons, and that's it. You know better because you've fought in a war. You know that the citizens of any given kingdom have different vested interests, jobs, and opinions. Not all citizens are soldiers, and in fact, one might support the country as a citizen but have nothing to do with the war. They might be a blacksmith or merchant who pays tribute to the government, but has no real implications in the conflict. Such are the ways of the spiritual war.

"Dorian was the steward of a planet much like this one. I played another role. Then Jacob used us. He thought he could pull off what the Morning Star failed to do so long ago. He had an unfortunate understanding of things, and now we're just another group of angels sentenced to Earth."

"Why sentence you to Earth? Are we God's jailhouse?"

"Nothing of the sort," said Nathan, "You must understand that this is the only planet on which we had hope of a chance at redemption. Most fallen angels seek such redemption and the rest that don't are usually too complacent to act on any resentment they might have."

"So, Jacob was the exception. Yet the Eternal One—God—didn't see it coming?"

"Jacob was the exception. As to the issue of what God does and doesn't know—well, you are delving into a complex territory."

"Try me," said Maynard.

"I don't fully understand it myself. I thought I used to, but the more time I'm here the less I seem to understand it. It's kind of like the universe was never meant to know this kind of pain, and after a few billion years, it still isn't equipped to understand it."

"I suppose not," said Maynard.

"Even if we could understand pain, it wouldn't change the fact that it still happens. In the end, we still have to face it. So, the question for us isn't why bad things happen or why God lets them happen. Leave that to the philosophers. The question is what we're going to do about it."

"And what can we do about it?" Maynard asked.

"We can hope. It's one gift that humanity gives back to the stars."

"We die anyway."

"Perhaps we will, but hope is something you pass on. I may have ulterior motives such as revenge or obligation, but those are auxiliary to something greater. I believe the same might go for you."

It might have been the beer, but the subject made Maynard's head spin a bit. Still, he pondered it, playing with the idea. There was such a thing as good for goodness' sake, after all. It was likely he was too broken, too damaged for such a thing, but if not for the desire of revenge, he could almost buy the notion that life was not about some simple and selfish survival, but about the greater solidarity of mankind. If that was the case, what was his life worth? Alone and dying, it was worthless, but if by the time of his death he had sacrificed enough, perhaps a few others might live a life fuller than his own. It was not about fixing the wrongs of the past, but rather preventing them in the future.

When he thought of Jacob, his temper burned. He recalled the betrayal, the stitches in his side, and the days of sleepless torture. Maynard breathed heavily. He could be no altruist. If nothing else, he wanted Jacob to burn.

"Are you all right?" asked Nathan. Maynard realized he was grinding his teeth and stopped.

"I'm fine," he replied. "Just thinking about Jacob."

"It's okay to want revenge," Nathan said. "Just remember that it won't satisfy you. It can consume you, and in the end, even with Jacob dead, he can still destroy you. Remember that you have greater motives."

"So they say," replied Maynard, "but it's all I can think about."

"I hope for your sake there comes a time when you recognize the change in yourself," said Nathan.

"Me too."

"There's something different about the people here," said Nathan, perhaps recognizing the need of a subject change. "The world took a strange turn when seven fallen started a war. Before that, there were people who didn't believe in God. Now the questions are if God is a good or bad deity. Which god is it? Of course, these days most people just pray to anything that will get them through the next drought. The world's even stranger with Jacob's return. I discovered a long-lost progeny, we pick up a demon, the prophet lives and his boy, Liam, he's something special too. I never met the prophet, but back then he had everyone's attention. At nine years old, he said something and it happened. He had the world watching. It's a wonder every single person wasn't rushing the gates of the City, but then again I think most simply couldn't make the move. He wanted to include as many as possible, unfortunately his financial backers were more interested in money, the thing that matters least at the end of the world."

"Is this really the end of the world?"

"Heavens, no!" said Nathan with a laugh. "That's a long way off, I can tell you that much. I meant it figuratively, which is why there's hope. We may have a dark time of it yet, but even if we don't succeed someone will."

"Dorian can do it, can't he?"

"He can," said Nathan. "But he needs to come around again and people like us to help him do it. He's the most powerful of us and the best leader we could have, but he has to rise to it. He's playing the part now, but he needs to own it. I fear he will have to witness Jacob's atrocities all over again before he really fills the role, though I think our encounter at Bronton made the necessary impression."

"What do you think of the demon girl?" asked Maynard.

"Callianeira? We had a talk about her the other day and we trust her."

"What's her story?"

"I'd like to know that as well, and I'd also like to know why she's here with us. That woman has caused us a lot of trouble across multiple galaxies. However, she's here, and I can't think of any reason that it's to her benefit. Have you talked with her?"

"I have," Maynard said, and thought he should talk to her more. Something else hid behind her sarcasm. She was here for a reason and he suspected it might help him better understand his own position.

"You know," said Maynard draining his mug, "I think more conversation would do us good. Any I idea where I might find her?"

Maynard knew that he was good at one thing and that was killing. That much was evident in the battles of the southern provinces, Jacob's skirmishes from town to town, and the random fights. The killings replayed in his head. He was no lover and nor could he find in his heart an honest contentment for a peaceful life. Deep within he wanted revenge, harboring a bloodlust. There inlaid a desire to take his sword and strike down an enemy. A man eats and is satiated, but soon he will be hungry again. Perhaps what Maynard really needed was a change of heart, but he could only want to want that. He was inadequate in all ways save for combat. Even the fact that it upset him catalyzed into the want to do it more. It was a bastard of a thing.

He sighed. There would be no redemption, though the shifting world demanded his competencies. He could yet use them for good. By helping Dorian and these strange people he could do something for the better, all the while vicariously doing what he did best, not to mention perhaps gain revenge. Well aware that he could never undo his past, that all else in him was damaged, Maynard decided that he was no longer the mercenary, no longer content to do anything for the sake of wealth or power. He had sought those things his whole life, and even at his wealthiest, he had nothing to show for it. He had still been discontent, happiness never quite within his grasp, always wanting more.

Jacob might have the best intentions for the City, but Maynard had seen the Graylands and the pile of bodies gathered as they crossed the desert. He had beheld the abominations and even come under Jacob's own wrath. Maynard shuddered. Whatever the case might be, Jacob needed to be stopped, and Maynard knew it was within his power to be integral in Jacob's undoing.

Still it nagged at him. A part of him wanted to aide in Jacob's fall, but he feared what it would do to him. Surely a demon had done things just as bad or worse. How did she overcome her nature?

The mansion was empty save for servants and the soft piano playing. The gentle arpeggios gave life to the rustic, floral atmosphere. He walked into the parlor and Callianeira sat at the piano with her back to him. Everything about her had a hardened gracefulness, as if what would have otherwise been a delicate lady had become a seasoned and perhaps bitter woman. She stopped playing.

"I'm sorry if I startled you," Maynard said.

She turned around with a little bit of a smile, "You can't sneak up on me." The moroseness had left and that sly humor had returned.

"If you had some time I was hoping we could chat." Maynard was no good at this sort of thing. "Maybe over a pint or something."

"Are you offering to buy a girl a drink? Who am I to refuse?" She got up and walked towards him. "Lead the way."

Maynard always seemed to pick the seediest of places, but it appeared nice enough on the outside, much like everything else in Mere. Goose's Wild looked to be the rough part of town, but there was no going back now, so they chose the quietest table they could find among the boisterous card players, detuned piano playing, and general rabble. Maynard had tasted better beer, but it was suitable. He should have taken her to Charis's own pub, but it seemed unoriginal and he preferred this be more inconspicuous.

"Sorry for the noise," Maynard said.

"No problem, just my kind of place," replied Callianeira. "So, you wanted to talk or is this your excuse for a date?" She looked around the smoky room.

"Right to it, I suppose. I can appreciate that." Yet, now that it had come to it, Maynard was not quite sure what he really wanted to talk about. Why was she here? What was her story? He could not help but feel a little self-serving, as if she was there to help him. He did not feel he deserved her help, and she was too clever not to know as much. Not to mention, the middle of a war was a bad time to get to know a girl.

"So," she said, breaking the awkward silence. "What is it?"

Perhaps it was this beer on top of the pints with Nathan, but Maynard decided to be honest. Regardless of what might have been better judgment, he let it all out. "Look," he said, "you and I, we don't really fit in. We're outsiders. Part of me is actually starting to believe in this crazy cause, and the other part of me just wants revenge, and knows the last thing I need is more bloodshed. But at the end of the day, well—"

"You wonder why you do it?" Callianeira asked.

"Yeah. I mean, why are you here? What's your story?"

"That deserves a longer and more complicated explanation than I care to give, but I'll try and give you the short of it. Demons are an interesting lot. Some manipulate people to do things out of fear and intimidation. Some get people to do things by pleasure. People can always push back when forced to do something. Therefore, getting a person to choose pleasure and complacency, even at the expense of others, is generally an easy route. To the men I tempted, I was just a girl at their side, a thing to bed when they felt like it. I'd hardly call it a paramour. But I was also the one whispering in their ear. Even the greatest of men can be bought. I had it all to offer. Sex, wealth, you name it. Suddenly, just and altruistic causes were replaced with selfish motives like greed, glory, and lust. I fed those things.

"Then one day, after hundreds of years, it occurred to me that it could work the other way around. Those preoccupied by their own selfish motives could come out of that. They could indeed learn to do things in the name of goodness and love. That bothered me. I was given an assignment, to tempt and corrupt a man. He already wasn't a good man, but it was imperative to my overseer that I drive this man to obsession with glory and wealth. When I looked into his soul, ready to feast on those carnal desires I saw something different. I saw a man who could love. He could go from self-serving depravity to altruistic self-sacrifice. At that point, I knew I couldn't do it anymore."

"And here you are," Maynard said.

"When I met the others, I joined them because I had little else to hope for and they offered a distraction from the temptation to go back. It has been a long while since I had an assignment on Earth. I didn't know much about what was happening at the time, but I knew that we—you, me, Dorian, and the others—were meant to come together."

"You found me covered in shit and tortured to near death. Even I might have left me for dead."

"No, Maynard. I've seen a piece of you that no one else has seen."

"I find it hard to believe that I'm the reason that you are here."

"I don't expect you to understand." He didn't. This fool girl thought he was someone who could really leave behind the terrible things he had done and do anything for the sake of good.

"Listen," Maynard said. "I've done bad things. And when I wasn't busy doing bad things I stood by while they happened, condoning it with my silence and inaction. I served Jacob, who apparently is almost as bad as the devil himself, and you think I have some potential for greatness? I'm a bad man and a fool, and you're a fool for not seeing that."

"Don't you understand? I know you've done bad things. You've left them behind, and because of it you will be that much greater. That's what gives you humans so much potential. You can push aside that instinctual desire to satiate yourself at the disadvantage of others. You can choose to not want the things you want. And you can act on that. I can't explain it. Just think about it. Pay attention to yourself."

"That's just it. All I want is revenge and I can't make myself want otherwise. "

"If I could take all of my demons and destroy them," Callianeira said. "I would. But we don't do what we do because of our past. We do it because of our future."

"Past dictates our fate," Maynard replied, but Nathan's words about hope returned to him.

"Don't you hear me? Human greatness is not in its fate. It is in its ability to spite fate, to reroute it, to change its trajectory."

Maynard sighed. Was there something wrong with these people or him? "Thank you for talking with me," he said, throwing some coins on the table as he started to get up to leave.

"Maynard," Callie said. The sardonic look was completely gone. This was Callianeira, the rogue demon girl, the one who gave it all up for some bizarre belief that he was something more than another man with a bad past. "There's a battle coming. Fight it and see how you feel. There's more to life than wealth, glory, or revenge. There's also more to life than self-pity and anger."

"Perhaps," Maynard said. "But with all of this hope you and Nathan talk about come risks, I've already disappointed people enough."

# CHAPTER TWENTY-EIGHT

## *The Invasion*

According to the scouts, Jacob's army was double their numbers. The difficulty was that abominations, no matter how ruthless, could not contend with trained soldiers. When Raven came to him with his task, Sol balked, but the plan made enough sense and in his shrewdness, Sol decided this was his sort of job.

To further pique his interest, Raven told him that he was not the only mortal to survive these past centuries. Not only had Raven seen Oliver in Bronton, but noted his use of a cane. Furthermore, a secluded and modest abode was found within the Pass and among many rarities an assortment of canes were discovered. It explained much that Oliver dwelt in the Pass during the hiatus. Judging by Oliver's writings and his choice of books, his resourcefulness had not waned.

The Pass far behind, the creature formerly known as Sachin Pendharkar rode beside Sol, their camels steadily taking them closer to Mere. Sachin took no food or water, nor said a word. "Do you know the way?" Sol asked. "What are you going to do once we get there? You got a cigarette?" He gave up after his next question. "What the fuck are you?" Sachin sat atop his camel with that shit-eating grin and eyes that stared into nothing a thousand yards away. He did little to shield himself from the elements, unlike Sol who now wore his customary robes, bandages and hat as he rode under the wretched sun. Even then his fingertips burned, a sensation to which he had grown accustomed, not that he preferred it.

This shell of a man, a shadower they had called him, was going to get them into the garden city. Sol's job was to wreak havoc wherever possible, avoiding direct confrontation, and doing as much damage as he could muster as a distraction. The shadower was going to assassinate as many of the important people as possible. Hopefully he would succeed with that little bastard Liam. Then again, Sol had a small respect for the boy. He was brave, bordering on stupidity, too curious for his own good, but he had fortitude as well.

The shadower seemed to know where he was going, but a few days later, Sol began to wonder if they were lost. However, when the fifth night neared, a city emerged on the horizon and as they got closer Sol knew there was no mistake that it was Mere. They would enter and leave the beauty that peaked from beyond those walls in chaos, retreating to wait at the Pass. Jacob and the others would be safely in the City, while Sol ensured their diversion at the Pass bought Jacob plenty of time and diminished their enemy's leadership and morale. Most important, it would lure them into action.

Back at the Pass, Captain Reed waited, who now looked more animal than human. Maynard and the lich women were to make their way from Bronton as well. Amelia left a few of her own nasty surprises at the Pass and there was the massive army of abominations. Jacob had made the Pass a strategic foothold that even the best trained soldiers could not hope to overcome without much greater numbers. *Our own little Battle of Thermopylae.*

The shadower held up a hand, motioning for them to stop, and pointed at the ground. They were far enough that it would have been difficult to spot them coming from the west, particularly later when the sun started to set. They needed to wait until nightfall. After dismounting, Sol erected a makeshift shade. One day he hoped to stumble upon a good parasol, but until then, the wooden tripod and a thick canvas would suffice. As he dozed in the afternoon heat, his hunger grew. If nothing else, this little invasion would give him plenty of sustenance for the coming battle at the Pass, assuming everything went according to plan.

When he roused from his nap, the gaunt face of the shadower greeted him, directing that haunting ear-to-ear smile at him. Their eyes met, but the shadower's pupils were bottomless pits of unseeing malice. Sol rubbed his own eyes, trying to shake the unsettling sight.

The man pointed at Mere, a shadow in the moonlight but visible nonetheless. Dark shapes jutted from the horizon, blotting out the stars splattering the sky. It seemed closer than it had by day. Sol disassembled his makeshift camp and they walked onward toward that shadow.

It must have been near three in the morning when they arrived. There were sentries along the wall, but they seemed oblivious to Sol and the shadower. The man who had been Sachin Pendharkar signaled Sol to remain and scaled the wall. His limbs moved with ease, like a spider, until he reached the top. Moments later, the figure peered over the wall, motioning for Sol to join him. What appeared to be a smooth wall proved an easy climb. Raven had hinted that such a being was quite powerful. By breaking the wards Sachin Pendharkar had protected, this thing could go on to break other wards and perhaps a little more. Perhaps the walls were more climbable than they looked, but if the ease with which Sol hoisted himself had anything to do with this thing's power, then it was potent indeed. What a terrible creature.

Sol almost laughed aloud when he reached the top. The crocotta part of him could see better in the dark, and the work of art before him was as glorious as it was disturbing. Sol turned and turned again, surveying the carnage. Each corpse, or what was left of it, lacked a tongue and jaw where the entrails had been shoved instead. These soldiers had been rid of their ability to make a sound and then fed their own intestines. Sol almost slipped in the blood. The man formerly known as Sachin Pendharkar still smiled.

Stairs led down from the wall, disappearing down an alley, dodging the multicolored lights. Between the shadows, they worked their way around every lamp and illuminated bulb. Past the trickle of water and the smell of honey, they crept in the bushes. Behind the stables the smell of dung repelled Sol's senses, but the scent of horse made him hungry all over again. They whinnied in unease, sensing his thirst. Tonight, he would taste more than horse meat.

When they came to the cottage, its windows dark, the shadower turned to him and nodded. Sol had his own work to do, but he sensed that he would know when it was his time. Shadows stretched from the man's hands lengthening into pointed, black talons. Silently, the cottage's door opened, and they entered the dark house. In the bedroom, a man slept alone. The Last Saint raised his shadow-clawed hand and brought it down.

They ripped through the man, too fast for him to let out a cry. They trenched down his body, slicing through flesh and bone. The sound was slick with the occasional crunch. When the shadower finished his head-to-toe gouging, he glanced at Sol before returning his attention to the corpse and continuing to belay it with his claws. The laughter started quiet, and though it never quite got loud enough to leave the little house, the shadower carried on ripping into the corpse until he decided that the walls and himself were adequately sprayed with blood. Sol was almost as shocked by the sound of the man's laugh as he was by the butchery itself. The man seemed to blur then, to become blacker than the night and divide as if out of focus. Then the dark men ran different directions. Most shocking of all was when it spoke. It was as dark and sinister as anything Sol had ever heard, "It's your turn."

Maynard the widowmaker slept restlessly. He smelled burning again and the words of the woman in the fire echoed in his mind. *Bane of wives. Maker of widows.* She was in flames, shouting at him, calling his name as the flesh fell from her body. He turned in his sleep, pushing it from his mind only to recall the torturing sisters. He startled awake, the sweat-soaked sheets clinging to his body. He was alone. Or was he? It was all a dream and the thick black figure of a man was a trick of the shadows, but then it moved. It seemed a wind in the curtains until the shadow raised a hand, its fingers stretching to sharp points. Maynard rolled from the bed just as it ripped into his pillow. The sheets stuck to him as he tumbled to the floor, his knees cracking against the hardwood. Upholstery rained down around him, tickling his skin. The sounds of scuffling emerged from the next room.

What little moonlight came through the window gave him a dim view of the shadowy figure coming toward him. Its blackness absorbed darkness around it, only something resembling a grin visible on its pit of a face. It ignored the sound of muffled fighting from the neighboring room. It raked its gangly talons on the remainder of the bed as it approached.

The creature evoked such trepidation in Maynard that he almost froze. He should die better than this. His eyes darted towards his sword leaning against the wall out of reach. If he could reach it, could it kill such a being? The shadow was closer now. The imminent smell of blood filled his nostrils and Maynard tensed. Before he could rise to defend himself, an explosion erupted.

Debris glinted in the moonlight, followed by a blinding flash. He covered his eyes and laid low as the heat washed over him and flecks of wood battered his skin. When his eyes adjusted he saw the detritus thrashing into his assailant, ripping into its blackness. Another dark body sailed through the air, crashing into the other figure.

Maynard's ears rang, but both of the dark men were down. Dorian ducked into the new gaping hole in the wall. "Are you okay?" he asked, holding up a glowing hand. Maynard nodded his head.

"Good," Dorian said. "Where's your sword? We're going to need your help." It seemed his decision was made for him. Maynard knew that if he fought now, he would continue fighting. Something about Dorian's eyes, the fire glowing in his pupils, reassured Maynard.

Maynard saw that his sword still leaned against the far wall. "I'll get it." Maynard crawled over, his body aching in protest, and found his sword. He gripped its handle and leveraged it to pull himself to his feet.

"These shadows are rare magic" Dorian said, "but steel will work on it as well as anything else. Let's go."

The dark figure was bent on cornering Liam. Liam attempted to dodge and maneuver around it, but it was fast and Liam had almost suffered fatal blows several times. It struck at him again and Liam moved more out of intuition than sight, thrusting his dagger forward. It sank into something like flesh. As Liam pulled it out, he put his shoulder into the dark man. The figure went down, but as Liam started to run from the room, he slipped on the blood, collapsing on the shadow. Liam's hands felt the sticky substance, empty of the dagger. A shadow that could bleed. What sort of thing was this?

The shadow rolled, twisting Liam under it and pinning him down. A strange hand locked around his neck, suffocating him. He kicked and punched to no avail. There was no sound from the figure as it raised its other hand, smoky claws ready to strike.

Liam gasped for breath until the grip tightened and he could inhale no more. Then only his heartbeat resounded in his ears. The room became even darker, the moonlight fading away.

His breath left him and so would his life. His nails dug into the wooden floor, the splinters coming to life in his hands. The muscles in his body failed him. Desperately he wanted air, but his lungs only ached. Pain became his world, from the discomfort of the floor to the agony in his chest. The creature raised a hand, each finger like a dagger and ready to fall upon him.

The silence broke with shattering glass. The figure jolted, its grip loosing, and Liam's world came back to him. The shards of glass flew into the air and clattered to the floor. A figure launched through the broken window. A silhouette against the moonlight, a girl, her hair blown back as she rushed at them, a gleam on her blade. The weapon came towards Liam's throat, but it went past him, digging into his assailants face. He felt the grip loosen and warm liquid gushed on him.

The figure toppled off, but recovered quickly. Liam's fingers found the dagger. The shadow rose without ceremony this time. Its claws flew in the air, and Liam ducked. He slammed the dagger into what would have been its ribs. It felt like the dagger sank into tar. In its thrashing, it knocked Liam to the ground. The girl plunged her own dagger down, striking the shadow's spine. It quivered, fell, and moved no more. As Liam recovered, the girl dragged it away. For a while he lay gasping. With help from the girl, he stood, and then saw that it was Aster.

"How did you know?" Liam stuttered, rubbing his throat. It would be bruised, another wound to add to all he had been through. As for Aster, he had avoided her, afraid that her odd knowledge of his past was a threat. Somehow, she knew to find him here, but apparently meant to help him.

"No time to explain," she said, putting the pommel of a sword in his hand. He looked down at it and realized this attack wasn't just a threat to him. He nodded at her and they left.

As they ran into the night, the scent of smoke plagued the air. Around the corner and out of the estate, the flames became more apparent. Cries of panic and pain rose, the wailing a dirge of destruction. After navigating the burning timber, Aster led him down another alley. The trees, their purple flowers once so beautiful, now glowed a devilish red.

Another dark figure emerged from behind the building. It rushed at them, but Liam had been ready and with a single slash stopped it. Gleaming blackness poured onto the ground until the figure fell into a melted mass.

"What are these things?" Liam asked.

"I don't know," Aster replied, "but I didn't like what I felt. We need to find somewhere safe."

"If the mansion isn't safe, I'm not sure where to go." Though he wanted to keep fighting, he was weary from his encounter. Even if Aster could take care of herself, and apparently him as well, he wanted to find safety for both of them.

Though short of breath, Aster spoke, "I think they primarily targeted the mansion and the parsonages of the consulate."

"But the whole city is burning," Liam said. "What about the church? If it's not safe, we at least stand a chance of saving Barker."

"The church it is then," Aster said. "I'll lead the way."

Maynard had first gone to Callianeira's room and found her with a stiletto in hand. Her shoulders relaxed when she saw him. "They sent one for everybody but me. They don't know I'm here." She really was a wild card, an unknown asset against Jacob.

When they got into the main area of the city, they entered the tumult. The once beautiful trees of vivid lavender and scarlet flowers now burned. Flame consumed houses, their residents screaming from within. For perhaps the first time, Maynard realized the gruesome reality as something more than the simple result of war. This was pain and suffering in its excess and it tasted bitter.

Soldiers worked to aid and restore order, ushering citizens one direction and looking toward the chaos for any oncoming enemies. A shadow jumped behind one of the soldiers, and with a swift gesture, cleaved the man in two. Maynard rushed over as two more dark men attacked the soldiers. He made quick work of one, a soldier took care of another, but the third shadow brought down two more soldiers before Maynard finished it.

"Where is Oliver? Where is Jaked Mari?" Maynard asked.

The remaining soldier, bloody faced, stood motionless and staring, the fire reflected in his blue eyes. Then the man turned and began to run. For a moment Maynard thought the man was afraid of him, until a great beast sideswiped the soldier.

*Sweet, sweet flesh.* This was something Sol gladly did for Raven. Amelia's dark man let him in and the slaughter began. The chaos started long before anyone realized it. He tore through the streets, shredding soldier and bystander. It was night and he was in his beastly element. He had seen—no smelled—a man coming at him and without having to look, clawed him down. It would take days for the man to die.

In this state, he contained all of the attributes of the crocotta. His bite was leaden with tetrodotoxin, a lovely chemical that left victims in paralyzed agony, able to feel but not move. If that didn't get the job done, the bacteria in his claws and teeth were sure to make for a painful death. After two hundred years of therianthropy, he still reveled in his existence, still loved every muscle movement, and every smell. He killed his way to a large square. There were people all around, but with whom to start?

There was a fight with the dark men, but it died quickly, a man with a big sword—likely more trouble than he was worth—taking the last dark man down. Sol concentrated his malice on the soldier whose shocked stare begged to have his traumatized state ended in death. Sol was happy to oblige. The man saw him first and ran. Sol leapt upon him, ripping out his arm.

The man cried in pain and Sol readied to end him when he heard the challenge. "Is that you, Sol, you bastard?"

He turned to see Maynard held the big sword. He didn't belong here. He was supposed to be a lich, but here he stood. With a growl Sol charged the traitor. Raven and Jacob would sing his praises when they found he laid the insolent *Nephilim* to waste. Maynard stood, legs apart, and sword outstretched. Sol ran at him, anticipating the look of surprise when his agile beast's body easily dodged the blade and he sank his teeth into the man. Maynard had tasted Sol's venom once under the lich women and now he would again.

Something slammed into Sol. The impact against the nearby building left him tumbling among clay and dust. He bit and clawed at the attacker, but it retreated too fast. Behind him came the feline snarl. Sol gained his feet and turned to face his assailant, letting out a small cackle. What could possibly oppose him? "That's the biggest fucking tiger I've ever seen," the woman with Maynard said. The tiger's size nearly matched Sol, solemn and menacing. The legendary Nathan had taken shape. Sol snickered again. In crocotta form, Sol couldn't talk but his grin said it all. *I'm going to kill you.*

Sol readied to pounce. His muscles tensed, his legs coiled, and he began to lunge. The tiger pounced first. Sol landed on his back, skidding on the desert sand. The cat growled and sank claws into his hide. Sol yelped, kicking Nathan off. Were fallen daemons susceptible to infection? Would one swipe do the job? The great cat lunged again, its orange and black coat rippling in the firelight.

Sol ducked and snapped his teeth barely closing down on the ends of the fur.

They paced back and began circling. Tigers were one thing, agile and vicious, but a daemon was another. Every muscle and reflex was at his command. Then again, Sol was a crocotta, the devil's own bastard animal. An abomination for sure, but a manifestation of all of the colorful ways of pain. And the geneticists had perverted it further.

The tiger snarled, pacing on the cobblestones. Sol had an idea. He drove at Nathan. He made a lunge, barely missing the claws. He lunged again, feline teeth snapping at Sol's neck. He played stupid, attacking and withdrawing. Then Sol feigned one such strike, and in his cunning, shifted. He outsmarted Nathan, playing stupid for minutes on end, and in a final feint, adjusted his momentum. He came at the tiger with such delightful bloodlust he never saw the tiger's maneuver. It pounced. With the weight of the tiger on his back came the claws piercing his shoulders, ripping down his torso. They streaked further down his back as he ran in panic, yelping in agony.

He darted into the dark. The pain seared down his spine and a deluge of blood soaked into his fur. *Must... escape... must hide.* A gutter, a trash bin, anything would work. It was too dark and he could feel the pain searing his hide, deep gashes running from shoulder to hip. He knew by smell that the tiger followed. Even if he evaded it, he would leave a trail of blood. He stumbled a moment, resumed his run, and came to the city wall. He careened up the stairs, almost slipping over the parapet as he came to the top. He looked down at the long drop. He could heal from all of this, but it would take time and the pain was great. He let out a whimper, it would do no good. Calming himself he finally resigned to jump from the wall. He leapt off the edge. In the dark, he barely caught himself as the ground came closer.

From the city wall, Oliver watched the crocotta race up the stairs. For a brief moment he feared an attack, but he saw the wounds entrenched down its back. It hesitated for a moment and jumped from the wall. He called for arrows, all of which missed. Moments later, Nathan came panting up the steps and took on his human form.

"What happened?" Oliver asked.

"The bastard got away," Nathan replied. Oliver would get the details later.

"Sir," Jaked Mari interrupted, "Grave news."

"Yes, captain?"

"It's Adivee and Obi, sir. They're dead."

Oliver cursed. "And the others?"

"Our medical facility was too small, so it has been extended to the baths. Charis is there currently. Liam, the girl, and the priest are at the church protected by a garrison."

"Maynard and Calli were fighting together last I saw them," Nathan said.

"And Dorian?" Oliver asked.

"I don't know."

"Damn it all," Oliver said. Organization was the key to surviving these things. So far they had lost half the city to the fire, an untold number of soldiers to these dark men and that damned crocotta, and they weren't any closer to getting control. "What about the tribesmen?"

"According to my men," replied Mari, "they've sent thirty soldiers to help us and the rest remain to guard their camp. There are unconfirmed reports of one casualty in their camp. Among the men fighting in here, none has fallen to my knowledge. They're remarkable fighters."

That was some good news. "They're more disciplined and will help us get this place back under control. See if they can help our men defend the walls and secure the premises."

"Already on it," Mari said and walked away. Maynard and Calli approached.

"How can we help?" Maynard asked.

"Hopefully the tribesmen can help us get things in order. I need anyone else to seek out these dark men and eliminate them." They left Oliver with two guards, as many men as he dared spare on his personal safety.

This was all wrong. They were supposed to meet in battle at the Pass. This might be the first wave of a far worse attack. Oliver should have anticipated it, should have prepared better. He might have lost his edge after two centuries. No amount of books could replace experience. Guilt crept in. He was responsible for these deaths, but he could not dwell on it. He was also responsible for getting them out of this. If Dorian had been present, he might have a better way of dealing with this attack, but he was missing. Surely he had his reasons.

The fires burned against the night sky, illuminating the once garden city. He prepared himself for the worst. Tomorrow it might all be ash and cinder. Who knew what was left of the army? If they lost half the men, it would ruin their chances at the Pass. They would be up against the abominations, but the real threat was the fallen angels.

He rapped his cane on the stone, unable to do anything further regarding the current circumstances, but also at a loss as to how to proceed once it was over. That helplessness made him more anxious.

A shadow moved and the guard to his left cried out. The other guard pushed Oliver aside, and with sword drawn moved the direction of the dark man. Oliver worked his way back, ignoring the pain in his leg. The second guard fell in a pool of his own blood and entrails. Oliver shifted on his cane and drew his sword. The shadow approached, stepping over the soldier, still alive in agony. The blackness of the creature's face gave way, flickering a sinister smile.

Through smoke and flame Dorian ran. He should have been on the wall with Oliver helping to command, but he knew—or at least had a suspicion—how to end this. Jacob perverted everything. The path of the dead at the Pass and now this. If it meant what Dorian thought it meant, Jacob had breached the ruins. He may not wait at the Pass for them to attack. He may march on the City.

Dorian sidestepped a burning pile and covered his face when he passed through the smoke. He came to the clearing, a town square that once held vivid vines and vibrant flowers. Those were reduced to ash and the shops and buildings along the ways burned. In the quadrangle sat the shadower. It was the body of Sachin Pendharkar, but it was not the Last Saint. The eyes and hollow smile said it all. A reversal of a ward was not unheard of, but such a perverse rebinding was truly a sign of Jacob's inventive malice.

The man then stood. "Hello, Dorian," said the hellish voice. Then the attack began.

A half-dozen shadows emitted from the man, coming all at once toward Dorian. His sword dealt with two, but he had to dodge a slash of dark claws. He brought his sword down in another blow. It slid through the black body with ease. The other three were upon him. He kicked one down while stabbing the another. The third nearly clawed him, but he leapt into the air, arching back. By the time he landed, the man emitted six more shadows. This might never stop and Dorian was no closer to the man.

He conjured a blast of fire that sent two reeling back in flames. He took a breath, increasing his speed, felling the remaining dark men and then he was upon the man himself. As his speed returned to normal, Dorian drove his blade toward the shadow.

The world tilted and Dorian struck air, but the shadower's fist slammed into Dorian's jaw. The man's other hand drove at him, fingertips extended in shadowed talons. The other dark men would soon be upon him. Dorian had to finish this now.

He ducked the clawed hand and launched himself upward. His jump arched over the figure and before the shadower could turn around, Dorian brought his sword down. The blade cleaved the apparition from shoulder to sternum. The opened body of the man once called Sachin Pendharkar fell to the earth. It was not bloody, but rather the insides looked as if they had rotted long ago. The shadows faded and Dorian stood among the burning city of Mere.

"Dorian," a voice said. Dorian looked down to find Sachin Pendharkar, the Last Saint, stretching an arm up to him. "Dorian," he said again. "What have I done?" The man should have been dead, but the magic lingered. Instead of a dead enemy, lay his dying friend.

Dorian knelt and took a hand. Sachin should have been allowed to finally rest in peace, but now his great sacrifice had been undone only to be used by the enemy. But it was not his fault. "It wasn't you," Dorian said. "It wasn't you, my friend. Your body was possessed, but not your mind."

"The Pass?" asked the dying man, his breath short.

Dorian only shook his head.

"It was—," the man broke off and took a few short breaths. "It wasn't—" his hand clenched Dorian's. "Not in vain." Then that final breath came. No breath was so tortured yet peaceful as the exhale of a man dying, that last rattle before the darkness comes.

The dark man damned near killed Oliver, but just as those claws would have ripped into him, the figure disappeared. Within moments everyone seemed to know it was over. Scouts reported no activity in the desert and the tribesmen remained undisturbed save for the rumor that one of their own had fallen. With the threat over, more tribesmen entered Mere to help stop the fires and tend the wounded. Their resourcefulness saved many lives.

Charis came and went, checking on him, and departing once she confirmed his safety. Oliver hurt for her. Her people and her city had been besieged. When she passed him moments later, bloody from tending wounds, her resolve was hardened, as if any distraction would break her will. She had gone so far as to extend the hospital to the mansion.

Dorian had explained these strange happenings. It was a dark subject and Oliver understood their magic too little to imagine how much was at stake. Since the chapel remained unharmed and so many had already rendezvoused there, they agreed to meet in the sanctuary, and Dorian went ahead to inform the others and make arrangements.

Maynard and the demon returned, covered in the black muck of the shadows. He sent them on to the chapel. They seemed to have a growing rapport, which Oliver considered a positive thing, though he retained a healthy fear that the two outsiders mutuality might lead to disloyalty. Whatever the case, he was glad to have them at the present.

Jaked Mari had commanded well and continued to organize their remaining troops. He set them up in shifts and strategic positions to prevent something like this from happening again. The rest of the troops helped the tribesmen with the fires that were mostly out by the time dawn broke.

As for Oliver himself, his leg hurt. It had twisted and turned in the fight against the dark man and now it bit at him with vengeance. Letting out a silent curse, he let himself down against the parapet and sighed. He needed a drink and he would kill Jacob personally if they had touched the stores. The mansion had not burned, so that was promising. At some point, he knew he had to get to the chapel. He might have felt guilty that he was so

tired when others had fought so much more, but he was too tired
to feel guilty.

# CHAPTER TWENTY-NINE

*Aftermath*

The chapel bustled, footsteps and voices echoing off the vaulted ceilings. Dawn emerged, faint at first, lighting the sanctuary through the stained glass windows. In morning dim, candles lined the walls between paintings. Some artworks were religious, but not all of them. Thanks to Ferrith's teaching, Liam recognized the Rembrandt portrayal of the Prodigal Son. At the front of the sanctuary, the pulpit sat on a risen platform, backed by a simple wooden cross. The large tome, presumably a Bible, sat atop the pulpit. Liam had seen it once, the handwritten annotations in the margins and illuminated pages a fascination to him. It was evidently common for towns to have a chapel and a priest, but like Novum, the lines between the long forgotten Protestant and Catholics were blurred. There were theological differences to be sure, but the past two hundred years had shown surprising compatibility, merging and morphing the various factions and denominations into something more singular and wholly unrecognizable from its prewar form. Liam had learned that from Master Ferrith. He had also learned how few practices of many former great religions remained, given the specificity of the City's religious parameters. But now there seemed two kinds of people: the devout and the apathetic. Liam thought of himself as caring, but dwelt on it little.

"It's complicated," Aster said after she explained everything. She sat next to him on a pew.

"So, you're saying that you knew this was going to happen?" Liam asked, scratching his head. "And that you can read minds?"

"Only by touch and only my family ever knew until now," she replied. "I didn't know about the attack until it was too late." When she handed him his glass back at Goose's Wild, had her hand brushed his? Or had she discovered it later? Whatever the case, she seemed to have known these things about him from the start.

The room lacked the rich metals and stones like the temple in the City. Rather it was wooden with ornate carvings. Its vaulted ceiling portrayed several paintings of men. The place remained untouched during the raid. Once Liam and Aster had arrived, Barker Stoke had prohibited them from leaving and then spent the time praying, his whispers indiscernible compared to the chaos outside. Now that the fighting was over, it was chaos in the chapel, as Dorian had started using it as their new base. Both of Aster's parents survived, though they had lost their house.

"How does that work exactly?" Liam asked. "Is that how you knew about me back at the lake?"

"I'm sorry I read your thoughts. I can tell a lot by just touching a person, but I'm mostly just looking for their happiest memory. I collect them. You, though, were just too damned interesting. I had to know more.

"I don't just read thoughts by touch." After brushing a blond strand of hair behind her ear, she clasped his hand. "It's like when you're between awake and asleep, not quite dreaming. I saw you trapped beneath a shadow. I had to come."

Liam pondered this girl. A few months ago the only magic he had experienced was the prophet's long age. Now he had met the angels themselves, a therianthrope, a former demon, and now this girl. The others made sense, but from where she came was a mystery. "How did you get this ability?" he asked.

"I don't know. It got me into trouble when I was young, but my parents saw that I was special. They taught me to be more 'circumspect' as my father would say. They also taught me to be a better steward of my ability, only using it for good, though sometimes I get curious."

"And when you got curious with me, what did you see?"

She smiled. "The best memories are never wholly happy. The happier the memory, the more heartache it takes to make it."

"And," Liam said. "What was it for me?"

"You have many lovely memories," Aster said. "That day at the top of the spire, finding Dorian, and those dear moments with your grandfather. But you, Liam, have yet to live your best memory."

She put a hand to his cheek, thumb brushing it as if wiping away an invisible tear. Liam didn't know whether to get lost in her eyes, or probe deeper at her meaning. His decision was short-lived. Dorian approached.

When Aster explained her abilities to Dorian he did not appear surprised. "Yes," he said, "I have spoken with her parents."

Her parents, their skin streaked by ash, approached. "Aster," her mother said, "We've talked to Dorian and he agrees that we should give you a choice."

"What do you mean?" Aster asked. It was a formality. She knew very well what they meant and so did Liam.

Her father cleared his throat. "What we mean, is that a girl with your abilities could serve well in this cause. If you wanted to go, you could."

"You would be kept out of battle," Dorian said.

"I want to go," replied Aster, "but who will stay and help you rebuild?"

"I think," said her father, "that you will be more valuable to them than to us."

"Your father's right," her mother said.

Aster looked to Liam, "I'll do it!"

"Good," said Dorian. "We will have a meeting in a few minutes and could use you for something specific. Otherwise, it may be some time before you see your family. Spend as much time as you can with them."

Dorian returned to his business and Liam let Aster go to her parents. He sat alone in the chapel pondering his current situation. He liked her quite a bit. There were previous interests and infatuations, but never before had he felt so close to someone in such a short amount of time. He considered her exotic compared to the relatively bland women in the city, not needing the expensive clothing and makeup to be attractive, nor wanting in personality.

Liam watched her excited gestures as she talked to her parents. He guessed that she told them about their night, expressing genuine grief at the loss of the city and so many of its people, but overcome with the new prospect of traveling with Liam. Her mother had a look of consternation, but her father appeared confident that she was in good company. They had to rebuild from the ashes, but she would go onto something new.

A pang ran up Oliver's leg and he winced. He wanted the pain to go away, he wanted a beer, he wanted to feel better. He wanted Charis's touch. When he arrived at the chapel, the helpers moved about, shifting the pews and chairs into a circle. Oliver lamented those that would not fill the benches. The tap of his cane on the tile echoed off the high ceiling as he approached a pew. He sat down with a sigh and to his great delight a servant brought him a beer. Even in the darkest of times there were glimmers of hope. The morning came, light shining a rich amber through his full glass. This was likely to be all the contentment he would find in the near future and he savored these moments. Oliver took in his surroundings.

Most of the townspeople focused on recovery from the attack, but a few sat in the chapel, eyes downcast and expressions despondent. A few seats over, Liam eyed a girl about his age. The Reverend Barker Stoke sat praying in inaudible whispers. Maynard and Callianeira were near, deep in their own conversation. Servants came and went with messages, trays of food and beverage. Charis was not in sight, a small disappointment. Dorian sat beside him, sighing with relief from the long night. "The meeting will start soon," Dorian said. "We lingered too long before and tonight we have to come to some decisions."

He was right. Their attempts at planning had been plagued by diversions. Not all of them were bad, but the apparent time to act had come.

"You want to lead this one?" Oliver asked. Dorian nodded. Oliver did not hold it against Dorian that he had been reluctant to lead. It was not like Dorian to assume power, rather he was more a steward of whatever power he was given. It was a quality that had been successful for few, but in Dorian it was inspiring. Dorian harbored other reasons for his hesitancy. Guilt was a plain insecurity, one that he seemed to have finally overcome. Oliver might have expected that a being who had led and lived for so long might be wiser, but Dorian was finally coming to understand that his inaction could cause more damage than tenacious proactivity.

Maynard was learning much the same lesson, though his trepidation had deep roots in his motivations. He was a unique man in that respect, not the typical warrior, but introspective. He may have only just now discovered such self assessment, but it served him well. Maynard finally saw his potential to do good. It also appeared that Callianeira was having an effect on him, but to what purpose it was hard to tell. If those two grew close and either was untrue—but no, he pushed the thought from his mind. Dorian held his own reservations, but trusted them, and on that much Oliver felt comfortable deferring to Dorian.

Charis soon arrived, greeting Dorian and sitting on the other side of Oliver. She reached over and touched his leg with her graceful fingers, relieving his pain. Like always, the discomfort remained, but the relief superseded it.

Dorian leaned over from Oliver's other side. "This won't be like it was before."

Anger emanated from all present. Liam and Aster looked amiable, but choler was apparent among the others. Even for Maynard, the idea—once an inkling—of commitment grew into zeal. Revenge had been for himself, to hurt Jacob like he had hurt Maynard, but now he experienced the very things he had done under Jacob. Mere burned and the people who had saved his life were hurting. Vengeance was no longer for himself but something he felt compelled to do for others. They deserved justice. And there was that word: *justice*. He could feel guilty for more bloodshed but he might feel guiltier for not preventing the future suffering of these people.

"Something has changed," Callianeira said to him. They sat next to each other in the bustling sanctuary, the meeting's start imminent.

"Is it that obvious?" he asked.

"Yes," she said, "and no. I've just been paying attention to you. That's all."

"How do you mean?"

"I realize that I hardly knew you before. You were nothing but a mission, an assignment. You were a sure man then, which is an intimidating thing. When I finally met you in person, you weren't a sure man. I didn't know what to think or do about you, but I hoped for something. You've been through a lot, so I knew I had to be patient. I listened to what you said, heard how you talked to others and myself. Tonight it seems you finally became a sure man again."

"A sure man?" Maynard asked.

"A person's greatness isn't necessarily in who they are so much as their choice to overcome who they are and their motives to do so. You're not doing this all for yourself are you?"

"At some point I was doing this all for myself, but you're right. Now I'm not. This attack isn't right, none of it is. The whole thing is so fucked, and while I'd find some satisfaction in bringing Jacob to justice, it isn't just about me anymore. I would do what the weak cannot, not for glory or my own revenge, but for all of our sakes."

"That's what I mean," Callianeira said.

"Don't mistake me," Maynard said. "I may only make a little difference. There are plenty of others, even those who lack my Nephilim abilities, that will do greater than I could possibly accomplish. Whatever small part I play, I hope it's part of the greater good. I don't care about the things I once wanted."

"What were those things?" Callianeira asked. Maynard almost felt he could not answer. He knew all too well what they were, but he dared not tell her. He had confided in others, but he knew how easy one could use them against him. Jacob knew what Maynard had done in the name of his shallow desires.

"Stupid things," he replied. "I wanted fame and glory and I thought it could be a path to something other than loneliness. I thought that by taking from other people that I would be worth giving to." In response Callianeira met his eyes. Behind her sincere and deep gaze, he knew that he could trust her.

"Do not let your talents become you," she said. "We must seek something higher. You may be gifted in battle, but you should not

be judged by such a gift without being judged for how you use it."
There was a breath's pause, "You were awesome out there
tonight." He seldom received compliments from women and
hardly knew what to say.

"Yourself as well." They had fought side-to-side and back-to-
back that night. The shadows had come, hardly distinguishable in
the dark, and with Callianeira, he had cut them down. She was
not primarily a warrior, yet she fought with a grace and finesse he
could never match. She was beautiful in battle. She was beautiful
outside of battle as well. He liked the soft brown of her tan skin
and the way it complimented with her straight brown hair. Her
smile was nice as well, not the one she put on when she was being
sarcastic, but the real one.

When Jaked arrived with Nathan, the Commander mentioned
that the tribesmen would arrive soon and that Argon had said not
to wait on them. "Jacob has taken everything from us. He twisted
my wards with a path of death and turned its protector into a
shadower. He has killed our friends and loved ones. He has taken
our homes. Father Stoke lost a city, Oliver lost a city, Charis has a
lost a city, and now Jacob threatens the last city. I'm almost sure
that he remains at the Pass waiting for us, and I intend to put an
end to this."

"Yes," said Charis, "but why is he waiting at the Pass for us?
Why hasn't he besieged the City yet? Why not send more men to
attack us?" Her tone was almost hopeless.

"She's right," said Oliver. "He would lure us into action so that
he can deal with us out here and not in the City, however he
intends to get into it. He may have done a lot of damage here, but
not as much as an army might have. This was meant to draw us
out. The Pass gives him the strategic advantage."

"I have considered this," said Dorian. "I think we have a few
advantages he may not have predicted. Maynard was right about
the tunnels. They are worth the risk. We put a force up front,

while our strongest make their way through the tunnels and take them from behind."

"It's going to take more than that," said Maynard. It had been Maynard's idea, but even he knew it was inadequate. He seldom had the privilege of sitting in on war councils but he knew when the odds were against them. There had been victories in such battles, but less had seemed at stake. These creatures claimed to have lived hundreds—perhaps thousands of years—built worlds, marched on the gates of hell, and this was the best they had? It resounded of desperation. There was another possibility. "Again, what about magic?" he asked.

Dorian looked at him for a moment before speaking. "We are outnumbered and the Pass gives them the strategic advantage. However, our soldiers are better trained. We can't depend on magic. It can destroy as much as it might save and we are well matched. And the stuff that we really need takes more time and energy than we have right now. Jacob is as powerful as me, but in an odd way. Through blood magic, he can apparently accomplish much, but previously his talents lay in manipulation. He also has a curious ability to diminish or block the use of the Darkworld. I'm powerful enough to overcome it, but I also have to be able to predict it. Amelia is a summoner and telekinetic. Most of Raven's work is already done as you've seen from his necromancy. The lich captain presents a certain threat. All of that against Charis the healer, Nathan the daemon, and you. Our best bet is in strategy."

"You're a worldmaker," Callianeira said to Dorian. "How about that ship in Bronton?"

"Now that's something I can do and likely prevent Jacob from undoing," said Dorian. "It will be worth the trip and give us a significant vantage point. That allows us to bring one more asset directly into the battle. Oliver, are you up for the task?"

"Give me enough men and arrows and we'll do as much damage as we can," Oliver replied. They worked well together.

The unspoken was already apparent. Oliver was previously unable to join in the battle, but Callianeira's idea for a ship would bring one of their strongest leaders into it.

"That brings up another question," said Dorian. "Are we adequately supplied after tonight?"

Charis looked to Oliver who answered. "Jaked tells me that our resources remain relatively stocked. A quarter of our fighters are gone, not to mention the two leaders we lost tonight. Furthermore, the problem is that the majority of Mere's population lost homes to the fire, meaning that our resources are spread thin. It is vital that we act soon so that we can also acquire whatever remains at Avianne." Oliver stopped a moment. Maynard realized this was a sensitive issue for him. His home had been taken and everyone there was surely dead or undead. That is why what Oliver said next surprised him. "Charis, if I may suggest, your home is lost but your people remain. My people are no more, but their homes are likely there. The Pass is smaller than Mere, but might it serve as a home until Mere can be rebuilt?"

Maynard noticed a flicker of endearment in her eyes. Perhaps everyone was being sentimental after such a tragic loss, but something seemed to be there. Was it odd that the angel would have feelings for the man? Nathan had fallen in love with a mortal, someone—unlike Oliver—doomed to die young. Oliver seemed to reciprocate what it was she felt towards him. It was strange how these things became evident on the brink of war. It was a common problem with camp followers, but rare among such a group. Of course, camp followers were whores and not lovers, but Maynard had often seen the attachment young soldiers could have for a girl they paid to like them. This was something more and he wondered if his thoughts on Callianeira were something more as well.

They had in some strange way evoked a change within one another. There were these fleeting moments of trust, but other times he feared there might be more to her. The meeting turned more coincidental to Maynard's thoughts. "May I borrow you, Aster?" Dorian asked. With a brief glance at Liam, she gave Dorian a nod and rose from her seat.

"Aster here is now a part of our company," Dorian said. "She has a unique ability to see into the minds of those she touches, something none of us here can do in the capacity that she can. It's a fraction of Amelia's power, but it's an asset to us. I would not presume to use her. In the same way that we all offer up our abilities, I would welcome her among us. Aster, dear, I'd rather not put you on the spot so soon, but you can be of help to us."

"I'm glad to be here," she said with a perky sincerity. Maynard had been too far away to know what Dorian and her parents spoke of, but he understood now. She was to join them, not for the battle, but for whatever came after. It must have been a small consolation that her parents would have homes at the Pass.

Maynard was surprised to find Dorian looking at him and then to Callianeira. "I'm sorry," Dorian said. "You will have to forgive me, but if you will allow this, we may remove all doubt from within our company."

"I don't understand," said Maynard.

"I do," said Callianeira. "If Aster can read minds, and Maynard and I are in the least bit suspect, we might as well clear it up now before we march off to war. Plus, she could learn all sorts of things about demons. What do we dress up as for Halloween? What's it really say when you play 'Stairway to Heaven' backwards? Did the Morning Star really invent Mondays?"

Some laughed, but for a moment Maynard bristled. After everything Maynard had been through, Dorian was in no position to presume any lack of allegiance on his part. Then again, Maynard had his own doubts about Callianeira, and however small and infrequent they were, he would rather be rid of them altogether than let them eat him away over time. He pushed the anger down as Dorian directed Aster toward him. It was completely fair as much as it chafed at him.

"Come, girl," Maynard said, "But don't go deeper than you need to. You don't want to see what I've been through." Aster laid a gentle hand on Maynard. He searched his mind briefly, making sure one last time that this was the right thing. "After tonight, my mind is made up. I am on your side and will stop Jacob and his followers at all costs."

"He's telling the truth," said Aster. She gave him a curious look and added quietly, so that no one else could hear, "You're a great man." He had little time to dwell on the curious line before Aster had moved onto the demon.

Callianeira gave that wry smile as she held out her arm.

"Why did you join us?" Dorian asked her. Had Maynard not seen the softness in Dorian's eyes he might have thought it a harsh question, but instead he saw that Dorian in some small way hated to ask it. It was necessary.

Callianeira's brow furrowed. She had not expected it. "I had nowhere else to go in a lot of ways. I was cast away from the Eternal One centuries ago and fell into the service of the Morning Star. I spent years bringing down the greatest of men. I brought down kingdoms and corporations alike. You know this. When I saw what I had left behind and what could happen again, I left. I knew I couldn't do what I was doing anymore."

"You couldn't have just quit," said Nathan with uncharacteristic seriousness.

"She's telling the truth," said Aster removing her hand from Callianeira's shoulder, freeing her to tell more without upsetting the poor girl.

"I can't explain everything," said the demon, "but I'm telling the truth. I did leave. They have come back for me several times. Vesuvia has come to me on behalf of Sagtyx in this very city. I turned her down."

Charis's eyes widened, but Dorian only nodded and said, "At least we got this part out of the way."

Three of the tribesmen entered. Argon, Belriah's closest counselor, had a greater presence than his chief or Serj. He would be a formidable opponent on the battlefield, intimidating even Maynard. Given the prowess that Belriah and Serj possessed, it was substantial to find Argon more daunting. "I apologize for our lateness," Belriah said. "We were delayed when one in our camp was taken." There was a stir before he continued, "I fear a crocotta took him away. Neither has been seen since. Our men are searching the desert as we speak, but there is little hope." They had a strange accent but spoke the common tongue well enough.

"It was no ordinary crocotta," Nathan said. "It was an ancient beast, cleverer and more capable."

"Please," said Oliver, "our condolences. Sit with us."

The tribesmen gave short bows and sat in one of the pews. Argon looked up at the cross on the wall, appearing to ponder it before returning his attention to the meeting. Maynard nodded at him and he nodded back. A servant offered them beer, which all three of the men took gladly. They had enjoyed the alcoholic pleasures of Mere for the past few days, but it was obvious they were still unaccustomed to the dry and bitter nature of the beverage.

"My friends," said Dorian to the tribesmen, "You are most welcome. We need you and request your aid."

Dorian informed them of the recent events and decisions, and they began to solidify the plan. There would be groups through the tunnels, *The Northern Lady*, tribesmen, and more to come Jacob's way. Maynard was unsure it would be enough, but he hoped that if he could kill just one of them—especially Jacob— that it would be worth it.

As the meeting broke, Nathan approached him. "I knew you would do it," he said.

"Then why do I still feel guilty?" Maynard asked. "Is killing all I'm good for?"

"It could probably be said of most men like you, but I think you're different. You should be proud of yourself. I know I'm proud of you."

That was a strange thing to hear. Maynard had certainly been proud of himself in battle or in bed. His superiors always seemed to appreciate his prowess and in the short time he commanded a company he accomplished good results, although that had ended badly. However, this sort of pride felt different. His ego felt smaller, not larger, yet he felt better about himself.

"I'll meet you in the middle," Nathan said. That was the plan.

"The middle," Maynard answered.

# CHAPTER THIRTY

## *The Path of the Dead*

The strange light filtered through the unnatural, shifting clouds. It desaturated the land, tingeing it in a gray shroud. Beyond the encampment, the slate walls of the mountains towered and between them the formless shadow of the Pass. Dorian should not have been able to see the corridor. It was not for his eyes. Yet, between the looming wall and rock he beheld the schism, like an inapposite phantasm. Kneeling, he picked up a handful of sand. The grains strained through his fingers. They sifted against his skin and whispered things.

*I miss the water,* one said.

*I was once the floor of the Coliseum,* said another.

*The dead walked here.*

He gazed at the Pass once more and it promised tribulation to all who entered.

"Are you ready?" asked Oliver.

Dorian nodded.

The jostling and hurried preparation for battle had ended and only the scraping of the whetstone on steel broke the silence. As the hour came upon them, all were silent save for the nervous murmurs and the sharpening of Maynard's sword. The ominous clouds shifted, letting through a shaft of sunlight. It glinted on his blade before the clouds rolled, recollecting and covering the sun once more. His thoughts eluded fear and anxiety, allowing the anger and bloodlust to possess him in the wild calm that preceded the coming tempest. His hand pushed the stone down the edge of the blade. It would taste the blood of his enemies. Again, it ran down the edge. It would be his vengeance. Each stroke sharpened the blade, perpetuating his wrath. The fire coursed through him.

Father Barker Stoke's cassock fluttered in the light wind. Months ago he had been a priest in Lavyn. In spite of his prayers, that place was no more. He had gone to Mere and it had fallen as well. Destruction reigned wherever he went and now he stood behind an army ready to besiege the Pass. He was a priest, but for all his piety he never seemed to make a difference. God never seemed to make a difference. But this was not a time to be discouraged. He prayed anyway for the very thing he had told Liam he prayed for. Hope. If he had nothing else, he at least had that, because without it there was nothing. But he felt tired, almost too weary to hope, but not quite.

Charis had brought him the boy on that fateful day. Liam had talked little of the City. In fact, he had not said much at all. But Barker saw that look in the boy's eyes. Underneath that adolescent curiosity was something else. He knew how the boy had come to be here, and that meant that something was at work. It may be the spirits who give prophecy, Dorian, or God himself, but something was at work.

Liam, who would eventually join the ranks, sat at the edge of their encampment, looking out over the army and the grayscape that led up to the foot of the foreboding mountains and the pass within. Aster, who might have been a year or two older than Liam was there as well. The priest whispered a prayer and when he stopped Liam looked up to him.

"Are you sure you want to do this?" Barker asked. He worried that Liam was too young. It would not do for a seventeen-year-old to see battle, much less die in it.

Liam nodded. He would say goodbye to Aster and join the battle. Barker would be here with her and a few guards until the battle ended. If it ended well, they would join the others in the Pass. If it ended poorly they would flee.

The priest continued whispering in prayer.

Callianeira sheathed the dirk in her boot and took a deep breath. She had known war, but seldom met in battle. The night in Bronton had surprised her, leaving her clumsy and afraid in the skirmish. It was a small consolation that she had been useful the night Mere was attacked. Perhaps it was because she better understood the dire circumstances, or maybe she didn't want to embarrass herself in front of Maynard. Prepared this time, she held her resolve, and donned her armor. It was light and flexible, mostly leather but with patches of mail in the most vulnerable places.

Whispers curled around her emotions, calling her back. Desperate murmurings tugged at her, a call to something safer, easier, less unknown. With hair pulled back and the armor fitted, she was ready. She sheathed her sword. She would never go back, never acquiesce to the lure of her old life.

That morning Argon made love to his wife and then prayed to his god. He bowed, relaxed his muscles, and whispered to Elah. "Send me your protection. Give me strength to fight bravely, and if necessary die nobly." His nose almost touched the ground, each breath disturbing the dirt. To his left bowed Belriah and to the right, Serj prayed to his god, Xu.

Argon did not fear battle, but he did worry for the lives of his comrades. They were his equal in battle, but even the mightiest fall. Only recently had he been reunited with Serj and Argon had always been Belriah's closest councilor. Most of all, he wanted to share in the promised rains with them. The anticipation of that raised his spirits. His hope, he knew, was not misplaced. They were meant to be here.

Oliver stood on the deck of the ship that was once *The Northern Lady*. They had renamed it *Jacob's Bane* and Oliver hoped it would be everything that it promised. It had taken Dorian days to solve Jacob's riddle, how he had gotten it to tread the desert sands. Once Dorian figured it out, it surpassed Jacob's magic, rising off of the ground, taller than a man on camelback. It presented a sure advantage, allowing them to sail over the heads of those afoot and fire arrows down on the enemy.

Spread below, the ranks of camels and soldiers awaited the time to march on his former home. He wished he was able enough to fight among the army, but while he had learned battle well enough despite his leg, he knew he was of more use above.

A horn sounded. Dorian had given the command. The ship moved forward, the air its own smooth current. Oliver called for the archers to ready themselves. The changing clouds ahead seemed to hang lower, a fog coming from them. His heart beat in his chest but Oliver's courage did not wane. He was ready to die, if need be, but he was more eager to put an end to Jacob's malice.

Below them the armies moved, Jaked Mari commanding one side and Dorian the other. The ship slowly entered the Pass. The bow tread the fog, breaking it apart, its wooden planks stretching out of the mists like a ghost in the dark of night. From the tendrils of smoky clouds the bow emerged, Oliver at the helm, the sides lined with dozens of archers. *Jacob's Bane* left the fog behind, hovering forward in dissipating mists. The abominations would come out at any moment.

It was time. Maynard strapped on his sword and checked his dagger. He looked to Callianeira, glad to have her in his company. She smiled at him, roguish cunning masking the trepidation he knew to be there.

"You look at me like I'm your knight in shining armor," he said, momentarily forgetting his bitterness before battle.

"Are you kidding?" she asked. "If you were a knight and if you wore anything shinier than those leathers, I'd worry. Knights are fools. Trust me."

Perhaps she had a point. The others in his company looked able enough. He had made it a priority to meet with every one of his men, ensuring that they were dependable, but also stirring confidence. Across the ranks, Nathan would lead the tribesmen, ready to enter the western tunnel. Between them, Dorian and Mari commanded the armies, camelries, and other tribesmen. The ship followed, its shadow looming over the army.

As if responding to the horn, the first roll of thunder echoed through the plains and lightning flickered in the clouds. It would rain soon. They began to march.

The clouds obfuscated the sun, making it difficult to tell the time, but it might have been daylight less than two hours. They had arrived early, eager for battle, but held back at the absence of abominations in the Pass, wary of a possible trap. Oliver sent scouts and they returned horrifically maimed, yet alive in their own way, reanimated in the way of the abominations. In his anger, Commander Jaked Mari nearly sounded the attack horn. Dorian, level-headed as always, deterred the notion.

If the battle was unfinished by sundown, Maynard feared that between fatigue and demoralization they might not survive the night. His company neared the Pass under a light mist haunting the gap. It did not reach so low that it hid their path, but *Jacob's Bane* disappeared into it. The ranks of Mere's soldiers lined the entrance, which was perhaps one hundred yards wide. On the western side, the river dipped into a low cave, flowing into the mountain. All along the walls the dark windows and doorways gaped. It all faded into the strange fog, a pewter shadow, almost as if the desert ground blurred into the air. The horn resonated again and they continued into the Pass, Maynard's company following him in uniform steps. "Where are they?" Callianeira whispered.

"Close, I think," Maynard said. There had been thousands of them. Where could they hide? He tried to conjure the map of the Pass in his mind. There had been an alley just short of the far side and it appeared that the homes were two stories. Yet, he feared they were using the tunnels. It would undo their entire strategy. He had never fought a battle in such a tight space, but it might work to their advantage that so many of the ranks were able to enter before the battle started.

"I know it's a trap," Maynard said, "but I can't see how."

Callianeira pointed to the mountainside. "Those are the homes and shops Oliver described. They could be hiding in there. I'd worry about an attack from the upper stories."

Maynard nodded. "Oliver knows to deal with that if it happens. Let's just hope we can get to those tunnels." *And that they're empty.*

The morning mists faded, leaving the Pass hollow and haunted. Jacob always waited until the last minute to show his hand. Had the delivery not always been grand, it might have been mistakable for procrastination, but it was of punctilious design.

The other regiments marched beside and behind Maynard's group. When they drew near to the tunnel's entrance, pale shapes emerged from the northern gap in the Pass. With quiet rapidity the abominations approached. Maynard signaled his company to run, to make for the tunnel before the abominations came upon them.

The first white shape fell from above. It came down on one of his men, beating him savagely. Maynard pushed through stunned soldiers, dispatching the creature with his sword. He called for the attack, the cry of battle overtaking his voice. A volley of arrows clattered against the walls, some striking the creatures reigning down from above.

Shrieks from above were followed by plummeting spears, striking his men. The man next to Maynard fell, lanced in the leg by a spear, crying out as blood spewed from the wound. The man would die.

As an arrow flew at Maynard, he struck an abomination down and then another, unable to free his blade long enough to block the arrow. Callianeira leapt into the air and deflected the shaft with her blade. She landed and resumed the battle. Fighting back to back, Maynard focused on the abominations coming at him.

The roar of war became deafening. First the organs and limbs of the long dead were thrown at them, an obvious attempt to demoralize the soldiers. Cries of horror rose as blood covered the men long before the battle came to a climax. "Hold steady!" Maynard commanded. White bodies fell from above, abominations jumping from the mountainside windows. They rushed from the first level homes. He had no time to react or command. For this brief moment it was every man for himself.

Maynard brought his sword down on one and felled another whose blade was within inches of piercing him. A shriek came from behind and a weak attempt with a mace hit his arm. He swung around, cleaving the creature in two. Callianeira—no longer so close—fought, her motions a dance, slaughtering the bastard abominations. He let out another battle cry as he butchered three more, working his way back to her.

The abominations were every shape and size. Male and female, naked or crudely clothed. They bore weapons of bones, honed and sharpened, or left dull for bludgeoning. Some carried steel spears and axes, other stones and staffs. They came. An abomination bit into the throat of a nearby soldier, ripping the man's life away.

Maynard cut once more, blood spraying from another wound and the creature's eyes dulled as it slumped to the ground. He glanced at the fallen men, at least a dozen casualties. The living were far overwhelmed. Then the dead found life again. The captain was close, invigorating their own fallen just like he had in Bronton.

Another abomination fell by Maynard's sword before he curved it toward the next attacker. He slashed, moving with ferocity. They kept coming. It became rhythmic. They came, they shrieked, he killed them. Even in the split second of a kill he sometimes remembered a face from one of the towns they had raided.

They needed to move forward. He struck another attacker and yelled for his company to regroup. His men fought their way toward him as Maynard and Callianeira tried to make a path. He motioned them forward and the slaughter continued, his men flanked on every side, trying desperately to reach the tunnel.

They came to the store called Last Chance Goods. Maynard motioned his men to enter. Callianeira led them in, hopefully finding the secret door and leading them to the tunnel. Meanwhile, Maynard continued to guard the entrance. The bodies began to pile before him, and the next wave of abominations tripped over his carnage. A soldier signaled that he was the last one. It felt all too soon, as if only a few had made it, but he followed into the tunnel, shutting the door behind him and slamming the wooden block down.

Callianeira's faint light glowed ahead. He walked by the soldiers in the narrow tunnel, taking the lead and counting them as he went. "You fought well," he said to one. "Wait for the real fight," to another. Of the eighty-five soldiers that had come with him, less than fifty stood. He hated losing so many men, but it could have been worse.

At the front, he joined Callianeira, her hand an amber glow in the dark. Maynard tapped the Darkworld and found his fire, matching his light to hers. They began the journey through the caves, rock wall muting the tumultuous battle outside.

Sol looked upon his army. For someone with so little experience in battle, he had done well. He had sent back Dorian's scouts in Raven's preferred form. There was always the element of surprise. Let them come into the Pass, think they had the advantage, and then hit them from all sides. He even had rope, anticipating that they might use the ship from Bronton, a marvel only previously known to Jacob. "I want all efforts on Dorian," he had told them knowing Dorian's powers would likely be the most taxed in this battle. Whatever the fallen angel had in mind, he needed to be distracted as much as possible.

The cravings had been perpetual. In his flight from Mere he had noticed the tribesmen. It had been luck on many levels. He was able to take one man, drag him into the desert, and consume him. It had been a disappointing meal, but the painful stripes down his back felt better afterward. He did want revenge. The brat Liam, the bastard daemon, all of them.

The Pass would be a success. Most of Jacob's army was right here, Sol at the lead. The Last Saint was finished, but that meant little. More aid had arisen in the ranks. Amelia's beasts, the crocotta Sol had gathered, the Infinite Bullets, and the captain. Sol was his own weapon. His skin stretched. Bones cracked and muscles bulged. Hair and teeth grew. With a light cackle, Sol joined the battle.

The fog had lifted and looking down, Oliver surveyed the battle. Man against monster, locked in tight quarters. Good men lay dying, bleeding out from their wounds among the fallen and fell creatures overcome by blade and determination. Oliver frowned at the bloody mess, hating that he was so far away. *Jacob's Bane* soon cleared the front lines and their confusion gave way to pale white enemies. But for a moment the yelling and clamor died.

"Archers," Oliver called. The bowstrings tightened. "Fire!" With a wave of Oliver's hand, the archers let their arrows loose. They rained down on a sea of abominations, striking down the enemy. "Steady! Starboard, aim for the windows and doors in the mountain's walls." The archers drew from their quivers, stringing another arrow. Soldiers, men and women alike, perched on the sides, looking down into the fray, marking their targets ready to strike.

The volley emitted from the ship, speeding toward the enemy. They appeared to have little effect on the swarm, but Oliver knew the real goal was to get to the rear, to help those coming from the tunnels. The howls arose, pain echoing in the towering rock walls of the Pass. The ship moved over the white masses and Oliver commanded the next release of arrows. The enemy lines began to break and in the distance Maynard and Nathan would soon emerge from the tunnels, leading their own soldiers to surround the enemy. The ship continued, unrelenting as arrows fletched and loosed on the abominations.

A rope sailed overhead, almost clipping Oliver. He dashed to the side as the hooked end locked onto the wooden deck. *How could they know?* The ship continued to move forward. Another hooked rope found the side of the ship. A soldier tried to pry the prongs from the railing, but it held fast. The abominations would climb the rope at any moment.

"Blades ready!" Oliver called. The soldiers shouldered their bows, each drawing a sword or dagger.

The abominations did not come. The ship lurched and Oliver almost lost balance. He inhaled sharply against the pain in his leg. Men stumbled, and the falling ship spun. The ropes held tight, anchored to the ground. The ship careened, starboard approaching the mountainside. Oliver barely let out a curse as

*Jacob's Bane* slammed against the wall. The sound resonated, a crack echoing in the Pass. Men fell overboard. Oliver himself lost his footing, sliding toward the damaged side. He let out a yelp as his leg bent. Pain shot from thigh to spine, and he thought he might lose consciousness. With another lurch his stomach lifted as the ship began to fall.

At first, this seemed less of a challenge than the skirmish at Bronton. Though Liam's inexperience earned him the occasional nick or bruise, it took some time before the battle thickened. He was deadly with the sword, intuitive and bold. Within moments the black blood of the slain stained his clothes and skin. The receding mists revealed a multitude of abominations under a darkening, cloudy sky. It thundered and this time a flash of lightening illuminated the glistening bodies of the abominations. Liam struck one across the chest. It howled angrily, bashing him with a closed fist. Liam faltered, but did not fall, and regaining his composure he beheaded the fell creature.

The opposing ranks gave an odd stir and the crocotta emerged, charging at his company. Liam abandoned his sword and pulled out a gun. The bullets lanced the giant hyenas. Cackles became yelps as they tumbled to the ground. Some ran undaunted. Liam fired at an oncoming crocotta. He didn't know if the shot struck, but the creature slammed into him, throwing him into the ground. It leapt atop him, its weight suffocating, its eyes gazing at Liam with anticipation. Liam knew those eyes. Sol. The nails dug into his chest and he let out a cry, assailing the beast with futile blows. It only cackled and gaped its rancid maul in a lunge. It was then that Liam saw that his gun was empty.

Hands aglow, Maynard and Callianeira led the group through the tunnel careful not to deviate down the mysterious paths. A wrong turn could land them in a cold and deep well or lost within the mountains. They pressed on through the passage, Maynard in the lead.

Maynard barely registered the smell of decay before it leapt on him from the dark. The slimy cold body smacked against his, pushing him down, flame extinguished. The slick hands groped at him, pulling scratching. The knee almost met his groin before he stabbed the creature in the stomach. He brought the flame back to his hand illuminating the withdrawing and wounded creature. Its horrible cry echoed down the tunnel before he silenced it with a final strike.

"That's an ugly little shit," Callianeira said wrinkling her nose. "If those bastards were ready for us here, they'll be ready in the other tunnel."

"That's for Nathan and the tribesmen to worry about," Maynard replied. "I think we're going to have our own problems."

The patter of feet reverberated, accompanied by subtle grunts traveling from down the way. The soldiers grew restless. Maynard called for them to hold steady. He intensified the light in his hand and saw the hoard, disfigured and stitched bodies coming from the dark tunnel. At the sight of the illumination they howled and came faster. He looked at Callianeira, but she kept her eyes forward in tense anticipation.

It was difficult in the narrow tunnel, but Maynard fought, careful not to accidentally hit Callianeira, deliberate in every strike. The men behind him were eager to help, but it was too constricted. The croaks and moans of the abominations echoed in the corridor among the clattering metal and human grunts. No longer methodical, Maynard fought blindly on the edge of chaos. He was slipping on blood, trying to block attacks while progressing with his own.

Between the fire and dagger they fought the coming abominations. Their ungodly howls echoed down the stone tunnel. The rubbery flesh ripped beneath his blade. Blunt objects fell upon him, sharp objects glanced off his light armor. Callianeira held her own but barely. They had not yet reached the other side of the tunnel and already they were weary. His dagger sliced a neck, then buried into a chest. Their howls were deafening.

The thicket of undead bodies became sparser and Maynard's company began to make more progress, only coming against the stragglers.

"Do you think we'll get another wave?" Callianeira asked.

"It's hard to say," Maynard replied. "I think they were meant to be a surprise attack through this tunnel, but I would have thought Jacob would use it more to his advantage."

Maynard led the soldiers on. Their armor rattled, their feet fell, and they continued down the passage.

Dorian's camel had fallen to the violent thrash of a crocotta. He fought afoot, the camelry scattered and fallen. The crocotta charged him but he brought such swift retribution that they had little time to cackle as he cut into their flesh. They came in close until Dorian found a spear and smote them from a safer distance. He impaled one beast through its throat, the spearhead ripping through the soft oral tissue, dousing the tip in dark red blood.

As he relinquished the spear, he put a boot to the head of one right before it could maul Liam. With Dorian's kick, Liam was freed. It appeared the boy was resisting panic as his fingers found a sword. Then he stood with Dorian and they continued the slaughter. More men came to their side.

They fought until Dorian's feet no longer found the ground, stepping upon the bodies of the fallen. Some were abominations, others the men who had fought alongside him. His sword swung with deliberate determination, dismembering and bloodying his attackers. How long had it been since he lost his camel? He could not remember, but fought on, pressing forward. The abominations were ruthless, unceasing, and zealous to kill. Dorian dodged a rusted dagger and sliced away the arm that wielded it. He struck one with a fist and another with his sword. Then something changed. Something more than abominations. The ship crashed.

Oliver slid down the deck, each plank chafing his leg. The ship tipped onto its side, plummeting against Dorian's magic. Oliver fell. It had started to rain, each drop racing toward the ground before him. Men tumbled down as well, their cries of pain resonating as they hit the ground. His cane was lost and he had no bow, just a sword he would soon find himself too useless to wield. The ground grew closer. He would crash into the side rail of the ship and beyond that the mass of violent white bodies and mud.

When he hit the bottom, the world around him faded and he only knew pain, but Oliver did not scream like so many men around him. For a brief moment he let himself close his eyes and forget the battle. Then the abominations, preceded by their howls, attacked him. *I'm dead*, he thought. *Leave me alone.* But they continued to come. Something blunt struck his chest and his eyes opened as he gasped for breath. He tried to roll away but they were too close, their bare feet kicking into him.

If only he could get up, but they smothered him. An abomination straddled him, fists beating into Oliver with ferocious malice. He might have cried then but he had no breath. He dropped his sword, attempting to raise his arms to block his face, but he was pinned.

His leg was free. His left leg. Screaming, he lifted it, kicking as torment ripped through his thigh. Whatever he struck shrieked as it tumbled back. It was all he needed to break free. His fingers searched the mud for anything to use as a weapon. They brushed the edge of a blade, cutting into his skin, more pain to distract him from survival. Ignoring his wounds, he found the hilt and gripped it. He drove up, thrusting his sword forward, slicing into the abomination on top of him. His mind cleared, and he did not know whether the pain had dulled or if it drove him to fight harder.

Several abominations managed dull blows, but he dispatched them and several others once he found his feet. This may be his death, but he would take as many abominations with him as possible.

After a moment, he realized that he did not fight alone. Steel rang cutting through the trickling rain and the gutturals of his attackers. He locked swords with an abomination, its size and muscle marking it as a warrior when it was once alive. It growled at Oliver, bringing its face close to his. It grimaced, its emaciated body, pointed rotten teeth, and black eyes menacing. Oliver prepared to disengage and strike at the abomination again, but the tip of a blade ripped from its chest. It stiffened and slumped to the ground, revealing Charis, one hand holding a katana at the ready.

They put their backs to the ship and took on their attackers together. They came, swift and maleficent. He parted them from their half-lives. Each movement and pivot tortured his leg, but his life depended on it. Charis fought with distracting grace and swiftness. The remaining men from the ship gathered about, helping fend off the abominations. They were at the heart of the enemy, too far from the front lines or where Maynard and Nathan were supposed to emerge. How Charis had come to his aid he did not know, but he did know that this was the last stand.

Maynard knew they neared the exit as the sounds of battle echoed down the corridor. Climbing over the corpses, he led them further into the tunnel, the following soldiers squishing and slipping through the carnage. If it was not for Callianeira, he might not have been able to defend their position. More abominations came, but it was sparse and they were more annoying interruptions than threats.

"We should almost be there," he said. He could hear the whispers down the line relaying the information. As Oliver had said, the tunnel emptied into a small cavern that appeared to have been a home. Through the windows the gray scene of abominations stood, ready for their turn in battle. The sight of their bodies sickened Maynard. They were charred, burned, and scarred. Their gnarled and twisted forms stood at the ready for the slaughter, their hateful eyes staring forward, awaiting their turn to rage into battle. These were not the men, women, and children of the towns, but their revenants, abominable undead mockeries. He would give them peace.

Maynard called down the tunnel in a low voice, "This is it. Don't worry about anyone else doing their part. Just make sure you do yours." The men gave an affirmative grunt. Callianeira nodded and together they rushed from the cavern and into battle. Just as he hoped, they took their enemy by surprise. In moments, they gained the advantaged and were making progress.

When the abominations fell back a moment, Maynard thought they had broken the ranks. He was wrong. A figure emerged on a black steed. Captain Reed had grown in size and his body bulged with unnatural muscle. The skin stretched over it, visibly ripping in parts, and the horns, grotesquely sown to his skin, had grown. This was Cain's sickness, his ill sense of humor, an intimidating vulgarity. It was Raven's lich. The captain roared and the abominations rushed anew, swarming them, and Maynard lost sight of the captain, save for his bulging head above the masses.

Maynard sliced a body in two, its top half still clawing at the mud. It howled and grasped. Maynard struck it dead. More came. They overran his men, hacking with crude weapons, mulling and clawing, they downed man after man. Then those men rose from the dead, their skin already turning sallow, the soul gone from their eyes, his own men resurrected and turned against him. Maynard yelled as he downed two in one blow. He cursed and spit and slashed, each lurch another bout of fury. All for the captain, Cain's prized abomination.

He made for the lich, but found himself pressed back against the wall of the Pass. He defended with each strike, too dire to worry about anything else. Grunting, he waved his sword in a full swing. Limbs fell from bodies, torsos slid from legs, thudding onto the ground. The creatures moaned, falling as well, or staggering on with missing limbs and exposed insides. He chopped, swinging with intensity, losing ground, increasingly pushed against the mountainside. Most of those who had fought alongside him had been killed and resurrected against him, and he couldn't see Callianeira. When he fended off another round, another wave came. They moaned, limbs groping, crude weapons flailing. He had to get to the captain.

A spear came at Maynard and he jumped. Something changed. The abominations charged at him, their marred bodies pressing in, and the spear struck under his feet. He could feel the world beyond offering something and acted with strange intuition. His feet found the side of the mountain wall and he pushed off, rising above the slaughter and the spears. Arrows flew past him, spears struck upward and missed, and sword held high he came closer to the massive sight of the captain and his horse. The horse was bulging, as if too bulky for its own skin, so black it was hard to distinguish anything more than its general shape. Maynard landed, bringing his sword down upon the stead, severing its head. Its limp body staggered to the ground, overthrowing the captain.

Then the barking and howls started.

Liam gained a sword, but found the time to recover and reload the gun. When Sol fled, he took on a bristling human form as he ran. Most of the other crocotta were struck down, but the abominations continued. And then *they* came. They were not dogs, but they held the form of a large canine. Rows of needle-like teeth protruded from their calloused snouts. As they emerged, Liam glimpsed the horror in Dorian's face. Liam's muscles ached and he could no longer distinguish the bodies or blood. The lightning flickered once again.

The hounds ran at him. Liam's sword stopped one short and a great fire swept aside the next one. Dorian's magic was no longer bound by the ship. He fought faster than anything Liam had ever seen. He could launch himself into the air, bringing his blade down and around killing four opponents without harming any of his allies.

A hound yelped as Liam brought a sword through its leathery skin. More blood flew into the air. His blade stuck in the flesh, but he wrenched it from the suction in time to deflect another attack. More abominations came with them, but no matter their numbers, Liam maneuvered around them. Not all of the soldiers shared his youthful agility. He had seen a leg ripped from a soldier, a serrated bone sank into another man's neck. The abominations themselves were grotesque. A little girl had bitten him but he struck her down, almost crying as he did.

He blocked a spear and beheaded an oncoming abomination. The clouds covered the world gray and black. With each step he nearly slipped, unable to find traction among the bodies and blood. A hound circumvented Dorian and Liam brought it down. Maynard and Nathan were supposed to bring relief, but it hadn't come. Oliver was on that ship and might be dead. Charis had been among the front lines, but she disappeared about that time. They were losing control.

The tribesmen lived up to their end of the plan while Maynard and Callianeira led their group up the eastern passage. The nomads had followed the tiger through the other side, forming a vanguard from the rear, surrounding their enemies. The enemy had planned to use the tunnels for a surprise attack, but Argon and his men saw to it that they littered the passage with the bodies of their adversaries.

Argon followed the tiger out of the caves and into the Pass. They took their opponents by surprise and began to slaughter the horrors. By spear and might the tribesmen fought their way to meet Maynard's company on the other side. Between each opponent he glimpsed the tiger bringing its claws easily upon his opponents. Argon felt cold hands upon him and hacked them off. Sweat beaded on his broad, muscled chest. He slit the neck of one abomination, and it still came for him, so he removed its head. He worked his way forward, leaving a trail of dismembered bodies behind. Argon and the following soldiers began to ford the shallows of the river, trying to form the line that would cut off the undead army from the rest. He fought at the shoreline, feet in the muddy shallows, surrounded. The progress was slow for the enemy was many.

The captain's three accompanying hellhounds attacked Maynard. They charged and lunged. One clasped onto his arm, jaws locking onto the leather. The teeth didn't pierce it, but the pressure hurt. Its claws scraped at him, cutting into his skin. The lacerations were shallow but frequent and painful as the beast kicked. A slash separated its body, and Maynard ripped the head from his arm.

The captain, having recovered from his fallen horse, came upon Maynard with surprising swiftness. Rolling, Maynard dodged the first blow and one of the hounds snapped at him. It only got his shirt, which tore as he pulled away. Before he could rise, the other hound pounced, knocking him back. He tumbled, pushing away the hound, as the captain brought his sword upon Maynard.

He kicked the captain's shin, the bone cracking, knocking Reed off balance, gaining Maynard enough time to find his feet. A dog pounced and he brought his sword around, slicing at the beast. *Two down*, he thought as each half hit the ground with a grotesque thud. The other hound cowered a moment. Maynard lifted his sword, blocking a parry from the captain and taking a swing of his own. The captain deflected it and then they locked in battle as the soldiers and abominations warred among them.

Whatever they had done to the lich gave it unexpected swiftness. Even Maynard's practiced hand could barely keep up with each strike. A gnarled grin spread across the captain's undead face. They exchanged quick blows, the resounding clashes split-seconds apart. Maynard blocked a hammering attack. The captain punched him. Sweat and blood flecked into the air, but Maynard held his ground and fought harder.

He blocked a down-stroke from the captain and maneuvered back just in time to avoid the hound. Maynard stood back a moment, breathing hard. One way or another, they would tear him apart. The surrounding battle raged, but all seemed to know that Maynard was the captain's prize and left them alone. None of the men dared oppose the beastly leader. Yards away, the abominations clustered around Callianeira.

The hound and the captain came at him. He would have to suffer a blow from one to defend against the other. He extended a hand, calling the Darkworld and the fire. It blazed from his palm, the Darkworld-amplified throw lacing his opponents. It was enough to deter the hound, which retreated pawing at its demonic snout. The captain stood, spots of flame glowing on his clothing, a multitude of burn wounds bleeding the blue black blood. Undaunted by the wounds, the captain smiled and charged at Maynard. It rained harder.

Serj and Belriah joined Argon, fighting with him back to back. Spears jutted at their formation and chains whipped at them. The rain's drizzle became torrential. Argon blocked and rolled, and soon lost his own spear. After regaining another spear from an abomination, he turned it on its opponent. He thrust it forward and pulled it back, swung it left, knocking down three more, and driving another down. A spear lunged at him and he deflected it with his own and brought the sharp edge of the tip on the wielder. He had been drifting from Serj and Belriah. Trying to work his way back, he brought the spear between two oncoming abominations and beat each of them down with it. They slipped in the mud and he trampled them, running back to his chiefs. Just as he was about to rejoin their hold, a group of abominations overtook them. The sheer numbers grouped over sword and spear and piled upon them in the river. Argon wrestled his way through and with his spear picked the abominations off the pile as quick as he could while fighting off other abominations which threatened to mound as well. A brown hand reached through the pale white bodies and Argon pulled Serj from the waters before thrusting his spear through another opponent. Belriah remained trapped in the river under the bodies and they fought to free him.

After seconds Serj and Argon found Belriah and pulled him, pale and cold from the water. Serj took down three more abominations as Argon turned from the battle. He dropped to his knees, looking to his chief. Belriah's chest lay still, the faintest pulse absent from his wrists and neck.

Argon let out a cry of anger and lamentation. He should worry about the battle, about survival. He should help Serj, but it could wait just another moment while he wept for his fallen chief. Belriah's eyes opened. Argon's relief was short lived as the living-dead Belriah locked fingers around Argon's throat.

He could not, would not kill his chief. In frantic lunacy he tried to pull apart the grip, but could not. "It is not him," Serj yelled over the clamor. "He's already dead. This is sorcery." Sanity returned and Argon took the dagger from his belt and drove it into the undead neck of his former chief. It spewed blood and those black eyes widened, the cold fingers tightened their grip and then Argon stabbed again into the skull. The fingers loosened and the body fell.

Serj cried a warning and Argon turned towards the oncoming hounds. Argon had seen nothing like it. It was as if they had been lacerated and burned. Their teeth showed, no lips to hide the jagged and sharp rows. More beasts arrived. They were all sizes, some like great lizards, others like menacing mutated apes. The tiger locked in battle with one. They rolled, a fury of claws and fangs. Argon began to lose momentum. Too many, too fast. The water was dark with blood and muck. They surrounded him on land and water. His brothers fell, their terrified screams piercing his ears. A hound jumped from the right, a lizard-like creature from the left. They charged him with indefensible swiftness. A new beast emerged from the river. Its great reptilian form curved up from the waters and in an elegant thrust locked the hound in its jaws. In a single moment the water flecked from its body, raindrops fell, and blood sprayed. He knew her, and for the short moment afforded him, Argon wondered how Taesa could be there. The crocodiles emerged from the river with violent lunges. They locked their jaws onto the hell-beasts and thrashed them about the shore. He heard the rallying cry from his soldiers and with restored morale they fought on.

Though weakened, the captain remained undefeated. Maynard fought with renewed vigor, each parry drawing him closer to victory. If he could just drive their duel closer to Callianeira, she might be able to help him. The rain had turned the sand to mud, and all of his might, all of his strength from the Darkworld, he directed to the melee. The captain's twisted smile faded for a more unsightly grimace. Those black eyes never wavered, nor did his defenses give purchase to Maynard's attacks.

Abominations did not grow weary, but Maynard hoped the captain's sentience would give him a crude desperation. Maynard counted on it. He parried an attack from the lich, but almost tripped on the carcass of the horse. Though his hands were slick with sweat and water, the sword was loyal to him and with it he blocked and advanced. Its large blade dwarfed the captain's and Maynard continued to gain ground, driving him closer to where Callianeira fought. Again he struck and the captain grunted. Reed, in all his mass, towered above Maynard, his armor digging into the undead flesh. He roared, his sallow cheeks revealing infected holes. The next strike almost knocked Maynard on his back.

With the fury of a demon, Callianeira emerged from the battle to face the captain. Together they fought him. Defending against two opponents, the captain had no time to attack. Callianeira and Maynard dealt fast and fierce strikes. The captain blocked an assault from Maynard, locking swords with him. Maynard looked into Reed's black eyes, matching their fury. Through rotten, clenched teeth it growled at him, holding firm against Maynard's steel.

Callianeira brought her blade upon the captain's sword arm. The well-placed slash fell between the plates of armor, cleanly severing the limb. As it fell to the ground those black eyes widened into horrific realization. Maynard gripped the captain by the neck and called the flame. It ripped out of his fingers, losing control, and enveloped the hulking captain entirely, the rain sizzling and smoking as it fell upon them. The lich howled and contorted but Maynard retained his grip, embracing the chaos of the fire, crushing the neck, burning the behemoth. Maynard realized he was yelling, bellowing a wordless scream, anger burning like the fire.

With the rear attack, the enemy's attention was spread thin. Liam had run out of ammunition some time ago and fought with sword. He had few moments to pay attention to Dorian, but what he had seen amazed him. Magic, but unlike anything Liam had imagined. Dorian possessed profound command of the elements. Mud swirled around him, confusing his opponents. Fire spurned an attacker. An abomination lunged at Liam and he stabbed it in the throat and pulled the sword back as the black liquid splashed in the air.

Just as Liam felt enlivened by the favorable turn of battle, a series of cracks reverberated in the Pass. They didn't sound so different from his pistol, but they were more numerous and rapid. It reminded him of that first night in Bronton. Abomination and soldier alike began to fall, writhing as they hit the ground. Their screams were met with laughter and hooting as several men, guns in hand—guns much bigger than Liam's—taking down all in their path.

One of them let off a series of rapid shots, felling a dozen soldiers, yelling as he did. "Infinite Bullets, motherfuckers!"

Liam pulled his own gun out and started firing. One of the men turned on him, and Liam rolled, dodging a shotgun blast. He kept moving, hoping the fog of battle would save him. Another booming shot sprayed dirt and dead flesh around him. A white hand gripped Liam's neck. After firing off a shot, the abomination released its grip and fell to the ground. Not wanting to waste any more bullets, Liam stowed the gun and redrew his sword. He took two abominations down, and turned, finding the shotgun wielder close and reloading. Within four steps, Liam's would reach the man.

Liam's sprinted, dodging one abomination and nearly slipping in the mud. Clicking the chamber shut, the shotgun-wielder raised the firearm. With a jolt, Liam's sword met flesh, and he tumbled into the man. As they fell, the shotgun fired, the end of the barrel well behind Liam, but the crack of its discharge in his ear. The man lay in the mud, Liam on top of him, sword deep in the man's flesh. As Liam pushed himself up, blood clung to his clothes.

The battle had gone quiet, but Liam looked around and it did not appear to have died down. A line of fire, as tall as a man, consumed two of the Infinite Bullets' outlaws. Dorian turned from them and focused his energy on an undead crocotta.

The ground trembled, and Liam realized that the sound of the shotgun's discharge had deafened him. He turned to see a group of abominations charging him. At least a dozen ran at him. After pulling out the gun, he took four down. The ground shook more as a dozen men on camelback stormed into the battle, Commander Jaked Mari at their lead.

Six or seven abominations took on one of the camels, pulling the rider down. Liam's hearing was returning, and he heard the screams over the ringing in his ears. Liam began to run to their aid. Commander Mari the remaining men into the foray, working their way towards Dorian, whose fire and earth bent the world around him. One man with a gun remained, its rounds firing in rapid succession. They never touched Dorian, but they took down five of the camels and their men.

As Liam ran, Commander Mari fought, but pale hands reached up, gripping him. With grace, the commander fought, sword hard at work on the probing limbs. When the commander had cleared most of his attackers, Liam slowed down. The captain turned and smiled at Liam, raising his sword. Dorian too saw the rally, and in unison they worked their way towards that area of the battle line.

A pale shape shot into the air, rising behind the commander. Liam shouted a warning, and it sounded like Dorian did too. Commander Mari maneuvered his camel around, turning, and reading his sword. The abomination landed on top of Mari, knocking him from his camel. The commander slammed into the ground as the revenant began to pummel him.

Why wasn't the commander resisting? What was happening? The camelry broke into disarray, more abominations seizing them. Liam got to the commander first. Too preoccupied with the commander, the abomination did not see Liam's sword falling upon it. Liam pushed the abomination's body from atop Commander Mari, ready to help the man up. Commander Jaked Mari lay dead, head at an unnatural angle, neck jutting sharply to the side. Liam had fallen from his camel at least twice, but the tougher man had died when he hit the ground.

A hand gripped Liam and he turned, ready to fight, but it was Dorian.

"I'm sorry," Liam said. He shouldn't have slowed down. He should have kept running. Between the sweat and blood and dirt, Liam hoped Dorian could not see that he cried.

"It's not your fault," Dorian said. "You have to understand that this is just how things are. But you can't let it keep you from fighting."

A camel nearly knocked him over as it careened by, its rider taking down more approaching abominations. Their disorganization at the commanders death was apparently short-lived and they had regrouped. Dorian put a hand on Liam's shoulder and then turned back to the battle.

Dorian continued to send waves of fire and earth upon their assailants, but he concentrated on reorganizing their line. Within minutes, after some sense of unification provided some resistance to the enemy, a man on camelback made his way to Dorian. The spirit made flesh smiled and he turned to Liam.

"They did it," he yelled over the noise of the battle. "They broke through."

The success of the rear attack caused more confusion and the assault from the abominations and hell-beasts seemed less concentrated. It surely could not be close to over, not even with nightfall so imminent. He had not seen any creature on the enemy's side that resembled a human, much less the descriptions he knew of Jacob, Amelia, and Cain. Did more await them into the night?

Oliver's sword arm grew pained, his leg hurt, and he was fatigued. Each breath brought a sharp agony to his chest. Charis never wavered, but tired as well and would likely rather be at her place in battle, tending the wounded. Too many of the soldiers around them had fallen and it was a matter of time before the remaining ten of them were overtaken. He did not relish the idea of their undead and barbaric arms clawing at his skin, ripping pieces of him away. How many soldiers had already fallen in such a horrific manner? There had been fifty on the ship at the start. He had seen the teeth sink into throats, entrails pulled from the bellies of the unfortunate, and the fear of that made him fight harder.

Shouts came from the north, distracting him, but the ship blocked his vision. He was already too busy trying to keep away the abominations. It crossed his mind to climb into the ship somehow, but sitting on its side it would be damn near impossible to scale. If the abominations carried ropes they could have fire as well, another terrible way to die.

He heard more shouts, closer this time, and not in the growls and moans of the abominations. A spear struck an abomination in front of him and then he was surrounded by tribesmen. Nathan, a great tiger, ripped into two attackers in one swipe. Maynard, faster than he could have imagined, swung his great sword, crushing all in his path. Callianeira was there too, making quick work of all who assailed her.

What had taken minutes felt like hours. They had almost formed with the soldiers on the other side when Argon saw a great flame in the distance. The man called Maynard had conjured fire, a soothing assurance of his faith in these people. The area to the north was mostly rid of foes, the majority of the threat between them and the frontlines. They had—more or less—surrounded the army within the Pass. Once trapped, they had made quick work of the abominations, and Nathan directed them toward the fallen ship. Once that was taken, the hard part was over, but Argon was weary and the task ahead was daunting. They had lost Belriah, and each abomination and hell-beast he struck down only made his anger grow.

When they met the soldiers on the other side, led by Maynard and Callianeira, no command was needed. They knew what to do. The undead army was trapped and the soldiers began the purging the abominations while rescuing any survivors from the ship.

When night had long fallen, the deed was done. Argon looked to Nathan—now in human form—and nodded approval. The old and dried stains of black and red blood covered the soldiers as they breathed their sighs of relief. Argon saw Serj solemn and distant as he surveyed the vast field of dead. He might lament Belriah more than Argon. Among the mounds of blue and white undead flesh, too many of his people lay dead. They would hold funerals for them soon. Argon said a silent prayer to Elah.

He found Taesa basking at the river's edge, her wet, scaled body lined by the moonlight. She gave a quiet bellow as he approached. It was a strange thing that she would find him and strike when the time was right. Her entire congregation was in tow, filed along the river in their fashion. Argon placed a hand on her scaled back and once again felt the reassurance of his kindred beast. He would have stayed there all night, content to be with her, but Nathan approached.

"Come," he said. "It's time we solved your riddle."

# CHAPTER THIRTY-ONE

## Enigma

Though tired, Dorian found the energy to trim his beard to its customary shortness. Long dark hair, a beard as short as he could manage, and the trench coat. He was not a man for change, but rather practicality. If something worked, it was unlikely he would amend it until something better came along. He was not flourished in his style, rather utilitarian, efficient, and comfortable. Of course, it had been a point of humor for Nathan, who—though never belittling—could not help but take some amusement from Dorian's dry sincerity. Oliver almost admired it, though his dichotomy of cynicism and optimism often rivaled Dorian's prevailing pessimism. Yet, Dorian was wise and learned from Nathan not to take himself too seriously and depended on Oliver for the reminder that there was hope. Indeed, Dorian was prone to get out of bed in the morning for no other reason than a sense of duty, as if the world rested on his shoulders, but Oliver's reminders had always been balancing to such delusions.

He was still needed, and this night after the battle would likely be as much rest as he could expect in the coming time. In spite of the mystery of Jacob's latest disappearance, and what was likely a rather desperate situation, they all agreed to clean up the mess and then take a rest.

Though he had anticipated a direct confrontation with Jacob, he was thankful to have avoided it, though it was probably not for the best. The battle left him both exhausted and restless. And so, after grooming, he paced the empty streets of the Pass, a world he created, but had not seen since its inception. On either end, the desert stretched, endless monotony to the south, the ruins and Novum to the north. The damned City was a fallen god, a monolithic obelisk, black and the object for which he had fought so hard.

Had he never met Oliver so long ago, he might not have come so far. Among the first, Oliver worked his way up in the ranks, one of the first to put faith in Dorian's resolution to stop Jacob. Yet, Oliver was not the blind believer like so many others, but a born leader. He was like a king's adviser, ready to say the hard things, and to risk everything for good. In those first days, Dorian had been cautious of Oliver. The man had just lost his wife and children, yet it was only in the brief personal moments that his professional and militaristic obligations fell to the wayside that Oliver had shown Dorian any real lamentation. He truly cared about his lost life and about the suffering of others. It came at a price, a disdain for wasted time, and with it a resentment for those who remained ignorant. From experience, Oliver learned that inaction was an action in itself, that complacency was a decision to not decide. Willful ignorance was to choose one's bliss over the bliss of others.

It wasn't long before Dorian and Oliver became fast friends, their mutual support crucial in those early days. The place was gone now, but for a time, they frequented a pub away from the enemy lines. Most of the time they had to catch up on sleep or other duties, but once in a while they had the luxury of meeting for drinks.

Many of their conversations lingered in his memory, but one particular recollection came to Dorian. Over one such pint in the tavern that started it all, Dorian sat next to Oliver at the bar. It seemed almost comical to Dorian then, and the resonance of that humor never quite waned, that alcohol—beer specifically—somehow served as a bonding agent to them. For Dorian, it was not the inebriation so much as the simplicity of it. When nothing else appeared certain, the simplicity of beer was a welcome distraction.

"Do you think we can really hold Jacob back in Chicago?" asked Oliver.

"Let's not talk about the war," said Dorian. "Can't we be two gentlemen having a pint?"

"I suppose we can," said Oliver

That sat in silence for a moment before Dorian spoke. "Why do we do it?"

"I thought we weren't going to talk about the war," said Oliver.

"Fine, but I just mean, why do we try?"

"Don't ask me, my friend," Oliver replied. "I'm the bitter one. You, the fallen angel, never thought to ask God that question?"

"It is a strange thing," said Dorian. "I was so certain, but I wasn't here long before I started to doubt it. It was so cut and dry before my fall. Now it is so gray down here."

"But you had to have some sort of dogmatic answer before. That should count for something. Come now, convince me that Talmas isn't right."

"It did count for something. And still does, but I need to be reminded."

"So, what was the answer?" asked Oliver.

In that moment Dorian's answer seemed so hollow. He recalled the taste of the hops, his dry throat, and the way the response seemed inexplicable to anyone unfamiliar with the way of the gods and the cosmos.

"The answer," said Dorian, "is beyond mankind, and I fear it becomes beyond me. Suffice to say, humans were not made to suffer as much as they have, and accordingly, they do not comprehend it. Our time is but what fate has woven and the occasional person strong enough to resist it."

"And God does nothing about it?" asked Oliver.

"The Eternal One? Perhaps he has done something," said Dorian. "Perhaps he set something into motion a long time ago, or maybe he is doing so now. Possibly, he is biding his time, and will enact some grand plan in the end. We muse on the fundamentals of life, frustrated at the cusps of our understanding. At the frays, what do we really know about anything? That's the interesting thing about humanity. They teeter on the line between fate and choice. Yes, the dominoes fall, but man can do something about it. He can overcome his fate."

"That's not very satisfying," said Oliver.

"I don't think a thorough answer would be all that satisfying either. Answers do not lead to contentment. Peace leads to contentment."

"I agree that answers don't lead to contentment," Oliver said. "However, humans have ruined every chance at peace ever given to them. And *you* didn't want to talk about the war." He sighed. "I see your point though. Not so long ago, we could leave this stuff to the armchair philosophers. You asked why we try. I would ask why we don't just retire on some distant island?"

"I'm pretty sure Jacob has destroyed most of them," said Dorian.

"He's a bastard. I'll admit it, but surely something remains." Oliver grew serious. "But, Dorian, I've lost so much. I've lost things I thought I cared about, but didn't. And I've lost things I wished I cared about more. If stopping Jacob means preserving the things—the people—that others care about, then it's worth it."

"What if we just handed it over to Jacob?" asked Dorian, "Let him rule."

"You know better than I do what would happen," replied Oliver. "You can't hold yourself responsible for losing to his warpath. Jacob laid D.C. to waste and he still has people convinced that it's a conspiracy and out of his control. *That* is fucking lie." Oliver held up a finger. "We stop him at all costs. Even if he takes us to the walls of the City itself, we stop him. If he succeeds in Chicago it might call for desperate measures."

"If he takes us at Chicago, there may be nothing else we can do," Dorian said.

"When all hope is lost, you fight anyway."

"Do you?" Dorian asked. The question was rhetorical. Dorian knew well that you do indeed fight, even when all was lost. At the loss of hope, he could do nothing and die, or he could die fighting for what he knew was right. He could not stand for Jacob's ways. Jacob could burn a hundred souls in a second, lay entire cities to waste, and thwart Dorian's every move with even more destruction, but only in Dorian's death would he cease to oppose the bastard.

The memory fading, Dorian now stood mere miles from the walls of the great pyramid. Jacob, as always, seemed one step ahead. It was either that or he had fled again, in which case, Dorian dreaded another wait, if he lived long enough to see it. Whatever the case, hope did indeed seem lost.

He pushed the thought from his mind. Liam, who had taken some crocotta wounds, was under Charis's healing. The girl Aster was presumably with him. Perhaps it was time for a pint. Nearby, Maynard, Nathan's curious progeny, seemed to be deep in thought as well. It was likely high time they both had a drink.

Maynard's nails dug into his palms as the rain came down. When the battle thinned, he left the Pass, working his way north. He had struck down any enemy that approached him, but most of all he fixed his eyes on the black object in the distance, midst the ring of mountains, barely visible under the rain. This had been it. Jacob was not there and would not come. The whole thing was a distraction meant to let him get into the City. Had he taken a force with him to besiege it? If that was the case, it appeared his force was out of sight on the north side of the City or already inside. Maynard wanted his chance to strike the fallen angel down, but that was not today.

The pride and altruism faded. The desire for revenge resurfaced and he had cried Jacob's name after the battle, only a few feet away from the Pass and among the flattened ruins. He held his great sword aloft, ready to take on any of the fallen who would meet his challenge, but nothing came. Even Sol, who had evidently been present during the battle, was nowhere to be found.

It might have been best to talk to Nathan, but once the battle was over and things under control, Nathan went elsewhere with the nomads. Callianeira was absent. It was perhaps better that she did not see Maynard when so much blood and dirt clung to him, the downpour doing little to wash it off. He had his share of bruises and one gash, but the rest of the blood belonged to something or someone else. He vaguely recalled an abomination clubbing the head of the man next to him. Maynard had barely wiped the brains from his face before another splatter of blood had come. It was not the part of battle that made him feel alive, but they were nuances to which he had grown accustomed.

He left the ruins, returning to the Pass. The rain lessened into a sporadic drip, but the river still ran high, crocodiles lining it much to Maynard's curiosity. Mud plastered everything. Men ran about. He could see the glow of a fire just outside of the southern exit in the Pass where they presumably piled and burned the bodies of the abominations. Even though the soldiers worked in shifts and Maynard's own obligations would come, he thought he should help, but he also felt tired. His mouth was dry and even his sword felt heavy. Dorian approached him and solved his dilemma for him. "Care for a pint?"

For a time they walked in silence, but there was something Maynard could not help but say, "You're not what I expected."

"I get that a lot," Dorian said with a small smile. Unlike Maynard, Dorian had cleaned up soon after the battle.

"None of you are. Jacob made you out to be some idealistic crusader."

"That doesn't seem far off," Dorian said.

"But you aren't an idealistic crusader," replied Maynard. "You fight because you care, because you have something worth living and dying for."

"And why did you decide to fight, Maynard?"

It was a good question. He may hold his motivations to certain ideals, but he had come to learn that they did not necessarily match. "Depends on the day," he said. "I'd like to say I do it for justice, but sometimes it's guilt, revenge, because I don't know my place otherwise." Dorian nodded in understanding. The fallen angel had struggled with these things as well. It was as if they were both moths desperately darting at the light, starving and dying for something so bright and real, yet unattainable.

"Aren't we driven by more than that?" Once again Dorian hinted that he identified with Maynard.

"Perhaps," replied Maynard. "It's all so new to me. I've spent most of my life looking out for myself, but now I think about others. Then again, maybe I just don't want to think about myself anymore and the terrible things I've done."

They stopped walking for a moment in the drizzling dark and faced each other. The river water trickled gently nearby and the warm air stood still.

"I tried to do good things," Dorian said, "and did a great deal of damage in the process. Does that make me any better than you? We've all done terrible things, and I'm not sure that what we do here will ever redeem that. A man who succeeds on his first chance is admirable, but a man that is given a second chance will try all the harder and give all the more to be worthy of it. You may do better than if you had never screwed up in the first place.

"You can go your whole life the victim of your own mistakes and circumstances, but that would be taking things for granted. Instead, you can take the sins against you and the sins you've committed and learn from them. Trust me when I say that it is those of us who have fallen hardest who have potential to rise the most, because we understand the costs. And you, Maynard, have a great deal of potential."

When they arrived at the inn, Oliver was there and asked for their help. Maynard nodded and followed him to one of the back rooms and down into the basement. It was dark and descending the stairs reminded Maynard of Bronton. He pushed the thought from his mind as they came into a cellar. Oliver had apparently lit a few wall torches prior.

Oliver paused a moment, his leg obviously bothering him. "It looks like Jacob stayed here and had his share of the beer and liquor, but he didn't make much of an effort to find my stores." In short order, they moved two kegs of ale upstairs.

Callianeira was still absent and Charis tended the wounded. Oliver, with unusual levity, elected a soldier to tend bar for them. The soldier seemed grateful for the job as it required him to stay indoors with minimal work, and soon Maynard and Oliver were enjoying their drinks. Dorian went behind the bar, concocting something of his own.

"I'd drink a bucket of this stuff," Maynard said, studying his glass of beer.

"It'd knock you on your ass," Oliver replied. They clinked glasses and each took a hearty sip of their libation.

"You look like hell," Dorian said to Maynard. Oliver and Dorian had taken the time to clean up.

"What of it?" Maynard asked. "Feel like hell too. Probably smell like it. I can't be bothered to get cleaned up right after that."

"Jacob wasn't there," Maynard said.

The others appeared disappointed as well. "Yes," Dorian said. "He and his followers seem to be missing. It is quite the cause for concern. We have put sentinels in every known crevice of this place."

"My bet," said Oliver, "is that he fled when the battle turned."

"Seems odd," said Maynard.

"I don't see why," replied Oliver. "He lost the battle."

"That he did," said Maynard, "but Jacob battles by strategy, not numbers. Getting us there was a matter of strategy on his part, but the battle itself was one of numbers. I'm not sure he was ever there. We shouldn't underestimate him. He could be camped out on the backside of the City."

"True," said Oliver. "Commander Mari was always the best at keeping me up to date, but he fell in battle today." Oliver raised glass and the others followed suit, toasting together. "Unfortunately, I have no intelligence on Jacob's whereabouts."

"Are we searching the caves?" Maynard asked.

"I'm afraid not," replied Oliver. "We might find ourselves on the other side of the mountains before we found him. I don't have enough men to seal off every entrance immediately, but we're working on it."

"Even if we do block him in," Dorian said, "we still have the Morning Star to deal with."

"It's possible Jacob is *in* the City?" Maynard asked.

"How?" asked Oliver.

"I witnessed the Morning Star first hand," Maynard replied. "Though I know nothing of his plans, I wonder if he could have something to do with getting Jacob into the City."

"I'd hope not," said Dorian. "But it is a possibility. I can't imagine how he got in. If he did, he might be days ahead of us in learning the place and hiding. He may rise just like he did when he first fell."

"Well," said Oliver, "perhaps we could put that off until tomorrow? We've had enough of it for today as it is. What say you we drink and be merry?"

They did until Maynard was good and drunk. They emerged from the tavern, perhaps too jolly, to find Nathan and the tribesmen emerging from a cave. They exchanged solemn words with Argon and Serj and parted respectfully. Maynard didn't bother with details. Oliver had paced himself, Dorian seemed to have a higher tolerance, but Maynard was in good spirits.

Maynard walked to his lodgings, made his way up to the mezzanine, careful not to stumble, and started for his room. It was the second door on the left they had told him, but his mind shifted in those few steps. Away from the others, he was no longer drinking to remember so much as to forget. He wished he could block out what lay before. For a moment he was Jacob's man again. At the time, he had claimed that he belonged to no man, but he knew better. Jacob had owned him and once again, perhaps drunkenly, he felt the guilt of it.

After grabbing a towel and a change of clothes, Maynard left his room and went in search for a shower. Once clean, and a bit more sober, he walked back to his room. He turned to the door and opened it. It was dark inside save for one candle, but he did not recall leaving a candle lit. The figure in the bed stirred and he realized he was in the wrong room.

"Maynard?" Callianeira, sat up, the sheets falling from her torso.

"I'm sorry, wrong room. I'm sorry." He closed the door.

That had been stupid. Perhaps the beer was still affecting him more than he cared to admit. He would have to talk to her tomorrow. He went to the second door—his door—and went into his room. In the dim, he found a chair and piled his things no it. Still sore from battle, Maynard eased into the bed.

It was only a matter of seconds in the dark before he knew that sleep could not come. The same thoughts plagued him. There was no improved or redeemed Maynard, only the same bastard who had killed anyone who stood in his way. He did not deserve a second chance, much less someone with which to share it.

There was a click and he opened his eyes. The door cracked and he reached for his sword. This was another one of Jacob's tricks, just like the darkmen and just like the Pass. But then he saw that it was her. Unlike him, Callianeira had not found the wrong room. Even her figure, a silhouette in the light from the hall, evoked feelings in him. Surely she had just come to talk, but Maynard thought he knew better.

She did not say a word as she closed the door behind her. The sound of her footfalls neared the bed. She sat down, near him and ran her fingers through his hair. For a moment he was simply grateful he had showered, but that fleeting thought gave way to his deep need of her to be here. Her fingers found the edge of the sheet and she eased herself in beside him. The bed was big enough for the two of them, even if they had not wanted to be so close. They did want to be close and she curled against him. His arms wrapped around her, his fingers searching her figure. He wanted more, but then he sensed something in her. Maynard had been with whores, the kind of women who always pretended to want him, but this was different. He held her tight, feeling the movement of her breathing, and he knew that they needed each other.

She turned, her hair tickling his face as she leaned near him, whispering in his ear. "I haven't done this since I came here. I've always done it for another cause. Never for the person I was with. Never for myself."

# CHAPTER THIRTY-TWO

## *Leviathan*

Into the dark tunnels Argon followed the tiger-man, fingers brushing against the stone. The fire ahead burned dimly, emanating from Nathan's palm, yet another strange testament to the power of these people. Argon, lamenting Belriah, wished his lost chief could have beheld this wonder. Pangs of guilt reverberated like their footfalls. Memories flashed of cold dead eyes, the choking grip, and then Argon's knife in Belriah's neck. It felt a disgrace leaving Belriah unburied while they followed Nathan into the caves.

"I'm sorry to part you from lamenting your dead," said Nathan, leading the way, "but I believe that this is our best chance."

"Where are we going?" asked Serj.

"I'm not really sure," said Nathan. "I'm just following the hum." Nathan continued ahead, leading them. Whatever the "hum" may be, Argon followed, but not without trepidation.

"This man speaks in riddles," whispered Serj.

"Trust him as you trust me," said Argon, not giving away his reservations. "I have spoken with him. Not only does he speak true, but he speaks of things beyond us."

Their path sloped downward yet again and Argon, wearied from the battle, stumbled. Catching himself against the wall, he took a breath of the stale air and moved on, following Nathan's dim glow. The light in Nathan's hand was a mystery, a phantasm before him, the amber flame laced by the darkness like the stripes of a tiger. They took a turn, followed another curve, descended a few more yards, and halted when the passage opened up. The light ceased to reach the ceiling or the walls, and the echoes grew louder and then farther. Nathan told them to wait. The light darted about as Nathan removed his shirt. To Argon's fascination, the lines along Nathan's back began to glow. Fire rippled in acute lines, curling and jutting around his torso and shoulders to form runes. They twisted and circled one another, arcane symbols beyond Argon's understanding.

A rumbling echoed in the cavern, like thunder harnessed by a vast chamber. Yet, it was not a thunder, but more like a great body dragging against stone. Cold water trickled at Argon's feet and dripped upon his brow. He looked up into the blackness, blinking away the rain.

"This is sorcery," said Serj.

Argon hid his unease. "Yes, my friend, there is magic afoot. The gods are at work."

A creature bellowed a deep exhale, and a wild decay filled the air. Nathan lifted his hand and his light burned brighter. In the cavern, rain dripping from its stone arches, was the crocodile. Its bulk filled the chamber, towering above them, and its eyes glowed afire reflecting Nathan's light, furnaces glaring at them from behind its toothed snout.

"I recommend that you be respectful," Nathan said. "And don't forget to grovel. These demigods love it when you grovel."

*"Who summons me to the mortal world?"* the Leviathan said, its voice a throaty bass.

Nathan knelt, "O Leviathan, it is I, Nathan. I bring your kindred beasts."

The Leviathan gave a low, croaking growl. *"And why would a degenerate* Grigori *bring them before me?"*

"Well," said Nathan rising, "I thought you might like to meet them."

"*And?*" The Leviathan gave what sounded like an amused chuckle that rattled the cavern.

"And," Nathan said, "we have some questions."

"*Ask then, mortals.*"

Nathan looked to Argon, who found himself unprepared. His mind raced with the questions he might ask, but he knew time was limited.

"We have at last completed our battle," Argon said. "I would ask when the promised rains will come."

"*Yes,*" it hissed, "*The promised rains. Follow the river beyond the City and to the mountains. There you will find what you seek.*"

"How are you connected to all of this?" Argon asked. It was a broad question that he hoped would gain a response to many questions.

"*I serve Elah. Yet, there are those who serve me and are sympathetic to the will of Elah. The nomads—Argon above all—have acted in great faith of me. In return, I have provided. I have guided my daughter's congregation through the underground waters to find you in a time of need. You will meet with them again in the promised rains.*"

Argon did not understand everything, but guessed much. His people, who had been so faithful to the moon god and respectful of his daemon had gained favor. They had, in essence, been respectful to the Leviathan by bonding with Taesa's congregation. They had not just believed, but acted on that belief, and had been rewarded accordingly.

"One last question?" asked Nathan, "We should not keep him longer."

"Yes," said Argon. "What is the will of Elah?"

"*Elah, first of the moon, does not serve the Eternal One or the Morning Star, but only her own will. High above in the cosmos she laments looking down on a soiled earth and longs for a day when dead things stay dead and life rises anew."*

"Thank you," said Nathan. "For your wisdom and answers, wise one."

*"Farewell, mortals."* The Leviathan faded in the darkness and his heavy breathing ceased to fill the cavern. Nathan's long red hair fell upon his shoulders, touching the fading glow of his tattooed back.

The return journey felt somehow shorter and they emerged out of the caves and into the Pass. Serj had been silent the entire way. When they came out, the dusk was a burning ridge on the western cliff above them. Down the way the great flame cremated the remaining bodies, and Argon could smell the foul smoldering of their flesh compounded with the remaining decay on the battlefield.

Dorian, Oliver, and Maynard met them as they emerged from the tunnel. Maynard stood slightly hunched, as if exhausted. Blood and mud were flecked upon his face and trench coat. Dorian and Oliver appeared to have found a bath.

"We have had the body of your chief taken to a safe place," said Dorian. "I'm sorry for what happened, but I heard he fought well. Did you find anything hopeful in the caves?"

"Aye," said Nathan, "As I suspected, our friend the Leviathan has been at work. And the bastard still claims he doesn't take sides."

"We're burning all the bodies," said Oliver, "but we figured your chief deserved a proper burial. It is tragic that we can't give all a proper funeral, but alas time is short. As far as we know, once you slay an abomination it's dead for good, but if Jacob has another lich, he could easily raise whatever of our own that weren't raised during the battle. Furthermore, we are moving camp to the Pass. The survivors from Mere will also arrive in the next couple of days. Presently, servants are arranging for your tribe to stay on the east side."

"That is kind of you," said Argon. "We must meet with our people and decide what lies ahead. I know we are to journey to the north side of the mountains."

"As you wish," said Oliver. "In the meantime, Jacob seems to have disappeared and we need to decide what's next as well."

Belriah's funeral was short, per the custom of the People of the Crocodile. They had the great fortune of being near a body of water, unlike so many who had passed on the dry desert journey. It was at the river's edge, Taesa and the other crocodiles present, that the nomads gave Belriah to the fire. Belriah's family attended, and his son, Baran, had an air of maturity he had not shown before. Perhaps there was hope. Dorian and many others paid their respects, Charis even shedding tears.

Argon, nor Belriah's son, cried. They did not weep, for though Belriah would be missed, they knew that he had only passed into the spirit world and they would see him when they passed as well. However, Argon was not so stoic as he appeared, and his heart ached over Belriah's death. The loss of his dear friend also came with much uncertainty. Could his son Baran take the mantel of chief? Would Argon retain his esteemed position? He felt selfish for wondering these things, but the thoughts plagued him as he later slept in restless anxiety.

The following meetings among the tribesmen ran together, and Argon felt like the more he cared, the more he was met with resistance. All agreed to follow the Leviathan's advice and go north, but Baran had attended the meetings late, hungover, and flippant. At last they agreed to leave sooner than later, but a date was not decided. Argon spent time on the riverbank with Taesa, but he did not have the will to swim and play with her as he had before, too sleep deprived and haunted by dark thoughts. The battle had detached him from his optimism and even those around him.

"You cannot fault the dead," Argon's father had once told him, but if Belriah had one flaw it was in his parenting. They gathered for council yet again and Baran might have still been inebriated from the night before.

"The People of the Fire leave tomorrow," Serj said. "Will the People of the Moon join us?"

Baran was young and strong-willed, but he was no warrior like his father. He was short, and where most of the tribesmen had muscle, he had a gut from too much food and drink. Even Belriah had been somewhat portly, but he could have bested Argon in single combat. "We only just got here," said Baran. "The promised rains will always be there. The river likely flows from them. I say we remain another week. I am not yet done mourning my father."

"The people from Mere have started to arrive. There is no room for us," Serj replied. "We were not meant to linger here. Scouts have confirmed that Jacob is not hiding behind the pyramid. The way is clear."

"Fine then," said Baran. "Take your people and go."

Serj stood, outraged. "You are a chief now and you have a duty. Don't you dare use your father as an excuse to stay here and drink with your friends. You know what your father would have wanted."

"My father spent too much time taking counsel from zealots."

That was enough for Argon. He was not a zealot and had always given Belriah good counsel. "Baran," he said. "Call me whatever you want, but do not disgrace your father. Listen to Serj."

"Who asked you?" Baran said. "In fact, what are you even doing here? I didn't invite you. You presume too much. Get the fuck out of my council."

"It is you who presume too much," Argon replied. "Your father held council with me and I never steered him wrong. Your lack of wisdom is unbecoming. You are not worthy to govern our tribe."

"Shall I get my whip or are you going to leave as ordered?"

"Listen to Argon," Serj begged.

"No," said Baran. "You listen to me. I am worthy. Argon is going to leave and you are going to leave, and I'm going to do whatever I want. This conversation is over. Argon, get out of my sight before I have you killed."

"Fight me in single combat," Argon said. It was perhaps too bold, but the boy needed to answer for his insolence.

"I don't have to fight you to prove that I'm worthy. I am the chief. Now, leave."

Argon had no choice but to depart and he found himself on the dusty road that spanned the Pass. Had he not been so loyal to way of his people, Argon might have called the tribe to hold the boy accountable to the challenge of combat. Given the chance, Argon did not know if he would simply put the boy in his place or kill him altogether, but he needed to be dealt with.

A few soldiers occupied the tavern, but Nathan and the others were nowhere to be found. Argon went to the tavern, found it mostly empty, and sat at a table. As he cleared his thoughts, Nathan approached.

"Greetings," Nathan said.

"Have a seat," Argon said.

Drink?" Nathan asked as he sat.

"No thanks," Argon said.

"I could always do with a pint for troubling matters such as yours."

"Is it that obvious?"

"Probably not. I just have a knack for such things."

It felt wrong to air the tribe's drama, but he could not lie to Nathan. "Sons are not always their fathers."

"Ah, trouble with your new leader."

"He wants to stay here."

"I see," said Nathan. "And what do you want?"

"I've lived my whole life hoping for the promised rains and at last there is a way, but my chief is not as excited." He could not let things go further, so he changed the subject. "How are things with you?"

"Frustrated. Everyone is frustrated. We fought this battle against all odds and damn near lost it. Those crocodiles of yours probably saved us more than anything. But as of our last meeting, we're all at a loss as to what to do next. The scouts confirmed that Jacob is not encamped behind the City, but that means we don't know where he is. He could be hiding in these tunnels, he could have never been here in the first place, but if he is somewhere south, he's far from here. The whole thing is fucked."

"What are you going to do?" Argon asked.

"We don't know. Jacob could be in the City. We expected him and the Morning Star and neither are here. If they had been, who knows how we would have fared. This was an ugly one."

Argon had known some battle, years and years ago, but it was nothing compared to this. It was one thing to fight man against man, but he had seen the undead and monsters. He had witnessed his friend and chief die twice.

"You've been through enough," Nathan said. "You should go. This river leads north and west and I imagine you'll find what you're looking for that direction."

Nathan seemed to be suggesting that Argon join Serj's tribe, the People of the Fire, and journey with them. Could he leave his own god, the one who commanded the Leviathan, who lead Taesa's congregation to their rescue?

"Are you saying I should join Serj?" Argon asked.

"No," replied Nathan. "It's just that these things have a way of working themselves out."

The conflict was resolved the next day, much to Baran's chagrin.

"Fuck this," he had declared after meeting with Dorian and his council. "Fuck them."

Serj, who had intended to leave that day decided to postpone it due to this news. As it turned out, the People of the Moon had been asked to leave. When word reached Dorian's council that Baran intended to stay indefinitely, they took the necessary action. The tribes were given generous provisions and animals to start them on their new life in the northwest in addition to a generous offer of alliance. The Pass, as it was made clear, was meant for the people of Mere.

As Baran went on in his childish harangue, Argon had to hide his satisfaction. Telling Nathan of his troubles was never meant to garner aid, but it seemed Nathan had little choice but to relay this information to his council. To Argon's benefit they had acted on it. The best part was when they sent Maynard to deliver the message, giant sword slung across his back, less patient than Dorian and less humorous than Nathan. Baran had shown a hint of defiance but it was pathetic against the bigger man.

Argon's thoughts were interrupted when midst-rant Baran had said his name. "This is your fault," Baran said, momentarily stunning Argon. Of course, it had indirectly been his fault, but he had only expedited the necessary and inevitable. Furthermore, Baran had no way of knowing of Argon's conversation with Nathan, much less that he had mentioned their troubles.

"How could it be his fault?" Serj asked.

Baran wrinkled his nose. "They knew we wanted to stay. Someone had to tell them. Do you deny it?"

Searching for an answer, Argon remained silent a moment. "I had not intended—"

"You had not intended what?" Baran interrupted. "You're nothing short of a treasonous fool. I should have you killed."

"That would be unwise," said Serj. "And while those beneath you in council cannot say it, you have been most unwise recently."

Baran dashed across the table. His knife flashed and entered Serj's stomach. Serj's wide eyes searched Baran, the betrayal deep in them. Serj's arms failed to push the younger man away. Argon stood to intervene but four men entered the room, spears pointed at him.

"You are the fool," Baran told the dying Serj. "When the news came to me this morning, I acted quickly. Not all of your men are happy with things and many have given me their loyalty. I'll leave like the council wants me to, but I'm going to have things my way. The People of the Fire are mine. As for your family, Serj, I haven't decided to kill your son. I may or may not raise him to hate you and follow me. You know exactly what I'll do to your wife."

Serj looked over at Argon, eyes wide and pleading. The expression begged Argon to do something, anything that might take this moment back, or at least restore his people. Argon could barely resist jumping forward, ripping Baran's head from his body, and slaying these four spearmen. If he tried, he would die too, and then nothing could be done for Serj's family and people. Hope may very well have been lost and Argon would soon suffer the same fate.

"Whose side are you on now, Argon?" Baran asked.

Argon thought of his wife and children, knowing their fate if he died, but he could not look his friend in the eye and turn his loyalty. Nor could his honor allow him to even fake allegiance to Baran. "The gods curse you," Argon replied. "You are unworthy of the People of the Moon, and the People of the Fire will never truly be yours."

"So be it," said Baran. "Kill him."

Argon looked at his executioners and met each set of eyes. He had known these men. Harsi, Nemsa, and the brothers Siah and Sera. Power was a curious thing. There had surely been threats if they did not follow Baran and generous concessions if they did. This had been in the works for a long time. Baran had wanted to stay in the Pass, biding his time until the right moment came, but when they had been asked to leave it forced his hand. Perhaps Gaezar's dissent was related, sowing dissatisfaction with Belriah. It would have come easier in the desert, when they were low on food and water, to talk these men into betrayal.

Argon then imagined the bodies of his children, and shuddered to think what would happen to his wife. He tried instead to remember them well, to die with their smiling faces in memory. The spears before him raised, ready to plummet down.

"Just what in the fuck is going on here?" a gruff voice asked. The men lowered their spears and Nathan stepped into the room. The mirth had faded from his eyes, their brown-green irises burning with anger.

"This does not concern you, angel." Baran said. The same man who had feared Maynard and should have feared Nathan more, but defiance remained.

"I demand an explanation," Nathan said pointing at Serj's body.

"You will not get one. You will go or we will kill—"

Baran did not finish his sentence. Nathan clasped a hand to his throat and lifted him from the ground. The man struggled with the grip, his feet kicking. The spearmen turned on Nathan who held up his other hand. "Don't bother," he said. "There's no need for you all to die."

Choking and clawing at Nathan, Baran managed a word: "Family."

"Let him go," Argon said with a sudden realization.

After coughing and gasping for air, Baran gave a chuckle, "Yes, you understand. You all thought I was unambitious, unwise, but as soon as I heard we would be meeting with our brothers in the desert I knew what to do. This moment came quicker than expected, but I already had plans in place. I just had to act sooner. If I don't walk out of this meeting unharmed, my men have leave to do whatever they want to Argon's family. The same goes for Serj's family."

"You son of a bitch," Argon said.

"Hear me out," said Baran raising a finger. "I am a man of compromise. You cannot save Serj's family, but you can save your own. I will guarantee their safety so long as you are not a threat. If you or your tiger friend here try anything, I will kill them."

Nathan looked to Argon. It was his decision and no one else's. He could let the traitor go free or lose his family. He would live in submission to this tyrant and maybe one day do something about it, but he could not risk his family."

"Promise safety for Serj's family," said Argon.

Nathan's growl convinced Baran. "Done," the young chief said.

"Let him go," Argon said.

"Very wise," Baran said. "Argon you are hereby sentenced to exile from the promised rains forever."

"No!" he said. "You cannot take me from my wife and children." He would never see them again, never feel his wife's body against his, never see his children come of age.

"What did you think I meant? You are a liability that I cannot afford. You have no place among us." With that Baran gave Nathan a sneer and left, spearmen following.

"We'll finish this before they leave," Nathan said after they departed.

"Please," said Argon, "do not. I cannot risk my family."

"We do not know if Baran will keep his word," replied Nathan.

"If we show any sign of attack he is sure to keep his word and kill them all. One day I mean to make this right, but for now we are powerless."

"So be it," said Nathan. "In the meantime, you are welcome to join our council."

The tribesmen assembled and made their way from the Pass, to the north and west. Serj was given to Xu that evening among the sparse funeral attendees. Serj was cremated upon the pyre, the smoke carrying the aroma of burnt flesh. Argon hoped the god was pleased.

He knew Taesa was loyal to the people and not just to Argon. He told her many things. He told her what had happened that day, he bade her to go to follow the people to the promised rains, and he said he would return one day and need her help.

His muscles strained in bitterness, knowing with profound despondence that he would be the outcast forevermore. Hours after the tribes' departure Argon still shook with fury, wishing he could see his family one last time, his hope of righting his world dissipating. His wife and children were surely with the procession that left the Pass, but Baran kept them out of sight. Argon worried they would be kept in chains, turned into slaves, or worse. Though he strained to think of what he could do, no plan came to him that was not too great of a risk.

That evening Argon was welcomed into the council with Dorian and the others. They talked into the night. Supper was served as they discussed their course of action, Argon learning more of these people and prior events. He had barely gotten to know anyone before Mere was attacked and they marched on the Pass, though Jaked Mari seemed to have been a great warrior.

"Why don't we just walk up and knock?" Argon asked. He had not expected a laugh, but he especially did not expect that anyone would take him seriously.

"There's an idea," said Nathan, but not in his usual jesting tone.

"How do these things work, Liam?" Dorian asked.

Liam looked a little surprised to be asked, though he surely knew better than anyone else. "I don't know," he replied. "I mean, there is at least one door, though there may be more. But the one door of which I am aware is a closed off. I can't see how that'd work, but if we did show up we'd surely be noticed."

"Are you saying we surround it?" asked Oliver.

"Well, it couldn't hurt," Liam said. "They don't have any harmful outer-defenses, just the glass itself."

"Can it be broken?" asked Maynard.

"Not even by the best of us," Dorian said. "It's as hard as it comes and thick too. That's what's so damned confounding about the possibility that Jacob is in the City."

"All the same," said Charis, "if he got in, so can we."

"That is a point," said Dorian. "If we can get in, I want to keep it quiet. We'll be seen approaching no matter what, but let's not draw any more attention than is necessary. I say the council goes and leaves a small and trusted governance here in the Pass."

"Given the situation with the tribesmen, do we have to worry?" Oliver asked.

"I don't think so," said Argon. "Baran has done what he meant to do."

"About that," said Dorian. "Are you confident that Baran is keeping his word and that your family is safe?"

"As confident as I can be," Argon said.

"I wish we could do something now," Dorian said, "but once this is all over, I intend to help you get your family back."

"I welcome any help," Argon said, "but I do not want to risk their lives."

"It will probably do to give it some time," Dorian said, "but Baran will need to be dealt with."

The meeting went on and they discussed at length any possible way into the City. Maynard found Argon after the meeting.

"Welcome," he said. The man had been mighty in battle and even intimidated Argon. "Listen," Maynard continued, "I know this must all be new to you, but I'm glad you're here, even if it's in these circumstances. We could use a man like you."

Argon pondered these words. Could he benefit from being among these people? Might they be what he needed to overcome Baran in the long run? Perhaps this was providential, but he felt overwhelmed. His family had been everything to him, and now they were captives among their own people.

"I seem to have found friends here," Argon replied. "I don't know what I will do without my family, my people, or the crocodiles, but I'm grateful to be here. I just wish I knew what lay ahead."

"I wish I knew as well," replied Maynard. They stood facing the City. The mountain pass ended into what remained of the ruins. Where the ruins ceased, the desert resumed, the ring of mountains encircling it. The tribesmen marched into the distance, soon to follow the river beyond the pyramid. The City itself stood, a black triangle in the distance. If Jacob was there and if they could find a way in, Argon knew he would see a new world unlike anything he had imagined, but within those walls was likely loss, destruction, and pain.

# INTERLUDE

## Agnys Negosta

*Beyond the Outlands hollow eyes survey the gray mists. The eyes might have belonged to a human once. The once-human no longer knows what it means to love or hope. It is the descendant of survival.*

*It does not know that just over two centuries ago its ancestors were bright and full of hope. They had been on the cusp of peace, a possible reality at the time and a delusion now. Weapons and arms were put aside. The powerful began to help the disenfranchised. Then a boy came along. The boy's words had been true, but they had also been bittersweet. Peace would end, not by the hands of men, but by the vengeance of the once divine. Those beings would awake the greed of men, they would conquer all, and then leave it a gray mystery.*

*The Graylands hold no memory of such a time. The feet of those lost souls do not know that they walk amongst the rubble of long forgotten monuments, factories, and farms. They do not know that life once thrived where ash accumulates. The Grayland's wanderers drift through the slate landscape, looking for something. Perhaps it is food. Perhaps it is the resonance of hope long forgotten. Perhaps they are lost in the mists.*

*There are places and islands far away, untouched by the nuclear ash, but even they have fallen from grace. The last hope was Novum, untouched by Jacob during the war.*

*However, almost a year before Jacob's second conquest, before the boy Liam was marked by fire, before any suspected that Novum was*

*compromised, the Morning Star possessed a man named Agnys Negosta.*
*There was a whisper in the man's ear, a goading to discretely befoul the*
*infrastructure of the City.*
　　*—Oliver*

Though Peter Hershel had no idea why he would be summoned
to the pinnacle of the City, a place long forgotten, he did know
that a man named Agnys Negosta awaited him. It was a name he
had heard in whispers, dissipating almost as suddenly as it was
mentioned. Yet, the rumors of Agnys were confirmed. The
message did not come by any of the customary digital routes, but
in a rather peculiar slip of fine paper. He could feel the grain
under his fingers, a stiff linen, a weighty summons to a place far
from memory.

Though Peter was unsure as to why he had been summoned
specifically to this floor of the central tower, he had a hunch as to
why he had been called. It was about time they recognized him
and heard what he had to say. There had been a stirring in the
party lately and it was high time that they temper their zeal for
reform and take more moderate steps. Whoever this Agnys
character was, he would set everything to right. If he would only
listen to Peter, they could straighten this all out. He had said as
much in periodicals—omitting the Agnys name, of course, as to
not draw unwanted attention—and some of the nobles in the City
certainly seemed to agree with Peter.

Anyone who had ever taken the third elevator to its utmost
floor knew that it seemed to stop short at least two stories from
that windowed spire, but after two hundred years, obscurity had
tangled its use and even how one got there. But that paper in his
hand told Peter Hershel what to do. He took the elevator to the
second level, the doors opening to a dark and deserted office.
Everyone had long gone home for the night and that piece of
paper alone had let him pass the guards into the building. They

had taken one look and ushered him on, their expressions unreadable.

He pushed the button for level two again and held it while he pushed the button for level eight. The doors closed and the elevator sat a moment. He took a nervous and deep breath before the elevator lurched upward. From the ground level it was over five thousand feet into the air. It took almost six minutes to get to the top and the elevator stopped with such a jolt that Peter's already tepid stomach lurched.

Was he shaken? He had nothing to fear. It was just a conversation and reason was bound to prevail. The elevator doors opened to a small, plain room with a single door. He opened it. Like all of the floors in the central tower, this one was round, but it was also smaller. The windows encircled the room, one of them open—no—shattered, the glass pieces sprawling across the floor nearby. *That's impossible.*

As a child, Peter carried a small paperback book called *The Wonders of Novum.* According to the book, the City's walls and all of the windows in the Central Spire were reinforced with palladium, the strongest glass in the world, stronger even than steel. The frame that held the glass would bend and break long before the glass itself. Yet, this same glass lay broken on the floor. He wondered if the book had exaggerated to fill his child's mind with wonder.

The strange man behind the desk awaited Peter's attention. Somehow that old face, sallow and dark seemed to fit the name. The worst part of all was when the man smiled. Peter lost his ability to speak and nervousness seized him. "Sir, I—"

"Peter Hershel," the man said, his lips curled into something resembling a grin, stretching into a horrible smile. "Pardon the window. I lost my temper a few days ago." This old man broke the window?

Peter regained his composure and looked the man in the eyes. It was everything he could do to maintain his gaze. "Mr. Negosta." Even that name seemed wrong. Who was this man?

Agnys spoke again, quoting words that Peter knew well. " 'The faster these bottom-feeders move, the sooner the city itself will collapse. They are so desperate to take shortcuts to power that when they at last have rule, they will possess power over nothing. This is beneath us as a civilized people. Will we return to the old days, before Novum, when political promises meant nothing, big false smiles won votes, and people gave up basic freedoms for so-called safety? Are our walls not enough? Shall we impose moral and ethical codes universally? These matters are beyond the scriptures and therefore beyond us. Embrace the preservation of the system we have built.' These are your words are they not?"

"Surely," Peter said and then paused. "Surely, you see, Mr. Negosta, that reform, as it is progressing at the present, will doom us all. We must—"

"We must," Agnys Negosta said, "play along, march to the beat—so to speak. Or cease to have any use at all."

This was surreal, this room of legend, the broken glass sprawling the floor, and an even more mysterious figure behind a desk. They were alone and this frail, old man had the audacity to make threats. "Beg your pardon, Mr. Negosta, bullying has no place here. If I'm so wrong, then I invite you to write your own periodical. Better yet, reveal yourself to the public—whoever you are—and I would be happy to reconsider. Until then, good day."

That was it. The trip to this tower, the paper he now clinched in his hand, the whole thing was a waste of time. He should have made the note public, exposing Negosta and calling for an accounting. Peter turned to the door and grasped the knob but it did not move. Cold and hard fingers grasped his neck, throwing him to the ground. Drawing quick breaths, he tried gather himself. Something gripped his ankle, sharp fingertips digging into it, pulling him along the floor. For one moment he fought, but then shock overtook his willpower as the carpet dragged beneath him. Terror followed confusion. "No, no, no, no—"

Broken glass began to trail underneath him. He screamed as it cut into his skin. Blood, his own, flowed onto the carpet, streaking it as he was taken along. A piece of glass slid into his skin and he wondered how the doctor would ever get it out. It was absurd to worry about such a thing in such circumstances. Another shard ripped through his leg. His cry barely surfaced.

Agnys's old hands, that had seemed so frail, had taken him. Peter tried to resist, but his futile efforts did not stop the old man from bending him over the broken window, face down, looking over the city. Shards of glass rimmed the window, cutting into his neck as the old man forced his head down. In the night, the lights gleamed below him. The tower flowed down to the ground level which gave way to the underground. Tears formed around Peter's eyes and they began to drop one by one into the abyss amid his dripping blood.

"Peter Hershel," the voice said, "an upstanding citizen and promising politician, behold your fate. I wouldn't normally explain such a thing, but it's a long drop and I'd rather you spend less time thinking about why and more time regretting your decisions. You were warned, multiple times, subtly and then less subtly. And now I'm telling you that it's too late. You are going to die. You were too bloody proper for your own good, too self-righteous, and now as you plummet you can know that the impact will be more than fatal, that your blood and body will splatter all over the first underground."

With that Peter Hershel's body left the floor to be hefted out the window and soon the only thing that existed was the air below him. A million thoughts came to him and he and tried to think another million thoughts before he landed. His political resolutions faded, the snobbery pointless. He might have talked to

God multiple times in fragmented begging. He could have done anything in his life differently and avoided this, but each decision, however small, led to this moment. He plummeted, like one of those damned fallen angels so long ago, but he was far more feeble and broken. He might have screamed, but he did not know how. It might have taken seconds to fall, perhaps a lifetime, but he would have traded it all to have groveled in that tower when he had the chance. And now he died.

# CHAPTER THIRTY-THREE

*The Messenger*

Perry climbed through the broken window, ignoring the long dried bloodstains. Once inside the round chamber, he lit a cigarette. The green-tinted glass crunched under his shoes as he crossed the room, passing the door, peering out one of the few windows. He put the cigarette to his lips and inhaled. This was the highest viewpoint of Novum and he wondered if anyone had been higher since the war. Master Ferrith had spoken of airplanes, but nothing other than the occasional bird had been seen in the skies. From below, the tinted panes of the sloping city walls looked clean, but with this closer view he could see the collected dust and buildup. He turned his gaze down to the City, its curving railways snaking below among the massive spires.

He had taken Liam to this place once, who had been far too timid to enjoy it. It was an enigmatic room, the apex of Novum, yet unused and strangely bloodied. The mystery was part of what Perry liked about it and as he lit another cigarette he wondered about Liam. His younger friend had started to come into his own just before his disappointing departure. Perry had wanted to go with him, but he knew it would be prohibited. It was a task for Liam alone, the eighth generation descendant from the prophet. Yet Perry expected something by now, and worried that if Liam was going to return at all he would have done so already.

Since Liam's leaving, Perry had been more diligent in attending Master Ferrith's lessons. The man welcomed him each afternoon. They spent one hour with the sword and another with history. He half-expected the lessons to run out, but there was always something new to learn. Perry improved with the sword, though he never had bested Liam and doubted he had improved enough to do so now. He also started to understand the world before the war. Some could be learned from the movies, but it helped to have Ferrith to separate the fact from fiction.

The jiggling door handle startled him. Regaining his wits he rushed across the room and climbed out of the broken window, pulling himself out of sight, and clinging on to the ladder rungs. He could hear voices and dared to peak back into the room.

"Our patience is about to pay off," said the tall dark-haired man. He was accompanied by a priest, a woman in all black, a massive bald man, a small man in odd clothes, and a sickly businessman.

"This man," he continued, "is our link to Novum. He is not the Grand Chancellor, he is not the head of their military, he is not a known face, yet they are all subservient to him. Agnys Negosta is the man behind the curtain. Agnys, these are my faithful."

The large, bald man was introduced as Cain. The woman was Amelia, and Raven was the smaller man, who introduced the priest as Sol. Perry knew his histories. That made the tall, dark-haired man Jacob. Perry nearly swore aloud. But who was this Agnys?

"The Morning Star has worked hard to give us this," said Jacob. "Until we learn how things work around here, we depend on him. This will be our base until we can work out something more accommodating. Furniture will be provided and we'll clean up that mess over there." Perry ducked out of view just as Jacob directed their attention to the broken window.

"What happened there?" asked Amelia.

Agnys laughed. It was a haunting chuckle. "Oh, that," he said in a raspy voice. "A small mishap, but nothing to speak of. I believe we are being watched." Perry did not think he had been seen but he knew they spoke of him and, ignoring the carabiner, began to rush down the ladder. His foot slipped but he caught himself. *Don't look down.* He reached the door two floors down and, opening it, slipped in. As he pulled himself in he looked up to see Jacob peering out the window.

He ran to the elevator and held a shaky finger to the button. They might be boarding it above him. If not, they may be able to stop it. He hit the down button and ran, searching for any sign of the stairwell. To his relief, he found it unlocked and began the descent. After the first floor, he was jumping down steps at a time, careening around the landings, feet carrying him swiftly downward. After ten floors, his bones ached, but he didn't slow. A dozen more floors later, it occurred to him that even at this pace, it could take more than hour to make the descent.

He exited the stairwell and ran among vacant cubicles and blank computer screens. After summoning the elevator, he ducked out of view from its doors and waited. Two minutes later, the doors opened to an empty carriage. Perry rushed in and took the elevator down to the tenth floor. Back at the stairwell, he continued his way down, hoping this was all diversion enough to escape.

He reached the ground floor, breathless, heart hammering in his chest, hands trembling. There were several elevators, and by the digital signs above their doors, none were at the ground floor. Once out of the building, and untroubled by the guards, he ran along the street. There were no cars in view, just a few cyclists, which was good. How fast could Agnys start a search for him? The situation had taken him by surprise and there was so much he didn't know. He looked up, surveying the building he had just left. The tallest building in Novum towered almost to the apex of the pyramid. He left the Central Building behind.

He did not return home, but rather went to his parents' apartment. Though sure that Jacob could not have recognized him, he had an uneasy feeling and decided to keep low for a few hours.

"You know, Perry," his mother said over dinner, "since you moved out, you have come here for dinner every Tuesday night. And you know that dinner is on the table at six o'clock every night. You could try and be on time for once." She said it in the same scolding tone that he had come to find endearing.

"Come on, Mom." he said, "You know how the train is late sometimes."

"It's never late," his dad said. Solemn as usual, the man was void of emotion.

His mother took some roast from the center plate and placed it on her own. For two hundred years people had eaten meat grown in a lab, but once in a while, Perry wondered how much it really tasted like the real thing.

"Another week and your friend Liam still isn't back," his father said. How many times had his father said it? Beneath the matter-of-fact tone was a hint of disapproval, that somehow Liam's failure to return had been a poor reflection on Perry. Sometimes Perry thought he understood his father's attitude, but other times he resented the old bastard. The afternoon's encounter had left Perry irritable and he was not in the mood for his father's typical passive aggressive jibes.

"I would think a man of the church would have more faith," Perry replied.

"The prophet's tenure has been long over. I don't know what happened the day of the fire, but if anything was going to come of it, it would have by now. It's time the Church was more in-step with the government."

"Are you going to eat those carrots, Perry?" his mother asked.

"As if they aren't similar enough," replied Perry, ignoring his mother.

"All I'm saying," his father said, "is that it would be better if the prophet retired."

Perry knew it was a pointless argument. After tonight, it wouldn't matter. He stabbed a piece of beef and finished his supper. After an awkward, quiet meal he said goodbye. His mother gave him the usual kiss on the cheek, and his father favored the television to seeing his son to the door. It was better that way.

Perry's loft was a mess, his things strung through the small studio apartment. A pair of jeans hung over the back of an office chair, dimly lit in the glow of his computer screen. He put a match to a cigarette, suppressing the anxiety of the fine for smoking in the apartment. The room was a spread of odds and ends, things lost under clothes piles, but he knew where to find everything. He pulled his backpack from among the clutter under his bed and began to stuff things into it. A small knife, a change of clothes. He had no idea what to bring.

Once ready, he cracked his apartment's door, peering through the slit. The hall lights were out. That was unusual. Climbing out the window was harder than it appeared, but he knew well the way to the rooftop and down the service ladder. He jumped between two more rooftops, and took a high fall to reach the street level. His pack shifted as he landed and he nearly sprained his ankle. Taking the rail was out of the question. He suspected that someone was onto him. What would have been a three-minute tram ride took him fifteen minutes of walking, keeping to the shadows. He had gotten good at this in grade school when he would sneak out of his parents' home and maneuver the alleys and rooftops.

"Master Ferrith," he whispered knocking. "Master Ferrith."

Indistinct mumbling came from the other side of the door. It opened. Ferrith was older than he looked, his dark beard graying and wrinkles creasing his brow. He gave Perry an incredulous look.

"At this hour? How did you even get here?" he asked.

"I climbed," replied Perry. "You have to let me in, it's an emergency."

The older man consented, though he did not appear alarmed or rushed. "Well," Ferrith said, "what is it?"

Ferrith made them tea and they sat under the single light in his kitchen as Perry told him of his encounter at the tower.

"You should not have been up there," said Ferrith.

"What do you mean?" said Perry. "If I hadn't been there we wouldn't have discovered any of this. Liam is somewhere out there. If he has found Dorian, we have to tell them."

"Perhaps," Ferrith said. "Give me a moment to dress and I will show you something."

Moments later Ferrith returned wearing black slacks and a black button-up shirt. He led Perry out of the apartment, up the stairs, and to the roof. At the southern corner stood a telescope. He gestured for Perry to look. He peered through the eye piece. At first, nothing, but then he saw lights and they came into focus as some sort of fire in the distance, perhaps at the Pass.

"You would be surprised what I can see during the day," said Master Ferrith. "All sorts of coming and goings. I'm pretty sure there was a battle two days ago. Thousands of figures. It was hard to tell much more."

"And you didn't tell me this?" asked Perry.

"No," Master Ferrith replied, "because I knew you wouldn't let it rest and I didn't want to act until we knew more."

"But we have to go out there," said Perry.

"Now that we know more, I agree. We could have gone out there only to run into Jacob, but now that we know he's here, there's a better chance that what we're seeing at the Pass are our allies. I don't know how Jacob got by me. I check this often enough, I should have seen him coming in the two days it takes to get here."

"When can we leave?" asked Perry.

"Well, now that we know more, that changes things too. If Jacob is in Novum, that means he may have won whatever battle it appeared to be. You may go out there, only to find the remnants of those he has defeated. Worse, he may have left a force behind, but I don't think that's the case. It will be faster if you go alone. You are young and swift. Standon and I can take care of things here."

"You want me to go alone?" asked Perry.

"I'm afraid so," said Master Ferrith, "but not ill-equipped. I saw the biggest hyena just a few days ago. I daresay we can't have you running into that unarmed. Some natives, a peculiar people, appeared to be headed to the northwest corner of the mountains, but you shouldn't have to deal with them."

The idea gave Perry pause, but he tried to act brave. "Fine," he said. "What now?"

His pack was now a more substantial. It contained dried fruits, jerky, and other morsels. He also had water, rope, a blanket, and matches. Ferrith gave him a more suitable outfit and a sword.

"Where do you get this stuff?" asked Perry.

"When you started tutoring under me we had to order your fencing outfit. When Liam was sent out there we had a special set of clothes made. I had a set made for myself and for you."

"You saw this coming?"

"Perry," said Ferrith, "I've seen this coming for a long time. It's why I've learned so much. The prophet saw it coming and naturally sent Liam to me. You, being a friend of Liam's, are just one more asset. Now, zip up that vest and let us be on our way before sunrise."

If Perry had mastered the rooftops, Ferrith had mastered the First Underground, which was the name of the top subterranean layer between the surface and the lower underground levels. Most of the utilities, factories, and other jobs lay well below the City. Some of the First Underground was residential, its poor tenants still comfortable relative to the more destitute quarters at lower levels. Most worked in a lower facility, a strange group of people who seldom had reason to come to the surface. Some said they preserved the old ways, whatever those were. Others said they had gone crazy from years in the dark. As for the First Underground, it was tunnels of pipes, cables, dim lights, and industrial transportation. Ferrith led the way, winding through the passages and Perry lost his sense of direction. At last they came to the stairs, followed them up, and entered a long, dark corridor.

"Imagine a world," said Ferrith, "in which the only place worse than being outside of it was being inside. Indeed, this place was designed with an evacuation plan. I have a feeling it's how Jacob got in, but the question is who let him in? My best guess is that this Agnys character has something to do with that.

"I will tell you this now, as I am confident that no ears or devices are listening to my words. The First Underground is home to a movement of sorts. It started as a guild, a secret society meant to keep the City safe. We are why swords are allowed in Novum and guns are not. Things have evolved. Shortly before rumor of this Agnys character, one of our louder and more arrogant members was killed. We've since grown into a resistance, suspecting that Agnys meant to work behind the scenes until he could rise to power. We did not correlate it with the prophecy regarding Jacob and assumed the very reason we had sent for Dorian was to keep Jacob from ever entering. We were wrong and Dorian is too late."

There was a click, which must had been Master Ferrith pulling a lever. A metal clang reverberated through the hall. The door rose, exposing the night sky. A flood of fresh air stimulated his senses. He was ready for this.

Master Ferrith took him by the shoulders. "Now listen," he said. "Go to the Pass and see what you can find out, but don't do anything stupid. Godspeed, young man."

With that, Perry left.

After two day's travel, Perry was exhausted. The initial novelty of the fresh air and trickling stream amazed him at first. Then the footprints in the sand had caught his attention. All massive, some three pronged and others like that of some large horse. No amount of water soothed the heat, even when he dipped his entire head into the stream. His legs felt like lead and the lack of sleep wore on him. Each step brought him closer to the Pass and he was almost too tired to be afraid. He willed himself to continue. His dirty, sunburned skin and aching muscles plagued him, but he walked on, each drudging step bringing him closer to the Pass.

The desert broke and he walked among old stone, broken glass, and steel. Then it gave way to the desert again, but a more packed, refined terrain. He looked up at the towering mountain walls around him. He had done it.

The river ran nearby and he drank from it. When he looked up, a man with auburn hair and a large sword strapped to his back stood over Perry. Still on his knees, face wet from his drink he just looked at the man, into his brown-green eyes.

"Jacob is in the City," Perry said.

# CHAPTER THIRTY-FOUR
## *The High Priest*

Everything smelled delicious. That is, *everyone.* If it had not been for strict orders, Sol might have dined on the next person he passed, but he walked on, suppressing his impulses. He sighed. At least in the City he could go about without his cassock. Cassocks were precarious things and he resented them almost as much as he disliked the sun. The sun shined through panes of the City, but for some reason he found it bearable, which Sol considered rather auspicious.

After the battle at the Pass, he fled to Novum, which he found full of surprises. Though somewhat dilapidated, the technology was unimaginable and he had yet to even explore the majority of the City's offerings. His first impulse had been to take to the underground portion, but the surface proved to his liking. Besides that, most of his business was on the topside. One could get just about anywhere by tram, so the streets were narrow. Most of the cars were small with some official logo, most likely law enforcement or people too important to use public transit. Bicycles were also a favorite mode of transportation.

Sol rounded a corner in a tight alley. Jacob might have established their headquarters at the top of that awful building but Raven preferred the shadows to Jacob's lofty aspirations. Not that either was any less arrogant, and though loyal to Raven, he detested the quality in both fallen angels.

Raven's quarters were dimly lit, simple, and lacking windows. The playing of a piano reverberated through the chambers and a woman lounged on a sofa, her pale face expressionless. She smelled dead. Sol removed his sunglasses as he entered and sat in a plush leather chair by the lit candelabra. As he did so, the woman rose and went into the adjacent room. The piano intonated an eerie melody, one he had heard Raven play before. The music stopped. Shortly thereafter Raven entered, wearing his customary robes like some eighteenth century Gothic Victorian.

"Why do you interrupt me?" asked Raven sitting in a nearby chair. Sol suspected his accent was also part of the whole thing. It sounded so proper.

"Me? I didn't say anything."

"Damn it all, Sol. You're such an ass?"

"I call it service with a smile. I see you have a new woman."

"I needed a new lich, but never mind that. What have you been up to?"

Sol smiled. "I went to church."

"And?"

"I didn't like it. Not one bit. Too much of the usual warm fuzzy stuff. Talk of hope, love, that kind of thing. A lousy bunch of extroverts too. They need a little more fire and brimstone if you ask me."

"We'll fix that soon enough," Raven said. "Religious fear is a powerful ally. Jacob claims that Agnys has instigated the deposition of the Great Prophet and the High Priest. Which means, my friend, that you will have a sermon to write."

"We never did figure out the Tartarus Project," Sol said.

"I have the feeling," said Raven, "that if the Tartarus Project-was of any consequence, we would have figured it out by now. If it was ever more than a rumor, it's likely a long lost failure."

"Fuck it," said Sol. "I'm hungry."

"There's plenty to eat," replied Raven. "Find that kid who was spying on us at the tower and he's all yours."

"Feeling regret for not letting me eat the last kid?"

"At least your wounds heal," said Raven holding up his hand. Raven was pale enough already, but his hand was ghostly white, jagged black lines working their way up his palm. Sol could indeed recover from a stab wound, assuming it did not pierce anything too important, but he doubted he could regrow a limb anymore than Raven could.

"So," said Sol, "we oust the entire priestly order. Then I suppose it is up to me to prime the people for Jacob's coming rule. Then what?"

"The battle at the Pass was successful in delaying Dorian, allowing us to establish ourselves here. However, Dorian is still a problem, and if he isn't dealt with, I fear what Jacob will do. He may destroy the City if he thinks he can't have it."

"That's no fun. I was starting to like it here."

"Who knows when Jacob will stop? I'm cosmically angry and all just like him, but this business tires me. Do you know how long it took for me to figure out the abomination thing, much less the lich? If all we leave in our path is a wake of destruction, there will be no reward left."

"If you remain in Jacob's company, that's sure to be our fate."

"There's something I want, and if he'll give it to me, I'll take it."

"And that is?" Sol asked.

"I want Mere and I want Charis," replied Raven. Sol had been to Mere in the dark of night. He had left it in ashes, though Raven must have some ambitions to restore it.

"You want Charis?"

"Charis and that city are the brighter side of creativity. I want to rebuild it and make it my own."

"Spoken like a true necromancer."

Raven chortled. "Come now, not all of my dealings involve the dead. I made you."

"That you did."

"What brings you here?" Raven asked.

"It's funny you should mention that kid."

"The one that got away from us?"

"Yeah," Sol said. "His name is Perry. He escaped the City. Watchers saw him walking for the Pass."

Raven didn't look concerned. "What are we going to do about it? Did we send someone after him?"

"No," replied Sol. "I heard from Amelia that Jacob means to use him as bait, to draw Dorian out."

"How did you hear that from Amelia?" Raven cracked a wicked smile.

Sol looked at the fallen angel insipidly. "I don't see why he won't just let Dorian and his folks stay at the Pass. Should have left them at Mere, at least for the time being."

"So he could gather his strength?" Raven asked. "No, that would be foolish. Draw him and his people out one step at a time, nip at their fringes, and then take them down one by one."

"Makes sense enough," Sol said. "Amelia says that Jacob has a plan, so I suppose that's the gist of it. I just don't how he means to deal with Dorian. As you've said, we should worry if he doesn't. We're fucked if they make it into Novum."

"Amelia doesn't know everything," Raven said. "Perhaps Jacob knows what he's doing after all. Now that we've established ourselves, gained the high ground to speak, we are at a better vantage by which to take on Dorian and his company."

"What if Jacob loses control?" Sol asked.

"I've made my own deals," Raven said.

They sat a moment in silence. Jacob had grand plans and Sol was beginning to wonder if they would benefit him.

"I should be on my way," Sol said. "I have a sermon to write, after all."

Raven gave him a nod and as Sol left, he heard the piano playing start again. The music was a thing of the darkest sort of beauty, haunting and elegant all at once. Sol departed, making his way back to his own quarters nearby, recalling the day Raven made him. The memory made him want to change now, to take the crocotta form His muscles tensed. Sol made himself relax. It would not do to make such a change for the whole city to see. Besides, he did not want to ruin yet another outfit. For that he had envied Nathan who seemed to be able to take on his form without the sacrifice of his clothing.

As he preferred, his rooms were dark. His primal eyes saw just fine where any other human would be blind. She sobbed in the corner, meek pleas begging to let her go. "I'm sorry," he said. Now in the privacy of his own home he disrobed and made the change. In he dark, she would not be able to see him like he could see her, but she would hear the crack of his bones and rustle of the growing hair. She would hear his breath become the huffing of a large animal's pant. She cried and begged more, so quiet and terrified. It was just one and Raven did not need to know.

# CHAPTER THIRTY-FIVE

*Hellspawn*

Once recovered, Perry told them all. Having arrived fatigued, dehydrated, and sleep-deprived, it was agreed that the boy needed rest, even if his message sounded dire. Maynard had been restless during the wait, perhaps more so than Liam, who, accompanied by Aster, sat anxious by his friend's bedside. The relief of Perry's awakening was short-lived, for he confirmed their worst fears. Jacob was in Novum.

Perry did not know how, nor did he know much more than what he had witnessed in the tower with the man he called Agnys. Jacob had not mentioned an Agnys in Maynard's travels with the fallen angel. In spite of Dorian's persistent questioning, Maynard was certain of it. Perry knew too little, but he carried one unanticipated hope: Ferrith, who Liam seemed to know as well, awaited them, ready to allow them into Novum. Even under such dire circumstances, Maynard marveled at that.

Time was short, much to Jacob's advantage, but the days of waiting had supplied them ample rest. With Charis's healing, Liam's crocotta injuries had been minor when they might had been otherwise catastrophic. Others had sustained wounds. Callianeira did not even notice the gash in her side until after the battle. Maynard was beaten and bruised, but nothing that warranted medical attention, though he thought wistfully of the baths in Mere.

With Perry's awakening, the time of rest ended. Meetings were had, lengthy discussions of the best strategies. Between Perry and Liam they came to obtain an ample grasp on the City, a place well beyond Maynard's understanding. All of the rumors of the old world seemed to have persevered there. They grew their own meat, whatever that meant.

The biggest problem was that of inconspicuously taking advantage of their way into Novum. Requiring two days of travel, entering unnoticed was unlikely. At this particular meeting, they gathered over lunch in the tavern and Maynard remained silent for most of the discussion. Instead, he enjoyed the beans and rice provided. Though not the most flavorful fare, it was sustenance all the same.

"We've been over this," Nathan said. "We're just going to have to walk right up to the walls. Let them see us if they will."

"Maybe so," Dorian said, "but had any of the fallen been at the last battle, we would not have won. We can't risk open conflict again."

"Then we will need to move swiftly," Argon said, his deep voice catching their attention. "Go by night. Light no fires."

"Yes," said Perry. "Jacob made it to Novum and we didn't spot him. He had to have done it by night."

"Impossible," said Oliver. "Other than what the tribesmen left, no hoof-tracks lead from the Pass, so they had to have gone by foot. It's a thirty mile journey. That's a hard day's travel and then some. Unless by some magic—"

"And what happens once we get there?" Dorian asked. "Even if we get in unnoticed, I doubt we can hide for long."

"That's where Ferrith comes in," Perry said in a dry croak, still recovering from his journey.

"What about Standon?" Liam asked.

"He wasn't there the night I fled," said Perry, "but I'm sure he will help."

Maynard wasn't so confident. From the sound of things, Jacob possessed all he needed to take and hold Novum to whatever end he desired. He had a head start on them, some sort of political presence through this Agnys, and a mysterious allegiance with the Morning Star. Furthermore, Jacob could see well in advance if any approached the City.

"Liam," Oliver said. "Do you have any other allies? What about your parents?"

"At the most, there is something to this Tartarus Project, but I have no idea what to expect." Liam looked to Perry who shrugged.

"Surely," said Nathan, "someone in the City sympathizes with us."

"They don't even know that they should," Oliver replied.

A look of realization crossed Liam's face. Too engrossed to notice, the others bantered on, circling the same arguments.

"I think I know how he did it," Liam said. Perry looked to his friend and Aster gave Liam a puzzled look. "I saw firsthand at the Pass what sort of creature Amelia could conjure. Can she conjure one big enough to ride?"

Maynard himself had been beyond the ruins to search for any sign of Jacob. "Other than the northwesterly trail, I saw no tracks of any beast." Maynard said.

"I saw tracks," said Perry. "They were all different, but they were huge."

"That is the most likely explanation," Dorian replied. "We wouldn't necessarily have seen them."

"What do you mean?" Oliver asked.

"All they would have to do is walk three miles, at the furthest," said Dorian. "There Amelia could do her summoning and they could ride the rest of the trip. Unless we went that far out for ourselves, the tracks would likely be too distant for us to see."

"Got to give them credit," Callianeira said.

"Aye." Nathan's expression soured.

"Then what now?" Oliver asked.

"They'll be watching for us to come from the south," said Dorian. "At thirty miles, the foot of the mountains might be difficult for them to see. We could work our way around. It would triple our travel time, but it might be our best bet."

"If Ferrith can see us from his roof, then so can they."

"We go directly there," Maynard said. "There is no other way."

Dorian sighed and looked at him. "He's right. We go straight there. But if we leave in the evening and ride hard by camel or horse, we can perhaps arrive early enough to remain unnoticed. It's our best chance."

It was agreed with some reluctance that the group of them would go, bringing no soldiers. Accommodating ten of them might be difficult enough. They would go by night, hoping that it concealed them.

Ten in all, they met the next evening, Dorian and Oliver at the front, surveying the evening before them. The sun dipped beneath the western mountaintops, the orange glow dissipating in the darkness. Charis stood next to Maynard and Callianeira, the worry plain on her face. Perry, Liam, and Aster appeared almost excited, though Maynard wondered how Liam felt about returning home. Argon peered into the northwestern corner towards the forest.

Nathan urged his camel over to Maynard, the usual grin reaching up to the red-haired man's twinkling eyes. Maynard could have sworn the stars reflected in them. "I'm glad you are here," Nathan said. "Both of you." He motioned to Callianeira. "There may only be ten of us, but this is the finest ten I've seen."

"You're not worried?" Maynard asked.

"Of course I am," Nathan replied. "But it doesn't mean I'm not optimistic."

"You angels," Callianeira said. "So bright-eyed. We're in a fucking desert and we're headed to a glass-walled pyramid city where true evil reigns. And you're smiling." But she too smiled that cunning grin of hers and endearment for her flared in Maynard. They had spent the previous night together, a night that was more than anything he had shared with another woman or with another soul.

Callianeira had traded her horse for a camel, matching the other nine mounts. Glad of her company, Maynard met her gaze before Oliver gave a call and they rode out, mounts trotting as swift as they dared in the night, the river muffling their hoof beats.

The hours passed and they spoke in whispers, as if the noise might somehow permeate the City's walls. There were occasional, short rests, but no fires were lit. They did everything by starlight and what little sliver the moon lent them. Argon seemed to always look toward the forest, but if the nomads lit their fires this night, they were deep into the woods. Scanning the desert, Maynard thought that he saw the imprints in the sand, graven remnants of the monsters that bore their masters to Novum. It was almost impossible to see the City in the darkness, but the stars reflected off its walls. They drew nearer, the great pyramid growing before them, far larger than it had appeared in the distance. Maynard saw that not all the lights were the reflected stars, but that the faintest glow came from within the pyramid, its obsidian facade unable to fully obfuscate the city lights. Whether Jacob hid behind them or not, those walls concealed a wonder.

Within ten miles of Novum they heard it. A clang echoed among the mountains, like a smith striking a giant anvil. They looked to each other, the dark hiding their expressions, but Maynard knew what they all thought. Something was coming.

"Any premonitions, girl?" Oliver asked Aster. She shook her head, watching warily.

The ground rumbled a terrible rhythm, growls and shrieking faint but growing louder. Dorian spoke, forgoing the whisper. "Lights."

All of the angels, Maynard, and Callianeira lifted their hands flaring the flames in the palm of their hands. The desert burned blue and orange with their fires and in the distance a dozen reptilian beasts of various shapes and sizes charged. Amelia's creatures.

Maynard led his camel around the company, unsheathing his blade. He positioned himself at the flank so that his sword posed no threat to the others. It left him vulnerable, but his camel, less skittish than a horse, did not shy from the oncoming beasts. He felt the Darkworld empowering him, taking his well-earned skills and enhancing his intuition.

A fireball flew from Callianeira's palm crashing into a charging creature, daunting it for but a moment before it resumed its rush.

Maynard faced his own monster, like a skinless crocotta with wings. The light in Maynard's palm illuminated it, glistening off its slimy, emaciated body. Maynard directed fire towards it, maneuvering his camel with one hand and bringing his sword around with the other. He struck the beast, his sword cleaving into it, but it embedded in hardy flesh, yanking the sword from his hand. Maynard reached for the handle, clumsily falling from the saddle, striking the earth. He heard an audible crack, pain sharpening with each inhale. A growl resonated in the darkness and the moonlight shimmered off the approaching being, the silhouette of Maynard's sword jutting from its side.

The others fought as well. The distant snarls and the sound of struggle met his ears, but they hardly registered amongst the creature's softest bellow. Through the haze of pain, Maynard raised his arm, conjuring the fire in his hand. It shied for but a moment, then lunged.

A figure leapt upon the beast, ripping the sword free of its flesh and cleaving the creature. Its charge halted, flinging the person from it, but the slim form gracefully twisted in the air, landing after a gymnastic twirl, sinking the sword through flesh and bone.

Weapon in hand, its blade through the animal's neck, Callianeira looked up at Maynard, the amber light smooth on her features. She smiled, and proffered his sword back to him, hilt first.

"You're better with it than I am," he said, taking it, ignoring the pain in his side.

"I'm better with this," she said, drawing her smaller sword.

"We need to protect the others," he said. He meant Oliver, Liam, and Aster, but it occurred to him that whether disabled, young, or inexperienced in combat, this was a company that could hold their own. It was fully realized when they found Oliver, having lost his camel, standing with sword at the ready. Liam guarded him closely atop his own camel, gun focused on a wary creature. It was birdlike, yet its six, taloned feet clamored at the ground spider-like. In the faint light, its gunshot wounds glistened.

With a squawk, it hammered a blow at Oliver. Pain clear on his face, Oliver moved swiftly, sword slicing away its appendage. It shrieked as Liam accosted it with four more gunshots, ringing deafening among the mountains. In its distraction, Callianeira maneuvered amongst its careening body and struck into its belly, dodging it as it fell to the ground, scrambling in pain.

"Friends of yours?" Nathan asked Callianeira as he ran for the beast that assailed Charis.

Maynard might have laughed, but he saw the solemn look on Callianeira's face, not for Nathan's jape, but for the scream that filled the night air.

"Where is Aster?" Liam asked.

They searched, the flames in their palms bright, looking for the girl. Nathan joined Charis, fighting two of the creatures, one like a large lizard and another a tortured ape. They fought in unison, dancing among one another with graceful synchronization. Nathan rolled, ducking the ape's swing, Charis following through with a slash to its eyes. It roared in pain as Nathan regained his feet, bringing his sword down on its neck. No sooner had he silenced it than Charis leapt into the air, gaining ten, then fifteen feet, the great lizard's jaws gaping at her. Its fanged teeth almost closed in on her but Nathan jabbed his sword into its foot. The newfound pain stopped it short as Charis landed atop its head and drove her katana down.

Dorian fought his own beast, something large and swift, like an emaciated cat. Ebony claws flashed and Dorian arced back, skidding as he landed. Argon, having just finished off his own adversary, approached Dorian's beast from the rear, but its tail knocked him aside. The momentary distraction gave Dorian a chance. He leapt, flashing upward, sword glinting to the left. The cat's eyes followed the distraction as Dorian curved his blow, bringing it in quick succession to the opposite side and driving it back at the creature's face. The beast failed to follow quick enough, the blade slicing through skin and skull.

Again the scream echoed and Maynard rushed among the others. The girl had no light, but their flames burned in the darkness, searching for her. A growl called them northward toward the City but they found Perry standing, sword deep into a dying beast.

"Killed that all on your own?" Nathan asked.

Perry's head wavered, then he fell, blood, black in the night, dripping from his back. Charis saw to him, but the others kept looking, wary that at least three more monsters remained, Aster possibly dead or wounded.

"Liam!" came Aster's cry. The company turned, Maynard near the forefront and he beheld three great beasts rushing toward them, pursuing Aster. He held his sword out, teeth gritted. As Aster gained safety among their small ranks, Dorian and Nathan ran to take on one of the beasts, their superhuman leaps carrying them up at the toothy creature. It's serpent like neck lunged at them, but their unified front made quick work of it. Argon charged another and it cringed and snarled as he unleashed his whip upon it.

"Looks like they have two handled," Callianeira said, the jerk of her head motioning Maynard to take on the third creature. He nodded at her and they ran toward it as a ball of fire erupted from its gaping mouth. A deep, gritty note shook the earth as flame spewed at them. They parted, rolling in opposite directions from the heat. Maynard found his feet, the sharp pain in his side jabbing at him once more. The light of the beast's flaming gust faded and Maynard found that Callianeira stood far from him, divided by its hellfire.

"A dragon?" Maynard asked, more to himself.

"No," Callianeira said. "It does not fly, though there are hell-creatures more similar to a dragon. However, it is fast." She leapt as another gout of flame scorched the desert sands. She soared into the air, flipping and twisting. It arched its neck jaws ready to catch her, but Maynard charged. Whether brave or stupid, his feet carried him swiftly. It snapped at Callianeira, missing her by inches. Maynard's blade sliced at the creature's chest. With a spasm, it diverted its attention to him. As he rolled, it snapped once more, close enough for Maynard to smell its fetid breath. It emanated another gout fire and Maynard thought that surely he would be burned. But no heat reached him and he turned. Dorian met the flame with his own power, hands warding it away.

The creature realized the unusual shield, but it was too late. With swift feet and a well arced strike, Callianeira lay its throat open, dodging as its boiling blood struck the desert stand and the beast slunk to the ground.

With help, Callianeira had dealt four deathblows, twice that of anyone else. Yet, Maynard was more astonished that Perry had conquered one of them on his own, even if it was smaller. Its carcass resembled something like a hellhound, but larger, bulkier. Perry, revived by Charis, called it luck, and Maynard didn't argue when he inspected the thing further, finding fresh burn marks. Whatever fiery creature Callianeira and Maynard had faced had clearly been indiscriminate towards its companions. The thing was wounded before Perry ever faced it. Still, it was impressive.

All in all, eleven devils were slain. Dorian claimed with certainty that a twelfth beast had emerged, but a brief search yielded no threat. It was, however, agreed that this might be the first wave of many and that they would do better to travel with caution.

"I guess someone knows we're coming," Callianeira said.

"I don't doubt it," Dorian said. "Where are the camels?"

"First thing those monsters did," Oliver replied, "was to start knocking them out from under us. I had the sense to dismount mine before it happened. Probably saved my leg a world of hurt." From the look on his face, it pained him now. Charis put an arm on his shoulder.

"What do we do?" asked Liam.

"Well," Perry said. "Ferrith was adamant that he would watch for us. Meet us at the western entrance by the river."

"How do we know that hasn't been compromised?" Liam asked.

"We don't even know if he spotted us in the first place," Oliver said.

"We don't have any guarantees," Charis said, "but our original plan remains our best option."

"And now we're fucked," said Perry.

"No," said Argon. "This Amelia sends a few petty beasts after us and we take them down with ease. If this is all she has, then I am not worried."

"There are more," said Charis. "Always."

"At least this isn't Chicago," Oliver said.

"What do we do?" asked Aster.

"What else is there to do?" asked Dorian. "We keep moving."

Maynard nodded in assent and they walked into the dawn.

The sun cracked the eastern ridge a few hours before they neared the pyramid's walls. By the time they arrived, the warmth of the afternoon sun amplified the desert heat. Staring up at the slopes of the great black pyramid, Callianeira wondered at what it held inside. She knew the old world, from the days of swords and stone to the era of computers. Now she would step from one such epoch into another. This may not have been her most epic endeavor, but it was her riskiest. She had always had more control, more certainty.

They stood, as in ceremony, waiting for the doors to open. A moment passed. Then a few minutes passed. Perry kicked at the earth, drawing in the sand with his foot. Liam and Aster grasped hands. Callianeira thought that it was, for lack of a better word, cute. When even Argon, serious as he was, looked cynical, Callianeira decided to give it up.

"Does anyone know the password?" she said. "Seriously, where's Gandalf when you need him?"

"Who's Gandalf?" Perry asked.

"Don't give him that look," she said regarding Oliver's disapproving glance. "That's the apocalypse for you. Gandalf, my dear Perry, was a wizard in a story."

"Sounds stupid," Perry replied.

"Every story is stupid until it's told right," Nathan said.

"They're fine books," Oliver said.

Callianeira laughed. "Next you'll tell us how great Narnia and Harry Potter are."

"Seriously," said Perry, "what is this shit?"

"Prewar stuff," Liam said to his friend. "You really should have paid attention to Master Ferrith."

"You've read them, have you?" asked Nathan.

"Well," answered Liam. "No."

"Kids these days," Callianeira said.

"To be fair," Nathan said, "you weren't exactly around during the late twentieth century, Calli."

"To be fair, Callianeira said, "I was a few galaxies away and still know those stories."

"So what do we do?" Aster asked, bringing the imminent topic to the forefront.

"We keep asking that question," Nathan said. "And no one knows the answer. It has gotten us into enough trouble this time."

"We wait," Argon said. He struck his spear into the ground and it stood upright. He put his pack down, and adjusting his robe, began to settle in.

"You thinking it might be a while, Argon?" Callianeira asked.

Charis, who had been silent up to this point, smiled. "He's probably right."

With a shrug of her shoulders, Callianeira unshouldered her pack. Oliver glanced at Dorian who shook his head in resignation.

Though Callianeira had tried her best to lighten everyone's spirits, the heat of the day weighed upon her. At first they passed the time telling stories, and while many of the tales were wondrous, the listeners grew distracted by the sun's ferocity. It was one thing to ride or walk in this weather, some trajectory or destination ahead, oftentimes a breeze to cool the harshest of weather, but out by the damned city with its black walls radiating heat, a sticky sweat and apathy plagued them. Their makeshift shade had been all too futile.

It was when Callianeira went down to the river to replenish her canteen that the stupidity of their discomfort struck her.

"Aren't we all a bunch of fucking morons?" she said.

There had been a laugh and then rush of excitement as they gathered at the river, childlike and eager, splashing in its shallows. The waters ran clear along the bank, uncluttered by anything more than sparse vegetation. Somehow it alleviated their anxiety, a brief and guiltless respite from their duty. Though the world inside Novum may crumble, there was nothing they could do about it, and so they reveled together in the river. Maynard splashed Callianeira in a rare act of playfulness. Oliver and Charis sat together, half immersed along the shoreline, like a couple grown old, and for a flash Charis's face showed how much she lamented the two centuries lost between the two of them.

After the group's initial jubilee, they quieted and gathered along the shore, letting the river run over their legs as they sat propped upon the bank. Dorian smiled, his usual dark disposition tucked away. His long dark hair was wet and beads of river water dripped from his short beard. Callianeira had rarely seen him without his trench coat, but he sat comfortable in his undergarments, the tattoos on his back a unique meandering of runes. She knew that her own tattoos enhanced her powers of persuasion, of strength if necessary, and they also amplified her communication with the deeper things, the spirits of the world, within and without her own dimension. Their power had diminished, but it reawakened in her with each battle. Dorian's own tattoos were almost unreadable. They were complex because he was a spirit meant to create worlds, not dwell within them.

Everyone dried in the remaining sun and redressed. By night they decided that a fire would not make things any more or less dangerous. As the cold set in, they gathered around its warmth. Oliver had talked to Callianeira then and she had told him her story. He seemed genuinely curious, but he also seemed the type to gather such information for some future anthology. Either way, she did not mind, and Maynard had heard it as well. It seemed to move him and he had drawn closer to her that night. Acting on their urges would have been inappropriate, but Maynard held her close nonetheless. Oliver and Charis had warmed up to one another, their romance more obvious. Liam and Aster hardly knew what to do with themselves, teenage love thriving between them, and Perry seemed content on his own. Callianeira slept close to Maynard and thought that she couldn't be happier anywhere else.

# CHAPTER THIRTY-SIX

## *Novum*

Oliver awoke to the clamor. Charis jerked awake, startling him even more as the earth trembled. He winced, feeling her quick comfort. "I'm sorry, I'm sorry," she said. As the pain in his leg cooled, he saw the source of the sound and his panic faded. A door opened and a man stepped out from its shadow.

"Master Ferrith?" Liam's voice called out.

"It is," the man said.

The young man rushed to his mentor, throwing arms around the older man. The company stirred, and started to gather their things.

"We have to move fast," Ferrith said, though his eyes shone with wonder at the company, lingering on Dorian. "Introductions and news will have to wait."

They disassembled their camp, leaving the river behind and allowed Ferrith to usher them into Novum. Oliver's first, uneven footfalls into the City were lost in shadow. He felt along with his cane. Dorian walked before him and lit the way, a flame flickering in his palm. Those who could, also lit their own fires.

"How many?" Ferrith asked.

"Ten," came Dorian's voice.

"Are more coming?"

"Not unless we send word to the Pass." Dorian said. "Can you accommodate more?"

"I don't know," Ferrith said. "The resistance is dwindling."

The resistance? There were people within Novum who would oppose Jacob?

Ferrith opened a door and led them through it. They took three flights of stairs, another two hallways, and an elevator. It opened into a massive underground commons where several groups of people came and went.

"Come on," Ferrith urged them.

"We should have done this at night," Oliver said.

"There are curfews by night," Ferrith said.

A group of ten people, battle-ragged and dirty from desert, walking in an underground metropolis gained the attention of the denizens. Many stopped to eye the company. The fashion had changed less than Oliver would have thought. Suits were still suits, if tailored a little odd. It was not the vision of the future one might expect.

The group entered a nearby set of doors. Flickering lights illuminated the cracked tiled flooring, but no light reached the steps Ferrith led them down. Oliver walked to the steps, leaning on his cane as the others made their way down. Charis came to his side.

"It hasn't been the same since the battle," he told her. "It has gotten worse. You'd think they'd have more elevators."

"Come, love. It's not so bad."

With her, it was not so bad. With one hand she held his arm, taking one step at a time. As they descended into the darkness, her other hand let out the usual green flame. It was not a neon green, but something more natural, as if the glow of a bioluminescent plant. She caught his gaze and smiled at him, and they were at the bottom of the stairs.

"In a city like this," Nathan said, "I'd think there was a more direct route."

"There is," Ferrith replied. "We came by a more discreet way."

"What about the surface?" Maynard asked. That one was surely awestruck, even without seeing the grandeur above.

Still leading them, Ferrith shot a glance back. "It houses perhaps twenty percent of the population. The rich and some of the upper-middle class, offices, and recreation. My partner worked for the government, so I was fortunate enough to live up there. The First Underground is what sustains the City. The working class lives down here, maintaining production, the food and water supplies, waste management. This was going to be a resort in the event that the worst didn't happen, so most of the accommodations are reasonable. But after two hundred years, even Novum has its slums."

Ferrith hit the button to summon an elevator. As they packed into the carriage, Oliver thought that they must be quite malodorous to Ferrith.

"Master Ferrith," Liam said. "What happened to Standon? Was he fired?" He looked to Perry who shrugged.

Ferrith swallowed. "He's dead. They took him right after Perry left."

Liam's shock was apparent, though he did not cry. The boy had become a man.

"There's a great deal to tell," Ferrith said. "I prepared for the worst, but some things were inevitable."

No one spoke again until they arrived at the base. The First Underground was a multileveled complex, a single shaft running from top to the bottom far below. Grated bridges crossed at odd intervals, spanning from one side to the other to shorten the walk around the balcony. They crossed one such bridge, and Oliver was thankful that Charis kept close. His cane shook each time he took a step. Height did not intimidated him, but the rattling bridge filled him with anxiety. They crossed safely, Oliver relieved to be on the solid concrete again. It was some time before they came to a single door, a small red light its only adornment. Ferrith waved a card before the light and it flickered green. With a click, the door opened.

The room might have been a warehouse, its ceiling so high it surely took up two stories. The concrete pillars that held it up, as well as the walls, might have been white once, but age and the lighting painted a dingy sepia tone. Cots lined the far wall, some occupied, others with tousled bedding. Another corner of the room was dedicated to weapons and practice. Real swords and assorted weapons lined the wall, but the few men and women sparring wielded practice swords.

Ferrith turned to face Oliver and the others. "Welcome to the resistance. Eponymous with its location, this place and these people are the First Underground. I'm sure you're all tired, but I don't have to tell you that there's much to be done. So, come, and I will debrief you."

Behind a partition stretched a table, mismatched chairs lining either side. A white board on the wall was littered with notes, many of them crossed out, ideas long deemed hopeless. They sat around the table, Oliver careful as he eased into a chair. Ferrith stood at the head. His hair and beard were more gray than black, accentuating his grim expression and slight hunch.

"It's a relief that you're here," Ferrith said. "We weren't sure you'd make it. Agnys and Jacob might know you're inside, but if they do, they've kept it a secret. I find it hard to believe that they didn't spot you this morning, but one of our men created a diversion, drawing most enforcer attention away from where you entered. They aren't stupid, though, so we are lucky that our strategy worked.

"As best we can tell, we are approaching the end of the third week since Jacob arrived. We didn't know it, but the Morning Star was already working ahead, perhaps years in advance. Per Perry's discovery, we believe that Agnys is either the Morning Star's vassal or the Morning Star himself. One way or another, he started gaining political power some time ago, though his name is just now known.

"Much has happened in the prior two days. An entire network of corruption was exposed by Agnys, who emerged as a supposed behind-the-scenes savior. He has already disputed the prophet's claim that Dorian is our hope. Transcripts of the prophecy show that he foresaw the need for aid from an angel, but that the angel was not named. We believe these to be revisions. Yesterday he installed his own man as the High Priest who has declared that Jacob is our best aid.

"Those that were in Agnys's pocket resigned from the council. Those that disputed it were hung from the Central Spire. Within a day, we became a dictatorship. I know what you're all wondering. Who let him get away this? Why did anyone trust Agnys? Persuasion comes in many forms, promises of power chief among them. Threats were sufficient for those too proud to take bribes. However, there are those who really believe that Agnys and Jacob will usher in a new age for the City.

"This new priest's speeches have been convincing. As he puts it, the Eternal One is hardly worth worshiping. After all, where did Elijah's prophecies come from if not God? In his foreknowledge, God didn't condemn the fallen, preventing the catastrophe. He sent them on their merry way, trusting the prophecy of a nine-year-old boy to be sufficient. He says that Jacob never intended to destroy the world, that it was a byproduct of Dorian's resistance."

Ferrith looked to Dorian. "You're not well liked." He cleared his throat, resuming his report. "Their methods are subtle. Agnys has allowed for unsustainable rations. Production will cease to exceed consumption before the year's end, and within another six months, will begin to result in drastic deficiency. Of course, so long as those up top are well-fed, who cares if we starve down here? Agnys has accounted for this shortage, claiming a plan to open the doors of the City and allow its inhabitants to pioneer the outside world. That doesn't sound so bad, but what concerns me is that he hasn't committed to any sort of trajectory. He's waiting for something.

"Standon," Ferrith paused with the name, "was trying to get to the bottom of their motives when he was killed. We also don't know what they've done with the prophet. I'm sorry, Liam. We don't know where he is. Most of the clergy has either been removed or killed. We suspect those who remain to be corrupt. At least three of them were pending investigation until Jacob arrived. Skimming the coffers, sexual predation, the usual. Tasrael voluntarily demoted himself. He has not expressed support or dissent regarding Jacob. As usual, the slimiest of them are beyond reproach. Jacob put his priest, this Solomon Glass, as the interim High Priest."

That caught Oliver's attention. Jacob had infiltrated the City on every level, and Sol's claim to the High Priesthood demonstrated just how deep Angys's roots went.

"Standon," Ferrith continued, "was attempting to find out more about this new priest when he was killed. They hung him from the Central Spire and he appeared as if ravaged by a beast. Standon believed that the Morning Star and Jacob would usher us into a world of darkness, but not in the most expected ways. We think that he is attempting to establish a world on his own terms. Solomon's sermons and Agnys's speeches have curious themes. They emphasize wealth and power. Appealing to base desires is nothing new, but Agnys is adamant that he is the source of that power, and that if anyone wants it dealt to them, they'll have to do whatever he asks, which among other things is to follow Jacob."

"They can't honestly believe that," Oliver said.

"The people that matter do," Ferrith said, "because he's demonstrated it. The rest do so out of fear. Agnys wants a society in which might makes right. To him, morality, love, and merit are weaknesses."

Dorian swore. "Does anyone here know about the Tartarus Project?" Everyone's expression was confused or blank. Dorian shook his head. "Carry on, I guess."

"Only certain people have immunity from the curfew," Ferrith continued. "Those found after are hanged from the spire. Those who express dissent are hanged from it. By the way, if he continues to hang everyone at this rate, our ration production might get us through the end of the year. He can do a lot in that time, like foster a virulent culture."

"Why would he do that?" Argon asked, who had been quiet since they entered the City.

"It goes against the very nature of the Eternal One," Dorian replied. "And while I have my own disgruntlements with God, I suppose it flies in my face as well."

"Yes," Ferrith said. "However, this isn't just a move against religion or an ideology. Four of our top scholars were killed, their throats slashed before they were defenestrated. It might have stalled years' worth of progress. Agnys wants to take us back to a more primal time and he wants to rule, surely with Jacob at his right hand.

"The resistance is around thirty people, most of them mustered as a precaution in the event that something such as this happened. Recruits have otherwise been sparse. The people on these subterranean levels are a simple folk. They've lived in fear most of their life, poverty and near-slavery eating at their souls. The people who might have joined us either lack confidence in our resistance or have fallen for Agnys's promises. Most find him benign, so long as they don't oppose him.

"We want to overthrow a government. Those in our resistance are thinkers, not fighters. We've tried dozens of ways to infiltrate the government or Agnys's defenses to no avail. I've been leading the First Underground, but I won't lie. Now that you're here, it's a relief to have some help. In fact, as far as I'm concerned, I'd rather someone else called the shots."

Oliver looked to Dorian. The reluctance was gone. Anger and surety remained. The angel stood. "I would not step on any toes, but I believe that you speak true, for I too have felt the burden of leadership. If you will allow it, it is a burden I will carry. For I intend to make sure that we make the best use of everyone here." Ferrith sat, extending his hand in invitation to Dorian. Dorian stood and faced his audience. "I'm tired of Jacob being one step ahead of us. We need to utilize our strength. We have fighters like Maynard and Argon and thinkers like Ferrith and Oliver. Let's use that to augment what we already have, to create a symbiotic relationship between our heads and our muscles. For the time being, let's take a day of rest. We could use it. I'll update Ferrith on our end of things and tomorrow we can tackle this. In the meantime, stay here and recuperate. Unless anyone has anything else, I suggest we adjourn."

No one expressed dissent and the meeting broke with a quiet murmuring. Liam said something to Aster and she smiled, shaking her head. Maynard looked at Callianeira, his usual, hardened expression soft. Charis put a hand on Oliver's shoulder, and he stood, the spasm of pain a faint nudging at his leg. As he left, he nodded to Argon, whose despondence was clear. The man missed his wife. Dorian and Ferrith remained behind.

"Liam!" a woman said. Liam looked over, seeing a dark-skinned woman and a man, his parents if the resemblance was any indication. Liam ran to them, giving a long embrace to his mother, tears streaking down her face.

When the embrace ended, Liam's father shook his hand stoically. "We weren't sure you would come back. It's good to see you, son." Not dispassionately, but perhaps awkwardly, Liam's father turned from his son and started directing the others. "There are a few private chambers," he said. "Office or industrial space we converted into quarters. It's a suite on the south side of the campus. I don't know if it will accommodate all of you, but you're welcome to make use of them."

Charis guided Oliver to the side, pulling him close so her lips nearly touched his ear. "Let's see if we can't find a place to have some time to ourselves."

# CHAPTER THIRTY-SEVEN

*Unraveling*

The City was not quite as Liam remembered it. Before, it seemed polished and opulent, and he had imagined that after weeks in the dusty desert, it would seem even more clean and otherworldly. However, upon return, the Central Spire was a little less radiant a spectacle. A haze hung about Novum, subtle to its inhabitants, yet obvious to fresh eyes. Furthermore, the First Underground was a place to which he seldom ventured, and the reality of it instilled a certain sense of guilt. His blindness to the poverty inside and outside Novum troubled him.

He held Aster as she slept, her calm breathing soothing his own anxieties. Much to his relief, his parents elected to continue in their usual duties. They kept to the safer routes, but they were the coordinators of a supplies acquisition team. He felt ashamed, but seeing them awoke the sense that the gap between himself and their life was only wider. They were participating in this rebellion, putting their lives in danger, but he could not reconcile the people he knew before with his parents now. Though they had changed, they were further from the people with which he had parental familiarity. More than anything, he needed to think, but the more he cogitated, the less he felt in control.

He wanted to leave this place, this dingy warehouse. Novum was his city and he knew it better than anyone else except perhaps

Perry. It was not that the prior three days had been unremarkable. There was his homecoming, the discovery of the resistance, and there was Aster. In their private times they had done, he supposed, as any teenagers would have. In a closed metropolis like Novum, population control was vital, and there was no shortage on readily available precautions to prevent the consequences of their doings. For a while, their amorous doings contented Liam, but he sensed that Aster grew restless as well.

He took his arm from around Aster and roused himself from the bed. Pulling on a shirt, he walked into the main room of the suite. It was austere with simple and utilitarian adornments. The room was empty of people, but Oliver's tapping cane approached from the hall. Oliver entered, slightly disheveled, but he appeared otherwise all right. He looked at Liam and gave a chuckle.

"A few days in the City," Oliver said, "and all we want to do is be with the people that we love."

Liam hoped he was not blushing. "I guess so," he said.

"I'm sorry," Oliver said. "I didn't come out here to talk about that. Apparently we've received a message. I was going to see what it's about. Care to join?"

Liam roused Aster and told her of the meeting.

"I had the strangest dream," she said, eyes still heavy from sleep. "There was sigil, a great seal, somewhere near here. It's a danger to Dorian and the other fallen angels."

"We can tell them at the meeting," Liam said as they returned to the commons. Charis arrived a moment later, trying to tame somewhat wild hair into a ponytail. Liam followed them out into the large room and towards the partition. The recording was already playing, a voice unfamiliar to Liam, though he knew it to be Jacob. Deep and resonant, the recording continued.

"You shouldn't be here, Dorian," the voice said. "I was arrogant to think that I had escaped you. I know that you think that you can hide from me. You have been traced down into the First

Underground. I have my people there too, vigilantly awaiting the sight of you. However, I may have little need of them. Novum is mine. The Morning Star will build an empire rid of the weakness of compassion and solidarity. He envisions a world where power unfastens the chains of morality. You stand in the way of that and I will remove you.

"So hear me now, Dorian. I know that you are the catalyst by which your rogue group operates. Convince your people to disband and turn yourself over to me, and I will let them live, so long as they leave and never return. I have already tracked down certain members of your group. Some I have captured. The hangings began at noon today, starting with someone very dear to your city boy, Liam. Is he listening? Liam, your parents are dead, strung up from the top of the Central Spire. You should be proud. They didn't peep a word of your whereabouts before Cain got overzealous with his torture."

As Jacob's voice paused, Aster looked to Liam, tears in her eyes. The recording continued, background noise to Liam's emotions. He did not remember parting from the company, but Aster had guided him to somewhere quiet. He was a grown man now, he wasn't supposed to cry, but the tears came all the same. Liam clenched his fists, nails digging into his palms. Aster's comforting hands rubbed his tense shoulders, but they did not soothe his anger. Through blurry vision, he saw that some of the others had come to comfort him. Looking at Liam, Ferrith must have understood something. "We should leave them alone," Ferrith suggested to Charis and Callianeira. The sound of their footsteps faded as they took his advice. Aster remained, still standing near to him.

"I'm so sorry," she said. He looked to her and saw that she continued to cry too.

His parents were gone. He had hardly known them and now it was too late. Their bodies hung from the Central Spire. For a moment he wondered if Jacob lied and that his parents yet lived, but something in Jacob's tone rang true. His parents had been taken from him, and worst of all, Liam did not know how much he had lost. Before leaving the City, his mother had cried, for the first time showing real affection for him. His tears now were the first affection he had known for her.

The prophet was missing, surely imprisoned by Jacob if not dead. Liam thought about the letter, about his grandfather's confidence, but in the end, Liam had not said goodbye nor arrived in time to save those he loved. He had not spoken with the man one last time.

The room grew claustrophobic, and his yearning to return above ground seized him like a madness. If he could have anything, he would have the fresh air of the Outlands, but he would be content to leave the stuffy warehouse. He knew every shortcut and dark alley in Novum. He could go anywhere he wanted undetected.

"Come on," Liam said. "I want to show you something."

"Liam, it's not safe," Aster said.

"I have my sword and no one will see us." Liam knew the ways of Novum. He and Perry had learned all there was to know about the upper-level. There were alleys that were always dark, covered in the shadows of the compact metropolis. At nightfall, two hours before the curfew, he led Aster from the First Underground and into Novum's upper-layer, winding and twisting through the streets, avoiding the main roads, avoiding the scrutiny of any pedestrians. He noticed that through sorrow and anger, Aster still beheld Novum with wonder. Even in the shadows, her head craned up at the buildings. As they passed between streets, she marveled at the lamp-lit sloping highways, towering platforms, and the hovercrafts that bustled among them.

They came to the building and Liam wheeled a dumpster over, scooting it into place. After climbing atop it, he helped Aster up, and began to ascend the ladder, hands gripping rungs in the dark. She followed. It was the spot, the one Liam and Perry frequented, taking in the view of the metropolis. It was a long climb, but if Aster tired, she said nothing. They reached the roof and he heard her breath catch as she beheld the City. From below it felt like a maze of clustering buildings, but from the rooftop, they had a vantage of its scenery.

It was not beautiful like Mere. Mere had an organic quality to it, a deeply rooted and floral character that demanded reverence. While Novum's aesthetic might only be surface-deep, it solicited a certain appreciation. Beneath the surface, the First Underground dove deep into a sordid, poor world. On top, crystal-lit gardens lined the southern wall and sprouted from rooftops. There was even a beauty to the sleek hovercrafts that gracefully glided in their comings and goings. The train passed nearby with a musical rumble.

At the center of Novum jutted the Central Spire, its pinnacle nearly touching the roof of the pyramid. The window at the top of the tower was broken, two ropes dangling from it, traveling nearly halfway down the building. The light of the tower's windows silhouetted the bodies hanging by the ropes. He knew he would see his parents there. He was thankful for the dark, not wanting to see what horrors Cain had inflicted on them.

More tears came. More rage.

Aster took his hand and they stood for a moment. Then she gasped. Liam saw it too.

In the distance the bodies of his parents spasmed, as trying to free the rope from their necks. Even from so far, it was obvious that they moved. "No!" *Not this, not Raven's sorcery.* "That bastard. That son of a bitch."

Aster pulled at him, turning him toward her, her arms wrapping around his waist. "Let's go," she said. "Let's go from this place."

594

Liam's shoulders heaved as he sobbed, burying his face in the crook of her neck. His tears wet her blonde hair.

"That was easy enough," said a familiar, raspy voice. Liam broke from Aster, wiping the moisture from his eyes and faced Sol, his black cloak hanging motionlessly.

"Aster," Liam said, drawing his sword. "Run. Don't let him touch you. You don't want to see his mind."

"Run to where?" she asked.

"Nowhere, kid," Sol said. "You know how this goes."

"Jump," Liam said.

"Bad idea," said another voice. Liam turned, heart sinking as a bald man gripped Aster. She gasped, as he put a muscled arm around her. At his touch, her eyes widened in horror. Liam raised his sword, but found nowhere to strike without risking her. He had never seen the man but he knew it to be Cain.

"Didn't see this coming, did you, bitch?" Cain asked. "Well, see this."

Aster cried out.

"Get out!" she screamed, her trapped arms straining. "Get out!"

"Hands off, asshole," a female voice said. Callianeira landed upon the roof with grace, ferocity in her expression.

Cain laughed, Sol jumped at Liam, and Aster pushed back.

They all fell from the roof at once, slamming upon a lower, slanted roof. They began to slide and Aster screamed. Liam looked down, trying to stop himself. Aster had freed herself from Cain, but he grappled for her as he descended as well. Sol dug in his claws and stopped himself. Aster caught herself short of the edge, but Cain fell into her, toppling them both over. Liam reached the edge and stopped his fall. Above, Callianeira came upon Sol. She seemed to keep her footing, thrusting her blade at him. He dodged an attack, but with another swipe she struck his shoulder. He grunted and swung a clawed hand into her. She cried out as they found their mark, and she lost her balance, sliding as well. Sol ran after her, animal-like on all fours.

Liam looked over to where Aster had fallen, scooting along the edge to the spot. Then he saw her fingers, gripping at the ledge. He worked his way over, extending a hand. "Aster!" He stretched his fingers, reaching for her.

"Liam!" she cried.

"I've got you," he said. She freed one hand and reached for his outstretched arm. They locked in a grip, her fingers on his wrist and his grasping hers. "It's going to be okay," he said.

With a rumble, Callianeira and Sol rolled down the roof. She struck the werecrocotta and he scratched her. Then they toppled over the edge. Liam heard a clang followed by a scream and a roar. Liam tried to find purchase as he pulled Aster up. She suddenly became heavier, jerking him part-way over the edge before her grip loosened. Liam beheld their height, a dizzying drop into the city streets. Cain perched upon a pipe, his hand on her ankle. *No.* Cain pulled harder. Aster's grip faltered, Liam nearly fell over the edge, his other hand failing to secure a grip on the smooth surface of the slanted roof. Then he lost her. She plummeted and Cain leapt from his perch after her. They descended and on instinct, Liam scrabbled back.

He needed to get down, to rescue her, to stop anything worse from happening. That was ridiculous. She would be dead when she hit the ground. Callianeira must have been sent to watch them, but she fell too. "Fuck!" Liam said. "Fucking shit!" This was his fault. He had to act. There had to be something, but he didn't even know how to get off of this particular roof. He frantically searched it, disregarding his balance. He climbed to the pinnacle and went down the opposite slope, finding a flat rooftop close enough that he could leap to it. He made the jump, rolling with the impact, ignoring the jolt of pain in his arm. He took the access stair down, rushing faster than he thought possible. He jumped to the next landing, spun around to the next flight, and flew through the first floor exit.

With the curfew coming soon, the streets were quiet, and there was no sign that anyone had hit the ground. That was hope enough, but it meant they had been taken. Should he go get the others? Surely her rescue was not something he could accomplish on his own. In his brief moment of hesitation someone called out.

"Liam!" He wheeled around, realizing that he was unarmed.

Dorian stepped from the alley followed by Nathan. "You look terrified." Nathan said. "What happened?"

"Aster," Liam said out of breath. "They took her. I think Calli too."

"The others have been looking for you," Dorian said. "They're set to rendezvous at the gardens. Go meet them there. Nathan and I will handle this."

"But—" Liam began.

"Go!" Dorian said.

Liam looked to Nathan. "As he says," the red haired man told him.

Liam ran back to the gardens, hoping to convince the others to help him. They would need more than Dorian or Nathan to track where Cain and Sol had taken the girls. Before he arrived at the gardens he heard the shout. "Dorian!" It was Jacob.

He arrived at the gardens. A form in all black stood over a body. Ferrith lay on the ground, blood trickling from his head. The figure standing over Ferrith turned, a thin dark-haired man, tall and charismatic. Jacob smiled. It was a terrible thing.

A shadow passed over, and something yanked at his dreadlocks. Liam's head snapped back and an arm wrapped around his neck, holding him. He kicked and squirmed, the nails of the person digging in. "Hold him there, Amelia," Jacob told his captor.

Maynard emerged, sword in hand, followed by Charis, expression just as fierce. Argon held back, eyes calculating the confrontation. He gazed at the fallen angel with a recognizable, wise apprehension.

"Wait," came a voice. From behind a tree, Oliver emerged, cane aiding his approach to the confrontation.

"No need for anyone else to die," said Jacob. "It's Dorian I want."

"Your promises are worthless," said Oliver. "You'd start with Dorian, then finish the rest of us."

The air grew cold and they fell silent until the sound of slow footsteps came through the grass. An old man approached, removing the hood from his black robe.

"The Morning Star," Maynard said.

"I am Agnys Negosta here, and am merely a representation of the one you call the Morning Star. I am him and I am not. Regardless, I carry his power. Jacob has promised you that if Dorian will give himself up and you will leave the City, that this can all end. I am here to see to the bargain."

"Bullshit," Maynard replied. "You've shown your hand, old man. You'd tell a falsehood if it got you what you wanted. Your agenda lies out there as much as in here, so you won't have us in any corner. But you'd make it easy on yourself, by eliminating Dorian and stripping us of the advantage we already have in here."

"I believe I already have the advantage," Agnys said. "I have Elijah, Aster, and Callianeira, the latter of which owes me greatly. However, as much as I'd like to begin her eternal suffering now, I'll even throw her into the deal. Even if I am lying, your only alternative is to die anyway."

The hairs on Liam's neck prickled and he tensed. Fear took hold as Agnys peered at Liam and in his mind he heard the whispers of the Morning Star. *You are not a man marked by fire. You are a boy.*

*You have wasted your time. Dorian will fall on this day and so shall your city. The only hope for you and your friends is to kneel to me.*

There was a cry. Perry flew from the bushes, landing on the turf with a thud. Raven came out behind him. "Found this one," he said with a smile as he put a boot to Perry's back, holding him down. Amelia had loosened her grip on Liam, as if she didn't fear that he would flee. Indeed, it seemed that the Morning Star held him captive more than her.

"Give us Dorian," Jacob said. Where Agnys had been matter-of-fact about it, Jacob's demand was filled with emotion. Wrath and hatred resonated.

"Yes," said the Morning Star. "Your reluctance to give up Dorian concerns me. If you forestall this conversation much longer I'm prone to take Callianeira and Aster off of the table."

"You'll let them all go," Dorian said, walking into the confrontation. Dorian was supposed to be with Nathan rescuing Callianeira and Aster. What was he doing here? Had they found the women and saved them? If Nathan and Dorian could find the girls, they would only have to go up against Sol and Cain.

"Ah," Jacob said. "Dorian."

Agnys smiled.

"How's this for a bargain? You and me, Jacob," Dorian said. "I win, you go. I don't care where, just away from here. I lose, you let everyone go, but they leave Novum to you."

Jacob looked to Agnys who said, "Why risk that when we have the advantage?"

"Because it's what Jacob really wants," Dorian replied.

Jacob unsheathed his sword, baring its steel toward Dorian who took out his own sword. The others stood back. Even Maynard relaxed his broad blade.

At first Dorian and Jacob sized each other up. Then, as if following the same rhythm, they raised their blades, striking at one another. Their swords met, testing the fight to come. Jacob struck next, a swing faster than Liam could see. Dorian deflected it, swiftly directing his own blow. After a series of parries, Jacob took the offensive, strike after strike slamming into Dorian's blade.

With a kick, Dorian twirled into the air, and by some agility, maneuvered around Jacob, faster than sight, and struck at Jacob. The other angel blocked it with ease, and then the fury began. Liam lost all concept of the fight as they twirled around one another, flashing their weapons in indecipherable motions. Dorian jumped, and landed to Jacob's side. Jacob nearly failed to block him, but no sooner had he swatted Dorian's attack away before avenging it. They skidded in the grass, churning it in chaotic flurries. Jacob kicked Dorian who arced into the air, back-flipping, and landing on his feet. He surged forward, and Jacob dashed to the side. They locked blades once, twice, broke apart and resumed their melee.

A hiss simmered in the air, as if the Morning Star grew excited. Jacob moved faster, every blow swifter, and every motion of Dorian's meeting it in dire defense. Jacob ceased to hold his sword two-handed, freeing a hand to direct blows at Dorian. The angel appeared undaunted by Jacob's mad rush, but each attack sent him back more. Liam looked to the others. Maynard was visibly worried, as was Charis. Oliver appeared confident. Argon, the warrior, watched with satisfaction. Perry remained on the ground, near Ferrith's body.

The hiss grew louder. Jacob struck Dorian, raised a boot and kicked him. Dorian twisted in the air, finding his feet and directing a slash at Jacob who slid back. Again Dorian swept his blade, followed by another attack, both times Jacob moving back agilely. Their weapons continued to move, the ringing of their swords accentuating the growing hiss.

"Come now, Dorian," Jacob said at a pause. "You're weaker than I remember."

Surely Jacob had suppressed the earthen magics of fire and rock that Dorian had demonstrated at the Pass, but Dorian had also proved himself adept. No matter how brilliant Jacob fought, Dorian should have possessed some advantage.

Dorian struck and Jacob hit him with the flat of his sword. Was Jacob playing with Dorian? It couldn't be.

"This is my world, Dorian," Jacob continued over the rattle of swords. "My city, my desert, my rules." Dorian came at him, teeth gritted. Jacob stepped aside. "Fuck you, Dorian, and fuck your ideals." He blocked another parry from Dorian and exchanged a series of dominating blows before backing away. "I've been one step ahead of you." Dorian struck, his blade fleet, and Jacob's sword met it. It was a casual twirl, but made Dorian's grip awkward. With a jerk, Jacob disarmed Dorian. The sword sailed into the air and Jacob caught it.

The look of surprise on Dorian's face turned to dismay. Both blades sank into his chest and Jacob lifted him, Dorian's feet rising above the ground. Blood seeped from the wounds, from Dorian's mouth, and his tears mixed within. "It's all mine," Jacob said. He threw Dorian down.

The angel thudded to the ground, twin swords jutting up from his chest, angling under their own weight. He choked, followed by a groan, eyes wide and terrified. Maynard stood shocked, chest heaving. Charis had fallen to her knees, reaching out to Dorian. Oliver stood, jaw clenched, eyes wide. Liam realized that Amelia no longer held him and he fell to his knees.

Charis reached out, surely attempting some healing on Dorian, whose breath fell shallower, but Jacob waved a finger at her. "As I promised," he said. "You are all free to go."

Liam began to crawl towards the others. Perry, more confused than sorrowful, had already made it over. Jacob ushered his followers to him. Agnys donned his hood, its shadows enveloping his face.

Dorian choked again, blue veins bulging along his face. Something wasn't right. Something changed. His beard grew longer, his hair redder. His arm reached out in his death throes and then the change settled. Nathan, not Dorian, lay dead. Maynard yelled.

Jacob looked up, shocked. "Bastard," he said. "Shapeshifting bastard. Pretending to be Dorian. The deal is off. I'll be taking Liam and Perry." Jacob took his sword from Nathan's chest. Nathan's own sword fell with it, clanging to the ground.

"No," said Charis, rising. "You won't. The deal regarded Dorian and he is not here."

Maynard found his composure and Argon stepped forward.

"We end this now," Maynard said, holding out his sword. The veins in his neck bulged.

Jacob smiled. "I'm smarter than that."

He walked away, followed by those loyal to him. Liam began to pursue them, but Oliver held out a hand. "We need to be smarter than that as well. If we fight them on an impulse now, we'll die. We need to be decisive, not impulsive. Jacob will surely have us followed. Liam, do you know a back way?" Liam nodded. Perry would know a way as well. They stood in the garden. Ferrith lay dead. Nathan lay dead.

There was sound of running and then Dorian arrived. "I know where they are," he said. Then he looked down at Nathan, his expression darkening. "No," he said and choked. "It's my fault," he said when he found his voice. "Fuck. God-fucking-dammit."

Liam thought Dorian meant it. Oliver went to Dorian and put a hand to his back. "You had no way of knowing."

"I told him to hold Jacob off. I told him not to fight him, just to stall him."

"It's not your fault, Dorian." Oliver had one hand on his cane, another supporting Dorian. "Hold fast."

Dorian broke from Oliver, kneeling before Nathan's body. He looked up, eyes piercing the city wall that sloped above. He cried. Lamentation came, the deepest of sorrows, as the tears fell from his eyes. He shook, choking on his sobs.

Liam watched Dorian break. This was the end of their hope.

# CHAPTER THIRTY-EIGHT
## *Phalaris*

Dorian looked up to the others' tear-streaked faces. He cradled Nathan's head in his hands, fingers grasping the red locks of hair. Maynard came over, kneeling before his forefather, and though he did not cry, Dorian knew that the man mirrored his sorrow. Dorian put a bloodstained hand on Maynard's arm, who remained silent, simmering in ire and grief.

"The girl," Dorian said, trying to sound strong. "Aster. I can sense her. North side of the city, first level of the Underground, there's a furnace for rubbish." He choked, knowing they needed to act, but he couldn't think clearly. He had known Nathan for over a thousand years. Now he was, what? Gone? What happened when they died? Was there an afterlife for them? Dorian didn't know. He had never known. It was a stupid thing not to know. He felt lamentation all over again and then stilled himself. "We'll get Calli and Aster back."

"They will need to wait," Oliver said. Dorian could sense his reluctance, but as usual he kept a level head. "The base is compromised and the resistance needs to be warned."

"Send one person," Liam protested. "Send Perry. He knows the way. It won't take all of us."

"No," Dorian answered. "Oliver's right. We're going to need more than just us. We need more people and we need a plan."

604

To Dorian's surprise no one protested. Dorian stood, holding Nathan's body between his arms, calling on the Darkworld to ease the burden. The power that coursed through him felt lethargic. Argon lifted Ferrith's body. Dorian walked toward the First Underground. It was Perry and not Liam who led the way, the latter perhaps too devastated by the day's events to guide them. Dorian could understand that much.

They arrived at the elevator and Dorian paused. He looked around, realizing that something was wrong. "Where is Maynard? Where is Liam?"

"They were at the back," Oliver said, turning and seeing that they were unaccounted for.

Dorian realized that Nathan's sword was missing. He had never picked it up. He looked to each in turn. Argon shook his head. Oliver and Charis didn't have it. Perry shrugged, but there was a knowing in his eyes. Dorian stood, stunned for but a moment. "Oh God…"

"You know where this place is?" Maynard asked.

"I think so," Liam said, hoping it was the truth. "I don't know exactly where, but I think I've been there before. Once maybe. A long time ago."

"Wait." Maynard raised a hand and they halted.

Liam stopped, irritated, but too winded to protest. He leaned on Nathan's sword, breathing heavily. He was thirsty, but hardly able to think about it. They needed to keep moving. Why couldn't Maynard see that?

"You don't know where we're going?" Maynard asked. He looked up at the buildings. He seemed less impressed than the others, as if the City weren't odd to him.

"I just know," Liam said. "Jacob thinks he has scared us off for the time being, that we're somewhere in the First Underground bickering over a plan. He probably knows where the hideout is

605

and he's heading there now, thinking that he can get to us before we can come up with a way to get to him. This is our chance to surprise them. If they know we're coming, they'll likely kill both Aster and Calli. This way they don't expect us."

Maynard shook his head. "I don't know, boy."

"I'm nearly eighteen years old, damn it." Liam felt the heat in his cheeks rising. "I fought my way through the Outland. I'm not a boy and I know what I'm doing."

Maynard opened his mouth to speak, then paused a moment. He looked past Liam. "You know how to use that?" Maynard asked, nodding at Nathan's sword.

"Well enough."

"Good."

Liam smelled something metallic, something that meant danger and he couldn't recall why. A cackle came and Liam froze. When he found the courage to turn, he beheld the crocotta emerging from the alley. Sol's eyes bore into him.

"He's a big fucker," Maynard said, his great sword ready to strike.

"He's a dead fucker," Liam said.

The crocotta lunged.

Callianeira awoke, hanging, arms bound by chains. The metal ground into her wrists and she worried at her binds until the world came into focus and she realized that it was the least of her problems. Her side and shoulder burned where Sol had scratched her. She and Aster were imprisoned on a grated, metal platform. Other chains hung from the ceiling on dark and grimy wheels. They had to be underground in some sort of manufacturing or waste facility. By the smell it was the latter. Either that or the odor emanated from her wounds. A few large, metal crates sat empty around the room. The chamber was illuminated by an orange light from which the dry heat seemed to come. Near the platform, a metal conveyor belt stood still, leading, she guessed, to the furnace that gave the room its light and warmth.

"Calli," a small voice called. She looked over to see Aster. "Calli, it hurts."

"I know," Callianeira said. "But you need to reach out. Reach out to the others."

"I have, but I can't forget him. I can't forget Cain. Such horrible thoughts."

"It's going to be okay," Callianeira told the girl. Could she have believed it less? If one of the others could find them, they might escape before things got much worse, but chances were slim. *Give it up, demon*, a voice told her. Was it her own or was it the whisper of the Morning Star?

"I saw," said Aster, "a girl. Maybe a couple of years younger than me. When he was finished with her, he gave her to the rats. Oh, God." Aster choked and bile dripped from her mouth. Whatever Cain had shown her of his twisted mind had taken the life from the girl.

Cain stepped in from an adjacent room, bearing a menacing smile. Bald and muscular he approached them, the furnace illuminating his bronze skin in orange hues.

"Callianeira," he said.

"You guys really struggle with pronunciation," she replied.

"I remember the old days, when you caused me so much trouble." He looked up wistfully. "I almost miss them. You were half clever then, but now it's all gone out of you." Aster struggled within her confines. He approached, leaning closer to the girl.

"What's wrong, Cain?" Callianeira asked. "I thought you'd prefer me." She pulled on her own chains, fingering the lock, trying to find a weakness. If she could dislocate her thumb she might be able to break free.

"I can handle you both," he said. Then he looked Aster deep in the eyes. "But I'll start with her."

"Come on, asshole," Callianeira said. "You've wanted me for a long time."

He looked over to Callianeira. "You," he said. "I've had enough women like you. I appreciate your maturity, your experience, your tenacity. Your desperation. But girls like this," he motioned to Aster. "So supple, so naive, young, for the taking." He put a hand on Aster's cheek, caressing her skin. "Do you see my thoughts?" he asked in a stage-whisper. Aster squirmed, her chains clattering. "Do you see," he continued, "what I do?"

"I've never known you to turn down a girl who begged for it first," Callianeira said.

"Then you haven't talked much with Amelia," he said.

Liam swung his sword at the coming crocotta. His blade glanced off, barely touching beneath the fur. It yelped. Maynard swiped his weapon but the beast dodged, leaping after him. Maynard rolled, angling his blade at the beast. It stopped short of the tip, saliva dripping from its jagged teeth.

The crocotta's toothy grin widened, Sol's cunning eyes so sure. The smallest bite and it was over. If Sol even clawed him, it could mean death. Charis would not always be there to heal him.

Maynard raised his sword, but Liam held up a hand, gripping Nathan's blade in the other. "Come at me, asshole."

The crocotta charged, swift and true, but not as agile as Liam. He leapt, blade striking down, feeling it sink into the snout of the beast. Sol toppled, clawing at his bleeding nose. Within seconds, Sol recovered, gaining his feet, growling at Liam. Even on all fours he stood above Liam who did not waiver. Sol jumped, claws out. Liam swung impulsively, driving the blade hard to the side. With a bark, Sol tumbled, his mutilated limb thudding to the ground. Sol groaned as black blood spewed from the stump of his forepaw. Sol attempted to rise, the missing appendage stealing his balance. Liam hacked down. His blade sank into the skull. Sol recoiled, sword wrenched from Liam hands, protruding grotesquely from the wound. The crocotta swayed, dumbfounded, as if something wasn't quite right. He tried to stand, but his bloody protuberance slid across the ground and he squealed. Liam approached Sol, drawing a dagger, and those black eyes met his. Sol attempted to scamper back, his cackle turned to a painful whimper.

"You're not going anywhere," Liam said, raising the short blade. "I have you."

The crocotta made one last attempt, jaws gaping lazily. Liam slammed the dagger into its gullet. Weapon sinking into its mouth, the beast wretched, and Liam pulled free, lest its toxic bite find him. Sol flinched for a moment and then slipped into death. Liam heard Maynard come up behind him. "Well done," the older man said. "If Sol is here, that means he's no longer watching Calli and Aster. Let's go."

Callianeira expected Cain to rape Aster, but instead he lightly brushed her cheek. At first she screamed, but succumbed to quiet sobbing. In a matter of minutes, the life had gone out of the girl, the trauma too much on top of the memories Cain had spilled into her. She hung limply, her eyes cracked open in dull horror.

"Don't hurt her further," Callianeira begged. "Not more. It's my turn." Her mouth soured at the prospect, but she knew how he could torture Aster. She shook, as if chilled, but hot sweat dripped down her brow.

"I'll be in the mood for you soon," Cain said with no real emotion in his voice. The relish for his deeds had gone out of his eyes and now a coldness took its place.

"You know why I do this," Cain said.

"Because you're a sick fuck who likes to torture women," Callianeira said.

"Come now, I don't discriminate when it comes to torture." Cain chuckled, and cocked his head as his eyes wandered over Aster's form. Aster's own eyes widened and her body trembled under his his gaze. "

The torture is just part of it. The real pleasure is in the breaking."

"You won't break me," Aster said meekly.

"May not," Cain said. "But in the end, it's Liam that I intend to break."

He drew a knife and held it up to Aster who shook. He flicked the tip of the blade down Aster's arm, drawing a gush of blood. She screamed.

"Look at me, love," Callianeira said. The claw wounds stretched, screaming in putrid agony, as she turned to Aster. "Look at me. Don't think about it."

Cain slapped Aster. "Ignore her," he said. He grabbed Aster by the neck and squeezed. She wheezed under the pressure. His knife searched her torso, sometimes merely a tickle, other times breaking the skin. She flinched, her eyes rolling into the back of her head. Then he let go of her neck, his hand trailing up her bare arm, over her bound wrists, his large fingers taking hers. Then he squeezed. They cracked. She shrieked, thrashing in her chains. Then he raised his knife and sliced at her hand. Blood gushed down on her blond hair, trickling from her fingers. He grabbed her by the neck again. "What do you see?"

She moaned, whimpering.

"What do you see?"

"I see heaven," she said.

He smiled.

"I see the throne of the Eternal One." For a moment she looked hopeful, the pain forgotten.

"Yes," he said.

Her expression turned to horror. "I see his court and the dead upon it."

He tightened his grip on her hands, then loosened it again. "Now what do you see?"

"Oh, God…"

"Wrong," Cain growled.

"Please," she begged.

"Cain," Callianeira joined.

"Shut the fuck up!" Cain looked back to Aster. "Tell us, dear. What is it you see?"

"The honey-covered man," she said. "He's bound. He's opened up. There are insects." She gagged, as if she might vomit, but there was nothing left in her stomach.

"You could live," he said.

"Please."

"You could carry my seed," said Cain.

"Kill me. Make it fast."

Cain smiled. "I do no such thing *fast*."

Liam's reeled, stumbling from his run. "She's hurt," he said.

"Then we have to keep moving," Maynard urged him.

Liam focused his energy, willing himself to hold steady. He felt her pull as images filled his mind. Horrific things. People eaten alive by abominations, rats, insects. Images of bloody rape barraged him. "Yes," Liam said. "Keep moving."

They called and boarded the elevator, a cylindrical apparatus that carried them down. The macabre visions continued, mixed with images of a great seal graven with runes. Liam recognized it the memorial commissioned by the prophet to remember the fallen world. He thought for a moment that the memorial was where she was held captive, but other images followed.

"I know where we're going," Liam said.

"Oh?" Maynard asked.

"I saw it, just now when I saw Aster's vision. This elevator takes us to a trash disposal in the First Underground. Dorian was right. There's a furnace. This is bad. Very bad."

The elevator neared the lower floor and the screams echoed down the shaft. Liam held Nathan's sword, recovered from the fallen crocotta, hoping it would be enough, hoping it wasn't too late. The elevator opened to a tall-ceilinged room. From an adjacent door came an orange flicker. In the middle of the room stood Jacob.

With a flick of his wrist, Jacob threw something. Maynard waived his sword, easily deflecting the dagger.

"I can feel you dampening the Darkworld," Maynard said. "I killed without for most of my life. I can kill you without it."

"Don't pretend like you haven't learned a thing or two," Jacob said. "And, Liam, I don't believe we have been formally introduced." Screams came from the adjacent room, then suddenly stopped. Jacob's eyes flickered to the door a few yards away.

"Liam," Maynard said. "Go to them. I'll take Jacob." He would. He would strike down this insolent, delusional, bastard of a fallen angel.

"Yes," Jacob agreed. "Why don't you?"

Liam looked at Jacob and then ran. Jacob showed no sign of stopping him. He only stared at Maynard.

"You would have been great, Maynard. You would have surpassed Achilles."

Maynard rushed him. Jacob's sword flashed from its scabbard and rang with Maynard's blow. They stood a moment, blades crossed, Maynard's hateful glare locked to Jacob's confident eyes. The melee began.

He blocked each of Jacob's strikes, their swift movements daunting. Maynard felt into the Darkworld, trying to find any enhancement, but Jacob only blocked any attempt to sustain himself with the magic. When Jacob came at him again, Maynard resorted to rolling away, hoping that he might come up in time to block Jacob's next attack. Steel rang, blow after blow almost too swift, almost his death.

"Come now, Maynard," Jacob said. "I killed Nathan. You think I can't take you?"

Maynard ignored him striking harder, grunting through clenched teeth. He did not have the breath or skill to retort. All of his efforts belonged to the battle.

"Oh," Jacob said with a smile. "So it *was* him. You were his bastard."

The melee accelerated. Jacob parried every blow.

"Well, then," Jacob said. "We'll end the family line that much sooner."

Liam burst into the room, the foul smell gagging him. Callianeira hung by chains, head turned away from the sight. Even in the dim firelight, her wounds appeared to fester. Liam vomited as he beheld the figure to Callianeira's left. It twitched, pieces of skin lumped on the floor before it, and Liam knew it was Aster. Bile in his throat, he approached, reaching out to her. Dead. Cain stepped in his way. Liam collapsed under the angel's blow, curling into a ball of pain.

"Easy enough," Cain said. "Just like the others."

The blindness receded and Liam struck, jumping up, blade coming at Cain. The man swatted it away, but Liam struck at him again, and Cain maneuvered just in time. "Whoa!" Cain said. "Got a fire in him."

Aster's bloody form hung from the chains, her blond hair soaked as red as her exposed limbs. Liam choked, swallowing a sob, letting the anger take over.

"She begged me, you know," Cain said. "Begged me to kill her."

Liam swung again at the fallen angel, but Cain stepped back. Staccato ringing came from the nearby room, Maynard and Jacob in a fierce battle. Liam found his focus just as Cain swung at him. The angel swatted the sword from his hand. Empty-handed, Liam looked dumbfounded. His resolve hardened and he charged the bigger being, colliding with his abdomen and taking him to the ground. Cain lurched, too startled to maintain his balance, his feet knocked from under him. They went down, but Cain rolled, pinning Liam. A blow and Liam's face became pain. Agony blinded him as his lip burst, tearing. He heard his teeth clattering to the floor. He might have cried out, but the blood from the wound filled his mouth. He flailed, trying to find a way out of the pain. Anger came upon him again. He slammed his own fist into Cain's jaw. The fallen showed no sign of injury.

Cain lifted a dazed and powerless Liam, and threw him. He landed in a pile of chains at the foot of one of the big metal boxes in the room, their reeking waste more apparent. Liam's fingers curled around the links. Cain approached him, but Liam jumped up, swirling a chain into the air. It struck high, battering Cain's temple. A fortunate strike.

"Run," someone called. Callianeira. "Liam! No! He'll kill you!"

Cain held a hand to his temple and Liam took advantage of his hesitation. The chain came down again whipping the man. Cain jumped at him, arms flailing wildly. Liam rolled out of the way, careful not to tangle in the chain. Cain barreled at him, but Liam leapt, jerking the chain up. It twisted around Cain's neck. Liam caught the opposite end and yanked at them. It was meant to pull Cain back, but he was too heavy. He let out a gurgling motion, trying to get to his knees. Liam twisted the ends in his hands and pulled again. The links clattered as they tightened and the bigger man fell back. Using the chain, Liam pulled himself up, drawing it tighter around Cain's neck. Liam had a close grip on the chain, and he held on, mounting to Cain's back.

Liam dug his knees in, wrenching the chain harder. Cain moved back, slamming Liam into the wall. The wind left his lungs, but he clung tight, the links digging into his hands. Everything hurt, more pain than he could remember. His lip continued to bleed and he felt it swelling. Cain slammed him into the wall again while grappling blindly behind him at Liam. Something cracked, and Liam yelled, but he held on. If he loosened at all, if Cain's fingers found purchase, he could easily rip free.

"You can't win this," Cain said with a dismaying effortlessness.

"Fuck you," Liam said through gritted teeth.

Callianeira continued to call his name, but he held onto the chain. It became his world, the only thing he could do in the agony. Each breath drew a sharp pain and his back felt out of place. Another crash against the wall. Pain shot into his groin. As he bit his tongue, his stomach roiled, projecting bile and blood over the angel's bald head. Cain lurched, arms flailing. He nearly grasped Liam's hand, but Liam jerked it back harder. Liam screamed, but he did not let go. There was a lurch and he braced himself for another slam against the wall. Then he was toppling. They spilled to the floor and the chain fell from Liam's hands. Cain's body crushed him, and he scrambled away, as much as his broken body would let him.

He readied himself for another attack from Cain, but found the fallen angel purple-faced on the ground, the chain still locked around his neck. All he wanted to do was curl into a ball. He wheezed, attempting to wipe blood from his face. His clothes were already so soaked that they merely smeared it.

"Free me," Callianeira said. "Then let's go."

Liam tried to stand, each movement a new pain. His heart beat and his hands shook, but he managed to gain his feet. Trying not to look at Aster's corpse, the missing skin, the exposed organs, he walked toward Callianeira.

"How?" The question came out convoluted by his broken lip. Something might have been wrong with his jaw as well. He spit red.

"Search for the key in Cain's pocket," Callianeira said. "Be careful."

He nodded and within moments he found the key.

"We have to go," she said, massaging her wrists.

Liam looked to Cain's body on the ground. "Cain," he said awkwardly. "Still alive?"

"Yeah," she said. "He's still alive."

He looked at her and then to Nathan's sword.

"Is that it, Maynard?" Jacob taunted him. "I thought you were one of us."

Maynard remained silent. He conjured all he could from the Darkworld, but Jacob thwarted the power, exercising his advantage. Jacob had known swordsmanship hundreds of years longer than Maynard had been alive. He was tiring and Jacob was not. Jacob struck at him and he jumped to the side. Jacob's next sword-thrust nearly caught him. By luck Maynard dodged out of reach. He came back up, knocking Jacob's blade away. The fallen angel continued, relentless.

"Come on," Jacob said. "Use that big sword of yours."

He was right. His sword had weight, it had reach. And no one could wield it like him. He struck harder this time. Jacob may know sword-fighting better than him, but he did not know this sword. It rang against Jacob's blade, knocking it lower. Jacob's eyes widened. "I guess," the fallen angel said, "that it's time I gave it all that I have."

Jacob came faster, his flippant remarks gone. Maynard fought harder, each strike parried, but Jacob moved back, a new seriousness in his expression. A side-blow, parry down, a twist. Jacob swung and Maynard, quicker than he thought himself capable, dodged, sliding behind Jacob. Adjusting to his newfound speed, he brought his blade down.

"Learned that trick did you?" Jacob asked, parrying with a flash of his blade.

Maynard attempted the maneuver again, tripping as he rolled and rose, another blow aimed at Jacob who dodged with similar speed. Twisting, Maynard tensed, ready to deflect from any direction. The air whistled to his side and his sword blocked Jacob's before the enemy's weapon descended again.

Maynard blocked, putting all of his force behind it, the meeting of their weapons vibrating down his arms. The resistance was but an instant before it relented. Jacob stumbled back, the grip on his sword undone. It clattered to the ground, sliding out of reach. The momentum carried Jacob off balance, Maynard falling with him, hands finding Jacob's neck as they hit the floor.

"Where's your Morning Star now?" Maynard asked, fingers finding Jacob's neck and clinching.

"I don't need him," Jacob croaked.

"I believe you do."

Jacob raised his hands, dampening all magic. He felt the fallen angel's energy pulse, resisting Maynard's call upon the Darkworld. Maynard pushed down on it.

"You remember who Nathan was?" Maynard asked. He felt the fire coursing through him. Jacob pushed back, resisting it. Maynard clenched tighter, willing it forward.

"He was a daemon," Maynard continued. "For the People of the Fire."

Jacob's eyes grew wide, the heat in Maynard's grip rising.

"You will not prevail against me," Jacob croaked.

But the fire grew and Jacob's resistance felt weaker. Maynard drew from the Darkworld. *Remember who you are,* Nathan's voice seemed to say. He pushed harder on Jacob. The fire began. Jacob screamed.

Cain stirred and Callianeira tried to keep balance. Liam offered her a shoulder and together they limped towards Nathan's sword. She steadied herself as Liam withdrew his support in order to pick up the weapon. Something slammed into her ribs, tearing at the crocotta wounds. She sank as agony screamed in her side.

"I'm just going to enjoy this all the more now," Cain said.

He kicked at her, but she rolled, a determination rising in her. By the time she stood, Liam lay in a heap on the floor, Cain having dealt a blow to the young man. She felt warm blood trickling down her forehead, warmer than the sweat that had collected on her brow. The weakness went out from her, an energy generating from her anger.

Cain walked toward her with little regard. He raised a hand to strike. She dealt a punch to his gut. Knuckles struck taut muscle, but when Cain pitched, bowing in pain, she knew he was already weakened and that she had struck well. With a kick to his groin, she sent him to the metal grate floor. He may have recovered swiftly, but Callianeira slammed a boot into his face, his head clanging against the metal. Before he could react, she straddled him and hit him. She struck him, fist after fist, until he no longer possessed the energy to try and stop her. His defensive hands went limp and when she ceased, his unrecognizable face lay still in a pool of blood and bruises.

She went to Liam, who though stunned had regained consciousness.

"Forget the sword," she said. "Help me carry him." Even with her enhanced strength, she wasn't sure they could pull this off. She wasn't sure if she should go through with it. It would have been better to put the son of a bitch to the sword and be done with it. But this was what he deserved. It was her idea and Liam seemed to have no reservations about it.

They pulled the pulp-faced bald man, lugging him across the floor, half carrying him. It took all of their effort to get him up to the metal case and she wondered how they would get him into it, if he'd even fit. It was stained with rubbish and ash. Where Liam found the energy, she didn't know, but apparently the adrenaline hadn't worn off. Sweat beaded down her face as she heaved at the body. Liam's straining came out in gurgles. Somehow Cain's body slouched into the container. They worked fast, wedging his feet and hands in. It was cramped, but the lid would shut tight. They looked down at him one last time, his muscles tense and veins bulging up to his glistening, bloodied face.

She grasped the lid, ready to lower it. "You deserve this, you sick fuck."

His eyes opened. Dark, terrible things, full of menace. She slammed the steel lid shut.

"Hold it down!" she said.

Liam jumped on top, for all the good it would do. Her fingers fumbled at the first lock. The lid rattled as she tried to latch it down. It lifted a little and she slammed it down. She found the lock and slid it into place. There were four other locks on the case. He rattled within it as she secured them.

"Can he get out?" Liam asked.

"I don't know," she replied. "Work fast. Here, give me that chain."

He handed her a chain and she took the time and heavy lifting to secure it around the metal tube, doubling the effort it would take to break through it.

They pushed the box, urging it closer to the conveyor belt, and she was thankful that the conveyor sat closer to the ground. It wasn't too difficult getting the container onto it. At the end of the line, it dropped into a deep, brightly burning furnace.

"All right," she said, stepping back once they had secured it, relieved that their plan had gone this far. "We're going to brazen bull his ass." This box lacked ventilation, but the resilience of the fallen angel was sure to prolong Cain's suffering.

Liam hit the button and the conveyor belt took the shaking container closer to the fire. The sound of muffled pounding resonated above the machinery. Then it tipped into the furnace. It plummeted, taking seconds to thud at the bottom. It was a matter of seconds before the screams began.

Joining it, screams came from the adjacent room.

They ran, entering to find Maynard hunched over Jacob, hands locked around his throat, swords well out of reach. Fire came from Maynard's hands, the glow bristling around Jacob's neck and the fallen angel screamed. He was trying to do what he had done to the captain, but this was different. This was Jacob. How potent was Maynard to overpower Jacob that much?

Callianeira picked up Maynard's sword and kicked Jacob's further out of reach. "Maynard," she said. He didn't look at her. Jacob spasmed, screaming as the flames licked his face.

"Maynard, you can't do this forever, and when you stop, he'll kill you."

She reached over, risking a tug at Maynard's shoulder. He looked at her, psychotic menace in his eyes. She could feel the energy around them, Jacob resisting Maynard's power, but unable to extinguish it.

"Maynard." She said it again, but this time more compassionate. They'd all die and she wasn't ready for that. She wasn't prepared to lose what they had just found.

"Strike him," Maynard said. She held Maynard's sword. This was the moment. She raised it, aiming true as to not hit Maynard or his hands. And she let the blade fall. Jacob's pale hands gripped Maynard, pulling him closer. Callianeira barely ceased her strike, the sword coming close the nape of Maynard's neck. Jacob kicked Maynard off, sending him across the room.

Jacob stood, the skin sloughing off the lower half of his burned face. His eyes bulged as he breathed heavily. There was a thrum in the air, his anger manifesting. She felt terror.

Maynard glared at Jacob, obsession boiling in his expression. "Kill him!" Maynard said.

She could see the edge of Jacob's sanity. He was too delusional with pain to fight, but provoking that could unravel all. She walked over to Maynard, taking him by the arm. "Please," she said. "If he comes to his wits, we will all die."

"Then go," Maynard said.

"You can die by his hand now," Liam said, "or live to defeat him another day." Lucidity had returned to Liam's eyes, and Callianeira thought he really might be the best of them.

Maynard nodded, as if not fully convinced, but wise enough to be wary of his own judgment. They ran, leaving behind Jacob, hoping he was too disoriented to pursue. *And what about the others?* Callianeira wondered. Amelia and Raven might be nearby. *Or worse.* The Morning Star. The elevator carried them up, her heart beating as each level passed.

Dorian tracked the smell of fresh blood and found the dead crocotta. Oliver's cane tapped close behind, making speed with the help of Charis. Perry followed as well. They stopped and stood over the carcass. In his death, Sol had kept his true form, the beast, the monster.

"One of them took it down," Dorian said.

"It was Liam," Oliver replied. "Look at the blade marks. Maynard's sword is too big to have made those."

"Damn," said Perry. "When did Liam start kicking so much ass?"

"The day he made it through the Pass," Oliver said. "I had confidence in him and even now I can see that I underestimated him."

"You sure Sol's dead?" asked Charis.

Dorian walked closer, blade at the ready. No breath crept from the beast's mouth, no heartbeat within. The smell confirmed as much.

"He's dead," Dorian said. "Small victory, that one."

"Small victory," Oliver said, "*if* Maynard and Liam are uninjured. Any sense of where they are?"

Dorian looked to Charis and she shook her head. He grimaced. "They went to find Calli and Aster but I don't know my way around here." Dorian pointed toward a cluster of buildings. "I'm getting flashes of things, which I believe are coming from Aster, but many are incoherent or dark. I know that they are to the north and through one of the First Underground entrances, in a room with chains and a furnace of some sort."

"How would they know where to go?" Charis asked.

"Liam knows this place better than anyone," Perry said. "Even myself."

"Any idea where this is, Perry?" Dorian asked.

"I might," Perry said. "There's a garbage processing station that might match that description, assuming it is the one on the north side as you describe."

Oliver leaned down, hand carefully reaching into the crocotta's gaping maw. He pulled out a dagger, slick with gelatinous blood.

Jacob emerged from his daze at Amelia's scream. He had been about to strike, to deal his death blow, but his own mortality daunted him. Where had his sanity fled? Had they struck at him, would have he had the wherewithal to defend himself? "Jacob!" Amelia fell before him. Her hands continued to feel his burned face, blood and puss covering them. Each touch awoke the flame within his skin. He blinked up at her, scored eyelids flickering. "Amelia," he said.

"Your face," she said.

"Damn them all," he said. He smiled, stretching the burned skin around his jaws. His power had faded before Maynard and he would have none of that. He had not waited on the Morning Star for two hundred years to suffer this. He would sacrifice the whole lot of them to the gods of the hells.

She knelt, and held out a hand. He took her hand and found the strength to sit up, squeezing his eyes shut at the searing pain.

There were tears in her eyes. "What have they done?"

"They have awoken something in me."

"They've destroyed you."

"Destruction is not the loss of something," Jacob said. "It is the rearranging of it, another manifestation of creation."

"We will destroy them," she said.

"No," Jacob said. "We will *unmake* them."

The burning sensation returned and he clenched his teeth in agony. His pain blurred his vision yet again. He winced, taking a moment to regain his composure. He opened his eyes once again and tried to stand. When Amelia didn't assist him he looked around the room. Amelia was gone.

"Cain!" he called. No answer came.

*If I am alone, so be it. All the more for me.*

Something felt wrong. It pulled at Dorian, beckoned him, but the pain that emanated from it disoriented him. It was Aster, he knew, but when it abruptly stopped, he worried that it was a trap. There was a whisper, something else, flirting with his mind. After two hundred years, he still knew that feeling.

They had started to walk again, to continue the search, but paces away from Sol's body, Dorian came to a stop and the others did as well. Oliver's cane ceased its tapping and Charis looked to him. Perry made to speak, but Dorian held up a hand, beckoning them to silence.

"Come out, Amelia," Dorian said.

She emerged from the alley, black-robed, expression as steeled as her bare sword. Raven followed, blade drawn, eyes wide at the sight of his dead pet.

Amelia looked down at Sol's carcass. The necromancer grimaced.

"I don't know what you're planning," Dorian said, "but you're outnumbered."

"No," Amelia replied. "There are two of you and you'll be too busy defending the cripple and the boy to match us. Besides, will you truly fight us when we have four of your own? Maynard and the boy. The demoness and the girl?"

"Lies," Charis said, a sureness in her voice that Dorian did not doubt. Whatever had happened, they held no hostages.

"Run, Perry," Dorian said.

Charis's sword was drawn when Amelia met her attack. Raven's weapon crossed Dorian's blade and the battle began. They clashed in an intersecting melee. Dorian blocked a strike from Raven, before deflecting Amelia's blade. She grunted with the collision before turning from him and exchanging a series of blows with Charis. Their combat accelerated until as each movement became a race of attacks and parries.

Intuitively, Dorian reached into Darkworld. Fire leapt from his hand and Raven dodged the flame. Amelia's blade met Dorian's, and he twisted it away with a grunt. Something flickered in her eyes and the smell of cinder filled the air. From the ground the beast emerged, leaping with outstretched talons and gnashing teeth. Dorian rolled from Amelia's next attack and struck down the hellhound with a gout of fire. No sooner had he dispatched it than another emerged. He twisted, his blade cutting through the beast before he rounded to deflect Amelia's blade.

Raven attacked, but Oliver joined the fray. Amelia rounded on the man, as he tripped backward, trying to keep balance with his cane. It clattered to the floor and Amelia knocked the sword from his grip.

*Not him too*, Dorian thought. *Not like this.*

Charis cried out. Dorian hardly found the time to deflect a blow from Raven. Another hellhound emerged, coming for Dorian, but Raven's next strike occupied him. Great jaws widened, blocking Dorian's view of Amelia's swift rush at Oliver. Steel rang in Dorian's ears and he wavered in shock.

Like liquid smoke the hound dissipated, its black muscle form slithering into the air. Raven stumbled from Dorian's block, and Amelia hung midair, lifted by Oliver. Sweat beaded off of his brow, the pain obvious on his face, but he lifted her, the hilt of the dagger in her chest as he thrust upward. The dagger, taken from the crocotta's toxic mouth, sank into her flesh once more. Through clenched teeth he spoke. "This is for being such a cunt." His hand drew back, the slimy, bloody dagger held tight in his hand, and he jammed it into her once again. Oliver released her and she fell as the tetrodotoxin took hold of her. She retained her wits a moment, struggling to rise before expelling black bile. It splattered onto the stone and Oliver leapt back, his face contorting in pain from his leg.

Amelia reached out a hand as she collapsed, her knees striking the hard ground with an audible crack. Blood seeped from her eyes like the night's tears, and no sound came from her gaping, desperate mouth. As trembling turned to convulsion, she collapsed, her body twisting and arcing in unnatural contortion. The violent spasms ended. Even perfectly still, her strain was palpable. A moment later, only her labored breathing remained until it turned to a short, wheezing gasp, rapid respiration falling into a tremulous struggle.

Black tears streaked from horrified eyes, the agelessness fading from them, as the realization of mortality grew with every diminishing of her flesh. The venom on the dagger boiled her life away. The breathing stopped, its rapid inhale and exhale giving way to sudden silence.

Dorian realized that Raven had fled. He also realized that he pitied Amelia. No such beauty could fade without sorrow, even if she had spent her long last days in wretchedness. He hoped that she had found peace, though he couldn't even hope for such a thing for Nathan who deserved it so much more.

Oliver swayed and Charis moved to support him, retrieving his cane and placing it in his hand. The man seemed to have aged a decade, though beyond his stunned expression, there was a newfound wisdom. "She's dead," Oliver said.

"No," said Charis, "her heart beats still. She will die. That much is certain, but she lingers and each heartbeat is agony."

"Shall I give her mercy?" Dorian asked. He would be no judge and jury for this pathetic woman.

They looked to Oliver. "No," he said, leaning on his cane. Though seconds earlier Dorian had some sympathy for Amelia, he could not fault Oliver. Dorian looked to Charis and saw no prosecution, but also no pity in her usually compassionate eyes. Dorian's own sympathy faded. Nothing so beautiful should fall, but nor should it be awful, so destructive, so lost. Had it been Dorian's decision he would have done the same.

They left Amelia, blood pooling out from under her black garments, eyes fixed up to the apex of the great pyramid. She looked as if she might reach out, as if she might say something, but not even a breath escaped her lips. With each of their fading steps, her heart beat softer and slower, the power of her Chernobyl soul decaying into seconds of pain that felt like centuries. She might have screamed in anguish, curled her toes in torment, and died a thousand deaths if it would have shortened this one. Charis felt her last, terrible heartbeat, and knew that it was mercy.

# CHAPTER THIRTY-NINE

*Raven's Song*

Over the years he had grown fond of Solomon Glass. Not even Raven's powers could resurrect the therianthrope. With tetrodotoxin, there was no hope for Amelia. She was gone as well. He had the lich woman, but to utilize her powers on Sol and Amelia seemed ignoble, although a viable last resort.

Something told Raven that all was not well with Jacob and Cain. Something wove into the air, a dread that he could not place. He sprinted toward that feeling, hoping it was not Jacob. That would be untenable fury.

Raven stopped in an alley, leaning against the concrete wall. Things were not going according to plan. They were not going well at all. He cursed, running the necrotic fingers of his left hand through black waves of hair. Two hundred years of work wasted. Jacob had told them to wait for the Morning Star. They could turn an uncertain victory at the foot of Dorian's mountains into an absolute win. Wait, Jacob had told them. For two hundred years they did wait, and Jacob's magic conjured the most peculiar figure. The Morning Star.

Then Raven had been told that he could do something new. The Morning Star gifted them the liches. What a marvel, but not quite worth the two hundred years. There was something else in store, but as it turned out, the old man, Agnys Negosta was hardly an indicative manifestation of the first fallen angel.

Leaving the alley, Raven began a brisk walk to the area that Jacob had established. Jacob always had a plan, but usually Raven could predict it. Jacob had always kept his promises, always retained an ace up his sleeve, one last gambit, but Raven's faith waned. Perhaps Raven's grief clouded his thoughts, but something, the song within his blackened soul, quavered at further trust in the fallen.

As he neared Jacob's alcove he heard the screaming. To his horror, he found Jacob burned from the neck up, his black shirt glistening with blood. He screamed, again, but not in pain. Outrage echoed in the pyramid.

"She's dead," Raven said, the adrenaline fading.

Jacob turned to him, eyes bulging from blistering, bloody sockets. Raven did not quaver, for not only had he beheld such marred familiar faces, but he suspected that Jacob had well-earned his disfigurement.

"What the fuck happened?" the burned man spat.

"They killed Sol. Whoever it was, covered the dagger in his toxin and stabbed her with it," Raven said, attempting to sound dispassionate. He couldn't give two shits about Amelia, but Sol's death was a growing anger in Raven.

"Where is Agnys?" Jacob asked, looking around frantically. "I'll burn this city to the ground." The fallen had gone mad. Not even Jacob could do such a thing as burn Novum, not in a place so well-built. The glass itself was impenetrable. Did Jacob think that the Morning Star would do it for him? Was the Morning Star's host, this Agnys Negosta, capable of such a thing, and if he could, would he? Raven doubted that. Their deal was to take the City intact. The Morning Star would not rule a ruin.

"I'm here," Agnys said coming from the shadows.

"Come," Jacob said, and he began to walk furiously.

"Where's Cain?" Raven asked. "Did you lose Calli and the girl?"

"Stifle," Jacob said. That was as good as an answer. Raven's clever surety was further undone.

Jacob led them to the foundation's edge of the great pyramid's northern side. They stopped in a small square, the gleaming waters of a fountain trickling at the center. Raven sat on its concrete side, waiting to see what Jacob would do. Better to watch. Inquiry always solicited riddles from Jacob.

"Burn it!" Jacob said.

Agnys looked to Raven. "He's surely not talking to me," Agnys said.

"Well," Raven said with a wry grin, "I doubt that he thinks that there's anything that I could do about it."

"Burn it!"

Agnys walked to Jacob, meeting his eyes. A shadow passed over Agnys's face, something sinister. Raven had a feeling he wouldn't like it.

"Listen, fool," Agnys said, "you forget who I am and you forget our deal."

"If you won't burn it," Jacob said, "I will."

"By what power?" Agnys asked. "I gave you everything you needed to succeed and you've made a very fine mess of it all. Dorian should have never been a factor, and yet here he is. But even then, you outnumbered him, but you squandered your forces at the Pass. You let the most powerful members of your team die, and all because of your bloody obsession."

The knife flashed, almost too quick for Raven's eyes. Agnys's eyes grew wide and so did the cut at his throat. Blood sprayed across Jacob's face as he muttered something.

Agnys sank to the ground, life spewing from his open neck. There was a crack and the ground began to quake. Raven stood, looking for anywhere to run. But he was trapped within the pyramid. If it had taken Amelia three deaths of mere humans to unblock the ruins at the north end of the Pass, what more could blood magic using the Morning Star's host accomplish?

Like the tearing of a curtain, the glass began to crack on the southern wall, a solid line running from the apex, trailing to the bottom. Shards fell, crashing down with ferocious speed. That's when the screams began. The City's people would be fleeing, running to the northern end of the pyramid.

The glass continued to fall until a solid, open line traveled vertical along southern wall. As the fresh air seeped into the pyramid and even from afar, Raven smelled it. Another crack, louder, deeper, resounded, fresh air turning to the smell of ruin. The Central Spire leaned forward and with the shaking earth it plummeted.

"Jacob," Raven called. Jacob turned his bloody, burned head toward Raven. He said nothing, but Raven saw the lunacy. It was the sort of madness that Cain had described. Ruthless desperation and obsession. Jacob's burns changed him.

Raven rushed at Jacob, pulling him to the ground. They fell next to Agnys's body, the earth turbulent as Raven attempted to pin Jacob down. There was blinding pain, and for a moment the world went blinding bright as the sharp stabbing sensation hammered the back of his head. What was Jacob doing to him? He regained his senses, the blurry vision coming into focus as the Central Spire collapsed. It fell away, crashing against the southern wall, debris breaking between the narrow gouge in its glass.

The sound deafened him.

Jacob's fist met his jaw, disorienting him again. He lay a moment as sound returned to his ringing ears. There were screams, not his own, distant cries from those caught in the devastation and those who fled from it. Another strike from Jacob and Raven found the wherewithal to fight back. He grappled with

Jacob trying to hold him down. Jacob muttered something, a chant sure to wreak more havoc.

"You have to stop," Raven cried out. "Leave something for us."

"The Morning Star is dead. By his blood, I can do what I want."

Raven had nearly pinned Jacob down, but his bad hand ached, numbness threatening to loosen his strength. "Agnys Negosta is dead," Raven said. "The Morning Star will not be forgiving."

"Fuck him," Jacob said. "And fuck you."

There was another distant rumble, a violent shake, and Jacob's hands found Raven's neck. He strained and then he screamed.

"Fuck," Dorian said. "I didn't think he would do it. I didn't think he could."

The dust had settled and they surveyed the wreckage. Charis had taken it harder than anyone else, the first to shed tears. The evacuation of the First Underground had ceased with the collapse, Dorian fearing that they would be no safer elsewhere. Callianeira, now recovering back in their room, had voiced her assent, though Maynard offered little more than a nod. Maynard's anger grew when the wreckage settled and they emerged to survey the damage.

A gouge tore down Novum's southern wall, the ruins of the toppled Central Spire a stream of destruction that trailed over half of a mile from Novum's boundaries. It had crushed everything in its wake sending dust into the air. The structure of the First Underground was compromised all along the southern side. Power was sporadic in parts of the City, but fortunately the reactor was buried deep and remained stable.

"How is this possible?" Charis asked.

"Through the Morning Star, perhaps," Dorian said.

"That doesn't make sense," Oliver said. "The Morning Star rarely resorts to outright destruction. He'd much rather people destroy themselves."

"This smacks of Jacob," Maynard said. He was sure of it. Had Liam witnessed this, it might have truly broken his mind. Liam's state, bedridden by his injuries, restless in his fever dreams, was no solace to Maynard, but he could be thankful at least that Liam wouldn't have to behold this so soon after encountering Cain. Maynard hoped the fucker was still roasting alive in that container. Another lifetime of suffering wouldn't suffice to punish the monster.

"What now?" Charis asked, looking to Dorian.

"I'm sick of being one step behind Jacob," Maynard said.

Dorian nodded, eyes flickering to Oliver. "I agree," Dorian said. "Our proactive strategy was supposed to be the battle at the Pass, but that was a trap, a distraction from what was happening here. There's nothing to be done for it now. We've spent too much time trying to come up with a plan, but anything short of a direct approach will be hopeless."

"And who will face the Morning Star?" Charis asked.

"I will," Maynard said. "Agnys is but a shell of the Morning Star. It's about catching him unaware."

"No," Dorian said. "We start by killing Jacob and Raven. That may be deterrent enough to send the Morning Star back where he belongs, in the shadows of his dimension, not so present in our world. He'll have no connections." Looking on the destruction before them, Dorian drew his sword. Charis's eyebrows rose, confirming that she had the same realization as Maynard. They should have recognized Nathan's disguise by his sword. Their attention had been too engrossed in what they hoped was the duel to end this. It had only prolonged it.

Maynard, like the others, followed suit, drawing his own large blade. He felt something stir in him. What had allowed him to break Jacob's barriers? Was it a matter of his will against Jacob's?

"Going somewhere without me?" a voice said. They turned to find Callianeira, standing with blade in hand. She should be resting, regaining her strength. Even if her nature gave her some sort of resilience, surely she was too traumatized to endure the sort of conflict they were bound to find. He opened his mouth to tell her to go back, but Dorian beat him to it. All the better since she was more likely to listen to him.

"I welcome you," Dorian said to Maynard's surprise.

Callianeira winked at Maynard and came to stand alongside him.

"How do we even begin to search for Jacob?" Oliver asked.

"There's something to the north that Liam told me about," Dorian said. "I couldn't tell if it was the fever talking, but I want to see it for myself. We can start there."

That seemed good enough for everyone, and in short order they followed Dorian. They were armed and Oliver even carried a gun. The northern side of the Novum had lost much of its shine to the detritus that settled on its former glory. It otherwise stood untouched, but for the grief of those who walked its streets. Maynard was surprised to find large crowds of people, sheep-like in their mourning. They were a people without hope, which troubled Maynard. He had no delusions that this stand or any resistance against Jacob would end well, but these were a people waiting for their own destruction. He wondered if there had been a group that escaped through the southern rent. If there was time, he imagined that Dorian would organize a full evacuation before pursuing Jacob, but things being what they were, their best hope was finding Jacob and Raven and killing them.

They passed a man-made pool, its once crystalline waters cloudy with dirt and dust. There was a small funeral nearby, held not by the high citizens of Novum, but by the likes of the First Underground. If nothing else, Jacob's destruction had not only leveled the Central Spire, but also the stratification with it.

Led by Dorian, they left what must have been a housing district or suburb and entered an area less populated. Though he had no concept of city-centers, the building central to this area must have been a temple, with its white columns and statuaries. A man preached from the dull, white steps, the crowd gathering to hear his words, the last small contingent of those who had any hope enough left to have faith.

"Even I, Tasrael, was once great," the man said. "But the Eternal One has humbled me." Maynard heard no more as they walked out of earshot.

"The more they talk about humility," Callianeira said, "the more arrogant they usually are."

"Oh?" Maynard said, breaking from his rumination.

"I've used pride against my fair share of mortals." She gave that wry smile, the one that made even Maynard's lip curve upward a bit.

They came to a large clearing, a strange sight in an otherwise packed city. It was a great stone disk, graven with intricate designs, perhaps twenty-feet across. It reminded Maynard of the tattoo on Callianeira's back. All of the fallen had them, she had told him. Dorian stopped at the sight of it."

"These symbols wouldn't normally mean much to me, but Liam was adamant regarding their importance. Before Aster died she sent me visions of this thing, but what is it?" Dorian said.

Oliver shrugged, walking jaggedly with his cane before stopping next to Dorian.

"Wait," said Dorian, and careful not to step foot into the seal, he walked around it. "From this angle I think I can guess at it. There's a symbol, right over there, that looks like a variation on a trapping ward."

"For us?" asked Charis.

"It could be for us," Dorian said. "However, it could potentially be for something more powerful. Let's move on and if anyone sees anything else like this, let me know. We might have solved the mystery of the Tartarus Project."

They left the mysterious circle behind, headed along the destruction on one side and what was left of Novum on the other. They came just north of the center, where the spire had fallen, when Dorian told them to stop and move close to the wall of a building.

"I think I glimpsed Jacob ahead," he said. "I need someone to come with me and scout it out. Callianeira."

He made it sound arbitrary that he chose her, but Maynard wondered if he had been intentional. Dorian had come to trust her, but it seemed strange that he wanted her to run reconnaissance alongside him. Obviously, Oliver would not have been much use and Charis didn't prefer battle. Perhaps Maynard was just too big, or maybe Jacob would sense him. Callianeira gave a nod and followed Dorian, crouching as they disappeared around the corner of the building.

There were a few tense moments as Maynard waited, exchanging anxious glances with the others, hoping that if things were going to go awry that at least it didn't start quite yet. To the company's relief, Dorian and Callianeira returned, both wide-eyed.

"Agnys is dead, throat cut." Dorian said. Callianeira looked relieved at that. "Raven is dead," Dorian continued, "head twisted around. There's an old man, hunched over on his knees and Jacob is standing over him with a knife."

"The prophet," Oliver said. Charis nodded in agreement.

Oliver held up his gun, nozzle still pointed in the air. "I can likely handle the knife before he sees us. If I have a clear shot and it won't risk Elijah, I might be able to get off another and kill him."

"Go for the hand," Dorian said. "You and Charis get Elijah to safety. If you think you can get off another shot, do it. The rest of us will go in for the attack, try and draw him off the prophet. Calli has special orders if things go bad. You are to trust her actions."

That befuddled Maynard, but he hardly had time to think about it. They were already springing into action.

Before rounding the corner, Oliver found an inconspicuous place from which to shoot. He took aim and Maynard thought that it felt unusually quiet. The silence was broken by the booming gun shot. As Oliver pulled the trigger they rushed Jacob. Maynard ran, accelerated by the Darkworld. The bullet struck Jacob's arm and the knife skittered across the tiled courtyard. The prophet looked to his would-be rescuers, terror on his face. He did not move or flee, but remained on his knees.

Jacob reacted slowly, his burned face turning to his injury, registering the bleeding wound. He then looked down at the prophet and turned, putting the old man between the others and himself. He put his hands on the prophet's head. They were not going to get to him in time.

"Is that you Dorian?" Jacob asked. "Do you see the city I have built on my destruction? Beautiful, isn't it? I killed Agnys, using his blood to do this. I killed Raven and nothing happened. I wonder what happens with the blood of a prophet."

"Jacob," said Dorian, stopping. Jacob looked up, and smiled at Dorian.

"Dorian," said Jacob. "It was Nathan and not you that I put a spear through, so I suppose that it has been some time since we last met." Maynard and the others were near.

"When is it too far for you? You're mad." Dorian said.

"And what would you have me do? What a silly notion that madness or the knowledge of it would compel me to stop."

"Is this what you really want?" asked Dorian, arm stretched to the broken world around them.

"It is now," said Jacob. "I wanted to rule everything, but the Eternal One stopped me. I wanted the world, but we destroyed it. I wanted to rule the City, but you won't let me. Now, I will see to it that I rule nothing."

Jacob looked down at the prophet as he pulled a slender knife from his belt with his uninjured hand. Charis let out a cry. Jacob raised the blade, and the prophet looked to them, and Maynard thought that the man looked calm, like someone who expected this long ago. They had all stopped, unable to get to him in time. Their best hope was another shot from Oliver, however risky it may be.

A black shape rose from the ground. Maynard couldn't make it out, but it appeared human, and to raise its hand in sync with Jacob. But its hand lowered first, before Jacob could kill the prophet. It sank something into Jacob's back. With a wheezy gurgling, Jacob's eyes grew wide as he fell to his knees. Charis, with inhuman speed and strength, reached the prophet, awkwardly helping him to his feet and fled.

Everyone else warily watched Jacob, blood pooling red on the white marble tiles. The relief at the prophet's rescue was short-lived, as the figure behind Jacob was revealed. Its face appeared as a shadow, but then Maynard saw that it was hair. Its neck contorted, an audible crack even from ten paces away, and its head twisted aright, Raven's bruised and slashed face sneering at them.

"You're not Raven," Jacob said, his tone pathetic as blood seeped from the corners of his mouth.

"Raven made his own deals," the thing that had been Raven said. "He never trusted you fully, never trusted me, but he knew that I keep my bargains."

"The Morning Star," Jacob said.

"Obviously." It was Raven's body, but his voice had taken a darker, edgier tone. "And I may keep my bargains, but you do not Jacob, and I will not abide insolence."

"No," Jacob said. If the fallen angel had possessed the energy, he might have screamed it, his horror plain in his expression.

It was like time had ceased, as if nothing existed outside of this moment between the Morning Star and Jacob. Maynard and the others had paused, witnesses to some end.

More blood spilled from Jacob's back, his complexion growing pale. "This isn't the end," Jacob said. "It can't be." He slumped over, pathetically lying on his side.

"It's not," the Morning Star said, twisting Raven's features into horrifying smile. "There is more to you than your dying body. You know that." He jerked the knife from Jacob's back and with a kick knocked him over so that he faced upward. He took a single step over Jacob and straddled him, looking down into the angel's dying eyes. "Your soul will not travel into the ether as it has for so many fallen before you. Nor will you be granted ascension by the Eternal One or a seat in my own courts. Your soul will be the engine by which I practice my greatest malice. You will suffer the price of your betrayal."

The Morning Star threw aside the knife and drew Raven's sword from its sheath. He stabbed down once, leaving the sword jutting straight up from Jacob's heart. From his vantage, Maynard saw Jacob's eyes, as if a brief moment before his death Jacob glimpsed his coming fate. The burned face went still, twisted in horror beneath eyes that endured eternal torment.

Like a broken spell, the Morning Star addressed them. "Dorian," the thing that had been Raven said. "Welcome."

Maynard saw that Charis was nowhere to be found. She had fled with the prophet while she had the chance and it appeared Oliver had gone as well. He looked to Dorian. "Run," Dorian said.

Maynard hesitated a moment, looking to the Morning Star and he felt fear. It was greater than the shadowy figure he had witnessed in the Darkworld. It was true fear, that if he died at the hands of this being, it would be the beginning of an eternity similar to Jacob's. He looked to Callianeira and she nodded. They should go.

Maynard ran.

# CHAPTER FORTY

## The Morning Star

*You must do as I tell you... The Tartarus Project.* Dorian's words to Callianeira filled her with an unshakable terror. For a time, she had run with Maynard, and when she was sure that he was unaware, she stopped. She stood still, in fact, at the center of the runic circle. Dorian had followed closely, the Morning Star in tow. Now, Dorian was on his knees before her, and she had pulled his head back by his hair, pressing the knife to his throat. The pit in her stomach roiled, but she stood fast, and waited.

"Can you really do this?" Dorian asked.

"Yes," Callianeira said, sucking in a breath. She exhaled, willing herself to calm. "At least it's not the end of the world."

The taps of boots echoed off of marble, softening as they came to rest on the edge of the stone circle. She looked up, cocking her usual half-smile at the thing that was once Raven. The Morning Star's amused eyes bore into her. Dorian didn't flinch at the presence of the oldest and most powerful of the fallen.

"You were to thwart the man Maynard," he said to Callianeira.

"Are you really going to bitch that I did you one better?" she asked.

"I'm impressed at your industrious betrayal," the Morning Star said.

"You know what this circle is?" Callianeira asked.

The Morning Star began to pace the outer ring, eying the etched runes and glyphs. "I can only assume that the only thing that keeps Dorian from incinerating you where you stand is that you have bound him to whatever design this is."

"That's right," Callianeira said. "So, let's bargain."

"What if I don't want Dorian?" the Morning Star asked. "I want to rule the world, enshroud it in darkness, all the usual stuff, but I don't give one fuck for his soul."

"Says the father of lies," Callianeira said, trying not to show the desperation in her voice. "If it wasn't for Dorian, you would have an easier time getting what you wanted. Novum would still be intact."

"And I'd still have to put up with that little shit Jacob."

"Now you have Jacob. Why not complete your vengeance against those who ruined your plans? You can't tell me that Dorian isn't chief among them."

"Still," the Morning Star mused, "why bargain with you? I can just take him. You are at my command."

"Stop trying to sweeten your end of the deal by pretending that you don't want him or that you could just take him. We have no arrangement and I am no longer subservient to you. I will cut his throat, relieving him of whatever torture you'd have for him, or you will reinstate me as your servant, and put me in Sagtyx place. We both know she's a pain in the ass. I'm sure to be more cooperative." The Morning Star's footsteps tapped behind her now as made his way around the ring. For the tense moments that he walked outside of her peripheral, she waited, cold fear running down her spine. If she couldn't hear his footsteps ten paces away, she would swear he was breathing on the nape of her neck.

"Fine," the Morning Star said. He faced her again now, eyes once again studying her. She rendered her emotions down to a single determination.

"I'll take Dorian off your hands and do you one better. I'll put you over Sagtyx. But I do want you to prove your loyalty to me first."

"Name it," Callianeira said.

The Morning Star walked into the circle. With confident steps he strode to Dorian and taking a handful of hair pushed Dorian's head back further. Callianeira held the knife at the ready.

"See, Dorian," he said. "She bargains you away cheaply, like Judas, but you're no savior. You're pathetic really." The Morning Star spoke in a hellish tongue and looked up to Callianeira. "It's done. If you kill him now, he will be bound to me.

"As you wish," Callianeira said, and she drew the blade across Dorian's throat. It sliced deep and easy, so that the darkest of blood poured out. Dorian held the Morning Star's gaze as the life faded from his eyes. Unlike Jacob, he showed no fear, no sorrow. Only confidence.

Callianeira let go of his head, leaving him to the Morning Star, who dropped his own grip. Dorian slumped over and the Morning Star crouched down. He began to whisper something, but she had backed away too far to hear. Far enough that she stood outside of the circle. Then she whispered something of her own, in a tongue she had not used since she had come to the Outland. When she had finished, the Morning Star looked up to her.

"Did you even bother to read the runes?" she asked.

For the first time since he had taken Raven's body, something of fear showed on his face.

"Maybe you couldn't," she said. "It's an old thing. Dorian himself barely worked it out. It's a banishment from this world."

He rose, fear turning to fury. "You think you can bind me? That you can betray me?" He walked briskly toward her, taking three steps before his legs gave out and he collapsed to the ground. "You can't force me to go anywhere!"

"It's just like the Last Saint," she said. "It was called the Tartarus Project. The magics are in place, the sacrifice is made, and there's no stopping them."

He began to drag himself away from her, reaching for Dorian's body. "I can take a new body," he said.

"It won't work," she replied. "Besides, I doubt the Eternal One will let you have this one."

"You don't know shit." Blood spat from his mouth. His hand fell short of Dorian's slumping form.

The Morning Star found the energy to look at her one last time. She met his eyes and she smiled.

"You—" he said, and then his form slumped to the ground. The tension in the air faded, and it was as if a rumbling had suddenly given way to silence.

She fell to her knees and wept.

# EPILOGUE

## *The Great Prophet*

Old as he was, the recent days had enlivened Elijah and he felt a
vigor that had been dormant for a century. He knew that his end
was soon, but he resolved to put his energy to use. The previous
days had been of great mourning and excitement. It was difficult
to suggest that Novum had been saved given its current state, but
that didn't seem to matter to anyone, least of all Elijah. What
mattered is that the world was now empowered to go about
restoring itself anew. They had spent so much time trying to
preserve Novum when what they really needed was to be free of
it. As if coming out of a great sleep, the people of the City seemed
to know it, and their complacency was exchanged for a newfound
determination to rebuild.

No one questioned what Callianeira had done, least of all
Oliver, who was apt to be the most cynical of the survivors. It was
perhaps helpful that Elijah had been able to add credence to her
claim by providing long forgotten details about the Tartarus
Project and attest that Dorian had requested this of Callianeira.
And he was also able to appease any concerns that Dorian was
under the wrath of the Morning Star, who had been deposed back
to his own realm. The very night it had all come to end, Elijah had
slept and dreamed what he knew would be his last dream. It was
a world, not unlike earth, but it had no moon. Instead it had great

silvery rings. He had drifted towards it in confusion, the thoughts coming to him not his own. *I should be dead, I should be in the dungeons of the Morning Star or part of the eternal ether of the dead* Grigori. He marveled at the celestial body before him, the scope of the planet and its rings belittling every petty fight and war that humanity had ever known. There was a voice, not that same as the first, but deeper and more resonant. It shook Elijah's spirit. *Well done, my servant, for here is your ascension, and your reinstatement to your rightful place.* Dor reigned over Elesonia once more.

Oliver and Charis had smiled at that news.

As for Nathan, Charis had noted a long-lost constellation had reappeared. From Earth it was nothing more than a cluster of stars, but from the vantage of where Charis had once reigned as goddess, it was known as Nataliel, a god that took the form of a tiger.

Charis and Oliver had consulted with Elijah. Why they would come to him for his senile wisdom, he didn't know, but all the same, he counseled them to the best of his ability. It seemed that some system of government was in order, and they wanted to know if he had foreseen some sort of monarchy or theocracy or democracy or the like. Elijah had delightedly told them that he had no such foreknowledge, and much to their surprise, he suggested that the establishment of rule and law be dealt by their hand.

"Don't you see," he had told them. "Novum was built as a place of a beauty for itself. If what I have heard is true, you built Mere as a place to spread beauty where it was otherwise absent. Why leave that dream behind now?"

A scout was sent to retrieve the folk from Mere who now dwelt at the Pass. They came in droves, hearing the spreading story of how Jacob nearly destroyed them all, and of Dorian's sacrifice. The people of Novum were skeptical of these strange new people at first, but they came to embrace the idea of the last of the fallen, Charis, and her wise companion Oliver, as leaders in their new world.

It had delighted Elijah, but nothing brought him so much gladness as reuniting with Liam. The boy had become a man, more than marked by fire. Elijah was later told that their reunion was the first flicker of joy from Liam since Aster's murder. Liam was, however, mostly solemn, though not without an appreciation for the sacrifices that had been made. However, in the passing weeks, Liam had done little to help the bustling restoration of their world. It seemed he had played his part, above and beyond his calling, and was eager to retire at the ripe age of eighteen. For a time, Liam had taken to raiding the communion stock of the temple, and in spite of the unhealthy coping mechanism, Elijah could not fault him for wanting to numb the pain. When at last Elijah—and the others—showed enough concern to confront Liam, he had appeared to them sober, with a backpack and a sword.

"I'm going," he said. And no one questioned him. They said their goodbyes and watched him as he disappeared on the horizon, heading toward the Pass. Had Elijah been concerned, he would have said as much, but he knew it would be good for Liam. Before leaving, the man marked by fire had confided in him.

"One day," Liam said, "I'll be ready to face all this again. Maybe when Charis and Oliver's restoration reaches wherever I end up, I'll be ready. But right now, I just need something simple." Elijah did not think that anyone else quite understood, but he did, and so he counseled Liam to go.

Maynard and Callianeira left as well, but on a particular business. They were to take back the Outland, going from town to town, establishing a new order. They were to cleanse the shoreline from the criminals who had dominated the better lands for so long. Argon and a small contingent went with them. They left in the night, heading first for the northwest forest. They finished their mission there, only Callianeira and Maynard returning to Novum long enough to tell the tale and continue their trip to the Pass and into the Outlands.

As it turned out, Baran had been a poor ruler. His tight-fisted reign had protected him on every side, and in his paranoia he kept the proverbial knife at the throats of Argon's loved ones. In the night, Argon had crept into the forest and secured his family. As Maynard told it, Argon killed six guards without raising an alarm, stole into his family's tent, and with Henmad's help guided them to the outskirts of the forest until Maynard and Callianeira were done with their business.

At dawn, Maynard and Callianeira entered as an envoy on behalf of Novum. Baran was suspicious at first, but caught off-guard by their early morning arrival, he allowed them in. He had been clever enough to send a runner to check on Argon's family. Henmad waited in the family tent and killed the runner. Callianeira and Maynard made quick work of Baran and his followers. Argon was well-received as their new chief and had sent word with Callianeira and Maynard that Novum had the full cooperation of the People of the Moon and the People of the Fire. The crocodiles congregated near the waterfall and so long as the weather permitted, Argon often ruled from the shores of the mountainside within the forest.

After Argon took his seat, the demon and the nephilim brought the news to the City, but shortly thereafter departed. Perry went with them, perhaps hoping to meet with Liam again. They left with a small contingency, the ambassadors commissioned to restore order as the new regency began its new nation.

Charis and Oliver sent a group of volunteers to the Mall to excavate their stores. The most brilliant minds were assembled, ready to make technology once again widespread. Novum had a token library, but the best books were within the temple, where

Oliver's collection from the Pass and what remained from Mere was also compiled.

As for the Great Prophet Elijah, he grew frail after the initial wave of energy swept over him. It had bore him for weeks, but as the dust settled and the people found their rhythm and routine in the clean-up and rebuilding, his own strength seemed to fade. He thought back on those prophecies two hundred years ago, on watching the baleful fire fall from the sky. He had seen war and apathy and fear, and at last, he witnessed peace. No more visions came to him. Charis had been kind, providing a parsonage for him in his last days. Oliver often joined him there, listening to Elijah's stories, taking vigorous notes.

When he knew his last breaths were upon him, he took to his bed, finding each breath shallower than the last. All of his doubt faded, and he rested assured, grateful to those who hoped when all was lost, who fought when it made more sense to give up, who held onto love and solidarity, that he had lived a life worth living.

# ACKNOWLEDGMENTS

There is a wealth of friendship in my life to which I am much indebted. I can only hope that it makes me a better person, and perhaps a better enough person that I empower and enable others to be better.

More than anything, I am grateful to my wife, Britt, who was there to support me even when this was just a shitty first draft.

I wrote this across three states, mostly on my couch, but often in the coffee shops and bars from Minneapolis to Miami to Chattanooga. I owe their cozy stools and booths and warm atmosphere my deepest gratitude.

I owe a big thank you to my first readers, who provided feedback, edits, and encouragement: Gary Lang, J.M. Thomas, Paul Smallman, Wesley Reitzfield. In addition to early feedback, Gary Lang and Matt Brown created artwork inspired by *Outland* which also inspired me to keep writing. And warmest thanks to Zane Seals, my first writing partner, as well as J.M. Thomas who spurred me to publish *Outland*.

Then there are those who made *Outland* real: Eryn Garcia of NeatPony for her brilliant cover and logo design, my editor Heather Linke for her keen eye, and Juliet Johnson at KapowCorp, Inc. for creating a brilliant website. My gratitude also goes out to Heather Jackson and Barley Chattanooga for hosting and promoting the *Outland* book launch party.

I am grateful to those who educated me: Barbara Coward, Warren Roberts, Randy Young, Jim Rehberg, Dr. Sophronia Grantham, Dr. Nicholas Barker, and Dr. Thomas Balázs. Additionally, I would like to thank Brad Hendrickson helping me write intelligently about firearms.

I owe an additional shout-out to Reddit's /r/Fantasy and /r/FantasyWriters.

Of course, I am very thankful for my family and friends, many who have already been named, and many others unnamed. Specifically, I am grateful for the support of Kimberly Collins, Emily Brown, C.J. Pitts, and Luther Cutchins.

12178152R10379

Made in the USA
Monee, IL
22 September 2019